WORLD'S END

LEFT BEHIND SERIES

THE REMNANT · ARMAGEDDON · GLORIOUS APPEARING

COLLECTORS EDITION IV

WORLD'S END

TIM LAHAYE
JERRY B. JENKINS

Tyndale House Publishers, Inc., Carol Stream, Illinois

Visit Tyndale's exciting Web site at www.tyndale.com.

For the latest Left Behind news visit the Left Behind Web site at www.leftbehind.com.

World's End: Left Behind Collectors Edition IV

World's End: Left Behind Collectors Edition IV first published in 2010 by Tyndale House Publishers, Inc.

Cover photography of outer space by NASA/courtesy of nasaimages.org.

Designed by Dean H. Renninger

Published in association with the literary agency of Alive Communications, Inc., 7680 Goddard Street, Suite 200, Colorado Springs, CO 80920, www.alivecommunications.com.

Characters in these novels sometimes speak words that are adapted from various versions of the Bible, including the King James Version and the New King James Version.

Scripture quotation used for epilogue in *The Remnant* is taken from the New King James Version. The message from Tsion Ben-Judah to the remnant at Petra in chapter 1 is adapted from Daniel 3:26 and Isaiah 48:10-21, New King James Version.

ISBN 978-1-61664-895-4

Printed in the United States of America

THE REMNANT

To the memory of Dr. Harry A. Ironside

Special thanks to David Allen for
expert technical consultation

1

RAYFORD STEELE had endured enough brushes with death to know that the cliché was more than true: Not only did your life flash before your mind's eye, but your senses were also on high alert. As he knelt awkwardly on the unforgiving red rock of the city of Petra in ancient Edom, he was aware of everything, remembered everything, thought of everything and everybody.

Despite the screaming Global Community fighter-bombers—larger than any he had ever seen or even read about—he heard his own concussing heart and wheezing lungs. New to the robe and sandals of an Egyptian, he tottered on sore knees and toes. Rayford could not bow his head, could not tear his eyes from the sky and the pair of warheads that seemed to grow larger as they fell.

Beside him his dear compatriot, Abdullah Smith, prostrated himself, burying his head in his hands. To Rayford, Smitty represented everyone he was responsible for—the entire Tribulation Force around the world. Some were in Chicago, some in Greece, some with him in Petra. One was in New Babylon. And as the Jordanian groaned and leaned into him, Rayford felt Abdullah shuddering.

Rayford was scared too. He wouldn't have denied it. Where was the faith that should have come from seeing God, so many times, deliver him from death? It wasn't that he doubted God. But something deep within—his survival instinct, he assumed—told him he was about to die.

For *most people,* doubt was long gone by now . . . there were *few* skeptics anymore. If someone were not a Christ follower by now, probably he had chosen to oppose God.

Rayford had no fear of death itself or of the afterlife. Providing heaven for his people was a small feat for the God who now manifested himself miraculously every day. It was the dying part Rayford dreaded. For while his God had protected him up to now and promised eternal life when death came, he had not spared Rayford injury and pain. What would it be like to fall victim to the warheads?

Quick, that was sure. Rayford knew enough about Nicolae Carpathia to know the man would not cut corners now. While one bomb could easily destroy the million people who—all but Rayford, it seemed—tucked their heads as close to between their legs as they were able, two bombs would vaporize them. Would the flashes blind him? Would he hear the explosions? feel the heat? be aware of his body disintegrating into bits?

Whatever happened, Carpathia would turn it into political capital. He might not televise the million unarmed souls, showing their backsides to the Global Community as the bombs hurtled in. But he would show the impact, the blasts, the fire, the smoke, the desolation. He would illustrate the futility of opposing the new world order.

Rayford's mind argued against his instincts. Dr. Ben-Judah believed they were safe, that this was a city of refuge, the place God had promised. And yet Rayford had lost a man here just days before. On the other hand, the ground attack by the GC had been miraculously thwarted at the last instant. Why couldn't Rayford rest in that, trust, believe, have confidence?

Because he knew warheads. And as these dropped, parachutes puffed from each, slowing them and allowing them to drop simultaneously straight down toward the assembled masses. Rayford's heart sank when he saw the black pole attached to the nose of each bomb. The GC had left nothing to chance. Just over four feet long, as soon as those standoff probes touched the ground they would trip the fuses, causing the bombs to explode above the surface.

+ + +

Chloe Steele Williams was impressed with Hannah's driving. Unfamiliar vehicle, unfamiliar country—yet the Native American, who had been uncannily morphed into a New Delhi Indian, handled the appropriated GC Jeep as if it were her own. She was smoother and more self-confident than Mac McCullum had been, but of course he had spent the entire drive across the Greek countryside talking.

"I know this is all new to you gals," he had said, causing Chloe to catch Hannah's eye and wink. If anybody could get away with unconscious chauvinism, it was the weathered pilot and former military man, who referred to all the women in the Trib Force as "little ladies" but did not seem consciously condescending.

"I got to get to the airport," he told them, "which is thataway, and y'all have got to get into Ptolemaïs and find the Co-op." He pulled over and hopped out. "Whicha you two is drivin' again?"

Hannah climbed behind the wheel from the backseat, her starched white GC officer's uniform still crisp.

Mac shook his head. "You two look like a coupla Wacs, but 'course they don't call 'em that anymore." He looked up and down the road, and Chloe felt compelled to do the same. It was noon, the sun high and hot and directly overhead, no clouds. She saw no other vehicles and heard none. "Don't worry about me," Mac added. "Somebody'll be along and I'll catch a ride."

He lifted a canvas bag out of the back and slung it over his shoulder. Mac also carried a briefcase. Gustaf Zuckermandel Jr., whom they all knew as Zeke or Z, had thought of everything. The lumbering young man in Chicago had made himself into the best forger and disguiser in the world, and Chloe decided that the three of them alone were the epitomes of his handiwork. It was so strange to see Mac with no freckles or red hair. His face was dark now, his hair brown, and he wore glasses he didn't need. She only hoped Z's work with her dad and the others at Petra proved as effective.

Mac set down his bags and rested his forearms atop the driver's side door, bringing his face to within inches of Hannah's. "You kids got everything memorized and all?" Hannah looked at Chloe, fighting a smile. How many times had he asked that on the flight from the States and during the drive? They both nodded. "Lemme see your name tags again."

Hannah's was right in front of him. "Indira Jinnah from New Delhi," Mac read. Chloe leaned forward to where he could see hers. "And Chloe Irene from Montreal." He covered his own name tag. "And you're on the staff of who?"

"Senior Commander Howie Johnson of Winston-Salem," Chloe said. They'd been over it so many times. "You're now the ranking GC officer in Greece, and if anybody doubts it, they can check with the palace."

"Awright then," Mac said. "Got your sidearms? This Kronos character, at least a relative of his, has some more firepower."

Chloe knew they needed more firepower, especially not knowing what they would encounter. But learning the Luger and the Uzi—which they knew the Greek underground could supply—had been more than enough to tax her before they left Chicago.

"I still say the Co-op people are going to clam up when they see our uniforms," Hannah said.

"Show 'em your mark, sweetie," Mac said.

The radio under the dashboard crackled. "Attention GC Peacekeeping forces. Be advised, Security and Intelligence has launched an aerial attack on several million armed subversives of the Global Community in a mountain enclave discovered by ground forces about fifty miles southeast of Mizpe Ramon in the Negev Desert. The insurgents murdered countless GC ground troops and commandeered unknown numbers of tanks and armored carriers.

"Global Community Security and Intelligence Director Suhail Akbar has announced that two warheads have been dropped simultaneously, to be followed by a missile launched from Resurrection Airport in Amman, and that the expected result will be annihilation of the rebel headquarters and its entire personnel force. While there remain pockets of resistance around the world, Director Akbar believes this will effectively destroy 90 percent of the adherents of the traitorous Judah-ites, including Tsion Ben-Judah himself and his entire cabinet."

Chloe's hand flew to her mouth, and Hannah grabbed her other hand. "Just pray, girls," Mac said. "We all but knew this was comin'. Either we have faith or we don't."

"That's easy to say from here," Chloe said. "We could lose four people, not to mention all the Israelis we promised to protect."

"I'm not takin' it lightly, Chloe. But we got a job to do here too, and this is no safer than a mountain under a bomb attack. You keep your wits about you, hear? Listen to me—we won't know what happened at Petra till we see it with our own eyes or hear it from our people. You heard the lies already, from the GC to their own forces! We know for sure there's only a million people in Petra and—"

"Only?!"

"Well, yeah, compared to several million like they said. And armed? No way! And did we kill GC forces—murder 'em, I mean? And what about commandeering those—"

"I know, Mac," Chloe said. "It's just—"

"You'd better practice callin' me by my GC name, Ms. Irene. And remember everything we went over in Chicago. You may have to fight, defend yourselves, even kill somebody."

"I'm ready," Hannah said, making Mac cock his head. Chloe was surprised too. She knew Hannah had warmed to this assignment, but she couldn't imagine Hannah wanted to kill anyone any more than she did. "The gloves are off," Hannah said, looking to Chloe and then back to Mac. "We've gone way past diplomacy. If it's kill or be killed, I'm killing somebody."

Chloe could only shake her head.

"I'm just saying," Hannah said, "this is war. You think they won't kill Sebastian? They very well already could have. And I'm not counting on finding this Stavros girl alive."

"Then why are we here?" Chloe said.

"Just in case," Hannah said, using the Indian lilt Abdullah had taught her in Chicago.

"Just in case is right," Mac said, hefting his bags again. "Our phones are secure. Keep the solar receptors exposed during the daytime—"

"C'mon, Mac," Chloe said. "Give us a little credit."

"Oh, I do," Mac said. "I give you more than a lot of credit. I'm impressed, tell you the truth. Comin' over here for somebody you've never met, well, at least you, Chloe. And, Hannah—er, Indira, I don't guess you got to know George well enough to give a—to, uh, care that much about him personally."

Hannah shook her head.

"But here we are, aren't we?" Mac said. "Somebody was here workin' for us, and best we can figure out, he's in trouble. I don't know about you, but I'm not leavin' here without him."

Mac spun and stared at the horizon, causing Chloe and Hannah to do the same. A black dot grew as it moved their way. "Y'all run along now," Mac said. "And keep in touch."

✢ ✢ ✢

Rayford's first inkling was that he was in hell. Had he been wrong? Had it all been for naught? Had he been killed and missed heaven in spite of it all?

He was unaware of separate explosions. The bombs had caused such a blinding flash that even with his eyes involuntarily pressed shut as tightly as his facial muscles would allow, the sheer brilliant whiteness seemed to fill Rayford's entire skull. It was as if the glare filled him and then shone from him, and he grimaced against the sound and heat that had to follow. Surely he would be blown into the others and finally obliterated.

The resounding *boom* sent a shock wave of its own, but Rayford did not topple, and he heard no rocks falling, no mountainous formations crashing. He instinctively thrust out his hands to steady himself, but that proved unnecessary. He heard ten thousand wails and moans and shrieks, but his own throat was constricted. Even with his eyes closed, he saw the whiteness replaced by orange and red and black, and now, oh, the stench of fire and metal and oil and rock! Rayford forced himself to open his eyes, and as the thunderous roar echoed throughout Petra he realized he was ablaze. He lifted his robed arms before his face, at least temporarily unaware of the searing heat. He knew his robe, then flesh, then bone would be consumed within seconds.

Rayford could not see far in the raging firestorm, but every huddled pilgrim around him was also ablaze. Abdullah rolled to one side and lay in a fetal position, his face and head still cocooned in his arms. White, yellow, orange, black roaring flames engulfed him as if he were a human wick for a demonic holocaust.

One by one the people around Rayford stood and raised their arms. Their hoods, their hair, their beards, faces, arms, hands, robes, clothes all roared with the conflagration as if the fire were fueled from beneath them. Rayford looked above their heads but could not see the cloudless sky. Even the sun was blotted out by the massive sea of raging flames and a pair of roiling mushroom clouds. The mountain, the city, the whole area was afire, and the fumes and plumes and licking flames rose thousands of feet into the air.

What must this look like to the world, Rayford wondered, and it struck him that the mass of Israelis were as dumbfounded as he. They staggered, eyeing each other, arms aloft, now embracing, smiling! Was this some bizarre nightmare? How could they be engulfed by the slaughtering force of the latest in mass-destruction technology yet still stand, squinting, with puzzled looks, still able to hear?

Rayford opened and closed his right fist, inches from his face, wondering at the hissing flarelike tongues of fire that leaped from each digit. Abdullah struggled to his feet and turned in a circle as if drunk, mimicking the others by raising his arms and looking skyward.

He turned to Rayford and they embraced, the fire from their bodies melding and contributing to the whole. Abdullah pulled back to look Rayford in the face. "We are in the fiery furnace!" the Jordanian exulted.

"Amen!" Rayford shouted. "We are a million Shadrachs, Meshachs, and Abednegos!"

+ + +

Chang Wong joined the other techies in his department as their boss, Aurelio Figueroa, led them to a huge television monitor. It showed the live feed from the cockpit of one of the fighter-bombers as it circled high above Petra, broadcast around the world via the Global Community News Network. Later Chang would check his recording of the bug in Carpathia's office to monitor the reactions of Nicolae, his new secretary Krystall, Leon, Suhail, and Viv Ivins.

"Mission accomplished," the pilot reported, scanning the target and showing square miles raging in flames. "Suggest subsequent missile sequence abort. Unnecessary."

Chang clenched his teeth so tight his jaw ached. How could anyone survive that? The flames were thick, and the black smoke belched so high that the pilot had to avoid it to keep the picture clear.

"Negative," came the reply from GC Command. "Initiate launch sequence, Amman."

"That's overkill," the pilot muttered, "but it's your money. Returning to base."

"Repeat?" The voice sounded like Akbar himself.

"Roger that. Returning to base."

"That's another negative. Remain in position for visual feed."

"With a missile coming, sir?"

"Maintain sufficient clearance. Missile will find its target."

The second plane was cleared to return to New Babylon while the first, its camera continuing to show the world Petra burning in the noonday sun, circled southeast of the red rock city.

Chang wished he were in his room and able to communicate with Chicago. How could Dr. Ben-Judah have been so wrong about Petra? What would become of the Tribulation Force now? Who would rally what was left of the believers around the world? And where would Chang flee to when the time came?

+ + +

It was four in the morning in Chicago, and Buck sat before the television. Leah and Albie joined him, Zeke having gone to collect Enoch. "Where's Ming?" Buck said.

"With the baby," Leah said.

"What do you make of this?" Albie said, staring at the screen.

Buck shook his head. "I just wish I were there."

"Me too," Albie said. "I feel like a coward, a traitor."

"We missed something," Buck said. "We all missed something." He kept trying to call Chloe, only imagining what she was going through. No answer.

"Do you believe this guy?" Leah said. "It's not enough to massacre a million people and destroy one of the most beautiful cities in the world. He's chasing it with a missile."

Buck thought Leah's voice sounded tight. And why not? She had to be thinking what he was thinking—that they had not only lost their leadership and seen a million people incinerated, but that everything they thought they knew was out the window.

"Get Ming, would you?" he said. "Tell her to let Kenny sleep."

Leah hurried out as Zeke and Enoch walked in. Zeke plopped onto the floor, but Enoch stood fidgeting. "I can't stay long, Buck," he said. "My people are pretty shaken."

Buck nodded. "Let's all get together at daybreak."

"And—?" Enoch said.

"And I don't know what. Pray, I guess."

"We've been praying," Albie said. "It's time to reload."

+ + +

Rayford could not keep from laughing. Tears poured from him and huge guffaws rose from deep in his belly as the people in Petra began shouting and singing and dancing. They spontaneously formed huge, revolving circles, arms around each other's shoulders, hopping and kicking. Abdullah was glued to Rayford's side, giggling and shouting, "Praise the Lord!"

They remained in the midst of fire so thick and deep and high that they could see only each other and the flames. No sky, no sun, nothing in the distance. All they knew was that they were kindling for the largest fire in history, and yet they were unharmed.

"Will we wake up, Captain?" Abdullah shouted, cackling. "This is my weirdest dream ever!"

"We are awake, my friend," Rayford yelled back, though Abdullah's ear was inches from him. "I pinched myself!"

That made Abdullah laugh all the more, and as their circle spun and widened, Rayford wondered when the flame would die down and the world would find out that God had once again triumphed over the evil one.

An older couple directly across from him gazed at each other as the circle turned, their smiles huge and wonder-filled. "I'm on fire!" the woman shouted.

"I am too!" the man said, and hopped awkwardly, nearly pulling her and others down as he kept one foot in the air, showing her the fire engulfing his entire leg.

Rayford glanced past them, aware of something strange and wondering what could be stranger than this. Here and there within his range of vision, which extended only about thirty feet, was the occasional huddled bundle of clothes or a robe that evidenced a person still curled on the ground.

Rayford pulled away from Abdullah and a young man on his other side and made his way to one of those on the ground. He knelt and put a hand on the man's shoulder, trying to get him to rise or at least look up. The man wrenched away, wailing, quivering, crying out, "God, save me!"

"You're safe!" Rayford said. "Look! See! We are ablaze and yet we are unharmed! God is with us!"

The man shook his head and folded himself further within his arms and legs.

"Are you hurt?" Rayford said. "Do the flames burn you?"

"I am without God!" the man wailed.

"That can't be! You're safe! You're alive! Look around you!"

But the man would not be consoled, and Rayford found others, men and women, some teenagers, in the same wretched condition.

"People! People! People!" It was clearly the voice of Tsion Ben-Judah, and Rayford had the feeling it came from nearby, but he could not see the rabbi. "There will be time to rejoice and to celebrate and to praise and thank the God of Israel! For now, listen to me!"

The dancing and shouting and singing stopped, but much laughter continued. People still smiled and embraced and looked for the source of the voice. It was enough, they seemed to conclude, that they could hear him. The cries of the despairing continued as well.

"I do not know," Dr. Ben-Judah began, "when God will lift the curtain of fire and we will be able to see the clear sky again. I do not know when or if the world will know that we have been protected. For now it is enough that we know!"

The people cheered, but before they could begin singing and dancing again, Tsion continued.

"When the evil one and his counselors gather, they will see us on whose bodies the fire had no power; the hair of our heads was not singed, nor were our garments affected, and the smell of fire was not on us. They will interpret this in their own way, my brothers and sisters. Perchance they will not allow the rest of the world to even know it. But God will reveal himself in his own way and in his own time, as he always does.

"And he has a word for you today, friends. He says, 'Behold, I have refined you, but not as silver; I have tested you in the furnace of affliction. For my own sake, for my own sake, I will do it, for how should my name be profaned? I will not give my glory to another.

"'Listen to me, O Israel,' says the Lord God of hosts, 'you are my called ones, you are my beloved, you I have chosen. I am he, I am the First, I am also the Last. Indeed, my hand has laid the foundation of the earth, and my right hand has stretched out the heavens. When I call to them, they stand up together.

"'Assemble yourselves, and hear! Who among them has declared these things? The Lord loves him; he shall do his pleasure on Babylon. I, even I, have spoken.'

"Thus says the Lord, your Redeemer, the Holy One of Israel: I am the Lord your God, who leads you by the way you should go. Oh, that you had heeded my commandments! Then your peace would have been like a river, and your righteousness like the waves of the sea. Declare, proclaim this, utter to the end of the earth that the Lord has redeemed his servants and they did not thirst when he led them through the deserts. He caused the waters to flow from the rock for them; he also split the rock, and the waters gushed out."

+ + +

As the Tribulation Force in Chicago watched, the fighter-bomber pilot acknowledged to GC Command that he had a visual on the missile originating from Amman. And from the right side of the screen came the thick, white plume trailing the winding projectile as it approached the flame and smoke rising from Petra.

The missile dived out of sight into the blackness, and seconds later yet another explosion erupted, blowing even wider the fire that seemed to own the mountainous region. But immediately following came a colossal geyser, shooting water a mile into the sky.

"I'm—," the pilot began, "I'm seeing—I don't know what I'm seeing. Water. Yes, water. Spraying. It's, uh, it's having some effect on the fire and smoke. Now clearing, the water still rising and drenching the area. It's as if the missile struck some spring that, uh—this is crazy, Command. I see—I can see . . . the flames dying now, smoke clearing. There are people *alive* down th—"

Buck leaped from his chair and knelt before the TV. His friends whooped and hollered. The TV feed died and GCNN was already into its apology for the technical difficulties. "Did you see that?" Buck shouted. "They survived! They survived!"

+ + +

Chang's brows rose and his chin dropped. His coworkers swore and pointed and stared, groaning when the feed was interrupted. "That can't be! That looked like—no, there's not a chance! How long was that place burning? Two bombs and a missile? No!"

Chang hurried back to his computer to make sure he was still recording from Carpathia's office. He couldn't wait to hear the back-and-forth between Akbar and the pilot.

+ + +

Rayford had reunited with Abdullah and was standing, listening to Tsion, when the earth opened with a resounding crash and a gush of water at least ten feet in diameter burst from the ground, rocketing so high that it was a full minute before it began to rain down upon them.

The flames and smoke cleared so quickly, and the refreshing water felt so good, that Rayford noticed others doing what he was. They spread their palms toward heaven and turned their faces to the sky, letting it wash them. Soon Rayford realized he was about a hundred yards from Tsion and Chaim, who stood at the edge of the gigantic abyss from where the water had burst forth.

It appeared Tsion was again trying to gain the attention of the masses, but it was futile. They ran; they leaped; they embraced, singing, dancing, shaking hands, laughing; and soon hundreds of thousands were shouting their thanks to God.

Still, here and there, Rayford saw people grieving, crying out. Were these unbelievers? How could they have survived? Had God protected them in spite of themselves, just because they were here? Rayford couldn't make it make sense. Was it important to know who was protected and who was not and why? And would Tsion speak to that issue?

After several minutes, Chaim and Tsion were able to call the people to order. Somehow the miracle of Tsion making himself heard by a million people without amplification was multiplied in that they could hear him above the rushing sounds of the volcanic spewing water.

"I have agreed to stay at least a few days," Tsion announced. "To worship with you. To thank God together. To teach. To preach. Ah, look as the water subsides."

The noise began to diminish, and the top of the column of rushing water slowly came into view, now three hundred yards above them. Slowly but steadily the spring shrank, in height though not apparently in width. Soon it was just a hundred feet high, then fifty, then ten. Finally it settled into the small lake caused by the initial eruption and crater, and in the middle of the pool the spring bubbled as if it were boiling, a ten-foot-wide, one-foot-high gurgling that looked cool and soothing and seemed capable of adding to the already miraculous water supply.

"Some of you weep and are ashamed," Tsion said. "And rightly so. Over the next few days I will minister to you as well. For while you have not taken the mark of the evil one, neither have you taken your stand with the one true God. He has foreseen in his mercy to protect you, to give you yet one more chance to choose him.

"Many of you will do that, even this day, even before I begin my teaching on the unsearchable riches of Messiah and his love and forgiveness. Yet many of you will remain in your sin, risking the hardening of your heart so that you may never change your mind. But you will never be able to forget this day, this hour, this miracle, this unmistakable and irrefutable evidence that the God of Abraham, Isaac, and Jacob remains in control. You may choose your own way, but you will never be able to disagree that faith is the victory that overcomes the world."

2

IN CHICAGO Buck tried calling Chloe, then Rayford, then Chang. Nothing. He tossed his phone away, but couldn't sit. "Where's Ming?" he said. "She know any of this?"

"She's gone," Leah said.

"Downstairs? Tell her to let Enoch's people sleep and to get up here."

"My people won't be sleeping now," Enoch said.

"She's not downstairs," Leah said. "She left a note."

"What?"

"Her brother told her something about—"

"Where's Kenny?"

"Sleeping, Buck. He's fine. Now listen. Her brother told her something about her parents, and she's determined to get to them."

"Oh, man!" Zeke said.

"She say something to you, Z?" Buck said.

"Nah, but I shoulda seen it comin'. I just finished her stuff this morning. Cut her hair, all that. Her papers are the best I've ever done. Made a guy out of her, you know. I mean, not really, just made her look—well, you know."

Buck knew all right. Ming was tiny to begin with. She was anything but boyish, but Zeke had cut her hair, showed her how to carry herself as a man, clipped her nails, removed the color from her face. From his stash of clothes and alterations on her old GC uniform, he had turned her into a young, male GC Peacekeeper.

"What name?" Buck said.

"Her brother's," Z said. "Chang. Last name Chow. I didn't know she was gonna be out of here as soon as I got her ready."

"Not your fault. How long has she been gone? Maybe we can catch her."

"Buck!" Leah said. "She's an adult, a widow. If she wants to go to China, you can't stop her."

Buck shook his head. "How long do you think we're safe here with everybody running around the streets whenever they feel like it? Chang's already told us the palace is starting to suspect something. If Steve Plank heard about it in Colorado, it won't be long before somebody comes snooping around."

"She probably didn't tell you what she was doing because she knew you'd try to talk her out of it."

"I might have tried to help. Find her a ride, something."

"Yeah, like you were going to arrange for a plane and a pilot."

Buck shot a double take at Leah's sarcasm. His father-in-law had groused that she was capable of it, but Buck hadn't been the brunt of it before. "This isn't helpful, Leah," he said.

"Helpful would have been to send Albie with her."

"I didn't know she was going!"

"Well, now you do."

"And I'm willing," Albie said. "But—"

"We can't spare you," Buck said. "Anyway, your cover's blown, and we don't have a new one for you yet."

"I can take care of that inside twenty-four hours," Zeke said.

"No! Let's just hope she checks in and keeps us posted." Buck kicked a chair. "How in the world is she going to sound like a guy? She's got that soft, delicate voice."

"Not when she was barking orders at the prison," Leah said.

"She'd better bark all the way to China, then," Buck said. "Imagine if she gets found out. They discover she's AWOL from Buffer, connect her with her brother, and bingo, he's history. And where does that leave us?"

+ + +

Chloe hadn't known what to expect, but it wasn't that Ptolemaïs would look like it had been through a war. For so long, the GC had largely left Greece alone. Its being part of the United Carpathian States contributed, she was sure. Nicolae would not have wanted the publicity that came with exposing Judah-ites in his own region. But the network of believers had so flourished that eventually it was too big to hide. Once the first wave of strong-arm tactics swept through and resulted in many facing the guillotine rather than accepting Carpathia's mark of loyalty, the battle between the GC and the Christ-following underground escalated. The administration of the mark of loyalty had begun with prisoners and had not gone well. The leadership had been infiltrated. Two young prisoners had escaped. And once the worst of the guillotining task was over, things got sloppier.

One of the strongest branches of the International Commodity Co-op, Chloe's own brainchild, was headquartered in town. It had become the clandestine meeting place for believers. But the ambush had cost the church there not only Lukas "Laslos" Miklos, but also one of its most beloved senior members, Kronos, as well as the teenager Marcel Papadopoulos. And if the girl who claimed to be Georgiana Stavros was indeed an impostor named Elena, as Steve Plank had heard, then for all Chloe knew Georgiana was dead too.

Few people were on the street in the light of day, and many of them were GC. They saluted politely the Indian and the westerner in high-level officers' garb and smart white caps piped in blue braid. Albie had taught Hannah and Chloe a proper salute, which they soon realized was crisper and more dead-on than most of the real GC used. Indifference was their mask. No eye contact, no talking to each other loudly enough for anyone else to hear. A serious look, close to a scowl, made them look all business. They had places to go and people to see, and their demeanor discouraged cordiality and small talk.

From the GC Palace complex in New Babylon, Chang Wong, through carefully placed confidential memos from pseudo high-ranking palace Peacekeepers, had sparked a rumor in Greece that the brass were sending a top guy to start cleaning up the mess there.

Chloe believed that GC forces who looked at Hannah and her twice were not just lonely men. She assumed they assessed the uniforms and put two and two together. Some had to assume these two were with the new guy, whoever and wherever he was.

Hannah had affected the perfect walk, and Chloe—had she not been so on edge—would have been amused at "Indira." They hurried to a dingy storefront, where a cracked window had been crudely taped. A dusty TV sat on a shelf and pointed to the street, and a half-dozen or so GC knelt or squatted in front of the window watching it. One noticed Chloe's and Hannah's reflections in the window and cleared his throat. The others quickly stood and saluted.

"Just make way, gentlemen," Hannah said, again with her practiced accent.

It was all Chloe could do to compose herself when first she saw Petra burning, and eventually whatever it was that had caused GCNN to pull the plug on the coverage. The milling GC leaned forward and stared at the TV, then at each other. "What was that?" one said. "Survivors?"

Others laughed and punched him. "You're crazy, man."

"Back to work, gentlemen," Hannah said.

"Yes, sir, ma'am," one said, and the others laughed.

"You know the difference between a male and a female officer, son?" Chloe snapped.

"Yes, ma'am," he said, straightening.

"You think that was funny?"

"No, ma'am. I apologize."

"Where's the nearest pub?"

"Ma'am?"

"Hard of hearing, boy?"

"No, ma'am. Three blocks up and two over." He pointed.

"You on duty, Peacekeeper?"

"Yes, ma'am."

"Where are you supposed to be?"

"Squadron headquarters, ma'am."

"Carry on."

The women had left their phones off, having agreed with Mac that they would not use them until after their first contact with the underground or in case of an emergency. Chloe knew her father and her husband would be trying to reach her after what she had seen on TV, but that would have to wait.

A few minutes later a young man in a chair in front of the pub—Chloe guessed him in his early twenties—glanced at them from behind his *Global Community Weekly*. Chloe wondered if the young man would believe her husband used to publish that very magazine. The boy appeared to casually shift position, pulling a corduroy cap lower over his eyes and resting his foot against a window at sidewalk level.

"Did you see what I saw?" Hannah said under her breath.

"Yep. Stick with the plan."

The women treated the lookout as if he were invisible and entered the pub. The shades were pulled, and it took a minute to adjust to the darkness. The place carried the stench of stale alcohol and an indifference to plumbing.

A couple of GC at a table in the corner immediately slipped out a back door on the street side. Chloe and Hannah pretended not to notice. The proprietor greeted them apologetically in Greek.

"English?" Chloe suggested.

He shook his head.

A nearby man in a turban rose and said something quickly to Hannah in an Indian dialect. Chloe was stunned at how Hannah covered. She looked the man knowingly in the eye and winked at him, shaking her head slightly. This somehow satisfied him, and he sat.

The proprietor swept a hand toward a row of liquor bottles behind him. Chloe shook her head. "Coca-Cola?" she said.

"Coca-Cola!" he said, smiling, and reached below the counter. Instinctively, Chloe rested her elbow on the handle of the Luger at her side, and she noticed

Hannah casually place her hand on the leather strap snapped over the grip of her nine-millimeter Glock.

The man behind the counter kept his eyes on them even when reaching, and now he smiled, bringing into view one ancient glass bottle of Coke. He held up one finger, pointing at the bottle and pushing two glasses across the counter. Chloe lay two Nicks in front of him and carried the stuff to a table.

After a sip, the lukewarm liquid biting at her dry throat, Chloe turned in her chair and quickly surveyed the room. People who had been gawking turned away. "English?" she said. "Anyone?"

A chair scraped and a heavyset man wearing several layers of clothing, his face moist from perspiration, approached with shy, small steps. He saluted politely, though he was clearly not GC. "Leedle Englees," he said.

"You speak English?" Chloe said. "You understand me?"

He made a tiny space between his thumb and index finger.

"A little?" she said.

He nodded. "Leedle."

"Downstairs," Chloe tried. "Where's downstairs?"

The man furrowed his brow, wrinkling the small *216* tattooed on his forehead. "Dounce?" he said.

She pointed down. "Downstairs. Basement. Cellar?"

He held up a meaty hand and shook his head. "Clean," he said. "Wash. Launder."

"A laundry?" she said, and felt Hannah's gaze. This was it.

He nodded.

"Thank you," she said.

"Tank ye," he said, but stood there, thick fingers entwined. Chloe dug half a Nick from her pocket and held it out to him. He took it with a bow and headed for the bar.

"Wonder what they know?" Hannah said quietly. "Rest of the place seems to be waiting for us to make a move."

"Uh-huh," Chloe said. "Let's just sit awhile, then mosey out. The laundry is a front, but people must actually take clothes there."

Hannah shrugged. "Do they have to come through here to get there? I have to think few believers would risk frequenting this place."

The women sipped their Cokes and glanced at their watches. No one but the two GC had left since they arrived, and no one had entered either. The young man from the chair walked lazily back and forth in front of the door twice. At least two passersby saw the women in uniform and apparently chose not to enter.

Chloe and Hannah stood and wandered out, looking for another entrance that could lead downstairs. "English?" Chloe asked the young man out front. He shrugged, staring at her. "Is there another entrance to this place?"

He shook his head.

"Not around back? Not through the alley?"

He shook his head again.

"I heard there was a laundry here," she said. "I need some cleaning done."

He stared at her. "I see no laundry." His accent was Greek.

"We don't carry it around," she said. "How do I get downstairs to the laundry?"

"Past the toilet," he said, his voice husky. "Back door, this side." He nodded toward the exit the GC had used. He tilted his chair back until it bumped the wall. "But they're closed."

"In the middle of the day? Why?"

He shrugged, pulling his cap lower and turning back to his magazine.

"Oh, well," Chloe said, sighing. Hannah followed her to the corner and out of sight. "I give him thirty seconds," she said.

After a beat, Hannah peeked around the corner. "You're right, as usual," she said. "Gone."

The women hurried back to the pub, went in the back door, past the washroom, and down rickety wood steps. A thin, middle-aged woman wearing a bulky gray sweater and a bandanna that covered her hair and much of her face stood terrified in the light from the window.

"Laundry?" Chloe said.

The woman nodded, a fist pressed under her neck.

"We can bring laundry here?"

She nodded again. Through the edge of a thick curtain hanging in a doorway behind the woman, Chloe spotted the young man. His eyes were wide. She pointed at him and beckoned with a finger.

"No!" the woman said desperately, backing against the wall.

The young man ventured out, a weapon showing under his shirt.

"Uzi?" Chloe said.

"Yes, and I'll use it," he said.

"Take off your cap," Chloe said.

"I'll shoot you dead first," he said, reaching for his weapon.

The woman moaned. "Costas, no."

As he brought the ugly weapon into view, Chloe and Hannah reached not for their guns but for their caps. Revealing their foreheads, they whispered in unison, "Jesus is risen."

The boy closed his eyes and exhaled loudly. The woman slid down the wall to the floor. "He is risen indeed," she managed.

"I almost killed you," Costas said. He turned to the woman. "Are you all right, Mama?"

His mother had buried her face in her hands. "You come disguised as GC?" she said, her English labored. "What are you doing here?"

"I am Chloe Williams. This is my friend, Han—"

"You are not!" the woman said, wiping her face and struggling to her feet. She rushed to Chloe and embraced her fiercely. "I am Pappas. I go by Mrs. P."

"This is my friend Hannah Palemoon."

"You are in the Co-op too?" Mrs. P. said.

Hannah shook her head.

"You are from India?"

"No. America."

"You disguised in disguise?"

Hannah smiled and nodded and looked to Costas. "Are we safe?"

"We should move," he said, leading them through the curtain to a huge concrete-walled storeroom full of supplies from all over the world. "The Co-op works as well here as anywhere," he said. "But we are suffering. Only a few of us are left."

"The people upstairs don't bother you?"

"We give them things. They ask no questions. They have their own secrets. Someday, when it serves them, they will turn us in."

"Head of the Co-op in my place," Mrs. P. whispered, her hand over her heart. "No one will ever believe."

"You can't stay long," Costas said. "How can we help you?"

+ + +

Two young GC Peacekeepers flashed an obscene gesture at Mac as they flew past in a small van; then Mac noticed the look on one's face when the uniform must have registered in his mind. The vehicle skidded off the asphalt and threw gravel as it backed toward him. "We waved!" the passenger hollered as the van stopped. He jumped out. "We waved at you, sir! Did you see us?"

"I did, and I thank you very much." The driver tumbled out as well, and Mac returned their salutes. "My support staff had an errand headin' the other way, and I have business at the airport."

"We can drop you. Do you need us to drop you? We'll drop you."

"I appreciate it," Mac said, as he shoved his bags ahead of him and climbed in back. "What's goin' on in Petra?"

"We got 'em, sir," the driver said, turning up the radio. Mac rested his forehead in his hand as if trying to listen carefully. He prayed desperately for his comrades. "Smoked 'em all. There'll be nothing left to bury."

"Let me hear it, boys," Mac said, and the two fell silent. Just before the connection was lost, Mac heard enough from the pilot to encourage him. "Well, that is good news, isn't it?" he said.

The passenger turned. "Sure enough. I don't know what to make of that last bit, but we got 'em; we sure did."

At the airport Mac could hardly believe the disarray. What was left of the GC force there looked undisciplined and lackadaisical. That could work only to his advantage. "I need wheels," he told the only Peacekeeper who rose and saluted him in the main hangar. "I need the key to those wheels, I want to store my stuff, and I want to see a Rooster Tail, if it's here."

"Oh, it's here, sir, and we've been expecting you. I'll take your stuff."

"Did I say I wanted you to take my stuff?"

"No, sir, you plain as day said you wanted to store it yourself." He ran to a desk where he dug keys out of a huge cardboard box. "The Rooster Tail's in Hangar 6. The car's the first one on the end. I can bring it to you."

"You do that."

"Oh, almost forgot. I've got to put your code into the computer and—"

"Not before you bring the car, you don't."

"Well, that's true enough." And he ran off.

Mac was aware of others staring at him, sitting straighter, looking busy. But nothing seemed to be going on, no planes coming or going.

"Gonna get us some help here, Commander?" someone called from across the room.

Mac glared at him. "Excuse me, officer?"

"I said, are you—"

"I heard what you said! Now get your seat out of that chair and address me properly!"

The man rose quickly and caught his foot on a wheel of the chair, stumbling before he righted himself and approached. Mac leveled his eyes at him. The man stopped and saluted. Mac ignored it. "You make it a practice to holler at your senior officers across the room?"

"I wasn't thinking, sir."

"You had a question."

"Just wondering if we were going to get some support here, sir. You see how shorthanded we are."

Mac looked from one side of the hangar to the other and out onto the runway. "You're overstaffed and underworked, and you know it."

"Yes, sir."

"Am I wrong?"

"No, sir. It's just that, well, we used to—"

"As you were."

The man saluted again and backed away. The younger officer skidded Mac's car to a stop in front of the hangar and opened the trunk. "You want some assistance with that high-speed Transatlantic, sir?"

"I need nothing but a toolbox and to be left to it. What'd you people find in it?"

"Nothing, sir."

"You're not serious."

"We were instructed to leave it for the brass. That would be you, I guess."

Mac pressed his lips together. Was there nothing Chang Wong could not accomplish with a few keystrokes? "Give me a toolbox and tell me who's handling the Judah-ite roundup."

"Sir?"

Mac cocked his head and squinted at the kid. "You tellin' me we had one of the most successful busts of the underground right under you people's noses out here, and nobody knows a thing about it?"

"Oh, that, no. Yeah, we knew. We know. I just, I mean, what are you asking?"

"Who's handling it? They took an operative alive and I want to see him. I'm under orders to see him."

"Well, I wouldn't know where they were holding him, sir. I mean, I—"

"I didn't expect you to know where they're holding him! Did I ask you that?"

"No, sir. Sorry."

"I expect whoever's handling the operation for us locally will know that. You follow?"

"Of course."

"So who is?"

"Guy with a funny name, sir. You'd have to check at headquarters in Ptolemaïs."

"Happens to be Nelson Stefanich. You in touch with him?"

"Yes, sir."

"Can you make sure he's expectin' me?"

"Yes, sir."

"Tell 'im I expect all the cooperation and information I need as soon as I get there."

"Yes, sir. Now could I get you to give me your six-digit security code for the—"

"Zero-nine-one-zero-zero-one," Mac rattled off, then took the toolbox and drove to the hangar where George Sebastian's plane had been quarantined. He knew where George hid his arsenal, and within seconds he had removed panels in the cargo hold and lifted a directed energy weapon and a fifty-caliber rifle with bipod into the trunk of the car. He could tell from the safety tab George had positioned on the cargo door that the GC had searched the hold. Clearly, they had not discovered the secret panels.

Mac rushed back to the main hangar. "Clean as a whistle," he told the young man, handing the toolbox out the window. "Ptolemaïs know I'm comin'?"

"Expecting you, sir."

+ + +

George Sebastian pretended to still be asleep. For the last several minutes he had been awake, hearing urgent staticky messages coming to his captors and their earnest, desperate replies, so quiet he could not make out the details.

He lay on his right side, his huge frame pressing into the packed dirt floor. He was cold, stiff, and ravenous. His right arm was asleep from the elbow to the tips of his fingers. He was handcuffed behind his back. George's head and face throbbed, and he tasted blood.

He heard soft snoring behind him. Oh, if only his hands were free. He would position himself to get blood flowing into that right arm again, would move silently into position. And if the sleeping guard was the only one with him, he could pounce, disarm the man, and silence him in a second. George turned painfully, his whole body aching and desperate for food and water. He rubbed his cheek against the soil enough to push the blindfold away from his eye—just enough to get a peek. Sure enough, the guard sat there asleep, one arm dangling, his high-powered weapon in his lap. Strange. Maybe he was wrong, but George thought he had figured out the hierarchy of this crew. The big man, who tried to cover a French accent, was not the leader. He talked a lot, but it was the other one—the Greek man George had not injured—who seemed to hold the cards. Yet, unless he was unusually cunning and was trying to fake George into trying something, he was the one who now slept just a few feet from his prisoner.

George's right arm tingled, but with his left hand he maneuvered enough to feel the handcuffs. Tight and strong. He had broken out of conventional cuffs before, but not ones applied this securely. He heard the door open at the top of the stairs, and the young woman—he'd heard them call her Elena, though she had originally posed as Georgiana—said, "I say give him one last chance, then do what we have to do."

The big man, George's double, clomped down the stairs with his handgun out. Elena followed, unarmed, but called back up the stairs, "Come now, Socrates!"

They've got a dog?

Elena's yell woke the leader, and he stood, clearing his throat and wiping his eyes.

"Anything?" the big man asked him.

"Nah. Hasn't moved."

"Still alive, isn't he?"

"Breathing."

The big man spoke into the ear of the just roused one.

"Really?" the smaller man said. "What time?"

"Nobody knows yet, but today or tonight."

The leader swore.

George hoped the moved blindfold didn't show. The big man put a heavy boot on his left shoulder and rolled him roughly onto his back. "Wake up, big boy," he said, and the leader added, "Last chance."

George wanted to say, "For what? Uncuff me and take this blindfold off, you coward, and I'll kill you unarmed." But he was determined to remain silent. No satisfaction for these amateurs.

Heavy, awkward steps resounded from upstairs, and the guard with the injured knee slowly made his way down. The big man handed his sidearm to Elena and straddled George. He dug his hands under George's arms, bent his knees, and lifted, grunting as he propped George up against the far wall. George let his chin drop to his chest.

"All right," the leader said, "Plato, over there, and Socrates, over here." George thought he was hearing things. He had been one of the few scholarship football players at San Diego State who'd read Greek history, but his mediocre performance on the exams had nudged him toward the military. His mind had to be playing tricks on him. So it was Plato and Socrates who stood six feet from him on each side, their weapons trained on his head? It was the hunger, he decided.

"He tries anything, kill him, but be careful of me."

The leader—George could only imagine his name—knelt in front of him and yanked off the blindfold. George blinked and squinted but kept staring at the floor. Now the man pressed the barrel of his handgun into George's forehead and lifted his face. "Look into my eyes and see how serious I am." George was tempted to spit at him.

"You have been brave, a model prisoner of war. But you have lost. You are down to your last chance. I am willing to waste no more time or energy on you. The only way for you to leave here and see your wife and child again is to tell us what we need to know. Otherwise, I will kill you with a point-blank round through your brain. You have ten seconds to tell me where the Judah-ite safe house is."

George could think of no reason to disbelieve the man. He was weak, wasted, at the end of himself, but he had succeeded. He had given away nothing, and he would not now. No way he would be allowed to go free even if he gave up Chicago. There was one option, but he didn't trust himself to choose it. He could make up a story—a long, rambling, nuance-filled tale anyone might believe. It could include a poisonous gas in the cockpit of his plane that would be triggered by someone trying to fly it who didn't first enter the proper code into the security system.

That might keep the GC from absconding with the Rooster Tail. It might even leave it available for the Trib Force if anyone came to try to spring him. But he was sure Captain Steele and the rest assumed him dead by now, and why not? And if he tried fashioning a story to delay his execution, in his present state he wouldn't be able to keep it straight—and he couldn't risk letting something slip that might be true.

George let his forehead rest on the muzzle of the gun and kept his mouth shut. He did not want to flinch, to grimace, to shudder. He merely clenched his teeth in anticipation of the shot that would deliver him to heaven.

3

"WE WERE WITH the group that had the leaders," Costas Pappas explained. "The pastor and his wife. The Mikloses. Old man Kronos. His cousin is still with us. You know who all these people are?"

"We know everything," Chloe said. "But how can you know so much and still survive?"

"Marcel told us the plan the night it happened," Mrs. Pappas said. "The girl was supposed to have been seen by people in the underground who knew her, but it was just a rumor. Everything seemed to add up. Help from the Tribulation Force, a military man, an operative from America, on his way back from the operation in Israel."

"But how did you learn what had happened? What did you do when Mr. Miklos and Mr. Kronos did not check back in?"

"We went looking," Costas said, his lips quivering. Chloe had thought him a bumbling lookout, then an angry young man. But he had to be brave, she decided, to live as he did. This softness touched her. "We knew the plan. We never found the stones at the side of the road. They had either been run over or brushed away. But those animals left that car right where it stopped, not far from there, in plain sight."

"But surely they were watching it," Hannah said, "lying in wait for you."

"We were sure of that," the boy said. "We drove past quickly, trying to appear as if we were not even looking. But we know K's car. It was just a few meters off the road—the lights gone dim, the engine off, a door open. We were desperate to search it, to find out what happened, but we didn't want to be stupid."

"And so . . . ?"

"We waited. We had to. There was no way to know when they would tire of waiting for someone to come, but after a few days, we could not stand not knowing anymore. Kronos's cousin lent us a four-wheel-drive truck, and from topography maps we plotted a way to get to the car from the fields rather than the road. We did it after midnight, slowly making our way from tiny trails through thick woods to the open, rocky plain. Cousin Kronos drove, and two others and I walked ahead in dark clothes to be sure no one saw or heard. It had to be three in the morning before we had brought the truck as close as we dared. We could not see Kronos's car yet, but we knew where it was. When we crawled over a rise where we thought it would come into view, we saw nothing.

"There is no longer money for streetlights, and the battery in the car had long since died. There was no moon and we didn't dare use our flashlights, so nothing illuminated the car. If the GC were waiting to ambush us, they would not have thought of our coming the hard way, especially that far. We were almost upon the car when we finally saw it in the darkness. We listened and watched and even fanned out to see if we could hear any GC. Then we felt in the car and found the bodies. Maybe we were foolish, but we dared shine our lights, just seconds at a time, our bodies hiding most of the light."

Costas quivered at the memory and broke down. He struggled to be understood. "All three of them," he managed. "Shot. Marcel in the face. Back of his head gone. We had to work to pull him from under the dashboard. K took one in the neck from behind. Probably cut his spinal cord. Laslos in the forehead."

"No sign of the American?"

Costas shook his head. "We dragged the bodies, one by one, all the way back to the truck. They stank and were stiff. It was awful. My friend, who was studying criminology before all of this, determined that whoever shot them was probably in the car with them. We also found Marcel's bag, one we had given him. It was under Laslos's body, covered with his blood. It still had a change of clothes and food in it. We do not know what happened to the American."

Chloe told him and his mother what Steve Plank had reported, that the GC boasted the successful thwart of an escape attempt. "There was an impostor for the girl and for our man. Something went wrong and all this resulted."

"The American is alive?" Mrs. P. said.

Chloe nodded. "Being held somewhere. They're probably trying to break him for information, but he's well trained. We're more worried he will get himself killed for not cooperating."

"You must think the GC is stupid," Costas said.

"Sorry?" Chloe said.

"You come here disguised as GC and you think they will just take you to him."

"It's risky, we know."

"It's suicide," Costas said.

"What would you do, son?" Chloe said, realizing that if Costas was younger than she, it wasn't by much.

He shrugged. "The same, I suppose, but I can't imagine it working."

"We have a man inside the palace in New Babylon, or we wouldn't dream of trying this," Chloe said. She began to outline the preparations and Mac's plans.

"Ah, excuse me," Hannah said. "A minute, please?"

Chloe glanced at her, then followed Hannah to a corner.

"Chloe, do they need to know this?"

"We can trust them! They're Co-op."

"But what if they are caught and forced to talk? Don't burden them with all this."

"Think of what they've been through, Hannah. They'll never cave."

"Well, if they do, it's more than just your funeral, you know."

They returned to Mrs. Pappas and her son.

"This works?" Costas said. "The GC falls for this?"

"Not for long," Chloe admitted, sneaking a peek at Hannah. "But with the right setup on the main database in New Babylon, we have bluffed ourselves into some remarkable places."

"We just met you," Mrs. Pappas said. "And we will bury you soon."

"We are people of faith," Hannah said, dropping her accent. "And we know you are too. We must also be people of action. We know the odds and we accept them. We don't know what else to do. Would you leave a comrade to a certain death?"

Costas was still emotional. He shrugged. "I don't know. I don't see that you have a choice, but you have a better chance going in with artillery than with disguises. I just can't see it working."

"But we don't know where our man is!" Chloe said. "How do we find that out without infiltrating?"

"What about your man in Colorado? He seems to know so much."

"He can tell us only what he overhears. If he asks for more details than seem appropriate, he'll soon be found out too."

"How does he get along in the GC without the mark?"

Chloe explained Steve's new identity and facial reconstruction, aware of Hannah's loud sigh and slight shaking of her head. "His forehead is plastic. The mark of loyalty would have to be applied under that, and no one can stand looking at him with his skull exposed."

"Please," Hannah said under her breath.

"I want to come with you when you go for your man," Costas said.

"Can't allow it," Chloe said. "We have our papers, our uniforms, and we're covered, for now, on the computer. It would take days to do the same for you."

"I could get a GC uniform, and you could cover for me. I—"

"No," Chloe said. "We appreciate it, but it's not going to happen. We have a plan, and we will follow it, succeed or fail."

"You need more firepower?"

"We do. It would have looked suspicious, bringing in heavy weapons that are not GC issue. Mr. McCullum is trying to get something, either from our man's plane or his car."

"Where is the car?"

"According to Plank, Sebastian's captors also have his car, which he talked his way into at the airport."

"And they wouldn't have searched it for weapons?"

"We don't know and we haven't heard."

Costas motioned the women to follow him to a corner where a large wood trunk was buried under piles of blankets. It was full of Uzis. "Don't ask," he said. His mother provided a large laundry bag into which Costas placed three cloth-wrapped weapons and several clips of ammunition. "Now, you'd better go."

\+ + +

George Sebastian had been told that you never hear the shot that kills you, but how could that ever be proved? He fought to remain composed, not wanting to give his captors the satisfaction of even tensing before the death blast. He held his breath way past what he believed were his final ten seconds, and then could not contain a shiver as he exhaled.

"All right," the leader said, "get him presentable, and fast. Food and water first, then the shower. And do something about this lip. Think of a story for that. We didn't do it."

George opened his eyes and blinked.

"You're still in trouble, California, but none of us is getting fried because of you. I'm taking the cuffs off, but you've got two weapons aimed at you, and all we need is a reason."

When his hands were free, George rubbed them together, making Plato flinch. George was tempted to scare him with a feigned swing or even a shout.

"Do something about his wrists," the leader told Elena. "Let's go, we've got to move."

They shoved George up the stairs and gave him two sandwiches stuffed with what tasted like summer sausage. The bread slices were nearly two inches thick and dry. He had to press them hard together over the meat to fit them into his mouth. His split lip stretched and bled as he chewed. He sucked eagerly from a bottle of warm, stale water.

George wanted to sit back and take a few deep breaths, but this was clearly not supposed to be a leisurely lunch. He gagged and coughed, but he made sure to force down all the food. His best chance to escape or do some damage would be when he was unbound and they were moving him. He didn't want to invest the mental energy guessing what it was all about, but he felt relieved to be alive and to have accomplished his one objective so far—silence.

When he finished, George quickly scooped bread crumbs from the table and pushed them into his mouth. He chased them with the last few drops of water, tipping the bottle all the way up. Elena snatched it from him and pointed toward a tiny room where he would just barely fit into a shower.

"Clothes there," she said, pointing to the floor. "You probably can't fit through the window anyway, but someone will be outside and armed."

She left and shut the door, and though he knew she and probably the others could hear what he was doing, he looked under a cot and found only dust. He yanked open three drawers of a spindly wooden dresser. Empty. There was nothing else in the room except a window he guessed faced west. He pulled back a paperlike shade, and Socrates leveled his weapon at him.

"Get going!" Elena called from outside the door.

He shed his clothes and edged into the shower. He turned on the left faucet first and was blasted with icy water. He stepped back out and reached in, trying the other. Also cold. He turned both on and let them run a minute. He tried angling the showerhead away from him, but it was rusted into place.

"The tap water is not drinkable!" he heard from outside. He wanted to ask if there was soap or a towel, but he would not speak. Gritting his teeth, George forced himself under the spray. His body jerked and shook, but he let the frigid water flood him from his short hair to his whole body. He vigorously rubbed everywhere for as long as he could stand it, and just as he was turning off the water, he heard the room door shut. He peeked out. Where his clothes had been lay a pile of clean stuff, clearly belonging to Plato, his supposed look-alike. *Great. He doesn't appear nearly as tall.*

A single hand towel lay on the bed. George made it work and threw on the clothes. A nondescript undershirt protected him from a prickly brown sweater. Military-issue underwear was tight. Gray wool socks started to warm him, and khaki pants with a canvas belt were tight around the middle and rode three inches above his ankles. The GC-issue boots were snug but okay.

George pushed the door open, and Elena motioned that he should follow her back to the table where he had eaten. Plato stood watching, weapon in hand, but George wondered how valued the girl was. He could have had her in a headlock before the others noticed, and he could have killed her before they fired.

She awkwardly dabbed at his lip with ointment and massaged his hands and wrists. He studied her face for any sign of weakness. The blood he had seen on her when he thought she was his underground contact was obviously not her own. She was a killer.

Elena pressed a bulge over his eyebrow that smarted, but George would not recoil. If he couldn't stand a little pain, how would he fight his way out of this? It seemed incongruous that she could find ice in that place, but she wrapped some in a cloth and held it against his swollen forehead. She did the same to a knot on the back of his head. Why couldn't she have spared a cube or two for his drinking water?

The food, whatever it was, lay heavy and troubling in his stomach, but he also felt a surge of energy from it. Part of him wanted to do some damage, to show these yokels what an American captive was capable of. Oh, he could do more than clam up. He had already broken one guard's knee, if he had to guess. And all during her administering to his wounds, George had sat close enough to Elena to have blinded her with a two-fingered shot to the eyes, broken her jaw with a punch to the chin, or crushed her to death by flipping the table onto her and dropping his whole body atop it.

Little would have been gained, of course, as he would have been shot. He fantasized about ignoring her and charging Plato, disarming him, butting him with the weapon, shooting Elena, and taking his chances with the two camped outside. That had better odds, but still not good ones.

They were making him presentable and moving him. Why? Someone above them must have wanted to try eliciting information. And they wanted to be sure he was being treated right. George was apparently as close as they had come to anyone connected with the Judah-ites, and that was why he was still alive.

He relished the idea of performing for GC brass. His silence would infuriate them. Better, from his perspective—the higher up you went, the less prepared they were for creative escape attempts. At some point these people would realize he was not going to help them. There would be no information volunteered or beat from him. Finally, at long last, he would be expendable. They would either use him as an object lesson, claiming he *had* ratted out the enemy, or they would execute him. Or both.

George's goal formed slowly in his mind. He wanted to stay alert, to be aware of every nuance. He wanted to know when the GC finally lost patience and realized he was a hopeless, lost cause. Because when they had finally had enough and his end had come, he wanted to be sure to take one or two with him into eternity. He knew from their marks they wouldn't be going where he was. But they'd get to their destination sooner than they thought.

George had to fight a smile as they led him to a Jeep. He was cuffed again, but not until after he had been fitted with a large pair of gloves. *How thoughtful,* he decided. *Protect my tender wrists.*

+ + +

By the time Mac rendezvoused with Chloe and Hannah at a clearing in the woods north of Ptolemaïs, all had been in touch with the rest of the Trib Force. "I can't wait to see how New Babylon spins Petra," Hannah said. "How can anyone remain an unbeliever now?"

"Who knows when Daddy and Abdullah will be able to leave?" Chloe said. "For all we know, Tsion will want to stay there, if they have the technology to let him continue cyberteaching around the world. I have to think the GC will kill anybody who leaves."

Mac told Chloe and Hannah that squadron headquarters in Ptolemaïs was expecting him, but that he wanted to downplay everything.

"How so?" Chloe said. "Sounds like your way has been paved."

"Yeah, but if I go in there, buttons shining, it's like I'm on display, tryin' to impress. I could give off the smell of a rat without even trying. Plus, if that headquarters is anything like the rest of this place, I'm gonna look suspicious if I don't start rippin' on anybody who's supposed to be in charge."

"Tell us about it," Hannah said. "I hated working at the palace, but the organization and decorum made this place look sick."

"If I was really a senior commander, I'd be pushin' paper to New Babylon for a week about this place. I had hoped to just rush in there, get what I needed, and get going. I wasn't even going to ask 'em for any support, 'cause I oughtn't need it. Now I'm of a mind not to even show up."

"What?"

"Myself, I mean."

"Us, then?"

"One of you."

"I'll go," Hannah said.

"Now, wait a minute," Chloe said. "I—"

"Frankly, I'm leaning toward Chloe myself, Hannah. I don't expect any suspicion, but if worse came to worst and they checked your iris or your handprint, you know you're on file in the palace."

"As a dead woman."

"Well, yeah, but then how would you explain an Indian lady havin' the exact ID marks of a dead Native American?"

"As long as it's not that you don't think I can pull it off."

"You kiddin'? Half the time I look at you and forget who you are. But Chang has entered Chloe's readings under her new name, so even if they got feisty and made a member of my executive staff prove her identity, she'd sail through."

"What do you want me to do, Mac?" Chloe said.

"I want you to be bored."

"Bored?"

"And irritated. You got grunt duty. While the fat-cat boss you came with and his other personnel are takin' a nap at a nice place—where is none of anybody's business—you got assigned to go get the info he needs. Any red tape, any holdup at all, and you're ticked off. Can you work that up?"

"What do you think?"

"Your approach is that this is bottom-end stuff—just give me the info and let me be on my way. Make sure the hostage takers know we're comin' so they don't get spooked, but they'd better have their man ready. The boss is none too pleased that they haven't gleaned anything from him yet, so make way for somebody who knows what he's doing."

"Gotcha."

"That flyboy friend of Abdullah's believes if everything goes well, we can take Sebastian—in cuffs, of course—right back to his own plane and fly out of here tonight."

"Does local have any idea you're planning to take the prisoner?"

"No, and by the time they find out, we oughta be out of here."

"Not going to be easy," Hannah said. "Even if they buy everything up to where we visit him."

"It never is, Indira," Mac said, smiling. "The key, though, is not trying to convince them of anything. You sting somebody by getting them to come your way. Follow?"

"Not sure."

"For instance, if I hinted to you that Rayford or Tsion wanted you to do something you didn't want to do, like head straight back to Chicago right now, your first reaction would be negative. You wouldn't want to do it, you'd refuse, and I'd say, okay then, I can't tell you the rest of it. You'd say what's that, and I'd say, no, you made your decision, so you don't need to know. Now I don't know for sure about you, but if I was in your shoes, I'd be all over me trying to find out what the whole story was and whether I made the right decision."

"You bet I would, and I'd wear you down too. You know I would."

"You probably would. But see, you'd be comin' my way then. It wouldn't be me trying to convince you of something. It would be you trying to drag it out of me. I tell you whatever I need to, to get you to do what I wanted in the first place, and you don't realize until later, when you realize I manipulated you, that you were stung and it seemed like your idea."

"Other words," Hannah said, "you're going to somehow make these people beg you to take Sebastian off their hands."

"You got it."

"And they're going to think you're doing them a favor."

"Exactly."

"This I've got to see."

"You will."

"And where am I while Chloe's doing her thing at headquarters?"

"Waiting in the Jeep, eyes and ears open. The impression is, yeah, there are two of you, but it takes only one to pick up directions for the boss."

"And where will you be?" Chloe said.

"On the phone to Chang and then to the kid at the airport. I want that Rooster Tail gassed up and ready to go."

"You going to tell him we'll have a prisoner with us?"

"I'll play that by ear. If we don't find a weapon in George's car, I've got one for him and one for me anyway. You've got your sidearms."

"Think we'll need them?"

"At least for show. There's nothing suspicious about a superior officer bringing armed staff with him on a visit like this."

+ + +

Chang hurried as casually as he could to his quarters during his afternoon break and flew across his keyboard, trying to track his sister. She was better at this than he expected. He wished only that she had let him in on it so he could have helped pave the way. Maybe if she arrived somewhere and discovered he had precleared her for transport on assignment, she would know he was watching.

Peacekeeper Chow was already in the system. Apparently "he" had gotten out of Chicago and found himself a ride to Long Grove, Illinois. Chang was glad his sister had avoided Kankakee and the old Glenview Naval Air Station. Though short-staffed like everywhere else, they had been burned by Judah-ites for the last time and were impossible to hoodwink. But Chang had never before seen anything on his system that mentioned even an airstrip in Long Grove.

He finally found an executive runway that had recently been reopened for limited commercial routes. With his break time running out, Chang contacted the tower there as a high-ranking official in the GC aviation administration, "requesting routine confirmation of a Peacekeeper from international sector 30 catching a ride on a commercial cargo plane bound for Pawleys Island, South Carolina."

Chang couldn't wait for the response and hurried back to his desk. There it became clear that Suhail Akbar himself was interrogating the first pilot to return from Petra. Chang could only assume that the second was also bound for Suhail's private conference room. With a few keystrokes, he activated the bug in that office to record, and later he would download it from the central system.

\+ \+ \+

Chloe appreciated that Hannah seemed sensitive enough to leave her to her thoughts on the drive back in to Ptolemaïs. "You're okay with my doing this, right?"

"Makes perfect sense," Hannah said. "If I was going to get checked, this would be the place."

Chloe tried to slow her pulse by breathing deeply and trying to doze. It didn't work, but she knew her life depended on what Mac referred to as her ability to play bored. Irritated was all right, if it came to that. But bored would play truest.

Squadron headquarters was on the top three floors of a four-story building with an abandoned first floor that appeared to have been some sort of business.

One of the men Chloe and Hannah had encountered on the street sat in the dark near the elevator at ground level, smoking and reading by the sliver of light from the street. He stood when he saw her and saluted. "Elevator's broke, ma'am," he said. "You want the stairs there behind you."

"As you were. This your assignment?"

"Yes, ma'am. Somebody's got to tell people or they'd wait all day for that thing."

"No one thought of a sign?"

"Yeah, but the commanding officer wants the personal touch."

She nodded. "He's the one I'm here to see. Could you tell him that I'm—"

The young man held up both hands. "I have no way to tell him, ma'am. There's a receptionist up there."

"Thought you people were understaffed."

He shrugged. "Doing what I'm told, ma'am."

The stairs led to a dingy, tiled room with about half the fluorescent lights working. No one was at the receptionist's desk, but another Peacekeeper began to rise from the end of a tired couch. Chloe stopped him with a wave. "What's your role here, son?"

"GC Morale Monitor, ma'am. And telling people the receptionist is not here."

"I can see that."

"Well, telling them she will be right back."

"How soon is 'right back'?"

He looked at his watch. "Supposed to have been ten minutes ago, so should be any minute now."

"Couldn't you just as easily inform Commander Stefanich that Ms. Irene is here from Senior Commander Johnson's staff?"

"Well, I could, ma'am, but I was instructed to—"

"Just do it. I'll take the heat."

"Yes, ma'am. Ms. who from what?"

"Never mind, I'll find him," Chloe said, reaching for the door.

"Oh, I can't let you do that, ma'am. Now, please. I'm sorry I forgot your information."

"Is your hand on your gun, Monitor?" she said.

"No, ma'am, well, yes, ma'am, it is, but not on purpose. I—"

"Read my name badge, son, and get that memorized. Now all you have to know is *Senior Commander* Johnson."

"Got it. One moment."

Chloe shook her head. It was a wonder the GC accomplished anything. The door had barely shut when it opened again and the Morale Monitor gestured her in with a nod. He pointed to a glassed-in office in a corner of the floor where the commander sat at his desk, a female underling stationed outside. "I have to get through her too?" Chloe said.

"Yes, ma'am. That is the commander's secretary."

Most of the other desks were empty, and the lights here were intermittent too. It seemed all this commander had were enough people to keep him buffered. Chloe strode toward the older woman in uniform. The woman smiled expectantly, but Chloe swept past her. "Irene, Johnson's staff, to see Stefanich."

The woman had no time even to protest. Nelson Stefanich looked startled and began to rise.

"Hi, sorry, sir, but Senior Commander Johnson doesn't have time for me to work my way through all your layers. You have some information for him?"

"Of course, but—"

Chloe whipped out her leather bifold and produced her GC ID card. "What do you need?"

"Well, I'd like to visit with Commander Johnson." Stefanich sounded eastern European, she guessed Polish.

"He sends his regrets. The GC brass would like this handled with dispatch, and we understood you were prepared to—"

"Sit down, Ms. Irene, please."

"I really—"

"Please, I insist."

Chloe sat.

"I had hoped to bring your commander up to speed on the ones we chose for this assignment. We are very proud of their—"

"Excuse me, sir, but we understand zero information has been extracted from the rebel operative."

"That's just a matter of time. He is highly trained military, and we have been patient to this point."

"Might I suggest that if your assignees were at the level you say they are, Commander Johnson would not have had to come all this way?"

"Perhaps. But I am happy with what they have accomplished thus far and plan to recommend them for—"

"Do whatever you like, sir, but please send me back to my boss with what he needs to make contact."

Stefanich made a show of pulling a file from his desk drawer, but he did not hand it to Chloe. "Are you not aware of what happened today? This prisoner became immediately less valuable with the success of the attack."

"I understood the results of that are not conclusive. If they were, wouldn't it be broadcast internationally?"

"There were technical difficulties. You will learn that millions of traitors are dead, including their leadership."

"We still don't know where their headquarters are," Chloe said, "or how much of the leadership might be left."

"We have them narrowed to the Carpathian States. Even the rebel would not refute that."

"Sir, are you refusing a senior commander access to your prisoner?"

"No, I'm—"

"Because if you are, I will be the first to fall under his displeasure. But you will be next." She rose. "I'm already late, but showing up empty-handed, well, I don't mind telling you, that is going to fall on you."

"Here you are," he said, offering the file.

Chloe was moving toward the door. "You can put in for commendations for the locals you hired, but you won't be in a position to award them if—"

"Here, no, please," he said, smiling apologetically.

Chloe stopped and looked at him with suspicion. "A folder? I don't want a folder. All I need to give the commander are directions to the prisoner."

"That's what this is! Now, here!"

Chloe stood with her hand on the doorknob, shaking her head. "And your people expect us."

"Of course!"

She stood with her lips pressed together, squinting at Stefanich. She had come this far; she wasn't going to return to him. "Let's have it, then."

He sat reaching, offering the file. She stared him down. Finally he sighed and rose and approached her. Chloe snatched the folder and left.

4

CHANG SAT FIDGETING at his desk, pretending to work, unable to concentrate. He was supposed to be coordinating flights and convoys of equipment, food, and supplies from production plants to the neediest areas. He had devised a way to make it appear his instructions were logical and complete, even efficient. But the actual transmissions caused no end of delays. Because of a glitch he had introduced into the system, shipments were held for days at remote locations, then delivered to the wrong places. Often the wrong place for the GC meant the right place for the Co-op or the Trib Force.

Chang had received a commendation for his work, somehow covering his tracks and avoiding having the problems traced to him. Something was niggling at the back of his mind now, though. Something didn't make sense.

Ming had left a note informing the Chicago Tribulation Force that she was on her way to see her parents in China. If that was true, why would she go east? It only made sense for her to find a flight to the West Coast. True, the major California cities were rubble and the big airports gone, but there were still many places to fly out of.

Chang considered feigning illness and taking the rest of the afternoon off, but he couldn't risk bringing attention to himself. Too many Trib Forcers were in precarious positions. He needed to be in place for them without suspicion. He watched the clock.

✣ ✣ ✣

Buck sat with Kenny on his lap and chatted with Zeke and Leah. It was just after eight in the morning, and Leah was riffling through stacks of messages and reports from Co-op people all over the world. Amazingly, the thing was largely working, even with the tragedy of the seas. The sheer audacity of people without the mark of loyalty transporting in their own vehicles gigantic shipments of goods to one another, no money changing hands, boggled the mind.

"Do you know what you have in that wife of yours, Buck?" Leah said.

Buck hadn't learned how to read Leah yet. He wanted to take that as a straight-out compliment, praise for Chloe. But did he detect a challenge? Was Leah implying he was insensitive, that he *didn't* know what he had in Chloe? "Yes, I think I do," he said.

"I don't think he does, Kenny. Do you? Do you think he does?"

"Does!" Kenny said.

"Do you?"

The baby giggled.

"Do you know what you've got in that mommy of yours, sweetheart? She's a genius. She—"

But Kenny heard "mommy" and began to squirm and repeat, "Mama. Mama."

"Thank you, Leah," Buck said.

"I'm sorry," she said, and sounded as if she meant it.

If she hadn't, Buck was prepared to add, "Brilliant. Real smart." That was the effect Leah had on him. She appeared to be trying to distract Kenny by changing the subject, but she should have tried with something that would interest him, not Buck.

"I'm serious," she said. "You know what I've learned here? Chloe knows how many one-thousand-ton or larger oceangoing vessels there were in the world before the seas turned to blood."

"You don't say."

"Say!" Kenny said.

"I do say," Leah said. "Can you guess?"

"I don't know," Buck said. "Thousands, I suppose."

"Can I guess?" Zeke said.

"Z!" Kenny shouted.

"I'm guessin' more'n thirty thousand."

"Ships that big?" Buck said. "Sounds high."

"He's right on the money," Leah said. "What, did Chloe tell you or something? How'd you know that?"

Z couldn't hide a grin. "Yeah, she told me. But that's a pretty good memory, right?"

Buck turned it over in his mind. "What happens to all those ships?" he said.

"Ruined," Leah said. "Dead in the water. Well, dead in the blood anyway."

"And if God lifts the judgment? The blood turns back to salt water, then what?"

She shook her head. "No idea. I can't imagine what it would take to clean a ship of blood throughout its works."

"And the dead fish," Z said.

"Fish!"

"Who could stand the smell? You don't see it on the news, but people who live on the coasts are trying to move. If nothing changes, the smell will only get worse, and the disease and all that. Ugh!"

"Ugh!"

Buck let Kenny run off. "I can't imagine how Carpathia deals with this. You can't spin it, can't gloss over it. Thousands are dying every day, and think of the crews marooned. They'll eventually all die. Hey, Leah, I did a piece a few years back on the surprising dependence Panama had on its shipping industry. What does this do to a country like that?"

She flipped through some sheets. "They're the only country with more ships than Greece," she said. "It's got to bankrupt them."

The mention of Greece made Buck check his watch. "Late afternoon there," he said. "If the plan is working, they ought to be ready to move in when it gets dark."

"Why are they waiting?"

Buck shrugged. "Mac thinks it gives them an advantage. He doesn't know what's going to unfold, but if they have to shoot their way out or try to escape somehow, he figures they're a leg up in the darkness."

Leah sat staring, as if she wasn't listening.

"Something on your mind?" Buck said.

"I was expecting a call or an e-mail by now. Chloe told me a businessman had something he wanted to ship to Petra. Cheap housing modules of some kind."

"Yeah?"

"Wealthy guy, made a killing in low-cost housing, then became a believer. He's really into the timing. Totally buys into Tsion's charts and graphs, figures the Glorious Appearing exactly seven years from the original agreement between Carpathia and Israel."

"Don't you?"

"Sure. If Tsion told me today was yesterday, I'd believe it." It was clear she had lost her train of thought. "I miss him, Buck. I pray for him constantly."

"We all do."

"Not like I do."

"Yeah, I know."

"What?"

"I know."

"You do?"

"'Course," Buck said. "Just thinking about him makes you forget what you were talking about."

She looked embarrassed. "That's not true!"

"Prove it."

"We were, uh, talking about ships. Panama and Greece."

"We were onto modular housing, Leah."

"We were, weren't we?"

"We were. Now who is this guy and what do we need to hear from him?"

Leah stood and looked out a pinhole in the black paint that covered the windows. "Not sure," she said. "He's from right here in Illinois. Something Grove. Says we've got less than three and a half years left, and he'd like us to help him figure a way to get his inventory to Petra. Says they could build the houses themselves in no time. You think he survived, don't you, Buck?"

"Survived what?"

"The bombing."

"This guy was in Petra?"

"Tsion!"

"Oh, pardon me. We're back to him. Well, I'm just as concerned about my father-in-law, and Chaim, and Abdullah, but yes, I do."

"Do what?"

"Think they survived."

"We won't be able to tell from the news, will we?"

"No. But Chang should know. He knows all."

+ + +

Chang had skipped lunch, so when his day was over he went back to his quarters by way of the central mess and filled a bag with food. There was so much he wanted to listen to, but top priority was tracking his sister. He didn't know if his parents were on the move or already in hiding, but they would be vulnerable regardless, without the mark of loyalty. He had sent them contact information on an underground church in their province, but he had never heard back whether they had or would try to make a connection.

How would Ming find them if he didn't even know where they were? And how long would it take her to get to China, heading east out of the United North American States?

The mood was somber in the palace complex. Everyone seemed in a hurry to get to their quarters. It had been a strange day. Who had not seen the attack on the rebels, and was anyone snowed by the so-called technical difficulties that suddenly swept the coverage from the air, just when the pilot clearly said he thought he saw people alive below?

Chang casually glanced up and down the corridor, quickly entered his quarters, and locked the door. He ran his computer through a quick program that checked his room for bugs. It showed his systems, installed by David Hassid and left for his use and safekeeping, still secure and running normally.

Chang wolfed down fruit and crackers, then checked his e-mail. There was his confirmation, addressed to the bogus name he used as an operative of the Global Community aviation administration. "Passenger, GC Peacekeeper Chang Chow from sector 30, riding with pilot Lionel Whalum, Long Grove, Illinois. Flight plan nonstop to Pawleys Island, South Carolina. Round trip for Whalum. Mr. Chow's papers in order, destination San Diego, California. Note: Whalum did not bear the mark of loyalty, but Mr. Chow asserted that he would see to it when they arrived in South Carolina."

Chang fired off a thanks, then searched the database for flights from Pawleys Island to San Diego. A flier scheduled for that route the next day rang a bell in Chang's mind. It was a Co-op pilot. So Ming was using Co-op people to get herself to China. Was Whalum Co-op too? He ran a search against Chloe's records. Nothing. If he was Co-op, he hadn't been used yet, or at least she hadn't logged him. Maybe he used another name, or maybe Chloe was behind in entering her records.

Chang checked the international GC database, and while the search engine looked for Whalum, he finished eating. He came back to the computer to find a photo of and an entire page on Lionel Whalum of Long Grove, Illinois. The man was black, of African descent. He and his wife and three kids had moved from Chicago to the suburbs when his business became successful. He had won many civic and business awards. His loyalty to the Global Community was listed as "unknown, but not suspicious."

Chang switched to another database and copied information for a loyalty oath administration center at Statesville in Illinois. Switching back to Whalum's records, he changed the loyalty designation to "confirmed," documented by the GC squadron in Statesville on the date Whalum had received his mark. If he *was* Co-op, that would take the heat off. And it ought to tip off Ming that Chang was watching out for her.

A tone sounded on Chang's computer and scrolling type informed him, and all other GC personnel, of "the unfortunate loss of both pilots involved in the attack on rebel forces today. Due to pilot error, their payloads missed the target by more than a mile, and the insurgents fired missiles that destroyed both planes.

The Global Community expresses its sympathy to the families of these heroes and martyrs to the cause of world peace."

Chang quickly flipped to the hangar manifests and found that both multimillion-Nick aircraft were back and accounted for. The morgue listed both pilots as "deceased—remains delivered from crash sites in the Negev." Their personnel records had already been flagged in red with the date of their deaths.

He called up the recording from Akbar's office around the time the first flier would have returned. There was clear conversation with Akbar's secretary and the pilot being escorted to the conference room. A few minutes later came the pleasantries, the invite to sit again. Then Suhail. "Good effort out there today, man."

"Thank you, sir," came the answer with a British accent. "Perfect execution. Felt good."

"I'm sorry. You're unaware then that your mission failed?"

"Sir?"

"That the outcome was negative?"

"I don't follow, Director. Both incendiaries were bull's-eyes, and the entire area was consumed, as ordered. When I turned for home, the missile had been launched, and according to what I heard—"

"You seriously don't know that you missed your target."

"Sir, if the coordinates were correct, we did not miss."

"There were no casualties, young man."

"Impossible. I saw people there before we launched, and I saw nothing but fire for several minutes before I left."

"The effort was there, as I said. Unfortunately, human error resulted in utter failure."

"I don't . . . I'm not . . . I'm . . . at a loss, sir."

"You will be demoted, and the party line is that you don't know how such a significant oversight could have occurred."

"Begging your pardon, sir, but I am not convinced it occurred!"

"I'm telling you it occurred, and that is what you will tell anyone who wants to know."

"I will not! Either you prove to me we missed our target or I will maintain to everyone I know that this mission went off without a hitch."

"You will see in due time reconnaissance photos that show no loss of life in Petra."

"You've seen these?"

"Of course I have."

"And you have no doubt as to their veracity?"

"None, son."

There was a long pause. The young man's voice sounded pitiful. "If there is one survivor on that mountain, it's a miracle. You know what we dropped there. You ordered it yourself! It can't be explained away, and I won't take the heat for it."

"You already have. You and your compatriot will be reassigned, and you know how to respond to—"

"I will not testify to something I don't believe, sir."

"Come, come, mister. I see the *2* on your hand and the image of our leader. You're a loyal citizen. You contribute to the cause, you—"

"Would the potentate want me to say I made a mistake when I didn't?"

"But you did."

"I did not."

"His Excellency is most disappointed in you, son."

"I'm not doing it, Director Akbar."

"Excuse me?"

"I won't play along. I take great pride in my work. I didn't question the order. I believed these people were dangerous and a threat to the Global Community. I did what I was instructed to do, and I did it right. No one can tell me we missed the primary target or that our 82s didn't waste that whole area and all those people. If you have evidence that proves concretely that they survived, then I'm going to call it what it is. I'll accept no demotion and I won't parrot a party line. If those people are still alive, they're superior to us. If they are still alive, they win. We can't compete with that."

"You realize you leave me no choice."

"Sir?"

"We cannot have personnel shirk responsibility for their own errors."

"You will not be able to silence me."

Akbar laughed and was interrupted by the intercom. "Primary pilot is waiting, sir."

"Send him in."

As soon as Chang heard the sound of the door, the Brit started in. "Tell him, Uri. Tell him we didn't screw up."

"What?"

And the conversation began anew, Akbar blaming the failure on the pilots, the Brit protesting, Uri silent for the moment. "Excuse me a moment, gentlemen," Suhail said. The door opened and closed.

"Kerry," Uri said, "listen to me. He's right. The—"

"He's *not* right! I saw what I saw and I will never—"

"Shh! Listen! You and I both know we launched perfectly. But I was there after you had gone. You heard my transmission. Those people survived the Blues and the Lance, lived through it all."

"Impossible!"

"Impossible but true."

"A miracle."

"Obviously."

"Then we must live with it, Uri. We must make the GC and the world face it. They are a more than formidable enemy, and unless we admit that, we'll never have a chance to defeat them."

"I agree. You heard me try to say it."

"They took you off the air! Now they want to make us the scapegoats. Demote us. Make us admit failure."

"Not me," Uri said.

"That's my man," the Brit said.

They traded encouragement.

"Be strong."

"Don't give in."

"Let's stick together."

Chang checked Akbar's phone.

Suhail had called the medical wing and asked for Dr. Consuela Conchita. Only the day before Chang had read the staff bulletin announcing her promotion to surgeon general of the Global Community. "Connie," Akbar said, "I need two heavy doses of sedative, the quick stuff. My conference room, ASAP. I'll have security here, in case the patients resist. And bring gurneys from the morgue."

"The morgue?"

"I want them cremated."

"You're asking for *lethal* doses?"

"No, no. I just want them out before they leave here, under sheets. The cremation will do the rest, will it not?"

"Kill them? Of course it will. You're asking that we execute two people?"

"This is from the top floor, Consuela."

A pause. "I understand."

Chang grimaced as he listened to the recording of Akbar trying to convince the fliers that he had asked for injections to help calm them. Both began scuffling and shouting, and Chang could tell they were held down and given the shots. And now they were gone. Anyone who had seen either of them land in New Babylon and make their way from the hangar to the palace and to Akbar's office would never admit it or mention it. They had been shot down by the enemy, and that was that.

Chang checked on the planes again. Already their serial numbers had been changed. And the original numbers were marked as lost in action. Somehow the total number of operative GC fighter-bombers in New Babylon did not change.

The story that had scrolled across Chang's screen would broadcast around the world that night. No doubt Carpathia himself would express abject personal sorrow over the losses.

Chang checked the records in Greece and found that Nelson Stefanich had forwarded location coordinates to "Howie Johnson's" team. It was a couple of hours yet till nightfall, when Mac planned to pay the visit. Chang had time to confirm Mac's instructions to the crew at the Ptolemaïs airport to refuel the Rooster Tail and entered into the computer that Senior Commander Johnson had been cleared at the highest levels to fly it to New Babylon.

That done, Chang found Stefanich's cell phone number and called it in to Mac. "Got everything else you need?" Chang said.

"Well, I'd still like to know the disposition of the Stavros kid."

"Nothing on that here, sir. Do you hold out any hope?"

"Always, Chang. But that's just me."

"Ask Stefanich."

"Oh, I will. Hey, Chang?"

"Sir?"

"Who's better than you?"

"Thank you, sir."

Finally, Chang was able to check his other recordings from throughout the day. He located the one emanating from Carpathia's office and backed up to several minutes before Nicolae, his secretary Krystall, Leon Fortunato, Suhail Akbar, and Viv Ivins sat watching the feed from the cockpit of the initial fighter-bomber. Suhail had just told the potentate he had arranged for him to watch live, and Carpathia had expressed excited anticipation. Chang sped through several minutes of setup and of Nicolae welcoming the various ones into the room.

Then, pay dirt. Akbar informed Carpathia that the fighter-bombers were set for takeoff from Amman, and that he could bring that up on the monitor, "if you wish."

"If I wish? Please!"

"Palace to Amman Command," Suhail said.

"Amman. Go ahead, Palace."

"Initiate visual coverage of takeoff."

"Roger that."

Several seconds of silence. Then Carpathia. "Suhail, these are fighter-bombers? Is it an optical illusion? They look *huge*."

"Oh, they are, Eminence. They have been in service only a few weeks. Notice how high they sit off the ground. The gear is the tallest of any fighter ever. It has to be to allow room for the payload."

"That is the bomb, underneath?"

"Yes, sir."

"Talk about huge. It looks massive!"

"Way too big to be carried internally, sir. It's four and a half feet in diameter and eleven feet long. The thing weighs fifteen thousand pounds."

"You do not say!"

"Oh, yes, sir. It's carried on what we call an underbelly centerline station."

"And what is it, Suhail? What are we serving the enemy today?"

"The Americans used to call these Big Blue 82s. They are concussion bombs. Eighty percent of their weight is made up of a gel consisting of polystyrene, ammonium nitrate, and powdered aluminum."

"Is it as powerful as it is large?"

"Excellency," Suhail said, "nothing but a nuclear weapon would be more so. These are designed to detonate just a few feet off the ground and generate a thousand pounds of pressure per square inch. It should kill everything—even the little creatures below the ground—in an area as large as two thousand acres. The mushroom cloud alone will rise more than a mile. And we're dropping two."

"Plus a missile."

"Yes, sir."

"Fire?"

"Oh, Your Highness, that's the best part. Each concussion bomb creates a fireball six thousand feet in diameter."

Chang recoiled at a loud hiss, and he imagined a nearly overcome Carpathia inhaling deeply through his nose and exhaling through clenched teeth.

Later, when the pilots let loose their payloads, Nicolae said, "Suhail! How quickly can we get this on television?"

"I'm sure it's just a matter of a few switches, Excel—"

"Do it! Do it now!"

Someone left the room.

The recording was interrupted only with occasional outbursts from Carpathia. "Ahh! Look! Ooh! Perfect! On target! Both of them. The best revenge is success."

"Absolutely."

"And victory."

"Yes, sir."

"Total and complete," Nicolae said.

Several grunted.

A loud sigh ended in a hum. It reminded Chang of a lion he had seen at the zoo in Beijing. It had just gorged itself on several pounds of raw beef, roared, yawned and stretched, settled its wide chin on its paws, and sighed like that, followed by a low rumbling from deep inside.

For several minutes they watched, and occasionally someone congratulated Nicolae. "Finally, Your Lordship." That was Viv Ivins. Carpathia did not respond, making Chang wonder if she was still in his doghouse.

To all the other compliments he merely said, "Thank you. Thank you."

The suggestion from the primary pilot to abort the missile launch was immediately rejected by Suhail. "Yes," Nicolae said in the background. "Very good, Director Akbar. The final dart."

When the pilot sounded insubordinate, Suhail immediately countered. Then silence, finally broken by Carpathia. "Was I hearing things, or did he dare cross you?"

"He came right to the edge, Excellency."

"Reprimand him!" Leon squawked.

"I do not believe he meant for me to hear it. He is watching in person what we are seeing on a screen. Of course it sounds like overkill to him."

"But still . . . ," Leon said.

Someone shushed him.

When the missile hit and the pilot began his halting, disbelieving commentary, Chang heard a chair roll back as if someone had stood suddenly.

"What?!" That was Nicolae.

"Impossible!" Fortunato.

"Cut the feed!" Carpathia said, and Akbar repeated it, loud.

Footsteps away from the table and, Chang assumed, toward the monitor. The door opening. The sounds of people leaving, evidently everyone but Nicolae and Suhail.

"Two of our largest incendiary bombs?" Carpathia whispered. "You said one was more than enough."

"It should have been."

"We saw the flames, watched them burn, for how long?"

"Long enough."

Several minutes of relative silence, during which Chang believed he heard Carpathia panting. And when the potentate finally spoke, he sounded desperate and short of breath. "Listen to me, Suhail."

"Yes, sir."

"Are you listening?"

"I am, sir."

"Deal with those pilots. They missed. They failed. Their eyes deceived them. Do not allow this victory to go to the Judah-ites. Do not."

"I hear you, sir."

"Then contact the other nine regional potentates, personally, on my behalf. Tell them the Judah-ites have raised arms against us and have dealt a severe blow. We shall retaliate. I told them this only recently."

"You did, sir."

"But the time is now; the budget is limitless. I will sanction, condone, support, and reward the death of any Jew anywhere in the world. I want this done as a top priority, by any means. Imprison them. Torture them. Humiliate them. Shame them. Blaspheme their god. Plunder everything they own. Nothing is more important to the potentate. Do you understand?"

"I do."

"Go quickly. Do it now."

"Yes, sir."

"And, Suhail?"

"Sir?"

"Send Reverend Fortunato in."

In seconds, Leon came bustling. "Oh, Highness, I don't know what to say. I can't understand it. What went—"

"My dear Most High Reverend Fortunato. Kiss my hand."

"How may I serve you, Potentate? I kneel before you."

"Be still and hear me. Are you still my most trusted devotee—?"

"Oh, yes, Supre—"

"Shh—my Reverend Father of Carpathianism?"

"I am, sincerely."

"Leon, do you love me?"

"You know I do."

"Do you cherish me?"

"With all my—"

"Do you worship me?"

"Oh, my beloved—"

"Stand up, Leon, and hear me. My enemies mock me. They perform miracles. They poison my people, call sores down on them from heaven, turn the seas into blood. And now! And now they survive bombs and fire! But I too have power. You know this. It is available to you, Leon. I have seen you use it. I have seen you call down lightning that slays those who would oppose me.

"Leon, I want to fight fire with fire. I want Jesuses. Do you hear me?"

"Sir?"

"I want messiahs."

"Messiahs?"

"I want saviors in my name."

"Tell me more, Excellency."

"Find them—thousands of them. Train them, raise them up, imbue them with the power with which I have blessed you. I want them healing the sick, turning water to blood and blood to water. I want them performing miracles in my name, drawing the undecided, yea, even the enemy away from his god and to me."

"I will do it, Excellency."

"Will you?"

"I will if you will empower me."

"Kneel before me again, Leon."

"Lay your hands on me, risen one."

"I confer upon you all the power vested in me from above and below the earth! I give you power to do great and mighty and wonderful and terrifying things, acts so splendiferous and phantasmagorical that no man can see them and not be persuaded that I am his god."

Leon sobbed. "Thank you, lord. Thank you, Excellency."

"Go, Leon," Carpathia said. "Go quickly and do it now."

5

GEORGE FELT PRETTY GOOD, considering. How long had it been since they had put him in the backseat of the Jeep? He was opposite the driver's side with Elena in front of him, Plato beside him. The leader slid in behind the wheel and told Plato to blindfold George again. George liked the fact that he was again sitting on his hands, giving him an excuse to bounce and tumble into Plato. If he timed it right, maybe he could even bang heads with him.

The leader backed up the Jeep and stopped, idling. "Where is he?" he asked, testy.

"There, by the road."

"What is he doing there?" A loud sigh. "Socrates! Come here!" George heard the hobbling footsteps. "Are you finished with the car?"

"Hidden, Aristotle."

"Give me the keys."

"Why? What if I need it?"

"That will ruin everything! Give them to me."

George heard the jangling as Aristotle took the car keys. "Think, man!" he said. "This way, no matter what happens, you have no keys to surrender. And stay away from the road! You have no reason to be outside. Just wait in there." Aristotle lowered his voice, as if thinking a blind Sebastian couldn't hear either. "Remember, the closer you come to the edge, the more believable you are."

"You know I can do it."

"You know I do! You can still produce tears at will? Take it right to the brink. It has to look like you tried everything before you crumbled. Now, I am sorry you are hurt, but this is just as important as what we are doing."

\+ \+ \+

Chloe could see why her father so admired Mac. He was earthy and plain, but he was also meticulous. He had spread the pages of the local GC's Sebastian file on the dashboard of his borrowed car. In the woods north of Ptolemaïs, with the other vehicle—the hot-wired Jeep—hidden deeper in the underbrush, they studied the record. Chloe leaned in from the passenger's side; Hannah peeked over their shoulders from the backseat. All three wore GC-issue camouflage, their faces streaked with grease.

"They were thinkin' when they got this gal that looks like the Stavros girl."

"Georgiana," Hannah said.

"Right. This one's real name is Elena, last initial *A.* Hmm, the only one whose actual name is given. Guess they don't feel any need to protect her. Then a couple of no-account locals, both of which it looks like tried to get out of Peacekeeping duty but wound up on this vigilante squad. Oh, get a load of these monikers."

"One of them's the leader, Mac," Hannah said, pointing.

Mac shook his head. "Aristotle. Other one's Socrates. Real creative. Given this, shouldn't Elena be Helen? Of Troy, get it? And the big guy, the one that's supposed to pass for George. Plato? Oh, for the love of all things sacred! Well, whatever you gotta do to keep track of each other. He's French. Brought in just for this. Sebastian would be insulted. This guy's heavy, but he's under six-two. He's no George."

Mac kept glancing at his watch, and as night fell, they kept reading, memorizing. They finally had to resort to the dome light and three tiny flashlights. "The original plan wasn't half bad," Chloe said. "Only somebody didn't cooperate."

"I don't know the boy or the other old guy, the driver," Mac said. "But from what I know of Miklos, my money's on him. Anyway, somebody smelled a rat. They were supposed to pick up the girl eight kilometers north of the airport, then have Plato, pretending to be Sebastian, show up just down the road."

"But Sebastian was expecting to hook up with them closer to the airport," Hannah said.

"They must've wanted to be sure the deal was done before he came looking," Mac said. "They're pretty proud of this change of plans. Looks like they originally wanted to take 'em all in, including George, and then threaten to kill the others if George wouldn't talk. Then, even if he did, they were gonna execute 'em together if they wouldn't take the mark."

Chloe had turned the page slightly. "Did we know this?" she said.

"What's that?" Mac said.

"The shootings, all three of them, were done by the girl."

Chloe had that tingling sensation inside as the zero hour drew near. Mac had studied the coordinates and determined they were about forty minutes from where George was being held. At 2130 hours he called Stefanich on his private cell phone with the number provided by Chang.

\+ + +

Early in the afternoon in Chicago, Buck and Enoch called their people together. "Quick update," Buck said. "Chang has a trace on Ming, and it appears she's probably on her way to San Diego. Then on to China. Problem is, he doesn't know where their parents are, so she couldn't either—far as we know."

"How'd she get to San Diego?" Albie said.

"The long way. Guess she got a ride with some private pilot out of Long Grove to South Carolina, then was able to—"

"Whoa!" Leah said. "Hold on! Long Grove?"

"Yeah. Then she—"

"Buck! Was the pilot this Whalum guy?"

"I don't know. The point is, she—"

"The point is, if it *is* him, he's the guy who wants to ship housing modules to Petra."

That stopped Buck. "I don't get it."

"She might be going to Petra."

"She'll never make it. Security's too tight."

"Tell me about it."

"Maybe she just caught a ride with a guy who's going on to Petra, but she isn't."

"That's worth praying about," Leah said.

"That's why we're here."

"So Ming used a Co-op contact . . ."

"Can we move on here, Leah?"

"Sure, but we haven't even checked him out yet. Don't know if he's legit. And here I thought when Ming was reading through all these records that she was just helping out."

Buck cocked his head at Leah. "Weren't you the one who said Ming was an adult and free to do what she wants?"

\+ + +

Mac was surprised when the phone rang four times. GC policy was that command officers always be available to the brass.

"This is Nelson Stefanich," he heard finally, "and the only reason I'm answering a call from a hidden number is because of a current operation, so state your business."

"Well, Nelly diggin'-a-ditch Stefanich, how in the world are ya?"

"Who—?"

"Sorry I missed ya today. Howie Johnson, here."

"Yes, sir, Commander. Have we met?"

"Naw, but I hear such good things about ya, I feel like I know ya, know what I mean?"

"Thank you, sir."

"'Preciate the info you gave my aide today."

"No problem."

"We're 'bout ready to roll here, Nels, and I just wanted to give you a heads-up so you can let your guy Aristotle know we're on our way. I'm assumin' your phone's secure."

"Of course, Commander."

"Good, good. Now I don't want them gettin' spooked. They should be expecting us and not start shootin' the minute they hear us. We want to protect them too, so we won't be drivin' right to their door. We'll approach on foot, and when we're within range I'll give out two loud whistles. They should respond with one, and we'll know it's safe to come on ahead."

"Got it. You whistle twice; they whistle once."

"And they understand that as soon as I'm on the scene, I am the ranking officer."

"Oh, yes, sir. Absolutely."

"Pretty creative, the code names, by the way."

"Thank you. I—"

"Listen, we keep forgettin' to ask about the original target, a G. Stavros, female, escapee from the pen there. What's the dispo on her?"

"Well, you know she was the source of much of what we know about the Judah-ite underground here, sir."

"So she's a valuable commodity."

"Yes, she was."

"Past tense?"

"Affirmative. Deceased."

"That so?"

"Yes, sir. Still refused the mark, even after providing a lot of information."

"Guillotine?"

"Actually, no, sir."

"You understand the blade is protocol, don't you, Commander Stefanich?"

"Under normal circumstances, yes, sir."

"And the difference here was . . . ?"

"She, ah, well, she began giving us false information."

"Such as?"

"Well, we never did get a straight answer on the location of the underground now. She was one of them caught in the raids of their original meeting places, so we know when she came back she had to know at least one of the new locations."

"Makes sense. Wouldn't give it up, eh?"

"No, sir. In fact, after the third wild-goose chase, that was when she was . . ."

"Executed?"

"Yes, sir."

"How?"

"Firing squad."

"It took a squad to shoot a teenage girl?"

"*Squad* is a euphemism we use, sir."

"I'm listening."

"Anyone past a certain level is authorized to attack enemy personnel with extreme prejudice."

"Shoot them dead?"

"Exactly."

"And then whoever did it shares the credit with the rest of the team? The squad?"

"Right."

"You shot her, didn't you, Commander?"

"Yes, sir, I did."

"Well, that showed remarkable, almost indescribable, fortitude there, Nelson."

"Thank you, sir."

"I know you did it on behalf of and with the deep gratitude of the Global Community, starting right at the top."

"Thank you very much."

"Don't thank me, Commander Stefanich. The fact is that I wish I could personally reward you for that act—"

"Merely doing my duty, sir—"

"Pay you back, as it were, for that service to the cause."

"Well, I don't know what to say. That would be just—"

"All right, Nelly, time's a wastin' here. You inform the Greek philosophers and their lady friend that we'll drop by to see 'em in a bit, hear?"

"Will do. Uh, sir?"

"I'm here," Mac said.

"We're hoping you can help, of course, but you need to know we're pretty happy with this operation."

"Oh, I can see how you would be."

"Well, I may have read something into it, but I got the impression from your aide that you might want to express some impatience with the crew because the prisoner has not yet been forthcoming. We're planning to honor them for what they've accomplished."

"I hear you, Commander. I wouldn't worry about that. I think it's fair to say that we want to respond proactively to their actions as well."

+ + +

"We'll want to give thanks also, of course, for the miracle at Petra today," Buck said. "That two experienced pilots could miss with such huge bombs at such close range, well, praise the Lord."

The others laughed. "Yes," Albie said, "and for the fact that somehow all the people caught fire anyway, well, talk about amazing."

"But seriously," Buck said, "God is acting in ways beyond description, and we never want to take for granted his power and sovereignty, his care for us, his protection of our loved ones."

And with that, several kneeling at the safe house began spontaneously to pray and praise the Lord. Enoch led in prayer for the safety of "our new friends, our brother and sisters Mac, Chloe, and Hannah, as they undertake a dangerous mission. Protect them, go before them, send angels to guard them, and may they bring our brother from California out safely so we can all thank him and rejoice with them."

+ + +

Chloe was grateful when Mac turned in his seat and held out an open palm to her and to Hannah. They both grabbed hold, and he prayed. It wasn't long, and it wasn't eloquent. But it was Mac, and he sounded as if he knew who he was talking to. And that settled Chloe. A little. Temporarily.

When Mac pulled to within what he said should be a half mile from their destination, Chloe was glad for the chance to get out of the vehicle. The ground was uneven but not bad, and she knew a short hike would be good for her nerves. They all turned off their cell phones and carried them in their left rear pockets. Tiny walkie-talkies were set to a unique frequency, set on Low, and carried in the right rear pockets.

Chloe took the safety off the ancient Luger on her right hip, and Hannah unsnapped the leather strap over the grip of her Glock. The three of them strapped loaded Uzis on their right shoulders so they hung near their rib cages.

Mac tossed Chloe the DEW from the trunk, and she angled it over her left shoulder. He handed Hannah a small, heavy canvas bag with extra clips for the

Uzi and several rounds for the fifty-caliber rifle, which Mac wrestled vertical, the feet of the bipod pointing away from him. He supported the four-foot-long, thirty-five-pound weapon by cradling the butt in his right palm and wrapping his left hand around the stock.

"Good thing I'm in reasonable shape for one of my vintage," he said. "Pushin' sixty, and I can still outrun either one of ya if the course is long enough."

"Not carrying that thing," Hannah said, and Chloe noticed the quaver in her voice. It was comforting to know she was not the only one scared to death.

"Don't bet on it," Mac said, deftly reaching up with his left foot and slamming the trunk. He held out his compass toward Hannah's flashlight and started off. "Follow me, ladies."

Mac's boots crunched a steady pace, and Chloe soon found herself perspiring and breathing heavily. But she felt good, and Hannah appeared able to keep up too. The work did not, however, take Chloe's mind off the danger. The bluffs had worked well so far. Maybe too well. If this were going to be easy, they wouldn't be so heavily armed.

\+ + +

Chang tracked Ming to San Diego and noticed she would not be flying out of there until early evening, West Coast time. He called her cell phone.

"Hello, Chang," she said.

"Where are you?"

"Is this a test? Do you think I'm going to try to convince you I'm at the safe house in Chicago?"

"You have to know I've talked to them."

"Of course. And I can tell from the benefits to my pilots that it didn't take you long to track me."

"But where are you specifically, Ming, and what are you doing?"

She sighed. "I am in a tiny charter terminal south of San Diego. My papers and my look are working perfectly. No one asks to see my mark because I am in uniform, and when the pilots see my believer's mark, they become very protective."

"You don't tell them who you are, do you?"

"Yes, Chang. I am a fool. No! Of course not. Why burden them with something that could bring them trouble? They cannot be held responsible for what they do not know. This is the perfect cover. They are helping the Global Community by transporting an employee. They know secretly I'm a believer, but they don't know I'm a woman, or former GC, or AWOL."

"Ming, you know Father and Mother are not at home."

"I assumed."

"Then how will you find them?"

"I will ask around, in my official capacity. Maybe I will arrest them."

"You have not thought this through."

"I have, Chang. More than you know. They have to contact you somehow before I get there. You can tell them I am coming and we can set a meeting place."

"Why didn't we try to arrange this before you left?"

"Because you would have refused. You think you know so much. Well, you *do*. But you don't know everything, or you would know that I cannot sit in a safe house while my parents flee for their lives. Do we know they are true believers, or have we just talked them out of taking the mark of loyalty? I must know. I must get them together with believers. I know I cannot save their lives or even my own. But I have to do something."

Chang was moved. So she *had* thought it through. Maybe not every detail. Maybe not strategy. But who could?

"You must let me know where you are as soon as you get there," he said.

"You love me, don't you, Chang?"

"Of course."

"We never tell each other. We never have."

"I know," he said. "But we know we do."

"You cannot say it."

"Yes, I can," he said, "but even thinking about it makes me emotional, and I must not allow that. Not right now."

"You, emotional? Impossible."

"Don't say that, Ming. If you say that, you don't know me."

"I'm sorry, Chang. I was teasing you."

"Well the truth is, sister, I do love you." Chang immediately teared up, and he felt a lump in his throat. "I love you with all my heart, and I worry about you and pray for you."

"Thank you, Chang. Don't now. It's all right. I didn't want to make you uncomfortable. And anyway, I know. I know, okay? I love you too and pray for you often. You *do* need to stay rational and practical, so don't worry about me."

"How can I not?"

"Because I go with God. He will protect me. And if he decides my time is up, it won't be that long before I see you again anyway."

"Don't say that!"

"Come, come, Chang. It's all right. You know it's true. There are no guarantees anymore, except we know where we are going. I will call you from China. I will be hoping for good news about Father and Mother."

\+ + +

After about ten minutes' walking, Chloe moved aside and let Hannah fall in behind Mac. Hannah gave her a long look in the low light, as if to ask if she were all right. "It's okay," Chloe said. "I'll be right behind you." She'd had a little trouble staying with Mac, but she decided if she was behind Hannah she'd be more motivated. If Hannah could stay with Mac, she could too.

And she was right. Chloe didn't want to give either of them the idea she was petering out. In fact, she didn't believe she was. They were on a gravel road now, and she had a rhythm going and her breathing was steady and deep. She was sweating through her clothes, but Mac and Hannah had to be doing the same.

Finally Mac held up his right hand briefly before having to get it under the fifty-caliber again. He slowed and stopped, moving to the side of the road and turning to face the women. "Everybody okay?"

They both nodded.

"Anybody need a breather?"

Though panting, both shook their heads.

"Almost there," he said, and they started uphill. Just over a rise Mac knelt and lay the fifty-caliber on the ground. He made a *V* with his fingers under his eyes, then pointed through a clearing to a small, wood shack. A faint light shone through the sliver between a shade and one window in the front. He took the directed energy weapon from Chloe and leaned it against a tree.

Mac motioned that they should follow him around back. Chloe was surprised how wide he made the arc, staying in the shadows and somehow walking so quietly she could barely hear his boots on the soil. When her Uzi brushed the handle of the Luger, it made a muted scraping sound and she held her breath. Mac stopped and half turned. Chloe had to resist the urge to raise her hand in acknowledgment and apology. She set herself again, and they crept around the back, where trees blotted any light from the stars and the shack was totally dark.

Mac squatted about forty feet behind the place. "I don't like it," he whispered. "Only one vehicle, and that looks like mine, so it's likely the one Sebastian got from the GC pool at the airport. And does that place look like it's got five people in it? I mean, I know they're hiding out, but . . ."

"You lost me already," Hannah said between gulps of air. "I don't see *any* vehicles."

Mac put a hand on her shoulder and turned her toward the side of the shack, where a small white car sat mostly hidden in underbrush. Hannah nodded. Chloe hadn't seen it either. "Maybe your eyes aren't adjusted to the light yet," Mac said, as if he meant it. Chloe nearly laughed aloud. They had all been traipsing around in the dark.

Mac slipped the Uzi off his shoulder and lay it on the ground. He pulled what looked like a utility tool from a vest pocket. "I know this is gonna sound like a cowboy movie," he said, "but cover me."

Before Chloe could ask where he was going, he moved quickly to the car and went to work on the trunk lock. Every time he made a sound loud enough for the women to hear, he stopped dead and remained motionless a few seconds. Eventually came the thump of the lock giving way, and the trunk lid sprung free. Mac kept a hand atop it so it wouldn't fly open.

He snaked his other hand in as far as he could, then finally had to let the lid rise another half inch or so. That triggered the trunk light, so he lowered the lid again. He set the tool on the back bumper, reached in, and held the lid down with his left hand, feeling around inside with his right. Once he found what he was looking for he quickly pulled his hand out, grabbed the tool, reached back in, let the trunk up enough to give himself room to maneuver, and—as the light came on—ground the tool into the bulb, breaking it and dousing the light.

Now he let the lid open all the way, silently, and felt around inside the trunk. From where she waited, it looked to Chloe as if the whole top half of his body was inside.

Suddenly he stopped and backed out, quietly shutting the trunk and hurrying back. "Just as I thought," he said. "Check it out."

"A twelve-gauge," Hannah said. "Learned to use one when I was a kid."

"These GIs love their shotguns," Mac said. "Leaves a DEW and a Fifty in the plane, brings his double-barrel on the job. And brilliant as this hostage team is supposed to be, they don't even search his car."

"We going in?" Hannah said.

"Yeah, but I still don't like it. Half of 'em take off when they found out we were comin', or what?"

He clearly wasn't expecting an answer. Mac handed the shotgun to Hannah. "Makes a lot of racket when you cock it, so do it when I whistle."

He picked up the Uzi, and they followed him back around to the front and the darkest area they could find, about twenty feet left of the door. Mac nodded to Hannah and whispered, "On three." He counted with his fingers and whistled shrilly twice while Hannah expertly, and noisily, cocked the shotgun.

From inside the shack came hurried movement, heavy steps, one louder than the other, like someone limping. The door squeaked open a couple of inches and someone whistled. Or tried to. It was mostly air. Then came the second try.

"All right!" Mac shouted, so loud Chloe jumped. "You know who it is, so show yourself and let us in."

The door opened in and struck the man or his weapon as he tried to get out of the way. "Right this way," he said with a heavy accent.

Mac marched straight toward the door, and Chloe noticed he had a finger on the Uzi trigger. "Senior Commander Howie Johnson comin' through with officers Irene and Jinnah. Stand aside, Peacekeeper."

The man, clearly favoring one leg, hopped back against the wall, warily eyeing them and nodding a greeting.

"So which one are you?" Mac said. "Hercules? Constantinople? Who?"

"Socrates, sir."

"Well, sure ya are. Awright, where is everybody, particularly my prisoner?"

"Not here, sir."

Mac looked as if he were about to explode. He tilted his head back till his chin pointed at the ceiling. "Not here, sir," he mimicked. He brought his eyes down to Socrates. "That's all I git? Where are they?"

"They told me to tell you to read the fine print." That took a second to register with Chloe, and from Mac's look, with him too.

Mac dramatically moved past Socrates, flattening him against the wall again. He strode to the front door and kicked it shut so hard the window rattled and an echo came back from the trees. Mac turned on the man. "The fine print in what? You think I brought the Sebastian file with me into the woods?"

"I am only telling you what they—"

"Why don't you just tell me what the fine print says?"

"They gave me this duty because I slow them down. I was attacked by the prisoner and he injured me with a kick to the—"

"I asked you about the fine print, man! What'd I miss? What's the message?"

"That they have the right to move the prisoner at any time without informing the GC until—"

"Where are they, Peacekeeper? Where did they go?"

"They do not have to inform their superiors until they have reached their des—"

"Do you know where they are?"

"They thought they heard something long before it should have been you, so—"

"You understand English, Socrates. I know you do. Do—you—know—where—they—are?"

"I believe the reason they did not tell me was because—"

"You want me to believe they left you here alone to greet me and didn't tell you where they'd be?"

"Because if I didn't know, I could not tell the wrong person."

"I hope you're lying."

"Sir?"

"I hope you're lying, because then you can change your mind about telling me before you die."

"Commander, I do not know!"

"Officer Jinnah, show Socrates what a twelve-gauge does to the front door."

Chloe wondered if Mac was serious. Apparently Hannah did not. She lifted the shotgun toward the door with one hand, and as soon as the barrel was parallel to the floor, fired. It was as if a bomb had gone off. Chloe was deafened, but nothing was wrong with her eyes. A gaping hole appeared in the door, and the entire thing blew off its hinges and landed several feet from the shack.

"The next one goes in your face, Socrates."

"But, sir!" he cried. "I—"

"Then get on your squawk box and tell your people I want to know where my prisoner is, and I want to know now!"

"But they—"

"Kill him, Jinnah."

Hannah raised the shotgun as quickly and forthrightly as she had before, and Socrates immediately tumbled to the floor, tears streaming. "Wait! Wait!" He dug a walkie-talkie from his pocket, dropping his weapon in the process. "Socrates to Plato, come in, come in. Hello? Plato? I know you can hear me! Please! I need you!"

Mac shook his head as if he had no choice. "Jinnah?"

"No! Please! Wait! Elena! Elena, are you there? Come in now, please. I am not joking! Answer me! Aristotle! Aristotle, they will kill me! I know I was not supposed to call you, but I don't care! Please, please come in or I die!"

Nothing. His shoulders slumped and he bowed his head, weeping.

Mac knelt and put a hand on Socrates' arm. "They're not that far away, are they?"

He shook his head, sobbing.

"They're close by, aren't they?"

He nodded. "You might as well kill me, because I die either way."

"What are you saying?"

"They said not to contact them, no matter what. Don't tell, no matter what."

"But they didn't mean not to tell me, did they? Surely not. They meant if they were right about the sounds. If the wrong people showed up. They're not afraid of GC, are they?"

The man shrugged. "I don't know. Maybe I do not understand. But I am a dead man."

"Then what difference does it make if you tell me?"

Socrates seemed to think about it. He scooted back against the wall and wiped his eyes. He put his walkie-talkie back into his pocket. When he reached for his weapon, Mac said, "Just let that lie."

Socrates seemed to be trying to catch his breath.

"Were they close enough to hear the shot?" Mac said.

"No. Maybe."

"How close?"

"Five hundred meters east. There is a lean-to garage."

Mac sat in an ancient stuffed chair. "Then they heard you calling for them."

Socrates nodded.

"And they left you to die."

6

THE CELEBRATING, SINGING, and dancing at Petra continued into the dark of night. People by the thousands filed into the new pool to submerge themselves and to drink directly from the wide spring in the middle. Manna covered the ground, and Rayford was nearly woozy from its refreshing taste.

"Eating directly from God's table," he told Abdullah, "was something I never expected in this lifetime."

Abdullah looked overwhelmed with joy. "How can this be, Captain? How dare we be so blessed?" The wording was lost on Rayford, but he knew what his friend meant.

A young woman, probably not yet twenty, approached. "Rayford Steele?" she said shyly.

Rayford stood. "Yes, dear."

"Two things, if I may," she said, speaking very slowly and holding up two fingers. "You understand?"

"Yes, what is it?"

"Is it true you speak only English?"

"To my shame, yes. Well, a smattering of Spanish. Not enough to converse."

"Do not feel bad, sir. I speak only Hebrew."

"Well, your English is lovely too, young lady."

"You do not understand."

"I understand you perfectly. You speak English beautifully."

She laughed. "You do not understand."

Abdullah leaned in, chuckling. "And you are funny, young one. Speaking Arabic and yet talking about knowing only Hebrew. And, Rayford, how is it you know Arabic?"

The girl threw back her head and laughed again. "We all speak in our own languages and understand each other perfectly."

"What?" Rayford said. "Wait!"

"Sir! I speak only Hebrew."

"And Arabic," Abdullah corrected.

"But no. I was forbidden to learn Arabic."

"I need to lie down," Abdullah said.

"You said there were two things," Rayford said.

"Yes," she said, holding up two fingers again. "Two."

Rayford put a hand over her fingers. "No need. I understand you."

She laughed. "The second thing," and now she spoke more quickly, "is that Drs. Rosenzweig and Ben-Judah request an audience with you."

"With *me?* I should request an audience with them! I'm sure they are very busy."

"They asked me to fetch you, sir."

Rayford followed her over piles of rock that had been blown to pieces by the bombs. Just inside a cave, by light from a torch lodged in the wall, Chaim and Tsion sat with several older men. Tsion introduced Rayford all around and said, "The one we have been telling you about."

The men nodded and smiled. "Praise the Lord, Rayford," Tsion said.

"Continually," Rayford said. "But forgive me if I am preoccupied."

Tsion nodded again. "I too await word from our compatriots in Greece, and yet even now, the Lord quiets me with his peace and confidence."

"He may be trying to communicate the same to me, brother," Rayford said, "but that one of them is my daughter may affect my faith."

Tsion nodded again and smiled. "Possible. But after what you survived here today, is it not fair to say that any breakdown in communication between you and the Lord has to be your fault?"

"Well, *that* goes without saying."

"Oh, by the way, I am speaking Hebrew, and you are—"

"I know, brother. I have been all through that with the young lady."

The others laughed and one said, "My daughter!"

"Lovely."

"Thank you!"

"Chaim and I have been talking with these brothers about plans," Tsion said. "We will be praying for the Tribulation Force members all over the world and are eager to see how God delivers them. But everyone needs accountability, and as Chaim and I are accountable to you, we—"

"Oh, Tsion, no! Surely we're way past that! You've been the spiritual leader of the Tribulation Force for some time, and of the worldwide church of Christ for almost as long."

"No, now, Rayford, hear me."

"Begging your pardon, sir, you always flattered me by deferring to me as the titular leader of the Trib Force, but please . . ."

"These men, Rayford, are a good start for us here. They are the core of a group of elders I hope will eventually arise to help Chaim with the daily decisions. But they are, naturally, new to the faith."

"As *I* am, Tsion. Surely you're not suggesting—"

"Excuse me, Rayford, but you forget. None of us is terribly mature in the faith. In years anyway. I am not going to insult your intelligence by implying that I will seek your counsel on the Scriptures, though I cannot deny I have learned from you. But God put you in a strategic place for me at a very dark time in my life. If you do not mind, I would like to run past you some thoughts regarding the immediate future and get your feedback."

"If you insist, but at least concede that it was not I who stood in the midst of a million people and saw God miraculously spare them from the fires of hell."

Tsion looked at him with a twinkle in his eye, then turned to the other men. They laughed uproariously.

Chaim pointed at Rayford and chortled. "Was it not you? Then my eyes fail me!" He turned to Ben-Judah. "Tsion! Did I not see this very man standing in the midst of us, and could he have not seen what God did?"

"Well, okay," Rayford said. "Point taken. But *I* was not the reason the enemy attacked, Tsion. You and Chaim were. And I was not preaching, not praying, not standing there full of faith when the bombs fell. Truth be told, my faith is stronger in the aftermath than it was in the fire."

Tsion fell serious and ran a hand through his beard, studying Rayford. "You would make a good Israeli," he said.

Rayford shrugged. "Zeke was going for the Egyptian look, but whatever."

"No, I mean you argue like my countrymen. We could debate all night. And even when you are wrong, still you argue!"

That brought more laughter from the others.

"All right, Tsion. I don't know why you would want to hold yourself accountable to one you find it so easy to ridicule—"

"All in good fun, my dear brother. You know that."

"Of course. But anyway, I'm listening."

+ + +

Mac pulled his phone from his pocket and turned it on. "What're they doin', Socrates, your pals? Checkin' us out?"

Socrates shrugged.

"C'mon, you won't hurt my feelings. They trying to make sure we're legit, that we're not gonna jump 'em, embarrass 'em, what?"

Mac punched in Chang's number.

"There are no cells out here, sir," Socrates said. "You won't get through to anyone."

"Well, I wouldn't if I had bad technology, would I? But what if I had a phone juiced by the sun and bounced by the satellites? Then I wouldn't care whether you've got cells in the woods here, would I?"

"But you won't be able to reach the commander unless—"

"This is Chang, Mac. You okay?"

"I'm fine, Supreme Commander, sir. Just checkin' in to see if my phone works all the way to New Babylon."

"Loud and clear, Mac. Talk to me. What's going on? You in trouble? What can I do?"

"Fine, sir. How's the weather there?"

Chang said, "I've got my screen open to the GPS, and I'm tracking you and, ah, Jinnah and Irene right to where you ought to be."

"Hang on, boss. Just a second."

Mac pretended to tuck the phone to his chest, but he held it lightly enough so Chang could hear. "What did you just say, Socrates? That I couldn't use my phone in the woods?"

"Yeah, well, obviously you can, with the satellite and all. But you couldn't talk to somebody unless they had the same thing is all I was saying."

"Who would I want to talk to here with my fancy phone who wouldn't have one?"

Socrates paled. "Well, like *I* don't have one."

"Who else?"

"My partners don't either. We have regular."

"Thought I was gonna call one of your partners, did you?"

"Well, no."

"'Course not. Not unless their boss gave me their number, right?"

"Right."

"But even then, I couldn't call them out here, could I?"

"No. That's all I was saying."

"You were saying something else, weren't you, Socrates?"

"No. I was just talking."

"You thought I was calling Commander Stefanich, didn't you?"

"No, I—"

"Didn't you?"

"Yes."

"But you didn't think I could reach him." Socrates nodded miserably. "But how would you know that?"

"I was guessing."

"I can't get through to him in Ptolemaïs, in the middle of all the cells?"

"You probably can."

"But he's not there, is he?"

"How would I know?"

"Because he's here in the woods, isn't he?" Silence. "Isn't he, Socrates?"

He shrugged.

"So, how did he let you and your team know I was coming? Couldn't call you, could he?"

"I am so stupid."

"I'll grant you that, Socrates. Not livin' up to that name anyway, wouldn't you say?" Mac turned back to the phone. "Sorry to keep you, Chief."

"I'm way ahead of you, Mac. I can beam a signal to that phone of Stefanich's that will make the bells and whistles blow, even if I can't talk to him on it. He'll get a readout that Deputy Commander Konrad, who reports directly to Security and Intelligence Director Akbar, wants to talk with him immediately."

"Sounds good, Chief. I'll talk to you later. Things are going fine here."

"When he calls, I will use the voice modulator that can make me sound like an old German, and I'll tell him that Akbar himself is holding him personally responsible for giving Howie Johnson access to Sebastian."

"Perfect."

"And if he doesn't call, I'll have that on his phone's readout in time to help you out. Got you covered, Mac."

"Ain't that the truth, Commander!" Mac slapped the phone shut. "Lemme have that walkie-talkie, friend."

"You're going to get me killed."

"Who, me? Nah. You're a dead man anyway. Said so yourself."

"Are you going to kill me? Or let her?"

Mac shook his head. "I'll leave that to your partners. Look on the bright side. If they're as effective as you are, you'll be eatin' breakfast in the morning as usual."

Socrates stared at him.

"You eat breakfast, don't you, Socrates?"

The man nodded.

"'Scuse me," Mac said, and pretended to mash the button on the walkie-talkie. "Now hear this, Plato, Aristotle, and Elena. I don't want to talk to any of you. I want Nelly Stefanich. Now, Nelly, I know you're close by, and I admire your creativity, goin' by the book and all. I'm not even insulted that you're checkin' up on me. I'll make ya a deal. When you get confirmation that me and mine are all we claim to be, I want you to personally bring Sebastian to me. You know where I am. And bring that team of philosophers out from under their rock so I can see 'em. If you can get that done, Nelly, I promise not to take your command. Oh, and Nelson? That's an order, and you've got thirty minutes."

Mac turned and gave Chloe and Hannah a look. "Now, Socrates, you're free to go."

"What are you saying?"

"You heard me. Go on. Get out of here." Socrates struggled to his feet, then bent to pick up his weapon.

"That stays," Mac said.

"My radio then?" he said, reaching.

"Uh-uh. I'll keep that too."

"Where will I go?"

Mac shrugged. "That's up to you."

Socrates sat on the edge of a flimsy table and rubbed his knee. "I am a man with nowhere to go."

"You wanna be here when—"

The man stood quickly, teetering. "No. No. But it is so far to town. And with no protection or radio . . ."

"I can't help you, friend. You're part of an operation that didn't follow orders. You're lucky to be cut loose, considering the options. If you want to be here when the rest of your team—"

"Ach!" Socrates hobbled to the front door. Mac signaled Chloe with a nod to watch him. He gingerly stepped through the wood chips and splinters and made his way out.

"Follow him," Mac said, "till you're sure he's headed toward town. Hannah, check the perimeter. I'll clear this place, and we'll meet by the weapons out front."

✣ ✣ ✣

Rayford felt a fool, sitting in a cave, high on having personally lived through an Old Testament miracle, worrying about Chloe, and entertaining even the possibility that Tsion Ben-Judah himself should seek his opinion.

He knew he would be reunited with his daughter regardless, but was it wrong to wish her spared from a painful, violent death?

"You and Abdullah need to decide what you will do, Rayford," Tsion said. "You are welcome to stay, of course, but I do not know how practical it is to expect you to oversee the Tribulation Force from here. Our computer people tell me that David Hassid and Chang Wong have somehow already put in place here the basis for a mighty technological center, and that the bombs had no effect on the hardware or the software."

"Are you serious?" Rayford said. "The electromagnetic pulse from the missile alone should have fried everything."

"Everything is fine. Praise the Lord. So, you could conceivably keep track of everyone from here, but that is your call."

"Oh, I will be leaving," Rayford said. "I can't say when yet. I do worry about your returning to Chicago, Tsion."

"That is precisely what we have been discussing, Rayford. We do not know if it makes sense for any of us from there to attempt to return. Would not you and Abdullah be under as much scrutiny as I? Without another miracle, how could we return to the safe house without giving away its location?"

The thought of finding a new safe house, of moving, wearied Rayford. "We'll worry about that, Tsion. What are your plans? You could transmit your daily teachings from here."

Chaim interrupted. "That is my wish and that of the elders here. And I daresay the rest of the people."

"I do not know," Tsion said. "I will do as the Lord leads, but I believe Chaim is God's man here."

"My work is done, Tsion," Chaim said. "God did it in spite of my feeble efforts, and here we are. I shall hand off the baton to you, my former student."

"I remain your student, Doctor," Tsion said.

"Gentlemen," Rayford said, "the mutual admiration is inspiring but doesn't get us anywhere. This place needs leadership, organization, mediation. If you stay, Tsion, you should be protected from responsibilities that interfere with your teaching—here and to your Internet audience around the world."

The elders nodded.

"Perhaps among us," Chaim said, "we can ferret out young people with these gifts. I am willing to administer, coordinate a bit, but I am not a young man. This is a city, a country unto itself. We need a government. God provides food and water and clothes that will not wear out, but I believe he expects us to manage ourselves otherwise. We must organize and build—admittedly only for the short term, but still . . ."

"Maybe," Rayford said, "that very work is God's way of occupying your time here. Living together, getting along, functioning in harmony will be a full-time job. Imagine the boredom of a million people just sitting around waiting for the Glorious Appearing."

Tsion warmed to this. "Oh, that is why I believe we need to motivate people to help the rest of the world from here. We are not blind to the prophecies, to the machinations of the evil one. Trying to blow us up is only the beginning. He will think he can starve us out by cutting off our supply lines. He will not know or will not believe that God feeds us. But we know we are safe. What we must guard against are his schemes to lure the undecided away from this place, out to where they are vulnerable, not only emotionally and psychologically, but also physically. I am jealous to keep them here and to persuade them."

"I don't understand," Rayford said, "how anyone could remain undecided after today."

"It is beyond human comprehension," Tsion said, "but God foretold it. Now my dream for the faithful here is that they be useful in the cause of aiding our brothers and sisters around the world. Peter warns us to be sober and vigilant because our adversary walks about like a roaring lion, seeking whom he may devour. 'Resist him, steadfast in the faith, knowing that the same sufferings are experienced by your brotherhood in the world.'

"The evil one will grow angrier, more determined, more vicious, and many will die at his hand. What better, nobler task could the million strong here undertake than to aid your daughter's Commodity Co-op and equip the saints to thwart Antichrist?

"I envision thousands of technological experts creating a network of resources for believers, informing them of safe havens, putting them in touch with each other. We know we will lose many brothers and sisters, and yet we should offer what we can to keep the gospel going forth, even now."

Rayford sat back. "Can't argue with that. And it's not a bad idea, Tsion, this becoming your new base of operation. We will miss you, of course, but it makes no sense to risk losing you to the cause when all you need is right here."

"I have been thinking," Chaim said, "and, Rayford, feel free to correct me, as I am out of my element on this topic. But I wonder if the day of a safe house for the Tribulation Force is past. We know New Babylon is sniffing around and that it is only a matter of time before Chicago is exposed. Yes, perhaps we need a central location for the coordinating of the Co-op, but if I were you I would worry for my little one, being moved hither and yon. I leave the details to you and your compatriots. But I ask you, is it not true that anyone who is asked to remain at the safe house quickly gets the cottage fever?

"The young man there, Zeke, who so masterfully equips us to venture out, might find moving around a nuisance. And the matter of record keeping and computers is difficult. But perhaps the safe house of the future will be in a thousand places, not just one. Perhaps the time has come to make your home in the hiding places of the believers around the world."

Rayford feared Chaim was right, and it must have shown.

"I am not saying it will be easy," Chaim said, "but I urge you to take the initiative. Make the hard decision. Disband the safe house and disperse your people before they are found out, for then you could lose everyone at once. Surely you all know you have stayed in one place long past a reasonable hour."

"Oh, I know that, Chaim," Rayford said. "In reality, we have not been at the Strong Building very long. Too long, no doubt, but not even as long as we were at our previous location."

Tsion stood and stretched. "We need to leave this with you. God will lead you. I intended to seek your counsel, and now we have tried to counsel you."

"I appreciate it."

"But please, Rayford, counsel me. Let me tell you what I believe God is impressing upon me, and see if it makes any sense to you. I know it will jar the sensibilities of many hearers, and yet I dare not casually disregard it. You see, because of what has happened since the Rapture of the church, I believe there is ample evidence of one part of God's nature and character. Clearly this is a time of judgment, even of wrath. We are in the middle of the last seven of the twenty-one judgments of God, and we even endured one he himself refers to in the Scriptures as the wrath of the Lamb.

"It would be easy for a preacher to illumine and drive home the truth of God's impatience, his judgment poured out on his enemies, his demand for justice for the blood of the prophets. But I have come to the conclusion that all this goes without saying. Yes, this is the last chance. Yes, everything has been telescoped into seven last years, and we are already well into the second half of that. God will do what God will do, but I am jealous to protect his reputation.

"Oh, I know he does not need me, does not require my assistance. I am humbled to the depths of my soul that he has seen fit to allow me *any* role in ministering to the nations. But a profound and seemingly contradictory message presses on my heart. I believe it is of God, but it is such a paradox, such a dichotomy, that I dare not run ahead of him without the counsel of and wisdom of my spiritual family."

Tsion massaged his temples and began to pace. "Gentlemen," he said, "walk with me."

"The crowds will press if you leave here," someone said.

"They will see we are engaged, I am sure," Tsion said. "Let us not make a spectacle. Surround me and let us move away from the masses."

The people still frolicked around the spring while others filled containers and gathered manna. Rayford joined the elders and Chaim and casually moved into a ravine and down a rocky slope.

When they were clear of others, Tsion talked as he walked. "I am not unaware that I have been bestowed a great privilege. I have a congregation here alone of a million souls. I have opportunity to teach the babies in the faith, offering them the milk of the Word. I also enjoy breaking the bread and carving the meat of the deeper things to the more mature. And I am blessed to preach the gospel, evangelizing, for even here, there are the undecided. We will not win all of them, a truth that astounds me, especially in the glow of an event such as we experienced just hours ago. But the point is, God daily refreshes me and allows me—expects me—to exercise all the gifts he has bestowed on a pastor-teacher."

When Tsion stopped, the rest stopped. He sat on a rock, and they gathered around him. "It may sound strange to you all, because I have said many, many times that this is the worst seven-year period in the history of mankind, but in many ways I count it an almost limitless benefit to be alive right now. Technology has allowed me a congregation, if the figures can be believed, of more than a billion via the Internet. Someday in heaven I will ask God to let me get my finite brain around that figure. For now it is too much to take in. I cannot picture it, cannot tell you how many one-hundred-thousand-seat stadiums it would take to house them all. Well, of course I know that ten thousand such stadiums would equal a billion people, but does that help you picture it in your mind? Me neither.

"Now, let me tell you what weighs on me when I think of the responsibilities I have to such a congregation. I believe the time has come to stop talking about the judgment of God. There is no denying it. There is no pretending that his wrath is not being poured out. But I have come to the conclusion that the whole message of God throughout the ages is an anthem to his mercy.

"Most of you know that this comes from a man who saw his beloved wife and children murdered. Am I saying that the holiness of God is less important than the love of God? How could I when the Scriptures say that he is love, but that he is holy, holy, holy?

"I am merely saying that I will let God's justice and judgment and wrath speak for themselves, and I will spend the rest of my time here championing his mercy."

It seemed to Rayford that Tsion took the time to look into the eyes of everyone who had heard him. He could have gone on, defended himself and his novel opinion. But he simply finished by saying, "You have until noon tomorrow to correct me if you believe I am a wayward brother. Otherwise, my teaching begins, and you know my theme."

✢ ✢ ✢

Buck was sympathetic to Albie. The diminutive Middle Easterner was wound tight, unable to sit still. "I can't live like this, Cameron," he said. "I'm going to spend this evening with Zeke and look through his files. Have you seen his inventory?"

"Of course."

"There has to be an identity in there for me. The GC thing probably won't work for me again, but I'll do anything. Anything but sit around here. You think he could make me tall and blond?"

Buck had to smile. One of two wasn't bad. "I might join you," he said. "Zeke's a master, and this sitting around is gonna kill me."

"But you write. You get to download all that stuff from Chang and get it out on the Net. I love your son, Cameron, but trading off babysitting, reading, looking out the window, and waiting for everybody to check in is going to drive me crazy."

"I know."

"Have you spent much time with Mac?" Albie said.

"Sure."

"Great man. Good mind. But we don't think the same. I can imagine all kinds of things he's doing in Greece right now that could get—oh, I'm sorry. I keep forgetting Chloe is right there with him."

"What? You think Mac won't look out for Chloe? She's probably looking out for him."

"I ought to be there is what I'm saying."

✢ ✢ ✢

"Deputy Commander Konrad?"

"That is correct," Chang said, his voice electronically modulated, "and this had better be Nelson Stefanich."

"It is, sir, and—"

"Commander, I want to know what in the world is going on over there."

"Yes, sir, we—"

"I sent my senior commander all the way from New Babylon to talk directly with your prisoner."

"And that will happen, sir. I—"

"I don't appreciate him getting jerked around when you had fair warning and plenty of time to make arrangements."

"I know. We—"

"I'll expect a full report transmitted to my office by noon tomorrow."

"I'll definitely do that, sir, because it *is* explainable."

"Is Johnson meeting with Sebastian now?"

"Not quite yet—"

"Even as we speak? Because if not, I want to know why not."

"There was some mix-up with our local team, sir. They thought they heard—"

"I'll look for those details tomorrow, Commander, but meanwhile I'm going to assume you're effecting this meeting."

"Yes, sir."

"And not making Johnson come to you."

"Sir?"

"He's gone as far as I expect him to have to go. Anywhere he is, is a secure environment, so you have your people get the prisoner to him."

"Yes, sir. Deputy Commander, could I inform you of some good news?"

"There is no good news until I know Johnson has access to Sebastian."

"I just wanted you to know that we have located the central underground headquarters in Ptolemaïs and plan to raid it at midnight."

7

CHLOE WATCHED SOCRATES from inside the shack until he disappeared, limping down toward the road. Then she tiptoed out, went ninety degrees into the trees, hurried past the Fifty and the DEW, which her quarry had passed some forty feet to his left. She found it no chore to keep up with the lame Socrates.

Chloe held tight to the grip on the Uzi, pulling the strap taut to keep it away from her body and from clacking into the Luger. She turned sideways and mince-stepped the decline, carefully crossing the gravel road. Stopping on the other side, she heard movement in the underbrush, someone heading left, east, hurrying and not worrying about snapping twigs and thrashing through the thick stuff. Chloe squatted and regulated her breathing, gauging direction and distance to keep from following too close and giving herself away.

There was no need for her to step into the overgrowth. She could easily keep pace staying at the side of the road in the soft, silent dirt. The only danger was overtaking her prey and being seen. It had to be Socrates. When he came even with the shack again, though he was below the line of sight from the front door, he stopped, apparently to listen. Hearing nothing must have encouraged him, because now out he came, maybe fifty feet ahead of Chloe and also choosing to stay on the quieter surface next to the road.

Chloe stood stock-still in case he decided to turn around. She couldn't imagine being seen in the darkness, but who knew what kind of vision the limping, unarmed man might have? Some people could see or sense shapes in the darkness. Mac had proved that. And maybe this character knew the area, would notice a silhouette between trees that should have provided a clear shot to the stars.

Chloe waited until he went around a bend, then hurried to where she could again hear the labored footsteps. She peeled her eyes and saw—or at least imagined—that he was testing the knee, trying to walk more upright, more normal, and not succeeding. Occasionally she heard a grunt or a moan. He was in pain, and he certainly was taking the long way to town.

No, Socrates was going to lead her to George Sebastian. Chloe just knew it. Should she attempt a quiet transmission, let Mac know Hopalong was headed the wrong way? How much of a lead could he get if that took thirty seconds? Mac and Hannah could catch up with her quickly, and they could overtake him in no time.

But Mac was double-checking the shack, and Hannah was outside alone, making sure no ambush was afoot. Chloe would never forgive herself if a needless transmission gave someone an audible target. If Socrates led her right to this lean-to or whatever it was, unless she was seen, she couldn't be in any danger. If the other three were there—even if Stefanich was there—she'd still have plenty of time to call for the others.

+ + +

Mac knelt in the cool dampness of the cramped cellar. The single bare bulb hanging from the ceiling revealed irregular shapes on the earthen floor. With his flashlight he tried to determine whether George had been mistreated. It was impossible to tell if those were flecks of blood among the footprints and indecipherable shapes. *It's where I would terrorize a hostage,* Mac decided.

He shined his light in every corner, flipped off the cellar switch, and was headed upstairs when his phone chirped. Eager to get outside to the rendezvous but hesitant to be on the phone in the open air, he paused on the stairs and flipped it open. Was it his imagination or had he heard a voice from out back? He assumed Hannah would have done her perimeter scan and would be waiting with Chloe by the tree in front.

Mac didn't dare say anything, so he just listened to the phone.

"Mac?"

It was Chang, but Mac didn't want to acknowledge. He pressed a button on the keypad.

"Mac? That you?"

He pressed the button longer.

"Okay, you can't talk, but neither can I until I can confirm it's you. One beep if the following is true; two if it's false: After the first book in the New Testament, the next four have exactly the same number of letters in their titles."

Now Mac for sure heard a voice from the back. Male. Chang's statement was true, but was it one for true and two for false or the other way around? He hesitated, listening while creeping to the top of the stairs.

"Mac would know this," Chang said. "One if true, two if—"

Mac pressed one quickly.

"Could have been a lucky guess," Chang said, and Mac closed his eyes. *Come on!*

"You have a contact in a very strategic location. Give me a beep for the number of letters in his sister's *maiden* name."

What? Chang would be so clever at a party. Okay, Chang's the contact. His sister is Ming Toy. Three. Wait! Maiden name. Same as Chang's. Wong. Four. Mac punched them quickly, now peeking out of the darkened shack toward the back. He could see nothing.

"Okay, Mac, right. Now listen. Talked to Stefanich as Konrad. He's going to make his guys bring Sebastian to you, so stay put but don't waste time. He claims they've found the underground headquarters and will raid it at midnight. I don't have any numbers on the Co-op people there. Do you? One if yes, two if no."

Mac pressed twice.

"I don't even know that they have phones. Can you send somebody to help? One if—"

Mac beeped once.

"Are you in immediate danger?"

Mac beeped twice.

"Okay, so you're somewhere where you can't talk. GPS shows you still where I talked to you last. Someone there with you?"

Twice.

"Outside?"

Once.

"See them?"

Twice.

"Okay, you hear them. Have you got personnel outside?"

Once.

"Both?"

Once.

"I'll let you go. You want me to stay on?"

Twice.

"Check in when you're clear. I want to know we're doing something for the Co-op there."

Mac put his phone away and crept outside. Half a dozen armed Peacekeepers milled about by the car.

"I say we take it. We've hiked for hours."

"No keys."

"So hot-wire it."

"Come on! Supposed to be only five hundred more meters."

The Peacekeepers headed east. Mac circled around to the front. *So Stefanich sent backup. Wonder if that's all of 'em?*

Neither Hannah nor Chloe was by the tree. Mac made a noise through his teeth, in case they were close by. Nothing. He knelt in the darkness. The Fifty was in place. The DEW was gone.

\+ \+ \+

It felt to George as if Aristotle had turned left onto the road and driven east for about twenty minutes before pulling off to the side and waiting. He had once been able to keep track of the passage of time, but now he had to fight sleep. If he had to guess, George would have said they sat, not moving, for more than an hour. But neither would it have surprised him if it were actually twice that long.

Finally Aristotle said, "What do you think?"

"We could have gone long ago," Elena said. "The place clears out early, and there aren't that many people there anymore anyway."

"Plato?"

"Yes, go! We've got to get back up here before long."

It seemed to George that they eventually made their way out of the woods and off the gravel road to a main road and were heading south. Then they went east, and he had the sense, from ambiance and sound, that they were in a populated area, maybe a town.

"Get him out of sight," Aristotle said a few minutes later.

Plato reached and grabbed George by the right shoulder and pulled him over to where his head now lay in the big man's lap.

Aristotle soon slowed and seemed to be parking.

"No, no!" Plato said. "Around back."

Once they finally stopped and parked, Elena said, "I'll see if we're clear." George felt a cramp in his lower back but could do nothing about it. She returned and got back in the Jeep, shutting the door. "About twenty minutes," she said.

"You got it?" Aristotle said. "Let me see it."

"And it goes where?"

"About a foot below the top of the right door."

"I never noticed before."

"Can I sit him up?" Plato said.

"Better wait."

\+ \+ \+

Chloe stopped fifty feet in back of Socrates and guessed they were close to five hundred meters from the shack. He was bent over, hands on his thighs, breathing heavily. His pace had slowed the last hundred meters or so, and maybe he was trying to come up with an approach to his comrades that would gain him sympathy rather than hostility.

She was watching him carefully when she froze at the sound of footsteps on the gravel. Several. Not hurrying. Not sneaking. Just coming. She backed into the underbrush about ten feet off the road and knelt, the knees of her camouflage pants immediately soaked through and cold. She fought the temptation to hold her breath, fearing she would exhale right when whoever was behind her came by. Chloe knew it couldn't be Mac and Hannah. There were too many.

She was out of sight of Socrates now and hated not knowing whether he was off again. If he was, he would find his team without her knowing where. And here came half a dozen Peacekeepers, weapons in hand. They were in no hurry, chatting, a couple smoking. Chloe tried to make it make sense. They seemed to have an idea where they were going. Same spot? She could follow them, and maybe more easily because of the noise they made.

They were ten feet past her, and she would wait another thirty seconds before venturing out. Her walkie-talkie gave two quick, staticky squawks, startling her. The Peacekeepers kept walking and talking, but she panicked. Though they hadn't heard the sounds, if someone started talking to her, they'd hear that.

She reached in her pocket to turn off the radio, but in feeling for the right knob turned it up. Frantic to shut it off, she lurched, lost her balance, and flopped onto her seat. "Johnson or Irene, come in, please."

Too loud!

Chloe leaped to her feet, yanked out the radio, squeezed the transmit button twice, shut it off, and set herself, readying the Uzi. The Peacekeepers had stopped and now crept her way.

+ + +

Mac pulled out his radio and whispered, "Johnson here, Jinnah. What's your ten-twenty?"

"One hundred yards northeast of rendezvous point."

"You okay?"

"Ten-four. GC troops in the woods, sir."

"Irene with you?"

"Negative."

"The DEW?"

"Affirmative."

"On my way. How many?"

"Guessing two dozen, sir."

"Come back?"

"Minimum twenty-four."

"Roger. Be sure you're clear, cease radio transmission, and return to rendezvous ASAP."

"Roger."

So much for bluffing Stefanich. Either he wasn't buying or he's royally stupid.

"Johnson to Irene . . . Johnson to Irene . . . Johnson to Irene. Do you read?"

Mac looked at his watch, kicked the ground, pressed his lips together, and waited for Hannah.

+ + +

Chloe stood in the bramble, finger on the trigger, feet spread in the mushy ground. The Peacekeepers stopped on the road, facing her position, close enough that she could hear their breathing. All six set their weapons at the same time. She could barely see them and assumed they could not see her. She held her breath and did not move.

"GC!" one called out. "Who goes there?"

Chloe entertained the hope that they would all six decide they hadn't really heard anything.

"Show yourself or we spray the area!"

"Friend!" she called out. "GC here too. Sister on assignment. Cool your jets."

"Armed?"

"Holding it over my head, Peacekeeper. Ten-to-one I outrank you, so don't do anything rash."

A big flashlight made her squint. Holding the Uzi over her head, she said, "Turn that thing off! We're all here on the same assignment."

The light went off. "Hand over the weapon, ma'am, and we'll sort this out."

"No, we'll sort it out first. Now I'm tucking it under my arm to show my papers. Stand down now. So far you've been by the book and I can't fault you."

"Thank you. I'm going to need to turn the light onto your docs, ma'am."

"Hold on, I got a smaller beam. Going into the pocket."

With the weapon tucked and pointing her small flashlight at her papers, Chloe's heart drumrolled against her chest.

"Superior officer, guys," the leader said. "Salute."

"No need," Chloe said. "Good job. A little sloppy on the march, but at least you're on time."

"What were you doing in the bushes, ma'am?"

"Following orders. Now wait here for my CO and another officer, and we'll go together."

"That Uzi's not official issue, is it?"

"Something to look forward to."

"Really?"

"At my level it is."

"Wow."

"We still reasonably on schedule?" she said.

"About twenty minutes early, ma'am."

"Stand by, gentlemen." Chloe pulled out her radio and turned it on. "Officer Irene to Senior Commander Johnson."

"Johnson! Oh, man!"

"Senior Commander!"

Chloe turned to the Peacekeepers. "A little decorum, please."

"Johnson, go ahead."

"Sir, I've met up with six Peacekeepers who will join us on the assignment. Standing by for you approximately 480 meters east of your position."

"Six?"

"Ten-four."

"Everything copacetic, Irene?"

"Ten-four."

+ + +

"For all I know, we could be surrounded," Mac told Hannah. "You sure you weren't seen?"

"Positive."

"What is going on?" He called Chang and filled him in. "What do you think Stefanich is up to?"

"I'm in his mainframe, Mac, and there's nothing there. Could be as bad as they're onto you, or he's still trying to cover."

"But what's he need all these people in the woods for? They mustering here for the midnight raid?"

"Seems out of the way."

"Sure does. Unless they're wrong about the location of the underground headquarters. We're not far from where the pastor hid out Rayford. You think they've finally discovered that?"

"You're a good thirty miles from there, Mac. I'll stay on it, but I don't know what to tell you."

\+ + +

Aristotle said, "All right, let's go."

Plato shoved George up. Someone opened his door, and it seemed Plato and Aristotle each took an arm and guided him, while Elena opened doors. They led him about fifteen feet, up three concrete steps, and inside. Then about twenty steps down a corridor that from the echoes seemed narrow. Finally into a larger room.

Aristotle let go of George and walked a few steps away. "Ach! I can't reach it. Plato?"

"Give me that."

George heard what sounded like metal being slotted into metal, then a couple of loud clicks. Plato grunted. "What's the secret here?" he said.

"Let me get the other side," Aristotle said, and he was replaced at George's side by Elena. *If only I weren't cuffed,* George thought. That was when he would have taken his chances. Coldcock the girl, whip off the blindfold, race back down that corridor and outside, and hope for the best. But not with his hands behind his back. Any hesitation and she would shoot him, he was sure.

Plato and Aristotle grunted, and Aristotle said, "Push him in, Elena. Come on, Plato and I have to get back."

Elena guided George forward, turned him sideways, and tried to force him through an opening apparently being held on each side by the men. He didn't fit. "Give me another couple of inches," she said, and they grunted louder. She pushed George through.

"Hold on now," Aristotle said. "I don't want him found cuffed and blindfolded."

Hands reached in and unlocked the cuffs. "Toss me the blindfold," Elena said.

George slipped it off and saw he was inside a dark elevator. Elena had a weapon pointed at him. *Good thing for them,* George thought, because Plato and Aristotle were totally occupied holding the doors open. Elena took the blindfold, shoved it in a pocket, and pulled a bottle of water from another. She tossed it in and said, "Cheers," as the doors slammed shut.

George let the bottle bounce on the floor and tried to get his fingers between the doors. Just when he had found purchase he heard the key slide into its hole again and the throwing of the lock. He heard water sloshing and felt around in the dark for the bottle. He uprighted it and decided to save what was left for as long as he could.

With his arms spread, George could touch the walls on each side, and as he made a quarter turn, he realized the enclosure was square. It didn't surprise him that the buttons on a panel were not working, but he could tell from the pattern that he was in a four-story building. The ceiling was less than a foot above his head.

George felt for loose panels, missing screws, anything. Everything felt secure. A thin, plastic panel had to be the cover for the light. He removed that and felt a small, circular double fluorescent tube. Next to that was a mesh panel. He pushed up hard on the side until it gave way, then ripped it down. Now he could feel the fan blades, dusty, oily.

His body was already heating, and his breath was short. Were these people crazy? A malfunctioning elevator might make a perfect prison cell, but did they want him to suffocate? George shed his sweater and boots and socks and sat down, his back against the door. He found a boot and began swinging it backward over his shoulder against the door.

"Knock it off or I'll put you out of your misery," Elena called out. So they had left her alone to guard him. He wanted to tell her that if they didn't want a dead hostage to show to the brass, they'd better at least get the fan running. But he was committed not to speak. Not a word. And so he kept banging.

+ + +

Chang had a bad feeling. Since the day he had been left as the only mole at the GC Palace, he had never felt so helpless. Was it possible Stefanich was playacting? They seemed to have him intimidated, eager to please. Even if he had checked on Mac, Chang had everything in place to make Howie Johnson look legit. He was certain Stefanich was embarrassed to find he had doubted this high-level Johnson character and should now be trying to cover that he had ever doubted him.

Chang was desperate to find out how vulnerable Mac and Chloe and Hannah were. Could they be walking into an ambush? Time was against him, but it might be wrong to just tell Mac to abort. Maybe they could hot-wire the car at the shack and get back to the airport, but Chang knew Mac wouldn't abandon Sebastian. What if he was already dead? If Mac had been exposed, there was no reason for the GC to keep him alive.

Chang slapped his forehead with both palms. *Think! If they're onto Mac, why are they? If you can find the connection, maybe you can figure out what they might do.*

Chang started a global search, asking David Hassid's superpowered engine to match anyone at high levels in the palace with the GC at Ptolemaïs. He even keyed in code breakers, in case the contact person feared someone within the palace was monitoring them. With the computer whirring away, darting through thousands of files in hundreds of locations, Chang fell to his knees.

"God, I have never asked you to override a piece of equipment. But you know a servant of yours designed this, and I want to serve you too. Help me think. Speed the process. Please let me protect these brothers and sisters. I know from what happened at Petra today that nothing is beyond you. We have lost so much to the enemy, and I know we will lose more before your ultimate victory. But don't let the Greek believers suffer more. Not tonight. Protect the Co-op. And help me get Mac and Chloe and Hannah and George out of there."

+ + +

Mac liked a clear mission, a black-and-white assignment. This one was infiltrate, then storm the gates, free your man, and hit the road. Now there was the underground complication. He wouldn't leave Greece without his man, and now he couldn't leave without defending the believers.

The original plan didn't figure he and his people would be outnumbered. There were four hostage takers. Mac, his two team members, and George made four good guys. Those odds he could live with. But to walk Hannah down the road to Chloe and six GC, knowing there were at least two dozen more in the area, well, that didn't make sense.

"Hold up," he told Hannah. "You know how to hot-wire a car?"

"Do I admit it or not?"

"Just say so. Time is not on our side."

"Yes."

"Do it."

While she trotted to Sebastian's car, Mac radioed Chloe. "Johnson to Irene."

"Irene, go."

"Unforeseen delay here. Need your assistance."

"Ten-four. Should I bring help?"

"Negative. Let them go on. We'll catch up."

+ + +

"You heard the boss, gentlemen," Chloe said. "We'll see you at the destination."

"We'd love to help the senior commander, ma'am."

"Thank you, no."

"Can we meet him later?"

"I'll see to it." And as she said it, Chloe was overwhelmed with a deep impression, and she had to express herself. "If you do me a favor."

"Anything, ma'am."

"Senior Commander Johnson's presence tonight is a surprise for Commander Stefanich. He's going to be compensated for some of his recent actions. So . . ."

"Don't let on he's coming?"

"Exactly."

"You got it, ma'am. And you know what? We didn't know Commander Stefanich was going to be here. Fact is, we don't know what we're doing here."

Chloe blanched. What if Stefanich wasn't there? "It's all part of the surprise, boys."

⁜ ⁜ ⁜

Chang knew God had protected him, probably more than he realized. But he had no reason to think God owed him anything or was obligated to act in this instance, just because Chang had asked. With zero confidence that his pleas had done any good, Chang wearily returned to his chair before the computer.

The screen was alive with red flashes. The search engine had reached secure files at the highest levels and was matching, comparing, translating languages, turning spoken word into written. A small box in the upper right-hand corner showed six matches already between some element of the GC operation in Ptolemaïs with top brass at the palace. Top.

Chang feared multitasking would slow the search, but he had to take the chance. Mac and the two women were in danger, outnumbered, without any idea what they faced.

He checked the first three matches and found they were routine interactions of Ptolemaïs administration reporting statistics to GC command. But the fourth was different. It was highest security interaction, a series of e-mails between TB and OT, plus more than one phone call, also between the same two, being reduced to typed transcription.

Chang keyed in, "Match logic?"

The response was immediate. "Meets broad, simple criteria: initials one letter removed from key personnel in GC Greece and GC Palace."

Chang squinted. That's what he had asked for: any connection based on standard search sequences and codes. TB was one letter away from SA. OT was one letter away from NS. Chang shot from his chair and stood hunched over the keyboard. He typed in, "Show interaction," and as the files cascaded onto the screen, he called Mac.

⁜ ⁜ ⁜

Mac heard the car running and footsteps jogging toward him from the north and the east. "Ladies?" he said.

"Yes."

"Yep."

His phone buzzed. "Stand by. Hey, Chang."

"Mac! I'll say this once and get back to you as fast as possible with details. Ready?"

"Go."

"Akbar and Stefanich have communicated personally several times today." *Click.*

"Busted," Mac said. "Listen up. No time for questions. Hannah, you're driving. Chloe, you're riding. Take the DEW, Uzi, and a sidearm each, phones on, radios on. Get to the Co-op now. Clear 'em out, including anything they don't want found in a midnight raid. Then straight to the airport and wait out of sight for Sebastian and me, ready to hightail it to his plane. If we don't show, that means we're dead and you're on your own."

Mac bent and heaved the Fifty up against his chest. "Time to go to work, big boy," he said.

Hannah and Chloe ran around the shack to the idling car.

8

"THANK YOU, LORD," Chang said, still standing as his fingers danced on the keyboard. In seconds he had opened the transcripts of four phone conversations on a line so secure that Carpathia himself had once said even he didn't have access to it.

But David Hassid cracked it, Nicky. Access that.

Chang also had copies of e-mails that showed up on neither the palace nor the Ptolemaïs mainframe and were supposedly guaranteed to disappear from every record after they had been read. Hassid's master disk probably had the only copies in existence, including the correspondents'.

Though he was curious, Chang knew it was irrelevant how someone at Stefanich's level had personal access to the director of Security and Intelligence. The way they interacted evidenced some history, but if the box in the corner had not begun flashing again, Chang would not have wasted the time tracking it down until the crisis was over. He quickly clicked on the box to find "100 percent primary match, no decode necessary."

He opened the manifest and sped read: "Straight correlation from List A to List B: Suhail Akbar and Nelson Stefanich registered at Madrid Military School, overlapping tenures."

From the years listed, Chang calculated they had been there together as teenagers, more than twenty-five years before. *That would get a phone call returned.*

Chang was flying now, his eyes darting over the copy, looking for how the ruse fell apart.

Stefanich had asked whether Howie Johnson was "a fair man."

Akbar responded that the name didn't ring a bell.

Stefanich told him, "Senior Commander under Konrad."

"I'll look him up."

Akbar found him and reported, "Stellar record, but our paths have not crossed. Unusual for someone at that level, but it happens."

"Don't want to be a pest," Stefanich had followed, "but does Konrad vouch for him? Want to be sure before exposing him to prisoner."

"What prisoner? And who's Konrad?"

"The Judah-ite, George Sebastian."

"Still nothing out of him?"

"We'll break him or kill him."

"Break him. I know you can."

"You're not Konrad's immediate superior?"

"No. Do I need to look him up too?"

"You'd better. He's supposed to be your top guy, deputy commander, office on your floor."

"Send documentation."

Later, Akbar told Stefanich, "You're being duped. Johnson and Konrad are in the system, everything adds up, except they don't exist."

"Permission to reverse sting them?"

"With my best wishes. Bring them in, dead or alive, and I'll move you to the palace."

As the phone calls and e-mails progressed, the women's identities proved phony too. "The one from Montreal was in my office."

By early afternoon, Akbar had decided, "If Sebastian is worth all this, they're tied in tight with the underground. Announce a raid and see if they reveal location."

Chang called Mac. "The raid's phony. If you warn the believers, you could give them away."

"Call Chloe or Hannah. I'm occupied."

"Your location is a trap too, Mac."

"All right, listen, Chang. You saved our lives. But whatever you do, find Sebastian. I'll get him out or die tryin'."

+ + +

Chloe answered her phone.

It was Chang. "Raid was a setup so you'd lead the GC to the underground. Abort."

"Hannah, you were right."

"What?"

"Hannah was right, Chang. She suspected we were being followed. I didn't notice a thing and thought she was paranoid."

"I told you!"

"Ditch them or lead them nowhere," Chang said. "From what I can tell, the GC has no clue where the Co-op is or that it's the meeting place. I gotta go. Mac is calling."

✣ ✣ ✣

"Go, Mac."

"Question. If this is a trap, why wouldn't Peacekeepers have come back with Chloe and taken me then?"

"I don't follow."

Mac told him of her encounter with the half-dozen.

"You got me. I'm still reading the back-and-forth between Akbar and Stefanich. Possible not everybody knows."

"That could be."

"It's to your advantage."

"Confirm if you can."

"Will do."

✣ ✣ ✣

Mac had moved east far enough to see the lean-to, if there was one. He saw nothing. Not even the GC Hannah or Chloe had seen. That meant the meeting place for the ground troops was at least a little farther on. If Chang was right, Sebastian wouldn't be within miles of there.

Brilliant military mind, Mac. Left yourself alone in the wilderness, way outnumbered.

Mac considered his options and few advantages. He was hard to see. He knew enough not to be lured to where Sebastian was purported to be. He had the Fifty. He was a long walk or a medium jog to the car, but the car had to already be under surveillance. It would be surrounded, so if he were stupid enough to try to get to it, he would be easily apprehended. "Lord," he said quietly, "I'm gonna thank you for keepin' me motivated to stay in shape, and I'm gonna ask you for more stamina than I've got. All I'm tryin' to do is get your man and my two partners out of here alive. Now I'm thankin' you as if you've already done it, 'cause I'm going to be busy here awhile. And if you've chosen not to, I figure you know best and I'll be seein' you real soon."

Mac made his way back toward the shack and stopped about a hundred yards above it. He removed his big, outer jacket, kept only three fifty-caliber shells and two clips for the Uzi, then wound the Uzi strap twice so the weapon was snug to his body.

He couldn't actually run carrying the Fifty, but he loped the best he could, staying high on the ridge and following the terrain, often as far as two hundred yards above the road. The air was cool on his arms and neck and face at first, but soon his body heat made him sweat. This, he knew, was only the beginning.

Mac's muscles ached and knotted and all but cried out, but he would not stop. He didn't even slow. He just kept moving, farther and farther west, trying to gauge the distance to where he had left the car. After traversing a rugged stretch with loose rocks that nearly made him fall several times, he finally decided to look for the vehicle.

Mac stretched out on the steep slant, facing down toward the road. He set the bipod, his arms shaking from effort and fatigue, popped open the telescopic sight, loosened the connection so he could scan with it rather than trying to move the heavy gun, and searched the road.

It seemed to take forever for his eye to adjust in the darkness. The gravel road was a ribbon of only slightly lighter gray against the blackness of the woods, but he knew what he was looking at. At the far right of his field of vision—far enough that he knew he would have to move the weapon nearly a hundred feet—he spotted something that picked up a hint of starlight. Only the white car would do that.

Mac gulped another minute's worth of the cool air, then forced himself up and over to where he could line the Fifty up with the car. He was nothing if not patient. While he tightened the sight and made several seat-of-the-pants calculations, he swore he saw movement on the north side of the road. If he was right, GC waited for him down there—and almost certainly on the other side of the road too.

He remembered from experience to tear cloth from his undershirt and stuff both ear canals. He set an extra round of ammunition next to the weapon, then dug himself footholds. It was a huge benefit to be pointing downhill, because the recoil could shove him up and back only so far. He had to remember to keep his knees bent.

Mac's plan was to fire two rounds into the car in as rapid a succession as possible, knowing that he would have to force himself to follow through, because no one who had shot this rascal once—and that included him—ever wanted to shoot it again, let alone right away.

He stretched out and settled in, leaving his finger off the trigger until he had drawn the butt of the rifle to his shoulder. He maneuvered it until it lay in a soft spot and not on bone, aware that the thing would still wreak havoc with his whole body.

Mac ran through the checklist. Steady. Relaxed. Pull firm to the shoulder. Trigger finger relaxed. Ears protected. Feet in holds. Elbows slightly bent. Knees flexed and ready to give. Barely visible crosshairs dead on the roof of the car, a tick left, allowing for wind. Distance just under two hundred yards. No matter what the thing does to me, reload and fire again, not worrying about accuracy the second time.

It warmed Mac as he silently counted himself down from three that he definitely saw movement through the lens. Unless someone was so spectacularly unfortunate as to step into his line of fire, no one would be hit, certainly not by the first round. By the second, even if he got it off inside a few beats, he expected the GC to be halfway back to the shack already.

When he got to one, Mac aborted. Better idea. Go for broke. Aim a little left, hope to hit the gas tank. Even if he missed, these guys had to think they were facing a tank or at least a bazooka. But if he got lucky, they'd think they were facing eternity.

He reset, just a smidge. Checklist. *Three, two, one, zero, oh, Mama!*

Mac thought he had been prepared. It was as if he had nothing in his ears. The sound was so massive it seemed to weigh on him. The woods had exploded, and yes, the erupting of that gas tank and the rebounding of that car on the gravel would have made a sound whether or not people had been there to hear it. The perverse nightmare of the sheer volume of it lay atop him longer than the orange ball rode his eyeballs.

The violence drove him back and onto his left side. As Mac struggled to gather his senses, he rolled back to his belly and slid back down into the same position. Fingers fluttering, he wrestled the extra round into the chamber, made sure the thing was generally facing away from him again, and forced himself against every instinct to pull the trigger again.

He should have run through the checklist again. One foot had not been secure. He was neither tight nor firm. The butt had been at least a half inch from his shoulder. The recoil sent it back seemingly at the speed of light and drove a ridge into the top of his shoulder he was sure would be there for weeks.

The sound was lessened only by the damage the first shot had done to his eardrums. His ears buzzed and rang, and he dumbly lifted his head to see trees falling, two on this side of the road, one on the other. His aim had been ten feet to the left of the now flattened and burning car, which prettily illuminated the carnage of machine and fauna—all wrought by two fairly simple pulls on a metal lever.

Mac wished only that he could have heard what had to be the frightened cries of the young Peacekeepers on the dead run. He awkwardly forced himself up on all fours like a spindly newborn colt and fought to keep from pitching down the hill.

When he was finally standing, arms outstretched for balance and to stop the woods from spinning, he waited. And waited. When his balance mechanism finally made the necessary adjustments, Mac caught his breath, shook his head, stretched each limb—even the one with the violated shoulder—and began to jog.

His intention was to jog what had taken him more than a half hour to drive. He would find his way back to where he and Chloe and Hannah had engaged in their sortie soiree that late afternoon that now seemed so long ago. There Mac would find the hidden Jeep, hot-wire it, and set off on what he truly hoped was his last caper of the day. Surely by the time he got there, he would have heard from Chang where he might find George Sebastian.

And after all this, may God have mercy—or not—on anyone who dared stand between them and freedom.

9

CHLOE DIDN'T KNOW the specifics of the directed energy weapon lying across the backseat, but she'd heard the effect it had on a target. And she was curious. She carefully lifted it into her lap, making Hannah alternate from watching the road to watching the DEW.

"Don't point that thing at me, Chloe."

"It's not even on!"

"That's like saying a gun isn't loaded. People get killed all the time with guns they swear aren't loaded."

"Looks pretty simple. You know the deal with these, right?"

"Yes," Hannah said. "Now, Chloe, please."

"Looks like you just turn it on, let it heat up or whatever it does, and fire away. It's nonlethal."

"Yeah, I know. But 130 degrees on soft tissue's going to make you wish you were dead."

"Bet I can get those guys to quit following us."

"Don't even think about it. You miss, they start shooting, and we're not going to help anybody."

"We're not helping anybody anyway," Chloe said. "We're sitting here with Uzis, sidearms, a shotgun, and a DEW, and we've left Mac up there by himself with all those GC."

"And how long are these guys going to let us lead them all over town before they realize we're playing them?"

"We've got to shake 'em before we head for the airport, Hannah. They'll never let us in there."

"*Shake* them? Chloe, their ranks may be decimated, but they've got other personnel, more cars, radios. We're not going to shake them."

"I'm calling Chang."

"What for?"

"I want to know how many people know where we are."

"Why?"

"Hang on."

\+ + +

Running was much easier without the cumbersome Fifty, but Mac had not run this far since . . . since when? Since never. No high school cross-country race was this far. This was longer than a marathon. With the slow but sure staccato of his steps, he repeated in his mind, "God, I'm yours. God, I'm yours. God, I'm yours."

If he was going to reach the Jeep, it would be only because God wanted him to. This was way past Mac's human capabilities.

\+ + +

Chang frantically read every tidbit of the communication between Akbar and Stefanich, hoping for something, anything, to help Mac. His secure phone chirped, and the readout told him who it was.

"You okay, Chloe?" he said.

"For now," she said. "Is there a way to know how many people are following us?"

"I can try to find out. What's your thinking?"

"If it's a bunch, we're dead. We'll run them around town, and we could try to outrun them or shoot it out with them, but you know the odds there. If it's just one car, waiting to tell everybody else where the underground headquarters is, I have an idea."

"Hit me with the idea before I start trying to access the Ptolemaïs mainframe again."

"Why? If you don't like my idea, you don't look? Is that it?"

"Chloe, don't do this. Mac is in more imminent danger, and we have no idea where Sebastian is yet, so I have to prioritize."

"Sorry. I'll make it quick. If they're looking to us to lead them to the underground, we'll lead them to one. Only it won't be the real one. It'll be some other unfortunate citizens who'll get raided soon."

"I like it."

"That's a relief."

"No, I really do. And I think you two are small potatoes to them. Not that you're in the clear. Getting out of that airport tonight is going to be next to impossible, but they probably assume you have nowhere to go anyway and they can round you up when you try to leave. They want the locals."

"And we're going to lead them to 'em, only not really."

"Back to you as soon as I can."

\+ + +

"Stop the racket or I'll kill you!" Elena yelled.

George heard no one else. He kept pounding. How was she going to reach the lock? unlock it? open the doors?

She swore, and he heard movement. She was dragging something near the elevator. He heard the key in the lock, then heard it turn over. It sounded like she had stepped down from the chair or whatever she had used to elevate herself. Now she was trying to open the doors. Not even Plato had been able to do it alone. George just sat there pounding.

"I'm trying to get to you!" she said. "But when I do, you're going to be sorry."

Thump!

Thump!

Thump!

"I'll shoot through the door!"

Thump!

Thump!

Thump!

"You'd better cut that out, and I'm not kidding!"

He could tell she was struggling with the doors. There was no way she could open them. If only he could get her to forget they were unlocked. He quit banging.

"That's better!"

He heard her step up again. The key was going into the lock.

Thump!

Thump!

Thump!

"No! I'm onto you! I'm locking it, and you can just thump all night!"

She locked it.

George stood and found the other boot. He put one on each hand. Now he leaned forward with his hands above his head, the boots pressing against the doors. He dragged them as he slowly slid to the floor and let them drop. George made sure his knee hit first, hard. Then his hip, then his side, then the boots, then his hands. He lay still.

"You finished playing around in there? . . . Huh? Are you? . . . You're going to get yourself shot! . . . You okay in there? . . . Hey!"

She swore again, and he heard her on the phone. ". . . was banging around in there. I threatened to shoot him and he quit, but now I think he's passed out . . . because it sounded like it . . . like he collapsed. You know there's no air in there. No ventilation. Where? I'll look."

She slapped the doors twice. "Hold on in there. I'll get you some air."

+ + +

Chang found the tape of radio transmissions among local GC Peacekeepers in Ptolemaïs, but the quality was so poor, the conversion facility couldn't turn it into readable words. He downloaded it into his own computer and tried listening through earphones.

"Chloe," he reported, "I'm guessing, so what you do with this is totally up to you. I believe there is only one car following you, and it's not official GC. They've farmed out your surveillance to two Morale Monitors. They're armed, of course, but all they're supposed to do is report who you warn about a raid."

"But you're guessing."

"I have to be honest, Chloe. I'm pretty sure that's what I heard."

"How sure are you?"

"Fifty-five percent."

She laughed.

"That's funny?"

"No. It's just that I was hoping for at least sixty. If I can get you to move to sixty, I'll buy this car today."

"Pardon?"

"Nothing. Could it be sixty-forty?"

"Max."

"We're going to give it a go."

+ + +

Elena was still on the phone, but George had to press his ear flat against the elevator door to hear, and unless she was shouting, he could barely make it out.

"On the wall next to the elevator?" it seemed she was saying. "Yeah. Gray door. Got it. There's dozens of them in here, man. . . . Well, like furnace, air, water heater—yeah, they sound like downstairs stuff. . . . How should I know? About twenty of them look like that stuff. Okay, twenty-one and further . . . okay, maybe this is first floor. . . . Alarm system, emergency lights, outside lights, stairwell lights, elevator. . . . Different one for vent, fan, or light? Doesn't look like it. . . . Yeah, all on one. . . . But I have to. He's going to suffocate in there. . . . No! Prop those open even an inch and I'd have to watch him every second.

"What if I turned it on but kept the doors locked? . . . Every floor? So I lock them on every floor. Then there's nowhere for him to go, right? . . . I'll call you."

George heard her leave the lobby and start up some stairs. He kept his ear against the door and could feel and hear her locking the outer elevator doors on the three floors above him. So she was going to flip on the circuit breaker for the elevator so the fan would run and he could get some ventilation. That wouldn't do. He had to somehow get her to open the doors.

She would be listening for the fan and for evidence of his being conscious. George reached up and felt the fan and the lights, pushing firmly around the sides. The panels were screwed on tight, but housings were hooked to wiring above the car, so those had to be the weakest panels in the ceiling. He pulled the gloves on and pushed hard. The metal was too tough and sharp in some places, even with the gloves on. Elena had to be nearly all the way back down.

George quickly slipped on the socks and boots, bent low, and stood on his hands, quietly walking up the sides of the car until the soles pressed against the ceiling. He toed around until he was sure he was pushing against light and fan, then stiffened his legs and pushed up from the floor with all his strength.

The fluorescents popped and fell; the fan blades bent and twisted and began to give way. His biceps shook and his chest ached, but he continued to push as if his life depended on it. He felt the panels tear away and the housing break away from the wires. The ceiling had to be a mess.

George tried to keep from gasping or making noise as he slowly brought his feet back down and lay panting on the floor, carefully brushing the debris into a corner. He heard Elena hurry past toward the circuit-breaker box and flip the breaker all the way off and then back on. The lights of the floor buttons on the panel came on, and he heard a hum in the ceiling where the light and fan should have been.

Trying to regulate his breathing, George turned himself around, laced up the boots and, catlike, moved into position.

"Getting any air in there?" Elena called out. She slapped the door. "Hey! Better?"

George got on all fours and crept backward until his feet were flat against the back wall. He reared up onto his knees until his seat was planted on his calves. Then he leaned forward and placed his palms on the floor, turned his face to the right, and lay his left cheek and ear flat on the floor. He fought to breathe deeply and slowly, preparing himself to hold his breath and appear dead.

Two more smacks on the door. "C'mon! That fan should be running. Is it? Give me a knock if you're getting any air!"

George lay there, crouched back against the wall, looking for all the world as if he had collapsed onto his face.

"All right! I'm unlocking these doors, but if you try anything, you're a dead man."

Now she was up on the chair. Metal into metal. The click. George was tempted to hit the Open Door button himself, but he knew she would be standing there with her weapon leveled at him. He blinked several times to moisten his eyes so he could lie there with them open, unblinking, hopefully able to see enough peripherally to know when to act.

"I'm opening the doors, so don't move! I'd rather the brass find you shot than dead by accident."

He heard her push the button, felt the car vibrate with the mechanism, and the doors began to separate. He wanted to drink in the cool, fresh air, but he dared not. In the faint light of the Exit signs and a light from down the hall, he saw her in his peripheral vision silhouetted before him, feet spread, both hands on the high-powered weapon.

She swore. She took a step closer. She took her left hand off the gun and reached for his carotid artery. As soon as her fingers touched his skin, he knew she would know he was alive. That touch would be his cue to spring.

+ + +

"I'll do whatever you say, Chloe," Hannah said, "but I've got a priority higher than our getting out of here alive."

"Mac?"

"Of course."

"Me too. And George."

"I just can't imagine he's still alive, Chloe. What's in it for them to keep him around?"

"Don't think that way."

"Come on! We're not schoolkids anymore. Not thinking about it isn't going to change whether it's true."

"I'm just hoping they think they can still get something out of him."

"Well, I had limited contact with him, Chloe, but let me tell you something. He looked like the kind of a guy who was going to do what he was going to do, and nobody was going to make him do different. I'll bet he hasn't given them diddly."

"Pull over there."

"You're sure this will work?"

"Sure? I have to be sure?"

"Let's just not be too obvious."

"That's why you're stopping here and not at the front door, Hannah. When I head for the store, you stand outside the car, like you're watching for nosey nellies."

"Nosey nellies?"

"You know, GC or Morale Monitors nosing around."

"Nosey nellies?"

"I didn't know that was so obscure. I forgot you grew up on a reservation."

"Well, I *will* be looking for GC or MMs. So what do I do if they show up?"

"They won't. They just want to raid whoever we're warning."

"Or at least there's a 55 percent chance of that."

"Sixty."

"So a 40 percent chance they arrest us, or worse."

"You're carrying an Uzi. I've seen what you can do with a shotgun, and I can only imagine what you might do with a DEW."

"I'm just telling you, Chloe. If anybody comes, I'm jumping back in the car, honking the horn, and coming to get you."

"Well, I should hope so."

+ + +

At the first sensation of skin on skin, George Sebastian called on all his years of training, football, and lifting. As he pushed off the floor with his palms and drove his heels into the back of the elevator, the massive quads and hamstrings in his thighs drove him up and into Elena, who had murdered her last believer.

George's 240 pounds slammed into her so fast and hard that as he wrapped his arms around her waist he felt the top of his head push her stomach against her spine. She projectile regurgitated over him into the elevator before her face banged off his back and her boots hit his knees.

He sailed four feet high and ten feet into the lobby with her body folded in two. When he landed, his chest pinned her legs, her torso whiplashed, and the back of her head was crushed flat on the marble floor. George pounced to his feet and ripped the weapon from her hand. He stuffed her phone and radio in his pockets, then grabbed her by the belt and slung her lifeless body into the elevator. He locked the doors and left the key on the chair she had used to reach the lock.

George laid a small rug from near the entry door over the gore where she had died and used the gloves to wipe up the blood trail to the elevator. He was about to charge out the back door to see if he could find a car to hot-wire when he heard keys in the entry door and looked up to see an old man smiling and waving at him.

The man wore a mismatched custodial uniform and carried two mops. As he entered, he said something in Greek.

"English?" George said, certain he was flushed and looked like an escaped hostage who had just killed his captor.

"I was wonder if elevator still to not work."

"Yes."

"Work?"

"No."

"Not to work."

"Right."

"Okay. Howdy, English, how are you?"

"Fine. Good-bye, sir."

"Bye-bye to you."

+ + +

Chloe set her Uzi, gripping it with her right hand, and reached with her left to open the door. As soon as Hannah stopped the car in the shadows of an alley three blocks from Chloe's target, she stepped out and moved quickly.

Tempted to look back or to glance from right to left for GC Peacekeepers, Chloe kept her eyes on the storefront, where earlier that day she had watched the bombing of Petra on television. The place was dark, but in the back were at least two apartments with lights burning.

She banged loudly on the glass door with the heel of her hand. It would be customary for the locals to ignore such a knock, assuming a drunk was stumbling around at that hour of the night. So she persisted until she heard someone call out, "Closed!"

She banged and banged some more. Finally a light and a door, and a craggy man in a bathrobe and slippers ventured out. "What is it? Who are you?"

"GC!" she stage-whispered. "Open up. Just a moment, please."

He came, scowling, but would not open the door. "What do you want?"

"I have an urgent message for you, sir, but I don't want to yell it aloud."

He shook his head and unlatched the door but would open it only a couple of inches. "What's so urgent?"

"I wanted to tip you off, sir, about a sweep through this neighborhood tonight, probably later."

"A what? A sweep?"

"A raid."

"Looking for what?" he said, pointing to his forehead and his *216*.

"For that," she said. "You are a loyal citizen, so we wanted to warn you early so you would not be alarmed."

"Well, you alarmed me!"

"I apologize. Good night."

He slammed and locked the door without a word, and Chloe hurried back to the car. "Well, that went well," she said. "Zap anybody?"

Hannah pulled away. "What?"

"With the ray gun."

"Is this how you cover your fear? Banter?"

"Must be. I'm numb all over."

"I saw no one, Chloe. I don't know what that means. Either they're very, very good, or we're paranoid."

"Probably both. We could hang around and see if the GC come looking for the underground."

"I hope you're not serious."

"Of course not, but you have to admit it would be fun. Especially when they ask that old guy if he was tipped off about the raid."

"Where to now, Batgirl?"

"I feel like we're sitting ducks, Hannah. We can't call Mac unless we know he's somewhere he can talk. Chang will tell us what he can when he can. I say we look for somewhere we can wait without being seen, and watch for Mac and George."

"You're dreaming."

✢ ✢ ✢

Rayford had been assigned a tent at Petra and was about to settle down for the night. He couldn't imagine sleeping after all he had experienced. As he studied the stars, he heard his phone, rolled up onto his side, and dug it out from his bag. He didn't recognize the calling number.

Rayford affected a Middle Eastern accent he was sure was awful. "This is Atef Naguib," he said.

"Ray?"

"Who is calling, please?"

"I memorized two numbers," the caller said. "Yours and Chang's. But this is not a secure phone, and I didn't want to expose him."

"Sebastian?" Rayford sat up. "They found you?"

"Who's *they*? I just busted loose. Is there a safe house around here? Somewhere I can crash until I figure a way out?"

Rayford was suddenly on his feet. He gushed the information about the Trib Force contingent in Greece and how Sebastian could get to the local Co-op. "I'll get to Chang and have him let the others know."

10

MAC LAY in the dewy grass next to the Jeep, overcome with gratitude though aware that neither he nor his team was out of the woods yet. His overheated body arched and drew in the night air, and he thanked God over and over for having given him the strength to run this far.

He had barely been able to respond when Chang told him all that had gone on, but it quickly became obvious that of the four fugitives in Greece, Chloe and Hannah were now in the most immediate danger.

They had been followed, were in a GC vehicle, were in Ptolemaïs, and did not dare try to get to the Co-op, even on foot. They were heavily armed, but also inexperienced. George Sebastian had gone from most precarious to temporarily most secure, provided he had found the Co-op.

Mac painfully sat up and leaned back against the car. He had longed for and yet dreaded this operation. He had wanted to spring George, but the odds were so bad. When it had started, he thrilled to how easy it had seemed to snow the locals. Then it had gone haywire and fallen nearly hopeless. Now, little credit to Mac, the whole multifaceted effort had become straightforward again. Mac now had one job: reunite with the other three and get out of Dodge.

Chang was inconsolable over not discovering the connection between Akbar and Stefanich before the operation started. Mac tried to tell him that the whole Global Community hierarchy was so new and spread out that no one could have anticipated that those two would know each other. Chang had redeemed himself by breaking through the security and the ostensibly indecipherable codes. He and Mac now knew more about Stefanich's and the hostage takers' plans than they did. For one thing, Mac knew Sebastian was on the loose. Of Stefanich, Aristotle, Plato, Socrates, and Elena, the only one who knew that was dead.

Through his fast yet thorough examination of the interaction between Akbar and Stefanich, Chang discovered they had hatched the plan to draw Mac and Chloe and Hannah into the woods. There they would get them to move to where they would be far outnumbered by GC forces, most of whom had no idea what was going on. Even if the tables had turned and Mac and his people had gotten the drop on the Peacekeepers, few would have known enough to give away the double cross.

The GC expected Mac's people to lead them to the Judah-ite underground, then eventually be apprehended themselves. Johnson, Sebastian, Jinnah, and Irene would be reunited at local GC headquarters, then carted off to New Babylon as feathers in the cap of Stefanich, the newest palace member of Akbar's staff.

"Stefanich is beside himself looking for you," Chang had told Mac. "They were worried when they couldn't get through to Elena for a while, but they have reached her now and have been assured everything is fine at headquarters."

"What do you make of that, Chang?"

"I don't worry about it. Sebastian confirmed the Elena kill, and he has her phone. Who knows how he bluffed them? I wouldn't put anything past him. My worry is for Chloe and Hannah. The Morale Monitors lost them after the women led them to what the MMs thought was the Co-op. They won't know that was phony till they raid it. But Stefanich had so many of his people in the woods to help bring you three back, he was short on help in Ptolemaïs. That's all changed now. Everybody's on their way back."

The problem for Mac, he realized as he hot-wired the Jeep, was that he could call Chloe and Hannah, but he couldn't reach the Co-op or Sebastian except in person. He had an idea of how they might all escape, but the women had to stay safe in the meantime.

✢ ✢ ✢

"How bizarre is that?" Chloe said. "We were probably walking distance from George when he came out the back door of GC headquarters. We could have driven him to the Co-op."

"And ruined it for everybody."

"Well, yeah, but I'm just saying. We've got to ditch this car and get where Mac can find us."

"The sooner the better," Hannah said. "I haven't noticed anyone for quite a while. Let's do it now."

"Let's at least get to the outskirts."

"Risky."

"Not as risky as parking in town and walking through the streets."

✢ ✢ ✢

Mac hated the thought of having to walk even a few blocks, but he couldn't risk parking anywhere near the Co-op. He left the Jeep about a mile north and set off on foot. The trick would be to get in without getting shot, with those at the Co-op on the lookout for GC.

He thought about just waltzing into the pub above, but for all he knew Socrates had described him, and the whole town was watching for him. He was still in camouflage and armed with an Uzi—not your typical Ptolemaïst out for a nightcap.

Instead, Mac went by what Chloe and Hannah had told him of the place and stayed in the shadows, coming the far way around, slipping in the back door and into the tiny bathroom. The pub was full and noisy, and that was to his advantage. He locked the door, tried not to inhale deeply, and scrubbed the grease from his face. Mac didn't look much cleaner in the dingy mirror, and he was struck by the fatigue showing around his eyes. *Some night,* he thought, *and we've just started.*

Mac studied the pipes. They ran straight down through the floor, probably just a few feet from George and who knew how many local believers huddled in the back room of the laundry. He sat on the floor and used an Uzi clip to tap in Morse code on the pipe. "Seeking friend from S. D."

He repeated the message twice more.

Finally, return taps. Mac had nothing to write with, so he had to remember each letter. "Need assurance."

Mac responded: "Amazing Grace."

The reply: "More."

He tapped out: "Let's go home."

Back came: "Favorite angel?"

That was easy. And only a compatriot would know that. "Michael."

"Welcome. Hurry."

Mac turned out the light before he opened the door, saw no curious eyes, and hurried down the stairs. He heard a "Psst" from the back room and ducked through the curtain, only to look down the barrels of two Uzis in the dim light.

A young, dark-haired man appeared ready to shoot. "Let me see your hands."

Mac raised them, his own Uzi—supplied from that very room—dangling from his arm.

"Is that him?" the young man asked.

"Could be," George said.

"If it's not," Mac said, "how do I know you're Costas?"

Then he realized why George had to be waffling and whipped off his glasses. "I used to work for Carpathia, man! The freckles had to go and the hair color had to change."

"That's him," George said, stepping forward to embrace Mac.

Several others—mostly men, all ages and all armed—emerged from under piles of clothing. Only three women were there—one middle-aged, one elderly, and one in her late teens. The first introduced herself as Costas's mother, Mrs. P. The older said, "My husband is K's cousin."

A thin, wiry man who looked to be in his late seventies said, "That would be me."

George pointed at the teenager. "This one answered Elena's phone a little while ago. Despite a very bad connection and a lot of static, she assured her partners I was still safely locked away."

"Nice to meet you," the girl said, adding the staticky sound as she spoke and causing the others to smile.

"Excellent work," Mac said. "Now, brothers and sisters, we have no time. There is a massive manhunt for me, and it won't be long before they find out Elena is dead and their prisoner gone. I have two compatriots on foot. K's cousin, are you also a Kronos?"

"I am, sir."

"Are you the one who lent your truck to the cause?"

He nodded solemnly.

"And is that truck available?"

"Two blocks from here."

"I want to buy it." Mac pulled a huge wad of Nicks from a pocket below his knee.

"No, no, not necessary."

"Actually it is, because by the end of the night, it will be well known to the GC, and you will be unable to be seen in it again."

"I do not need the money."

"Does the Co-op? the underground?"

"Yes," Mrs. Pappas said, and she stepped forward to take it.

"Tell me about the truck. Four-wheel drive?"

"Yes. But not new, not fast. Five-speed manual transmission, very heavy and powerful."

"As soon as I connect with my other two team members, George and I will take the truck and pick them up. The GC expects us to head for the Ptolemaïs airport, but that's a suicide run. We have a plane at an abandoned strip eighty miles west of here. If we can head that way without attracting attention, that's where you'll find the truck tomorrow. If we draw a tail, pretend you never saw that truck."

"I want to come," Costas said.

"I'm sorry, no. Unless you are going all the way to America with us, there would be no way for you to help us and to also escape."

"But I—"

"We will accept all the ammunition you can spare. I would say if we leave now, our chances are only about fifty-fifty. Agree, George?"

"No, sir. I think that's optimistic. But I agree it's our only option and that we need to go now."

Mrs. P. held up a hand. "There is nothing wrong with working while someone is praying. Someone put extra ammunition clips in a bag while I pray.

"Our God, we thank you for our brothers and sisters in Christ and ask you to put around them a fiery ring of protection. Give them Godspeed, we pray, in the name of Jesus. Amen."

George took the bag and got the keys and directions to the truck, while Mac huddled in a corner and tried to bring up Hannah and Chloe on his walkie-talkie.

+ + +

Chloe was on the phone to Chang when she heard Hannah take a radio message from Mac and give their location—off the road and behind underbrush north of the city.

"This is urgent," Chang was saying. "I don't have time to call everybody individually, so get this. All Ptolemaïs GC Peacekeepers and Morale Monitors are on high alert. They have abandoned the woods and are beginning a sweep of the entire town. We're talking hundreds of personnel and all working vehicles.

"They've found Elena's body, know they were the victims of an impostor on her phone, and are tracing that phone with GPS. If George has it, they'll know where he is, and if he ditches it, it needs to be far from the Co-op.

"The airport is crawling with GC, and though the Rooster Tail is sitting on the tarmac as if it's ready to go, it has been drained of fuel. If you can't get back to Mac's plane, the best I can offer is to try to get Abdullah's pilot friend to Larnaca on Cyprus tomorrow."

"Thanks, Chang," Chloe said. "Hannah tells me Mac and George are on their way. Forget Larnaca. We'd never get there. It sounds like the net is being drawn in all around us. Tell everyone we love them and that we're doing our best to get home."

+ + +

Mac was driving toward the north road with George in the passenger's seat when he got the call from Chloe about Elena's phone. "That's easy," he said, stopping in the middle of the road. "Stick Elena's phone under the front tire, George," he said.

The truck flattened the phone.

As they reached the north road, Mac saw a sea of flashing blue lights in the distance. "We're toast," he said.

"They're not looking for this truck," George said. "Don't do anything suspicious."

"Like picking up two armed women?"

"Drive on. The women will see the GC and know we'll have to come back."

"When would we have time to do that?"

"What are you going to do, Mac?"

"They're setting up a roadblock. Stick the weapons and ammo under the seats and get a cap on. There's a better description of you than me out there. You can't hide big but you can cover blond."

+ + +

Chloe and Hannah lay on their stomachs, watching the long line of GC cars, lights flashing. "There's the truck," Hannah said.

"Most of the GC are driving by them. Guess they don't need all those for a roadblock."

One GC car stopped on each side of the road, and a Peacekeeper held up a hand to stop the truck and wave through the rest of the squad cars.

"Hannah, if you can hear me, give me one click."

Chloe looked at her. "Was that George?"

Hannah nodded and clicked her walkie-talkie.

"All right, I've got Mac's radio on the seat here, and I'm staring straight ahead and pretending not to be talking, so I may be hard to hear. Listen carefully. If you have the DEW with you and can turn it on, give me a click."

Hannah turned on the weapon and gave another click.

"These guys are going to check us out. I'll leave the radio locked open. If it sounds like they're going to look closer, incapacitate both of them. Understand?"

Click.

"Here they come. Stand by. If one comes to my side of the truck, please use very careful aim."

Click.

+ + +

Chang was exhausted and wished he could call it a night like most everyone else at the palace except Suhail Akbar and the literally indefatigable Carpathia himself, who did not require sleep anymore. Chang would not, however, be able to sleep anyway until Mac and Chloe and Hannah and George were safely in the air. He stayed at his computer, available to help. Meanwhile, he tapped into Carpathia's office.

"I really must stay on top of this Greece thing," Akbar was saying. "I'll return as soon as I can."

"Is it not something you can do from here, Suhail? The nights are so long, and there is much to learn from the daylight regions."

"Forgive me, Potentate, but we have had a serious breach of security. I am on a secure phone to Ptolemaïs and on a secure e-mail connection. The situation is about to be resolved, and I will hurry right back."

"And we can see how the morale effort is going in Region –6 and in Region 0?"

"Of course."

"There should be audio and video feeds where I see the last holdouts taking the loyalty mark, worshiping my image three times a day, or suffering the consequences. They are suffering, are they not?"

"I'm sure they are, Excellency. I don't know how you or I could have been clearer on that."

"And the Jews? There are many Jews in both those regions who might be enjoying the sunshine right now, but who do not know that this is their last chance to see it. Am I right?"

"You are always right, Highness. However, few people anywhere are truly enjoying anything with the seas as they are. I don't know how the planet can survive such a tragedy."

"This is the work of the Judah-ites, Suhail! They tell the Jews they are God's chosen. Well, they are my chosen ones now. And what I have chosen for them will taste bitter in their mouths. I want to see it, Suhail. I want to know my edicts are being carried out."

"I will see to it, my lord. By the time I return, someone will hook up the monitor to reporting stations in those regions so you may be brought up to date."

"This security breach, Suhail. It is here, inside the palace?"

"That's all we can conclude, sir. If such misleading, wholly false information can be planted on our main database from a remote location, we are much more vulnerable than we imagined. Bad as it is, we are most certain it is coming from inside, and that should not take long to trace."

"You remember, Suhail, what I have asked for in the way of treatment of the Jews, not to mention the Judah-ites. That would be retribution far too lenient for one under my own roof who would deceive me in such a way."

"I understand, sir."

"The perpetrator must be put to death before the eyes of the world."

"Of course."

"Suhail, have we not combed our entire personnel list?"

"We have."

"And are there any employees of the Global Community, here or anywhere in the world, who have yet to receive the mark?"

"Less than one thousandth of one percent, Excellency. Probably fewer than ten, and all loyalists with valid reasons, and all—to the best of our knowledge—with plans to rectify the situation immediately."

"But should they not be our primary suspects?"

"We have them closely watched, sir. And there is not one employee in the palace or in New Babylon without the mark."

After Suhail was finally able to excuse himself and get back to the situation in Ptolemaïs, Chang kept listening to Carpathia's office. Nicolae mumbled under his breath, but Chang could not make it out. Occasionally he heard banging, as if Carpathia was pounding on a table or desk. Finally he heard a clatter that sounded like Carpathia had kicked a wastebasket and stuff spilled out.

After a few moments, Chang heard a faint knock and Carpathia calling out, "Enter."

"Oh, excuse me there, Potentate, sir. I'm to get your monitor hooked up to the United North American States and the United South American States."

Carpathia ignored him until the man was on his way out. "Clean up this mess," he said.

\+ \+ \+

Mac decided to take the initiative with the GC Peacekeeper in charge of the roadblock and not wait to be asked for his papers. George was slouched in the passenger seat.

"Wow, whatcha got goin' tonight there, Chief? I haven't seen this many of you guys on the streets since I started workin' road maintenance. All these guys are makin' it hard on our construction zones, but you gotta do what you gotta do. What're ya lookin' for, anyway? Something I can be watchin' for?"

"Confidential matter, sir. High-level manhunt. Long day for you guys, huh?"

"Tell me about it. We're hardly ever out this late. Had to come back around the long way from the airport. That part of this deal? That place is locked up tight. Went through the roadblock there too. They cleared us even though we don't have our papers on us, 'cause we had to work so late, asphalt and all. Goin' back to the work shed now."

"That's no excuse to not have your papers. Everybody is supposed to have their papers all the time."

"We know, and we both feel terrible about it. But we'll have 'em with us on the way home."

"They let you off down by the airport?"

"Yeah, nice guys. I mean, we aren't Peacekeepers, but we're all working for the people anyway, right?"

"That's not by the book."

"You know, I thought that very thing and really appreciated it that he wasn't one of those hard guys that gives the workingman a bad time."

"Well, I don't want to make your life miserable either, sir, so we can make this real easy. How about you two just show me your marks of loyalty, and you can move it along."

+ + +

Chloe thought Mac had nearly talked his way out of the situation. But if he was no threat, showing his mark would not have been a problem.

"Don't hesitate, Hannah," Chloe said.

"I wish that other guy would get out of his car."

From the walkie-talkie: "You just want to see our marks?"

"Yes, sir. Hand or forehead?"

"Mine's on the forehead here, under the cap. My partner's is, ah, where is yours, bud?"

"Hand," Sebastian said.

"Let's have a look," the Peacekeeper said.

"Where's yours, by the way?" Mac said. "You got the image of the potentate too?"

"Nah. Just the number. I'm kinda military that way."

Chloe glanced at Hannah, then back at the truck, where Mac slowly unlatched his seat belt and took off his cap. He leaned forward.

"I don't see anything."

"What? Look!"

From the walkie-talkie, George in a quiet singsong: "Now would be the perfect time."

The Peacekeeper spun in a circle, slammed back against the cab of the truck, and dropped, screaming. As he slowly started to rise, Mac said, "Say there, fella, what was that all about?"

"I don't know, I—ah, fire ants or something." He rubbed his back gingerly, now standing. He motioned to the officer in the other GC car, who quickly stepped out.

"What's the trouble?"

"Pain in my back, like I backed into a hot pipe or something. I think a blister's rising."

He leaned toward Mac again, then grabbed the back of his leg and howled, falling and writhing. The other officer drew his weapon. "What are you guys doing?"

"We're not doing anything!" Mac said. "What's his problem?"

The inside light of the truck came on, and George got out and went toward the front with his hands raised. He must have had the walkie-talkie in his pocket now, because Chloe could still hear him on Hannah's radio. "Can I help in any way?" he asked.

"Stay right where you are," the second Peacekeeper said, just before he flopped in the road, dropping his weapon and trying to cover his face.

+ + +

Mac jumped out to help George. "Yank the radios in their cars," he said. "I'll get the ones on their uniforms."

By now the officers were delirious, glassy-eyed, and wailing. "Ladies," George radioed, "come help us with these cars."

Mac disarmed the officers and tossed their weapons into the bed of the truck. He took their radios and put them in the front seat. "Once you've got those car radios disconnected," he told George, "pop the trunks."

Chloe and Hannah came running. "Chloe," Mac said, "you two are going to give us an escort. Once I get this guy in the trunk of his car, I'll pull the truck in behind you. Hannah, you fall in behind once we get the other guy in his trunk."

The GC were whimpering. "You boys hush now," Mac said. "You're gonna hurt awhile, but you're not gonna die unless you make us shoot you. We're just going for a little ride."

With the GC ensconced in their respective trunks, Mac carefully turned the truck around and told George to give the women extra ammo from the bag they had gotten at the Co-op. With the truck and the two GC squad cars pointed west, one of the GC radios crackled. "North roadblock, acknowledge, please."

"North roadblock," Mac said, while only half mashing the transmit button.

"Repeat?"

"North roadblock here," he said, careful to make sure he was heard, but not perfectly.

"Status?"

"Busy."

"Carry on."

George hopped back into the truck, and as Chloe pulled away and Mac followed, George said, "Looky here. I knew there was something about that old gal I really liked." In amongst the ammunition, Mrs. P. had had Co-op people pack bread, cheese, and fruit. "Chloe and Hannah took most of it," George said. "And I'm gonna take most of what's left unless you grab now."

Mac grabbed. And the unlikely convoy rolled west into the night toward their ride home. How long the ruse would hold was the mystery. For now, Mac enjoyed the food and the hope that they had beaten the odds.

11

THE REPORT FROM MAC allowed Chang to breathe easier for the first time in hours. He checked back in to Carpathia's office, where Akbar was debriefing the big boss.

"We've had a setback, but there's no way this bunch can—"

"A setback?"

"Without going into all the details, sir, the hostage killed one of our people—a woman—and has escaped. We assume he's on the run with the three who—"

"He killed one of his captors?"

"Yes, Highness. We assume—"

"My kind of a man. Why cannot he be on our side?"

"We assume, sir, that he is reconnecting with the three who came for him, and we're hoping they will be foolish enough to try to get back to the airport. We have that sealed tight."

"Yes, well . . ." Carpathia sounded distracted, as if the rest of the story was not as interesting. "Suhail, how was damage control today?"

"Too early to tell, sir."

"Come, come, I count on you as one who does not try to simply appease me. They heard the pilot's report, and my telling them he was mistaken, that the bombs had missed their targets. Well, what are people saying?"

"I honestly don't know, Excellency. I have spent my entire day between your office and my own, trying to ride herd on this Greece thing."

"Let me tell you this, Suhail: The disc from the plane clearly shows direct hits and those traitors burning! Whatever is the magic that allows those people to survive simply cannot extend outside that area."

"Begging your pardon, but not that long ago we lost ground troops outside—"

"I know that, Suhail! Do you think I do not know that?"

"Apologies, Potentate."

"I want us to find the safe place surrounding that area, where we have not seen our weapons of war swallowed up by the earth, and from which we can stop all traffic in and out. They will need supplies, and we must see that they do not get them."

"Our armed forces have been so decimated, sir—"

"Are you telling me we have no pilots or planes that can cut off supplies to Petra?"

"No, sir. I'm sure we can do that. Ah, on another matter, sir, our ancient-text experts say that the next curse could be that the lakes and rivers of the world fall into the same predicament as the seas."

"*Freshwater* sources all turn to blood?"

"Yes, sir."

"Impossible! *Everyone* would die! Even our enemies."

"There are those who believe the Judah-ites will be protected, as they have been against our forces recently."

"Where will they get their water?"

"The same place they got their protection. Perhaps there is wisdom in negotiating with their leader to have the curses lifted."

"Never!"

"Not to be contrary, sir, but we cannot survive long with this devastation. And if the rivers and lakes do also turn—"

"You are not aware of everything, Suhail. I too have supernatural power."

"I have seen it, sir."

"You will see more. Reverend Fortunato is prepared to match the wizardry of the Judah-ites blow for blow, and he has designates who can do this around the world."

"Well, that—"

"Now show me what I want to see, Suhail."

\+ + +

"North roadblock, this is Central."

"Roadblock," Mac said. "Go ahead, Central."

"Disposition of suspicious truck?"

"Repeat?"

"One of our squads reported that your first stop after they passed was a truck."

"Affirmative. Clean."

"Traveling west to east?"

"Affirmative."

"We traced a cell phone to the west side of the city and then east before losing it."

Mac looked at George. "What do they want to hear?"

"You know nothing about that."

Mac transmitted. "Can't help you there."

"Truck proceeded east?"

"Roger that."

"You reported lots of traffic."

"Ten-four."

"Busy?"

"Affirmative."

"Squads said they saw nothing but the truck when they passed."

"Busy now."

"What's your ten-twenty, roadblock?"

Mac looked at George again. "They're onto us."

George pulled the weapons from beneath the seat and Rayford's walkie-talkie from his pocket. "Jinnah, Irene, be advised. We'll soon have company."

Mac clicked the GC radio button a few times. "Repeat," he said.

"Your ten-twenty, roadblock. What's your location?"

✠ ✠ ✠

Chang froze. He had been nearly dozing, listening to Carpathia and Akbar's sparring while they watched reports from the United North American States and the United South American States. He had not kept up with the Ptolemaïs project.

The local GC had traced Elena's cell phone to the west side of the city, and it had remained in one location for more than an hour. Commander Nelson Stefanich and the survivors of the philosopher team were personally leading the raid on a pub in that area.

He phoned Mac.

"Talk fast, Chang. We may be in deep weeds here."

"How far west of the city are you?"

"Not sure. I've had this thing floored, but I don't think it goes faster'n fifty. They chasin' us?"

"Are you too far from the Co-op to help them?"

"Depends. What's up?"

"GC's raiding the pub right now. You know the next thing to go will be the Co-op."

"Any chance they got out?"

"Can't imagine. I couldn't warn them."

"I'm guessing we're less than thirty minutes from our plane. We'll go back if you think we can help."

"Hang on, a report's coming through. Judah-ite underground discovered beneath pub. Firefight. Sixteen GC dead, and another dozen injured. Building grenaded and torched. Several adjacent buildings destroyed. No enemy survivors."

+ + +

While Mac filled in George, the GC continued to try to reach Mac on the radio, asking for some kind of a code. "We've blocked off both ends of the north road due to the raid, so wrap it up," they said. "Still need your all-clear code."

George looked devastated and tried to grab the GC radio from Mac. "I'll give 'em an all-clear code."

"Take it easy, friend."

"This was *my* fault, Mac! What was I thinking, hanging on to that phone?"

"I wish we could have gone back," Mac said. "I'd like to have taken out a few of them myself. But our brothers and sisters are in heaven, and it sounds like they put up some kind of a fight."

"That's it?" George said. "We're supposed to feel good because I got a bunch of people killed and now they're in heaven?"

"Need the all-clear code now," the radio said.

"I ought to tell them it's Psalm 94:1," Mac said.

"I know what I'd like to tell 'em. Have the women stop and we'll get those GC to tell us the code."

"They'd probably give away where we are."

"Not with the DEW starin' 'em in the face. Let me get it out of 'em, Mac. Please. I've got to do this."

"Chloe, pull it over," Mac said.

"Right now?"

"Right now."

"We okay?"

"Temporarily."

Mac's phone chirped. Chang. "Stefanich and Plato and a bunch of GC are looking for the truck and the two GC squads. They're heading west."

"Let's make this quick," Mac said, jumping out as Chloe emerged and Hannah pulled up behind.

"Pop that trunk, Chloe," George said, "and Hannah, let me have the DEW."

Chloe opened the trunk, and Mac shone a flashlight in on the nearly wasted Peacekeeper. George pulled him from the trunk with one hand, and he lay crying on the ground. "Blisters," he sobbed. "Careful, please. Or kill me."

"You'd like that, wouldn't you?" George said, wielding the DEW. "See this?"

The man opened one eye and nodded miserably.

"This is what cooks your flesh, and there's plenty more juice in it."

"Please, no."

George turned it on, and the thing whirred to life.

"Please!"

He aimed it at the man's ankle, and the man stiffened, whining. "Give me your all-clear code."

"What?"

"You heard me. Give me the all-clear or—"

"It's in the glove box! In my book!"

Chloe went to check. She brought back a small, black leather ring binder. "It's full of all kinds of notes," she said.

George took it and dropped it onto the man.

"We've got to get rolling," Mac said. "They're never going to buy the all-clear from us now anyway. They're on their way."

"These guys are deadweight," George said. "Maybe we can slow the others by leaving them here in the road."

The man was ripping through the pages. He gingerly held the notebook up to the light from the truck's headlamp. "It's one-one-six-four-eight!" he said.

George dragged him onto the road while Mac brought the other from the other car. The men lay writhing. "Just kill us," the second one pleaded.

"You don't know what you're asking," George said. "Bad as this is, trust me, you should prefer it."

"Leave one of the cars here," Mac said. "Block the road with it and the truck. It won't take the GC long to get around them, but any slowdown has to help."

Chloe maneuvered one car nose to nose with the truck across the highway; then they ripped out the distributor caps from both vehicles and took the keys.

"Last call for clear code," the radio said.

Mac hollered it into the mike. Then, "Chloe, you drive. And keep it to the floor. I'll ride shotgun. I don't expect them to catch us now, but everybody stay armed and ready."

George put the DEW in the trunk and climbed in the back with Hannah. The economy car was too small for the four of them and seemed to groan with the weight, but Chloe soon had the thing chugging along at over seventy miles an hour.

George said, "So, Mac, what's Psalm 94:1?"

Mac turned as far as he could in the seat. "'O God,'" he said, "'to whom vengeance belongs, shine forth!'"

The GC radio came to life again. "We need an immediate ten-twenty. Personnel on the north road report zero traffic and no sign of you."

"Give me that," George said, pulling it from Mac's hand. He mashed the button. "Yeah, you'll find us at Psalm 94:1."

+ + +

Chang fixed himself some tea, adding a strange concoction that included instant coffee with the highest concentration of caffeine he could find. He would crash when this ordeal was over, but he couldn't risk dozing now. It was clear the Greek GC had a bead on his people, and it wouldn't be long before they figured out Mac must have a plane at the abandoned strip not twenty minutes more up the road. He certainly wasn't going to escape into Albania. How long would it take Mac and his people to board, and how far could they get before needing to refuel?

Meanwhile, from what Chang could hear, Carpathia was at least entertained—if not totally distracted—by feeds from his regions where it was still daytime. The potentate for Region 0, the United South American States, announced an event he said his wife, "the first lady," was personally attending right then.

"And where are you while she is doing your work?" Carpathia asked.

"Oh, my revered risen one, you may rest assured that I am doing the greater work. We have taken you at your word regarding the effort to root out infidels here, and I am working closely with our Peacekeepers and Morale Monitors, as well as with civilian undercover groups. We expect to have dozens more face the guillotine or take your mark within twenty-four hours."

"Dozens? My dear friend, we are hearing from your compatriots around the world that some are finding hundreds, even thousands, who will suffer for their disloyalty. Some are stepping up efforts even in our part of the world, in the dark of night."

The South American sighed. "Sir, sadly, we are so dependent on the seas that our forces have been dramatically reduced."

"But surely so have your dissidents, have they not?"

"That is true. But please, allow me to take you live to Uruguay, where my wife attends the public ceremony culminating in loyalty enforcement."

Chang switched quickly to Mac and his crew—nothing new—then tapped into the video feed from the United South American States. The first lady was receiving enthusiastic applause. She had her arm around a shy-looking middle-aged man. "This gentleman is finally getting his mark of loyalty to our risen potentate!"

More cheering.

"And tell us, Andrés, what took you so long?"

"I was afraid," he said, smiling.

"Afraid of what?"

"The needle."

Many laughed and cheered.

"But you will do it today?"

"A very small *0*, yes," he said.

"You are no longer afraid of the needle?"

"Yes, I am still. But I fear the blade much more."

The crowd cheered and continued to applaud as Andrés sat stiffly for the application of the mark. His forehead was swabbed, someone held his hand, the machine was applied, and he looked genuinely relieved and happy.

The first lady said, "You may now return to what you were doing when you were discovered without the mark."

The camera followed Andrés as he ran back to the image of Carpathia and fell to his knees before it. The first lady told the crowd, "Andrés avoided detection for so long because he obeyed the decree to worship the image, and no one suspected."

Carpathia did not seem impressed. "He worships me and yet he is afraid of a little pinprick. Agh!"

"But you will be most pleased, Potentate," the South American leader said. "Following the leads of several loyal citizens, we have uncovered a den of opposition. Six were killed when they resisted arrest, but thirteen have been brought to this worship and enforcement center."

"How many will take the mark now?" Carpathia said. "How many have had their attitudes adjusted by the very presence of the loyalty enforcement facilitator?"

"Well, uh, actually none so far, sir."

Chang heard a fist slam. "Stubborn!" Carpathia said. "So stubborn. Why are these people so resolute? so stupid? so shortsighted?"

"Today they will pay, Highness."

"Right now, even as we speak?" Carpathia's voice evidenced his excitement.

"Yes, right now."

"What is the music?"

"The condemned ones hum and sing, my lord. It is not uncommon."

"Shut them up!"

"One moment. Excuse me, sir." He called to someone in the background, "Jorge! Communicate to the officers at the site that the supreme potentate does not allow the music. Yes, now! Your Highness, it will be stopped."

"These have definitely chosen the blade?"

"They have, sir. They are in line."

"What are we waiting for?"

"Only to carry out your wish to stop the music, sir."

"Get on with it! The blade will silence them."

Chang recoiled when he saw a guard with a huge rifle and bayonet nudging the first person in line, a woman who appeared to be in her late twenties. She was singing, her face turned toward heaven. The guard yelled at her, but she did not acknowledge. He bumped her and she stumbled, but still she sang, eyes upward.

He jabbed her in the ribs with the butt of the rifle, and she dropped to one knee, then rose and continued singing. Now he set himself to her side, planted his feet, and drove the bayonet through her arm and into her side. She cried out as the bayonet was removed, and she reached with her other hand to press it over the wound. Her singing now came in sobs as the people behind her fell to their knees.

"What is she singing?" Carpathia demanded.

The sound was enhanced, and Chang found himself breathless as he listened to the woman's pitiful, labored singing. She could no longer hold up her head, but she stood wobbling, clearly woozy, struggling to sing, ". . . did e'er such love and sorrow meet, or thorns compose so rich a crown?"

The guard was joined by others, swinging the stocks of their rifles at the heads of those who bowed.

"Tell the guards to stop making a spectacle of it!" Carpathia raged. "They are playing right into these people's hands. Let the crowd see that no matter what they do or say or sing, still their heads belong to us!"

The guillotine was readied as the woman continued to force out the lyrics, though she had long since lost the tune. As she was grabbed by guards on each side and wrestled into place, she cried out, ". . . demands my soul, my life, my all!"

The blade dropped and the crowd erupted.

"Aah!" Carpathia sighed. "Can we not see from the other side?"

"The other side, sir?" the South American potentate repeated.

"Of the blade! Of the blade! Get a camera around there! The body does not drop! It merely collapses. I want to see the head drop!"

The next several in line approached the killing machine with their palms raised. The guards kept grabbing their elbows and pulling down their arms, but the condemned kept raising them. The guards slashed at their hands with bayonets, but the people instinctively moved and mostly avoided being cut.

The guards moved in behind them and prodded them with bayonet points in the lower back. Now the camera moved around behind a man who held a safety lever with one hand and used the other to grab the hair of the victim and pull the head into place. He lowered the restraining bar onto the neck, let go of the lever, and nodded to a matronly woman. She yanked at the release cord.

The blade squealed against the guides as it dropped in a flash, and the head fell out of sight, blood erupting from the neck.

"That is more like it!" Carpathia whispered.

✣ ✣ ✣

"We're home free, aren't we?" Hannah said.

Mac turned to look at her. "My plane has about enough fuel to get us to Rome. There's a small airstrip south of there manned by Co-op people who stockpile fuel. I'm not going to feel safe until we take off from there."

"But these people, I mean," she said. "They'll never reach this airport before we do, will they?"

"Not in cars."

"What're you saying?" George said.

"It won't take 'em long to guess where we're going. They won't think we're trying to beat 'em to the border by car."

"Your plane hidden?"

"From auto traffic, sure. From the air? No."

"How long would it take them to fly here?"

"Out of Kozani, in a fighter? They could beat us there."

"Could they destroy your plane?"

"Only if they get there first."

"How much personnel could they bring?"

"Not many if they use a small, quick plane."

George sounded irritated. "This has been too much work to see it fail now, Mac. Let's get it all on the table. You hoping we just show up, climb aboard, and take off?"

"That's the only plan I've got," Mac said.

"We've got to figure they'll beat us there," George said, "and decide what to do about that."

"You want to assume the worst?"

"Of course! We have to. You think I got away from those idiots by hoping they'd let me go? Tell me about this airstrip."

"Runs east and west. I'm at the east end, facing west."

"If they can get a plane in there before we take off, all they have to do is get in our way."

"Let's get in their way first," Mac said. "I'll dump you guys at the plane; you get the engines warm while I drive out onto the runway and sit directly in our path. They're going to have to be pretty crafty and flexible to avoid hitting me on landing. When we take off, we angle enough to miss the car and them, and we're gone."

George shook his head. "And when do you board? You're leaving a lot to chance."

"Leaving it to God, George. I don't know what else to do."

Mac's phone buzzed. "Go, Chang."

"They're in a jet ten minutes from touchdown. Stefanich, the three philosophers, and a pilot. Plane does not appear to be offensively equipped, but they are heavily armed."

"We're closer than that," Mac said. "We just have to beat 'em, that's all."

He asked Chloe if she could get any more out of the little car, but it was whining as it was, speeding along on a bad road. "When we get there, get off the road and come in on the east end."

Mac was giving Sebastian instructions about the plane when he thought he heard the scream of jet engines in the distance. He and George rolled down their windows to listen. "That's our clearing, Chloe! Easy!"

She whipped off the road, down into a ravine, and up the other side. The car bounced and jerked, and Mac's head hit the ceiling. "Use your brights! I have no idea what's out here."

"Am I going to be able to get through those trees?" she said.

"Assume you will. Just get us there."

Chloe hit a rocky patch that threw the car into the air. When it landed, the left rear tire blew. "Great!" she said.

"At least it's in the back," George said. "Stand on it!"

+ + +

With the brights on, Chloe saw only uneven, rocky terrain up to a thick grove of trees. She couldn't imagine a way through, but there was no turning back now. The left rear side was dragging from the flat as if someone had dropped an anchor. It didn't help that Sebastian, the biggest person in the car, sat back there.

With the jet looming, Chloe wished she could kill the lights and just plow on through. But it had all come down to timing. And determination. These were the people who had killed her comrades and who would now snuff out this little surviving band of Trib Forcers without a thought.

Chloe had wanted action, to be in the thick of it. And though she would do whatever it took to get back to Buck and Kenny, she was already long past any option but recklessness. Caution, diplomacy, trickery—that was all out the window now. She had to get to that plane and they had to take off, or none of them would see the sun rise again.

She picked her way through the trees, only occasionally lifting her foot from the accelerator. The little car had front-wheel drive, a small blessing in a bad situation. Making her own path, she smacked the car against a tree first on one side, then the other, and kept going.

Now she could see Mac's plane, but a three-wire fence was in the way. Slowing even a bit could make the car get tangled in it. She glanced at Mac, who braced himself with a palm on the ceiling. He merely nodded at the fence as if she had no choice. Chloe kept the accelerator down, and the car caught the lower wire, made the top two slip over the hood, pulled a wood post from the ground, and snapped its way through to the edge of the runway, forty feet from the plane.

Banking at the other end came the GC jet, landing lights illuminating the strip all the way to the car.

12

FOR THE FIRST TIME since he had been running the point for the Tribulation Force at the palace complex, Chang wondered if he had been found out. His computer screen was suddenly ringed with a red border, meaning an outside source was testing his firewall.

He immediately switched to a screen saver that scrolled the date and time and temperature, cut all the lights in his apartment, disrobed, and jumped into bed—prepared to look as if he had been sleeping, should Figueroa or one of his minions come knocking. There was really no way of knowing what the warning meant, but David Hassid had told him he had built the security in just to alert the operator that someone was nosing around.

Maybe someone was checking to see every computer that was turned on. Who knew whether the search was capable of hacking in and finding out who the mole was?

The latter didn't seem possible, if David could be believed. He had rigged the system so elaborately that it seemed there wouldn't be enough years left before the Glorious Appearing before someone could decode it. Chang's mind began playing games. Perhaps Akbar had instructed Figueroa to sense every computer running, eliminate the mainframe that ran the whole place, isolate the laptops and personal computers, and do a fast door-to-door search to see what people were up to.

Chang's computer would show no record of what he had been doing during the hours since he got back from his office. For that reason, he hoped someone would show up and check.

As he lay there in the darkness, heart galloping, Chang was frustrated at having to quit monitoring Greece. Ironic, he thought, that with all the technology God had allowed them to adapt for the cause of Christ around the world, he was suddenly left with nothing to do to help, except old-fashioned praying. He wished he could check the bugs in Carpathia's and Akbar's offices once more to see if the computer recording showed them giving a directive. It wouldn't be long before someone at the highest level ran out of patience with all the hacking going on.

Chang eased out of bed and onto the cold floor, kneeling to pray for Mac and Chloe and Hannah and George. "Lord, I don't see how they can escape now, outside your direct help. I don't know if it's their time to join you, and I have never assumed our thoughts were your thoughts. Everything happens in your time for your pleasure, but I pray for them and the people who love them. Whatever you do I know will prove your greatness, and I ask that I be able to know soon what it was. Also, please be with Ming as she searches for our parents, and may they be able to communicate with me somehow."

Chang felt the urge to let Rayford know what was going on. He looked at his watch. It was well after midnight, but would the people in Petra be sleeping after all that had gone on there that day? Nothing indicated that his phone was not still secure, so he dialed.

+ + +

"Out! Out!" Mac hollered as the doors flew open. "Let me over there, Chloe. I've got to get in the way of that jet."

"I'll crank 'er up," Sebastian told Mac, "but I'm not inclined to leave without you."

"Listen, George. You do what you have to do. Worrying about me might distract 'em long enough for you to get in the air. If that's what it takes, I'll see you at the Eastern Gate."

"Don't talk like that!"

"Don't get emotional on me now. Get yourselves on home!"

Mac waited a beat for George to back away from the car, and when he didn't, Mac just floored it and wobbled down the runway, in line with the jet that was just about to touch down.

+ + +

Rayford was not asleep, but he had finally settled and was breathing easier, gazing at the stars through a slit in the tent. His phone indicated Chang was calling.

"Give me good news," he said.

"I wish I could," Chang said, "but I think the Lord just wanted me to let you know so you could pray."

Rayford didn't feel as glib as he sounded, but when he heard the story, he said, "God protected a million people in a fiery furnace; he can get four out of Greece."

He slipped on his sandals and hurried to where Tsion and Chaim were to bed down. If they were sleeping, he would not wake them. It didn't surprise him to find them awake and huddled around a computer with some of the other elders. At the keyboard was the young woman, Naomi, who had summoned him earlier.

"Tsion, a word," Rayford said.

Dr. Ben-Judah turned, surprised. "I thought you were sleeping, as we all should be. Big day tomorrow."

Rayford brought him up to date.

"We will pray, of course, right now. But get back to Chang and tell him the computer warning was a false alarm. Naomi has been exulting in the hundreds of pages of instructions David built into the system here, including one that allows us to check the palace computers. That is what she has been doing, and that sent Chang's computer a warning."

Tsion hurried back to the elders and asked them all to pray for the safety of the Tribulation Force contingent in Greece. To see a dozen and a half people immediately go to their knees for his people warmed Rayford, and he couldn't wait to get back to Chang.

+ + +

When George Sebastian's foot hit the first step up to the plane, he heard the engines whine and then scream to life. He had not realized either of the women knew how to fly. So much the better. He squatted to pull the door up behind him, but when he turned toward the cockpit, he noticed both Chloe and Hannah strapping themselves into the back two seats. They looked as surprised as he felt.

George set his Uzi and pressed his back up against the bulkhead that separated the cabin from the cockpit. He slowly edged around to where he could peer up front to see who was there. The surprise pilot, in brown and beige Bedouin-type robes, was working from the copilot's chair. Without turning, the man raised a hand and motioned George toward the pilot's chair.

George pulled back and faced the women. "Who is that?"

"We thought it was you," Chloe said.

"We've got to get him off here or we won't have room for Mac. Cover me."

Chloe unstrapped and knelt behind George with her Uzi ready. Hannah raised her weapon and stood on the arm of her seat so she could peer over George's head into the cockpit.

Sebastian hopped into view of the copilot's chair. Empty. "All righty then," George said, exhaling loudly and climbing over the back of the seat to take the controls. He jammed on the earphones. "Why doesn't God just let these guys do the flying?"

"I can do that too," a voice said.

George jumped and saw the reflection of the man in the windshield. But when he looked to his right, the copilot's chair was still empty. "Quit that!" George said, his pulse racing.

"Sorry."

"Michael, I suppose."

"Roger."

George saw Mac and the rattling GC car struggling down the runway in the face of the oncoming jet. He wanted to ask Michael if he wouldn't be more help riding next to Mac.

"Illuminate landing lights," he heard.

"For takeoff?"

"Roger."

Sebastian wasn't about to argue. He flipped on the landing lights, which merely shone into Mac's back window. "Should I start the taxi, angling away from Mac, like he said?"

"Stand by."

"No?"

"Hold."

+ + +

For an instant, Mac thought the GC jet didn't see him. He slammed on the brakes and stayed in line between the two craft. When the jet finally stopped, about fifty feet in front of him, he realized it could easily go around him. Why wasn't Sebastian rolling? With the right angle, he could get past Mac and the GC and be in the air in seconds.

Not wanting to give the GC a chance to cut George off, Mac hit the accelerator and pulled to within ten feet of the jet. He realized someone could open the door and have a clear shot at him, but they couldn't do much to his plane if he sabotaged their aircraft. Not wanting to give them time to think, he raced forward and lodged the front of the car under the nose of the jet, banging into the landing gear. He had raised the plane off the ground a few inches but couldn't tell if he had done any damage.

Mac rolled down his window and leaned his torso all the way out, firing his Uzi at the tires. He was amazed how resilient they were, and he heard bullets bouncing off and hitting the fuselage and the car. Reaching farther and experimenting with angles, he finally got one of the tires to blow. But where was George? Why weren't they advancing? Was something wrong with the plane? Sebastian just sat at the end of the runway with those lights on.

Mac expected the GC to come bounding out any second, weapons blazing.

Could they not see he was the only person in the car? What were they afraid of? He was a sitting duck, lodged under their jet.

Mac tried to open the door, found it hopelessly stuck, and tried getting out the other side. It too was out of shape and not moving, but he thought he sensed a little more give on that side. He lay on the front seat and pushed with his hands on the driver's side door while pressing against the passenger door with his feet. It finally broke free and he scrambled out.

He crouched beneath the jet, Uzi trained on the door. He would take them as they came out, if they dared. Maybe they were waiting for him to make a break for his own plane or for Sebastian to come and pick him up. But opening the door for him would slow George too, and all of them would be in danger.

As he waited, locked in a bewildering standoff, Mac didn't know what to do. Should he try to shoot through the skin of the jet and take them all out? If it was armor plated, which was likely, he would waste ammunition. Why weren't they coming after him? And why was George still waiting?

The GC jet shut down. Now what? Nothing. No movement inside or out.

Frustrated, Mac grabbed his walkie-talkie. "Chloe or Hannah," he whispered desperately, "come in, please."

"Chloe here, Mac."

"What's going on?"

"Got me. George is at the controls."

"What's he doing?"

"You wanna talk to him? Here."

"Kinda busy here, Mac. What's up?"

"You can see what's up! What're you doing?"

"Waiting for clearance."

"You're clear! Go! Go now! Angle to your right! These guys are hung up and I've got one of their tires blown. They've shut down their engines."

"Waiting for you, partner."

"Don't be silly. I'd run right into their line of fire. Go to the other end of the runway, and I'll meet you there. But if they come after me, just keep going."

"Yeah, I know, and you'll see me in heaven."

"Exactly—now quit being stupid and go!"

"I'm not being stupid, Mac. I'm obeying."

"You're supposed to obey *me,* so do as I say."

"Sorry. You've been superseded."

"What?"

"You're supposed to put down your weapon and walk this way."

"You got GC on that plane!?"

"Negative. Come unarmed, and you will be safe."

"Have you lost your mind?"

"God is telling you to come."

Mac shook his head. "Ah, stand by."

"Come now."

Mac sighed, his eyes darting back and forth between the jet door and his own plane. He pushed the transmit button. "Lord, if it is you, command me to come that way."

"Come."

The voice had not been George's.

"Unarmed?"

"Come."

Mac waited a beat, then unstrapped the Uzi and laid it on the ground. He turned off the walkie-talkie and jammed it into his pocket. He walked past the car and stood directly under the cockpit. He felt exposed, vulnerable, indefensible. If that jet door opened now, he was a dead man.

He heard nothing above him, saw nothing beside him. Mac stepped out from under the plane and headed directly in front of it. He kept imagining he heard movement behind him—the engines roaring to life, footsteps from the cabin to the door, the door opening, weapons firing.

He prayed urgently as he strode along, "Lord, save me!"

Immediately he felt as if God's hands were upon him, and he barely felt his feet on the ground. "O you of little faith, why do you doubt?"

The voice was clear as crystal, but the walkie-talkie was off and George had his engines roaring. Mac broke into a trot, then a run. Every step sounded like a gunshot. Hannah was lowering the door when he got there, and he leaped in.

"Flyin' or backseat drivin'?" George said, unstrapping as if ready to take the copilot's chair.

"Here is fine," Mac said. "I don't think I could ride a bike right now."

+ + +

Chang was relieved to hear from Rayford and eager to meet Naomi even if only online. He was tempted to scold her for scaring him, and so decided to wait until the next day to try to make contact. Meanwhile, he checked in on Mac and his team, fearing the worst despite all the praying that had been going on.

Mac answered his phone, sounding exhausted.

"I need to meet this Michael someday," Chang said, after hearing the story. "You guys get all the fun."

"I could use a little less fun, frankly," Mac said. "And you might as well know, Sebastian here doesn't call him Michael anymore. Calls him Roger."

"Roger?"

"Says he told him he assumed he was Michael, and the guy said, 'Roger.'"

"So Stefanich and those guys are just sitting on the runway with a wounded plane?"

"Yeah, and they're gonna need some repair work before they can take off again."

"Why didn't they shoot you?"

"I thought you could find out. What was going on in that cockpit when I strolled out from underneath, unarmed?"

"I'll let you know."

Within half an hour the rest of the Tribulation Force had heard the good news out of Greece, and Chang had paved the way for George to land south of Rome for the refuel. They were on their own for getting back to the safe house without going through Kankakee, Illinois, and without arousing more suspicion. That should be the easiest part of their ordeal.

When Chang was finally able to hack back into the Ptolemaïs GC system and find transmissions between the plane and the Kozani tower, he could only shake his head. The pilot had reported seeing the plane at the end of the runway, putting down, and seeing a car approaching. But at the same time Chang figured Michael had instructed George to turn on his landing lights, the pilot reported a light so blinding that "we have lost visual contact with the plane and the auto."

A few minutes later the pilot reported being struck—by what, he did not know. His jet was being jostled and the front end lifted, but no one aboard could take his hands from his eyes because of the intense light. They heard shooting and feared for their lives, heard one of their tires blow, and shut down the engines. In essence they sat in fear, unable to peek out of the cockpit for the next several minutes, until they heard the plane thunder past them and rise.

Chang listened as they finally ventured out, shoulder radios left on, weapons ordered at the ready, only to find their damaged plane, wounded landing gear, flat tire, beat-up squad car, and an Uzi on the runway. Only now they were being rescued by a fleet of GC in cars, who reported that others had picked up the injured officers at the side of the road on the way. They were being treated for severe burns they claimed were caused by a ray gun.

It was still a couple of hours before Ming was to leave San Diego for the Far East. Chang was finally finished with his night's work. He dropped into bed, spent. How strange, he thought, to feel so pivotal and indispensable and then discover that the entire success of an operation was out of his hands. In fact, he had been out of commission when God worked his miracles.

There were victims to grieve, martyrs to praise, and much work ahead. Chang didn't know how long he could evade detection. He was willing to hang in and work in the office during the day, doing his real work after hours, for as long as God chose to protect him.

✢ ✢ ✢

Rayford stirred at dawn's first light, amazed he had been able to sleep at all. Petra was already humming, families gathering the morning's manna and filling any container they could find with the pure springwater God provided.

Thousands were working on the caves, thousands of others erecting more tents. On everyone's lips were stories of the miracle from the day before and the promise of live teaching from Dr. Tsion Ben-Judah himself later in the day.

From the elders and organizers came word that building materials were on their way and that the people should pray for the safety of pilots and truckers who would begin delivering materials. Volunteers were sought with expertise in various crafts. Rayford knew the current spirit could not last forever. The memory of the miracle would fade, inevitably, though he could not imagine it. And people, regardless of their shared faith, would find living elbow to elbow taxing after a while. But for now he would enjoy this.

Rayford would have to get back to the Tribulation Force at some point, but Carpathia's people would target anyone coming or going from Petra. Perhaps if the supplies were able to get in, that would be a clue it was prudent to try to get out.

Naomi and her team of computer gurus already reported that *The Truth* cyberzine had been transmitted from Buck Williams, recounting stories from around the world. The whole episode of what had gone on in Greece the day before was played out in detail, as was the truth about what had happened at Petra.

A team of computer experts from Israel said they had the technology to project *The Truth* onto a giant screen, if one could be fashioned. And among the various supplies already in the camp was enough white canvas to be stretched several stories high. Thousands gathered to read the stories.

Rayford loved the idea that it was not just believers, not just the so-called Judah-ites, who read *The Truth.* Many undecideds and even some who had taken the mark of Antichrist risked their lives by downloading Buck's magazine from the Tribulation Force site. All over the world the believers' underground and Co-op personnel translated it and printed it and distributed it. Carpathia could get away with nothing.

Sadly, Rayford knew, there were hundreds, if not thousands, of uncommitted people right there in Petra. Tsion had already promised to address them too, going so far as to say many of them would *still* be deceived and eventually spirited away by liars and charlatans. It was hard to understand or believe. How could someone have survived what Rayford had lived through and even question the one true God of the universe? It was beyond him.

Late in the morning, nearly twenty-four hours since the bombing, the people began to gather. Word spread that Dr. Ben-Judah would begin his teaching on the mercy of God. Throughout the crowd, however, stories also spread from around the world that persecution had intensified against believers and particularly against Jews.

Chang had tapped into the feeds to Akbar's and Fortunato's and Carpathia's offices and had set on automatic the utility that sent to Buck Williams's computer the reports from the sub-potentates around the world. As the sun rose in various countries, news of the bloodshed and mayhem of the night before and the relentless daytime raids was transmitted not just to New Babylon, but also from Chang to Buck and from Buck to the world through *The Truth.*

As the crowds gathered to hear Dr. Ben-Judah, they were riveted to the giant screen, set on a wall away from the sun for best viewing. Buck had transmitted the visuals Chang had sent him from the United South American States, and the masses booed and hissed as the shy man accepted the mark of loyalty. They cheered, then wept, then sang and praised God for the testimony of the brave martyrs who faced the blade with such peace and courage.

The remnant at Petra seemed outraged en masse at the reports from Greece about a midnight raid that had destroyed what was left of the small contingent of underground believers. Buck had added audio to that video report, reminding his readers and listeners and watchers that it had fallen to Greek believers to be among the first to give their lives rather than accept the mark of the beast.

Now, it seemed, on every continent the Morale Monitors and the Peacekeepers had been revitalized, financed, equipped, and motivated to more than turn up the heat. From every corner of the globe came reports of the end of the patience of the Global Community for dissenters or even the undecided. It was either accept the mark now or face the consequences immediately. Even many who had already taken the mark of Carpathia were punished for not bowing to worship his image three times a day.

Leon Fortunato came on—in full regalia and introduced by every title and pedigree he had ever enjoyed—to warn that "those of Jewish descent who are as stubborn as the Judah-ites and insist on worshiping a god other than our father and risen lord, Nicolae Carpathia, shall find themselves receiving their just reward. Yea, death is too good for them. Oh, they shall surely die, but it is hereby decreed that no Jew should be allowed the mercy of a quick end by the blade. Graphic and reproachful as that is, it is virtually painless. No, these shall suffer day and night in their dens of iniquity, and by the time they expire due to natural causes—brought about by their own rejection of Carpathianism—they will be praying, crying out, for a death so expedient as the loyalty enforcement facilitator."

Those in Petra appeared to Rayford shocked by the lengths New Babylon would go to, to take revenge on its enemies and humiliate Jews. But their greatest wrath and derision were saved for the report from GCNN about what had happened the day before, right there in the red rock city.

An anchorman intoned that the attack on Petra—two incendiary bombs and a land-based launch missile—had missed their target and that the enemy encamped there had swiftly struck back and downed the two fighter-bombers, killing the pilots. The laughter began with that report and turned to waving fists and hisses and boos as Carpathia came on to mourn the deaths of the martyred airmen.

"While there is no denying that it was pilot error, still the Global Community, I am sure, joins me in extending its deepest sympathy to the surviving families. We decided not to risk any more personnel in trying to destroy this stronghold of the enemy, but we will starve them out by cutting off supply lines. Within days, this will be the largest Jewish concentration camp in history, and their foolish stubbornness will have caught up with them.

"Fellow citizens of the new world order, my compatriots in the Global Community, we have these people and their leaders to thank for the tragedy that besets our seas and oceans. I have been repeatedly urged by my closest advisers to negotiate with these international terrorists, these purveyors of black magic who have used their wicked spells to cause such devastation.

"I am sure you agree with me that there is no future in such diplomacy. I have nothing to offer in exchange for the millions of human lives lost, not to mention the beauty and the richness of the plant and animal life.

"You may rest assured that my top people are at work to devise a remedy to this tragedy, but it will not include deals, concessions, or any acknowledgment that these people had the right to foist on the world such an unspeakable act."

In the middle of that newscast, from Chang through Buck, came a reproduction of the conversation between Suhail Akbar and the two pilots from the Petra bombing raid. Though the GCNN tried to speak over it and stream words in front of it saying it was false, a hoax, anyone listening heard the pilots defending themselves to Akbar, and his order for their executions.

Rayford could not fathom how Carpathia could have a supporter left in the world, and yet it was clear that Scripture foretold he would. At Petra the crowd grew restless and murmured among themselves about both the lies and the truth they had just been exposed to. But the rumor was that Micah, the one who had led them out of Israel to this safe place, was about to emerge and introduce Dr. Ben-Judah.

Spontaneously, the entire crowd fell silent.

13

CHAIM ROSENZWEIG HELD both hands aloft and addressed the assembled in a huge voice that could be heard everywhere.

"It is my great pleasure and personal joy to once again introduce to you my former student, my personal friend, now my mentor, and your rabbi, shepherd, pastor, and teacher, Dr. Tsion Ben-Judah!"

The only reason Rayford did not applaud and cheer was that he knew Tsion hated personal adulation. Yet he hoped the rabbi would appreciate that these people were merely trying to express their love for him.

When Dr. Ben-Judah was finally able to quiet the crowd, he said, "Thank you for the warmth of your welcome, but I ask that in the future, when I am introduced, you do me the honor of merely silently thanking God for his love and mercy. That is what I will be talking about primarily, and whether you pray, raise your hands, or just point to the sky in acknowledgment of him, your adoration will be properly directed.

"In the fourteenth chapter of the Gospel of John, our Lord, Jesus the Messiah, makes a promise we can take to the bank of eternity. He says, 'Let not your heart be troubled; you believe in God, believe also in me. In my father's house are many mansions; if it were not so, I would have told you. I go to prepare a place for you. And if I go and prepare a place for you, I will come again and receive you to myself; that where I am, there you may be also.'

"Notice the urgency. That was Jesus' guarantee that though he was leaving his disciples, one day he would return. The world had not seen the last of Jesus the Christ, and as many of you know, it still has not seen the last of him.

"Think with me now of the five paramount, pivotal events of history. From Eden until this present moment, God has given us in the Bible an accurate history of the world, much of it written in advance. It is the only truly accurate history ever written.

"The first pivotal event was the creation of the world by the direct act of God.

"Next comes the worldwide flood. This flood had a catastrophic effect on the world and still boggles the minds of scientists who find fish bones at altitudes as high as fifteen thousand feet.

"The third pivotal event in history was the first coming of Jesus the Messiah. That event made possible our salvation from sin. Jesus lived a perfect life and died as a sacrifice for our sin. He died for the sins of the world, for all those who would call upon him.

"But that is not the end of the story, as we all know, because none of us here called upon him to forgive our sins until after the fourth pivotal event in history—when he came back.

"Most of us have since rectified that situation, and it is a good thing. Both the Old and the New Testaments of the Bible point to his coming one last time—the fifth pivotal event in world history. This glorious appearing will signal the beginning of the millennial kingdom, true utopia.

"Imagine paradise on earth with Messiah in control. Many believe that during his thousand-year reign, which will begin less than three and a half years from now, the population will grow to greater than the number of all the people who have already lived and died up to now. How can that be? Because ours will be a world without war. Imagine a globe in which government will not be responsible for killing the nearly 200 million it has slain to this day.

"Serving God has never been the choice of mankind. But when Messiah returns, he will establish his kingdom and people will live at peace. We will live in righteousness. We will have plenty. It is difficult to describe what an incredible time it will be. Everyone will have enough.

"God wants this kind of a world, and he wants it for us for one reason: He is gracious. In the Bible, Joel 2:13 says he is merciful, slow to anger, and abundant in loving-kindness. He relents from doing harm. Jonah, 125 years after Joel was born, described God in the same words. And Moses, fifteen hundred years before these men lived, said the Lord is merciful and gracious, long-suffering, and abundant in goodness and truth.

"Those are the prophets' views of God. Where do you get your view of God? What better picture of him could we have gotten than what we lived through yesterday? When you kneel to pray, remember that event and what the prophets have said. Yes, we have an august God—the only supreme, omnipotent potentate. But if the Bible teaches one thing about God, it is that he is for us. He is not against us. He wants to bless our lives, and the key to the door of blessing is to give your life to him and ask him to do with it as he will. How could you not love the God the prophets describe? How could you not love the God Jesus the Messiah refers to as our Father who is in heaven?

"How wonderful it is that we can come as children into the presence of God himself, the creator of everything, and call him our Father.

"We find ourselves enduring the worst period in human history. Sixteen of the prophesied judgments of God have already rained down upon the earth, each worse than the last, with five yet to go. The Antichrist has been revealed, as has the False Prophet. That is why Messiah referred to this period as the Tribulation, and the second half of it—in which we now find ourselves—as the Great Tribulation.

"How can I say this judging, avenging God is loving and merciful? Remember that during this period he is working in people to get them to make a decision. Why? The millennium is coming. When Jesus makes his final glorious appearing, he will come in power and great glory. He will set up his kingdom exclusively for those who have made the right decision. That decision? To call on the name of the Lord.

"Does that sound exclusivistic? Understand this: The Bible makes clear that the will of God is that all men be saved. Second Peter 3:9 says, 'The Lord is not slack concerning his promise . . . but is long-suffering toward us, not willing that any should perish but that all should come to repentance.'

"God promised in Joel 2 that he would 'show wonders in the heavens and in the earth: blood and fire and pillars of smoke. The sun shall be turned into darkness, and the moon into blood, before the coming of the great and awesome Day of the Lord. And it shall come to pass that whoever calls on the name of the Lord shall be saved. For in Mount Zion and in Jerusalem there shall be deliverance, as the Lord has said, among the remnant whom the Lord calls.'

"Dear people, *you* are that remnant! Do you see what God is saying? He is still calling men to faith in Christ. He has raised up 144,000 evangelists, from the twelve tribes, to plead with men and women all over the world to decide for Christ. Who but a loving, gracious, merciful, long-suffering God could plan in advance that during this time of chaos he would send so many out in power to preach his message?

"Remember the two supernatural witnesses who preached the Word of God in Jerusalem and on global television? After three and a half years they were murdered in full view of the whole world. And then after their bodies lay in the streets for three days, God called them to heaven. Why? Because as a loving and merciful God he wanted to manifest his power and glory so men and women could see and make the right decision about him.

"Here we have the supernatural God of heaven fulfilling his promises of ages past, preserving the children of Israel while Antichrist tries to persecute you.

"Whom will you serve? Will you obey the ruler of this world, or will you call on the name of the Lord?

"God has done all these great and mighty things because he wants to save mankind. Many will still rebel, even here, even after all they have seen and experienced. Do not let it be you, my friend. Our God is merciful. Our God is gracious. He is long-suffering and wants all to be saved.

"If you agree that God is using the period we now live in to get people ready for the millennial kingdom and for eternity, what will you do with your life? Turn it over to Messiah. Worship Jesus, the Christ. Receive him as the one and only Lamb of God that takes away the sins of the world. Receive him into your life and then live in obedience to him. He wants you. And a God who will go to such lengths to save to the uttermost anyone who will call on him is one worth trusting. *Will* you trust a God like that? *Can* you love a God like that?

"Messiah was born in human flesh. He came again. And he is coming one more time. I want you to be ready. We were left behind at the Rapture. Let us be ready for the Glorious Appearing. The Holy Spirit of God is moving all over the world. Jesus is building his church during this darkest period in history because he is gracious, loving, long-suffering, and merciful."

All around Rayford, people had bowed their heads, and many began praying. They prayed for friends and loved ones in Petra and in other places in the world. They had to have heard, as Rayford did, the emotion in Tsion's voice as he pleaded once again for all to make the decision to follow Christ.

"The time is short," Tsion cried out, "and salvation is a personal decision. Admit to God that you are a sinner. Acknowledge that you cannot save yourself. Throw yourself on the mercy of God and receive the gift of his Son, who died on the cross for your sin. Receive him and thank him for the gift of your salvation."

+ + +

"Major, major problem," Aurelio Figueroa said, steepling his fingers as he leaned back in his chair. Chang sat across the desk from him, praying silently. "It's not just the bogus entries in the palace database, the phony personnel and checks and balances that have allowed the enemies of the GC to fool local leaders. Now we clearly have bugs in offices as high as the director of Security and Intelligence. Do you know that earlier today, while the potentate was trying to properly mourn our dead pilots, someone superseded the feed with a bogus conversation Director Akbar was supposed to have had with the pilots?"

"Bet you're glad it was bogus."

"I don't follow, Wong."

"If it was real, it could have been catastrophic. We all heard it, sir. Akbar lecturing the pilots, their disagreeing, and his having them executed."

The tall, bony Mexican studied Chang. "Where would someone have gotten that kind of a recording?"

"You're asking me?"

"I don't see anyone else in the room."

"I'm sorry. I should have said, '*Why* are you asking me?'"

This was zero hour. If Figueroa accused him, Chang might have to be out of New Babylon within hours to avoid execution.

"I'm asking everyone, of course. Don't take it personally. You wouldn't believe what's been planted on the main database."

"Tell me."

Figueroa stood. "I'm not telling everyone this, but Akbar himself began to suspect something shaky in Chicago. You know the place was hit more than once during the war. The city was evacuated and declared off-limits, and we have virtually ignored it for months. Years."

Chang nodded.

"We didn't fly reconnaissance planes over it, didn't take pictures, didn't check heat sensors, anything."

"Because?"

"Because someone planted on the computer that the place had been nuked and would be radioactive for years. Akbar didn't remember it that way. He thought the city had been virtually destroyed, but not by nukes. Every time he had somebody check, they went straight to the database, checked the current levels, and said, 'Yup, it's radioactive all right.' Not until recently did anybody check the archives to find out if the readings could be right. Of course, they can't. The place is clean."

"Wow."

"Wow is right. You know as well as I do that there is only one reason someone would plant such information: to have the city to themselves. We've been able to bypass the phony readings, finally, and have tried to get a bead on what's happening there. Precious little, of course, because everyone else was getting the same info we were. But there has been activity. Water and power usage. Planes, choppers, coming and going. Jets from an airstrip on the lake. That would be Lake Michigan."

"Really?"

"Yes. There is evidence of both vehicular and pedestrian traffic. Very little, of course, but there could be up to three dozen people in the city."

"Hardly enough to worry about," Chang said.

"Oh, on the contrary," Figueroa said. "These people are going to wish they'd never been born."

Chang was dying to ask but desperate to appear remote. He waited.

"You'd think we'd just send a team of Peacekeepers sweeping in there and round them up, wouldn't you?"

Chang shrugged. "Something like that, sure."

"Akbar has a better idea. He says if somebody wants it to appear radioactive, let's nuke it."

"You can't be serious."

"Totally."

"Waste technology like that at a time like this?"

"It's brilliant, Chang."

"It's a solution, I'll say that. But has he thought of the freshwater that flows through there?"

"We're harvesting Lake Michigan from northern Wisconsin. We don't have to worry about the Chicago River."

"People living downstream from it do."

"Well, anyway, word is the big boss loves the idea."

"Really."

"You kidding? Carpath—uh, the potentate loves stuff like this."

"We've got an atomic bomb we can spare?"

"Come on, Wong! Whoever these people are, they're up to no good. If they were loyal citizens, wouldn't they say, 'Hey, we didn't know this place was off-limits and we mistakenly settled here, and you know what, we're okay'?"

Chang shrugged, wanting to know how much time he had to warn the Trib Force but not daring to ask. "I guess."

"You guess? There's no record of a loyalty mark application site there, of course. And nobody who's registered with us would live there without telling us."

"You're right."

"'Course I'm right. Hey, Chang, you don't look so good."

Chang had been surreptitiously holding his breath and not blinking. His face had reddened and his eyes watered. "Just tired," he said, exhaling finally. "And I think I'm coming down with something."

"You all right?"

Chang coughed, then pretended he couldn't stop. He held up a hand as if to apologize and say he was okay. "Didn't sleep that well last night," he managed. "I'll be fine. I'll go to bed early tonight."

"You need a nap?"

"Nah. Too much to do."

"We're okay. Take a break."

"I couldn't."

"Why not?"

"Want to do my share, pull my weight, all that." He disintegrated into a coughing spell again.

"Just knock off early. You've got sick time left, don't you?"

"Just used some during the, you know, plague thing."

"Boils? Yeah, didn't we all? Take the rest of the day off, and if you're not in tomorrow, I'll understand."

"No, now really, Mr. Figueroa, I'll be fine. See? I feel better already."

"What is it with you, Wong? I mean, I'm all for gung ho, but—"

"Just don't like being a wimp."

"You're anything but that."

"Thanks," Chang said, covering his mouth and coughing longer than he had before.

"Stop by Medical and get something."

Chang waved Figueroa off. "I'm going back to my desk," he wheezed.

"No, you're not. Now that's a directive."

"You're *making* me leave work early?"

"Come on! You think I'm thinking only of you? Get over yourself. I don't want a department full of coughers, and I think you've contaminated my office enough too. Get going."

"I really—"

"Chang! Go!"

+ + +

It was the crack of dawn in Colorado, and Steve Plank, aka Pinkerton Stephens, was asleep in his quarters. He had spent until midnight firing off warnings to his friends in the Tribulation Force that something big was coming for Chicago and that if they knew what was good for them, they would escape, and fast. He had reached Rayford Steele by phone in Petra and urged him to stay there and not let Abdullah Smith or anyone else go back to Chicago either.

When the insistent banging on his door woke him, his first thought was that in his haste he had not used a secure phone or that his computer had been bugged. If they caught him, they caught him. Warning the Trib Force was the most productive thing he'd done since becoming a believer—or at least since helping them get Hattie Durham out of his custody and to a place where she became a believer.

Plank tried to call out to see who it was and what they wanted, but his facial appliance was next to the bed, and without it, he could not make himself heard. The best he could do was grunt, and he felt for the plastic pieces in the dark.

"Mr. Stephens, sir, no need to open the door." It was Vasily Medvedev, Steve's second in command. "I just wanted to give you fair warning. New Babylon is cracking down on the handful of employees around the world who have not yet received the loyalty mark. You're expected to have yours applied by noon mountain time at Carpathia Resurrection Field. Just acknowledge that you got that."

Steve slung himself into his motorized wheelchair and rolled to the door, then tapped twice on it.

"Thank you, sir. This puts me in an awkward spot, but I've been ordered to accompany you and see to it."

Steve rolled back to the bed stand and quickly snapped on his appliances. "Hold on a second, Vasily!" He opened the door and waved him in.

"I'm sorry, sir," the Russian said. "What could I do or say?"

"Tell them I already have it."

"There's no record of it."

"You know it cannot be applied to synthetic. You want to see it?" Plank began to unsnap the forehead piece.

"No! Please! Now, sir, I'm sorry, but I tried looking once, and that was more than enough. Forgive me."

"Well, I'm going to see if the administrator of the marks wants a look," Steve said.

"Come, sir, there'd be a record, wouldn't there?"

"I should be exempted. Can you imagine the pain of having it applied to the membrane—"

"Please! I was told to inform you and to—"

"See to it, yeah, I know."

"Sir? Why don't you just have it applied to your hand?"

"My hand? My hand, you say? You forget my hand was also donated to the cause?"

Steve held up the stub, and Vasily recoiled. "I am so stupid," he said. "Can you forget I—"

Steve waved him off. "Don't worry about it."

"When would you like to leave, sir? They open at eight and we're about an hour away."

"I know how far away we are, Vasily."

"Of course."

"I'll let you know."

When Medvedev left, Steve bowed his head, weeping. "God, what should I do? Bluff them? See if I can get a waiver? Is this it? Is it over? Can I be of no more service to the believers around the world?"

Steve spent the morning communicating with Chang in New Babylon, where it was late afternoon. They worked frantically to come up with suggestions as to where the Chicago-based Trib Force might go. No one anywhere could take them all. The Strong Building had been perfect, if only briefly.

Neither Chang nor Steve had yet been able to ascertain when the bombing of

Chicago might commence, but clearly speed was of the essence. Only after they had informed everyone and made their recommendations did Steve tell Chang what was happening with him.

"I knew they were cracking down," Chang said, "but I had no idea how soon. Let me put in the database that you've had the mark applied. I can copy you on the documentation."

"Can't let you do that, brother."

"Why? I just did it for a Co-op flier the other day. He didn't even know till it was done."

"With the way they're watching at the palace right now? I go from no documentation one day to totally clear the next?"

"It doesn't have to be at Resurrection. I could say it came from anywhere."

Steve paused. It was intriguing, enticing even. But it didn't resonate. "Maybe if you'd thought of it before—if it had just showed up, like an accident, like you did with the other guy. But this would be like my choosing the mark. I couldn't do that."

"Then you're getting out of there, right? Where will you go and how will you get there? Should I send someone for you? appropriate a ride?"

"It's not going to work, Chang. That'll make you vulnerable. And you know they've got to be watching me."

"No one's on to me yet," Chang said. "I don't think they're even suspicious."

"You need to keep it that way."

"Can you get to Petra? There's a Co-op flight out of Montana today. I could have him—"

"I'll let you know, Chang. I appreciate it, but it may be time to take my stand."

"What are you saying?"

"You know."

"Oh, Steve, at least make them catch you. We need you, man."

"On the lam? What good would I be?"

"We need everybody we can get."

✣ ✣ ✣

Buck debated waking the Greek contingent and decided against it, though it meant more work for everyone else. Chloe, Mac, Hannah, and Sebastian had staggered in during the wee hours.

Buck could tell Kenny was fascinated by all the activity. People scurried everywhere, deciding what they absolutely had to have, packing small boxes, ignoring printouts, notes—anything that was in a computer anyway. The person allowed to take more than anyone else was Zeke. There were things he simply could not do without: his files, his wardrobes, the tools of his trade.

Leah spent most of her time on a secure phone to Co-op people all over the country. She told Buck, "Everyone is resigned to the fact that they may have to take a few people in, and they honestly seem honored, but no one is excited about it. They are stretched to the limit for space and necessities as it is."

"We have no choice, Leah. It's time to call in the chips. I hate to say it, but a lot of these people owe us nothing less. We have run the Co-op from here and provided them with stuff that keeps them alive."

Albie seemed glum. And why not? Buck wondered. The only place Albie could think of to go—and wanted to go—was back to Al Basrah. "But I don't want to take a plane when so many of you have places to go."

"Do what you have to, Albie," Buck said. "See if Leah can get you a ride with someone delivering supplies to Petra. You know we'll be calling on you frequently."

"You'd better," Albie said.

Enoch's people were under the building, checking vehicles, seeing how many were in running condition. He had traded the privilege of choosing cars and SUVs as a concession against trying to get all thirty of the others from The Place onto planes. Leah had already lined up for them several underground centers within driving distance, Enoch himself in Palos Hills, Illinois.

"You know the danger of a caravan pulling out of here in broad daylight," Buck said.

"I sure do. But we also know the danger of being here when the GC hits."

\+ + +

Steve Plank had communicated to Vasily that he wanted to leave the GC compound at 11 a.m. He spent much of the rest of the morning behind closed doors, agonizing in prayer. Finally he called Buck. *What a strange turn,* he thought. Seeking solace and counsel from a young man who had once been his best—and most challenging—employee. The glory days of *Global Weekly* were long gone.

Steve's news was met with silence. Then a subdued Buck: "Steve, don't do it. Please."

"You think I want to? C'mon, man! Don't get personal with me now, Buck. I just wanted to say good-bye."

"Well, I don't want to, all right? I've said enough good-byes for one lifetime. Anyway, we need you. This is no time to be giving up."

"Don't insult me."

"I'll do what I have to, to keep you from this, Steve."

"I had hoped for more from you."

"I could say the same," Buck said.

"You think I'm taking the easy way out? Don't do this to me."

"What're you saying, Steve? That I'm supposed to just support you, wish you the best, say I'll see you on the flip side?"

"That would help. Tell me you trust my judgment."

"When I think you've lost your mind?"

Steve sighed. "Buck, I've got no one else to call. If I tell you that you can't talk me out of it and that's why I'm calling, will you just tell me you're with me?"

"Of course I'm with you, but—"

"I'm not a coward, Buck. You've seen me. You know I should have died. I was buried underground for almost a week. I live in pain every hour of every day, but I've misled, I've conspired, I've finagled, I've double-crossed the enemy every way I know how. Well, there's something I won't do. I won't run like a child and I won't deny Christ."

"I know you won't."

"Well, that's something. That wasn't so hard, was it?"

"Don't tell me I have to like this, Steve."

"Will you pray for me?"

"Of course, but I'd pray you come to your senses."

"I'm going through with this, Buck. And I won't pretend I'm not scared. The GC considers this an oversight, a timing thing, something to do with my limitations. But when they make it official, make me make my decision and take my stand, I don't want to fail God."

"You won't. He promises grace beyond measure and a peace that passes understanding."

"I gotta tell ya, Buck, I'm not feeling any of that yet."

"God," Buck began, but Steve could tell he had to compose himself before he could continue, "please be with your child. Give him your grace, your peace. I confess I don't want him to do this. I hate it. I'm tired of losing people I love. But if this is what you're calling him to do, give him courage, give him words, give him power over the enemy. I pray that people who see this will be so moved that they will make the same choice."

+ + +

Buck was so shaken that his comrades seemed to gather round him spontaneously. When they learned what was going on, they knelt and prayed for Steve. Buck called Chang.

"He'll be going to the center at Resurrection south of the Springs," Buck said. "Any chance they monitor that visually?"

"They do."

"Could that be transmitted here?"

"I can do it."

"I don't know why I want to see it, but I'll feel like I'm there with him."

\+ + +

Steve was aware of Vasily's double take when Steve rolled up in the parking lot in casual clothes. In fact, less than casual. He wore slip-on shoes, khaki pants, and a white undershirt.

"You're wondering about protocol," Steve said as Vasily lifted him into the car.

Vasily nodded. "I've learned not to question you, Chief."

"Are you armed, my friend?"

"Of course."

"I'm not."

"I can see that."

Steve reached out a hand to Vasily, who looked at it. "Shake," he said. "Sorry the hand isn't what it used to be." Vasily touched it gingerly. "The name's Steve Plank."

"Excuse me?"

"You heard me."

"Steve Plank?"

"So, you *were* listening, as usual. You know *Global Weekly*?"

Vasily appeared to have trouble concentrating. "What? The magazine? Sure. We get it from New Babylon."

"You remember when it was independent, before the disappearances?"

"Of course."

"I was on the masthead."

"The—?"

"Masthead. That list of the staff. I was the boss—the editorial boss, anyway." And Steve told Vasily his story. They were fifteen minutes from their destination when he finished.

Medvedev shook his head. "What am I supposed to do with that?"

"Well, you don't need to arrest me. You already have me in custody, and you're following orders. You're taking me to the center."

"And you will take the mark, continue to live as a secret enemy of the Global Community, and I am to look the other way because we have become friends?"

"Have we, Vasily?"

"I thought we had, but of course you have not trusted me with the truth until now."

"If we are friends, you could do me a favor."

"Let you go? Let you make a run for it? Where would you go?"

"No. I was thinking you might rather shoot me."

"You're joking."

"I'm not. It would look good on your record. Say what you want. You found me out, worried I would escape, whatever."

"I could not."

"Well, I couldn't either. Do myself in, I mean. Not that I didn't give it some thought."

"What are you asking me to do, short of shooting you? I am supposed to watch you die?"

"You are to 'see to it,' aren't you? Isn't that your assignment?"

Vasily sighed shakily and nodded. "You are not really going to go through with this, are you?"

Steve nodded. "I am. Running would only put off the inevitable. And you have to admit, I'm fairly recognizable."

"That is not humorous to me."

"Nor to me. Vasily, I regret only that when you came to me it was already too late for you. You had taken the mark, and proudly."

"I'm not so proud of it anymore."

"That is the tragedy of where we find ourselves."

"I know."

"You do?"

"You think I do not sneak a look occasionally at the Ben-Judah Web site? I know my decision is irreversible."

"You wish it wasn't?"

"I don't know. I am not blind, not deaf. I can see what's happening. If I had to say right now, I would say I envy you."

14

IT WAS TIME to wake Chloe, at least. And once she was up, the others soon followed.

Chang had called. The Trib Force needed to be packed and prepared to relocate at a moment's notice.

Chloe worked quickly, though bleary-eyed, with Kenny wrapped around her neck most of the time. George and Mac collected large quantities of canned and boxed foods, then started loading cars. Hannah, who helped Leah get the Co-op stuff in order, looked like she could use several more hours of sleep.

George told Buck he had arranged for someone to come and get him in Chicago but agreed he should reroute them, possibly through Long Grove, and meet them there. "We've got room for you and Chloe and the baby in San Diego, and I'd love to be your pilot."

Buck had to think about that one. He could think of worse scenarios. Leah had tentatively arranged for him and his family to move in with Lionel Whalum and his wife. Buck didn't know the man—but he wouldn't likely have personally known anyone they might stay with. Whalum had agreed to the setup, telling Leah he had a large suburban home but that he was planning to be gone frequently with runs to and from Petra.

"Leah," Buck said, "maybe you and Hannah ought to move in with the Whalums and let us take this opportunity George is offering. That way, you'd have a pilot, and so would we."

"Why don't you just take over and do this job, Buck, if you're going to make all my work a waste of time anyway."

"Chloe's up now anyway, Leah. Why don't you just get yourself ready to go."

She looked stricken and hurried away. Buck intercepted her. "Listen, let's forgive each other under the circumstances. Think about this: Whalum is transporting stuff to Petra all the time."

"I know, Buck. Chloe and I have been helping coordinate that."

"Are you thinking?"

"Are you insulting?" she said.

"You're not thinking."

"What?!"

"Catch a ride over there with him sometime, Leah. Anybody in Petra you want to see?"

That stopped her, briefly. "Oh, Buck, you can't be serious. I don't deny I'm enamored of Tsion. Who isn't? But he's not going to have the time for a friend with all he has going over there."

"So, what, are you afraid Long Grove is going to be too close to Chicago when the bomb hits? It may be."

"No. I—"

"You want to go with George to San Diego? They might need medical help out there. And there are private quarters. Nobody's sharing a house. They're in underground shelters, like Quonset huts."

"No, that sounds perfect for you and your family. I'll talk to Hannah about Long Grove."

"Did I hear my name?" Hannah said. "I prefer the Southwest."

"Got a contact?" Leah said. "Need one?"

Within a few minutes Hannah had agreed to stick with Leah. Zeke and Mac were the only two left without arrangements. "I got to be somewhere where people can get to me to take advantage of my services," Zeke said. "Someplace safe but central."

"Workin' on it," Chloe called out.

"I want to be where I can make runs to Petra," Mac said on one of his trips in for more boxes. "Maybe get Rayford out."

"Rayford ought to stay there," Buck said. "Might drive him crazy after a while, but he's got everything he needs to safely keep track of everybody."

By the time they were set to pull out if and when the word came, Albie had invited Mac to Al Basrah, and Zeke was set up with an underground unit in western Wisconsin, a city called Avery, not far from the Minnesota border. Buck called Chang. "We're gonna be noisy parading out of here," he said, "but I don't guess we have any choice."

"Go in the wee hours," Chang said, "only a few at a time over the next few days. I'll be able to tell if anyone's on to you. It's a risk, but you know the odds if you wait."

The entire group—all forty of them, including the thirty-one from The Place—met in a huge circle. They wrapped their arms around each other and prayed for each other and wept. All of them. Even George and Mac. And seeing all those tears made Kenny cry, which made the others laugh.

"It seems as if we just got here," Buck said. "And now we don't know when we might see each other again. I have a list here of what order we'll go in, and my family and I will be the last ones out."

The Strong Building had been safe for only so long. And now it would disgorge a few of them at a time into a hostile world that belonged to Antichrist and the False Prophet, the Global Community, and millions of searching eyes that demanded a sign of loyalty none of these had.

+ + +

"I could lose you," Vasily said. "Misplace you. What can I say? You escaped."

Steve sat with him in the parking lot at Resurrection Airport. "What, I raced away in my chair, and you couldn't keep up? Too late. Let's go."

It wasn't easy, and Steve wasn't going to pretend it was. He had often wondered, when reading or seeing a movie about a condemned man, what it must have felt like to make that last long walk. It wasn't long enough, he felt, especially in a chair.

As they approached the loyalty mark application site in the north wing of the airport, Steve noticed the line was longer than he had seen it in ages. The crackdown, the intensifying—whatever New Babylon wanted to call it—was working. Hundreds milled around the statue of Carpathia, bowing, praying, singing, worshiping. For the moment, the guillotine was silent. In fact, Steve didn't know if it had ever been used in this part of the state. Some had been martyred near Denver. Others in Boulder. Maybe he would be the first here. Perhaps no one was trained to use the facilitator. But there it stood, gleaming and menacing, and those in line for the mark laughed nervously and kept glancing at it.

Steve was still in the part of the line that snaked its way to the decision-making point. No one was expected to make the "wrong" choice, of course. The stocky, sixtyish, red-haired woman with the documents and the files and the keyboard barely looked up as people identified themselves and chose what they wanted tattooed and where they wanted it. As they were administered the mark, they raised their fists or whooped and hollered. Then they made straight for the image, where they paid homage.

Steve had lived for his daily encouragement and education from Tsion Ben-Judah. It had been his only form of church. There was interaction between him and Rayford and him and Chang, and occasionally him and Buck or one of the others. But he was starved for live contact with other believers. That would be quickly remedied.

Steve debated whether to use his real name, to finally come clean and tell the GC he had been undercover for a long time. But his name would easily be linked with Buck Williams from their days at the *Weekly,* and how long would it take to progress from there to the link with Rayford, then Chloe, then the Co-op, and—who knew?—maybe even Chang?

He couldn't risk that kind of exposure, especially for people who didn't know it was coming. When it was finally Steve's turn, the woman noticed Vasily in his dress uniform and said brightly, "We've been expecting you two. This must be Pinkerton Stephens."

"In the flesh, Ginger," Steve said, studying her badge.

"How about a nice *–6* and a tasteful image of the supreme potentate?" she said, looking him up and down, clearly puzzled by his garb.

"And where would you put it?" Steve said.

"Your choice."

"Well, this won't work," he said, showing his stump. Ginger's smile froze, and she searched his eyes. She had not found that amusing and looked as if she wanted to say so. He had put her in an uncomfortable position, and she clearly didn't like it. "And I understand it doesn't work on plastic."

"That is true," Ginger said, appearing relieved to move on.

"Then we can't put it here, can we?" he said, knocking on his fake forehead.

Snap, snap, snap. He popped off his combination nose and forehead appliance, exposing his eyeballs and brain sac. "Guess this would be the only option, Ginger," he said in the nasal voice resulting from no covering on the nose.

"Oh! Oh, my—! Mr. Stephens, I—"

"Who wants to put it there?" Steve said. "Who'll volunteer for that chore? And when I wanted to display it, would I just pop my face off?"

She turned away. "I'm sure that will work. It's totally hygienic and should cause no problem."

"I could take my mouthpiece off too, Ginger, if you want the full effect."

"Please, no."

"Well, anyway, I'm in the wrong line."

"Pardon me?"

"I'm not accepting the mark of loyalty."

"You're not? Well, that's not really an option."

"Oh, sure it is, Ginger. I mean, the other is a much shorter line—in fact, I'll be the only one in it. But it's most definitely an option, isn't it?"

"You're choosing the, uh, the loyalty enforce—"

"I'm choosing the guillotine, Ginger. I'm choosing death over pretending that Nicolae Carpathia is divine or ruler over anything."

She looked to Vasily. "Is he putting me on?"

"Sadly, he's not, ma'am."

Ginger studied Steve, then reached for her walkie-talkie. "Ferdinand, we need someone to run the facilitator."

"The what?"

"You know!" she whispered. "The *facilitator.*"

"The blade? You serious?"

"Yes, sir."

"Be right there." A tall, balding man with red cheeks hurried over. "You're not taking the mark?" he said.

"Yes," Steve said, "but I thought I would try the blade first. Please, can we just get on with this? Do I have to go through the whole ordeal again?"

"This is no joking matter."

"It's no redundant matter either, so could you just do what you have to do and get me processed?"

"There is no processing. You just sign, stipulating that you made this choice of your own free will, and we, ah, you—"

"Die."

"Yes."

"Do I get some last words?"

"Anything you want."

Cheeks found the proper form, Steve signed "Pinkerton Stephens," and the man said, "You realize this is your last chance to change your mind."

"About Carpathia being Antichrist, evil personified? About Leon Fortunato being the False Prophet? Yes, I know. No changing my mind."

"Dyed-in-the-wool, aren't we?"

"Let's just say I've thought it through."

"Clearly."

Steve glanced at Vasily, who had paled and held a hand over his mouth. Others in the line murmured and pointed, and now all eyes were on the strange-looking wounded man in the undershirt.

Ferdinand slipped between a couple of chairs and went to study the guillotine. "They say it can be run by one person," he said. He looked up. "Over here, Mr. Stephens."

Steve rolled to a line four feet in front of the contraption. His belly began to tighten and his breath came in short puffs. "God, be with me," he said silently. "Give me the grace. Give me the courage."

The grace came. The courage he wasn't so sure about. He wished he were at a facility with more experience. Ferdinand had raised the blade to its full height, but as he worked with the elements at the business end of the shaft, he looked tentative and kept peeking up and pulling his fingers back.

"I think if that safety lever is set, you're okay," Steve said.

"Oh, sure enough. Thank you."

"Don't mention it. You can owe me."

It took Ferdinand a second, but that elicited a wry look. He set the restraining bar in place, none too easily, then found the release cord and surveyed the whole scene once more.

+ + +

Kenny was asleep. Buck sat hunched before the TV, to which he had hooked his phone. Chang had devised some digital marvel to transmit the images from Colorado. A TV camera in a corner showed the entire area, and Chloe pointed. "That's him, Buck. He's right there."

Buck's chest felt heavy and he was short of breath. Steve was the only one before the guillotine, and a man seemed to be fiddling with it.

+ + +

"Do you have a basket of some sort?" Steve said.

"Excuse me?" Ferdinand said.

"A container? Unless you wanted to just chase after my—"

"Yes! Thank you. One moment."

Steve wanted to say, "Happy to be of service."

Ferdinand found a corrugated box that for some reason had been lined with tinfoil. Steve didn't even want to think about why. "Now," the man said, looking up, "if I can get you to come here."

Steve rolled close.

"Can you get down, or—"

"I can get myself in there," Steve said, "though it seems a little lacking in customer service that I should be expected to—"

"I will get assistance."

"No! I will get situated, once I've had my say."

"Oh yes, your say. Now is the time. Feel free."

"Will this be recorded?"

The man nodded.

"Well, then . . ."

Steve spun halfway around to face those in line for the mark of loyalty. Their eyes would not meet his, but he sensed a hunger on their faces for what they clearly felt privileged to soon see.

"I don't expect you to believe me or to agree or to change your minds," he began. "But I want to go on record for my own sake anyway. I have chosen the guillotine today so that I can be with God. I am a believer in Jesus Christ, the Son of God, the maker of heaven and earth. I renounce Nicolae Carpathia, the evil one, Satan incarnate. When you take his mark today, you once and for all forfeit your chance for eternal life in heaven. You will be bound for hell, and even if you want to change your mind, you will not be able to.

"I wish more of my life had been dedicated to the one who gave his for me, and into his hands I commit myself, for the glory of God."

Steve spun back around, launched himself out of the chair and into the guillotine. "Please just do it quickly, Ferdinand," he said.

+ + +

Buck could not take his eyes from the screen. Chloe sat next to him, her face buried in her hands. The picture disappeared, but Buck sat there for almost an hour. Finally his phone chirped. It was Chang, who also sounded shaken.

"A confidential note was added to the report from personnel at the loyalty center," he said. "It tells Suhail Akbar, 'You will no doubt be hearing from the Global Community command center in Colorado, which will need not only a replacement for the deceased Pinkerton Stephens, but also for his second in command, Vasily Medvedev. The latter was just found in his GC automobile. Medvedev died of a self-inflicted gunshot to the head.'"

Of course, neither death was reported on the Global Community News Network.

+ + +

By the time Ming Toy landed in Shanghai after flying all night, she was more than exhausted. She had made the seemingly interminable flight many times before, but she could not sleep this time because she was getting to know the pilot. He was an acquaintance, if not a friend, of George Sebastian's. And while she had not met George, they had many mutual friends by now. Her pilot, a South Korean named Ree Woo, had been a naturalized American citizen at the time of the Rapture and was stationed at the same base as Sebastian.

"Everyone knew George," Woo said. "He was the biggest man most of us had ever seen, let alone the biggest on the base. There was nothing George couldn't do."

Woo had been a pilot trainer specializing in small, fast, maneuverable craft with high-fuel capacity and thus long-distance capability. "I was unusual for a Korean-American, Mr. Chow, because I acted more American than Asian, even though I did not move to America until after I was a teenager. I had no religion. I would have made a good Chinese. You grew up atheist, I bet."

"I did," Ming said, "but Korea, especially South Korea, is about half Christian, half Buddhist, isn't it?"

"Yes! But I was neither. I wasn't really an atheist either. I was just nothing. I didn't think about religion. My feeling was, there might be a God; I didn't know and didn't care, as long as if there *was* one, he left me alone. I worshiped me, you know what I mean?"

"Of course. Didn't we all?"

"All my friends, we all worshiped ourselves. We wanted fun, girls, cars, things, money. You too?"

"I want to hear the rest of your story, Ree," Ming said, "but it's time for me to use my real voice and tell you the truth."

He leaned toward her and squinted in the darkness at the change in her tone.

"No," she said. "I never wanted girls. I wanted boys."

He recoiled, smiling. "Really?"

"It's not like that," she said. "I am a girl. In fact, I am a grown woman. I have been married. I am a widow."

"Now you are putting me on!"

"I'm telling you the truth." And she told her own story for the next hour or so.

"Would you believe I have heard of your brother?" Woo said.

"No!"

"It's true! No one mentions his name, but many in our underground group in San Diego know he is there, inside the palace."

Woo then finished his own story of how scared he was when the disappearances occurred. "I did not know such fear existed. Nothing ever bothered me before. I was a daredevil. That's why I wanted to fly, and not big commercial jets or helicopters or props. I wanted to fly the fastest, most dangerous. I had many close calls, but they only thrilled me and never made me cautious or careful. I couldn't wait to live on the edge of danger again.

"But when so many people disappeared, I was so scared I could not sleep. I went to bed with the light on. Don't laugh! I did! I knew something terrible and supernatural had happened. It was as if only an event that huge could have slowed me down and made me think about anything. Why did these people vanish? Where did they go? Would I be next?

"I asked everybody I knew, and even many people who were just like me and had never even been inside a church started saying that it was something God did. If that was true, I had to know. I began asking more people, reading, looking for books in the chaplain's office. I even found a Bible, but I couldn't understand it. Then someone gave me one that was written in simple language.

I didn't even know for sure there was a God, but I prayed just in case. This Bible called itself the Word of God, so I said, 'God, if you are out there somewhere, help me understand this and find you.'

"Ming—now that *is* your real name, right? No more surprises?"

She nodded. "No more."

"Ming, I read that Bible the way a starving man eats bread. I devoured it! I read it all the time. I read it over and over, and if I found books and chapters that were too puzzling, I skipped and found ones I could follow. When I found the Gospels and the letters from Paul, I read and read until I collapsed from exhaustion.

"In the back of the Bible, it listed verses that showed how a person could become a Christian, a follower of Christ, and have their sins forgiven. It said you could know you were saved from your sins and would go to heaven when you died or be taken to be with Christ at the Rapture. I was heartbroken! I was too late! I believed with all my heart that this was what the disappearances were all about, and I cried and cried, regretting having missed it.

"But I followed the verses the salvation guide listed, and I prayed to God and pleaded for him to forgive me. I told him I believed he died for me and would receive me to himself. I felt so clean and free and refreshed, it was as if I had not missed anything at all. I mean, I wish I had been a believer in time to have been raptured, but I have no doubt that I am saved anyway and that I will be in heaven someday."

Hours later it seemed to Ming that she and Ree had been lifetime friends. Exhausted as she was, she would rather hear him talk and watch him respond to her than sleep. As the sun rose on the Yellow Sea, Ming was sickened by the vast expanse of blood that extended all the way into the harbors. The lower they flew, the more she could see the devastation, the rotting wildlife. When they landed they were issued face masks that did little to filter the stench.

Ree was delivering goods for the Co-op in Shanghai, but he agreed to take her on to Nanjing, two hundred more miles west. Chang had told his parents of an underground church there, and though it was a big city, Ming prayed God would lead her to them.

Ree stayed with her as she carefully sought out secret believers. It was not easy. They would sit in small eateries, and she would carefully tip back her cap occasionally so a fellow believer might see her mark. It was not until Ree did this at a small grocery that an old woman approached and did the same to him. The three of them met in an alley and quickly shared stories. Ming understood the woman's dialect and translated for Ree.

The old woman said that the underground church was almost nonexistent now in Nanjing and had largely relocated to Zhengzhou, yet another three hundred-plus miles northwest. Ming finally slept on the last leg of the journey, but even unconscious, she worried Ree might doze at the controls. In the days of tighter aviation rules, he would never have been allowed to fly on so little rest.

The GC seemed on the rampage in Zhengzhou, hauling the unmarked to loyalty mark centers, rounding up Jews to take to concentration camps, and shouting through bullhorns every time a new session of worshiping the image of Carpathia came due. Even the thousands who already boasted his mark appeared weary of the constant requirements and the treatment of the undecided.

Ming and Ree found a cheap hostel that asked no questions and rented them tiny individual rooms, not much bigger than cots, where they paid too much to sleep too little. But the rest took the edge off, and when they met up again they set off to find the underground believers.

Ming finally connected with a small band of Christ followers who hid in the basement of an abandoned school. Ree had to get back to the airport and eventually to San Diego, and parting with him—though they had just met—felt to Ming like an amputation. He promised to come back and to be sure that the little church in Zhengzhou was added to the Co-op list, though they had little with which to barter.

Ming had been able to connect with Chang in New Babylon and learned of the gradual dispersion of the Tribulation Force from Chicago and the soon relocation of the Williams family to San Diego. "You must get to know them, Ree," she said, "and become more than acquaintances with Sebastian. My dream is to find my parents and take them back there with me one day."

It was more than a week before Ming found anyone who had heard of any Wongs, despite the popularity of the name in that area. It was a weary old man with liquid eyes who sadly told her, "We know Wongs. Late middle-aged couple. He very loyal to potentate but never took mark."

"That's him!" Ming said.

"I so sorry, young one. He was found out."

"No!"

"He die with honor."

"Please, no!"

"He was believer. Your mother grieving but okay. She with small group about fifty miles west in mountains."

"And she is a believer too?" Ming asked through tears.

"Oh yes. Yes. I take you to her when time is right."

15

CHANG NEVER FELT so isolated, so alone, as over the next five months. He grieved for his father but rejoiced that he was in heaven. He prayed for his mother and his sister, urging Ming to stay there and not try to bring the old woman out. It was, he knew, a horrible time to be in China, but escaping was more precarious.

Chang was intrigued by Ree Woo and helped Chloe arrange Co-op flights and connections for him. But for the most part, Chang lay low, especially on the computers. Suhail Akbar had made it a personal quest to ferret out the mole in the palace. All employees were interrogated again and again, but Chang was certain he had aroused no more suspicion than anyone else. He longed for the day when he could be as free to keep up with the Trib Force as he once had.

The day was likely over when he could pave the way for them with phony credentials. And he had to ask Buck to go easy with what he provided him from the palace for *The Truth.* It was one thing for Buck to write what he knew, but quite another to prove it with recordings and video feeds that could have come only from bugs in New Babylon itself.

Chang was thrilled that the dark-of-night relocations of the Trib Force had gone smoothly. So far they had lost no one since Steve Plank, who had never officially been part of the Force but was mourned as if he were.

Leah and Hannah were staying close to their new home in Long Grove. Their occasional missives about Lionel Whalum and his wife proved them to be the type of couple the Trib Force, and the Co-op, needed.

Albie and Mac flew recklessly all over the world in aircraft Albie seemed to trade on a new black market. Chang worried that they didn't have solid phony credentials anymore, but Mac, at least, seemed to feel invincible after the triumph in Greece.

Zeke, from what Chang could tell, flourished in a country environment the GC seemed to have forgotten. Many secret believers traveled for miles to be transformed by the young man with the master's touch.

Word from Enoch and his charges from The Place was less encouraging.

The group had been split up and parceled out to various underground homes, individuals, and families. Most of them were still active in trading via the Co-op, but many despaired of ever having the kind of camaraderie they had enjoyed in Chicago.

That city had been devastated again, this time by the real thing—a nuclear bomb that hit three days after Buck and Chloe and Kenny had rendezvoused with Sebastian and flown to San Diego. GCNN reported a thousand casualties, all Judah-ites, but viewers realized that confirming the deaths or numbers would have jeopardized the very people who claimed the count.

Most thrilling to Chang was keeping up with Buck and Chloe and Kenny, who now lived literally underground in a bunker near San Diego. Sebastian and his family had smoothed the transition, and the secret church there seemed one of the most vibrant Chang knew of. There Kenny was just one of several babies born since the Rapture.

With the military technology still mostly intact, Buck was able to re-create the setup he had enjoyed in Chicago, and he broadcast his cyberzine every few days. He had been careful to stay close to home but envied Rayford's getting to live at Petra.

Now there was where the real action was.

\+ + +

Four Years into the Tribulation; Six Months into the Great Tribulation

While the atmosphere was still festive and the daily messages from both Tsion and Chaim inspiring, Rayford would not say Petra was entirely cocooned from the real world. The million there were reminded daily of the havoc wrought by Carpathia all over the globe. From everywhere came reports of miracles by thousands of deities who seemed loving, kind, inspiring, and dynamic. It was easy to watch them live on the Internet, reattaching severed limbs, raising the dead, taking blood from the sea and turning it into water so pure and clear that many stepped forward to drink it without harm.

"False!" Ben-Judah preached every day. "Charlatans. Fakers. Deceivers. Yes, it is real power, but it is not the power of God! It is the power of the enemy, the evil one. Do not be misled!" But many were, it was plain.

Jews were mistreated, persecuted, tortured, and killed on every continent. They were paraded across the screen of the Global Community News Network and trumped-up charges leveled. They were traitors, commentators said, enemies of the risen potentate, would-be usurpers of the throne of the living god.

Over the months, New Babylon's policy on those found without the mark of loyalty changed from one that gave violators one last chance to have it applied immediately to one of zero tolerance. There was no longer any excuse to have neglected one's duty. Most barbaric to Rayford was the vigilante law that now allowed a loyal citizen with a valid mark to kill an unmarked resident on sight. The act was the opposite of a crime. It was lauded and rewarded, and all that was required was to deliver to a local GC facility the body of a victim who clearly bore no mark on forehead or hand.

Pity the citizen who was mistaken, however. The murder of a loyal Carpathianite was itself punishable by death, and trials were unheard of. If you could not produce an alibi against a charge of murdering a marked loyalist, you were dead within twenty-four hours.

Rayford terribly missed his family and the other Trib Force members, but what was good for one was good for all. They had relocated and were staying put for a time. He knew it would not, could not, always be that way. He wanted so badly to get to San Diego, he could taste it.

The highlight of his day, beyond hearing the teaching and keeping up with the scattered Force, was the evangelistic message delivered every day by one of the two preachers. Had he been asked if he would enjoy a daily diet of preaching that laid out the plan of salvation and gave unbelievers the chance to receive Christ, he might have predicted it would wear thin.

But every day, day after day, Tsion insisted on either Chaim or himself delivering just such a message—following the normal teaching for the majority who were already believers. And every day, Rayford found himself thrilled to hear it.

It wasn't only because someone was saved every day—and usually more than one. But also, the defiant ones and the undecideds often fell in anguish, battling, fighting God. Rayford marveled to watch the spiritual warfare as selfish, sinful men and women couldn't evade the preaching and yet would not give in, even for their own benefit.

Every evening Chaim would ask new believers to identify themselves and talk about their old lives and their newfound faith. This gathering always culminated in singing, praying, and celebrating.

One night, still high from the meeting that spotlighted the new believers, Rayford was enjoying a lesson taught by Naomi, the young computer whiz. She was teaching anyone who wanted to learn how to access the various databases and get news from around the world.

Rayford was just one of several gathered to learn what they could, but he was summoned from the session by none other than Chaim himself, who wanted to introduce a new friend.

Rayford followed Chaim a couple of hundred yards, and all along the way, people reached out to "Micah," blessing him, thanking him, telling him they were praying for him and appreciated his leadership. "Thank you, thank you, thank you," Chaim said, gripping hands and shoulders as he went. "Praise God. Bless the Lord. Blessings on you."

Finally they reached a clearing where several young people of different races and cultures sat chatting. They appeared to be in their late twenties or early thirties. "Ms. Rice?" Chaim said quietly, and when the short black woman excused herself, the others watched with interest as she joined Chaim and Rayford.

"I know you, don't I?" Rayford said, bending to shake her hand. "Don't tell me. You're a friend of—no, you've been on television."

"Bernadette Rice," she said, with a clipped British accent and a gleaming smile. "Reporting from Petra, but no longer for the GCNN."

Rayford didn't know what to say. So she was here on assignment—or not?—or what? He smiled at her and glanced at Chaim. "I'll let her tell you," Chaim said.

The three sat on rocks. "I was at the Temple Mount for GCNN the day that Micah, well, Dr. Rosenzweig, first emerged. I didn't recognize him. None of us did. I don't know what I would have thought had I known who he was. It was well known, of course, that he was the one who had assassinated Carpathia.

"But I was not even thinking of that when I was called to the scene. A woman, a GC Peacekeeping corporal named Riehl—forgive me, but I remember everything and talk this way as a means of organizing my thoughts—pulled me away from a story I was doing about families visiting the Temple Mount that day. To tell you the truth, I was none too pleased when she insisted that Rashid—that was my cameraman—and I wrap it up and come with her. I demanded to know what was going on.

"As she dragged me across the plaza, she said Rashid and I were about to get a rare privilege. A high-ranking Morale Monitor was about to carry out an order from the potentate himself. When we got there, the tall young man, dressed as the MM do—dressy casual, you know—was standing with what looked to me like a frail, little old man. Forgive me, Dr. Rosenzweig, but that is my recollection.

"Well, sometimes non-journalists have different ideas of how exciting a particular story is. I didn't even know if they expected this to show live or if we were to record it. This MM gentleman just wanted to get on with it, so I asked central control—who was producing the broadcast—what I should do. They wanted to know who the MM guy was, and before I knew it, he was insisting that we roll.

"He said he was Loren Hut, new *head* of the Morale Monitors, and that he had been ordered by Carpathia to execute this Micah person for refusing to take the mark and for resisting arrest. I do a fast lead-in, Rashid focuses on the pair, and it goes live over GCNN.

"You'll recall that everyone was starting to get the boils around this time, and Hut was suffering. He was wriggling and scratching and making me do the same just watching. Did you happen to see it, Captain Steele?"

"No, but I heard about it from my—"

"Then you know what happened. Hut shot Micah several times from point-blank range, and except for the deafening sound, the bullets had no impact. The crowd laughed and accused Hut of using blanks. He shot a man through the heart for saying that, proving he was using real bullets. The crowd dived for cover and I fell right to the ground, scared to death. Then Carpathia himself showed up. When I could compose myself at all, I crawled away—toward the loyalty mark application lines, in case anyone was looking.

"But from there I went straight to my hotel. I was so glad I had not gotten around to accepting the mark yet. This man was an enemy of Carpathia's, and he had some sort of supernatural protection I wanted. My superiors thought I was suffering from the boils like everyone else, but nothing was going to keep me from following Micah. I watched from my hotel room, learned about the meeting at Masada, disguised myself, went there, and came here as part of the airlift. Only recently did I finally pray for salvation."

"Praise God," Rayford said. "May I ask what took you so long? You were here when the bombs were dropped. You were protected by God though—"

"Set afire."

"Yes! I'm really curious. What could give you pause after that? Surely you did not still doubt God."

"No, that is true. I don't know how to explain it, Captain Steele. All I can say is that the enemy has a stronghold over the mind until one surrenders it to God. I was a pragmatist, proud, a journalist. I wanted control over my own destiny. Things had to be proved to me."

"But what more proof—?"

"I know. It mystifies me still. I suppose what comes closest to explaining the lunacy is the verse that both Dr. Rosenzweig and Dr. Ben-Judah have often quoted—how does it go, Doctor? Something about wrestling not with flesh?"

Chaim nodded. "'We do not wrestle against flesh and blood, but against principalities, against powers, against the rulers of darkness of this age, against spiritual hosts of wickedness in the heavenly places.'"

"Yes, that's it! And that's why we have to wear the armor of God, right?"

"'That you may be able to withstand the evil day, having done all, to stand.' Amen."

"I appreciate very much hearing your story, Ms. Rice," Rayford said. "You know my son-in-law was—"

"There, yes. Dr. Rosenzweig told me. That's why he thought you might like to hear it."

Rayford looked to Chaim and back at Bernadette. "Please tell me Buck hasn't heard this yet," he said.

"Not from me," Chaim said.

She shook her head.

"Then, if you'll excuse me . . ."

Rayford hurried back past where Naomi was finishing her computer class, down through the tent area where many of the younger people preferred to sleep, and finally to a small encampment of prefabricated modular homes. They were tiny but well built, had been provided almost wholly by Lionel Whalum, the new Co-op member, and had been assembled by a team of volunteers who seemed to reshape the landscape of Petra nearly overnight.

Rayford, hoping and planning that his stay in the rock city would be only temporary, chose one of the smallest—but for him, efficient—units not far from where Abdullah stayed. Smitty liked an open fire and had opted for a tent, not much smaller than Rayford's enclosure, on the edge of one of the bivouac villages.

Before Rayford ducked into his place, which was barely big enough for his bed and an area for his computer and transmitting equipment, he peered down the way to see if Abdullah was still awake. The Jordanian, silhouetted behind a smoky fire, waved at him, then beckoned him.

"I will join you in an hour or so, my friend!" Rayford called.

He sat before his computer with two glass jars, one containing water, the other manna. No preservative or storage was necessary for the manna. It would spoil overnight, but there was always a fresh supply every morning anyway—so saving it was considered a lack of faith, and forbidden.

Rayford entered his code, keyed in the coordinates that allowed him to interact securely with San Diego—some ten hours earlier on the clock—and typed, "Praise God for David Hassid and Chang Wong."

He waited. Buck and Chloe's machine would signal them that he was trying to communicate, and when one of them typed in their code, the units could talk to each other. Not only that, but they also had video capability. Sensors around the edges of the respective screens stored and interpreted digital images and transmitted them back and forth, so—unless the sender turned off that feature—both parties could see each other on the screen.

A minute later Chloe came on with twenty-month-old Kenny squirming on her lap. She had to block the boy from reaching for the keys. Seeing them both made it even harder for Rayford to wait to get to San Diego.

"Hi, Dad," Chloe said. "Say hi to Grandpa, sweetheart."

Kenny said, "Gampa!" and stared at the screen. Rayford tried to situate himself for the best light and transmission and waved.

Kenny smiled and opened and closed his hand before the screen.

"I miss you, Kenny!"

"Miss! Big boy!" Kenny threw his hands over his head and arched his back, forcing Chloe to hold him tighter to keep him from slipping off her lap.

"Are you a big boy?" Rayford said.

But Kenny had already lost interest. He wriggled until Chloe let him down. "You need to come see him," Chloe said.

"Maybe soon," Rayford said. "I miss you all so much."

They brought each other up to date. Buck was somewhere with Sebastian and Ree Woo, so Rayford told Chloe Bernadette Rice's story.

"Buck will be thrilled," she said. "You know Ree is headed back to China. Ming's still not aroused any suspicion. She comes and goes as she pleases, but she sure wants to get out of there and bring her mother with her. Maybe this time."

"They would come to San Diego?"

"Yes. I think she's sweet on Ree."

"Doesn't surprise me. I got to meet him, you know, on one of his runs here."

"Nobody told me that!"

"Yeah, he talks about her. Seems preoccupied with her. I thought I told you."

"No. 'Course I'm buried with Co-op stuff most of the day. It's getting harder and harder, Dad. Has Tsion said anything about the lifting of the plague? Or are these things permanent?"

"The previous ones haven't been. But this has held the longest. Tsion thinks the Bowl Judgment on the lakes and rivers is imminent. That one is for sure not permanent."

"It's not? How does he know?"

"He says there's a later judgment, one of those that ushers in the Battle of Armageddon and the Glorious Appearing, that calls for the drying up of the Euphrates River. And it clearly says it dries up its waters."

"That's a relief, but if the rivers and lakes turn to blood soon and don't happen to turn back to water until almost Armageddon, I don't know. Should the seas clear up before the rivers and lakes turn, or does that even make sense?"

"No one knows, Chloe. And what happens if the seas do turn back to salt water? How long would it take to replenish them?"

"And what would we do with everything that's dead now? The cleanup alone would take a hundred years. At least we might be able to treat salt water and make it potable, because if the lakes and rivers turn too—and if the seas are still affected—I don't know how anybody or anything stays alive."

"Tsion says God will winnow out many who have the mark of the beast so they can't continue to evangelize for the evil side. I guess he wants to even the odds a little for the last battle."

"As if he needs to do that, Dad."

"How are you holding up, honey?"

"Exhausted, that's all. But we love the Sebastians and the body of believers here. If you have to live through this time, this is the place to be."

+ + +

It was well after midnight in Zhengzhou, and Ming was homesick. For where, she was uncertain. She had no home anymore. She wanted to be with Ree Woo, though they had never so much as held hands. He had visited her—more than once—as he had promised, and they had become dear friends, a brother and sister in Christ.

Ming didn't know whether it made sense to think of him in romantic terms anyway, with only three years left before the Glorious Appearing. Besides, Ree had a ridiculously dangerous job, and who wanted to risk being widowed twice within a few years? On the other hand, what might it be like if they both survived? She would have to study what Dr. Ben-Judah had to say about married couples entering into the millennial kingdom.

Though Ming was with her mother, still she did not feel at home. Sure, she understood the language, even some of the more obscure dialects, because she had grown up in China. But the believers lived in constant fear, slept in communal rooms with little privacy, and never knew who might come knocking in the dead of night.

Her mother seemed remarkably at peace in spite of the recent loss of her husband, though she told Ming she wished she could have died with him. Though Mrs. Wong was a new believer, she was a worrier by nature, and she had grown fatalistic over the past several weeks. Ming tried to talk her into sneaking out of China and going to live in San Diego, but her mother would not hear of it. This was her home—such as it was—and California sounded like a different planet. She worried about Chang, and she worried about Ming, both playacting as employees of the Global Community.

Ming, still masquerading as Chang Chow and living essentially as a man when away from the underground shelter, was constantly on edge. Her brother offered to set it up in the computer that she was a full-fledged employee, entitled to a paycheck and benefits. She refused for his sake, knowing how intense the scrutiny had to be in New Babylon. A little money would allow her to complete the ruse and live in her own small place, but it would not be worth it if it left Chang vulnerable at the palace. And so she scraped by on the meager pool of resources among the believers.

Ming tried to keep her distance from other Peacekeepers, though some wanted to be chums and invited her to various places with them. She always found excuses. Hardest for her was being randomly assigned duties by anyone superior to her in rank. She herself had been a top official at the Belgium Facility for Female Rehabilitation (BFFR), a women's prison better known among the GC as Buffer. But now, in her male Peacekeeper uniform, Ming was just a grunt, someone for most of the others to boss around.

At least this gave her some access to information, and she was able to warn fellow believers about raids and surprise canvasses.

At two o'clock one morning the local GC had planned a raid not of Christ followers but of a small Muslim contingent who lived in the northeast corner of the city in caverns where the subway once ran. Ming was surprised to hear of this group, as she had been largely unaware of holdouts against Carpathianism besides the so-called Judah-ites and the mostly Orthodox Jews. At a meeting rallying the GC troops to root out the dissidents, Ming learned that these "zealots" still read the Koran, wore their turbans, almost totally covered their female population, and practiced the five pillars of Islam.

She had not seen anyone bowing toward Mecca five times a day, but Intelligence had determined that this group still followed that dictum in private. They also contributed alms—a communal giving and sharing of resources that would have been necessary anyway, given the current political climate. It was not known whether these adherents—more prevalent in western China—still fasted during Ramadan. It seemed everyone was fasting in one way or another since the seas had turned to blood. There was no getting to Mecca at least once in a lifetime anymore either, not since the Global Community and Carpathianism had leveled the Muslims' sacred city.

The pillar of their faith that so enraged the potentate and thus the Global Community Peacekeepers and Morale Monitors was the first and foremost tenet of the Islamic religion. Their profession of faith declared a monotheistic god—"There is but one God, Allah . . ."—and the high status of the founder of the religion—". . . and Muhammad is his prophet."

Of course, that flew in the face of Carpathianism, which was also monotheistic. Neither were the Muslims idol worshipers, so not only were there no statues associated with their practice of faith, but they were also loathe to pay homage to the image of Carpathia.

"That will be their choice in about half an hour," the local leader, a thick man named Tung, told the GC troops. "We'll storm their little enclave, fully armed and prepared to shoot unmarked people on sight. But our wish and our hope are that they do not resist. I have it on good authority from high levels in the Global Community Palace that a certain someone at *the* highest level wants these people used as living examples.

"We will march them to the loyalty mark application site about six blocks from their hideout, and there they will spend the night deciding what they will do in the morning. As the sun rises on the beautiful, jade, life-size image of Supreme Potentate Carpathia, these infidels will either bow the knee to him—prepared to accept his mark of loyalty—or they will be executed in full view of the public. Little do they know that regardless of their decision, they will be executed anyway. GCNN plans to air this live."

The GC all around Ming burst into cheers and applause. They then lined up to be issued weapons; hers turned out to be a grenade launcher she would not use, no matter what. If that meant the end of her life too, so be it.

+ + +

Rayford found Abdullah Smith warming himself by his fire. Smitty, who had become much more expressive and emotional over the past few months, rose quickly and embraced Rayford. "It is as if I am already in heaven, my friend," he said. "I miss the flying, but I love all this teaching. And the food! Who would have guessed that the same meal three times a day would be something I so looked forward to?"

Rayford didn't know how Abdullah could sit so flat and comfortably cross-legged. He made it look normal and easy, yet Rayford seemed to creak and groan going down, and cramped up as he sat. He always gave way to unfolding himself and leaning on one hand with his legs out to the side. This amused Abdullah to no end.

"You westerners brag so much about working out, and yet it has not made you limber."

"I think you sit on a magic carpet," Rayford said.

Abdullah laughed. "I wish Mac were here. He inspires me to think of earthy . . . of earthy what? Comebacks? Is that what he calls them?"

"Probably. With Mac, you never know. Did you see him today?"

"Of course. He and Albie always look me up when they get here, tease me about getting fat on the manna, and want to know when I will join their little band of fliers. The day will come soon, I hope. For now, the elders think it is too dangerous, but my guess is that you too are eager to get going."

"More than you know," Rayford said. "And while I am content to submit to the authority here, still I wonder."

"So do I! God is clearly supernaturally protecting those who fly in and out of here, despite all the efforts of the enemy. You would think that would give the GC an idea to stop wasting bullets and missiles. Have they hit anyone or anything?"

Rayford shook his head. "Not yet. And the stories. Have you heard the stories?"

Abdullah let his head fall back and gazed at the stars. "I have heard them, Captain. I want to be part of one. I want the Lord to once again protect me from harm and death by sending one of his special visitors. The flight here, when the GC were shooting right through our craft? That was like living in the Bible days. I felt like Daniel in the den of the lions. I could see the missiles coming and I knew we were in the way, yet they passed right through.

"Captain, what must the GC think when they see this happen in the light of the sun almost every day?"

16

MING MARCHED through the streets with the other local GC to the northeast corner of Zhengzhou. Few citizens were out and about, but the Muslims were known to have one of their worship and lecture periods at this time of the morning.

The GC leader, Tung, fanned out the armed group of around thirty Peacekeepers and sent them to four entrances to the old subway that marked the borders of the area the Muslims occupied. Apparently the group had never been bothered after midnight, because it was guarded merely by a lone man at each entrance at the bottom of the stairs. The guards were quickly and quietly overtaken, and none could produce a mark of loyalty to show the GC. They were taken to the surface by a couple of GC who would walk them to the mark application site. The rest of the Peacekeepers silently moved in on the meeting of about four dozen men and women. The Muslims immediately realized their security had been breached and no resistance was possible.

So they simply stayed where they were, listening to a speaker, one of their own. Tung had foreseen this possibility and had instructed his people to merely wait and listen themselves, gathering evidence of treason and disloyalty to Carpathianism.

The speaker seemed to quickly assess the situation and began to close his remarks. But often looking directly at his captors, he was devout and defiant to the end. "And so," he said, "we view god as more than the creator of all things, but also all-knowing, full of justice, loving and forgiving, and all-powerful. We believe he revealed the Koran to our prophet so he could guide us to justice and truth. We are his highest creation, but we are weak and selfish and too easily tempted by Satan to forget our purpose in life."

He paused to gaze at the GC once again. "We know that the very word *Islam* means to submit. And those of us who submit to god, repenting of our sins, gain paradise in the end. Those who do not will suffer in hell."

The Muslims then bowed toward Mecca and began to pray—all but three. These sat together at the back of the assemblage, and when Tung stepped forward to call a halt to the proceedings, one of the three stood and pointed at him and held a finger to his lips. "Wait," he said quietly, but with such strength of character and—Ming couldn't put her finger on it—conviction, perhaps, that Tung stopped. His people looked at him and back at the standing man.

The Muslims looked up from their prayers and turned to sit again. The three men carefully stepped through the crowd and made their way to the front where the speaker had been. "This meeting is not over yet," one of them said.

Ming was puzzled. The three were not armed. Though they wore garb somewhat similar to the Muslims, it was not the same. They wore sandals and robes, no turbans. Their beards and hair were relatively short. They did not look Asian or Eastern. In fact, Ming realized, she would not have been able to guess their nationalities from their look or the speaker's accent. He spoke just loudly enough to be heard, but again, with a certain quality everyone found riveting.

"My name is Christopher. My coworkers are Nahum and Caleb. We visit you on behalf of the one and only true God of Abraham, Isaac, and Jacob, the Holy One of Israel and the Father of our Lord and Savior, Jesus the Messiah. We come not to discuss religion, but to preach Christ and him crucified, dead, buried, and resurrected after three days, now sitting at the right hand of God the Father."

Suddenly Christopher spoke with a voice so loud that many covered their ears, yet Ming believed they could still hear every syllable. "Fear God and give glory to him, for the hour of his judgment has come! Worship him who made heaven and earth, the sea and springs of water!"

Christopher seemed to let that settle with everyone, then in more muted tones said, "Christ died for our sins according to the Scriptures; he was buried, and he rose again the third day according to the Scriptures. Now if Christ be preached that he rose from the dead, how say some among you that there is no resurrection of the dead?

"If there be no resurrection of the dead, then is Christ not risen. And if Christ be not risen, then is our preaching vain, and faith in Christ is also vain. We testify of God that he raised up Christ. If Christ be not raised, men and women are yet dead in their sins."

Ming searched the faces of the Muslims, whom she expected to rise in protest. Perhaps it was because their captors were at hand, or because they realized that this preaching also defied Carpathianism, but they did not object. They appeared mesmerized, if only at the audacity of an outsider disregarding their beliefs and preaching his own.

Christopher stepped back and Nahum stepped forward. "Babylon shall fall," he said. "That great city, because she has made all nations drink the wrath of her fornication, shall surely fall. Hers has been a system of false hope not only religiously, but also economically and governmentally.

"God is jealous, and the Lord will have his revenge. He will take vengeance on his adversaries, and he reserves his wrath for his enemies.

"The Lord is slow to anger and great in power. He will have his way in the whirlwind and in the storm. The clouds are the dust of his feet."

The GC seemed to tremble, and Ming looked to Tung, whose lips quivered. He gripped his weapon tighter, but he did not move.

Nahum continued: "God rebukes the sea and makes it blood. He can dry up all the rivers. The mountains quake at him, and the hills melt, and the earth is burned at his presence, yes, the world, and all that dwell in it.

"Who can stand before his indignation? Who can abide the fierceness of his anger? His fury will be poured out like fire, and the rocks shall be thrown down by him.

"The Lord is good, a stronghold in the day of trouble. He knows them that trust in him. But with an overrunning flood he will make an utter end of the place that opposes him, and darkness shall pursue his enemies."

Everyone in the underground sat or stood unmoving, arms close to their sides. It was as if they were folded in upon themselves, made fearful by Nahum's pronouncement. When he stepped back, Caleb moved up, but rather than address everyone, he turned and stared directly at Tung.

"If any man worships the beast and his image, and receives his mark on his forehead or on his hand, that one shall drink of the wine of the wrath of God, which is poured out into the cup of his indignation. The one with the mark shall be tormented with fire and brimstone in the presence of the holy angels and in the presence of the Lamb, who is Christ the Messiah.

"The smoke of his torment ascends forever and ever, and he will have no rest day or night, he who worships the beast and his image and receives the mark of his name."

At first no one moved. Then one GC and another, then one more, raced from the underground, taking the steps to the street two at a time. Tung shouted after them, called them by name, threatened them. But two and then three more followed.

The Muslims had not moved. Finally some stood, but the GC who watched Tung did not know what to do. He raised his weapon toward the three outsiders but appeared unable to speak. Finally finding his voice, he said, "To the center!"

The GC began surrounding the Muslims, who, except for a half-dozen, allowed themselves to be led out and up the stairs. Tung nodded to two of his men and signaled that they should join him to round up the final six. But as they approached, Christopher merely leaned toward the GC and said, "It is not yet their time."

Ming stalled and maneuvered in such a way that she was the last one out, trailing the main group. It was clear that Christopher, Nahum, and Caleb were talking with and praying with the six stragglers. Christopher told Tung, "These will come when it is their time." And to Ming's astonishment, the GC leader beckoned the last two guards, and they left.

Ming had been so moved, she realized she had not noticed whether the three strangers had the mark of the believer on their foreheads. They had to, didn't they? She wanted to know, but she did not expect to see them again.

As the petrified group of Muslims was led through the streets to the loyalty mark application site, Ming allowed herself to hang back far enough that, despite her small stature, she could see past them for several blocks.

Huge klieg lights lit up the center, but no one in the area knew of the raid, and few spectators were there—only the GC who had first rousted the four Muslim guards. But unless her eyes deceived her, Ming believed she saw three more strangers in robes with short hair and beards and no turbans. They could have been a matched set with the other trio!

But as the GC and the Muslims drew closer, they all began to point and talk among themselves. It was the same three! They stood at the head of the line, ignoring the vociferous GC clerical workers who told them to move aside.

As the Muslims were herded into line, Ming got a closer look at the three. They did not have the mark of the believer on their foreheads! She didn't know what to make of it. Were they underground rebels, charlatans, what?

Tung rushed them, brandishing his rifle. "Where are the others? We will hunt them down, and you will be responsible—"

"They will come when it is their time," Christopher said again. And somehow that shut Tung up.

The Muslims were instructed on how to be processed. When Tung asked how many would be taking the mark of loyalty to Carpathia, about half raised their hands. The others groaned and argued with them.

Tung laughed. "It makes no difference! Don't you see? You waited too long. You were discovered this very morning, months past the deadline for taking the mark. You will die at dawn with the rest."

He turned to the others. "And how many of you are *choosing* the guillotine, as if there was a choice?"

The rest of the Muslims raised their hands, and yet Ming noticed that none of them had the mark of the believer either. Christopher addressed them. "Resist the temptation to choose the guillotine without choosing Christ the Messiah. You will die in vain."

"We will die for Allah!" one shouted, and the others raised fists of defiance.

"You will die all the same," Tung said.

His attention was diverted to the street, and everyone turned to see the last six Muslims striding purposefully toward the site. Ming could tell Tung had not expected to see them again. When they arrived, they seemed to assess the layout, then headed directly for the area that led to the guillotines.

"I am glad you are so decisive," Tung said. "But we are closed until daybreak. Then you will be television stars, and a live audience will enjoy the show as well."

Christopher and Nahum and Caleb sat before the undecideds, each talking to a small group, pleading, explaining, urging them to receive Christ before it was too late. Finally Tung had had it. "Enough!" he shrieked. "You are finished here! These people made their choices long ago, and punishment will be meted out in the morning. Now, begone!"

The three ignored him. But he would not be put off.

"In five seconds I will open fire on you and instruct my people to do the same."

Ming panicked. She would not fire on these men of God! Could she pretend, hide, somehow go unnoticed?

Tung waited a few beats and raised his weapon. He was six feet from Christopher's head when he released the safety and squeezed the trigger, calling out, "Peacekeepers, open fire!"

Ming moved into position and made a show of readying her grenade launcher. Surely Tung did not expect her to deposit an explosive in the middle of everyone, Muslims, GC, and all. But she quickly realized she was the only one moving. Everyone else appeared frozen. Tung's face was set in the grimace of a man about to blow another's head off.

Ming tried to stop moving but was off balance and tripped on the foot of the man next to her, having to catch herself on yet another on her other side. She feared she had been exposed now, the only one not under the spell of the holy men.

But Christopher addressed her directly. "Do not fear, dear sister."

So she had been given away! Now all would know she was not even a man!

"God is with you," Christopher said. "None of these can hear us, and none will remember what happened here, except that their offensive against the spokesmen of the Lord was futile. Be encouraged. Be of good cheer. Your Father in heaven looks upon you with pleasure, and you will not see death before his Son returns again."

Ming felt a glow as if she were flushed from head to toe. A warmth rode through her that enlivened her, gave her strength and courage. She was curious. If Christopher knew the mind of God, could he tell her more? Ming could not open her mouth, yet she had so many questions.

Christopher answered even the unasked. "Neither will your mother see death before the glorious appearing of the King of kings. But you will be separated soon. You will return to your friends, not all of whom will remain on this earth to the end."

Ming wanted to ask who, but still she could not make herself speak. Her limbs, warm and liquid, felt heavy and immobile. All she could do was stare at Christopher. She felt as if she were smiling, in fact as if her entire body was.

Christopher stood, and Nahum and Caleb joined him. As she watched, they seemed to grow larger until they towered over the area. Christopher reached out an open hand to her, but she could not move to take it and feared anyway that her body would be enveloped by it.

"And now," he said, "may the God of peace who brought again from the dead our Lord Jesus, that great Shepherd of the sheep, through the blood of the everlasting covenant, make you perfect in every good work to do his will, working in you that which is well pleasing in his sight, through Jesus Christ, to whom be glory for ever and ever."

The three were gone, and suddenly it was morning. The sun was bright and warm. Tung and his people acted as if they knew they were on the air, serious looks plastered on their faces. They strode about through the crowd of onlookers and Muslims.

All the victims of the raid were in line for the blade, and to Ming's surprise and great joy, at least twenty-five of them bore not only the mark of the believer, but also a look of assurance and deep peace that said they would have the grace to accept the consequences of their decision.

+ + +

It was nearly half a year later before Chang began to feel the pressure had lightened, if only a bit, at the palace compound. He tried a little something new every day, tapping in here and there, checking the memory disk David Hassid had buried deep within the system. It was all there, everything that had gone on in the place since Chang began to lie low. He had not listened in to anything live, but he could check his calendar for specific events and go back to hear what had gone on behind closed doors on those days.

His sister had finally escaped China, their mother insisting that Ming go back to the United North American States "with your young man. I will be fine here." Ming told Chang she had not told their mother of Christopher's promise that neither of them would see death before the Glorious Appearing, but that "Mother seems to get along as if that is her intention anyway—to make it to the end."

Ming rhapsodized to Chang about how wonderful it had felt to finally get on board with Ree, to fly all day, to get past easier checkpoints and wind up in San Diego, finally able to get rid of her male GC Peacekeeper's uniform and let her hair grow out . . . to be a woman again.

"For Ree?" Chang had asked via secure phone.

"For me!" she said. "Well, maybe a little for him."

"How's that going?"

"None of your business."

"Of course it is."

"It's safe to say we're an item," she said, "but it's awfully hard to concentrate on that with him gone almost all the time. The people here tease me about it, even Captain Steele. But Ree and I are not really romantic yet."

"He hasn't kissed you?"

"I didn't say that."

"That sounds romantic."

"It was a kiss good-bye before his last run and a kiss of greeting when he returned. It was in front of people, so no, romantic it was not."

Chang was curious about how Rayford was getting along, relocating once again.

"It's been hard for him, Chang. He's thrilled to be back with his family, of course, and you should see him with that grandson! But he still feels isolated from much of the Tribulation Force, even though Sebastian has had a techie in here giving him—all of us—whatever we need to carry on as before. Living literally beneath the ground can get depressing. And I know he misses many of the advantages he had at Petra."

To Chang's mind, the one who had benefited most at Petra was Abdullah Smith. He was flying again, making regular runs in and out of the place, many of them with his old friends Mac and Albie. But he had chosen, and they had agreed, that he should continue to live in Petra. He had become expert on the computer and frequently regaled the rest of the Trib Force with his latest escapades, many of which happened right there at Petra. He had just filed a long account with Rayford and copied everyone else. He wrote in English for everyone's benefit, and was still learning. It read:

> *Late yesterday after the noon we had a very special time here as Dr. Ben-Judah instructed us on living in the Spirit. That is the Holy Spirit, which I knew some about from his previous teachings, but not nearly enough.*

Captain Steele, you will recall that just before you left, there had been some trouble here. Nothing too major, but people getting on each other's nervousness and complaining to the elders about this and that. Well, do you know who straightened all that out and got people to get along better? No, not Dr. Ben-Judah, but Chaim. Yes, it's true. He has become quite a wise leader and very belovered by everyone here. My spell checker is making belovered *blink madly, but that is what he is, most certainly.*

Anyway, today Dr. Ben-Judah talked about Chaim, who many here still like to call Micah. His Bible passage was Ephesians 5:18-21, which talks about being filled with the Spirit, having a song in your heart (I liked that especially), having an attitude of thankfulness, and submitting to one another. He said those were characteristics of Chaim, and from the reaction of the people, I would have to say they agreed enthusiastically.

He also referred to Galatians 5:22-23, which list the nine fruits of the Spirit. I know you know this, Captain Steele, but as my messages to you also go into my personal journal, let me list them here: love, joy, peace, patience, gentleness, goodness, faith, humility, and self-control. I don't know about you, but many of these were not part of my nature, culture, or background. But again, they have become part of the personality of Chaim, making him a great leader here.

It was such good teaching, Captain Steele. I took many notes. Dr. Ben-Judah told everyone that if we could all learn to walk in the Spirit, we would have an easier time getting along for two and a half more years. He told us that besides the nine characteristics and the joyful, thankful, submissive heart, we will know we have the Spirit when we have the power to tell other people about Christ. He took that from Acts 1:8, where Jesus told his disciples that they would have power after the Holy Spirit came upon them and that they would be witnesses to him to the ends of the earth.

Believe it or not, we have to be witnesses even here. There are still some among us who have not chosen Christ. The trouble now is that there are rumors of miracle workers in the Negev, not far from here. Many have said they heard about this from friends outside. Some even said they read of it in Mr. Williams's The Truth. *Well, I know they could have, because it was in there, but he made it very clear that these people were fakes, pretenders. Even if they can perform some magic tricks, they were put in place by Carpathia and are not to be trusted.*

But can you believe it? There are groups here who plan to venture out and hear these people! I must have the Spirit, Captain Steele, because I myself—and you know how shy I am—am preaching against this, pleading with people not to go.

Have you heard the rumors that the head of Carpathianism, the one we know to be the False Prophet, is himself challenging Dr. Ben-Judah to a televised debate? I cannot believe his foolishness! Does he not remember that it was Dr. Ben-Judah's television message about Jesus being the Messiah that first brought him to the attention of the world? Why does he think Dr. Ben-Judah has such a big following yet today?

No thinking person would allow Leon Fortunato inside Petra, of course, and neither would any of us advise Dr. Ben-Judah to venture out to some Global Community–approved site. So if this is to happen, Tsion will probably be on camera from here, and Leon from who knows where? Frankly, I hope the GC is foolish enough to follow through with this and that they have the courage to air it live and not censored.

I continue to be thrilled to be able to serve God under his divine protection. And though it happens nearly every time I fly, I never get tired of seeing the GC threaten and warn and even try to blast us out of the sky and then waste their missiles and bullets, missing us from point-blank range. Many of them must be among those who would change their minds about God and about Nicolae Carpathia, if only it wasn't too late for them.

✢ ✢ ✢

Rayford always loved hearing from Smitty. There was a youth and innocence about him that had nothing to do with his age. In fact, he was still in his early thirties, but Rayford loved him like a son.

He was shutting down his computer when Chloe came knocking. She was alone. "Got a minute?" she said.

"For you, are you kidding? Where are your men?"

"Doing Kenny's favorite thing."

"Wrestling on the floor," Rayford said.

"Exactly. I'm telling you, Dad, since a little before his birthday, we've been finding out what the Terrible Twos are all about."

"It's not that bad, is it? He's naturally going to be a little rambunctious, having to play inside all the time."

"We'll survive. Roughhousing with his dad takes a little of the steam out of him. He's all boy, I can tell you that. But, hey, this is a business call."

"Really?"

"I need to call in a favor. Do you owe me anything?"

"Let's pretend I owe you everything. Give me an assignment. Co-op, I assume."

"Oh yeah. One of our biggest trades ever could happen in about three months, but it has to be done by air, and we need a larger than normal crew. I'd like you to head it up on the western side. Mac's going to run things from the east."

"That big, huh? I'm all ears."

"I've been sitting on this awhile, trading off bits of it here and there, but both parties have too much inventory. They don't need what they've got, but they're ready to trade with each other. You know how water has become as valuable as wheat?"

"Sure."

"Our Argentine friends are willing to prove it. We've got a contingent, run by a Luís Arturo, at Gobernador Gregores on the Chico River. They've harvested thousands of bushels of wheat. Naturally they are worried they're on borrowed time, with the size of the operation. And they're worried about water. The Chico is getting more polluted all the time, and they are suspecting it's intentional on the part of the GC."

"They've got wheat and need water. Who's got water?"

"The most unlikely place. Well, maybe not as unlikely as the middle of the desert, but this isn't a place you normally think of for bottled water. Probably the biggest underground church outside of America. Bihari's group at the Rihand Dam."

"You're not saying . . ."

"I am."

"India?"

"That's the place. They've got about as much volume of water as the Argentineans have wheat, and they're willing to trade straight up."

"You need more than a big crew, hon."

"Tell me about it. We need big planes. Albie got something lined up out of Turkey, of all places, and he's having it retrofitted to hold the skids of water."

"Regardless, it should work fine for the wheat."

"Thing is, Dad, we can't wait. We've got to do this almost simultaneously. The wheat's got to be heading toward India while the water's on its way. Albie and Mac are going to pick up Abdullah and bring Bihari with them. I'd like you to choose three other guys from the States—"

"Well, Buck and George—"

"Not including Buck this time, if you don't mind. Don't look at me that way. It's just a feeling."

"That this is a doomed mission? Thanks for sending me!"

"Not at all. I just think Kenny needs him right now, and frankly—I may be self-serving or prejudiced or whatever—I don't think he has the time to take away from *The Truth.*"

Rayford leaned back and looked at the ceiling. "George and Ree from here, if you can spare 'em."

"We've got time to work around their schedules, sure."

"And I'd look first to Whalum for a plane that big. And if he's got one, he ought to bring it here to pick us up and serve as our fourth."

"I'm for that," Chloe said. "That'll get Leah off my back."

"Still wants a ride to Petra?"

"Yeah. Which is not all bad, except we haven't been able to work it out yet, and I think she's taking it personally."

"What a shock, eh?"

"Well, we both know what she's up to, and I'd almost like to get Tsion's permission before I send her over there to start stalking—that's overstated—shadowing him."

When the time came for the project, Lionel Whalum was en route to San Diego, sans Leah, who was none too happy.

17

"IF YOUR WIZARDS can do all these tricks, Leon, why can they not turn a whole sea back into salt water?"

Chang sat listening through headphones.

"Excellency, that is a lot to ask. You must admit that they have done wonders for the Global Community."

"They have not done as much good as the Judah-ites have done bad, and that is the only scorecard that counts!"

"Your Worship, not to be contrary, but you are aware that Carpathian disciples all over the world have raised the dead, are you not?"

"I raised *myself* from the dead, Leon. These little tricks, bringing smelly corpses from graves just to amaze people and thrill the relatives, do not really compete with the Judah-ites', do they?"

"Turning wooden sticks into snakes? Impressive. Turning water to blood and then back again, then the water to wine? I thought you would particularly enjoy that one."

"I want converts, man! I want changed minds! When is your television debate with Ben-Judah?"

"Next week."

"And you are prepared?"

"Never more so, Highness."

"This man is clever, Leon."

"More than you, Risen One?"

"Well, of course not. But you must carry the ball. You must carry the day! And while you are at it, be sure to suggest to the cowardly sheep in Petra that an afternoon of miracles is planned, almost in their backyard, for later that same day."

"Sir, I had hoped we could test the area first."

"Test the area? Test the *area?*"

"Forgive me, Excellency, but where you have directed me to have a disciple stage that spectacle is so close to where we lost ground troops and weapons and where we have been unsuccessful in every attempt to interrupt their flying missions, not to mention where, my goodness, we dropped two bombs and a—"

"All right, I *know* what has gone on there, Leon! Who does not?! Test it if you must, but I want it convenient to those people. I want them filing out of that Siq and gathering for *our* event for a change. And when they see what my creature can do, we will start seeing wholesale moves from one camp to the other. You know who I want for that show, do you not?"

"Your best? I mean, one of your—"

"No less. Our goal should be to leave Petra a ghost town!"

"Oh, sir, I—"

"When did you become such a pessimist, Leon? We call you the Most High Reverend Father of Carpathianism, and I have offered myself as a living god, risen from the dead, with powers from on high. Yours is merely a sales job, Leon. Remind the people what their potentate has to offer, and watch them line up. And we have a special, you know."

"A special, sir?"

"Yes! We are running a special! This week only, anyone from Petra will be allowed to take the mark of loyalty with no punishment for having missed the deadline, now long since past. Think of the influence they can have on others just like them."

"The fear factor has worked fairly well, Potentate."

"Well, it *is* sort of a no-more-Mr.-Nice-Guy campaign, one would have to admit. But the time is past for worrying about my image. By now if people do not know who I am and what I am capable of, it is too late for them. But some blow to the other side, some victory over the curse of the bloody seas—that can only help. And I want you to do well against Ben-Judah, Leon. You are learned and devout, and you ask for worship of a living, breathing god who is here and who is not silent. It takes no faith to believe in the deity of one you can see on television every day. I should be the easy, convenient, logical choice."

"Of course, Majesty, and I shall portray you that way."

+ + +

Lionel Whalum turned out to be a compact black man, a tick under six feet and about two hundred pounds. He wore glasses and had salt-and-pepper hair, and was a skilled pilot of almost any size craft. He brought a transport lumbering into the clandestine strip in San Diego, and within an hour was airborne again with George and Ree in the back and Rayford in the copilot's seat.

"Chloe has told me so much about you," Rayford said, "but it's all been business. I think I know the basics of that story, but how did you become a believer?"

"I love when people ask," Whalum said. "A big reason I was left behind had to do with how I lived. I know there's nothing wrong with being successful and making money, but in my case, speaking just for me now, it made me deaf and blind somehow. I had tunnel vision. Don't get me wrong. I was a nice guy. My wife, she was a nice lady. Still is. We ran in our circles, had nice things, a beautiful home. Life was good.

"We were even church people. I had grown up going to church, but I was a little embarrassed about it, to tell you the truth. I thought my mama and my aunties were a little too emotional and showy. And about the time I should have figured out what the whole church thing was about, I was old enough to not want people knowing I even went. When Felicia and I got married, we didn't go to church in Chicago regularly. And when we did, it was to a higher sort, if you know what I mean. Very proper, subdued, not demonstrative. If my people had visited that church, they would have said it was dead and that Jesus wouldn't even go there. I would have said it was sophisticated and proper.

"That's the kind of church Felicia and I found in the suburbs too. It fit our lifestyle to a T. We could dress the way we did for work or socializing. We saw people we knew and cared about. And we definitely were never hollered at or insulted from the pulpit. Nobody called us sinners or hinted that we might need to get something right in our lives.

"Now our kids, on the other hand—two girls with a boy in between—they went the other direction. They got off to college and wound up, every *one* of them, in the kind of church I grew up in. Wrote us. Pleaded with us to get saved. Asked why we hadn't exposed them to this when they were kids. Flabbergasted me, I have to tell you.

"But did it reach me, change my mind? Not on your life. But then somebody in our neighborhood invited us to a Bible study. If it hadn't been for who it was, we never would have gone. But this was a cool guy. This was a guy who had made it, and big, in real estate development. He made this deal sound as casual as a golf game. No pressure. No hassle. They just read the Bible and talked about it, and they traded off meeting in about six different homes. We said sure, put our house on the list, and never missed.

"I was kind of bemused by it. After a while they started adding prayer to the thing. Nobody got called on or had to pray, and so Felicia and I didn't. But people starting telling prayer requests, asking for prayer for their families and themselves, their ailments, even their businesses. I mentioned a couple of prayer requests now and then, but still I never prayed.

"One time the guy who invited us the first time asked if he could talk to us afterward. When it was just the four of us—his wife didn't say anything—he kind of put it to us. Wanted to know where we were spiritually. I thought he meant where did we go to church, so I told him. He told me that wasn't what he meant. He laid out how to become a born-again Christian. I had heard it. I knew. It was just a little overboard for me, that's all. I told him I appreciated his concern and asked if he would pray for us. That always got 'em, was my experience. But he thought I meant right then, and so he did.

"He wasn't pushy. Just a little intrusive. I forgave him. That's sort of what it felt like. I thought it was good to feel so strongly about something and feel so deeply that you felt you should tell your friends and neighbors about it. That was it for me, end of story. No big deal.

"Two days later, millions of people all over the world disappeared. Including—are you ready?—every last person in that Bible study except us. And all three of our kids were gone.

"Saved? We got saved in, like, ten minutes."

* * *

Abdullah was so excited about the operation with his old friends that he had been packed and ready for several days. He didn't know or care how much of the actual piloting he would get to do. It would be enough to be together with Mac and Albie. To him the idea that the International Commodity Co-op could pull off such a huge trade, given the stepped-up persecution of believers around the globe, was just one more proof of the sovereignty of God.

When he knew Rayford and the other three from San Diego were in the air, he could barely contain himself. They would head directly to Argentina to load the wheat, which meant Mac and Albie would soon be on their way to pick up Abdullah. They were often spied upon and followed, so the plan was that they would bring some supplies into Petra and stay the night, not leaving for India until the next day. That way, if everything worked according to plan, the three of them plus their Indian fourth, Bihari, would be in the air toward Argentina at the same time the Americans were on their way from Argentina to India.

Abdullah felt a spring in his step as he moved about Petra, singing more loudly with the mass congregation, trying to pay attention and listen as Tsion and Chaim taught the Scriptures. This was the day that the computer and television technology center in the city would beam a signal of Tsion to Global Community headquarters at the palace in New Babylon, and a large monitor in Petra would receive the GC's transmission of Leon Fortunato. Abdullah, for one, believed Leon didn't have a clue what he was up against in a man as scholarly as Tsion—especially considering Tsion was a man of honor and truth.

Early in the afternoon Abdullah scaled the heights and peeked down from one of the high places onto the airstrip that had been built just for runs in and out of Petra. When Mac and Albie arrived, Abdullah would pilot a chopper to the end of the runway and bring them into the city.

As he scrambled back down, looking for something to occupy him until the great debate, he was surprised to see yet another gathering of thousands, with Chaim and Tsion trying to quiet them. Were they early for the telecast, or was something amiss? As he drew closer, he could see that several hundred of these did not bear the mark of the believer on their foreheads. They were jostling for front position for the debate because, one of them hollered, as soon as it was over, they were leaving Petra for a few hours to hear another speaker. "He will be right close by, and many believe he is the Christ. Jesus come back to earth to perform miracles and explain the future!"

"Please!" Chaim called out. "You must not do this! Do you not know you are being deceived? You know of this only through the evil ruler of this world and his False Prophet. Stay here in safety. Put your trust in the Lord!"

"Who are you but the second in command?" someone demanded. "If the leader will not beseech us to stay, why should we stay?"

"I *do* beseech you," Tsion began, but Chaim interrupted.

"Why would you trouble the mind of this man of God on the very day he has been anointed and called to counter the False Prophet? You are being used by the evil one to wreak havoc in the camp."

To Abdullah's dismay, he noticed that some of the dissidents rose up before Tsion and gathered themselves together against him and against Chaim, and said, "You take too much upon you. Why do you put yourselves above the congregation?"

Tsion slowly covered his face with his hands, fell to his knees, and pitched forward onto the ground. Then he raised his head and said, "The Lord knows who are his and who is holy. For what cause do you and all those gathered here speak against the Lord? And why would you murmur against Chaim?" Tsion called on two among the assembled and said, "Please, come to your senses and stand with me against this shortsightedness!"

But they said, "We will not stand with you. Is it a small thing that you have taken us from our motherland, our homes where we had plenty, and brought us to this rocky place where all we have to eat is bread and water, and you set yourself up as a prince over us?"

Abdullah had never seen Tsion look so stricken. Tsion cried out to God, "Lord, forgive them, for they know not what they do. I have neither set myself over them nor demanded anything from them except respect for you."

Tsion continued, "God is telling Chaim and me to separate ourselves from you to save ourselves from his wrath."

Many fell on their faces and cried out, "O God, the God of all flesh, must we die because of the sins of a few? Would you take it out on all of us?"

Tsion spoke to all the assembled and said, "Unless you agree with these, it would do well for you to depart from the presence of these wicked men, lest you be consumed in all their sins. From this point on, let it be known that the Lord has sent me to do all these works; I do not do them in my own interest. If these men do what is in their minds to do and God visits a plague of death on them, then all shall understand that these men have provoked the Lord."

As soon as he finished speaking, the ground under hundreds of the rebels opened and swallowed them. They went down into the pit, screaming and wailing as the earth closed upon them, and they perished from among the congregation.

Thousands around them fled as they heard the mournful cries from beneath the earth. "Run!" they said. "Run or the earth will swallow us also!"

But Abdullah heard many grumbling and saying, "Tsion and Micah have killed these people. We will stay with our plan of leaving from this place to hear the man who would be Christ."

Abdullah went to comfort Tsion and Chaim, but as he drew near them, he heard them. "Lord," Tsion said, "we pray an atonement for those left. Spare them your wrath so that we may yet reach them with your truth."

+ + +

By now Chang was bold. Not only was he tapped in to GCNN to monitor the great debate between Tsion and Leon, but he was also prepared to override New Babylon control. He was so tired of hearing the advertisements for Leon's special envoys and their "Miracle Fairs" that when he noticed Tsion was speaking to the assembled at Petra just before the debate was to begin, he patched him through and put him on the air early.

Tsion was telling the several hundred closest to him that they should repent of their plan to leave Petra and go into the wilderness to hear the charlatan who claimed to be Christ. Once Chang had Tsion on the air, he switched to Carpathia's office for the expected outrage.

Tsion was saying, "I would ask that all pray during the broadcast that the Lord give me his wisdom and his words. And as for you who still plan to venture away from this safe place, let me plead with you one more time not to do it, not to make yourself vulnerable to the evil one. Let the Global Community and their Antichrist and his False Prophet make ridiculous claims about fake miracle workers. Do not fall into their trap."

Carpathia shrieked, "What are we doing? We *want* these people to come and to hear and to be persuaded! Get him off the air!"

Tsion said, "Messiah himself warned his disciples of this very thing. He told them, 'Many false prophets shall rise, and shall deceive many. And because iniquity shall abound, the love of many shall wax cold. But he who endures to the end, he shall be saved. And this gospel of the kingdom shall be preached in all the world for a witness unto all nations.

"'If any man says to you, "Lo, here is Christ," believe it not. For there shall arise false Christs and false prophets, and they shall show great signs and wonders—so much so that if it were possible, they would deceive even you. If they say to you, "Behold, he is in the desert," do not go. "Behold, he is in the secret chambers," believe it not.'"

+ + +

Abdullah stood in the midst of the million or so in Petra, thrilled to see that Tsion was already on the air and that he was speaking against the thousands of false Christs springing up everywhere. They claimed power from Carpathia himself and from the leader of Carpathianism, the Reverend Fortunato. They taught heresy, and yet multitudes were taken in by them.

Resounding off the rock walls, a woman's voice came from New Babylon GCNN control. "Dr. Ben-Judah, please stand by as we switch to our studios, where the Most High Reverend Father Fortunato waits to engage you in respectful debate."

"Thank you, ma'am," Tsion said, "but rather than stand by, as you flip your switches and do whatever it is you have to do to make this work, let me begin by saying that I do not recognize Mr. Fortunato as most high anything, let alone reverend or father."

Fortunato appeared on the split screen in one of his elaborate outfits, all robed and hatted and vested in velvet and piping. He was behind an ornately carved pulpit, but it was clear he was seated. His smile looked starkly genuine.

"Greetings, Dr. Ben-Judah, my esteemed opponent. I heard some of that and may I say I regret that you have characteristically chosen to begin what has been intended as a cordial debate with a vicious character attack. I shall not lower myself to this and wish only to pass along my welcome and best wishes."

He paused, and Tsion did not respond. After a few seconds' silence, Tsion said, "Is it my turn, then? Shall I open by stating the case for Jesus as the Christ, the Messiah, the Son of the living—"

"No!" It was the moderator, the woman from central. "That was merely a welcome, and if you choose to ignore it, we shall begin."

"May I ask a question, then," Tsion said, "if we choose to be so formal? Is one of the ground rules that the moderator is permitted to editorialize about the statements from this end of the argument? Such as concluding that my ignoring a greeting from an enemy was rude?"

"May we begin, sir?" she said. "The Reverend Fortunato has the floor."

"My premise is simple," Leon began, looking directly into the lens. Abdullah was rattled. He had always considered Fortunato a bit of a buffoon. But the man on the screen, though Abdullah knew better, seemed so warm and kind and loving that it had to give him credibility among the uninformed.

"I proclaim Nicolae Carpathia, risen from the dead, as the one true god, worthy of worship, and the savior of mankind," Leon said. "He is the one who surfaced at the time of the greatest calamity in the history of the world and has pulled together the global community in peace and harmony and love. You claim Jesus of Nazareth as both the Son of God and one with God, which makes no sense and cannot be proven. This leaves you and your followers worshiping a man who was no doubt very spiritual, very bright, perhaps enlightened, but who is now dead. If he were alive and as all-powerful as you say, I challenge him to strike me dead where I sit."

"Do it, Lord," Abdullah prayed. "Oh, God, show yourself right now."

"Hail, Carpathia," Leon said, still smiling, "our lord and risen king."

Leon looked as if he were about to continue, but Tsion took over. "I trust you will spare us the rest of the hymn written by and about the egomaniac who murders those who disagree with him. I raise up Jesus the Christ, the Messiah, fully God and fully man, born of a virgin, the perfect lamb who was worthy to be slain for the sins of the whole world. If he is but a man, his sacrificial death was only human and we who believe in him would be lost.

"But Scripture proves him to be all that he claimed to be. His birth was foretold hundreds, yea, thousands of years before it was fulfilled in every minute detail. He himself fulfills at least 109 separate and distinct prophecies that prove he is the Messiah.

"The uniqueness and genius of Christianity is that the Virgin Birth allowed for the only begotten son of God to identify with human beings without surrendering his godly, holy nature. Thus he could die for the sins of the whole world. His Father's resurrecting him from the dead three days later proves that God was satisfied with his sacrifice for our sins.

"Not only that, but I have discovered, in my exhaustive study of the Scriptures, more than 170 prophecies by Jesus himself in the four Gospels alone. Many have already been literally fulfilled, guaranteeing that those that relate to still future events will also be literally fulfilled. Only God himself could write history in advance—incredible evidence of the deity of Jesus Christ and the supernatural nature of God."

Fortunato countered, "But we *know* our king and potentate arose from the dead, because we saw it with our own eyes. If there is one anywhere on this earth who saw Jesus resurrected, let him speak now or forever hold his peace. Where is he? Where is this Son of God, this man of miracles, this king, this Savior of mankind? If your Jesus is who you say he is, why are you hiding in the desert and living on bread and water?

"The god of this world lives in a palace and provides good gifts to all those who worship him."

Tsion challenged Leon to admit to the number of deaths by guillotine, that ground troops and weapons of war were swallowed up by the earth outside Petra, that two incendiary bombs and a deadly missile had struck Petra with full force, yet no one had been injured and no structure jeopardized. "Will you not also admit that Global Community Security and Intelligence Peacekeeping forces have spent millions of Nicks on attacking all traffic in and out of this place, and not one plane, flier, or volunteer has been scratched?"

Leon lauded Carpathia for the rebuilding effort around the world and added, "Those who die by the blade choose this for themselves. Nicolae is not willing that any should perish but that all should be loyal and committed to him."

"But, sir, the population has been cut to half what it once was, the seas are dead from the curse of blood—prophesied in the Bible and sent by God. Yet the believers—his children, at least the ones who have survived the murderous persecution of the man you would enthrone as god—are provided water and food from heaven, not just here, but in many areas around the world."

Leon remained calm and persuasive, soldiering on, praising Nicolae. At one point he disparaged "disloyal Jews, of whom you are one, Dr. Ben-Judah."

"You say it pejoratively, Mr. Fortunato, and yet I wear the title as a badge of honor. I am humbled beyond measure to be one of God's chosen people. Indeed, the entire Bible is testament to his plan for us for the ages, and it is being played out for the whole world to see even as we speak."

"But are you not the ones who killed Jesus?" Fortunato said, grinning as if he had parried the killing dagger.

"On the contrary," Tsion said. "Jesus himself was a Jew, as you well know. And the fact is that the actual killing of Christ was at the hands of Gentiles. He stood before a Gentile judge, and Gentile soldiers put him on the cross.

"Oh, there was an offense against him on the part of Israel that the nation and her people must bear. In the Old Testament book of Zechariah, chapter 12, verse 10 prophesies that God will 'pour upon the house of David, and upon the inhabitants of Jerusalem, the spirit of grace and of supplications; and they shall look unto me whom they have pierced, and they shall mourn for him.'

"Israel must confess a specific national sin against the Messiah before we will be blessed. In Hosea 5:15, God says he will 'go and return to my place, till they acknowledge their offense, and seek my face; in their affliction they will seek me earnestly.'

"The offense? Rejecting the messiahship of Jesus. We repent of that by pleading for his return. He will come yet again and set up his earthly kingdom, and not only I but also the Word of God itself predicts the doom of the evil ruler of this world when that kingdom is established."

"Well," Leon said, "thank you for that fascinating history lesson. But I rejoice that *my* lord and king is alive and well, and I see him and speak with him every day. Thank you for being a quick and worthy opponent."

"You call me that and yet never answer the claims and charges I have made," Tsion said.

"And," Leon continued, "I would like to greet the many citizens of the Global Community who reside with you temporarily and invite them to enjoy the benefits and privileges of the outside world. I trust many will join one of our prophets and teachers and workers of miracles when he ministers in your area less than an hour from now. He will—"

Tsion interrupted, "The Scriptures tell us that many deceivers are entered into the world, who confess not that Jesus Christ is come in the flesh. Such a one is a deceiver and an antichrist."

"If you'll allow me to finish, sir—"

"Whoever abides not in the doctrine of Christ, has not God. He who abides in the doctrine of Christ, he has both the Father and the Son. If any come to you and bring not this doctrine, do not receive him into your house, neither bid him Godspeed, for he who bids Godspeed partakes of his evil deeds."

"All right then, you've worked in all your tiresome Bible verses. I shall be content to merely thank you and—"

"For as long as you have me on international television, Mr. Fortunato, I feel obligated to preach the gospel of Christ and to speak forth the words of Scripture. The Bible says the Word shall not return void, and so I would like to quote—"

But he was cut off the air, and much of the multitude at Petra cheered and applauded his presentation. A remaining rebellious faction, however, even after hearing all that Dr. Ben-Judah said, began its exit. "We shall return," many of them shouted when confronted by the majority, who chanted and pleaded with them not to go.

Tsion cried out, "'Be sober, be vigilant; because your adversary the devil walks about like a roaring lion, seeking whom he may devour.'"

"There is amnesty for us!" one said. "No one pays for missing the mark of loyalty deadline, now so long past!"

Abdullah could not make it compute. Surely these had to be among those who waited too long to consider the claims of Christ. Their hearts had to have been hardened, because there was no logic in their behavior.

He hurried back to his quarters and took binoculars that had been delivered with the last shipment from the Co-op. He climbed again to a high place to watch for their emergence from the Siq and their two-mile walk to where the Global Community had already erected a platform.

18

MAC HAD LEARNED to ignore the warnings of the GC when he flew into restricted airspace over the Negev. They came on the radio, they sent reconnaissance planes, they even tried to crowd him out of the sky. Often the threatening GC planes flew close enough to reveal the pilots' faces. The first few times, Mac recalled, they looked determined. Later, when their mounted rifles missed their targets without explanation, they looked scared. When their heat-seeking missiles found their targets but seemed to pass through, the GC had backed off so as not to become targets themselves.

Today they went through all their typical machinations: the radio warning, the fly alongside, the shooting, the missiles. When Mac could see the pilots, they looked bored or at best resigned. They seemed as puzzled as the Co-op pilots why the GC continued to waste such expensive equipment, munitions, and warheads.

Mac looked at Albie and they shook their heads. "Another day, another deliverance," Albie said.

"I'll never take it for granted," Mac said. "I'm glad it doesn't hinge on clean living."

"You live clean enough," Albie said.

"Not by any virtue of my own, friend."

As they went screaming over the desert to the Petra landing strip, Mac looked for the oversize plane Chang had appropriated from New Babylon. It sat at the end of the runway, big and plain as day. "How do you figure that?" Mac said. "God must be blinding these guys. You can see it from a mile away, maybe more."

"Look there," Albie said.

Almost directly below them was a serpentine line of several hundred exiting the mile-long Siq that led into and out of Petra. They were headed for the concertlike setup in the middle of the desert. As Mac focused on the airstrip and began his descent, he saw the chopper hopping from inside Petra to the end of the runway from where Abdullah would ferry them in.

"You think Smitty would want to get a closer look at this deal?" Albie said.

"Why? Would you?"

"Sure."

"I'm game. We protected that far out?"

"In the air we are. Might be takin' a chance on foot."

"Let's go in the copter."

\+ + +

"This is an answer to prayer," Abdullah said a few minutes later. "I so want to see what is going on out there."

"It's a risk though, Smitty," Mac said. "You've got a pretty good cover, lookin' like you belong out here. Albie and I have had our covers blown, and we got no disguises, no aliases, no fake marks, no nothin'. You'd better decide if we're worth being seen with."

Abdullah could not hide a smile.

"You rascal," Mac said, grinning. "I set myself up for a shot there, didn't I? And you almost took it."

"I was not about to shoot you, Mac."

"Verbally you were. You sure were."

"I guess I have decided I would rather not be seen with you when we get back to Petra."

"Cute. But seriously now . . ."

"I believe God will protect us. We should stick together, look official, but not make it plain that we do not have marks."

"Your turban covers you, and we've got caps. You think that's enough? Should we be armed?"

"I have no idea how many GC will be there," Albie said, "but I'm guessing once we get there we're going to be vulnerable. Guns won't help is what I guess I'm saying."

Abdullah rubbed his forehead. "We should stay in the chopper. If we can see and hear from there."

"And if we're approached?"

"You speak Texan at them and they will be puzzled long enough for me to lift off."

"Oh, you're hot today, Smitty."

"Who would want to come close to a helicopter when the blades are turning?"

Abdullah studied his friends. It was clear they were as curious as he was.

"Should we check in with someone?" Mac said.

"Who?" Abdullah said. "Your mommy?"

Mac nodded, conceding that Abdullah was developing a sense of humor, but not rewarding him with more than that. "Rayford's in the air somewhere. It's on us. What're we gonna do?"

"I'm in," Albie said.

Abdullah nodded.

Mac climbed in the back of the chopper. Abdullah slid in behind the controls. Albie sat next to him.

When they were in the air, Abdullah shouted over the din, "We could check with Chang. Have him put something in the computer."

Neither responded, so Abdullah abandoned the idea. He wondered if they were being foolish. Down deep he knew they were. But he could not stop himself from going.

\+ \+ \+

It was clear to Mac that this show was set up exclusively for the rebels from Petra. He tried to get out of Abdullah why anybody would want to leave the safety of that city, but it was an unanswerable rhetorical question.

Abdullah was clearly taking his time, but the chopper quickly overtook the walking masses and set down about a hundred feet from the stage, whipping up a cloud of dust that a light breeze carried directly to the people on the platform. They stared at the chopper.

Mac saw several armed GC looking and talking among themselves. One approached, a young, thick-chested man who would have been stocky even without the bulletproof vest that became apparent as he drew near. Abdullah had shut down and the blade had just stopped.

"Just sit here and look at him," Mac said. "Make him make the first move."

Vest Chest stood with his weapon dangling, totally nonthreatening, but he looked expectantly at Albie, who sat in the second seat by the door. "You going to open up?" the young man said.

"Not if we don't have to," Albie said. "The AC still has this thing cooled."

"You have to," the Peacekeeper said.

Albie looked back at Mac. Mac nodded. Albie opened the door.

Mac leaned forward and spoke in a gruff voice, "You don't want to be too close to this machine, son! Engine's still hot, and she's been known to spit some oil. And we might want to fire her up again, just for a little air."

"What's your business here?"

"Same as yours. Security. Monitoring. Now I'm going to have to ask you to back away from the craft."

It was gutsy, but after what Mac had been through the last year, to him it was like a walk in the park. If the guy wanted to get into a contest of wills, Mac would stall him long enough for Smitty to get the engine roaring again, and they would be out of there. Of course, even small-weapons fire could bring down a chopper from close range, but maybe planting in his mind about the spitting of hot oil would give the GC pause.

Mac's ruse worked. The man just nodded and backed off.

"Start 'er up, Smitty," Mac said. "Got to give him a reason to concede."

The dust blew again. Abdullah shut down quickly. The GC returned. Mac took the offensive. He leaned past Albie and opened the door himself. "Don't worry," he said, "that's the last time we do that till we leave. We don't want to get people dusty or keep 'em from hearin' or anything, okay?"

"Just what I was going to say, sir."

Mac gave him an index-finger salute, and the people began showing up, already looking exhausted.

It took only a few minutes for the crowd to gather, and it appeared that an otherwise normal-looking guy, whom Mac thought looked like a younger version of Leon Fortunato, grabbed the microphone. He wore white shoes, white slacks, a white shirt, and sounded like a motivational speaker, all peppy and crisp. He said he was the whole show—announcer, performer, everything.

"But I'm not typical. No, folks. People have called me a type of Christ. Well, you be the judge. All I can tell you is that I am not from here. That was not a joke. I am not even from this world. There's no music today, no dancing girls, just me, a wonder-worker. I come under the authority of the risen lord, Nicolae Carpathia, and I have been imbued with power from him.

"If you are skeptical, let me ask you to look at the sky. I know the sun is still high and hot and bright, but would you agree with me that there are no clouds? None. Not one. Anyone see one anywhere? On the distant horizon? Forming somewhere in the great beyond? Shade your eyes, that's all right. But do me the favor of removing your sunglasses, those of you who have them. You're squinting, and that's all right. Some of you are frowning, but you won't be in a moment.

"Would you like a nice cloud? Something to block the sun for just an instant? I can provide one. You're skeptical, I can tell. Don't look at me; you'll miss it. You'll think it was a trick. But what do you call that?"

A shadow fell over the crowd. Even the GC gawked at the sky. Abdullah leaned over. Albie bent forward. Mac turned his body between them and looked up. A thick, white cloud blotted out the sun. The people oohed and aahed.

"How does he do that?" Abdullah said.

"He already told you," Mac said. "Power from Nicolae."

"Too quick?" the miracle worker said. "Did the sudden change in temperature chill you, even out here in the desert? Maybe that's enough shade for the moment, hmm?"

The cloud disappeared. It didn't move, fade, or dissipate. It was there, and then it was gone.

"How about half shade, but still enough of the sun coming through to keep you warm?" It was instantaneous.

A woman near the stage dropped to her knees and began worshiping the man.

"Oh, ma'am, thank you ever so kindly. But what is the cliché? You have seen nothing yet. How about this microphone stand? A solid steel base, long two-piece shaft, separate microphone and cord, attached at the top. Anyone want to come up and prove it is what I say it is?"

An older man limped up the steps to the platform. He felt the mike and stand and then rapped on the upper shaft, causing thudding noises through the sound system. "Oops, look at that!" Miracle Man said. And the mike stand and mike had been replaced by a snake that led from his hand all the way to the transformer box.

The people recoiled and some cried out, but as quickly as it had appeared, the snake disappeared and the mike and stand were as before.

"Magic tricks? You know better. Had trouble getting enough water lately? Or shall we believe the stories coming from inside Petra? Think a spring in there was an act of God? Then what does that make me?"

He pointed into the middle of the crowd, and a spring gushed from the ground, splashing over their heads. "Cool, crisp, and refreshing, no?" he said. "Enjoy! Go ahead!" And they did.

"Hungry? Tired of the fare in your new home? How about a basket of real bread, warm and chewy and more than enough for all?"

He reached behind him and brought out a wicker basket with a linen napkin in it. Five popover-sized chunks of bread, warm and golden brown, were piled in it. "Start that around. Here you go. Sure, take one. No, a whole one! Take two if you'd like. There's more where that came from."

The basket passed from hand to hand and everyone took at least one piece, several two, and yet the basket was never depleted.

"Who am I? Who do you say that I am? I am a disciple of the living lord, Potentate Carpathia. Have I persuaded you that he is all-powerful? His patience has run out with you people, however. He would like me to administer the mark of loyalty to you, which I can do without technology. You don't doubt me anymore, do you?"

People shook their heads. "Who will be first? I will do four simultaneously. You, you, you, and you. Ask your friends what they see."

Even Mac could see that they had Carpathia's mark on their foreheads.

"More? Yes, raise your hands. Now those of you who have your hands raised right now, hear me. No, no new ones. Hands down if you did not have them up when I said that. Why have you waited so long? What was the holdup? The one I serve wants me to slay you, and so, you're dead."

More than a hundred dropped to the desert floor, causing the rest to shriek and cry out.

"Silence! You do not think I could slay the lot of you? If I can slay them, can I not also raise them? These six, right up here, arise!"

The six stood as if they had just awakened. They looked embarrassed, as if they didn't know why they had been on the ground.

"Think they were merely sleeping? in a trance? All right, they're dead again." They dropped again. "Now if you know them, check their vital signs."

He waited. "No breath, no pulse, correct? Let that be a lesson to those who remain. You see that, in the distance? Yes, there. The little cloud of dust, what appears to be tumbleweed rolling this way? Those are vipers of the deadliest sort. They are coming for you."

Some turned and began to run, but they froze in place.

"No, no. Surely you do not think escape is possible from one who can create a cloud to cover the sun? If you want the mark of loyalty, raise your hand now and receive it."

The rest of the crowd raised their hands, frantic. "But more of you should die before the vipers get here." About three dozen keeled over.

"Why do the vipers keep coming?" a woman cried. "We have all obeyed! We have all taken the mark!"

"The vipers are wise, that is all," he said. "They know who was serious and loyal and who acted only out of fear for their lives."

The spring turned to blood, and the people near it backed away.

"Fools!" he said. "You're all fools! Do you think a god like Nicolae Carpathia wants you as his subjects? No! He wants you dead and away from the clutches of his enemies. You are free to run now, and it is entertaining to me to see you run as fast and as frantically as you can. But let me warn you. You will not outrun the vipers. You will not reach Petra in time to save yourselves. Your bodies will lie bloated and baking in the sun until the birds have their way with your flesh. For as I leave, I take with me the shade I provided."

The people burst from the scene, screaming and staggering madly in the sand toward Petra. The GC guards seemed apoplectic and stared as the vipers changed course to chase down the people. The spring dried up, the cloud disappeared, and dozens of chunks of bread lay in the sand.

Mac looked at Albie and Smitty and they all shook their heads, trembling. Suddenly the wonder-worker stood directly in front of the chopper. Though he did not open his mouth, Mac heard him as if he were inside the craft. "I know who you are. I know you by name. Your god is weak and your faith a sham, and your time is limited. You shall surely die."

Mac had difficulty finding his voice. "Let's go," he croaked, and Abdullah started the engines. The cloud of sand blew up and then away, and as Smitty lifted off, Mac looked down to see nothing but a long stretch of undisturbed sand, dotted only by the dead who had dropped at the site. No GC. No miracle man. No platform. No bread. No vehicles.

What about the snakes? He didn't see them either. But stretched for a quarter mile were the rest of the people, still and flat and grotesque on the desert floor, limbs splayed.

+ + +

Tsion was troubled in his spirit by a deep sense of foreboding. He knew he would not be able to shepherd all the way to the Glorious Appearing every person who had arrived in Petra. And yet he believed that when they had seen the mighty and miraculous hand of God, many of the undecided would be persuaded.

Many had been; of that there was no doubt. That was what Chaim and the other elders were saying as Tsion despaired, deep in one of the caves. It was as if the Lord had told him that the rebels would not be returning—not any of them. But he didn't know if God would slay them, as he did in the Korah rebellion in the days of Moses, or whether Antichrist would kill them after luring them into the desert with his great deception.

He looked up when Naomi hurried in from the technology and communications center and went directly to her father. She stole a glance at Tsion as she whispered in her father's ear, and when Tsion saw the slump of his shoulders and the sad shaking of his head, he knew.

The young woman left, and her father made his way up to Chaim. Tsion leaned over. "Tell us both. I must know of this eventually anyway."

"But, sir," Naomi's father said, "could you not be spared the totality of this until even one day after your triumph over the False Prophet? Why must your rejoicing be tempered?"

"I am not rejoicing, my friend. I was unable to keep the False Prophet from enticing the rebels to go their own way, no matter what I did or said. Tell me the whole of it. Spare me nothing."

"Three of your friends from the Tribulation Force were eyewitnesses and are just now returning. They request a moment with you."

Tsion stood. "Of course! Where are they?"

"On their way from the helipad."

As he and Chaim neared the entrance to the cave, Mac, Albie, and Abdullah were coming in. They all embraced. The elders maintained a respectful distance as the five huddled and Mac told the story.

"You should not have attended," Tsion said sadly.

"If we'd known what we were gonna see, we wouldn't have," Mac said. "But you know, sometimes us pilot types are as curious as little boys. This just mighta cured us."

"That man was not even human," Tsion said. "Surely he was a demonic apparition. Revelation 12 says that when Satan, who will deceive the whole world, was cast down from heaven to earth, 'his angels were cast out with him.' And of course it is no surprise that these people were not even recruited for the Global Community. John 10:10 says Satan wants only to steal and to kill and to destroy."

"I have a question, Dr. Ben-Judah," Albie said. "Is it okay not to like this? I mean, everybody's outraged about what happened, but just when I think I have an idea what God might be up to, he lets something like this happen, and I don't understand him at all."

"Do not feel bad about that, my brother, unless your questioning of him makes you doubt him. He is in control. His ways are not our ways, and he sees a big picture we will not even be able to fathom this side of heaven. I too am distraught. I had so wished that some of these might run back to us, pleading that we intercede for them before God, the way the wayward children of Israel did in Old Testament times. I would have loved to pray for atonement for them or to hold up an image of a bronze snake so that those bitten could look upon it and be healed.

"But God is doing his winnowing work. He is cleansing the earth of his enemies, and he is allowing the undecided to face the consequences of their procrastination. You know as well as I do that no one in his right mind should choose against the God who can protect them against weapons of mass destruction. But here were these fools, venturing out into the desert, outside of God's blanket of protection, and there they lie. As the apostle Paul put it, 'O the depth of the riches both of the wisdom and knowledge of God! How unsearchable are his judgments, and his ways past finding out! For who hath known the mind of the Lord? Or who hath been his counselor? . . . For of him, and through him, and to him, are all things—to whom be glory for ever.'"

+ + +

Mac was up before dawn, eager to get going. But as he waited for Albie and Abdullah, he was aware of a buzz throughout Petra. An announcement was going out, through an elaborate word-of-mouth system, that Tsion and Chaim were calling for everyone to assemble after they had eaten their morning manna.

Abdullah and Albie ate quickly and packed, joining Mac with the million others before the three of them were to lift off.

Chaim addressed the crowd first. "Tsion believes the Lord has told him that no more indecision reigns in the camp. You may confirm that by looking about you. Is there anyone in this place without the mark of the believer? Anyone anywhere? We will not pressure or condemn you. This is just for our information."

Mac made a cursory pan of the people within his vision, but mostly he watched Tsion and Chaim, who waited more than ten minutes to be sure.

Then Tsion stepped forward. "The prophet Isaiah," he said, "predicted that 'it shall come to pass in that day that the remnant of Israel, and such as have escaped of the house of Jacob, will never again depend on him who defeated them, but will depend on the Lord, the Holy One of Israel, in truth.

"'The remnant will return, the remnant of Jacob, to the Mighty God. For though your people, O Israel, be as the sand of the sea, a remnant of them will return. . . .' And of the evil ruler of this world who has tormented you, Isaiah says further, 'It shall come to pass in that day that his burden will be taken away from your shoulder, and his yoke from your neck, and the yoke will be destroyed.' Praise the God of Abraham, Isaac, and Jacob.

"The prophet Zechariah quoted our Lord God himself, speaking of the land of Israel, that 'two-thirds of it shall be cut off and die, but one-third shall be left in it. I will bring the one-third through the fire, will refine them as silver is refined, and test them as gold is tested. They will call on My name and I will answer them. I will say, "This is My people." And each one will say, "The Lord is my God."'

"My dear friends, you remnant of Israel, this is in accord with the clear teaching of Ezekiel, chapter 37, where our barren nation is seen in the last days to be a valley of dry bones, referred to by the Lord himself as 'the whole house of Israel. They indeed say, "Our bones are dry, our hope is lost, and we ourselves are cut off!"'

"But then, dear ones, God said to Ezekiel, 'Therefore prophesy and say to them, "Thus says the Lord God: 'Behold, O My people, I will open your graves and cause you to come up from your graves, and bring you into the land of Israel. . . . I will put My Spirit in you, and you shall live, and I will place you in your own land. Then you shall know that I, the Lord, have spoken it and performed it.'"'"

* * *

It had been a long time since Rayford had done such hard physical labor. Even at Mizpe Ramon, the building of the airstrip for Operation Eagle had largely been done under his supervision but by others with heavy equipment. He was in charge of this operation too, but there was no getting around that every pair of hands was crucial.

Lionel Whalum had landed almost without incident at Gobernador Gregores. The only trouble was that the main runway had been destroyed during the war, and the Co-op had rebuilt it by duplicating it a hundred feet parallel to the original. The GC were unaware of the rebuilding or of the huge encampment of underground believers who had been harvesting wheat and trading through the Co-op ever since.

But when the destroyed runway was discarded, which Rayford's main contact there—Luís Arturo—later told him had taken weeks to haul away, what was left was a smooth, dark depression in the ground. From the air, it looked as if the runway was still there.

Luís had spent his high school and college years in the United States and spoke fluent, though heavily accented, English. He had had enough exposure to campus ministry groups that when he returned to Argentina and suffered through the disappearances, he knew exactly what had happened. He and some friends from childhood raced to their little Catholic church, where hardly anyone was left. Their favorite priest and catechism teacher were gone too. But from literature they found in the library, they learned how to trust Christ personally. Soon they were the nucleus of the new body of believers in that area.

Luís proved to be an earnest, fast-talking man, and while he took especially to Ree Woo and was friendly and cordial to everyone, his top priority was getting the plane loaded and these men on their way again. "All we hear are rumors that the GC is polluting the Chico and that they are onto us," he said. "I have many reasons to believe that is only the talk of the paranoid, but we cannot take chances. The time grows short anyway, so let's move."

He seemed to like Ree so much because, though the South Korean was the youngest and smallest member of Rayford's crew, with the exception of George Sebastian he proved to be in the best shape of everyone—Americans and Argentineans combined.

Big George's reputation preceded him, and while he worked, lifting heavy sacks of wheat aboard the plane by himself, many of the South Americans tried to get him to talk about his imprisonment in Greece and his escape.

Rayford noticed that George tried to downplay it. "I overpowered a woman half my size."

"But she was armed, no? And she had killed people?"

"Well, we couldn't let her keep doing that, could we?"

Rayford worked mostly alongside Lionel, each of them able to handle one sack of wheat at a time. Ree helped too, but he was young and fast and wouldn't feel it in the morning like Ray and Lionel would.

After two solid days' work, thanks to hydraulic-lift loaders and six aluminum pallets that held up to thirty thousand pounds each, the wheat was nearly loaded and the plane partially full when Luís came running. "Señor Steele, to the tower with me, quick. I have field glasses."

Rayford followed the young man to a new, wooden, two-story tower that had been designed to blend into the landscape. Aircraft had to watch for it, but nosy types unaware of it might not see it at all.

Rayford had to catch his breath at the top of the stairs, but when he was ready, Luís passed him the binocs and pointed into the distance. It took Rayford a few seconds to adjust the lenses, but what he saw made him wonder if they were already too late and their work had been wasted.

19

THOUGH IT WASN'T a long flight from Petra to India, Mac was sound asleep when Albie put the cargo plane down at Babatpur. With the delay at Petra, losing a couple of hours to time zones, and the cumbersome plane, it was the middle of the night when they arrived.

It took Mac a moment to get his bearings, but within seconds he and Abdullah and Albie were rushed from the plane by the man known only as Bihari. Serious and no-nonsense, he said, "Hurry, please. We remain about a hundred miles north of the Rihand Dam."

"A hundred miles?" Mac said. "How we gettin' this water back to the plane?"

"Trucks!"

"The GC asleep over here, or what?"

"The GC, my friend, enjoy the drinking water."

Bihari averaged more than seventy miles an hour in a minivan that had no business going that fast on roads that may never have seen that speed before—especially in the dead of night. Ninety minutes later, in a swirling cloud of dust, he swung into a clearing near a small processing plant and showed Mac and the others towering skids of bottled water that looked as if they would fill two large trucks.

"Where's the rest of it?" Mac said. "We got us a big, big plane."

"I wondered if you would notice," Bihari said. "Did you not hear me honk at passing traffic on the way?"

"Occasionally, I guess."

"All but two trucks are already on their way to the plane. When we heard you were in the air, we got started. The prospect of real wheat to eat has motivated all of us. With you gentlemen and forklifts, we can load the last two trucks by dawn and be on our way."

A few minutes later, as Mac backed a forklift toward a stack of skids, he passed Albie. "These people make me feel like a lazy old fool," he said. "Our job is cushy compared to theirs."

"They wouldn't want to worry about the missiles and bullets," Albie said. "They get away with this by supplying the GC with a little water?"

Bihari interrupted the last of the loading by waving his hands over his head at Mac. "Will your people be discouraged by a setback?" he said.

"Depends," Mac said. "We still gonna be able to take off and get outta here?"

"Yes, but I believe *we* are doomed."

"That wouldn't make our day. What's the trouble?"

"We will drive by the dam on our way back to the airport. It is a little out of the way, but you must see it."

"I've seen dams before. Somethin' wrong with yours?"

"My people tell me the next curse from the Lord has fallen."

"Uh-oh."

"I cannot imagine what blood looks like, being forced through the control doors of a dam."

"Me neither," Mac said. "How's your water inventory, minus what we're takin'?"

"Maybe six months. But the GC will surely raid us when they discover we no longer have sources either."

"They know where you are?"

"They have to have an idea. It will not take them long."

"Hidin' this place oughta be your top priority."

\+ + +

The sun was going down, and yet heat still shimmered off the plains of Argentina. Rayford tried to hold the binoculars still enough to make out what all the commotion was about. It could have been anything, but none of the options hit him as positive. There were an awful lot of people out there, that was sure. But he couldn't quite tell if they were military, GC, Morale Monitors, peasants, people from the city, or what.

He handed the glasses back to Luís. "Do we just get in the air? Or had we better check this out?"

"You know what I think."

"Do we go armed? How many go with us?"

Luís shook his head. "How about I supply the vehicle, and you supply the ideas?"

"Fair enough," Rayford said. "Sebastian and I will go. And we will be armed but not on the offensive. We're just seeing what's going on and keeping you and yours out of it."

As they descended from the tower, Luís said, "Oh, dear Lord, I pray it hasn't already happened."

"What's that?"

"Do you smell that, Captain Steele?"

Rayford sniffed the air. Blood.

* * *

Mac was preoccupied on the drive from the processing plant. Would the huge shipment of wheat have to be trucked all the way down here too? Did they have enough trucks? And where would they store it?

On the one hand he worried about it, and on the other he was glad it wasn't his problem. Better thinkers than he had put this deal together. It was their concern.

When Bihari stopped at the dam, the other loaded truck pulled up behind. At first no one disembarked. Then all four of them did.

They just stood and watched for a minute. Two of the great doors in the wall of the dam were open, both disgorging huge arcs of liquid, splashing into a ravine and sweeping past them. Blood was so much thicker than water that it sounded and acted differently. It smelled awful, and Mac found it frightening somehow. It reminded him of a nightmare and chilled him.

A man stood several hundred yards from the dam, downstream from the rushing blood. He looked familiar. "Who is that?" Mac said, pointing.

"Who is who?" Albie said.

Mac turned him the right direction and pointed.

"I don't see so well this time of the morning, Mac. Who do you see?"

"No one sees that man by the rock down there? He's close to the river."

No one said anything.

"I'm going to check him out. He's looking right at us! Waving us down there!"

"I don't see him, Mac. Maybe this is one of your cowboy marriages."

Mac cocked his head at Abdullah. "One of my *what?*"

"One of those things you cowpokes see in the desert when you're thirsty. It looks like water but it's just a cactus or something. A marriage."

Albie threw back his head and laughed. "I grew up ten thousand miles from Texas and I know that one! It's a *mirage,* Smitty. A mirage."

"Well, this ain't a marriage or a mirage," Mac said. "I'll be right back."

He drew within a hundred yards of the man, who watched him all the way. "If you're going to come," the man said, "why not bring an empty bottle?"

"What do I want a bottle of blood for? Anyway, I don't think I have an empty one."

"Empty one and bring it."

Mac turned around, as if it was the most normal request and he had no choice.

As he hurried back, Abdullah said, "So what was it, pod'ner? A marriage?"

"Very funny, camel jockey."

Mac pulled a bottle from one of the skids, drank half of it on his way back, then poured out the rest.

"Hey!" Bihari called, "that stuff's as valuable as wheat, you know."

Mac watched his footing as he reached the rushing crimson tide. "You get around, don't you, Michael?" he said. "You omnipresent or something?"

"You know better than that, Cleburn," Michael said. "Like you, I am on assignment."

"And coincidentally in the same part of the world as me. I never got to thank you for—"

Michael held up a hand to silence him, then reached for the bottle. He sighed and looked to the sky. He spoke softly but with great passion. "Great and marvellous are thy works, Lord God Almighty; just and true are thy ways, thou King of saints. Who shall not fear thee, O Lord, and glorify thy name? For thou only art holy: for all nations shall come and worship before thee; for thy judgments are made manifest."

Michael carefully walked among the rocks, down to the edge of the rushing river. The surging blood was so loud that Mac worried he would not be able to hear Michael if he spoke again. And as if he knew Mac's fear, Michael turned and beckoned him closer. Mac hesitated. Michael was being spotted with blood. His brown robes were speckled, as were his beard and face and hair.

"Come," he said.

And Mac went.

Michael stood with one foot on a rock and the other just inches from the river. He said, "Thou art righteous, O Lord, which art, and wast, and shalt be, because thou hast judged thus. For they have shed the blood of saints and prophets, and thou hast given them blood to drink; for they are worthy."

Then another voice, Mac did not know from where: "Even so, Lord God Almighty, true and righteous are thy judgments."

Michael bent low and thrust the bottle into the current. The rushing blood pushed against his arm and soaked his sleeve and filled the bottle. And when he drew it from the river and turned toward Mac, there was no blood on him. His robe was dry. His face was clean. His arm was clean. The bottle was full of pure, clean water.

Michael handed it to Mac. "Drink," he said. Mac put the cold bottle to his lips and tipped it straight up. As Mac closed his eyes and drank it all, Michael said, "Jesus said, 'Whosoever drinketh of the water that I shall give him shall never thirst; but the water that I shall give him shall be in him a well of water springing up into everlasting life.'"

Mac opened his eyes and exhaled loudly. Michael was gone.

+ + +

"All due respect, sir," Sebastian said, "but you realize it's just you and me, a couple of guns, and a few rounds of ammunition, and we don't have a clue what we're driving into?"

"I was hoping you'd protect me," Rayford said. "This military stuff is fairly new to me."

"We're not really going to take these people on, are we?"

"I hope not, George. We're hopelessly outnumbered."

"Sorta what I was getting at, sir."

"Let's just play this out and see what we find."

"Uh, hold on. Could you stop a second?"

"You serious?"

"Yes, sir."

Rayford stopped and put the vehicle in park.

"You didn't read that in some military strategy book, did you?"

"What's that?"

"The see-what-we-find gambit?"

"George, listen. Nothing is as it used to be. We improvise every day. You're a living example of that. We have no choice here. We've got a whole bunch of our brothers and sisters trying to survive out here, and now something could be threatening them. If I went back and got all of them and armed them all, they would be no match for the GC if they decided to advance. So let's see what this is. We shouldn't have to get right into the middle of it before we know we should turn back. Use the binocs. You see armed GC, say the word, and we turn around. Fair enough?"

George looked like he was thinking. "Consider this," he said. "See over there? Over your other shoulder. There's a big group of somebody heading toward the gathering place. Let's go wide around the back way and get into that group. They aren't military and they aren't threatening."

"Makes sense."

"Always does. Make use of your resources."

"Like your mind, you mean?" Rayford said.

"Well, I wasn't going to say that."

+ + +

Mac looked around, his heart stampeding as if he'd run up a mountainside. He scampered down to the rushing river of blood and plunged the bottle into the current. Blood splashed all over him, but when he pulled the bottle out, it was pure freshwater again.

He laughed and shouted and charged back toward Albie and Abdullah and Bihari. But they had apparently never seen Michael and quickly tired of Mac's antics. "You didn't see him! You didn't, did you?"

They looked at him gravely from the trucks.

"Did you see me pour the water out? Well, did you? Bihari, you did, 'cause you told me it was worth its weight in wheat. Remember? Well, then where did I get this?"

Bihari got out of the truck. "Where *did* you get that?" he said.

"From that river right there! And do you see any blood on me?"

"I don't!"

"Still think you're doomed? The GC is going to leave you alone when they see what's happened to your water source. But you send your people and your equipment down here like usual. God takes care of the ones he's sealed, amen?"

By now Albie and Abdullah had come to see as well.

"Try a taste of this, gentlemen. You'll want to drink it all, but it's for sharing."

+ + +

Rayford and George found themselves in the middle of a pilgrimage of some sort. Almost everyone else was on foot. From their clothes they appeared to be both town and country folk, and some peasants. "English, anyone?" George said.

Two more times he said it, and finally a man—who appeared to be with his wife and perhaps a couple of other family members—came alongside the vehicle. "English? Yes," he said.

"Where are we going?" George said.

"We are going where we have been invited," the man said.

"All of you? Invited?"

"I do not know about the others. We were invited."

"Who invited you?"

"Three men. They came to the door and told us to meet them out here and they would tell us good news."

"But you are not Carpathia loyalists," George said. "I see no mark."

"On you either, sir," the man said. "And yet you seem no more afraid than we do."

"You don't even seem concerned," George said.

"The men told us not to fear."

"Why did you believe them? What gave you such confidence?"

"They were believable. What can I say?"

"Ask some others why they are here."

The man spoke to another group in Spanish. Then to another.

"We were all invited by the same men," he said.

"And who are they?"

"No one knows."

"And yet you all risk your lives to be here."

"It is as if we have no choice, sir."

Rayford stopped and the crowd surged past him. "What does this sound like to you, George?"

"The same thing it sounds like to you: Ming's story."

"Exactly. And we'll know for sure from the first words that come from their mouths. If the one . . . Christopher—?"

"Right."

"—starts out with the gospel, and the next one predicts what's going to happen to Babylon . . ."

"Nahum."

"Right. And Caleb warns about taking the mark, well, that's all we need to know."

"But where's the GC, Rayford? These guys got people saved in China, but the Peacekeepers still killed 'em."

Both men turned in their seats to watch for the enemy.

"Maybe God and these guys work differently in different parts of the world."

+ + +

Leah Rose worked in the basement of Lionel Whalum's huge home in Long Grove, Illinois. She and Hannah were making an inventory of medical supplies and a list of what was needed at various Co-op locations. They were working with printouts from Chloe Williams.

"I'm looking for a place that needs more than supplies, frankly," Leah said.

"I hear you. Is anything more exhausting than being idle? I don't know if I want to be in the middle of combat again, but I've got to be somewhere I'm needed."

"Problem is," Leah said, "Petra doesn't need medicine *or* nurses. But I'd like to at least stop by there on the way to my next assignment."

"Hmm, really? Wonder who? I mean, wonder why?"

"Shut up, Hannah."

Suddenly, Leah's knees buckled and she almost fell.

"What was that?" Hannah said. "You all right?"

"Yeah. I don't know. I just went weak all of a sudden, but it passed."

But as soon as she had said that, she dropped to her knees.

"Leah!"

"I'm okay. It's just—it's just that I . . . oh, God, yes. I will, Lord. Of course."

"What? What is it?"

"Pray with me, Hannah. We're supposed to pray for Mr. Whalum."

"Should I get his wife?"

"We're supposed to do it right now. Lord," Leah said, "I don't know what you're impressing upon me except that Mr. Whalum needs prayer right now. We trust you, we love you, we believe in you, and we know you are sovereign. Do whatever you have to do to keep him safe, and all those who are with him. He and Rayford and George and Ree should be leaving soon, so give them whatever they need, protect them in whatever way they need protection, and go before them into India."

+ + +

"Here they come," Rayford said, pointing past the west end of the crowd to show George the GC. They pulled up in Jeeps and vans, maybe a hundred troops, uniformed and armed. They had bullhorns.

While Rayford drove to the other side of the crowd and parked where he could see the people, the GC, and the front of the assembly, a GC officer announced, "This is an unlawful assembly. You are violating the law. There is no facility here for administering the mark of loyalty, and you are so many months past now that you will not be allowed to rectify that oversight. Appearing in public without the mark of loyalty is punishable by death at the hands of any law-abiding citizen, but if you will disperse now and go directly back to your homes, we will offer a brief extension and allow you to take the mark within twenty-four hours. An application site is available as close as Tamel Aike or Laguna Grande, both within sixty miles of here."

The people did not stop, did not look, did not appear troubled. The GC began again. "This is your last warn—"

"Silence!"

The commanding voice came from the front, from one of the three, and without amplification.

"My name is Christopher, and I speak under the authority of Jesus Christ the Messiah and Son of the living God. He has determined that those of this company who receive his everlasting gospel today shall enter into his millennial kingdom at his glorious appearing, just over two years from now."

The people began to murmur, and the GC were on their bullhorns again, but the horns malfunctioned and no one could hear them.

"My coworkers Nahum and Caleb are here with me only to proclaim that which the Lord has assigned us to proclaim. And then God's message of salvation as found in his only begotten Son will be presented by one of the 144,000 witnesses he has raised up from the tribes of the children of Israel.

"And now begone, you workers of iniquity, you servants of the evil ruler of this world. You shall come nigh unto these people and this place never again. Begone lest the God and Father of our Lord Jesus Christ strike you dead where you stand!"

The GC ran for their vehicles and for their lives. Christopher said, "Fear God and give glory to Him, for the hour of His judgment has come; and worship Him who made heaven and earth, the sea and springs of water."

Nahum followed with his curse on Babylon, and Caleb warned of the consequences of accepting the mark of the beast. Then a white-robed evangelist strode to the front and said, "There shall be signs in the sun, and in the moon, and in the stars; and upon the earth distress of nations, with perplexity; the sea and the waves roaring; men's hearts failing them for fear, and for looking after those things which are coming on the earth: for the powers of heaven shall be shaken.

"And then shall they see the Son of Man coming in a cloud with power and great glory. And when these things begin to come to pass, then look up, and lift up your heads; for your redemption draweth nigh."

+ + +

"Wheat's a-comin' and you've got water galore, Bihari. 'Scuse me while I make a phone call." Mac punched in Rayford's number. "Ray? Where you at, man? When you guys headin' this way? Good! Listen, you've seen the rivers? That's right, you're *on* the Chico. Let me tell you, it doesn't affect the believers. At least it doesn't here." He told him of his encounter with Michael and what had happened to the blood. "We're about an hour from takin' off, so tell those brothers and sisters the water is comin'! Well, that's right, they don't need it that bad now, do they? Bihari here's lookin' at me like I've just lost it. Well, hey, you tell 'em a deal's a deal."

+ + +

"Can I tell him, Captain Steele?" George said.

"Tell who what?"

"Luís. About the GC having to leave this area alone. And about the water."

"Like to share good news, do you?"

"You bet!"

"Knock yourself out."

When they got back, Luís jogged up to the car. "Well?"

"George wants the privilege," Rayford said. "We roll in ten minutes."

Lionel would take the first four hours, then Ree would take over, but Rayford would land the craft. Ray was strapping into the copilot's chair when Lionel fired up the engines, but as he put his headphones on he sensed something wrong. "You okay?" Rayford said.

Lionel pressed his lips together. "Did all my preflight."

"Me too. So?"

"Doesn't feel right."

"Long flight, big plane, lots of cargo, friend. We don't go till you're happy, hear?"

"I appreciate that, but I can't put my finger on it."

"Wanna do preflight again, check every box from top to bottom, just to be sure?"

"Nah, just let me think a minute."

Rayford turned in his seat. "How you doing, Ree?"

Ree gave him a thumbs-up and laid his head back, as if ready to sleep.

"Here comes your last crew member, Mr. Pilot. Should he shut the door, or are we holding?"

"Aw, nuts. Hold a second. I'm checking the cargo."

"Need help?"

"Nah, I got it."

"Cold back there."

"Don't I know it!"

Rayford waited just past ten minutes. Ree and George were strapped in and dozing already. Ray unstrapped and started back to the cargo hold when he met Lionel coming the other way. "All set?"

Lionel gave him a look. "Tell the tower we're ready."

As they strapped back in, Lionel looked at Rayford again. "Praise God, is all I've got to say."

"No, it isn't. Tell me."

"Had a whole pallet that never got secured. First bank, it would have shifted."

"Could have put us down."

"'Course."

"Surely you'd checked the cargo on preflight."

"I did. I always do. Hardly anything's more important than keeping that load centered and secure."

"What made you think of it?"

"I have no idea. I double-checked every lock. All were up. I just got a feeling I should check again."

"Well, buddy," Rayford said, "if we land in India, that feeling will be the reason."

20

Five Years into the Tribulation

CHANG SPENT HOURS monitoring the palace, his ears always pricking up when he heard Carpathia.

"Something in the atmosphere of that ancient Edom region interferes with our missiles, our flights, our artillery," Nicolae said one evening. "The entire area has become a Bermuda Triangle. Ensure the peace but do not waste another Nick on armory that does no more than what we can accomplish diplomatically."

Chang knew Global Community diplomacy was an oxymoron. Standard operating procedure no longer included any semblance of public relations for the potentate. Someone was trying to protect the potentate from it, but from all over the globe came evidence that even the millions of citizens who bore marks of loyalty to him now knew that the risen god of the world had become a despot king. Hundreds of thousands were dying everywhere for want of drinkable water.

One report from Region 7, the United African States, showed a woman railing in public before a small, obviously fearful crowd: "Justice, fair play, even juries are relics from another time! We obey the GC and bow to the image of the supreme ruler only because we all know someone who has been put to death for failing to!" She was shot to death where she stood, and the crowd scattered for its life.

From the same area came a sham of a recording depicting a programmed parade for the benefit of the Global Community News Network. The people marched listlessly, their faces blank, as they held aloft placards and chanted, "Hail, Carpathia" in monotones.

Chang both suffered and benefited from the chaos at the palace. In many ways New Babylon had become a ghost town. Citizens could no longer afford pilgrimages to the gleaming edifices. He knew from the real figures—not the cooked books whose summaries were announced to the populace—that half the world's population at the time of the Rapture had now died.

The capital city of the world didn't work very well anymore. Factions and minikingdoms sprang up, even around Carpathia—top people threatening, cajoling, surrounding themselves with sycophants. Everyone was suspicious of everyone else, while all were obsequious and cloying around the big boss. Revolt was out of the question. Theirs was a ruler who had proved himself impervious to death. What was the point of killing him again? You could take power for three days, but you had better loot the place and be gone when he resurrected.

The sad state of services in New Babylon was nothing compared to everywhere else in the world but Petra. Trib Force and Co-op fliers reported that everywhere they went, they saw that things simply wore out and were not replaced. The huge depletion of the population cost society half the people once employed in service jobs. Few were left to transport fuel, fix cars, keep streetlamps and traffic lights working, maintain order, protect businesses. Buck recounted in *The Truth* that the GC, especially at the local level, used their uniforms, badges, and weapons to get more for themselves. "Pity the shop owner who doesn't grease the palm of his friendly neighborhood insurer of security."

Chang watched all this from his spot as a journeyman techie in Aurelio Figueroa's computer department—but mostly from the system so expertly designed and installed by his predecessor, David Hassid. Ironic, Chang thought, that it was the one thing still humming along perfectly.

Carpathia himself was a madman, and no one around him even pretended otherwise—except to his face. Everyone seemed to cater to his craziness, competing to see who could be first to curry his favor by carrying out his latest directive—which usually came in a fit of fury.

"Insubordination!" he shrieked late one night as Chang listened to his weary lieutenants trying to stay awake with him. "My sub-potentate in Region 7 must wake up tomorrow to find that the heads of both Libya and Ethiopia and their entire senior cabinets have been assassinated!"

Suhail Akbar said, "I'll talk with him, Excellency. I'm sure he will realize that—"

"Did you not understand that to be a directive, Suhail?"

"Sir?"

"Did you not understand my order?"

"You literally want those leaders and their cabinets dead by morning?"

"If you cannot accomplish it, I will find—"

"It can be done, sir, but there would not be time to send our strike force from here—"

"You are director of Security and Intelligence! You have no contacts in Africa who can—"

"I'm on it, sir."

"I should hope you are!"

The deed was accomplished by an S & I force of African Peacekeepers and Morale Monitors. Akbar was lauded the next day, then suffered in Carpathia's doghouse for more than three weeks because the boss was having trouble "getting useful information out of Region 7."

\+ \+ \+

Rayford lived in an underground hut, like everyone else who worked out of the former military base in San Diego. And like Mac and Albie out of Al Basrah, Rayford flew missions directly between San Diego and other International Co-op centers—places so remote and well hidden that if the fliers could elude GC radar—and even that was crumbling with the loss of personnel all over the world—there were no pesky airport details they had to bluff their way past. The head of the Tribulation Force worried that he and his people might lower their guard and see their whole network come crashing down. He actually had felt more in control and careful when the GC had been at full strength. The world had become a cauldron of individual free-market systems.

When he was "home" in San Diego, Rayford studied the reports that came to Chloe from Co-op workers all over the globe. Hardly anywhere in the world escaped the evil influence of the GC-sponsored deceivers. Magicians, sorcerers, wizards, demonic apparitions, and deputies of Leon Fortunato preached a false gospel. They set themselves up as Christ figures, messiahs, soothsayers. They lauded the deity of Carpathia. They performed wonders and miracles and deceived countless thousands. These were lured away from considering the claims of Christ himself, usually by the promise of drinkable water, but once they had made their decisions for the evil ruler, either he snuffed them out as he had done in the Negev or God slew them. Tsion Ben-Judah continued to maintain that God was continually evening the score, removing from the earth those with the sign of the beast, because a great war was coming.

"It is not as if the God of gods could not defeat any foe he chooses," Dr. Ben-Judah taught, "but the stench of the other side evangelizing for evil has offended him and kindled his wrath. Yet the wrath of God remains balanced by his great mercy and love. There has been not one report of death or injury to any of the 144,000 evangelists God has raised up to spread the truth about his Son."

Though weary of the battle and longing for heaven or the Glorious Appearing—sometimes Rayford didn't care which came first for him—still he thrilled to the reports from all over the world. The Tribulation Force saw many of these 144,000 brave men venture into public, calling the undecided from their homes to confront them with the claims of Christ. The men were powerful preachers, anointed of God with the gift of evangelism. Often they were accompanied by angels, guardians to protect them and their listeners. GC forces were incapable of stopping them.

"The archangels Gabriel and Michael have been seen in various parts of the world, making pronouncements for God and standing in defense of his people," Tsion and Chaim told the people of Petra and thus the world via the Internet. Rayford thanked God silently as he read that the angel with the everlasting gospel, Christopher, often appeared in remote regions where Christ had never been preached. Nahum continued to warn of the coming fall of Babylon, sometimes with Christopher, sometimes by himself. And Caleb was reported somewhere else almost every day, warning of the consequences for anyone accepting the mark of the beast and worshiping his image.

Besides these, it was not uncommon for the Tribulation Force to see or feel the presence of angels protecting them wherever they went. Often, even outside of the routes to Petra, GC planes would intercept theirs, warn them, try to force them down, then shoot at them. Never knowing when and where they might be protected outside of the Negev, Tribulation Force pilots took evasive action. But thus far God had chosen to insulate them, to the frustration and astonishment of the GC.

With less than two years to go before the Glorious Appearing, Rayford met with Buck and Chloe to assess the current state of the Tribulation Force. "Where are we," he said, "and where do we need to be for maximum benefit to the entire body of believers around the world?"

Chloe reported that Lionel Whalum and his wife had somehow been able to keep their home in Illinois, "though Leah and Hannah have developed serious cases of cabin fever. I mean, I think they're encouraged by God's work in their lives. Lionel was, of course, thrilled by Leah's story of having been compelled to pray for him before he ran the final check on the cargo out of Argentina. You know, Dad, he's one of our busiest pilots now, delivering supplies all over the world."

"How bad is it with Leah and Hannah?" Buck said. "I don't know either of them that well, but Leah would get on anybody's nerves. She still pining for Tsion?"

"They keep low profiles," Chloe said, "and say they feel as if they live only at night. They don't dare venture out during the day. GC activity is spotty in that area of the suburbs, but all it would take is one report of someone without the mark, and one of our major thrusts would be jeopardized."

"I hardly ever hear from Z anymore," Rayford said.

Chloe shook her head. "Of all people, Zeke has probably changed the most. There's almost zero call for his services there in western Wisconsin. No uniforms to tailor, no disguises to invent, no undercover agents to transform."

"Could we better use him out here?" Rayford said.

"Not when you hear this," Chloe said. "Zeke has sort of settled into a new persona. He's taken such an interest in studying the Bible that he's become the de facto assistant to the spiritual leader of the underground church there."

"Zeke an assistant pastor?" Rayford said. "Push me over with a feather."

"Chloe's been keeping up with Enoch and some of his people," Buck said.

"Yeah, I apologized for intruding on their lives and their community, because I felt responsible for the split-up of much of The Place congregation. But Enoch reminded me that if I hadn't discovered them, they never would have known of the coming destruction.

"On the other hand, Dad, I know that if I had not been traipsing around Chicago in the middle of the night, there might never have been that secondary destruction."

\+ + +

One morning in Petra, the assemblage awoke to the news that all the seas of the world had spontaneously turned from blood to salt water again. "God has given me no special knowledge about this," Tsion announced. "But it makes me wonder if something worse isn't coming. And soon."

Little changed except that Carpathia tried to take the credit for the cleansing of the seas. He announced, "My people created a formula that has healed the waters. The plant and animal life of the oceans will surge back to life before long. And now that the oceans are clear again, all our beautiful lake and river waterways will soon be restored as well."

He was wrong, of course, and the blunder of his bluster cost him even more credibility. God had chosen, in his own time, to lift the plague from the seas, but the lakes and rivers remained blood.

Just before being executed, a Swedish insurgent announced, "What our so-called potentate ignored in exulting over the revived seas is that there is still an international mess. Dead, rotting, smelly fish still blanket the shores around the world and still carry the diseases that have driven most of the coastline populations inland. And where are the refining plants to turn the seas into potable water? We die of thirst while the king hoards the resources."

\+ + +

Sixty-Eight Months into the Tribulation

Chang was intrigued to hear of an unscheduled meeting in Carpathia's conference room. Leon had actually called the meeting, much to Carpathia's frustration, but Suhail Akbar, Viv Ivins, and Nicolae's secretary Krystall all quickly came to

Leon's defense. "This is about water, Excellency," Leon began. "Because you no longer need nourishment, including water, perhaps you don't underst—"

"Listen to me, Leon. There is water in food. Are you people not eating enough food?"

"Potentate, the situation is dire. We try to harvest water from the seas and convert it. But even getting new ships out there is a chore."

"It is true, unfortunately," Akbar said, "and our troops everywhere are suffering."

"I'm suffering," Viv said. "Personally, I mean. There are times I think I should die if I don't find a swallow of water."

"Ms. Ivins," Carpathia said, "we shall not allow the administration of the Global Community to grind to a halt because you are thirsty. Do you understand?"

"Yes, Highness. Forgive that selfish expression. I don't know what I—"

"In fact, do you have a whit of expertise in this area?"

"Sir?"

"In the matter before us! Do you bring anything to the table that helps get us to a solution? Are you an expert? a scientist? a hydrologist? There is no need to shake your head. I know the answers. If you do not have pressing business in your office, why do you not just sit and listen and be grateful that you draw a paycheck here?"

"Would you prefer I leave?"

"Of course!"

Chang heard her chair push back from the table.

"A little tie with my family," Nicolae said, "and you ride that horse as if it is your own! Do not turn from me when I address you!"

"I thought you wanted me to leave!" she whimpered.

"I do not cater to subjects, employees, friends, or otherwise who disrespect their sovereign. This same attitude made you think you could sit on *MY THRONE* in *MY TEMPLE*!"

"Your Lordship, I have apologized over and over for that indiscretion! I am humiliated, repentant, and—"

"Excellency," Leon said softly, "that *was* more than two years ago. . . ."

"You!" Carpathia roared. "You call this meeting and now you counter me as well?"

"No, sir. I apologize if it sounds as if I am c—"

"What would you call it? Would you like to join *Aunt Viv* and return to your office to work on what you have been assigned? You are head of the church, man! What happens to Carpathianism while you worry about water? Where are the scientists, the technologists who have something to offer here?"

Leon did not respond.

"Ms. Ivins, *why* are you still here?"

"I—but I thought you—"

"Go! For the love of all—"

"Sir," Suhail began, as if the voice of reason, "I did consult the experts before coming, and—"

"Finally! Someone who uses the brain I gave him! What do you have?"

"If you'll notice here, Your Highness . . ."

Chang heard the rattle of paper, as if Akbar was spreading a document.

"Satellite photography has detected a spring in the middle of Petra that has apparently been producing freshwater since the day of the bombings."

"So we are back to Petra, are we, Director Akbar? The site of so many billions of Nicks poured into the desert sands?"

"It has been a boondoggle, sir, but notice what the aerial photography shows. Apparently the missile struck an aquifer that supplies thousands of gallons of pure water every day. It only stands to reason that the source of this spring extends far outside the city of Petra, and our people see no reason why we could not access it as well."

"Where do they believe it extends?"

"To the east."

"And how deep?"

"They are not able to tell from this kind of technology, but if a missile could tap into it in Petra, surely we could drill—or even use another missile—east of there."

"Use a missile to tap into a spring? Suhail, have you heard of using too much equipment for a job?"

"Begging your pardon, sir, but two daisy cutter bombs and a Lance missile produced only drinking water for a million of our enemies."

\+ \+ \+

Mac had called Abdullah to tell him of the news of the finishing of a new Co-op airstrip, "beautifully hidden" just east of Ta'izz, north of the Gulf of Aden in southern Yemen. "Albie's got a shipment he'd like to deliver to Petra, if you could run it down there sometime in the next day or so."

"Me?" Abdullah said. "By myself?"

"Need me to hold your hand there, Smitty?"

"No. It is not that. It is just that such errands are so much more fun with company."

"Yeah, I'm a barrel o' laughs, but that's a quick one-man run you can do with one of the lighter planes."

"One of Mr. Whalum's people left a Lear here. Can the new strip take a Lear?"

"Sure. A 30 or smaller. Anyway, watch for us around noon. When do you think you'd do this?"

"Probably today. If I finish with my hair and nail appointments in time. I was going to have my face done too, but—"

"What in heaven's name are you goin' on about?"

Abdullah laughed. "I finally got you, Mr. Mac! I was doing a joke on you!"

"Very funny, Smitty."

"I got you, didn't I, cowboy?"

+ + +

Abdullah was checking the weather at the communications center when Naomi called out to him. "Mr. Smith, could you tell me what you make of this?"

He hurried over.

"What does that look like to you?" she said.

Abdullah's stomach dropped. Dare he say it? Dare he not? "That looks like incoming."

"That's what I thought! What do I do?"

"Get Tsion and Chaim. Code red."

"May I tell them you said that, sir?"

"Tell them whatever you need to, but quickly."

She pushed a button and spoke into a microphone. "Communications central to leadership."

"Leadership here. Morning, Naomi."

"I need Drs. Ben-Judah and Rosenzweig here ASAP on a code red, authorized by Mr. Smith."

"I will not ask you to repeat that if you can confirm what I thought you said."

"That's affirmative, Leadership. Code red."

Abdullah met Tsion and Chaim at the entrance. Several grave-looking elders accompanied them. "Abdullah," Chaim said, "code reds are reserved for threats to the well-being of the whole."

"Follow me."

He took them to Naomi, where they formed a half circle behind her and stared at the screen.

"A missile?"

"Looks like it," Abdullah said.

"Headed for the city?"

"Actually no, but close."

"From?"

"Probably Amman."

"Time?"

"Minutes."

"Target?"

"Looks east."

"Where they have been drilling?"

Abdullah nodded.

Tsion said, "They have been drilling for weeks, and we have seen nothing. No oil, no water, no blood. Now they are going to bomb the place? It is not like Carpathia to take up arms against his own forces, depleted as they are. Do we have time to watch? Would it be prudent?"

Abdullah studied the screen. "I was at ground zero for two bombs and a missile two years ago. I would not fear another missile at least a mile from here. We have field glasses on tripods at the high place north of the Siq."

"Shall I warn the people?" Naomi said.

Tsion thought a moment. "Just tell them," he said, "to not be alarmed by an explosion within—when would you say, Abdullah?"

"Fifteen minutes."

"This is not a surprise to the drilling crew," Abdullah said a few minutes later, bent to look through high-powered binoculars.

"They have moved," Tsion said.

"Quite a ways, actually. More than a mile. Maybe two. And the drill rigging has been disassembled. That tells me that they don't want it destroyed by the missile. It is probably programmed internally for a specific coordinate."

Chaim sat on a rock, breathing heavily. "Is it just my age or is it particularly warm today?"

"I am perspiring more than usual myself, my friend," Tsion said.

Abdullah pulled up from the binocs and shaded his eyes with his hand. "Now that you mention it, look at the sun."

It seemed larger, brighter, higher than it should have been.

"What time is it?" Tsion said.

"About ten."

"Why, that could be a noonday sun! You don't suppose . . ."

Abdullah heard a whistling sound in the distance. He looked north. A white plume appeared on the horizon. "Missile," he said. "It will be hard to follow with the glasses, but you could try."

"I can see it with the naked eye," Tsion said.

"I am warm," Chaim said.

They watched as the winding missile streaked into view and began to descend. It appeared aimed for the original drilling site. It soared past the disassembled drilling rig on the desert floor, then slammed a hundred yards south of it, raising a huge cloud of sand and soil and digging a deep, wide crater.

The rumble of the explosion reached them in seconds, and the cloud slowly dissipated. Abdullah readjusted the binoculars to study the crater. "I cannot imagine it went nearly as deep as the hole they had already been drilling," he said. "Regardless, so far it has produced nothing."

"I am amused," Tsion said, "but I wonder what they thought they might accomplish. If they were hoping to strike water, would they not have simply produced a geyser of blood anyway?"

21

CHANG TOOK an unusual risk and surreptitiously followed the missile-for-water effort from his desk at work. He listened through headphones but kept an eye out for anyone walking by.

Nicolae swore. "What did that little project cost, Suhail?"

"It wasn't cheap, Excellency, but let's not assume failure just yet."

"Assume? The Lance we sent to Petra immediately produced a gusher that flows to this day! This is a disaster plain as day!"

"You may be right."

"I am always right! Face it. You are going to have to attack this water thing another way."

Chang heard a knock and Krystall's voice. "Begging your pardon, sir, but we are getting strange reports."

"What kind of reports?"

"Some kind of a heat wave. The lines are jammed. People are—"

Chang heard shouting and realized it came from his office and not from the surveillance. He quickly exed out and removed his earphones. He followed his coworkers to the windows, where they crowded to look outside.

"Get back!" Mr. Figueroa screamed as he burst from his office. "Get away from the windows!"

But like toddlers, these people wanted to do whatever they were told not to, and anyway, they were curious. What was causing all the explosions outside? Fortunately for the crowd around the window Chang peered out from, it wasn't the first to go. But two of their coworkers—the cocky, condescending Lars and a young woman—were impaled with shards of glass when the window before them gave way.

As they lay writhing, pale and panicked, the steamy desert air blew in. The first woman who knelt to aid the injured immediately reddened from the heat, and as she surrendered and tried to evade it, her hair curled, produced sparks, burst into flames, and was singed off.

Others tried to drag the first two to safety, but they too had to scamper from the heat.

"What *is* this?" someone shrieked. "What's happening?"

Those in front of Chang quickly backed away from the window, and he saw what was going on below. Car tires exploded. People leaped from their cars, then tried to get back in, burning their hands on the door handles. Windshields melted, greenery turned brown, withered, then became torches. A dog yanked loose from its leash, raced in circles, then dropped, panting, before being incinerated.

"To the basement!" Figueroa shouted, and to people who seemed reluctant to leave the fallen injured, "It's too late to help them!"

People watched over their shoulders as they hurried away, and by the time they reached the door, they saw Lars and the young woman flailing at flames that would soon consume them.

Chang was one of the last out of the room, because he was only faking the effects of the heat. He saw the results, but aside from being aware that the temperature outside seemed higher than normal, he was impervious to the killing force.

He was glad to reach the elevator just as the doors were closing. "I'll catch the next one," he said and ran to his quarters instead.

+ + +

At midnight in San Diego, Rayford was awakened by insistent tones from his computer. He dragged himself out of bed and turned on the monitor. Tsion was informing his cyberaudience around the world that the terrible fourth Bowl Judgment had struck, as prophesied in the Bible, and would affect every time zone on the earth as the sun rose. "Here in Petra," he wrote, "by ten in the morning, people out in the sun without the seal of God were burned alive. This may seem an unparalleled opportunity to plead once again for the souls of men and women, because millions will lose loved ones. But the Scriptures also indicate that this may come so late in the hearts of the undecided that they will have already been hardened.

"Revelation 16:8-9 says, 'Then the fourth angel poured out his bowl on the sun, and power was given to him to scorch men with fire. And men were scorched with great heat, and they blasphemed the name of God who has power over these plagues; and they did not repent and give Him glory.'"

Rayford keyed in a request to interact privately with Tsion or Chaim; he did not care which. "I know both of you will be terribly busy just now, but if either can spare a moment for the sake of the Tribulation Force, I would appreciate it."

+ + +

Three Quonset huts away, Ming Toy had been awakened by a call from Ree Woo. Ree had promised to look up her mother, so maybe this was his update, but Ming was alarmed at the hour. She rested in the promise Christopher had given about her and her mother surviving until the Glorious Appearing, but that—she knew—was no guarantee that her mother might not live out her days imprisoned.

"Is everyone all right?" she said.

"Better than all right," Ree said. "Although I was not so sure when I arrived. I was warned to stay away from the underground shelter, because rumor had it that the GC had found them out and were planning a raid. The believers were busy packing and were going to sneak away in the night. They were praying the GC would raid them later—as is the custom—when they were supposed to be sleeping.

"But as the sun rose, they realized they heard very little noise from the street. Some ventured out and saw the damage from the sun. Everything is scorched, dried up, burned, melted, wasted. No one was on the street, though charred remains were scattered. The believers are protected, but the GC and the Carpathian loyalists cannot face the sun. The underground moved by the light of day, and if the GC come for them in the night, they will be disappointed. The believers did not move far away, but it is a better hiding place.

"Something they saw along the way would have been amusing, had it not been so sad. A small faction of GC had apparently tried to use fireproof suits and boots and helmets to protect themselves from the enormous heat. They lasted long enough to travel about a hundred yards; then they split up as their suits caught fire. Piles of burning material are dotted here and there in the streets."

"Will you hurry back, Ree? I miss you terribly."

"I miss you too, Ming, and I love you. This will allow me to leave during the daytime, so I should be back early."

"Be safe, love," she said.

+ + +

Rayford sat on the edge of his bed, head in his hands, enveloped in the unmatched darkness provided by an underground shelter. Rayford was tired and knew he should get more sleep. But he would not sleep. This plague, perhaps unlike any leading to it, might provide unique opportunities for him and his team.

Finally the signal came, and Tsion was on the other end of the private messaging system. "Forgive me for not turning on the video," Rayford said, "but it's the middle of our night here."

"Quite all right, Captain. Let me ask, need this be a private conversation? I am in the tech center and others may overhear."

"No problem, Tsion. Is everyone all right there?"

"We are fine. We feel some extra warmth and some are fatigued, but we are apparently protected against the real effects of this plague."

"I know you're busy, but I need confirmation. Do you believe those of us with the mark of the seal of God are immune to the heat?"

"Yes."

"Do you see what this could mean for the Tribulation Force, Tsion? We could do what we wanted during the daylight hours. As long as we are hidden again by the time the heat of the day subsides and the GC venture out again, they would be powerless to interfere."

"I see. I would caution that God has never been predictable with these things. We know the sequence, and we used to think that one plague began and ended before another started. But the curse on the oceans lasted well past when the same curse hit the lakes and rivers, and the oceans turned back not too long before this one hit. I would not want to see you some bright day when the curse ends. You would be most vulnerable."

"Point taken. I'd like to think this would last long enough to allow us some elbow room. I've never seen the world in worse shape or more people in need of help."

"Oh, Rayford, the world is a spent cartridge. Even before God unleashed this curse, the globe was in the worst condition imaginable. It makes me wonder how the Lord can tarry until the end of the seven years. Really, what will be left? Poverty is rampant. Law and order are relics. Even Global Community loyalists have lost faith in their government and their Peacekeepers. The Morale Monitors are all on the take, it seems. The people who are to be out and about do not even dare venture into the streets without being armed.

"Cameron tells me he does not know one common citizen who does not own and carry a weapon. I hardly hear from countries where there are not marauding bands of thieves and rapists, not to mention vandals and terrorists. The best things we have out there are the 144,000 evangelists and the increase in angelic activity the Lord has so graciously allowed.

"Remember, Rayford, we are down to three kinds of people now: those of us with the mark of God, those who bear the mark of Antichrist, and the undecided. There are fewer and fewer of these, but they are the ones we must reach out to. They are suffering now, but oh, how they will suffer as the sun rises each day. Imagine the turmoil, the devastation. Power shortages, air conditioning overloads, breakdowns. And all this coming with half the population already gone.

"We are not far from anarchy, my friend. The GC does not care to crack down because they benefit. I am amazed there remain any loyal to Carpathia. Look what he has wrought."

"Dr. Ben-Judah, how does this square with your contention that these judgments are as much about God's mercy and compassion as they are about his wrath? The angel that announced the rivers and lakes turning to blood said it was to avenge the blood of the prophets."

"God is just and God is holy, Rayford, but I do not believe he would send any more judgments on the world now if he weren't still jealous that some repent. No doubt some will. I know the majority will not, because of what the Scripture says about their blaspheming the name of God. Obviously, by now everyone knows these judgments are from God, yet many refuse to repent of their sins."

"I agree with you, Tsion. No one could possibly argue that God doesn't exist. There's overwhelming evidence of his presence and power—yet most still reject him. Why?"

"Captain Steele, that is the question of the ages. You remember the Old Testament story of when Moses grew up and refused to be called the son of Pharaoh's daughter, even though he could have? The Bible says he chose 'rather to suffer affliction with the people of God, than to enjoy the pleasures of sin for a season.'

"Well, these people certainly are not Moses. They will suffer torment and lose their souls, all to enjoy the pleasures of sin for a season—and what a short season. I applaud your thinking that this may be the time for the Tribulation Force to step up its efforts, to help struggling believers, to find the remaining undecided and help the evangelists and the angels bring them in before it is too late. I wish you Godspeed with whatever you decide."

+ + +

Buck hurried to George Sebastian's underground quarters, where George's wife played on the floor with their child.

"I've got to get out and see this," Buck said.

"Got to be careful of radar," Sebastian said. "The GC would be astounded to see anybody in the air during the day."

"What do you recommend?"

"Chopper."

"You up for it, George?"

"You don't have to ask twice."

Buck had seen vapor appear above the water inlets on cool mornings, but he had never seen the Pacific emit steam as far as the eye could see. "Do you believe this?" he said.

"I'll believe anything now," George said.

Buck was reduced to silence as fires broke out all over what was left of San Diego. The closer it got to midday, the brighter the sky became. Houses and buildings no longer began smoking and smoldering and finally kindling. Now they shimmered and shook, windows bursting, roofs curling, then whole structures exploding and sending flames and sparks showering about.

George cruised back over the ocean, where Buck saw the sand change colors before creeping carpets of flame began dancing about. The waves brought the bubbling water in, and it hissed and boiled as it touched the blistering shore. Without warning, the entire ocean reached the boiling point and became a roiling cistern of giant bubbles, sending a fog of steam that blocked Buck's view of the sky and sun. The chopper was engulfed in white so pure and thick that Buck feared Sebastian would lose control.

"Totally on instruments now, friend," George said.

The helicopter bounced and shook in the soup as they *thwock-thwock-thwock*ed toward the shore. Sebastian was half a mile inland before they escaped the steam cloud and peered down on the burning grasses and neighborhoods.

"What's the boiling temperature of blood?" Buck asked.

"Not a clue," George said, but he immediately banked and headed toward the San Diego River.

"Whatever it is," Buck said, "we've reached it." He gawked at the huge crimson bubbles that formed and burst, emitting a fine spray that rose with the steam. "Agh!" he said, grimacing and holding his nose. "Let's get out of here."

The Tribulation Force was free to come and go, as long as they were careful to plan their travel into time zones that kept them in daylight as long as possible. The only relief for the Global Community forces and citizens with the mark of loyalty was to stay inside below ground level and invent ways to take the edge off the suffocating heat. Even then, hundreds of thousands died when their dwellings burned and fell in on them. Homes and buildings were largely allowed to burn themselves out, as firefighters could not venture out until well after dark.

Gardens, crops, grasses died. The polar ice caps melted faster than at any other time in history, and tsunamis threatened every port city. Shores and coastlines were buried under floods, and the dump of dead sea creatures washed miles onto land. Had it not been for people having moved inland to avoid the stench and bacteria in the first place, more lives would have been lost.

In the midst of such turmoil and grief, Rayford and Chloe worked harder than ever to rearrange their storehouses of goods and products traded through the International Commodity Co-op. Knowing their time was limited, they took advantage of everyone's obsession with finding shelter and relief from the sun. They strategized with Chang to move equipment and aircraft around and created new warehousing and distribution centers, preparing for the last year of existence on a wounded planet.

+ + +

In New Babylon, Carpathia himself insisted the heat did not bother him. Chang overheard people in maintenance repeatedly ask whether he wanted draperies over the second story of his penthouse office. Even the ceiling was transparent. The sun was magnified through the glass and roasted his office for hours every day, making the entire rest of the floor uninhabitable. Krystall was relocated deep in the bowels under Building D and had to communicate with him via intercom all day. No meetings could be held in his conference room or office, but he spent most of the day there, ordering people about via telephone or intercom.

Executives on lower floors had their windows replaced, then taped and coated and even painted black, and most other employee offices were moved to the basement of the vast complex. Chang's department worked only at night, so he was often able to listen in as Nicolae hummed or sang softly as he worked in his office all day.

"I will sunbathe in the courtyard while the mortals eat," he told Krystall one day at noon. Chang snuck to a corner window where he scraped a hole in the coating. He was appalled to see the potentate strip to his trousers and undershirt and lie on a concrete bench, hands behind his head, soaking in the killer rays.

After an hour, as flames licked at the concrete, Carpathia seemed to think of something and pulled his phone from his pocket. Chang sprinted back to his quarters and listened in as Nicolae told Leon he was on his way to Fortunato's temporary underground shelter.

Later, Chang recorded Leon's call to Suhail.

"I'm telling you, the man is inhuman! He had been outside, sunbathing!"

"Leon . . ."

"It's true! He was so hot I could not stand within twenty feet of him! The soles of his shoes were smoking! I saw sparks in his hair, which was bleached white—even his eyebrows. His shirt collar and cuffs and tie had been singed as if the dry cleaner had over-ironed them, and the buttons on his suit and shirt had melted.

"The man is a god, impervious to pain. It's as if he prefers being outside in this!"

One day Chang overheard Carpathia call Technical Services. "I would like a telescope set up that would point directly at the sun at noonday."

"I can do that, Your Highness," a man said. "But of course I would have to do it after dark."

"And might it have recording capability?"

"Of course, sir. What would you like to record?"

"Whether the sun has grown and if bursts of flame from its surface would be visible."

The instrument was set up and calibrated that night, and Chang watched the next day as Carpathia hurried outside at noon. He actually peered at the sun through the lens for several minutes. An hour later the lens had melted, and the entire telescope stood warped and sagging in the heat.

The technician called Carpathia that evening to report that the recording disc had also melted.

"That is all right. I saw what I wanted to see."

"Sir?"

"That was a very nice piece of equipment. It provided me a crystal-clear image of the noonday sun, and indeed, I could see the flares dancing from the surface."

The techie laughed.

"You find that humorous?" Carpathia said.

"Well, you're joking, of course."

"I am not."

"Sir, forgive me, but your eyeball would be gone. In fact, your brain would have been fried."

"Do you realize to whom you are speaking?"

Chang was chilled at his tone.

"Yes, sir, Potentate," the techie said, his voice shaky.

"The sun, moon, and stars bow to me."

"Yes, sir."

"Understand?"

"Yes, sir."

"Do you doubt my account?"

"No, sir. Forgive me."

+ + +

Seventeen Weeks Later

Chang was idly monitoring various levels and temperature records at his desk one evening when he realized that the third Bowl Judgment had been lifted. He called Figueroa. "You'll want to see this," he said.

Aurelio hurried from his office and stood behind Chang. "Look at this reading."

"'Boiling water overflowing the Chicago River,'" his boss read quietly. "'Overheated and radiation contaminated.' Nothing new, is it?"

"You missed it, Chief."

"Tell me."

"It doesn't say blood. It says water."

Figueroa was trembling as he used Chang's phone to call Akbar. "Guess what I just discovered?" he said.

+ + +

"The waterways will now heal themselves over time," Chang heard Suhail Akbar tell Carpathia the next day.

Maybe, Chang thought, *if there were decades left.*

It seemed to Chang that Carpathia was less concerned about water and heat because neither plague had affected him personally. What occupied most of his time was the failure, particularly in Israel, of his master plan for taking care of the Jewish "problem." In many other countries, the persecutions had had relative success. But of the 144,000 evangelists, those assigned to the Holy Land had had tremendous success seeing the undecided become believers. And then, for some reason, they had been able to evade detection. Just when Carpathia and Akbar thought they had devised a sweep to rid the area of Messianic Jews, the sun plague had hit and the GC were incapacitated.

Now, though Carpathia rarely saw Suhail Akbar face-to-face during the day, they were constantly in touch. Chang was amazed at how much firepower was still available to Global Community forces after all they had lost and had wasted in many skirmishes with the protected Judah-ites.

The United African States threatened secession because of what Carpathia had done to their ruling elite, while a rebel group there was secretly scheming with the palace about taking over for the disenfranchised government.

"Suhail," Chang recorded one day from Carpathia's phone, "these plagues have always had their seasons. This one has to end sometime. And when it does, that may be the time for us to pull out the half of our munitions and equipment that we have in reserve. Would you estimate that the confidentiality level on that stockpile remains secure?"

"To the best of my knowledge, Excellency."

"When the sun curse lifts, Director, when you can stand being out in the light of day again, let us be ready to mount the most massive offensive in the history of mankind. I have not yet conceded even Petra, but I want the Jews wherever they are. I want them from Israel, particularly Jerusalem. And I will not be distracted or dissuaded by our whining friends in northern Africa. Suhail, if you have ever wanted to please me, ever wanted to impress me, ever wanted to make yourself indispensable to me, give yourself to this task. The planning, the strategy, the use of resources should make every other war strategist in history hang his head in shame. I want you to knock me out, Suhail, and I am telling you that resources—monetary and military—are limitless."

"Thank you, sir. I won't let you down."

"Did you get that, Suhail? Lim-it-less."

+ + +

Six Years into the Tribulation

Chang arose at dawn, as usual, but he realized immediately that things had changed. He had not been vulnerable to the damage of the sun, but he had been aware of the difference in temperature and humidity. This morning, the air felt different.

He hurried to his computer and checked the weather. *Uh-oh. Show's over.* The temperature in New Babylon was normal.

Chang ate, showered, dressed, and hurried out. The palace was abuzz. Windows were open. People streamed in and out. He even saw smiles, though most of the depleted employee population was overworked, undernourished, and looked pale and sickly.

The brass announced that the noonday meal would be served picnic-style, outside. Little was accomplished that morning as everyone anticipated lunchtime. Then the mood was festive and the food plentiful. Many got a peek at Carpathia, striding purposefully about as if he had a new lease on life.

Chang hurried back to his quarters after work that day, eager to check on the rest of the world. The Tribulation Force had trimmed its sails and pulled in its cannons. They were back in hiding, picking their spots, strategizing for returning to an after-dark schedule.

Carpathia remained tireless and expected the same of others. He held another high-level meeting with the brass that had spent much of the day moving back to his floor. Even Viv Ivins was invited, and from what Chang could hear, all had been forgiven.

"For the first time in a long time," Nicolae said, "we play on an even field. The waterways are healing themselves, and we have rebuilding to do in the infrastructure. Let us work at getting all our loyal citizens back onto the same page with us. Director Akbar and I have some special surprises in store for dissidents on various levels. We are back in business, people. It is time to recoup our losses and start delivering a few."

\+ + +

The new mood lasted three days. Then the lights went out. Literally. Everything went dark. Not just the sun, but the moon also, the stars, streetlamps, electric lights, car lights. Anything anywhere that ever emitted light was now dark. No keypads on telephones, no flashlights, nothing iridescent, nothing glow-in-the-dark. Emergency lights, exit signs, fire signs, alarm signs—everything. Pitch-black.

The cliché of not being able to see one's hand in front of one's face? Now true. It mattered not what time of day it was; people could see nothing. Not their clocks, watches, not even fire, matches, gas grills, electric grills. It was as if the light had done worse than go out; any vestige of it had been sucked from the universe.

People screamed in terror, finding this the worst nightmare of their lives—and they had many to choose from. They were blind—completely, utterly, totally, wholly unable to see anything but blackness twenty-four hours a day.

They felt their way around the palace; they pushed their way outdoors. They tried every light and every switch they could remember. They called out to each other to see if it was just them, or if everyone had the same problem. Find a candle! Rub two sticks together! Shuffle on the carpet and create static electricity. Do anything. Anything! Something to allow some vestige of a shadow, a hint, a sliver.

All to no avail.

Chang wanted to laugh. He wanted to howl from his gut. He wished he could tell everyone everywhere that once again God had meted out a curse, a judgment upon the earth that affected only those who bore the mark of the beast. Chang could see. It was different. He didn't see lights either. He simply saw everything in sepia tone, as if someone had turned down the wattage on a chandelier.

He saw whatever he needed to, including his computer and screen and watch and quarters. His food, his sink, his stove—everything. Best of all, he could tiptoe around the palace in his rubber-soled shoes, weaving between his coworkers as they felt their way along.

Within hours, though, something even stranger happened. People were not starving or dying of thirst. They were able to feel their way to food and drink. But they could not work. There was nothing to discuss, nothing to talk about but the cursed darkness. And for some reason, they also began to feel pain.

They itched and so they scratched. They ached and so they rubbed. They cried out and scratched and rubbed some more. For many the pain grew so intense that all they could do was bend down and feel the ground to make sure there was no hole or stairwell to fall into and then collapse in a heap, writhing, scratching, seeking relief.

The longer it went, the worse it got, and now people swore and cursed God and chewed their tongues. They crawled about the corridors, looking for weapons, pleading with friends or even strangers to kill them. Many killed themselves. The entire complex became an asylum of screams and moans and guttural wails, as these people became convinced that this, finally, was it—the end of the world.

But no such luck. Unless they had the wherewithal, the guts, to do themselves in, they merely suffered. Worse by the hour. Increasingly bad by the day. This went on and on and on. And in the middle of it, Chang came up with the most brilliant idea of his life.

If ever there was a perfect time for him to escape, it was now. He would contact Rayford or Mac, anyone willing and able and available to come and get him. It had to be that the rest of the Tribulation Force—in fact, all of the sealed and marked believers in the world—had the same benefit he did.

Someone would be able to fly a jet and land it right there in New Babylon, and GC personnel would have to run for cover, having no idea who could do such a thing in the utter darkness. As long as no one spoke, they could not be identified. The Force could commandeer planes and weapons, whatever they wanted.

If anyone accosted them or challenged them, what better advantage could the Trib Force have than that they could see? They would have the drop on everyone and everybody. With but a year to go until the Glorious Appearing, Chang thought, the good guys finally had even a better deal than they had when the daylight hours belonged solely to them.

Now, for as long as God tarried, for as long as he saw fit to keep the shades pulled down and the lights off, everything was in the believers' favor.

"God," Chang said, "just give me a couple more days of this."

ARMAGEDDON

To the memory of A. W. Tozer, who pursued God

Special thanks to David Allen for
expert technical consultation

1

FOR THE FIRST time since takeoff, Rayford Steele had second thoughts about his and Abdullah Smith's passenger. "We shouldn't have brought her, Smitty," he said. He stole a glance at Abdullah behind the controls.

The Jordanian shook his head. "That's on you, Captain, I am sorry to say. I tried to tell you how important she was to Petra."

The darkness enveloping only New Babylon, but visible from more than a hundred miles, was unlike anything Rayford had ever seen. By the time Abdullah initiated the descent of the Gulfstream IX toward Iraq, the clock read 1200 hours, Palace Time.

Normally the magnificent structures of the new world capital gleamed stunningly in the noonday sun. Now a stark and isolated column of blackness rose from New Babylon's expansive borders into the cloudless heavens as high as the eye could see.

Chang Wong was Rayford's mole inside the palace. Trusting the young man's assurances that they would be able to see where others could not, Rayford traded glances with Abdullah as he guided the craft into the dark from the whiteness reflecting off the desert sand. Abdullah flipped on his landing lights.

Rayford squinted. "Do we need an ILS approach?"

"Instrument landing system?" Abdullah said. "Don't think so, Captain. I can see enough to fly."

Rayford compared the freakish darkness to the beautiful day they had left in Petra. He peeked over his shoulder at the young woman, whom he expected to look afraid. She didn't. "We can still turn back," he said. "Your father looked reluctant when we boarded."

"That was probably for your benefit," Naomi Tiberias said. "He knows I'll be fine."

The teenage computer whiz's humor and self-confidence were legendary. She seemed shy and self-conscious around adults until she got to know them; then she interacted like a peer. Rayford knew she had brought Abdullah up to speed in computer savvy, and she had been in nearly constant touch with Chang since the lights went out in New Babylon.

"Why is it dark only here?" Naomi said. "It's so strange."

"I don't know," Rayford said. "The prophecy says it affects 'the throne of the beast, and his kingdom became full of darkness.' That's all we know."

Rayford's every visit to Petra had found Naomi growing in influence and responsibility among the Remnant. She had emerged early as a technological prodigy, and as she taught others, Naomi had become the de facto head of the vast computer center. Quickly rising from go-to person to the one in charge, she'd finally become the teacher who taught teachers.

The center that had been designed by Chang's predecessor, the late David Hassid, was now the hub that kept Petra in touch with more than a billion souls every day. Thousands of computers allowed that many mentors to keep up with Tsion Ben-Judah's universal cyberaudience. Naomi personally coordinated the contact between Chang in New Babylon and the Tribulation Force around the world.

Having her join the flight to rescue him from New Babylon had been Chang's idea. Rayford had initially rejected it. He had enough trouble assigning himself the task of traveling more than seventy-five hundred miles from San Diego to Petra, then having Abdullah fly him the last five hundred miles to New Babylon. Combat-trained George Sebastian was better suited, but Rayford thought the big man had been through enough for a while. There was plenty for him to do in San Diego, and anyway, Rayford wanted to save George for what Dr. Ben-Judah called the "battle of that great day of God Almighty," now less than a year off.

Mac McCullum and Albie, stationed in Al Basrah—little more than two hundred miles south of New Babylon—stood ready. But Rayford had other things in mind for them.

Rayford's son-in-law and daughter, Buck and Chloe Williams, both wanted in on the extraction of Chang from the enemy lair—no surprise—but Rayford was convinced Buck would soon be more valuable in Israel. As for Chloe, the International Commodity Co-op always suffered when she was away. And somebody had to be there for little Kenny.

"Store and grab all the equipment you need while I'm en route, Chang," Rayford had said, the phone tucked between his shoulder and ear as he packed. "Smitty and I will come get you in a couple of days."

Chang had explained that the job was too big and that he and Naomi working together could get him out of there that much faster. "I don't want to miss a thing. She can help. I want to be able to monitor this place from anywhere."

"Don't worry," Rayford said. "You'll get to see her face-to-face soon enough."

"I don't know what you're talking about."

"Her father is one of the Petra elders, you know."

"So?"

"Only the two of them are left in the family. He's very protective."

"We both have too much work to do."

"Uh-huh."

"I'm not kidding, Captain Steele. Please bring her along. It's not like I haven't seen her on-screen already."

"So, what do you think?"

"I told you. We have a lot of work to do."

✣ ✣ ✣

Rayford felt a tug on the back of his copilot's chair as Naomi pulled herself forward. "Can Mr. Smith see to land?"

"Not sure yet," Rayford said. "It's as if someone painted our windows brown. See if you can raise our boy."

Chang was to be sure the New Babylon runways were clear, but he couldn't talk by phone from there for fear someone would overhear. Naomi pulled a small, thin computer from an aluminum box and attacked the keys.

"Avoid runways 3 left and 3 right," she said. "And he wants to know which you choose so he can be there to meet us."

Rayford glanced at Abdullah. "He's serious, Naomi?"

She nodded.

"Tell him the tower is closed, and it's not like we were going to announce our arrival anyway. We can't see which runway is which from up here, so he's going to have to give us coordinates and—"

"Hold on," Naomi said, keyboarding again. "He's attached everything you need." She passed the machine to Rayford and pointed at the attachment. "It is voice activated. Just tell it what you want."

"It'll recognize my voice?" Rayford said, studying the screen.

"Yes," the computer intoned.

Naomi chuckled.

"Attachment, please," Rayford said.

A detailed grid appeared with an aerial view of the New Babylon airfield.

"I'll set the coordinates for you, Smitty," Rayford said, reaching to program the flight management system.

"This thing will do everything but cook a meal for you, Captain Steele," Naomi said. "You have an infrared port?"

"I assume. Do we, Smitty?"

Abdullah pointed to a spot on the control panel.

"Here," Naomi said. "Let me." She leaned over Rayford's shoulder and pointed the back of the computer at the port. "Ready to land, Captain?" she said.

"Roger."

"Initiate landing sequence," she said and hit a button.

"Runway choice?" the computer asked.

Naomi looked at Rayford, who looked to Abdullah. "Does that thing recognize even my accent?" the Jordanian said.

"Yes," the computer said. "Congestion on runways 3 left and 3 right. Please select from runways 11 or 16."

"Eleven," Abdullah said.

"Left or right?" the computer said.

"Left," Abdullah said. "Why not?"

Abdullah engaged the left autopilot and lifted his hands from the controls. "Thank you," he said.

"You're welcome," the computer said.

Six minutes later the Gulfstream touched down.

+ + +

At just after one o'clock in the morning in San Diego, Buck bolted upright in bed.

Chloe stirred. "Go back to sleep, hon," she said. "You stood watch three straight nights. Not tonight."

He held up a hand.

"You need your sleep, Buck."

"Thought I heard something."

The tiny walkie-talkie on the nightstand chirped. Sebastian's telltale code. Buck grabbed it. "Yeah, George."

"Motion detector," Sebastian whispered.

Now Chloe sat up too.

"I'll check the periscope," Buck said.

"Carefully," Sebastian said. "Don't raise or rotate it."

"Roger. Anybody else aware?"

"Negative."

"On it."

Chloe was already out of bed and had pulled on a sweatshirt. She unlocked a cabinet, removed two Uzis, and tossed one to Buck as he headed for the periscope next to Kenny's tiny chamber. He set the weapon on the floor, dropped the walkie-talkie into his pajama pocket, and bent to peer into the viewer. As his eyes adjusted to the darkness he was aware of Chloe opening and closing

Kenny's door. Going on four years old, Kenny slept longer but less soundly than he used to.

"He out?" Buck said, eyes still glued to the scope.

"Dead to the world," Chloe said, draping a sweater around Buck's shoulders. "As you should be."

"Wish I was," Buck said.

"I should think so." She rested her palms on his shoulders. "What do you see?"

"Nothing. George doesn't think I ought to rotate the scope. It's facing west at ground level. I'd love to elevate it about six inches and let it give me a three-sixty."

"He's right, babe," she said. "You know it's got that whine when it moves. Anybody out there could hear it."

"I don't think anybody is out there," Buck said, pulling away and rubbing his eyes.

She sighed. "Want a chair?"

He nodded and returned to the periscope. "Could have been an animal. Maybe the wind."

Chloe pressed a chair behind his knees and guided him into it. "That's why you should just let me—"

"Oh no," he said.

"What?"

He put a finger to his lips and pulled out the walkie-talkie. "George," he whispered. "Six, seven, eight, nine. Nine uniformed, armed GC directly above to the west."

"Doing?"

"Not much. Kicking at the vents. They look bored. Maybe something caught their eye on the way by."

"Vehicles?"

"I'd have to raise or rotate."

"Negative. Any more?"

"Can't tell from this angle. No more coming past. Only three left in sight now."

"Listen for engines."

Buck sat silent a moment. Then, "Yeah, there's one. And another."

"I hear 'em," George said. "Must be leaving. Can I come over?"

"Tell him no," Chloe whispered.

\+ \+ \+

What palace personnel Rayford could make out in the eerie sepia-toned landscape through the cockpit window appeared to be in agony. Chang had told him that the people writhed and moaned, but a jet screaming onto the runway also clearly terrified them. They had to think it was about to crash, as some had on runways 3 left and 3 right.

It was as if the people had given up trying to see. Anyone near the Gulfstream IX had stumbled in the darkness to get away from it, and now they huddled here and there.

"That has to be Chang," Rayford said, pointing to a slight Asian hurrying toward them and gesturing wildly to open the door.

"Let me get that, Miss Naomi," Abdullah said, unstrapping himself and climbing past her. As he pushed the door open and lowered the steps, Rayford saw Chang turn to a small group of men and women in dark jumpsuits feeling their way along behind him.

"Keep your distance!" he shouted. "Danger! Hot engines! Leaking fuel!"

They turned and hurried away in all directions. "How did it land?" someone shouted.

"It's a miracle," another said.

"Did you all remember rubber-soled shoes?" Chang said, reaching to help them off the plane.

"Nice to meet you too, Mr. Wong," Abdullah said.

Chang shushed him. "They're blind," he whispered. "Not deaf."

"Chang," Rayford began, but the boy was shyly greeting Naomi. "All right, you two, get acquainted back at the ranch. Let's do what we have to and get out of here."

+ + +

"Should I change?" Buck said when he saw Sebastian in fatigues.

"Nah. I always wear these on watch. Let me have a look." He peered through the periscope. "Nothing. Want to raise and rotate it, Buck?"

"Be my guest."

"Clear. False alarm."

Chloe snorted. "Don't be saying that to put me at ease. At least nine GC were out there, and for all we know there were more, and they'll be back."

"Hey," Sebastian said, "why not assume the best and not the worst?"

"Maybe I am," she said. "Priscilla and Beth Ann sleep through this?"

He nodded. "I might not even tell Priss, so I'd appreciate it—"

"If I didn't either? Makes sense, George. Let the little woman carry on, oblivious to the fact that it's time to move," said Chloe.

"Move?" Buck said. "I can't even imagine it."

"Then we sit here and wait till they find us, which they may already have?"

"Chloe, listen," Buck said. "I should have let you take a look at those guys. They weren't even suspicious. They were probably talking about how this used to be a military base. They weren't tense, weren't really looking. They just saw the vents and checked them out, that's all."

Chloe shook her head and slumped in a chair. "I hate living like this."

"Me too," Sebastian said. "But what're our options? GC found an enclave of people without the mark yesterday in what's left of LA. Executed more'n two dozen."

Chloe gasped. "Believers?"

"Don't think so. Usually they'll say if it's Judah-ites. I got the impression it was some militia holdouts, something like that."

"Those are the people we're trying to reach," Chloe said. "And here we all sit, unable to show our faces, raising babies who hardly ever see the sun. Isn't there somewhere in the middle of nowhere where the GC wouldn't even know we were around?"

"The next best thing is Petra," Buck said. "They know who's there, but they can't do a thing about it."

"That's starting to sound more attractive all the time. Anyway, what are we going to do about what just happened?"

Buck and Sebastian looked at each other.

"Come on, guys," Chloe said. "You think Priscilla doesn't know you're gone and isn't going to ask where you've been?"

"She knows I was on watch."

"But you don't come over here unless something's up."

"I'm hoping she slept through it."

Chloe stood and moved to Buck's lap. "Look, I'm not trying to be cantankerous. Buck, tell him."

"Chloe Steele Williams is not trying to be cantankerous," he announced.

"Good," Sebastian muttered. "Coulda fooled me."

Chloe shook her head. "George, please. You know I think you're one of the best things that's ever happened to the Trib Force. You bring gifts nobody else has, and you've kept us from disaster more than once. But everyone living here deserves to know what you guys saw tonight. Not telling people, pretending it didn't happen, isn't going to change that we came this close to being found out."

"But we didn't, Chloe," Sebastian said. "Why stir up everybody?"

"We're already stirred up! I'm with these wives and kids all day. Even without bands of GC nosing around right over our heads in the middle of the night, we live like prairie dogs. The kids get fresh air only if they happen to wake up before the sun and someone herds them out the vehicle bay door. You guys have to sneak around and drive thirty miles, hoping you're not followed, to get to your planes. All I'm saying is that if we're going to have to defend ourselves, we have a right to be prepared."

+ + +

Rayford would have to ask Tsion about this one. What was it about the darkness that was so oppressive it left victims in agony? He had heard of disaster scenes—train wrecks, earthquakes, battles—where what haunted the rescue workers for years had been the shrieks and moans of the injured. As he and Abdullah and the two young people tiptoed across the massive runways, around heavy equipment and between writhing personnel, it was clear these people would rather be dead. And some had already died. Two crashed planes lay in pieces, still smoldering, many charred bodies still in their seats.

As he moved from the dead to the suffering, Rayford was overcome. The wailing pierced him and he slowed, desperate to help. But what could he do?

"Oh! Someone!" It was the shriek of a middle-aged woman. "Anyone, please! Help me!"

Rayford stopped and stared. She lay on her side on the tarmac near the terminal. Others shushed her. A man cried out, "We are all lost and blind, woman! You don't need more help than we do!"

"I'm starving!" she whined. "Does anyone have anything?"

"We're all starving! Shut up!"

"I don't want to die."

"I do!"

"Where is the potentate? He will save us!"

"When was the last time you saw the potentate? He has his own concerns."

Rayford was unable to pull away. He looked ahead, but even he had but twenty feet of visibility, and he had lost the others. Here came Abdullah. "I dare not call you by name, Captain, but you must come."

"Comrade, I cannot."

"Can you make it back to the plane?"

"Yes."

"Then we will meet you there."

Abdullah was off again, but their muffled conversation had caused a lull in the cacophony of agony. Now someone called out, "Who is that?"

"Where is he going?"

"Who has a plane?"

"Can you see?"

"What can you see?"

The woman again: "Oh, God, save me. Now I lay me down to sleep—"

"Shut up over there!"

"God is great; God is good. Now I thank him—"

"Put a sock in it! If you can't produce light, shut your mouth!"

"God! Oh, God! Save me!"

Rayford knelt and touched the woman's shoulder. She wrenched away with a squeal. "Wait!" he said, reaching for her again.

"Oh! The pain!"

"I don't mean to hurt you," he said quietly.

"Who are you?" she groaned, and he saw the United European States' number *6* tattooed on her forehead. "An angel?"

"No."

"I prayed for an angel."

"You prayed?"

"Promise you'll tell no one, sir. I'm begging you."

"You prayed to God?"

"Yes!"

"But you bear Carpathia's mark."

"I despise that mark! I know the truth. I always have. I just didn't want to have anything to do with it."

"God loved you."

"I know, but it's too late."

"Why didn't you ask his forgiveness and accept his gift? He wanted to save you."

She sobbed. "How can you be here and say that?"

"I am not from here."

"You are my angel!"

"No, but I am a believer."

"And you can see?"

"Enough to get around."

"Oh, sir, take me to food! Get me inside the terminal to the snack machines. Please!"

Rayford tried to help her up, but she reacted as if her body were afire. "Please, don't touch me!"

"I'm sorry."

"Just let me hold your sleeve. Can you see the terminal?"

"Barely," he said. "I can get you there."

"Please, sir." She struggled to her feet and gingerly clasped the cuff of his sleeve between her thumb and forefinger. "Slowly, please." She mince-stepped behind Rayford. "How far?" she said.

"Not a hundred yards."

"I don't know if I can make it," she said, tears streaming.

"Let me go get you something," he said. "What would you like?"

"Anything," she said. "A sandwich, candy, water—anything."

"Wait right here."

She chuckled pitifully. "Sir, all I see is black. I could go nowhere."

"I'll be right back. I'll find you."

"I've been praying that God will save my soul. And when he does, I will be able to see." Rayford didn't know what to say. She had said herself it was too late. "In the beginning," she said. "For God so loved the world. The Lord is my shepherd. Oh, God . . ."

Rayford jogged toward the terminal, stepping between ailing people. He wanted to help them all, but he knew he could not. A man lay across the inside of the automatic door, not moving. Rayford stepped close enough to trip the electric eye, and the door opened a few inches and bumped the man.

"Please move away from the door," Rayford said.

The man was asleep or dead.

Rayford pushed harder, but the door barely budged. Finally he lowered his shoulder and put his weight behind it. He bent and drove with his legs, feeling the pressure on his quads as the door slowly rolled the man away. Rayford heard him groan.

Inside, Rayford found a bank of vending machines, but as he reached in his pocket for Nick coins, he saw that the machines had been trashed. Enough people had felt their way here to tear the machines open and loot them for every last vestige of food. Rayford searched and searched for something, anything, they had missed. All he found were empty bottles and cans and wrappers.

"Who goes there?" someone demanded. "Where are you going? Can you see? Is there light anywhere? What has happened? Are we all going to die? Where is the potentate?"

Rayford hurried back outside. "Where're you going?" someone shouted. "Take me with you!"

He found the woman on her stomach, face buried in her arms. She was wracked with sobs so deep and mournful he could barely stand to watch.

"I'm back, ma'am," he said quietly. "No food. I'm sorry."

"Oh, God, oh, God and Jesus, help me!"

"Ma'am," he said, reaching for her. She shrieked when he touched her, but he pulled at the sides of her head until he could see her hollow, unseeing, terrified eyes.

"I knew before everybody disappeared," she said pitifully. "And then I knew for sure. With every plague and judgment, I shook my fist in God's face. He tried to reach me, but I had my own life. I wasn't going to be subservient to anybody.

"But I've always been afraid of the dark, and my worst nightmare is starving. I've changed my mind, want to take it all back. . . ."

"But you can't."

"I can't! I can't! I waited too long!"

Rayford knew the prophecy—that people would reject God enough times that God would harden their hearts and they wouldn't be able to choose him even if they wanted to. But knowing it didn't mean Rayford understood it. And it certainly didn't mean he had to like it. He couldn't make it compute with the God he knew, the loving and merciful one who seemed to look for ways to welcome everyone into heaven, not keep them out.

Rayford stood and felt the blood rush from his head. And that's when he heard the loudspeakers.

"This is your potentate!" came the booming voice. "Be of good cheer. Have no fear. Your torment is nearly past. Follow the sound of my voice to the nearest loudspeaker tower. Food and water will be delivered there, along with further instructions."

+ + +

"I'll make a deal with you," Chloe said. "I'll take over the rest of the watch, and you agree that we tell everybody in the morning that we had visitors tonight."

Buck looked to George, who pointed at him. "You're in charge when your father-in-law is away, pal."

"Only because of seniority. I defer to you on military stuff."

"This isn't combat, man. It's public relations. If you want my advice, I'd say do what you want but do it right. Tell them, 'It's only fair we tell you people we saw GC around here last night, but as far as we know there's nothing to be concerned about yet.'"

"Fair enough, Chlo'?" Buck said.

She nodded. "I'd rather pray and pass the ammunition, but yes. Treat everybody like adults and you'll get the best out of them."

"If you're really taking watch, Chloe," Sebastian said, "I'm going home and turning off my walkie-talkie."

"Deal."

2

WHOEVER HAD FIGURED out how to rally the panicked souls in New Babylon thought playing music over the sound system would draw them to the loudspeaker towers.

So while Nicolae Carpathia's right-hand man, Leon Fortunato, spoke soothingly—"Tread carefully, loyal subjects. Help one another. Avoid danger."—a recorded version of "Hail Carpathia," sung by the 500-voice Carpathianism Chorale, played in the background:

Hail Carpathia, our lord and risen king;
Hail Carpathia, rules o'er everything.
We'll worship him until we die;
He's our beloved Nicolae.
Hail Carpathia, our lord and risen king.

+ + +

Rayford hated that song and the infernal penchant of the Global Community Broadcasting System to play it over the radio at least every two hours. Carpathia insisted upon its performance at his every public appearance. The staged parades and rallies in his honor always began and ended with it.

Something strange was happening here, though. While the people seemed to rouse and slowly, agonizingly move toward the sound, no one sang along.

"Remember," Fortunato intoned, his words pinched when he grimaced from his own pain, "those of us servicing you, bringing you water and food, are also following the sound to the right places. Please be patient and allow pushcarts to pass. There is plenty for everyone if we all work together. Now, sing along with the chorale. This takes the place of your worshiping our supreme potentate's image, currently not visible."

The people around Rayford were not encouraged. "I'm not singing," one said. "Death to the potentate!"

"Watch your mouth," another said. "You'll get yourself killed."

"Carpathia can't see any more than we can! He doesn't know who's talking."

"He's no mere mortal. I wouldn't be tempting fate."

"What has he done for *you* lately?"

Personnel inside the palace had a better time of it, Rayford assumed. They could at least feel their way to familiar places, including showers, beds, and refrigerators. Many outside couldn't even find their way back in. Rayford could only imagine the disorientation of zero light anywhere. It was frustrating enough to have been granted even diminished vision.

"There are twelve separate loudspeaker towers," Fortunato said, the music mercifully subdued as he spoke. "When supplies have arrived, please be as orderly as possible. State your name so our personnel can record it on audiodisc, and take your ration of food and water."

"We want answers too!" someone shouted as if Fortunato could hear. "What is this? How long will it last? Why does it hurt?"

+ + +

Chloe knew what Ming Toy's response to this new danger would be in the morning. She and Ree Woo would want to marry right away. Everyone but Chloe had been trying to talk them out of it, but Ming had it all planned. She wanted Tsion Ben-Judah to officiate from Petra via video cam. "I know it's a lot to ask of such an important and busy man," she confided to Chloe. "But I have designed the ceremony to last just a few minutes."

"I think he'd do it," Chloe had told her. "I would if I were him."

The same people who urged Ming and Ree not to marry, given where things stood on the prophetic calendar, were the ones who had advised against Chloe and Buck having a child during the Tribulation. But certain matters were private issues of the heart. Chloe couldn't imagine not having married Buck, despite knowing how little time they had. And she couldn't get her mind around the concept of life without their precious little one.

If Ming and Ree wanted a year of marriage before the Glorious Appearing, whose business was it but theirs? It wasn't as if they were unaware of the hardships. Starting a family at this stage was another thing, of course, but Chloe figured that was none of her business either, unless Ming asked.

It seemed Buck was asleep again in seconds. She assumed George was right about his wife sleeping through his leaving their quarters. Priscilla was one of the busiest people in the compound, always up before dawn and rarely fully healthy. She often appeared groggy soon after dinner and was usually in bed by nine.

Chloe was glad to stand watch, if for no other reason than to keep Buck from having to do it for the fourth night in a row. She enjoyed the routine—checking the motion detector, surveying the area with the periscope. Her daily job was hectic and demanding, spent almost entirely at the computer, contacting and coordinating suppliers and shippers of supplies and foodstuffs around the globe.

That was also her way of keeping up with the news, only the news kept getting worse. More and more of her contacts were being found out, caught by the GC in nighttime raids or at surprise checkpoints. As soon as it was discovered that these delivery people did not bear the mark of loyalty to Carpathia, they were executed.

One eyewitness reported that the Co-op driver of an eighteen-wheeler, laden with copies of Buck's *The Truth* magazine translated into Norwegian, refused to let his cargo fall into GC hands. Distracting checkpoint guards long enough for his backup driver to escape, he set the rig to roll out of control and plunge down a hundred-foot embankment into a deep fjord. Morale Monitors shot him to death.

Chloe also heard of dissidents around the world, Jews mostly, who, rather than being put to death, were transported to concentration camps where they were mercilessly tortured while purposely kept alive.

Occasional reports of miraculous interventions came, like an angel appearing at a guillotine site to warn the uncommitted of the consequences of choosing Carpathia's mark. Besides the fact that by now even the last-minute decision to take the mark was futile—tardy ones were put to death anyway—the angel had pleaded with the undecideds to choose Christ and be saved. And many did.

Chloe wrapped an afghan around her shoulders and moseyed to Kenny's room. His breathing was still deep and slow, and she draped another blanket over him. He did not stir.

Closing his door, she checked the motion detector, then sat before the periscope. With no evidence of anyone in the area, she could raise and rotate it for a full view. She rather liked having the contraption in the middle of her home. It satisfied some inner need to protect—control, Buck would have teased—her friends and loved ones, the more than two hundred who now lived underground in San Diego. All hoped to survive until the Glorious Appearing, but more than that, to also somehow make a difference from their claustrophobic warren.

A unique feature of the periscope was that the viewer did not have to move when it did. A simple control on the handgrips raised and lowered the contraption, as well as made it scan in a circle in either direction. Chloe didn't want to think about the series of mirrors required for that.

As she rested her forehead on the eyepiece and relaxed, letting her eyes adjust to the low light outside, she noticed that George Sebastian had left the scope at ground level and pointing west. The topside lens was camouflaged with fake shrubbery. It could be raised as much as five feet, but it was crucial to do a 360-degree scan at ground level first to be sure no one was in the vicinity who might notice.

The scan could be done all in one smooth motion at virtually any speed, but of course the San Diego Trib Force had learned that slower was better and easier on the eyes and equilibrium. Chloe's method of choice, however, was to move the mechanism one inch at a time. With each mash of a tiny red plunger on the left-hand grip, another one-inch turn of the lens brought a new 45-degree view; thus eight moves covered 360 degrees.

Seeing nothing due west, Chloe began her incremental scan to the right. It was just past three o'clock in the morning in California.

+ + +

Rayford had walked perhaps a quarter of a mile north from the terminal, easily slipping past men and women clearly younger than he but who shuffled along with the painful gait of the elderly.

"In our effort to keep you totally informed," Fortunato announced, "we bring some encouraging news. While it remains true that no light is being emitted in New Babylon, this puzzling phenomenon has not affected telephone or radio transmission. Our heating and cooling systems remain functional. Your stoves even work, unless they are solar powered. Electric and gas stoves will still burn and radiate heat, though you will not see it, so be extremely careful.

"Pilots flying from New Babylon or toward her when this darkness occurred report that it is confined to the city. As we do not know how long this will last, be assured that if you can follow a path that leads you beyond our borders, you will eventually reach light."

From all around, Rayford heard determination on the parts of the sufferers. "I'm going," one said.

"Me too. I don't know where or how, but I'm getting to the light somehow."

"Does anyone have a Braille compass? We'll wander in circles without one."

"Attention," Fortunato broke in again, "all senior command personnel are to meet in the potentate's office at 1500 hours."

Rayford studied his watch. *It's one fifteen. How are they going to pull that off by three in the afternoon?*

"Use audio clocks," Fortunato said. "It is now 1315 hours. At 1430 hours we shall turn off all loudspeakers except for the ones on the tower near the west entrance of the palace. Follow the sound there and you should be able to make your way to the meeting. Elevators are operational. The bottom right button is the top floor. Attendance is mandatory but limited to command-level personnel."

"I'm going anyway," someone said.

"So am I. Get to the bottom of this."

"Find out what the deal is."

"He's supposed to be god incarnate; why can't he do something?"

Rayford blinked, then blinked again. In the distance he thought he saw light. He was getting farther from the plane and from where Chang and Naomi and Abdullah were, but if worse came to worst, he could follow command personnel to the palace entrance at two thirty and find his people from there. For now, he had to investigate the light.

✣ ✣ ✣

Chloe was four clicks into her intermittent scan now, looking due east. As she studied the dark landscape she detected a pair of pinpricks of light. She held her breath as they became larger. Whatever they represented was drawing closer. Soon it became clear it was a car or truck. It rolled to within a block of the compound, stopped, and turned around. Now she saw only the red taillights. And there it sat. For ten minutes, then another five.

Chloe hurriedly scanned the rest of the way around. Nothing. One more click and she was back to the east section and the idle vehicle. No way she was going to wake Buck for this. It wasn't as if those in the compound expected no traffic outside. But there wasn't much else in the area, certainly nothing worth stopping for at this time of the night.

Chloe wished the periscope had a telescope feature so she could home in on the vehicle and see whether anyone was emerging. The compound's hidden vehicle bay, used only at night when they knew the area was clear, opened to the east. Dare she head that way for a closer look? An individual service door, hidden next to the big one, would allow her to peek out if she kept the inside lights off. She would be a hundred yards closer. And it wasn't like she was planning to actually venture outside.

Chloe pulled a black sweat suit with a hood from the closet and put it on over her pajamas and sweatshirt. Over thick woolen socks she laced high-top hiking boots. She took the Uzi but not the walkie-talkie. She didn't want any unintended transmission to give her away. And she did not intend to get herself into a situation where she'd need to call for help. The Uzi was just for peace of mind. So was the prayer: "Lord, help me or forgive me, one of the two."

Chloe quietly opened Kenny's door yet again. He hadn't moved. She felt his cheek. Moist with sleep but comfortably warm. She kissed his forehead. Cool and soft.

Shutting his door, she made her way to where Buck slept and planted a knee on the mattress next to his midsection. She leaned to kiss him, holding his head. If he were anything but sound asleep, that would have roused him. In the darkness Chloe was struck by the contrast between her dark clothing and her skin, which hardly ever saw the sun.

She found gloves and a ski mask, and by the time she was in the corridor that led past other underground quarters to the vehicle bay, Chloe was sweating. Their place was in the center of the complex, and four wings led to everyone else's places. She crept past the Sebastians', three other families' places, a bank of single men's residences—including Ree Woo's and her own father's—two more family places, then a mixture of family and single quarters, including Ming's.

Everybody knew Big George was on watch tonight and that Buck Williams, in charge when Rayford was gone, was first alternate. That must have been why everyone seemed to be sleeping so soundly.

\+ \+ \+

Rayford broke away from the tentative crowd and headed toward the light. Was it his imagination? Past twenty feet all was foggy anyway, and no one near him seemed able to see anything, let alone what he saw. The closer he got, the more the light appeared to be the silhouette of a person, but he saw nothing else and guessed it was still fifty yards away. When he had worked at the palace and lived nearby, the garages and motor pool had been in that area.

Had someone figured a way to produce light? Rayford had passed through small groups of limping people, and now it appeared nothing stood between him and this . . . this what? Apparition? It looked merely bright from a distance, but soon the color became more distinct. First red, then yellowish, and finally, a deep burnt orange. Yes, clearly a person, specifically a man, tall and lithe. And moving.

Others were within a few feet of the man, using his light to work on vehicles. They seemed in pain like everyone else, but they worked with dispatch, as if invigorated by the light. The glowing man appeared to be able to see as far as he radiated, about three feet. Anyone who needed light had to be that close to him.

Rayford realized it was Carpathia. Dr. Ben-Judah had often taught that this same person came first as a lying snake, then as a roaring lion, and finally as an angel of light. Rayford had to stifle a chuckle. The devil in Nicolae surely wished he could emit more than this pathetic glow that allowed him to identify only those within a few feet of him.

Rayford moved until he was among a small crowd just outside the circle of mechanics trying to ready several vehicles for some purpose he did not yet understand.

"All systems are functional?" Carpathia said.

"Yes, Potentate. The Jeep is operational."

"Turn on the lights."

The mechanic did. "You can hear the drain on the electrical system, so juice is flowing, Excellency, but as you can see—"

"As we can all see or not," Carpathia said, "no lights. Well, if I must, I will walk ahead of the convoy until we pass through the darkness on the way to Al Hillah. I do not care how long it takes."

What kind of a strategy was this? The brass will meet in Carpathia's office, and then he will lead them to Al Hillah? For what? And what about the thousands remaining in New Babylon? Wouldn't they want to follow, to find relief?

"What's in Al Hillah?" Rayford said.

"Who is asking?" Carpathia said. "And why do you not address me with a title of honor?"

Nicolae was looking in Rayford's direction, but it was obvious he could see no farther than anyone else within range of his hellish aura. As Nicolae moved forward, Rayford moved back and to his left, then circled around behind Carpathia.

"Yeah," Rayford said in a slightly different tone. "What is in Al Hillah, O Great One?"

Nicolae whirled around, and Rayford slipped away again. "I was speaking to the original questioner! Who is asking?"

"Perhaps he fled in fear," Rayford said with a gravelly voice, "Excellency."

This could be fun.

+ + +

Chloe had known the long passageway to the vehicle bay to be cold and damp most of the time, and perhaps it was now. But in her getup and in her state of mind, moving quickly up the incline past the vehicles and toward where the doors opened to ground level, she had grown uncomfortably warm. She removed her gloves and ski mask, chiding herself for having them on before she needed them anyway. Chloe lowered the zipper on the sweatshirt, then squatted to cool down and catch her breath with her back against the dirt wall between the bay door and the service door.

Being that close to the surface and the outside gave Chloe a delicious feeling of freedom. *Less than a year to real freedom.*

Her knees soon burned, so she slid to the earthen floor and straightened her legs. Setting her weapon aside, she reached for the toes of her boots, alternately stretching her right and left sides. Despite her many serious injuries, she was proud that her duties in Greece had proved she was still in remarkable shape. She zipped her sweatshirt to her neck, pulled the ski mask over her face, raised the hood over that, tugged on her gloves, put the strap of the Uzi over her head so the weapon rested on her right hip and in her right hand, then stood and turned to the service door.

There could be no slight opening of the bay door. That was an all or nothing deal. The glued-on sand and dirt and greenery moved as one, and the thing was either fully open or shut. But the service door, though camouflaged the same way, she could open as slowly and slightly as she wanted. She flipped off the light and gripped the doorknob.

+ + +

Rayford hurried toward the palace. He wanted to check on the others and tell them of his plan. He had experienced more bizarre events in six years than he ever could have imagined, and while many had been bigger and louder and wilder, this was unique. These poor people! Yes, they had made their choices, and yes, they had had their opportunities to turn to God. But what a price!

They were in agony. Everywhere he went, more and more people came into the twenty-foot limit of his visibility. Many were dead. More sat rocking or lay weeping. All had given up looking for ways to see anything but a blackness so thick it disoriented them. Those who tried to follow the music or Fortunato's voice limped or shuffled with arms extended to the front or sides, tipping one way and then the other as if drunk or dizzy. They ran into each other, into buildings, tripped over debris, and many simply seemed to run out of gas, slowing, stopping, and tumbling. Rayford wished he could help, but there was nothing he could do.

On his way to Chang's quarters, Rayford came up with an idea and changed course. He stayed on the elevator and reached the top floor of the palace. There he tiptoed past several executives and their aides, who talked on phones or sat before computers, trying to dictate but unable to see whether their messages were getting through.

The phone calls all had the same theme and tone.

Carpathia had a new assistant since the time when Rayford had worked with him. Chang had told him her name. He assumed she was the one on the phone at the desk outside Carpathia's new office. Rayford noticed her double take when she heard him sit on a couch across from her area, but he said nothing and she continued her conversation.

"I don't know," she said with a whine. "He wants me to try to carry on as if I am not suffering like all the others. But I am, Mom. There are little things I can do when he is in here, because he emits this glow of some sort and I can at least find a few things. But he's called a meeting of the brass and they're planning some sort of a pilgrimage. . . . No, I don't get to go, and I don't want to. He's not even telling the rank and file that their bosses are leaving.

"Ooh! Ouch . . . oh, I don't know how to describe it. Cramps, I guess. A headache like nothing I've ever had, and I've had some doozies. . . ."

She sounded American, but her back was to Rayford and he could not see the number on her forehead or hand.

"And it feels as if I'm carrying a huge weight on my shoulders, pressing on my spine. My hips hurt, my knees, ankles, feet. Like your arthritis, I suppose. But, Mom, I'm thirty-six years old. I feel like I'm seventy-five. . . . Yes, I'm eating. I feel my way back to my apartment and I can manage, but when I lie down, I want to sleep for a hundred years. But I can't. . . . Well, because of the pain! No position relieves it. It's like this darkness itself is pushing on me and causing all this, and it's the same for everybody."

Rayford shifted his weight and the woman froze. "Hold a minute, Mom." She turned and Rayford saw the *–6* on her forehead, confirming his guess. The United North American States. "Is someone there? May I help you?"

He was tempted to tell her he had some questions about the meeting but that he would wait until she was off the phone. But he knew she knew who was left on the decimated senior staff, and she would not recognize his voice. He wished he could speak soothingly to her, to say something Jesus would say. But she was beyond help now. Rayford had never felt so hog-tied.

"Sorry, Mom," she said. "Now I'm hearing things. I'd better get off. This meeting's coming up, and I don't even know what he's going to want. No one will be able to read anything unless they hold it up to his light, and there are twenty expected. . . . Yes, twenty. . . . I know. . . . Yeah, we're down from thirty-six. Imagine.

"Exciting? No. Not for a long time. He is not the man I thought he was. . . . Oh, in every way. Mean, cruel, vicious, egotistical, selfish. I swear, I'd need a thesaurus. . . . Well, I can't! . . . No! Of course I can't! Where would I go? What would I do? He knows what I know, and he wouldn't be able to let me out of his control. . . . No, now I just have to live with it. . . . I don't know, Mom. It can't end well. I don't care anymore. Death will be a relief. . . . Well, I'm sorry, but I mean it. . . . Now don't, Mom. I'm not planning anything rash. . . . I know you have. We all have. All but Uncle Gregory, I guess. He's still holding out, is he? . . . How does he live? You know what happens if he's found out. . . . No, don't tell me. I don't want to know. That way if somebody asks, I'll be able to tell them I don't know. Just tell him I'm proud of him and keep it up, but be careful. You and Dad be careful too. If you're caught aiding him in any way . . ."

Rayford heard footsteps in the hall, and it was clear she did too. "Gotta go, Mom. Stay well."

She hung up and turned when the door swung open. A big, bony man of about fifty looked wide-eyed at Rayford and his mouth fell open. He pointed at Rayford's forehead, and Rayford noticed the mark of the believer on him too.

"May I help you?" Carpathia's assistant said. "Who is it?"

Rayford held a finger to his lips and pointed down the hall. He mouthed, "Five minutes," and the man shut the door and ran off.

The woman shrugged. "Thanks for dropping by," she muttered, "whoever you were."

"Whoever it was has left," Rayford said.

She jumped. "And how long have you been here?"

"Long enough to know about Uncle Gregory."

"I'm so stupid! I don't know you, do I?"

"No."

"You're not senior staff."

"I'm not."

"Is anyone with you?"

"No, Krystall."

"How do you know my name?"

"I can help your uncle."

"Tell a soul, I'll deny every word."

"Don't you want him helped?"

"You're trying to trap me."

"I'm not. If I was GC, I would not be able to see, would I?"

"You can't see."

"I can. And I can prove it. Your colors don't match."

"You couldn't prove that by me, idiot. I can't see them either. I dress by sense of touch these days, like everybody else."

"My mistake. Hold up some fingers; I'll tell you how many. . . . Three, and your right hand is facing me, and the three fingers are your pinkie, ring, and middle."

"How do you know that?"

"You mean how can I see?"

"You can't see."

"Then how do I know you're showing me six fingers now, all five on your left and the index on your right, the backs of your hands toward me? I can see by your face you're starting to be convinced. You're hiding your hands under the desk now."

Krystall pressed her lips together and looked as if she was about to cry. Rayford stood.

"Stay where you are," she said, voice quavery, hands in her lap.

Rayford slipped around behind her. "That would be no fun," he said, and she jumped and spun in her chair. "Now I can see your hands again," he said. "They're balled in your lap, thumbs pointing."

"Okay, so you can see me. How?"

"Because this darkness is a curse from God, and I am one of his."

"Are you serious?"

"I can help your uncle, Krystall."

"How?"

"Were you implying he has not yet taken the mark?"

"What if I was?"

"Then it's not too late for him. Is he a believer in Christ?"

"I don't think so. I think he's just a rebel."

"A lucky one, if he acts quickly."

"If you think you're going to trick me into telling you where he's hiding, you're—"

"I don't need to know that. You'd be foolish to risk telling me, and anyway, didn't you tell your mother not to even tell you where he was?"

She didn't respond.

"If you really want to help him, tell him to log on to the Web site of Dr. Tsion Ben-Judah. Can you remember it if I spell it for you?"

"You think I don't know that name and how to spell it?"

"Sorry."

"It's from his Web site that I know it's too late for me and my parents, my whole family . . . who were so proud of me."

"I'm sorry, Krystall."

"You're sorry? How do you think I feel?"

"Ma'am, you're not going to tell anyone I was here, are you?"

"Why would I? They couldn't see you anyway, and what would they do? Feel around for you?"

"Good point."

"What are you doing here?"

"Business. The prospect of helping your uncle was just a bonus."

"Well, thanks for that. You're a Judah-ite, eh?"

"A believer in Christ, to be more precise."

"Tell me something then: what's the deal with it being too late for people who already took Carpathia's mark? We don't still have our own free will?"

Rayford felt his throat tighten. "Apparently not," he managed. "I don't quite understand it myself, but you have to admit, you had plenty of reasons to choose the other way."

"For years."

"You said it, Krystall."

"So the statute of limitations ran out on me when I made the big choice."

"Well, then for sure. Maybe even before that. Who knows the mind of God?"

"I'm starting to, sir."

"How's that?"

"This hurts. It hurts worse than the pain from the darkness. Just learned it too late, I guess, that you don't mess with God."

3

THE PROBLEM with the camouflaged service door open just a sliver was that it did not give Chloe the view she needed. While the door faced east, where the suspicious vehicle had stood idling just a block away last time she looked, the opening in the door gave her only a northeast view. The door would have to swing open to at least forty-five degrees to confirm that the car or truck or whatever it was was still there. Dare she risk the door catching a glint from a streetlamp or making a sound or triggering some portable motion detector the GC might have brought along?

Chloe allowed herself to wish that the vehicle brought good news rather than bad. Maybe it bore a band of other underground believers who had heard about the Trib Force contingent that had burrowed itself beneath a former military base. Wouldn't that be heaven, to discover more brothers and sisters who could come alongside to help, encourage, and defend? It was Chloe who had stumbled upon The Place in Chicago with its exciting band of self-taught believers. On the other hand, all that activity, their moving in with the Trib Force, was the first step in compromising the safe house. That many warm bodies moving about in an area the GC had believed was quarantined tipped them off and brought them sniffing. If Chloe was to take credit for the new friends, she had to accept the heat for the end of a great safe house.

She couldn't let that happen again. There were too many here, and though the place was under the earth, it had all the advantages the Strong Building had. For one thing, it had George Sebastian, who had expanded on what Chloe—and anyone else who was interested—had learned about combat training from Mac McCullum on their mission to Greece. The rickety exercise equipment George and Priscilla had salvaged from the military base was anything but state-of-the-art, but George thought that was an advantage.

"The newfangled machines do all the work for ya, anyway," he said. He had refurbished and lubricated what was available, and within six weeks several Trib Forcers had spent enough time in a makeshift workout room to start toning neglected muscles. That was just a prerequisite, of course. What Chloe enjoyed most was George's training. A lot of it was just common sense, but a lot of it wasn't.

He had been trained at the highest levels and proved to be an excellent teacher. Chloe felt she could handle herself and a weapon in almost any situation.

That training was what niggled at the back of her brain now and told her she was making a fundamental mistake. Not only was she away from her post, but no one would have a clue where she was. She had no way of communicating from a remote location. So if she was going to open the service door wide enough to see a potential enemy a block away or—for all she knew—standing directly in front of her, she had to make a decision. Was she opening the door quickly to step outside and shut it again, or was she going to keep a hand on the doorknob in case she needed to retreat fast?

She pressed her ear against the door to see if she could detect movement nearby, but her Uzi clattered against it, and her ear was covered by her sweatshirt hood and ski mask anyway. She pulled back, feeling like an idiot. *Deep breath. Calm down. Let's just step outside in one smooth motion and shut the door behind us.* Referring to herself in the collective *we* made her feel less alone, but she knew she was kidding herself.

Careful to take full, quiet strides, rolling heel to toe, Chloe pushed the door open, moved out, and shut it behind her. Was the vehicle still there? She'd have to wait a beat. If it was, its taillights were off. Chloe moved to a row of tall bushes that hid her from the east, then spun silently to be sure no enemy had flanked her from another direction. She paused for a moment to drink in the freedom of simply being out in the crisp wee-hour air.

As her eyes adjusted to the dim light provided only by streetlamps, Chloe peered through the shrubbery and saw the white GC personnel carrier parked where she had seen it from inside. Not only were its lights off, but it also didn't appear to be idling.

The question was whether it was empty, and if so, how many troops had it brought, and where were they?

+ + +

Rayford quickly tiptoed to the end of the corridor and found the big man rocking on the balls of his feet and wringing his hands. "English?" he said with a thick German accent.

"Yes. I'm an American."

"Brother, brother, brother!" the man whispered, grabbing Rayford in a fierce embrace. "Who are you? What is your name? What are you doing here?"

The man felt solid, as if he could have been a manual laborer. "I have the same questions for you, friend," Rayford said, extricating himself. "But let's make sure we won't be overheard."

"Good, good, yes. Where?"

"I have colleagues in private quarters here. You need to meet them. We can talk there."

"I'm not sure I can wait that long! This is so exciting. How far?"

"Six stories down and a wing the other way," Rayford said, leading him toward the elevator.

"You live here? In the palace, I mean? You work here?"

"Used to." Rayford looked around and then leaned close. "I'm with the underground in San Diego with connections in Petra. We're getting our mole out of here while we can."

"I was going to ask if *you* were the mole!"

"Used to be one of several. We are down to just this one, or at least that's what we thought. You're from here?"

"Not six miles away, can you believe it?"

At the bank of elevators three executives stood lightly touching each other and feeling for the buttons. Rayford and his new friend looked at each other knowingly and merely moved behind them into the first available elevator car.

"Got to be back up here on time," one executive said.

"Yes," another said. "Wish I had an audible watch."

"I took the crystal off mine. I'm learning to feel what time it is. Problem is, I keep snagging the hands on who knows what, and for all I know, I don't have the right time anymore myself." He pressed two fingers lightly on his watch. "I'm guessing 2:50. Gives us ten minutes."

Rayford noticed the German check his own watch and raise his eyebrows. The elevator stopped two floors down, and the three felt their way off. But as the doors were shutting, Rayford's companion reached out with both hands, tapped the timekeeper on a shoulder, and rubbed his thumb against the man's watch at the same time. The tap made him hesitate, which made the man behind him bump into him. He said, "Hm?" and the third man said, "What?"

The big man pulled his arms back in, in time for the doors to shut unimpeded, and when it was just he and Rayford on the elevator, he burst into laughter. "I think that was the last time he'll have the time right, you know? Now, may I introduce myself?"

"Not just yet," Rayford said. He mouthed, "Most of the elevators and corridors are bugged."

\+ + +

Foolhardy or brave? Chloe knew that was a matter of opinion and that she would likely hear from many who assumed the former. But she was desperately curious about that personnel carrier, and even more, about the personnel. Keeping to the tree line and away from streetlamps, she circled left and headed a block west, moving silently in the night as she had been taught.

She slowed as she came even with the vehicle from about thirty yards to the left of it, chastising herself for not bringing binoculars. And the walkie-talkie. She could have left it off until she needed it, avoiding an inopportune transmission while still having the ability to communicate with Buck or anyone else in a pinch.

So far though, no pinch. Chloe moved closer, telling herself that if anyone sat in the truck the engine would be running or one or more windows would be open. None of that was so, but she didn't want to think she could simply advance past it without knowing for sure. First turning in a slow circle to be sure no one was approaching or that she had not missed anyone, Chloe finally reached the truck and peered in the back windows. No one.

But from there she could not tell if anyone was in the front seat. If anyone was waiting, he or she would most likely be behind the wheel. She approached from the other side, staying below the window level until she could stand quickly and take her prey by surprise, if necessary.

+ + +

Rayford was stunned by the increased number of ailing residents who filled the halls as he and his new buddy left the elevator and headed toward Chang's quarters. Couples huddled in corners, weeping. Others crawled, feeling their way to various rooms, pulling themselves up by door handles and running their fingers across numbers before knocking, pleading with friends to be let in.

"This breaks my heart," he whispered to the German.

"Not mine," the man said, "but I'm working on it."

Rayford knocked lightly on Chang's door and heard the conversation inside die. "It's me," he said, just above a whisper. "And don't be alarmed. I have someone with me."

Abdullah opened the door just wide enough to accommodate one eye and the barrel of a .45-caliber Glock. That eye, satisfied with seeing Rayford, surveyed the German side to side and head to toe. Apparently noticing the mark of the believer on the man's forehead, Abdullah swung the door open.

Once inside, it seemed the man couldn't be still. After looking at everyone and the computers and stacks of miniature disks, he said, "I can talk? We are okay here?"

Chang nodded and, though he seemed overwhelmed by the man's effusiveness, he and Naomi kept working.

"Otto Weser is my name," he said. "German timberman, Judah-ite, head of a small band of believers right here in New Babylon."

He embraced Abdullah. "Watch that sidearm now, would you?" Otto said, laughing. He nearly lifted Chang off the floor. "Look at us! You are Asian. Our turbaned friend is, what, Egyptian?" Abdullah corrected him. "Ah, Jordanian. I was close. I am German. Mr. Steele, your name is Western and you told me you were American, but your appearance is Egyptian also."

"A disguise."

"And the young lady, you are Middle Eastern too, are you not? Of course you are. I will not hug you without the permission of your father."

Otto pointed first to Rayford, who shook his head, and then to Abdullah, who looked insulted. "Oh, you are old enough even if she is not yours." He turned to Chang. "I know she does not belong to you, unless by marriage."

Naomi approached him, arms spread. "My father is not here, but if the permission is mine to give, you have it."

"Ah, I love the young ones who appreciate the old movies."

When he had learned everyone's name, Otto said, "I will be brief. I know you are on a mission and you must go. I did not know if I would find any brothers or sisters inside the palace, but I am so glad I did. My friends and I, we consider ourselves fulfillments of prophecy. Do you want to know why? We were holed up in Germany, hiding mostly but fighting the GC when we could, and God—who else?—led me to Revelation 18. It dumbfounded me; what else can I say? You know the passage. I have it memorized.

"I'm no scholar, no student, no theologian, but I try to stay a step ahead of my people so I can teach them a little. Well, Revelation 18 talks about the coming destruction of this city, this one right here. Beginning at the fourth verse it says, 'I heard another voice from heaven saying, "Come out of her, my people, lest you share in her sins, and lest you receive of her plagues. For her sins have reached to heaven, and God has remembered her iniquities. Render to her just as she rendered to you, and repay her double according to her works; in the cup which she has mixed, mix double for her. In the measure that she glorified herself and lived luxuriously, in the same measure give her torment and sorrow; for she says in her heart, 'I sit as queen, and am no widow, and will not see sorrow.' Therefore her plagues will come in one day—death and mourning and famine. And she will be utterly burned with fire, for strong is the Lord God who judges her."'

"Well, you could have knocked me over. 'Come out of her, my people'? What were we to make of that except the obvious? People of God—at least some—were going to be here until just before this happens! Who were they? I could not imagine believers being here, and if they were, not for long. How could they be? If the GC and the Morale Monitors are killing people all over the world for not bearing the mark of Carpathia, what chance would someone stand here?

"We didn't know, but we wanted to find out, and I tell you, playing hide-and-seek with the GC in Germany was getting old. Nearly forty of us packed up and headed this way—no easy trip, I want to say. It has not been easy living here either, but we knew it would not be when we came. We have lost six of our members since we have been here—four all at once, and two, I have to say, were my fault, to my eternal shame. But we will see them again, will we not? And I cannot wait.

"Something else I could not wait for was this plague of darkness. When it came and we realized that everyone was blind but us, I got it in my head I wanted to see this place—the compound, the courtyard, the palace and all—especially the potentate's office. I could not get any of the others to come with me, so here I am, and who should I run into but you? Well, if we are fulfilling prophecy by being at least some of God's people who must come out of here before the end, you are an answer to prayer if I ever saw one. We need a place to go if we are to come out, and what better place than where we will finally be safe? If you have connections at Petra, that is where we want to be, if they will have us."

"Excuse me, Rayford," Chang said. "This is all very interesting and exciting, but I need to show Naomi the, you know, inner workings David set up here, and then I think we need to get going."

"Right," Rayford said, "and I'll feel more comfortable if Abdullah stays with you two. I want to head back to Carpathia's office and see if Otto and I can crash the big meeting and see what's going on."

"Oh! I'd love that! As I said, I wanted to see his office anyway. That's why I was there when you were, but I was so startled to see someone with the mark of the be—"

"Otto," Rayford said, "we've got to move."

+ + +

Chloe had crouched by the passenger-side door long enough to almost talk herself out of what she planned. What if she rose into view of a driver waiting for his charges? She likely had the drop on him, and then what was she going to do? Disarm him? Keep him from the radio? Make him tell her where his people were and what they were up to? That would do nothing but give away the underground compound unless Chloe was willing to kill the man and try to run off the rest of them—provided he told the truth about where they were.

She finally told herself that if the truck was empty, she would merely make one wide reconnaissance loop around the compound to make sure the GC weren't close or on to them or about to be; then she would head back for help.

Chloe released the safety on the Uzi, put her right index finger on the trigger, cradled the barrel in her other palm, and rose quickly.

Empty.

And so was she. She had been unaware of the effects of the adrenaline on her since she had ventured out of the service door, but the resultant crash of her system left her nearly immobile. She slumped by the truck to gather herself. Her arms and legs felt rubbery, and had Chloe's senses not been on such high alert, she believed she could have tucked her chin to her chest and slept.

Though she couldn't escape the feeling she was being watched—she imagined at least nine GC with scopes trained on her—she felt remarkably lucky, given how serendipitous her plan had been. That is to say, she hardly had a plan. And while she agreed with the Tribulation Force's motto—"We don't do luck"—it was difficult to attribute her safety so far to God when she felt so foolish for how she had again tested her destiny.

Chloe rose and began her scouting ring of the perimeter. As she moved silently in the darkness, feeling vulnerable and trying to be more thorough than quick, all she was aware of was the pace of her breathing and her thundering pulse.

+ + +

By the time Rayford and Otto reached Carpathia's suite of offices, the meeting had begun and the stragglers spilled out of the doorway of his conference room. Rayford saw Carpathia's wretched glow, but it was obvious that only Leon Fortunato stood close enough to the man to take advantage of it.

Rayford gently put his hands on men in the doorway, and they gave way to let him slip through, Otto following. To be safe, they moved to the far end of the room, away from Carpathia. The potentate asked Krystall to call the roll, which she did almost entirely from memory. When she drew a blank on the last three names, she asked if she could read the rest of the list in Carpathia's light.

"Better simply to have those whose names have not been called identify themselves," Nicolae said.

As they were doing that, Otto touched Rayford's arm and mouthed that he was tempted to call out his own name and see what kind of havoc that might wreak.

"If you gentlemen would kindly attempt to keep your outbursts to a minimum," Carpathia began, "Director of Security and Intelligence Suhail Akbar has the first item."

"Thank you, Excellency. Oh! Forgive me, sir, but I am in pain as well. Ah!"

"Suhail, please!"

"Apologies, Highness, but I don't know what to—"

"Control yourself, man!"

"I shall try, sir. Our primary concern, ladies and gentlemen, besides the obvious, is that a—"

"What's more important than the obvious?" someone with an Indian accent said. "We've got to find a solution to this—"

"Who is that?" Carpathia demanded. "Raman Vajpayee, is that you?"

"Yes, sir, I simply want to know—"

"Raman, I simply want you to be quiet. How dare you interrupt a member of my cabinet?"

"Well, sir, it is most important that—"

"What is most important is that the only response to your offense is an abject apology, and it had better be immediately forthcoming."

"I am sorry, Potentate, but—"

"That was hardly abject. At a time of international crisis, I cannot imagine such insubordination. I am of a mind—"

"To what?" Vajpayee said. "To put me to death as you do anyone who speaks his mind? I tell you, I would rather be dead than to live like this! In the dark! In pain! No relief in sight. And yet you carry on—"

"Show yourself, Raman! Do it now!"

The Indian rushed forward, pushing others out of his way. It was clear to Rayford that he was simply following the sound of Carpathia's voice, unable to see even the glow. "I am here, within arm's length of you! Kill me for daring to speak my mind, or reveal yourself as a coward!"

"Suhail," Carpathia said, "take this man out and execute him!"

"So you *are* a coward! You will not do it yourself! At least give me that much respect."

"I have only contempt for you, Raman. You have disgraced your position with the Global Community and I—"

"Kill me yourself, you impotent—"

And with that, Carpathia thrust himself toward the Indian, finally allowing both to see one another. As the others listened in horror, the two men struggled, and Carpathia succeeded in getting the man's head in his hands. With a violent twist he broke Vajpayee's neck, and the dead man slid to the floor.

"Any other dissidents?" Carpathia said. "Anyone who would rather be dead than suffer for the cause? Hmm? If not, Suhail, proceed, and when you are finished, get this corpse out of here."

Somehow a shaken Akbar was able to control his own outcries of pain as he reported that an aircraft had landed at the New Babylon airstrip that very afternoon. "We can only assume it was a miracle of autopiloting," he said, "but we have no record of what plane it is and urge caution on everyone's part, as we may have subversives among us."

"If we cannot accomplish having the occupants of that plane identify themselves," Carpathia said, "I will personally inspect it at the end of this meeting."

"That's our cue," Rayford whispered to Otto. "We've got to be out of here before then."

As they began to surreptitiously make their way out of the room, Carpathia continued. "As you know, I am determined to put an end to our Jewish problem, and if that includes the cowardly Judah-ites who remain hidden in the mountains, so much the better. I am hereby calling for a meeting of all ten heads of the global regions in six months' time. We shall meet in Baghdad to map our strategy to rid the world of our enemies. Meanwhile, we will move our command post into the light at Al Hillah. As many of you know—and if this is news to you, I expect full confidentiality—Al Hillah is the location of our vast storehouse of nuclear weaponry, voluntarily surrendered to us by the rest of the world as a condition of my accepting my position. That will prove most useful to us in this ultimate effort and final solution.

"Until the rest of the world is on the same page with me, I plan to begin amassing fighting forces in Israel. All available military personnel in the United Carpathian States who are not already assigned as Peacekeepers or Morale Monitors will be expected to report for duty in the Jezreel Valley for combat training.

"As for our relocation to Al Hillah, be ready to move out in twenty-four hours. Take anything that will assist you in this transfer."

"What about our workers, our departments?"

"They will stay, and they must not know where we are going or even that we are going. Is that understood?"

Rayford was just outside the door when he heard that no one had responded.

"Understood?"

"Yes," a few muttered.

"Then go about your business. Mr. Akbar, Reverend Fortunato, and I will make our way to the airstrip."

Rayford motioned for Otto to follow, and he began running toward the elevators. "Call every car and push every button on each. Stall those elevators for as long as you can. I'll take the stairs. I have no idea where my friends are, but I need to leave a note at Chang's place in case they head back there. We have to be out of here before Carpathia finds out the identity of our plane and where we are. Got it?"

"Got it. Thanks for trusting me."

"Were you hoping to come with us? Because unless you can get—"

"No, we'll arrange that later. I wouldn't come without my people anyway."

"If you happen to see any of my friends before I do, send them to the plane."

Rayford bounded down the stairs, drawing screams and squeals from people suffering in the stairwells. They called out, asking how he could run like that in the dark. He hated ignoring them.

He reached the main level, vaulted over several people, and zigzagged between others. He burst out the door and sprinted across the runways toward the plane. If he could get it started and turned around, all he could do was hope and pray that Chang, Naomi, and Abdullah were on their way.

\+ \+ \+

Buck had been sound asleep for hours before something began troubling him. He grew fitful and was suddenly wide awake. It was guilt. Letting Chloe take watch duty when she worked so hard all day with the Co-op and their son. What kind of a husband was he?

He ran his hands through his hair and sat up, calling out. "How's it going, babe?"

Maybe she was checking on Kenny. Or getting herself some tea in the kitchen. He padded out of the bedroom, stretching. "Chlo'!" he called out. "You've got something on the motion detector here!"

He bent over the periscope and scanned quickly. He saw nothing until he got to the southwest, where he saw a lone figure, armed. He scowled. "Chloe!" he called. "Better call George. I've got a bogey at eight o'clock. Chloe?"

He froze. He stood and moved toward the kitchen. It was dark. And Kenny was crying. Buck grabbed the phone on his way to Kenny's room and punched in Ming's number.

"Hey, big boy," Buck said, finding the boy standing in his bed, quickly going from crying to smiling.

"Mama?"

"In a minute," he said. "Why don't you lie down and go back to sleep. It's still night."

Ming answered.

"I'm so sorry to wake you, Ming, but I've got a little emergency here."

"Anything, Buck."

"Could you watch Kenny for a little while? I think Chloe is outside."

"Be there in less than a minute."

He thanked her and got on the walkie-talkie. "George, you up?"

4

RAYFORD HAD THE ENGINES started and the plane turned around when he saw Carpathia's glow in the distance. The potentate seemed in a hurry, but he was apparently leading Suhail Akbar and Leon Fortunato, and he had to go slowly to light the way for them a few feet at a time. That would not have been as much help without the sounds of the jet engines, however, so Rayford shut down and prayed that this mostly blind threesome would veer off course before his own trio found him.

Rayford turned on his cell phone and called Mac McCullum in Al Basrah to debrief him. "Can you and Albie leave for Al Hillah today?"

"We been sittin' here like a past-due hen."

"I'll take that as a yes. You're pretty hot since Greece. How are you going to get around?"

"With bluster, charm, and only at night, of course. I figure you pretty much just want to know what NC and his boys are up to."

"Ideal would be your finding out where they're meeting in Baghdad and bugging the place for us."

"Oh, sure. I'll just tell 'em I'm his new valet and can I have a few hours in the meeting room before everyone else gets there."

"If I thought it was easy, I'd do it myself," Rayford said.

"Albie knows everybody. If it's gonna get done, he'll get it done."

Chang, Naomi, and Abdullah appeared, each laden with boxes and cases. Naomi looked ashen. Rayford opened the door and lowered the steps. "Good timing," he said.

"We were on it all the way, Captain," Abdullah said. "Thanks to this young genius."

"Just showing off," Chang said, handing cargo in and helping Naomi aboard. "I wanted to show her how David had bugged the whole place and that we could actually listen in on Carpathia."

"So you knew he was coming," Rayford said, letting Abdullah edge past to the pilot's chair.

"Could we please talk about something else?" Naomi said.

That made everyone uncomfortably quiet. Rayford sneaked a peek. The pale orange silhouette was moving more quickly now. He must have abandoned Akbar and Fortunato or they were ailing anew. The pain didn't seem to reach Carpathia. Maybe God was saving his best till last for him.

Rayford and Abdullah eschewed a formal checklist for a quick confirmation of the cockpit flow by checking the critical switch positions. "Crank 'er up," Rayford said.

But Abdullah just sat there, craning his neck to watch the glow grow larger as it neared the plane.

"What're you waiting on, Smitty? Let's move out."

"A moment, please, Captain. How far do you assume he can see?"

"About as far as he glows. Now let's go."

"A moment, please."

"What are you doing, Mr. Smith?" Naomi called out. "Isn't that Carpathia?"

"He does not know where he is going. But I do."

"Once we start up, he can do nothing," Rayford said. "But I'd rather he not know who we are."

"He won't," Abdullah said.

Rayford leaned past Abdullah and saw Carpathia hurry across the runway about twenty feet behind the craft.

"Here we go," Abdullah said, firing up the engines and blowing the orange glow to the ground over and over until Nicolae was just an ember in the distance.

Once in the air, Naomi leaned forward. "Can I talk to you?" she said. Rayford removed his headphones.

"Is that stuff normal for you guys?" she said.

"Nothing's normal anymore, Naomi. You've been through a lot yourself."

"I never heard a man being murdered before. And I've never walked by so many hurting people without a thing I could do for them. We're isolated in Petra, and I wanted to be where the action is. But if I never see anything else like this, it'll be all right with me. And we can do more from our computer center than anywhere I can think of."

"I'm sorry it was hard," Rayford said. "It was for me too." He told her of the woman he had tried to help and of his conversation with Nicolae's assistant.

"We'll watch for her uncle's name on the system," she said. "And I suppose we'll hear from Mr. Weser too."

"Hope so. What a character."

She leaned closer, and while she had to raise her voice over the engines,

Naomi seemed to speak so only Rayford could hear. "Chang's not doing well, you know."

"Why's that?"

"This has been his home, crazy as it's had to have been. It's got to be strange leaving."

"I should think he'd be glad to be gone."

"I wish I could have met Mr. Hassid, the one Chang talks about so much. What they did in the palace and the setup at our place . . ."

Rayford nodded. "You going to be able to do the same thing—monitor this place—from Petra now?"

"With Chang, yes. It's going to be wonderful to have him in our shop."

"Is he going to be competition?"

"Hardly. I'll just let him do what he wants. He likes the technical stuff, keyboarding and inside the box, more than managing people. But he can teach if he wants to."

Rayford's phone chirped. It was George Sebastian. "Been trying to get hold of you. Your phone down?"

"Had it off for the palace mission. I was going to report in when I knew you guys were up. It's still early there, isn't it?"

"We've got a situation."

"Why are you whispering? Where are you?"

"Outside."

"What time is it there?"

"Just before five in the morning. We can't find Chloe."

+ + +

It hit Buck that the figure on the periscope had been Chloe, so where was she? It was just like her to be out without a walkie-talkie or a phone, which he attributed to strategy rather than impetuousness. He would have a hard time convincing anyone else of that, though.

He and George had split up, fully armed and in constant touch with each other. George had found the empty GC personnel carrier—which had to be some sort of a decoy—but no GC or Chloe. Buck hoped he wouldn't have to call for more help and further expose his people or their location.

Two hours later, when the sun left Buck and George with no choice but to retreat inside, they had covered two square miles with nothing to show for it. In the compound, everybody was up, worried, praying, and eager to be brought up to speed. Ming Toy took Kenny and George's daughter, Beth Ann, to her place "for as long as is necessary."

George and Priscilla set up a command center in the workout room. Ree Woo sat at a small folding table in the corner, digging through files to see if any of their aliases had been underused or uncompromised.

Buck admitted he was going to be of little help. "I'm paralyzed."

"Snap out of it," George said. "You do Chloe and us no good that way."

Buck glared at him, knowing he was right. "Easy for you to say, Sebastian. It's not your wife out there."

Priscilla looked away. George let his papers fall on a table and approached Buck. He put a hand on each arm of Buck's chair and leaned close to his face. "I'm only gonna say it once. If it was my wife out there, I wouldn't be sitting in here with my hands in my lap. I owe your wife big time. She risked her life for me in Greece. I can only imagine how you feel. Not knowing anything is worse than knowing the worst, but we know nothing. Maybe you're just a little mad at her because she didn't seem to follow protocol and skipped a lot of steps here.

"Maybe you're feeling guilty about being angry with her because you're scared to death she's into something over her head. I don't blame you. I don't. I'm telling you, we need everybody on this, especially somebody with your brain. Now, you want to find her so we can get her back safe and sound, or you want to assume the worst and start grieving now?"

"George!" Priscilla scolded.

"I'm not trying to be a hard case," George said. "It's just that there's nothing we can do outside in the daylight unless we know the coast is clear and we've got someone with a good disguise and alias. Meanwhile, we've got to rest and strategize, and we don't need Buck sitting here feeling sorry for hims—"

"All right, George, I got it! Okay?"

"You and I are all right then?"

"Of course."

"I mean, you think I was out there in the middle of the night for my health?"

"Not so good news," Ree said. "Chloe's 'Chloe Irene' and Mac's 'Howie Johnson' are no good after Greece. Hannah's 'Indira Jinnah' might still be okay, but only she can use it and she's too far away. Rayford and Abdullah's Middle Eastern brothers IDs may still be okay, but Abdullah is staying in Petra and Rayford will need R and R when he gets here."

"Don't be so sure," George said. "He'll go till he drops."

"Tell me about it," Buck said.

"Has Albie's 'Commander Elbaz' been exposed yet?" Ree asked.

Buck nodded. "Unfortunately, yes."

"Too far away too," George said. "What else have we got?"

"One more. Ming's guy persona, 'Chang Chow.'"

"Let's not risk Ming," Buck said.

"Why not?" George said. "She's still got the uniform. She can cut her hair and—"

"Hey!" Ree said. "You're talking about my fiancée."

"So?"

"She at least ought to be consulted."

"No, Ree," George said. "I thought we'd just drag her in here, hold her down, and cut her hair."

"Cool down, boys," Priscilla said. "Nobody knows who I am. I could be given an alias and—"

"No you don't," George said.

"Shoe's on the other foot now, eh?" Buck said. "Prospect of sending your wife out there—"

"Stop it!" George said. "I'm just saying she's inexperienced and not all that healthy."

"Ming is not very physical," Ree said. "Not trained in weapons."

"Don't give me that," Buck said. "She worked at Buffer."

"Handling inmates at a women's prison is not like rescuing one of our people from the local GC."

"We wouldn't be looking for her to do that anyway," George said. "Buck and I and maybe you, Ree, would have to go get Chloe. We need Ming, or somebody, just to find out where she is."

+ + +

Chloe had caught sight of two more GC vehicles, both moving, to the south as she was in the middle of her loop around the compound. As she watched, both trucks stopped and more than half a dozen troops disembarked from each. It became clear that they were walking a carefully planned grid to check for hidden encampments. And the underground safe house was in their path. They may have looked bored to Buck through the periscope a few hours before, but something had sent them for reinforcements.

These guys were serious. They had metal detectors, probes, and what appeared to be Geiger counters. Chloe debated whether she had time to race back to the compound to alert the others. If she erred, she could lead these guys right to her door.

Determined to distract them and knock them off course, she started moving again. She had to make them see her without appearing to want that. She moved stealthily, but with a purpose.

Rather than take a right at the edge of the property and circle back to the entrance, Chloe continued west on the south side. When she heard at least one of the vehicles heading her way, she broke into a trot, then a jog, then a full run. She was not going to outrun a truck, but maybe she could go where it couldn't.

The Uzi, light as it was, weighed her down. Unless she believed she could take on an entire platoon or two of GC with it, it made more sense to ditch it and come back for it later. She would never be able to explain a weapon like that. With the sound of a truck, and maybe two of them, just a block south and closing fast, Chloe detoured and flung the Uzi and her ski mask behind some trees. She picked up her pace and sprinted about a quarter of a mile, succeeding in getting both trucks to bear down on her.

Chloe was out of sight of the underground complex and decided the best approach was indifference, so she kept her head down and kept running. The lead truck pulled up beside her, but she didn't even turn to look. From the passenger-side window a young woman called out, "Need a lift?"

"No thanks."

"Get in."

"No thanks. I'm good."

"We want to ask you a few questions."

"Go ahead."

"C'mon, stop and let us talk to you."

"Talk to me anyway."

"Where you from?"

"About six miles west."

"That was underwater from the tsunami not that long ago."

"How well I know."

"What're you doing down here?"

"Running."

"How'd you get here?"

"Ran."

"Where you going?"

"Home."

"What's your name?"

"Phoebe." *It sounds biblical.*

"Phoebe what?"

"Phoebe Evangelista."

"Ethnic?"

"Husband is." *He's a WASP.*

"Have any ID?"

"Not on me."

"Okay, ma'am, I'm going to have to ask you to stop and let us talk with you a minute."

"No thanks. You can follow me home if you want." *I'll run as far from the underground as I can until I drop.*

"I need to know your original region and see your mark."

"I'm not taking off my hood or my gloves in this weather after working up a sweat."

"What, you've got marks both places?"

Chloe waved her off and kept running. The truck veered off the road in front of her and stopped. Chloe swerved around it and kept going. She heard doors opening and boots on pavement. Soon armed GC in full uniform flanked her, a man on each side, keeping pace.

"Okay," one said, "fun's over. Stop or we'll have to put you in the truck. Come on now, ma'am, you know we can take you down, and there's no need for that."

Chloe kept running. The man on her right tossed his weapon to the one on the left, and the next thing she knew he had both arms around her neck and was drawing his knees up into the middle of her back. He had to weigh two hundred pounds. She staggered and fell. He shifted his weight just before she hit the ground and drove her face into the dirt. Chloe knew she had been scraped deep, and blood ran down her forehead. He slid up and pressed his knee behind her neck, pulled her hands behind her, and handcuffed her.

Desperate to stall them, Chloe let herself go limp. "Have it your way," one of the men said. He grabbed the cuffs to drag her toward the truck. She purposely kept her face down, letting sand and pebbles and pavement tear at her face.

On her stomach next to the truck, she could not be lifted by the handcuffs without wrenching her shoulders out of place, which the GC almost did. "There's an easier way," a young guard said, "if that's what she wants."

He grabbed her feet and bent her legs up to where he could bind her ankles to the handcuffs with a plastic band. He tossed her into the truck.

Chloe was sure she had cracked a rib. During the twenty-five-minute ride to the local GC headquarters, Chloe began to pray. "God, give me strength. Let me die before I give away anything. Be with Kenny and Buck and Dad."

She remembered George regaling them with stories about how he had said absolutely nothing to his captors in Greece. If only she had that kind of fortitude. She would rather banter, anger them, mislead them. Was it better to sit and take it or to shoot back, to let them know she was no pushover?

Torture. Could she handle that? "With your strength, God. Let me trade my body for the ones I love."

At headquarters she was uncuffed, searched, and again asked her name and home region. Chloe said nothing. She gingerly pressed a palm against her face and felt the abrasions on her forehead and cheeks.

"She already told us. Phoebe Evangelista, American."

"Then there ought to be a *–6* somewhere under that blood. Get a wet cloth and wash that off."

Someone held Chloe by the back of her head and dragged the cloth across her face. She cried out.

"I don't see anything. Doesn't mean it's not there. We running her name and description?"

"Yeah. Nothing so far."

"Jock will be in at nine. Get her cleaned up and in a jumpsuit. And fingerprinted."

Chloe was tempted to go limp again and make the GC undress her, hose her down, and dress her, but she did what she was told. She came out of the shower with her face stinging, changed into the dark green jumpsuit, and clenched her fists.

When she was led to the photo area and printing station, she kept her hands balled. Chloe looked so different from the girl who had been at Stanford six years before, she wasn't worried about her photo giving anything away.

A matronly Mexican guard reached for Chloe's hand and said, "Right first, please."

Chloe shook her head.

"Come on, honey. You don't want to fight me. You're going to get yourself fingerprinted, so you might as well just let me do it."

Chloe shook her head again.

"I'm going to do this, so how's it going to happen? Do I have to get a couple of guys in here to hold you down? Because if I do, here's what I'm going to use."

The woman showed Chloe an ugly adjustable metal cord similar to the tool dogcatchers use at the ends of poles to snag puppies. "I wrap this about three inches above your wrist. When it tightens, your hand comes open. I don't know who you are or why you're in here, but you don't want to endure this."

Chloe shook her head again, and the woman spoke into her radio, asking for help. Chloe resisted the two young men, but as the matron had said, it was hardly worth the effort. When that metal loop tightened around her arm, her fingers popped open, and the GC had fingerprints that were sent via the Internet to their databases all over the world.

"We also read your eyes with the camera, honey. If you've ever had a driver's license, been to college, gotten married, anything, we'll find a match."

Chloe only hoped the GC were as shorthanded as everyone else. Maybe it would take long enough that Buck and George and the rest could bust her out. *Who am I kidding?*

\+ + +

Rayford had hoped for a day or two of rest before jetting back to San Diego, but he had no choice but to leave Petra as soon as he could refuel. He was stunned to find Mac McCullum waiting for him.

"Got the word from Buck," Mac said. "Thought Tsion and Chaim ought to know so they could get the folks here praying. Albie's already got a contact on the Al Hillah thing, so he doesn't need me. I'll be your pilot."

"Mac, I can't ask you to—"

"You didn't. I volunteered. Now unless you're gonna be a mule and pull rank on me, saddle up."

Rayford was more grateful than he could express. In the air Mac told him, "You can think, pray, sleep, or talk. I've got this baby on a path to San Diego, and I'm looking forward to seeing those people again and meeting some new ones. My prediction is that Chloe will be there waiting for us."

"I was with you right up until that last," Rayford said. "I've got a bad, bad feeling about this. If Buck and George don't find her soon, or if they find out the GC has her, we've got to get those people out of there."

"And take them where?"

"Petra is the only place I know anymore."

"Chloe ain't gonna give the GC a thing. Unless they saw her coming out of the underground, what've they got?"

"She had to be in the area. Unless she can convince them she came from somewhere else, she sure gives them a place to start looking."

Rayford buried his head in his hands and tried to sleep. No dice. All he could do was pray. Chloe had been Daddy's girl from day one. She loved school, was inquisitive, single-minded, stubborn. She was the last person in the family to come to Christ, and Rayford had no illusions that he was responsible for that. He had taught her to believe only in what she could see and smell and touch.

Chloe always wanted to be in the middle of the action, and if someone wouldn't put her there, she'd put herself there. He wanted to resent her for it, especially now, but he was overwhelmed with worry and fear. All he wanted was to know she was safe and back with Buck and Kenny. He knew that no matter what happened, they would be reunited someday, and that it would be less than a year from now. But somehow that wasn't as comforting as he thought it might be.

They were destined to be with Christ when they died, and should they survive, they would be with him on earth for a thousand years. But the prospect of dying was still a fearful thing. It was likely that any of the Tribulation Force who died during the next year would be martyrs to the cause of Christ, but their loved ones would still mourn them, still miss them. Worst of all, Rayford realized, he didn't want to think about how his loved ones might die.

The suffering might be short-lived, but no one wants to think of his beloved going through anything terrifying or torturous or agonizing. "Father," Rayford said, "let this be a mission of relocation at worst. I have no reason more valid than anyone else to deserve special treatment, to have my daughter supernaturally protected. You don't need her; you don't need any of us. But we have pledged ourselves to you and trust you know what you're doing."

✢ ✢ ✢

Jock turned out to be a tall, heavy man with a uniform that may once have fit him but now encased him like a sausage. He had his underlings bring Chloe from a small cell to a slightly larger room. He pointed to a chair and she sat directly across from him at a metal table.

Jock dropped an accordion file on the table and took off his jacket, draping it over the back of the chair. He sat wearily and let out a loud sigh. "So, Phoebe Evangelista. Where'd you come up with that one?"

Chloe stared at him. She detected an Australian accent and noticed the number *18* on his forehead. On the back of his right hand was a tattoo of Nicolae Carpathia's face.

"Mind if I smoke?"

Chloe raised her eyebrows and nodded.

"Well, what do I care whether you mind or not? I've got a lot of work to do today, young lady, and you're keeping me from it."

"Go do it," Chloe said.

"So, she talks," Jock said, pulling a small cigar from his pocket. "I thought you were going to be one of those name-rank-and-serial-number types, minus the last two. Well, you are my work, and you've been a bad girl. You've been lying to my people, haven't you?"

"Yes."

"You want to fess up, or you want me to tell you what we found?"

Chloe shrugged.

"We're not getting a thing out of you, are we?"

"No."

"Took a while, but we got it. Besides being short of people, our systems are crashing, and—"

"You're breaking my heart."

Jock reached for his file. "Yeah, well, from what we found, I can imagine. I have good news and bad news this morning, Mrs. Williams. Which would you like?"

So, there it was. In a matter of hours, the prints or the eye reading had given her away. "Nothing you can say will be good news."

"Don't be rash. We're reasonable people, much as you and yours would like to think otherwise and persuade all the sheep who follow that kook Ben-Judah."

Tsion has more brains in his eyebrows than any ten GCs I've ever met.

"I have a proposition for you, ma'am."

"I don't want to hear it."

"Sure you do."

"Let me guess. My freedom for a few leads?"

"Well, you can play high-and-mighty all you want, Mom, but I'd think you'd be open to hearing me out when the benefit to you deals with your own child."

5

ALBIE'S BLACK-MARKET WORLD was a shadowy landscape of operators who largely went by nicknames and initials. Albie himself had fashioned his name from his hometown, Al Basrah. People who needed to know who he was knew enough to reach him. Before he became a believer, Albie had been one of the top three black marketers in the Middle East. His conversion to Christ had left only two, and the death of one of them, reputedly at the hands of the other in a deal gone bad, left one. And that was who Albie needed to get ahold of.

He had never liked Double-M, or Mainyu Mazda, even when Albie was of the same ilk and character. Killing was nothing new for Mainyu. It was how he maintained his reputation and control. You wanted something, anything, he was the man. But pity anyone who ever, ever tried to swindle or even shortchange the man. Legend had it that he had personally murdered a dozen people—one of them one of his own wives—who had not lived up to their end of some bargain. None dared calculate how many he may have hired others to eliminate.

Those who claimed to know said Mainyu celebrated each personal killing by adding a tattooed double-M to his neck. He had begun twenty years before when he had strangled a guard in a Kuwaiti prison. He applied the first tattoo himself, the ink a concoction of rubber shavings from the soles of his shoes, paint chips from the prison bars, and blood. A sharpened paper clip heated by a cigarette lighter was his applicator. He put that first double-M directly under his Adam's apple. He added one on either side of the original for each subsequent murder, so people could tell whether he was on an odd or even number by whether or not his tattooed necklace was even on both sides.

The last time Albie had seen Mainyu, his necklace had one more double-M on the left than on the right and his count stood at twelve. The more recent tattoos were clearer and more professionally done, and supposedly the one for his wife had a feminine flair.

Albie put the word on the street that he wanted an audience with Mainyu, and within two hours a note was slipped under his door with an address deep in the street markets on Abadan Island on the Shatt al Arab River in southwestern Iran.

It was like MM to follow the money. Pipelines connected Abadan's huge refinery to the oil fields of Iran. Of course Mainyu did his black marketing in the city's underbelly.

Like anyone anywhere who didn't bear a mark of loyalty to Carpathia, Albie had become nocturnal. He and Mac shared a flat in a forsaken corner of Al Basrah, where the landlord didn't know or care about one's loyalty to the Global Community provided the rent envelope was full and waiting the first of every month. Albie had taught Mac that the best way to get around was on motor scooters small and light enough to be stored indoors or hidden in the woods near where they hid their small plane.

Albie would wait for the sun to disappear before venturing out to a ferry that would get him and his scooter to the island, where he would find the address some thirty miles from home.

\+ + +

When big Jock said something about it probably being past Chloe's breakfast time, her mouth watered. "But as you can understand, ma'am, we don't feed uncooperative prisoners. Oh, at some point, you'll get some sort of nutrition bar that'll keep you alive until your execution." He patted the big file. "I can't say for sure until I hear from International, but this has all the makings of a spectacle. Wouldn't you say?"

"That's not my call."

"But your baby—what's the name?"

Chloe leveled her eyes at Jock and pressed her lips together. How she loved to say her baby's name. *Kenneth Bruce Williams. Kenny Bruce. Kenny B.* But she would not tell this man. There was no official record of Kenny's birth, and the GC didn't even know whether she'd had a boy or a girl.

"Surely there's no harm in my knowing the name."

"Phoebe Evangelista Jr."

Jock looked at the ceiling. "You know what? I am not the least bit amused. I'm not surprised either, because I've dealt with enough of your type. Some say there's something admirable about you people, sticking with something this long even though in the end you're going to lose, and you know it. But I would have thought a religious person—and come on, that's what you are, isn't it?—I would have thought you'd care a little more about the disposition of your child. Is it a girl? How old is she now?"

"Look," Chloe said, "you know who I am and what I am and what I'm not, which is a Carpathia loyalist. That's punishable by death, so why don't you just—"

"Oh, now hold on, ma'am. These things are still negotiable. Don't be jumping to concl—"

"I will not be providing you any information to reduce my sentence. I'm not interested in life in prison. I would not take the mark even if you promised freedom for my family. And everybody knows that even those who take the mark now are executed anyway."

"Oh, where did you hear that? That's terrible. And a lie."

"Whatever you say."

Jock leaned back in his chair and called out, "Nigel?"

"Sir?"

"Could you open a window? It's stuffy in here."

The young guard entered and opened a window behind heavy bars. There would be no escaping.

"It's only fair that I outline what I have to offer," Jock said. "You see, we know more than your name. We know you dropped out of Stanford University six years ago. We know you're the daughter of Potentate Carpathia's first pilot. We know that you know that your father became a subversive and may have either conspired or participated in the assassination of the potentate.

"Your husband is also a former employee of His Excellency and now publishes a contraband magazine. They're deeply connected with Tsion Ben-Judah and the traitor assassin Rosenzweig. And you, Mrs. Williams, are no retiring bride either. No. You run the Judah-ite black market, keeping alive millions without the mark, who have no legal right to buy or sell.

"No ma'am, you should be offered nothing, no plea bargain, no break, nothing even for your child. Because more than that, you were involved in an operation in Greece where you impersonated a Global Community officer."

"How did you know that?" It was out before Chloe could think. Was there a mole in their own operation? She couldn't have been recognized.

"I'll tell you if you'll tell me something."

"Never mind."

"It's the beauty of iris-scan technology. Normal security cameras, like the ones in our headquarters in Ptolemaïs, can get a good enough read on your iris to match it with the one recorded when you enrolled at Stanford. It has four times as many points of reference as a fingerprint, and there has never been a recorded error. Lucky for the one among your number who murdered one of our operatives in that very building that we weren't able to trace you to him. But he's from right here in town, isn't he? How far away can he be? How far from where you were jogging?"

+ + +

Buck could barely believe what he was hearing. And from Sebastian, of all people, who was sitting there because of the selfless, heroic efforts of the Tribulation Force, Chloe in particular.

"It's not easy to say, Buck," George said. "But we have to weigh the welfare of two hundred people against springing one person in the face of almost impossible odds."

"First," Buck said, "you're assuming the GC has her. She could be anywhere. But even if you're right, how is that any more impossible than the situation you were in?"

"Buck, I know, okay? And there's no way I want to just do nothing. But there's one big difference here too. The prisoner in that situation was a very big and strong man, trained to kill. And, you'll recall, for all Mac and Hannah and Chloe did on my behalf, it came down to me against one of my captors. Even then the odds were bad, and it could have gone either way. Let's say I'd failed and the three of them had been compromised. We lose four people. We blast into local headquarters here, we could wind up giving away everything."

"So, what, we let her rot while we move to Petra?"

+ + +

"Here's what I have in mind for your child, Mrs. Williams," Jock said, "in the event you come to your senses and help us a little. I'm guessing you would prefer your son or daughter to remain in the tradition you and your husband have begun. Obviously, that would be counterproductive to our aims. We would like to see all children enrolled in Junior GC before they start school.

"But in your case, we're willing to treat your child as a nonentity until he or she is twelve years old."

"And who would raise him?" Chloe said, wincing, realizing hunger was an effective tactic after all.

"So we're talking about a boy, then. Fair enough. Want to give me a name to make it less awkward to carry out negotiations?"

Chloe didn't answer. These weren't negotiations. All she had to do was protect Kenny for one more year and the GC wouldn't have a chance at him.

"Come now, Mrs. Williams. You're a bright woman. You have to see what a prize you are to us. We have been inconvenienced and, I'll admit it, embarrassed by the Judah-ites. There is little doubt you people are somehow behind our little problem in New Babylon right now. You can help us. I'm not naïve enough to think you want to do that, but I'm trying to give you a reason. You have some huge bargaining chips."

"May I stand?"

"You may, but I need to warn you that we are locked in. I'm three times your size, but just for smiles, let's say you overpower me, get the drop on me. You could break my neck and kill me, but you're not getting out of here."

"I just want to move a little, sir."

"Feel free. And call me Jock."

Yeah, you're my best friend now.

"Hey, you want some breakfast?"

"Of course."

"Me too. What do you like?"

"I'm not fussy."

"I am. I go for the old artery-clogger special. Eggs, bacon, sausage, toast, pancakes with lotsa syrup. Want some?"

He had to be kidding. Chloe stood with her arms folded and turned away.

"Come on! Can't get you to call me by my first name. Can't get you to tell me what you want to eat. How 'bout it? Will you join me? Will you have what I'm having?"

"I told you, I'm not fussy."

"You also told me you were hungry. I'll order for us, eh, Chloe? You mind if I call you Chloe?"

"Actually, I'd rather you not."

"Oh, well, then, by all means. It's all about you. Just let me know all your desires and preferences. If the pillow in your cell is not soft enough, give me a holler. Or call the front desk."

So the gloves were off. Chloe had convinced him she wasn't going to cooperate, so he was done playing good cop.

Or was he? Jock moved past her and summoned Nigel again, and she overheard him ordering the very breakfasts he had described. He turned back to her.

"Food service here is about the same as at any jail, Chloe, but even a hash slinger is hard-pressed to mess up breakfast. Now listen, while we wait . . . I can see you're no pushover. I didn't expect you to be and wouldn't have respected you if you had been. Here's the deal. You know nothing you give us is going to set you free. How would we look to the public? But I can get your execution commuted to a life sentence, and I can get that in a livable facility. You'd have my word on it. It'd be maximum security, of course, but you would have full custody of your son until he's twelve years old."

The fact was, Kenny was safe with Buck, and if she could maintain her sanity, that might not have to change. If only she could get word to Buck to get everyone out of there and to Petra.

Chloe felt light-headed, and hunger gnawed. "And that deal is in exchange for . . . ?"

"Taking the mark of loyalty would be a given. No way we would have any credibility otherwise. That gets you life instead of death. But what gets you the nice facility and custody of your son is information."

"You think I'm going to flip on my people."

"I do, and you know why? Because you're a loving mother. You think your people wouldn't give *you* up in a second to keep their necks out from under that blade? Give me a break."

+ + +

Albie shuddered, tooling through Abadan on his scooter, cap pulled low over his eyes. Al Basrah was no better, but this had to be what Sodom and Gomorrah had been like before God torched them. Every form of sin and debauchery was displayed right on the street. What was once the seedy side of town now was the town. Row after row of bars, fortune-telling joints, bordellos, sex shops, and clubs pandering to every persuasion and perversion teemed with drunk and high patrons. Hashish permeated the air. Cocaine and heroin deals went down in plain sight.

The GC Peacekeepers and Morale Monitors had once made a noisy bust or two weekly to keep up appearances. But with their ranks shrunk, they now concentrated on crimes against the government. Skip one of your thrice-daily bowings and scrapings before the image of Carpathia and you could be hauled off to jail. Caught without the mark of loyalty? Zero tolerance. They enjoyed playing with people's minds and telling them they had one last chance. When a gratefully weeping soul eagerly approached the mark application site, he or she was pushed or dragged screaming to the guillotine as an example.

Bad as Abadan had become, there was a worse part of town, and it was where Mainyu Mazda and his kind plied their trade. In the open-air market, where loud haggling and swindling were the daytime sport, were makeshift dens of clapboard squares, which consisted of just walls and a locking door, no roof. A tarp in the corner could be hastily attached to corner posts in the event of rain, but otherwise, black marketeers and their henchmen (one always standing guard outside) held court inside, meeting with people who wanted something, anything, and were willing to pay a lot to get it.

Albie cut the engine but stayed aboard his scooter, straddling the seat and pushing it along with his feet through the narrow alleyways. Amid the sleeping drunks were also crazy men, women of ill repute, men and women with all kinds of wares for sale. All beckoned to the leather-clad, smallish man walking the quiet scooter.

Albie looked neither right nor left, catching no one's eye. He knew where he was going and wanted it to appear so. He couldn't avoid a modicum of pride that his business had never sunk this low. What he had done for years was illegal, of course, and no circumstance justified it. But compared to this, he had had class. He had run an airstrip—that was his front. And his clientele had been made up as much of wealthy businessmen and pilots as it was lowlifes and crooks.

But he knew this world and its language. He needed a bad guy, someone who knew someone. Someone who had an inside track at the palace and knew where the meetings were to be held in Al Hillah. Someone who might even know where the largest ever cache of nuclear warheads was stored. Someone who, before Carpathia and his minions arrived, could get into the meeting room and bug the place, transmitting everything to a frequency accessed by only one person in the world. Only Albie and his people knew that would be Chang in Petra.

Had he more than a day to get this done, Albie might have been able to do it himself with his own contacts, people less risky, less volatile. But there were times in a man's life when he had to weigh his options and throw the dice. And while that analogy was foreign to his new life, this was one of those times.

+ + +

"Please sit at the table while the door is opened briefly, Chloe," Jock said. The smell of the breakfasts overwhelmed her, and she sat with her back to the door.

"Right over here, Nigel, if you would."

Jock sat facing her. He tossed her a cloth napkin and made a show of tucking his over his tie and spreading it to cover the expanse of his chest and belly. Chloe opened her napkin and laid it in her lap as Nigel set the heaping tray between them.

Nigel put a stack of pancakes in front of Jock. A pitcher of syrup. A plate of toast with butter and jelly. A large coffee cup, into which he poured steaming black coffee, and he left the pot there too. A massive plate of scrambled eggs with bacon and sausage links. He set Jock's silver on either side of his main plate, then put knife, fork, and spoon in front of Chloe. And there she sat, only silver before her and napkin in her lap. Nigel removed the tray and left, locking the door.

Jock rubbed his hands together, grinning. "Does this look great or what? I hardly know where to begin." He pulled each plate a little closer, then picked up his knife and fork and began manipulating the eggs into a huge first bite.

"I'm sorry," he said. "Where are my manners? Did you want to say grace? Ask a blessing? No? I will then. Thank you, Excellency, for what I am about to enjoy."

Jock shoveled the bite of eggs into his mouth, stored it in his right cheek, followed it with half a link of sausage, and spoke with his mouth full. "Nigel must have forgot yours, eh, Chloe? Oh, that's right. You haven't been a cooperative prisoner yet, have you? Well, that's your call."

The big man sat there, knifing, forking, spooning, smacking his lips, chugging coffee, and grinning. "Sure you don't want some? Huh? It's good. I mean it. 'Sup to you. Otherwise, Nigel will keep an eye on you and that energy bar will be delivered to your cell, oh, I'd say about an hour, maybe two, after you've given up on it. And *energy* may not be the right word. It's designed to keep you alive until we can put you to death. There's nutrition, but not energy per se. You'll get to love it though, look forward to it. I mean, come on, it's not bacon and eggs, but it's going to be your only treat."

\+ \+ \+

Albie rolled up in front of a tiny structure that appeared to be a mass of incongruously faded yellow boards wired and nailed together. The padlock was conspicuous on the door, which was guarded by a tall, thin rasp of a man Albie recognized from years before. In fact, if he wasn't mistaken, the name was Sahib and he was Mainyu's former brother-in-law. Former because he was the brother of the wife Mainyu had murdered. Talk about loyalty.

Albie stepped off the scooter and thrust out a hand. Sahib ignored it and squinted at him in the darkness. "Looking to sell that bike? You came to the right place."

"No. I want to see Mainyu, Sahib."

That provoked a double take. "Albie?"

And now the man shook his hand. He held up a finger, unlocked the door, and disappeared. Albie heard a low, intense conversation. A stranger emerged, hard and cold eyes darting before he hurried off.

Sahib came out, shutting the door behind him. "Two minutes, Albie," he said, and made a motion indicating Mainyu was on the phone. "Fifty Nicks to guard your bike."

"Twenty."

"Twenty-five."

"Deal. And if it is not as I left it, I split your skull."

"I know, Albie. Pay in advance."

"Ten now, fifteen later."

"Fifteen now."

Albie peeled off the Nicks. The negotiation, even the threats, was expected. A throat clearing from behind the door spurred Sahib to usher Albie in, but as Albie followed, he saw a small woman striding their way from a similar cubbyhole a hundred feet away. "Wait," he said. "Sahib. Watch the bike."

"I said I would. Oh, this is just a guest who will be joining you."

The young woman, robed head to toe, big eyed and severe looking with a *42* on her forehead, carried a satchel. Sahib pulled her in as he slid out, locking the door.

Mainyu, illuminated by a battery-powered lamp, sat behind a flimsy wood desk, a mug of something before him, his smile exhibiting surprisingly white teeth. "Albie, my friend, how are you?" he said, reaching with both hands.

"I am well, Mainyu. But I must insist that my business with you is private."

"As usual, of course. Please, sit."

Albie sat in a rusted metal folding chair while the woman went around the desk and pulled a wood box from a corner and sat on it, opening her satchel. Albie looked into Mainyu's eyes and cocked his head at the woman.

"Her?" Mainyu said dismissively. "Tattoo artist. She has neither ears nor tongue."

The woman smiled as she removed her instruments and reached in front of Mainyu to direct the lamp more squarely toward him. He lifted his chin, and she swabbed a small area on his neck where a tattoo would even the number on both sides.

"You know what they say about my tattoos, do you not, old friend?"

Albie smiled. "Everybody knows what they say."

"So, true or not, it is effective, no?"

"Effective. Is it true, Mainyu?"

"Of course."

"Who was your latest victim?"

"You mean who will be?"

"Sorry?"

"Sometimes I get the tattoo in advance."

\+ \+ \+

In spite of himself, Rayford had been dozing. And as the Gulfstream rocketed toward the States, he began digging through his bags.

"What's up, Ray?" Mac said.

"What time is it in New Babylon?"

"Coming up on ten o'clock in the evening."

"That makes it late morning in San Diego, and still no word. Buck promised to call even if they just found out where she was. You remember the main number at the palace?"

"Never knew it. Did you?"

"Once upon a time."

"Should be easy enough to get. But no one is still there, Ray. Need someone at Petra?"

"No. Now do you remember what David or Chang said about making these phones impossible to trace?"

"That I do remember." He told Rayford the combination of symbols and numbers that made the satellite phones appear to be coming from anywhere.

Rayford punched in the number for an international operator. "The Global Community Palace in New Babylon, please," he said.

"I'm ringing it for you," the operator said, "but they have no light there just now, and you may encounter delays."

"Thank you."

"You have reached the Global Community Headquarters Palace in New Babylon. Please bear with us as technical difficulties may make it impossible to answer your call immediately."

And there came "Hail Carpathia" by the big choir again. "Agh!"

"Global Community, how may I direct your call?"

"Krystall, please."

"In the potentate's office?"

"Of course."

"Sir, it's after hours here. Those offices are closed."

"I know that. Her quarters, please."

"Who may I say is calling?"

"I'll tell her."

"I need to know, sir, or I won't ring someone at this time of the night."

"If you have to know, it's her uncle Gregory."

"One moment."

Mac shot Rayford a look. "Uncle Gregory?"

"Long story."

"Long flight. I'll look forward to it."

"Uncle Gregory?" Krystall said, her voice thick from sleep.

"Is this line secure?" Rayford said.

"I think so. I don't know. This isn't my uncle, is it?"

"You know who it is."

"You never told me."

"You know I'm a friend."

"I'll know for sure if you can really help my uncle. I passed along your message."

"You did? Is he following up?"

"I think he is."

"Believe me, if he makes contact, our people will get him everything he needs."

"I'm grateful, but why are you call—"

"A favor."

"I knew it. I can't—"

"Hear me out. I had no idea I would need anything when I talked to you. I just need information that only you can give me."

"I can't be giving you inf—"

"I'm not asking for much, but I don't want to get you in trouble."

"Oh, what's the difference?" she said. "Being in trouble is no worse than being in his good graces around here."

"I need to know if there's been any talk of an important arrest in the United North American States. It would be a young wom—"

"Yes! Yes! Late in the day, a couple of hours after quitting time—we were still working because of the move tomorrow afternoon—Mr. Akbar came in excited about some break in San Diego. Local GC there arrested someone connected with the Judah-ites."

"Any idea whether they are planning to—"

"That's all I know. Really."

"I appreciate this more than I can say, Krystall. Is there anything I can do for you?"

"What could you possibly do for me?"

"I just wish—"

"If you can't send me a pair of eyes, I can't think of a thing."

6

THE TATTOO ARTIST snapped on her rubber gloves and asked Mainyu Mazda in an Indian accent if he wanted anesthetic. He pulled back and looked at her.

"You never do," she said. "Head back, chin up."

Albie did not expect a meeting with this man in this part of this town to be other than bizarre, but neither did he dream he would have to compete with a dermatological procedure.

"Go ahead, my friend," Mainyu said, gesturing. "You come to me why?"

Albie leaned forward, forearms on the desk, and told MM of his urgent need in Al Hillah. The woman's battery-powered applicator emitted a loud, rapid clicking as she worked. Mainyu winced but managed to encourage Albie with "Uh-huhs" and "Hmms." Finally he said, "A moment, Kashmir." The woman pulled away and busied herself with the needle in the glow of the lamp.

"It is no secret that you are not a friend of the potentate," MM said.

Albie smiled. "I hope it is a secret in some places."

"Why do you not let me have Kashmir give you a loyalty mark? Any number you wish."

"You know I cannot do that, Mainyu."

"Oh yes. You are now a Judah-ite and believe in the evil spirits."

"The evil sp—?"

Mainyu waved with the back of his hand. "Don't you people believe that anyone who takes the mark of Carpathia goes to hell, something like that?"

"More important is where our loyalty lies."

MM looked at Kashmir, then leaned back and grinned at Albie. He laughed loudly. "You are not going to start in on me now, are you, old friend? I wondered."

"No, you have made your choice. I am curious as to why you have a *72* and not a *216,* though."

"You think I am a friend of the international regime?"

"Well, I wond—"

"You think my mark is real? You know me better than that." He spat.

"But the penalty for a fake mark is worse than death," Albie said.

"Public torture, I know," Mainyu said. "But the GC is not interested in me except in how I can benefit them. If I were to bear the mark of the one to whom I am loyal, it would have to be the number *1*. What is it our Mexican friends say, Albie? 'Look out for *número uno!*' And if I was not a benefit to the GC, I would be assigned to the Plain of Jezreel like so many millions of others. What kind of business could I do there?"

"How do you benefit the GC?"

Kashmir dabbed at a tiny stream of blood on Mainyu's neck.

"I am a businessman, Albie. I look for the biggest profit for the smallest expense, and right now that is bounty money."

"You—"

"Deliver the disloyal to the Peacekeepers. Of course I do. Tell me, what is the cost of doing that kind of business? Twenty thousand Nicks a head, same price dead or alive. I find the dead more manageable. Once the victim is still, there is no danger, no escape attempt, nothing messy. With the right size plastic bag, even the car stays clean. Follow?"

"So, you are a supplier—"

"To the GC, yes, of course. If low overhead and high profit is the businessman's mantra, what better business is there than something for nothing? They are willing to pay for something I can provide."

Albie wondered how many unmarked victims of Mainyu's were Judah-ites. "My request, then," Albie said, "does it constitute a conflict of interest for you?"

"Of course not, my friend! Not if you brought the money. I am not a friend of the GC. I am merely a business associate. My interest is profit."

"I wasn't sure what such services would cost."

"Oh yes, you were. You are not out of the business that long. And surely you didn't expect me to commit to this without all the money up front, not when it has to be done almost immediately."

"You have the people, the hardware, the—?"

"You know I have everything. It will be done. Provided you have the money."

"Such a job would have cost twenty thousand Nicks a few years ago," Albie said.

"So I assume you brought more, due to inflation and the urgent nature of the request."

Albie hesitated.

"Sure you did, and you will not make the mistake of holding out on me, because you know how easy it would be for me to find out how much you have with you."

"Of course. I brought thirty thousand Nicks."

"Hmm."

"Surely that's enough. Fifty percent more than before has to cover inflation and the rush."

"It's not enough," Mainyu said. "It's twenty thousand short."

Albie assumed the deal was about to go down. They were in the haggling stage, and anything other than a vigorous argument from both sides would show disrespect. "Thirty thousand is all I brought, and all I am willing to pay."

"Uh-huh. And is it all on your person or did you leave some on your bike?"

"You know better than that, Mainyu. Who leaves cash in the alley here?"

Mainyu laughed. "Sahib!"

The tall man unlocked the door and entered.

"How much is our friend paying you to watch his bike?"

"Twenty-five."

"How much does he owe?"

"Ten."

Mainyu turned to Albie. "Do you have thirty thousand plus the ten you owe Sahib?"

"Yes."

"Any more?"

"Spare change for the trip home."

"Let me see the thirty thousand."

Albie reached inside his jacket and produced a brick of bills wrapped in cellophane.

"Now the ten you owe Sahib."

Albie slapped a ten on the table.

"Now your spare change."

From his left pocket Albie produced a wad of bills and coins. "Maybe another fifteen-plus," he said.

Mainyu pressed his lips together and cocked his head, arching his eyebrows at Albie. "We are still twenty thousand apart," he said.

"I said thirty thousand is all I'm willing to pay."

"Then we have a problem. What are we going to do about the other twenty?"

Albie fought a grin. Mainyu had always driven a hard bargain. "You're serious," Albie said. "You won't do it for thirty? You want me to take my business elsewhere?"

"Oh no! And pass up what's before me? No!"

"It'll be done, then?"

"It's already done, my friend. Something for nothing. Fifty thousand and change for virtually no overhead."

"Fifty?"

"Kashmir, call the palace for me, will you? Get Mr. Akbar. Sahib? Remember what I have been teaching you about the business? Creative solutions for getting to where a deal makes sense?"

Sahib nodded. "Yes, Mr. Mazda."

"Your handgun, please."

Sahib produced a .44 revolver.

Mainyu Mazda hefted it and turned it over in his hands. "My old friend and I are twenty thousand Nicks apart, and he is the solution. What is the bounty on unmarked citizens again, Sahib?"

"Twenty thousand."

"That makes fifty. And we don't even have to do the job."

He pointed the barrel between Albie's eyes and pulled the trigger.

+ + +

Her cell, Chloe thought, was in a strange location. It consisted of a cage in the corner of a larger room. A metal shelf protruded from the wall. Her bed, she imagined. And a combination sink and toilet stood in plain sight. It was what wasn't there that concerned her. Nothing was movable or removable. There wasn't so much as a toilet seat, a blanket, or a pillow. No reading material. Nothing.

Faint from hunger, Chloe crawled onto the shelf and lay on her side, facing the door. She was supported by woven strips of metal about four inches wide that might have given a bit if she weighed a hundred more pounds. Not even the formerly ubiquitous Nigel was anywhere to be seen. The outer room was bright enough, the sun streaming through the windows and bars. But the room was otherwise drab, all tile and linoleum and steel in institutional greens.

Chloe wanted to call out, to tell someone she was hungry, but her pride overcame her discomfort. She sat up quickly when she heard the door open, and a man in a custodial-type uniform hurried in. Cleaning bottles hung from his belt next to his cell phone. He carried a rag and had another in his back pocket.

"Oh, hi," he said. "Didn't know we had somebody in custody."

"You're not supposed to," she said, dying to be charming.

"Pardon?"

"I just wandered in here. Locked myself in like an idiot."

He laughed, a smile radiating. "And you had the bad fortune of wearing a jumpsuit today that makes you look like an inmate too. Unlucky."

"Yeah, that's me," she said.

"Maybe they locked you up for your taste in clothes, huh?"

"Must have."

"Well, I'm just getting a bucket over here. Best of luck to ya."

"Thanks."

He grabbed a bucket from the corner under a suspended TV set and headed back toward the door. Then he stopped and turned on his heel. "They gave you your phone call, didn't they?"

"Oh, sure. I've been treated like a queen. I called Santa Claus."

He set the bucket down and moved to within a few feet of the cage. He looked over his shoulder at the door, then turned back and lowered his voice. "No, I'm serious. That's the one thing I don't like here. I mean, people get what they deserve, not taking the mark and all, like you. I'm not so naïve as to think there'd still be a trial for that after all these years, but what ever happened to one phone call? I mean, this is still America, isn't it?"

"Not the one I remember."

"Me either. Hey, you wanna make a phone call?"

"What?"

"You gotta promise not to tell. I'd be in a lot of trouble."

"What, with your phone?"

"Sure. Here." He slid it from his belt and angled it so it would fit between the wires of the cage. "But just one, and you gotta make it quick. Then hide it. Or slide it across the floor like I dropped it or something. I'll come back for it in a while."

"You're serious?"

"Sure. What's the harm? Go ahead. Knock yourself out. Pretty little thing like you. I'll be back."

Chloe's hands shook as she went to a corner with her back to the door. *How dumb do they think I am? Thing probably doesn't even work, and if it does, not from here.* She didn't care. It was worth a try. She had to talk with someone. She didn't dare risk calling the safe house, assuming this was a setup and that any call would be traced.

Chloe dialed her dad's phone number. He had to be back in Petra by now.

* * *

Rayford had awakened Krystall in the palace yet again. "I've been thinking about your request," he said.

"My request?"

"For eyes."

"Don't play with me."

"No, it kept working on me, and I might just know of a pair you could use. You remember, just before you and I spoke, someone opened the door, then shut it again and ran off?"

"How could I forget? That's when you scared the life out of me."

"He's a believer too, and he can see in New Babylon."

"I'm listening."

"I might be able to talk him into coming back and helping you when everyone else is gone. He can tell you where stuff is, do all sorts of things for you."

"What's in it for you?"

"There might be things in the files I'd like to know about."

"More than you know."

"See? He helps you for a few days, or for however long you want, and you give him access to things that might help me. Deal?"

"What's in it for him?"

"I'll take care of that. In fact, I'll call him right now and see if I can set it up. Well, I'll call him tomorrow. No sense waking him."

"No, why should I be the only one up at this hour?"

"Sorry." Rayford heard a tone that told him he had a call coming in. "Hang on just a second, Krystall." He checked the caller ID. A San Diego area code, but a number he didn't recognize. "I'd better take this. If I can get this deal arranged, I'll have the guy call you."

He punched his call button twice, ending one call and picking up the other. "Steele here."

"Daddy, it's me."

"Chloe!"

"Please, just listen. You still have that record feature on your phone?"

"Yes, but—"

"Turn it on right now. Do it. Did you? Is it on?"

"Yes, but—"

"I know this call is being traced and your phone is going to be useless after this, but I couldn't call anyone else. I'm in the San Diego GC jail, and they're trying to bargain with me to get to the others. Tell Buck and Kenny I love them with all my heart and that if I don't see them again before heaven, I'll be waiting for them there. Dad, this was all my fault, but I was jogging within thirty miles of our place and, oh, listen, I just wanted to tell you that I'm all right for now.

I've just been sitting here reminiscing about that wonderful trip you and Mom and I took to Colorado when I was five or six. Remember?"

"Vaguely. Chloe, listen—"

"Dad, I don't dare stay on long. It's important to me that you remember that trip!"

"Honey, that had to be more than twenty years ago. I—"

"It was! But it was so special, and I wish everybody could go there again. If I had one dream, it's that we could all go there right now, as soon as possible."

"Chloe—"

"Dad, don't. You know they have to be listening. Just please give my love to everybody and tell them to pray that I'll be strong to the end. I will give nothing away. Nothing. And, Dad, think of the Colorado trip so I know we'll both be thinking of the same thing at the same time. I love you, Dad. Don't ever forget that."

"I love you too, honey. I—"

"Bye, Daddy."

And she was gone.

+ + +

"You're supposed to be the combat guy, George," Buck said. "And all you want to talk about is packing."

"I just want you to know, Buck, that I'm not going to hold you responsible for any mean thing you say to me until Chloe is back safe and sound. Then I'm going to tell on you."

"Yeah, and she'll ground you," Priscilla said.

Buck owed George a smile, and it never ceased to amuse him when Priscilla vainly tried to add to or improve on her husband's humor. It was just that Buck's spirits could not be lifted. His father-in-law had confirmed where Chloe was through his contact at the palace, and the local GC headquarters simply was not a place vulnerable to a raid.

"The best thing we have going for us," Sebastian said, "is that as soon as they determine who she is, she's most valuable to them alive."

Buck knew it was true, but talking about his beloved as a commodity of war left a bad taste.

Late in the afternoon Ming brought Beth Ann Sebastian and Kenny into the workout room. Ree leaped to his feet and uncharacteristically embraced Ming. Buck knew the Chloe situation had sobered him. He wondered if it had even given Ree second thoughts about marriage.

Beth Ann ran back and forth between her parents, showing off. Kenny, frowning, trudged to Buck and climbed in his lap.

"He didn't nap," Ming said.

Buck nodded and held Kenny's cheek to his chest. "Sleepy, bud?" he said.

Kenny shook his head. "I want Mommy."

"She'll be back later."

The boy closed his eyes.

Buck looked at Priscilla, biting his lip and unable to stanch the tears. "This is the part I'm going to hate," he mouthed, his chest convulsing. Kenny roused, but Buck tucked the boy's head under his chin and wrapped both arms around him, rocking. And weeping.

Priscilla pushed Beth Ann toward her dad and leaned close to Buck. "Don't you dare give up, Buck. None of us are."

+ + +

Chloe wanted to call everybody she knew, but she had little question she'd been set up. It had all been too easy. The global positioning system in her father's phone would tell the GC right where he was. She had assumed Petra, but from the ambient sounds, he was in the air. How long had he and Abdullah been in New Babylon if he was just heading back now? It didn't compute. Of course he would have been informed of her disappearance. Maybe he was on his way home. She only hoped he could get rid of the phone before getting close to California. The last thing she wanted was to lead the GC right to the safe house.

Chloe reached as high as she could and pushed the phone through an opening in the cage. It flew about eight feet before landing on the floor and breaking into pieces. "Oops," she said. "And after that nice man entrusted it to me."

Inside a minute Custodian returned, still dressed the same but this time with no props. No bucket, no cleansers, no rags. No smile either. He knelt to pick up the pieces.

"Thanks for the use of your phone. That was most thoughtful. Maybe you could smuggle me in a cake with a file in it or get word to my people. Sorry about the damage."

"That's all right, doll," he said, not looking at her. "We got what we needed. Looks like Daddy's just off the East Coast. Gotta think he's due to refuel by now. Should be able to alert the most likely airports. You wanna do yourself a favor, work with Jock. He's a fair guy. No, he really is. I'm not saying he's got your best interests at heart, but he's a realist. You've got what he wants, and he knows that's going to cost him."

"Well, then by all means, friend, tell Jock I'm ready to wheel and deal. I'll give him everything he wants, now that I know he's fair. I mean, I heard that from you, and I've known you long enough to trust you completely."

"Be as much of a smart aleck as you want, kid. See where it gets ya. Oh, by the way, Nigel's got your energy bar. Should I tell him you're hungry?"

Chloe sat on the metal bed. She was famished but still more proud than desperate. "Nah. I had a big breakfast. I couldn't eat another thing just yet."

"Maybe some television then."

"Spare me. I've heard enough propaganda to last a lifetime."

"But it's time for the news."

"Oh yes, the eminently objective Global Community News Network. Hey, okay, all right! That's plenty loud enough!"

He ignored her, leaving the volume up and heading for the door.

"Turn it down, please! Sir?"

"Can't hear you," he said. "TV's too loud."

Jock must have been choreographing everything. The five o'clock news was just coming on, Anika Janssen anchoring live from Detroit.

"Good evening. Darkness continues to plague Global Community International Headquarters in New Babylon at this hour. It is confined to the borders of the city and is believed to be an act of aggression on the part of dissidents against the New World Order.

"GC Chief of Security and Intelligence Suhail Akbar spoke with us by phone earlier from the beleaguered capital. In spite of the turmoil there, he reports good news, constituting our top story tonight."

"Yes, Anika," Akbar said, "following months of careful planning and cooperation between the various law-enforcement branches of the Global Community, we are happy to report that a combined task force of crack agents from both our Peacekeeping and Morale Monitor divisions has succeeded in apprehending one of the top-echelon Judah-ite terrorists in the world.

"The arrest was made before dawn today in San Diego after months of planning. I'd rather not go into the details of the operation, but the suspect was disarmed and arrested without incident. Her name is Chloe Steele Williams, twenty-six, a former campus radical at Stanford University in Palo Alto, California, from which she was expelled six years ago after making threats on the lives of the administration."

"Thank you, Chief Akbar. We have further learned that Mrs. Williams is the daughter of Rayford Steele, who once served as pilot for Global Community Supreme Potentate Nicolae Carpathia. He was fired some years ago for insubordination and drinking while on duty, and GC intelligence believes his resentment led to his current role as an international terrorist. He was implicated in the conspiracy to assassinate Potentate Carpathia and is a known associate of former Israeli statesman and now leading Judah-ite Dr. Chaim Rosenzweig.

Both are known to serve on the cabinet of Rabbi Tsion Ben-Judah, head of the Judah-ites, the last holdouts in opposition to the New World Order.

"Mrs. Williams is the wife of Cameron Williams, formerly a celebrated American journalist who also worked directly for the potentate before losing his job due to differences in management style. He edits a subversive cyber and printed magazine with a limited circulation.

"Williams, his wife, and her father are international fugitives in exile, wanted for more than three dozen murders around the world. Mrs. Williams herself heads a black-market operation suspected of hijacking billions of Nicks' worth of goods around the world and selling them for obscene profits to others who cannot legally buy and sell due to their refusal to pledge loyalty to the potentate.

"The Williamses, who have amassed a fortune on the black market, have one child remaining after Mrs. Williams apparently aborted two fetuses and an older daughter died under questionable circumstances. The son, whom they have named Jesus Savior Williams, pictured here, is two years old. Acquaintances report that the Williamses believe he is the reincarnation of Jesus Christ, who will one day conquer Nicolae Carpathia and return the globe to Christianity."

Chloe sat staring at a toddler, clearly not Kenny Bruce, who had a Bible in his lap and wore a tiny T-shirt that read "Kill Carpathia!"

"Chief Akbar reports that his forces traced the leading cell of the Judah-ites in the United North American States to San Diego, where Mrs. Williams was apprehended today. Local GC operatives there say she is already, quote, 'singing like a bird, offering all kinds of information on her colleagues, including her own family, to avoid a death sentence.'

"Here's San Diego GCNN reporter Sue West with Colonel Jonathan 'Jock' Ashmore. Sue?"

"Thank you, Anika. Colonel Ashmore, how important would you say this arrest is?"

"It's almost inestimable," Jock said, nervously tugging at his uniform jacket, which came short of covering his middle. "And Mrs. Williams has proved to be the typical terrorist who knows when it's time to bargain. When the reality hit her that she had been positively identified and we informed her of the overwhelming charges against her, it was only a matter of minutes before she began offering various deals to save her skin."

"Are you at liberty to say what some of those might be?"

"Not entirely, though she has already pledged to enroll her son in Junior GC as soon as possible. She did reveal the whereabouts of a low-level Middle Eastern black marketeer named Al Basrah, after the Iranian city of the same name."

"I believe that's in Iraq, Colonel, but go ahead."

"What?"

"Al Basrah is in Iraq, sir."

"Whatever. Anyway, this character shot himself to death rather than be arrested."

"We are about to show a picture of the dead Al Basrah," Sue West said, "but we warn you that the picture is very graphic."

Chloe stood and stared as the photo was displayed. It showed Albie with a black hole between lifeless eyes, a pool of blood behind his head. It was clearly him. But was it real or doctored?

Chloe shouted, "Jock! Jock! Nigel! Get Jock!" Her screams became sobs, and she demanded, "Is that true? I want to know if that's true! Is Albie dead? Tell me Albie's not dead!"

But no one came. No one responded. As the TV blared, Chloe slid to the floor, wailing, "God, please! No!"

7

"GOT ME A FRIEND in Florida," Mac said. "Jacksonville. Co-op guy. We can refuel there and avoid the normal spots."

"And I can put this phone under one of the wheels before we take off," Rayford said. "If they find a mass of metal and plastic on the tarmac, what're they going to do with it?"

"Wouldn't you rather drown it? Won't take but a minute to drop it in the drink."

"What'm I going to do, Mac, roll down my window and toss it out?"

"Nah. There's a dandy little thing we used to do in the military when we wanted to drop something from altitude. You stick it in the speed brake well, which is, of course, closed on the ground. When we get back in the air, I'll activate the speed brake—"

"Which will open the panel. Beautiful."

"Yes," Mac said. "You just take her up, throttle up, activate the brake, and send that phone into the wild blue yonder."

"I don't want to lose any time fooling around."

"Gimme that thing. I'll do it. Won't take more'n sixty seconds."

"I've got to copy Chloe's message first. She's trying to tell me something, that's for sure."

"It's about my turn for a break anyway, Ray. Once you get it ciphered, switch seats with me and I'll study it."

+ + +

Chang had arrived at Petra in the middle of the afternoon, and Naomi offered to give him his first look at the place. "I will leave word at the computer center to let us know when they learn anything about Chloe," she said, "but I don't want you to see that place until the end, okay?"

He shrugged.

"Abdullah got someone to take your things to your new quarters, which are not far from his. He will take you there so you can get settled, and then I will come by to give you your first day's tour."

Chang had been determined not to let anyone immediately pair him off with somebody. Especially not Naomi. She had to still be a teenager, which was all right. He was just twenty himself. And while there was no question about her intellect and technical brilliance, they were going to have to work closely over the next year. Why complicate things?

And yet . . . in person she was stunning. Olive skin and welcoming dark eyes were set off by her long, black hair. Chang found it difficult not to stare. She had a beautiful, shy smile, and she seemed so friendly and selfless. He had never even had a girlfriend, only girls he had been interested in in high school but whom he would never have dared let know it.

On the way to Chang's prefabricated quarters, Abdullah seemed to know everybody and wanted them to meet him. They treated Chang like royalty, but he was so ashamed of bearing the mark of Carpathia that he kept his baseball cap pulled low. His instinct was to remove it and bow each time, but he could not.

"Our man inside the palace," Abdullah called him, and people embraced him or shook his hand, and many blessed him.

To Chang it was a foretaste of heaven. "I wonder what the chances are of meeting Dr. Ben-Judah and Dr. Rosenzweig," he said.

"Oh, I am so sorry," Abdullah said. "I was supposed to tell you. They send their most abject apologies for not greeting you appropriately. They have been meeting with the elders about the issue of Chloe's disappearance, and they have a council meeting later. They request that you join them over manna in the morning."

"Good, yes. Thank you, Mr. Smith. I have something I must consult with Dr. Ben-Judah about."

"I believe Naomi's father would like to meet you too."

He could tell from Abdullah's inflection that he was trying to say something, but Chang would not bite. "Well, I will look forward to meeting him as well."

When they reached the dwellings, shipped in and assembled by a team led by Lionel Whalum, Abdullah first showed Chang his own place. "You can see that I like to live close to the ground. I sit outside near a fire when I eat my manna. And inside, I sleep on the floor. If that is not your custom, you need not do that. Your place is not much different in size from what you had at the palace, but of course it is much plainer and simpler."

"It's perfect," Chang said when they arrived. His luggage lay next to his cot, and his computers and file boxes sat by the door. "I will sleep tonight a free man, worried about nothing but the welfare of our comrades."

"I'll leave you to unpack. If you need anything, you can see my place from here. Do you need anything at all?"

"Just one thing. I am a little nervous about the manna. Does everyone care for it?"

"Yes, they do. I am confident you will enjoy it. Imagine, being fed by the King. Yes, it is just sustenance, and yes, it appears to be merely bread. But it comes from the kitchens of heaven. How can it be anything but glorious? We are due a portion just before sundown, so you will know before you join the doctors for breakfast whether you like it or not."

Half an hour later, when Chang had his place situated just the way he wanted it, he heard a knock. "Come in!" he said, but no one did. As he approached the door, he said, "It's open!" Still nothing.

He opened the door to Naomi. "Come in, come in!" he said.

"Oh, I must not," she said. "In my culture it is improper."

"I'm sorry."

"You'll learn. Come, let me show you Petra."

"No word yet on Chloe?" he said as they ventured out.

She shook her head. "It's not going to come to a good end, you know."

"That's my fear," he said. "But we can hope and pray."

Naomi explained that the city was so spread out that it would take days to see it all. "We'll get ATVs near the tech center. Then let me take you to the Treasury first, then to a few of the nearby tombs—there are many. Finally I'd like to take you to the high place where the missile hit and the spring still bubbles, providing daily water for more than a million people. If I have timed it right, it should then be close to sundown, and we can enjoy our manna with water directly from the source."

Chang was not used to this much walking and climbing, so he was glad when they were finally aboard four-wheelers. He was stunned by Petra's beautiful architecture and wondered how anyone could have carved such structures out of solid rock.

When they finally reached the crest of the high place, where the spring cascaded into cisterns and aqueducts to the entire area, Naomi cut her engine and signaled Chang to do the same.

"Are you thirsty?" she said.

"Always. But mostly I'm trying to get used to not worrying who is watching."

"I cannot imagine. Are you willing to drink from my hands?"

Chang, usually quick and flippant, only smiled. "Whatever is proper in your culture."

She knelt and washed her hands in a brook, shaking them dry. Chang did the same. She took him as close as they could get to the center of the spring. "Ready?" she said.

He nodded, and she thrust her cupped hands into the water, bringing them up to just under his chin. "Hurry," she said, laughing. "My hands are not watertight."

He lowered his face into her hands and took a huge gulp. His throat had been more parched than he knew, and though the water could have been only a few degrees cooler than the air, it felt almost icy. He coughed and laughed and said, "More."

He drank from her hands again, and she said, "My turn."

Chang made a bowl of his palms and let her drink. "Enough?" he said, when his hands were empty. She nodded, and he cupped her face and wiped the dust from under her shining eyes. He spread his fingers and extended his hands, brushing through her hair.

Naomi closed her eyes and lifted her face to the setting sun, spreading her arms and holding her hands palms up. "Here it comes, Chang. Receive your daily bread from the God of heaven."

Chang stepped back, looked up, and extended his arms as the skies seemed to snow bits of soft bread that covered the entire area. Below, the million strong emerged from their quarters with jars and baskets, and gathered what they needed for dinner.

"Just like in the Bible," Naomi said, "we are to take what we need but not store any. It will spoil and we will have shown our lack of faith in God to provide every day."

Chang sat beside her and scooped manna into his hand. "Do you ask God to bless food that he has just personally delivered?" he said.

She laughed. "Would you like me to?"

"Please." He quickly removed his cap as she began.

"To the great God of Abraham, Isaac, and Jacob, and to the Father of our Lord and Savior Jesus Christ, we offer our humble thanks for everything you provide."

Her young voice was so pure and sweet and her words so perfect, Chang found his face contorting as tears welled.

"Thank you for safety for our mission today and for allowing us to bring Chang here. May he find refreshing peace and rest in you. In the name of Jesus we ask you to bless to our nourishment this gift you have given. Amen."

With tears streaming, Chang turned away and tugged his cap back on. He sat with the warm manna in his hand, unable to eat for crying. He felt Naomi caressing his shoulder. "God bless you, Chang," she said. "Bless you."

He gathered himself and wiped his face with his free hand. "Don't wait for me," he managed. "Go ahead."

"I just might," she said lightly. "I never grow tired of this."

"What does it taste like?" he said.

"Oh no, that is not for me to tell you. I know only what it tastes like to me."

Chang picked two of the small, white disks from his hand and laid them on his tongue.

"Well?" she said.

It was as if he had been struck dumb. "Oh," he said. "Oh."

"That's all you can say?"

He took several more at once. "Oh!"

"I'm guessing you approve."

"I taste honey. Honey for sure."

"Yes."

"Almost like cookies, those sweet wafer things. And they're so filling. I want more and yet I've had enough."

"Imagine," Naomi said. "Everything we need for twenty-four hours comes in three helpings of this."

"Miraculous."

"Exodus 16:31 says, 'And the house of Israel called its name Manna. And it was like white coriander seed, and the taste of it was like wafers made with honey.'"

"I'm impressed," he said. "What, you have the whole Old Testament memorized?"

She laughed. "Hardly, but you know for all of my childhood, I didn't call it the Old Testament. It was my Bible. I studied it every day. I still do, but it's a whole different thing now, now that I really know God."

"I memorize Scripture too," Chang said. "But I've never owned a Bible. I was raised an atheist, so I have to memorize off the Internet."

"But you do memorize?"

"Doesn't everybody? I mean, Dr. Ben-Judah only reminds us to about five times with every daily message."

"What are you memorizing?"

"New Testament. John. I'm up to chapter three. I'm slow."

"But you have it memorized up to there?" she said. "That's good."

"Well, yeah, I think. But don't test me. I mean, you could test me on chapter three, because that's right where I am, but . . ."

His voice trailed off. Chang could have sat there next to Naomi all night, but she stood and took another drink from the spring. "Let me show you something," she said, reaching for him. He offered his hand and she pulled him up. "You see my garment?"

He shrugged and nodded. Did he see her garment? He had been stealing glances all day. He wouldn't have known what to call it. It was more robe than dress, like something he imagined women wearing in Bible times.

"It is the only thing I have ever worn here. I had it on when we arrived."

"It looks brand-new."

"I wash it out every night, and it is new every morning, like the Lord's compassion."

"Another memorized passage?"

"Yes. Only that was one my father led me to after we survived the bombs."

"You were here for that?"

"We were among the first."

"What was that like?"

"Like a dream, Chang. Sometimes I cannot imagine it really happened."

"What was the passage?"

"Lamentations 3:22-24: 'Through the Lord's mercies we are not consumed, because His compassions fail not. They are new every morning; great is Your faithfulness. "The Lord is my portion," says my soul, "Therefore I hope in Him!"'"

"That's beautiful."

"Isn't it? Well, I promised my father we would be back at the tech center at least by sundown. It's near the amphitheater, so we'll have to hurry."

"Am I going to get to hear your story?" he said.

"Of course. And I want to hear yours. Maybe after breakfast tomorrow."

Chang found the tech center much as he might have expected, except that it was so incongruous to see the massive network of computers in a building cut from rock. By that time, however, he was much more impressed with Naomi than with hardware and software.

"Can you find your way to your quarters?" she said. "We retire early here and rise with the sun."

"I can, but I'd rather not," he said. "I think I need a guide just one more time, you know, being my first night here."

"I can find you one. Hold on."

"Naomi!" he said. "I'm kidding. Of course I can find it. I'd just rather you walked me there."

"In my cul—"

"Inappropriate, of course. How about my walking you home?"

"That would be acceptable and even chivalrous. My father is waiting for me, and it will be dark by the time I arrive. He will appreciate that I had an escort."

Like Abdullah, Naomi's father tended a small fire outside their place. He was a tall, rotund man with a thick, curly beard. Chang approached shyly, took off his cap in the darkness, and bowed. "Chang Wong," he said.

Naomi's father grasped him by the shoulders and pressed his right cheek to Chang's, then his left. "Eleazar Tiberias," he said with a great, deep voice. "Perhaps you know my lake."

Chang scratched his head and looked at Naomi, which seemed to bring no end of mirth to her and her father.

"I have heard so much about you, young man," the elder said. "I am grateful to you for looking after my daughter, and I look forward with great anticipation to getting to know you better."

Chang breathed deeply of the crisp night air on his way to his quarters. Abdullah's fire was just smoldering now, and the smoke permeated Chang's clothes. He felt so free, so happy, and so enamored that he was sure he would not be able to sleep. He knelt by his bed, hardly knowing what to pray. He tried to remember the verse Naomi quoted, but all he could come up with was "Great is Your faithfulness," so he repeated that over and over as he climbed into the cot. Through the open window he stared at skies so clear he felt as if he could see every star in the universe. But after fewer than sixty seconds he saw nothing but Naomi in his dreams.

+ + +

Mac studied Rayford's scribblings. "You copied every last word of this conversation, didn't you?"

"I didn't know what else to do," Rayford said. "Clearly the clue is in that Colorado business."

"What do you remember about it, Ray?"

"It was so long ago, Mac. Just one of those summer things you do when the kids are little. Raymie wasn't even born yet. It was just the three of us."

"Yeah, but after she tells you what to say to Buck and Kenny, she says something about this being her fault. And then the jogging stuff, she's not serious about that, is she?"

"Being thirty miles from home? Nah. Trying to mislead the GC, no doubt, but they're not going to fall for that."

"She promises not to give anything away, and you know, I believe every word of that."

"Me too. They won't get anything out of Chloe."

"So she says the trip was 'so special and I wish everybody could go there again.' But you say it was just the three of you."

"Right. So she, what, wants everybody in San Diego to go to Colorado?"

"Can't be," Mac said. "She says herself she knows the GC is listening in. But she says her dream is that 'we could all go there right now, as soon as possible.' Where did you go in Colorado, Ray?"

Rayford shook his head. "I don't remember. Where do you go there?"

"Been there lots of times," Mac said. "What cities were you in?"

"Just the Springs and Denver, I think."

"You do the cog railway thing?"

"Pikes Peak, sure."

"The place with all those big rock formations?"

"Yeah, Garden of the Gods."

"That cowboy place, the ranch?"

"Flying W, of course. Wouldn't miss that."

"Air Force Academy?"

"Drove by it but didn't have time. We were going to a concert."

"Where?"

"Outside of Denver. And it was outside too. Seemed like we climbed forever, and I had to carry Chloe. I was so out of breath at that altitude."

"Red Rocks?"

"Yes! That was the place. Some country-music deal. Chloe loved it."

"You got it yet, Ray?"

"Got what?"

"What she's trying to tell you."

"No, but apparently you do, Mac. Spill it."

"Red Rocks."

"That's what I said."

"Mm-hm."

"Oh! Petra! The GC is on to the safe house, and we've got to get those people out and to Petra."

+ + +

In the morning Abdullah ushered Chang toward an area near where the elders' council met daily. Fresh manna covered the ground all along the way, and many were out gathering their breakfasts. "I will not be joining you today," Abdullah said, "as Miss Naomi has need of me in the computer center. She requests that you come and help when you are free as well."

"Is there a problem?"

"I'm afraid there is."

Chang stopped. Abdullah sounded so sad, so ominous. "What is it?"

"I'd rather not spoil your breakfast, Master Chang."

"It would spoil my breakfast? I am meeting with my heroes, and I am here where I can go where I please and do what I want, and still there is news that intrudes enough to ruin my day?"

"Please hurry. Let us not be late."

"I need to know, Mr. Smith. Tell me it's not Chloe Williams."

"She is alive for the moment, and except for the fact that the Global Community News Network is spreading the most heinous lies about her, everyone involved speculates that the GC will not execute her as long as they think they can get information from her."

Chang shook his head as they continued walking. "So she would be better off to pretend to be about to cave, to at least be considering giving them something, than to make plain from the beginning that she will not."

"Have you met Mrs. Williams?"

"Of course not."

"But you have dealt with her by phone and via the Internet enough to know—"

"Her personality. Yes. Not only will she not be betraying a thing, but she will also enjoy telling them so."

"My fear," Abdullah said, "is that this will shorten her potential benefit to the GC and thus shorten her life."

"Surely the San Diego Trib Force is planning a raid."

"I do not know. Knowing Cameron, it must be all he can do to keep from trying to blast in there on his own. George Sebastian will want to lead such an effort, and he's the man for it, but this is not like surprising a band of amateurs in the woods, as they did in Greece. You can imagine that the San Diego GC is alert to just such an effort."

"You're not telling me everything, are you, Mr. Smith?"

"I should save some for you to learn at the tech center, not that Naomi is eager to tell you either."

Chang stopped again and put a hand on Abdullah's shoulder. "Forgive my familiarity, but there is no point in withholding information. Please, I must know. Don't make me go in there unprepared."

Abdullah appeared to study the ground. He stooped and scooped a handful of manna but just held it. "The GCNN says Chloe gave up Albie and that he committed suicide rather than be taken in."

"Come on, Mr. Smith. We know that's not true. She would never—"

Abdullah took Chang's elbow and urged him to keep moving. "No one suspects Chloe of having anything to do with it, and anyone who knows Albie does not believe he killed himself."

"Then what is the probl—?"

"There is evidence that Albie may be dead. He and Mr. McCullum had grown close, as you know, and when word reached Mac, he tried several different ways to get in touch with Albie."

"It could be coincidence. He may have been away from his phone. Maybe he—"

"He is never away from his phone. Mac has always been able to reach him."

"But Mac and Captain Steele should be in San Diego by now. Maybe the satellite phone acts up at that distance and—"

Now it was Abdullah's turn to stop. "We are almost there. Around the next bend, Drs. Ben-Judah and Rosenzweig await you. Mr. Tiberias will make the introductions and attend to the meal. Meals are short here because we eat only one food and enjoy springwater with it."

"Thank you, Mr. Smith. I am going to go believing that Albie will still call back."

"All right, if you insist on knowing. . . . Albie's phone was answered, but not by Albie. As you may know, he was on a dangerous mission and may have erred terribly by going alone. The man who answered the phone told Mac that if he wanted to see his friend one more time, he should watch the news. We have watched and recorded that newscast, Master Chang. Naomi will show it to you after breakfast. Now go."

✣ ✣ ✣

At 9 p.m. in San Diego, Chloe lay whimpering on the steel bed in her cell. With the setting of the sun the big room had faded to darkness, and now the only light came from the blaring TV. No one had visited her since the phony custodian had come back for what was left of his phone. She had heard her segment of the news a dozen more times—only because she had no choice—but she refused to watch again.

She didn't care about the lies. No Judah-ites would believe any of that, and if they did, Buck could straighten them out in the next issue of *The Truth.* But Albie, poor precious Albie. She hoped and prayed that was a lie too, but how could they have so quickly concocted such a vivid image of a dead man who looked so much like him?

Chloe had not eaten since seven o'clock the night before. She drew her knees up to her chest and wrapped her arms around her shins. She rocked, trying to ease the pain in her stomach. She tried to comfort herself by imagining the operation George and Buck and her father had to be planning that very minute.

Chloe tried to force from her mind thoughts of Kenny, because she so longed for him that her arms ached. Would she ever see him again? How would Buck answer their son's questions about her? Who would take care of Kenny when Buck was away?

She wondered if sleep would ease the hunger pangs and whether it was possible to sleep. She had learned enough about such things from George to know that any attempt to free her would have to come when the GC least expected it, so it could be days, maybe longer. She had to learn to sleep. Somehow Chloe had to keep her sanity in spite of how she was treated.

Any vestige of prisoners' rights had disappeared with the rise of Nicolae Carpathia. *Here we are, a year to go to the end of history, and I could be shot in my cell for not bearing the mark.*

Lonely, hungry, aching for her loved ones, grieving for Albie, Chloe closed her eyes in the darkness, covered her ears, and hummed to drown out the TV. That, she realized, was why she didn't hear the night matron until she was standing at the cage. Chloe flinched and sat up quickly, terrified of the stocky silhouette.

8

NAOMI'S FATHER GREETED Chang the same way he had the night before, cheek to cheek, and while Chang bowed, he did not remove his cap in the light of day. "A word to the wise," Elder Tiberias rumbled in his ear during their embrace, "just about any culture considers it impolite not to remove one's hat in the presence of one's elder."

"Forgive me, sir," Chang whispered, "but removing it would reveal a disgrace."

Eleazar Tiberias shut his eyes and nodded knowingly, as if remembering that he had been told of Chang's dual marks. "I understand."

The older man reached for a basket filled with manna. "Dr. Ben-Judah will be a few moments, but let me introduce you to Dr. Rosenzweig. Come, come."

Chang followed the big man into his quarters, where he was surprised to see the diminutive Chaim Rosenzweig, who looked more like Albert Einstein than the famous Micah who had stood up to the potentate. Rosenzweig had apparently been in Petra long enough for his hair to grow back, his pigmentation to return to normal, and to look like his old self.

Rosenzweig leaped to his feet, a bundle of energy for such an elderly man. "So you are Chang Wong, the genius mole!"

"Well, I—"

"Do not feign modesty, my young friend. God has used you. Oh, he has used you so mightily! Ah, the rewards that await you in heaven." He took Chang's arm and pressed it against his own side. "Come, let us wait outside for Dr. Ben-Judah. Eleazar, join us, please. Dr. Ben-Judah, as you know, is the leader here, though he is my junior by many years. Oh yes, at least twenty years. He was a student of mine many, many years ago. It is true. Well, Mr. Wong, welcome, welcome, welcome. It is unfortunate you join us on a day of sadness over the loss of one of our members and the capture of another, but we are happy that you are with us."

From a distance, Chang saw the commotion as Dr. Ben-Judah approached. He was flanked by several of the other elders, and they were coming from the direction of the tech center.

Dr. Rosenzweig confided, "Those men will not be joining us, and they are not bodyguards per se. None are needed here, of course. But Dr. Ben-Judah is so popular and beloved, if he is not surrounded by the elders, he would never get anywhere. Everyone wants a moment of his time, but those moments add up. They just want to express their appreciation and their love, but he has so much to do and such a heavy schedule."

"I'm honored that he would take a little time with me," Chang said. "Like everyone else, I want a moment of his time."

"Oh, trust me, young friend, I know him well, and he has been looking forward to this."

The other elders peeled away as Dr. Ben-Judah arrived. "I am so sorry to have postponed and then to be late on top of that," he said. "But it could not be helped. Well, someone introduce me to our newest resident."

Eleazar Tiberias chuckled loudly as Dr. Rosenzweig said, "Oh, I believe you know who this is. Dr. Tsion Ben-Judah, may I present Chang Wong."

Dr. Ben-Judah eschewed the customary Jewish greeting, first returning Chang's bow, then stepping forward to embrace the boy tightly. "Sit, sit," he said. "Sit right here between Dr. Rosenzweig and me. You know, years ago he was my prof—"

"I have told him all about it, Tsion," Chaim said. "Let us pray and eat."

Tsion leaned close and whispered, though loud enough for Chaim's benefit too, "The elderly have no patience!"

Tsion held one of Chang's hands and reached across him to take one of Chaim's too. "Eleazar, join us and take a hand, please."

As the four sat holding hands, Dr. Ben-Judah lifted his face and Chang bowed his head. "Great Father, creator, master, and friend," he began, "as we begin yet another day leading to the glorious appearing of our Lord and Savior, we bless your name. We thank you for our daily bread. And we are humbled as we think of where we were so few scant years ago. Mr. Tiberias, a businessman and devout man of religion. Dr. Rosenzweig, a statesman and scholar and agnostic. I, a student of the Bible but blind to the truth. And Mr. Wong, a brilliant young atheist. Who but a good God would give us all a second chance and redeem us by the blood of your precious Son? We praise you in his name."

Tsion held out the basket of manna to Chang, who took a small handful. The older men all took goodly portions, and Tsion said, "Allow me to show you how I eat my daily provision. I am grateful that mealtime does not consume the time it once did, though I confess there are days when I miss everything that used to go with it. Often my meals here last but five minutes."

He allowed the manna to settle in his right palm, wrapped his fingers gently around it, and formed a circle with his thumb and forefinger. "Like peanuts, no?" he said, smiling, and tapped his thumb knuckle on his chin until the wafers popped into his mouth. "A handful," he said, chewing, "and I am nourished."

Mr. Tiberias stood and gathered leftovers into the basket, then tossed them to the wind, where they scattered on the ground.

"Tell me, Dr. Ben-Judah," Chang said, "is it true about Albie?"

"That he is dead? I am afraid so," Tsion said. "Self-inflicted, no, none of us believes that."

After a few moments, Chaim said, "Tsion, we really must be going."

"Oh, sir," Chang said, "I hesitate to ask because I have been told by everyone how busy you are and how everyone wants a bit of your time. . . ."

"Please, Chang. We feel so indebted to you. Ask anything of me, and if I can comply, I will."

"I need just a moment alone, sir. No offense, Dr. Rosenzweig."

"None taken. Mr. Tiberias and I will prepare for our meeting."

Tsion took Chang behind an outcropping of rock. "What can I do for you?"

Chang took off his cap, exposing the *30* emblazoned on his forehead and the thin, pink line where the Global Community biochip had been inserted. He caught the pity in the older man's eyes.

"I confess it *is* strange, Mr. Wong, to see that when I also see the mark of the believer on you."

"I can't stand to look in the mirror," Chang said. "I don't dare take off my hat here. Yes, it may have kept me alive and yes, I had access where no believer would have dreamed. But it mocks me, curses me. I hate it."

"It was forced on you, son. It was not your choice or your fau—"

"I know all that, sir, but I want it gone. Is that possible?"

"I do not know."

"Sir, I study your teachings every day. You say that with God all things are possible. Why would he not remove this now?"

"I do not know, Chang. I just do not want to promise that he will."

"But what if I believe he will? And if you believe?"

"We can agree in faith on this, Chang, but as much as we believe and trust and study, no one can claim to know the mind of God. If you want me to pray that God will remove it, I will. And I believe he can and will do what he chooses. But I want you to pledge that you will accept his decision either way."

"Of course."

"Do not say that glibly. I can see how much you want this, and if God does not grant it, I do not want to see your faith threatened."

"I will be disappointed and I will wonder why, but I will accept it. Will you pray for me?"

Dr. Ben-Judah seemed to study Chang's face. He pressed his lips together, then looked away. Finally, he said, "I will. Come, sit over here and wait. Much as you want to do this in private, I prefer having men of God agree together in prayer. Do you mind?"

"Of course not. I just hate to have them see me with this—"

"There is no getting around that. It may be part of the price."

Chang nodded, and Tsion moved away to call for Eleazar and Chaim. They came, looking somberly at Chang, who sat on a rock and had begun to weep. Tsion briefed them and asked them to join him in the effort of prayer. The three approached, Ben-Judah in the middle, Tiberias on his left, and Rosenzweig on his right.

Tsion placed his left hand behind Chang's head and the heel of his right hand on Chang's forehead. The other two each took one of Chang's hands and put their free hands on his shoulders. Chang shuddered at the gentle touch from these three men of God, and he felt loved by them and by God. His body stiffened and then relaxed.

"Creator God," Tsion began, so softly Chang could barely hear him, "we acknowledge that you made this young man. You have known him and loved him since before the earth was formed. You, who are rich in mercy, loved us even when we were dead in trespasses, made us alive together with Christ and raised us up together, and made us sit together in the heavenly places in Christ Jesus, that in the ages to come he might show the exceeding riches of his grace in his kindness toward us in Christ Jesus. For by grace we have been saved through faith, and that not of ourselves; it is the gift of God, not of works, lest anyone should boast. For we are his workmanship, created in Christ Jesus. . . .

"Now, Chang Wong, knowing that you were not redeemed with corruptible things like silver or gold but with the precious blood of Christ, as of a lamb without blemish and without spot, believe in God. He raised Christ from the dead and gave him glory so that your faith and hope are in God. We now come together in faith, believing. We pray to the God for whom anything is possible, the God who spared us like Shadrach, Meshach, and Abednego of old from the fire of the enemy and made it so that we were people on whose bodies the fire had no power; the hair of our heads was not singed, nor were our garments affected, and the smell of fire was not on us.

"God, according to your will, we ask that you remove from this boy any sign of the evil one."

Chang went limp and felt as if his limbs weighed a hundred pounds apiece. He perspired profusely from every pore and felt sweat run down his face and arms and torso. The men's hands were wet, but they remained still, unmoving in the silence.

Just when Chang felt that if the men let go he would slide off the rock, Tsion said, "Thank you, gentlemen."

They squeezed Chang's hands and shoulders and stepped back. Now he was supported only by Tsion, who still cupped the back of his head and had his right hand over Chang's forehead. He pressed with that hand and let it slide around to the right so that now he had both hands behind Chang's head.

Chang opened his eyes, blinking against the sun and studying the face of Dr. Ben-Judah as Tsion studied his.

Tsion smiled. "Gentlemen," he said, "what do you see?"

Tiberias leaned in from one side and Rosenzweig from the other.

"Praise God!" Chaim said.

Eleazar lifted his head and roared with laughter in his deep bass voice. "I see only the mark of the believer! I have a mirror in my house. Come, see for yourself!"

* * *

Rayford had never seen Mac so despondent. Or so resolute.

"If somebody's killed that old boy, I'm gonna have to do something about it, Ray," Mac said. "Find me something to do that puts me right in the middle of it, and I'm not kidding."

"Albie and I go way back too," Rayford said.

"I know you do. And I feel like I've known him forever."

"What's your gut tell you, Mac? This just part of the GC's propaganda, or is he gone?"

Mac sighed. "Well, no way he killed himself, but I feel like they got him."

Rayford used Mac's phone to call Buck and tell him they would be putting down at about 10 p.m., San Diego time.

"Buck's phone. Hey, Mac, this is George."

"Well, this is Mac's phone, but it's Rayford. How's it going there, George?"

"Like you'd imagine. Buck's in pretty bad shape. It's all we can do to keep him from heading to GC headquarters by himself."

"Can you guys come get us at ten?"

"Ten? You made good time."

"Not bad. Only stopped once, then detoured a bit to drown my phone. Make Buck come with you. Maybe we can all help keep him cool."

"*You* make him come with me. He's not listening to me, and he shouldn't have to."

"Is he there?"

"He's down with Kenny. The little guy's having trouble getting to sleep without his mom."

"Well, tell Buck I said it's a directive. The four of us need to talk as soon as we hit the ground. Can somebody watch Kenny?"

"Sure. For right now we've got more babysitting volunteers than we can use."

"Hey, you think it's too late to call Lionel Whalum in Illinois?"

"Nah. He's a night owl. 'Sup?"

"I figured out Chloe's message. She's convinced we've got to get everybody out of San Diego and to Petra."

"I was afraid of that," Sebastian said.

"Lionel's the only guy I know with enough planes, enough contacts, and enough experience to pull off something like that—and fast."

"This place was so perfect."

"Every safe house we've had has been perfect until it all of a sudden wasn't safe, George."

"Can't argue with that."

"Call Lionel for me, would you? I need to try to get hold of Zeke. See if he's ready to come out of mothballs and help us in Petra."

"What're you thinking, Captain?"

"Something for Buck to do so he doesn't go crazy, and something for Mac and me to do so we feel like we're doing something for Albie."

"Hope I'm part of that."

"We wouldn't dream of trying anything without you, George."

+ + +

"Tired of that TV?" the night matron asked Chloe.

"Yeah. I hope I don't miss it though." Chloe had been watching the congregating of armies from every country in the United Carpathian States, excluding only the city of New Babylon, which was largely ignored on the news. In the flickering light of the TV, Chloe could see the woman was black.

"I'm Florence," she said, jangling to the TV and turning it off with her nightstick. "I'll be the one feeding you tonight if you've been good. You been good?"

"I'm officially hungry, if that's what you mean."

"That's not what I asked you, but I do have your daily energy bar in my pocket if you want it."

"I want it."

"Didn't take long for your tune to change. I heard you was all uppity and smart-alecky before, like nobody had nothin' you needed or wanted."

"I'd like to stay alive."

"For how long? You better be coming up with something Jock can use or you won't make your first hosing down."

"And when is that?"

"Once a week. A week from now."

"I don't bathe for a week?"

"Bathe all you want in that sink. How's that water taste?"

"Not like water."

Florence cackled. "Ain't that the truth. You'll get to like it though. You got to have it. That two hundred fifty calories a day will keep you alive, but you won't be good for much else."

"What else is there in here?"

"Oh, you know, a guard or two might take a liking to you, want a date. You know what I mean."

Chloe laughed. She couldn't help it.

"You think it's funny? What you going to do?"

"That would be worth dying for," Chloe said. "They'd have to kill me first."

"You say that now. But you ain't going to kill me. Look at the size I got on you."

"One of us wouldn't come out of here alive."

"Big talk. You'll be singing a different song when your body weight drops and you be stinking and that jumpsuit is falling off you."

"I'll warn you right now, while I'm lucid, you and anybody else around here would regret trying anything with me."

"That so?"

"That's so, and that includes Jock."

"Jock don't do that kind of thing, but he knows when to look the other way."

"Well, he'll look back to find somebody dead. One of his people or his star prisoner."

"Why don't you just give a little, girl? Tell Jock something. He's not asking for much. And you'd be getting breaks nobody else has got for months. Come in here with no mark and still be alive? That should tell you something. You're in a bargaining position."

"They might as well kill me now."

"Don't think I wouldn't like to."

"You? You don't even know me. I wouldn't want to kill you."

"You just said you would, missus. If I came in that cage."

"Well, yes, if you intended me any harm, I'd defend myself."

"I mean you all kinds of harm. You're either with us or against us now, honey."

"Well, I'm against you," Chloe said.

"Tell me something I don't know."

"Tell me what form these two hundred fifty calories come in."

"You know. The energy bar."

"And that's all I get?"

"That's it. Once a day."

"A person can't live on that."

"You said it, not me. 'Course, the more you tell, maybe the more you get."

"Maybe?"

"But not likely. Like since you didn't earn it today, I'm in charge of it tonight. And you only get one every twenty-four hours. Way you been sassing me, I might just pass it on to Nigel for tomorrow."

Chloe wanted to beg for it, but she would not. She would just fall silent and hope Florence would get some fun out of being the one in charge of the food each day.

"If you're still awake and don't tick me off anymore, I'll bring it by about midnight. Now, in case you want to read or do your makeup, paint your toes, whatever, I'll turn the lights on. And since the TV's off, I'll pipe in a little music to help you sleep."

Oh, please, leave the lights and music off.

Florence waddled to the door, elbows resting on her leather equipment belt, which had everything but a gun—nightstick, can of Mace, ring of keys, empty holster, and for whatever reason, a supply of bullets. She flipped the lights on, all of them, and it seemed to Chloe it was brighter than when the sun had shone through the windows.

She could deal with that. She would turn her face to the wall. And despite her deep, private regret that she had cost herself a bit of food for a few more hours, Chloe would handle that as well. She would pray, think of her loved ones, rehearse her Bible memory verses, and hope to drift off to sleep.

But then came the music, louder than it needed to be. Much too loud. And of course it was "Hail Carpathia" on a loop that would no doubt play all night.

Buck had taught her his alternate words. That might amuse her for a few minutes. What were they again? She walked them through her mind, then began to hum along, then softly sing:

Fail Carpathia, you fake and stupid thing;
Fail Carpathia, fool of everything.
I'll hassle you until you die;
You're headed for a lake of fire.
Fail Carpathia, you fake and stupid thing.

+ + +

Chang had raced from Eleazar Tiberias's mirror to the tech center, where he leaped and shouted, exulting with Abdullah and Naomi.

Eventually, however, they showed him the tape of Albie, which sobered him. And despite being fresh from the palace, even Chang was stunned at the gall of the GC to air a so-called news story about Chloe that was so patently invented. He wondered how even GC sympathizers could buy such poppycock. But Naomi showed him samples of e-mails coming in from Judah-ites around the world that showed many were going to need reassurance and to be reminded that the devil is the father of lies.

"Our writers," Naomi told Chang, "here in this section, are composing boilerplate responses, answers to the most common questions. These will be transmitted to the keypunch people, who can pick and choose and shoot them out immediately."

She asked a writer to print out his current list of responses, then pulled it from the printer to show Chang.

The only thing the news seemed to get right was Chloe's name and age and the fact that she is the daughter of Rayford and the wife of Cameron "Buck" Williams. While it's true she attended Stanford University, neither was she a campus radical nor was she expelled. She dropped out after the Rapture but had a grade point average of 3.4 and had been active in student affairs.

Rayford Steele did serve, while already a believer, as pilot on the staff of Nicolae Carpathia, providing invaluable information to the cause of Christ's followers everywhere. He was never fired and never charged with insubordination or drinking while on duty. He left after his second wife was killed in a plane crash.

The Judah-ites are anything but "the last holdouts in opposition to the New World Order." Many Jewish and Muslim factions, as well as former militia groups primarily in the United North American States, still have refused to accept the mark of loyalty to the supreme potentate and must live clandestinely in fear for their lives.

Cameron Williams was indeed formerly a celebrated American journalist who also worked directly for the potentate, but he quit rather than "losing his job due to differences in management style." As for his subversive cyber and printed magazine's "limited circulation," that, of course, is a matter of opinion. The Truth *is circulated to the same audience that is ministered to daily by Dr. Tsion Ben-Judah, at last count still more than a billion.*

Rayford Steele, Cameron Williams, and Chloe Williams are not "wanted for more than three dozen murders around the world." The Tribulation Force acknowledges one kill for Cameron Williams and two for Rayford Steele, both in self-defense.

The International Commodity Co-op, headed by Mrs. Williams, has never hijacked any goods, nor does it sell for any kind of profit, but rather trades for the benefit of its members.

The Williamses have amassed no fortune on the black market or otherwise. In fact if not for the generosity of its members, no such Co-op could exist.

Mrs. Williams has never had an abortion or lost a child, and has had but one pregnancy, resulting in a son, now three-and-a-half years old. The Williamses have never claimed deity or special powers for their son, though they do believe Nicolae Carpathia is the Antichrist and that Jesus Christ will one day conquer Carpathia and bring his own kingdom to earth.

Limited contact with Mrs. Williams since her capture has confirmed that she is committed to not bargaining with the GC, and that is the policy of the Tribulation Force. Not only is she not offering anything to avoid a death sentence, but she has also been on the record many times in the past regarding her willingness to die for the cause of Christ.

There is no evidence that Mrs. Williams provided any information about Tribulation Force activist Al Basrah, and neither is there evidence to support that he committed suicide.

"Will this do any good?" Chang said.

"Among our people it will," Naomi said. "Even people who know better want to be reassured. Everybody else is preoccupied with troop buildup in the Jezreel Valley anyway."

"What's happening in San Diego?"

"Not much until Captain Steele and Mr. McCullum get there, which should be any minute now. We are gearing up for at least two hundred new arrivals over the next few days, so that should tell you something. Have you talked with your sister lately?"

"No. But I've been meaning to, and now, of course, I have news for her."

"Well, she has news for you too."

"What?"

"Oh, I can't spoil it for her."

"Naomi!"

"Now, no. I can't wait to meet her, and I don't want to start off on the wrong foot by breaking her confidence."

"She told you something she hasn't told me?"

"Not exactly. But my job makes me privy to information I might not otherwise know."

"Such as . . ."

"Such as messages to the leadership. Rather than have them come and read them off the computer, often we print them out and deliver them ourselves."

"And so from one of those you learned something about my sister that she would want to tell me herself."

Naomi nodded.

"Well, I can take care of that in short order," he said, pulling out his phone. "And then when will you have a few minutes?"

"Right now," she said. "But only a few. It's going to be a hectic day."

"You owe me a story."

"My story, you mean? It's really my father's and my story, but it's not a long one, so yes, I'll have time to tell it."

"I'll see you in ten minutes then," Chang said, punching his sister's number.

"Hello, Chang," Ming said when she answered. "Forgive me for whispering, but I am babysitting Kenny Bruce, and he is finally asleep."

"Just wondering how you were and how things are going out there."

"I'm sure you know."

"Yes. I have news for you."

"Tell me, Brother."

"God has removed the mark of the beast from my forehead."

"Praise God! Tell me all about it! I can't wait to see you."

He told her what had happened.

"That's too wonderful for words, Chang. Too bad it had to happen on an otherwise unhappy day."

"Yes, and you have news for me, no?"

"What are you talking about?"

"I have no idea. It's just a hunch."

"Oh, Chang. Ree has asked me to marry him, and I have asked Dr. Ben-Judah to officiate when we arrive."

9

"LET ME SCOUT the area," Buck said, "make sure they're clear to land."

George, behind the wheel of the Hummer, shot Buck a sideward glance. "Nobody was in the area when we left the compound, there's been no one suspicious along the way, and no one followed us. We came the last half mile in the dirt, using the lights only to make sure we were on track. Buck, the airstrip is as secure as it's ever been."

Buck sighed and shook his head. "When did I become the cautious one? You're the military guy."

"There's cautious and prepared, and there's paranoid," Sebastian said. "I know they've got Chloe, but that wasn't because of some vast stakeout. It was her fault. I'm sorry, but your father-in-law said she admitted that herself. And she has a history of venturing out—"

"But *why* was she out? I saw guys. She must have seen 'em too. And they got her."

"Routine reconnaissance. You said yourself they looked bored."

"Well, they're not bored now, are they?"

"No, Buck, they're not bored now. I'm parking at the end of the runway. You want to go traipsing around in the woods till they get here, be my guest."

"You're not coming?"

"You're the boss. If you tell me to come, I'll come. But you distinctly said, 'Let me scout the area.' Well, I'm letting you scout the area."

"Come with me."

"You're making me?"

"I'm asking you as a friend."

"That's not fair, Buck. Don't play that card."

"Come on. What if I find something? You'll never forgive yourself."

"You're incurable."

Buck knew Sebastian was right. The fact was, he was frazzled and needed something to do. He was ready to head straight to San Diego GC headquarters, guns blazing, and bust Chloe out. "You know Rayford will be up for going after

Chloe," Buck said as they tramped through the woods in their fatigues, Uzis at their sides.

"C'mon, he and Mac will have just spent nearly sixteen hours in the air, probably splitting the piloting duties. These guys are going to need to sack out."

"You know Mac's heard about Albie. He'll be wired and ready to go."

"He'll be looking to get back to Al Basrah and find out what happened. Anyway, Buck, even if we do plan a raid, when are we going to do it, and who's going to get our people to Petra in the meantime?"

"I thought Rayford was getting Lionel on that."

"Lionel will organize and supply it, sure. But we've got to lead these people and see the work gets done."

Buck slapped a mosquito. "What're we doing? There's nothing out here. Whose idea was this anyway? You hear a jet?"

"No. Now we're out here like you said, so let's do a job."

"Now you *want* to look for something?"

"I just don't want to waste time, that's all. Let's not get too far from the landing strip."

Buck was suddenly swarmed by bugs. He let his Uzi dangle and smacked his head and face with both hands. "Let's get out into the open."

They emerged at about the midpoint of the strip.

"Now we're going to have to go all the way down to that end when they get here," George said.

"Let's head that way now," Buck said. "You can occupy your time helping me plan the attack."

"On GC headquarters?"

"Where else?"

"What do you know about the place?"

"What do you mean? We've been past there. You've seen it."

"Buck, neither of us has ever been inside. I know it's four floors plus a basement, but I don't even know if they use the basement for prisoners. Do you?"

"Nope, but I remember they have bars on the windows down there."

"Well, that's good. That's helpful. But the more you know, the more you should realize you don't know."

"What kind of GI mumbo jumbo is that?"

The big man stopped. "All right," George said, "look. Here's my take on San Diego GC headquarters. I know it's one of the biggest in North America, but I have no idea how many personnel they have. Do you?"

"No."

"Of the four floors and the basement, I don't know which houses the jail. Do you?"

"No."

"I'm guessing they segregate men and women prisoners, but I don't know for sure. Do you?"

"No."

"Well, if they do, are they all on the same floor or different floors?"

"Couldn't tell you."

"You see where we are, Buck? Nowhere. A military operation, especially a surprise first strike, is a complicated, highly planned maneuver. We'd have one objective and one only, and that is to get Chloe out alive. To accomplish that, we'd have to have someone inside."

"We can't get someone inside!"

"Then how are we going to do this, Buck? Think, man. Think what we'd have to know before we go charging in there. Do they keep high-profile prisoners separate from the general population, and if they do, where?"

"All right. You've made your point."

"I haven't even started, Buck. You guys are all enamored with my military training, but you don't know the half of it. Most of this is just common sense. Besides knowing exactly where Chloe is, we'd have to know the shortest distance in and out. We'd have to know what doors or windows might be vulnerable. We'd have to know how much firepower we'd need, and, Buck, you tell me what that means. What will determine our munitions needs?"

"The size and strength of the doors and windows?"

"Well, that, yeah. But it's their personnel, buddy. How many of them are we going to run into, and what will their resources be? If you could tell me Chloe was in the northeast corner of the second floor and how many GC I'd have to get through to get there, then how many are guarding her and what kind of weapons they are toting, I might be able to plan a mission for you. Otherwise, we're messing around, guessing, and we're likely to get a strike mission force wiped out."

They reached the end of the runway and sat in the grass in the darkness. "Then how does anybody ever pull off a raid like that?"

George cradled his weapon in his lap. "It's never easy, but there are prerequisites, and in the good old days when people weren't identified by a mark, you could usually get somebody into a place. Somebody has to have a thorough working knowledge of the building, maybe even access to the blueprint, the floor plan, the utility systems."

"I can't just do nothing, George. What're we going to do?"

Buck saw the landing lights before he heard the roar of the Gulfstream's engines. He signaled with a powerful flashlight that the area was clear, and within minutes the plane was down and hidden, and Rayford and Mac were disembarking.

The four shook hands without a word; then Buck and Rayford embraced. Neither was much for showing emotion, but they held each other tight for longer than Buck could remember doing before. They loaded the Hummer, but before they got in, Mac said, "I feel twenty years older. Do we have to sit in a cramped space again right away?"

"We're in no hurry," Rayford said. "Stretch your legs."

"I don't mind getting back a little late anyway," Buck said. "We've had no GC activity today, but they'll be snooping around later for sure."

Rayford said, "You don't suppose Chloe got them started in a whole new direction by claiming she was thirty miles from home?"

Buck chuckled. "Hardly, but you got to hand it to her for trying. Actually, it'll be interesting to see where they are tonight. That should give us an idea where they picked her up."

"Now you're thinking," George said. "It'll also give us an idea how long it'll take them to discover the compound and how much time we've got to get out of there."

+ + +

"I really mustn't be gone too long," Naomi said. Chang sat with her beside a pillar that made up part of the portico in the courtyard of the Urn Tomb. "Now if I had someone like you who could fill in for me, I could be gone longer."

"But with who?" he said, and she laughed. "Seriously, though, I'm curious about your background."

"I love remembering, Chang, though it is also a sad story. My father was a businessman, a restauranteur. He owned several eateries in the area around Teddy Kollek Stadium. Do you know Jerusalem?"

"No."

"He was honest and good and people liked him, respected him. That is very important in my culture."

"Mine too."

"I suppose in all cultures a person's reputation is paramount. But my father took great pride in his many friends and his successful businesses. He provided well for my mother and me. He was also a devoutly religious man, and so our family was too. Synagogue every Sabbath. We knew the Scriptures. We loved God. I believe my father was proud of that, but not in a bad way—you know what I mean?"

Chang nodded.

"About eight years ago—this was when I was eleven—my mother fell ill. Cancer. Cancer of the . . . well, you'll forgive me if I am too shy to mention it. We do not know each other well enough for me to be comfortable about it."

"It's all right."

"She was very ill. My father was so good to her. He had the money to hire help for her, full-time help. But he would not do that. He hired part-time help, but he cut his workday in half and spent every afternoon and all night with her. He was a wonderful example to me and made me want to help even more. We loved my mother, and my father said we should consider it a privilege to serve her the way she had served us for so many years. He made her happy despite her pain."

"He seems like a wonderful man."

"Oh, he is, Chang. He always has been. Even before. Well, just after my twelfth birthday, my mother, she took a turn for the worse and he had to put her in the hospital. The doctors told him there was no hope. But my father did not believe in 'no hope.' He believed in God. He told the doctors and anyone who wanted to grieve my mother too early that we would show them—he and his little girl would show them. And how were we going to show them? We were going to pray, and God was going to work, and my mother was going to be healed."

Chang heard the anguish in Naomi's voice, and then she fell silent. "It's okay," he said. "You can finish another time."

"No," she said, wiping her eyes. "It's just that it does not seem so long ago now. I can finish. I want to. One night my father came home from the hospital late, and he was upset. I did not go with him on school nights, only in the afternoons. I asked him, 'Father, what is it? Is Mother worse?' and he said, 'No, but she might as well be.'

"That frightened me. He had never had a cross word with her, never said a bad thing about her, at least not in front of me. But she told him something that he said was only because of all the drugs she had been prescribed. She wept and told him that wasn't true, that she really believed it. I said, 'What, Father, what?' But he burst into tears and said he had raised his voice and told her that she should stop talking nonsense.

"'I made her weep,' he told me, crying, crying his eyes out. 'The woman I love with all my soul, who is dying before my eyes, I upset her.' And I said, 'But, Father, she upset you too. What did she say?' He said, 'She told me, "Jesus is Messiah." I demanded to know where she had heard such heresy, but she would not tell me for fear I would get someone in trouble, which I would have!'

"I did not know what to think. I gasped when he repeated what she had said. He told me that he had told her that he would not allow me to see her again if she kept up with such nonsense, but that only made me cry. That very night we were called to the hospital, told that if we wanted to see her alive, we must come now.

"All the way he wept and blamed himself for being cross with her. 'I caused this!' he said over and over. He pleaded with God to spare her, made promises to him. I had never seen him so pitiful. We were with her when she died. Her last words to us—and they were to us both, Chang, because she looked directly into my eyes and spoke, and then she looked at my father and said the same thing—her last words were, 'I go to be with God. Study the prophecies. Study the prophecies.'"

"Wow!"

"I did not come to Jesus in the way you might think. The tidy conclusion might be that my father and I went home and studied the prophecies and came to believe the way my mother did. But it didn't happen that way. My father was so heartbroken that he became angry with God and quit studying the Scriptures at all. We stopped praying. We stopped going to synagogue.

"He still loved me and took care of me, but he tried to lose himself in his work. His friends only pitied him, because he was not the same man he had been.

"I could not get my mother's last words out of my head, but my father forbade me to study anything in the Bible, let alone the prophecies. I was sad, so sad, because my life had changed radically with the loss of my mother and, really, the loss of my father as I had known him. Whenever I suggested that God could help us or the synagogue might comfort us or we might find some answers in the Bible, he would not hear of it.

"I was thirteen when the disappearances happened. That got everyone's attention, even my father's. Scared to death, we turned back to God, back to synagogue, back to the Scriptures. I began studying the prophecies, and though I was young, I couldn't avoid seeing what Mother had seen when someone pointed them out to her. My father wouldn't admit it, but I think he started to see it too.

"When we heard that the renowned biblical scholar, Dr. Tsion Ben-Judah, was going to speak on international television about his conclusion about Messiah from the Bible prophecies, we watched it together. The next day everyone was talking about the trouble Dr. Ben-Judah had gotten himself into by declaring that Messiah had already come, but my dad and I were excited about more than that. He found a New Testament, and we began reading it every night.

"When we got to the story of the Jewish man Saul, who became Paul, my father was overwhelmed. We read faster and faster and more and more, and we came to believe that Jesus was Messiah and that he could save us from our sins.

We memorized First Corinthians 15:1-4: 'Brethren, I declare to you the gospel which I preached to you, which also you received and in which you stand, by which also you are saved, if you hold fast that word which I preached to you—unless you believed in vain. For I delivered to you first of all that which I also received: that Christ died for our sins according to the Scriptures, and that He was buried, and that He rose again the third day according to the Scriptures.'

"All my father and I wanted to do was what Paul had done. Receive. Receive that truth by which Paul said we could be saved. We didn't know what to say or do, so we just prayed and told God we believed it and wanted to receive it. It was weeks before we read enough and knew enough to understand what we had done and what it all meant. Father finally found in the back of the New Testament a guide to salvation that talked about accepting and believing and confessing. We studied what it called the road to salvation—all those verses that tell that all have sinned and come short of the glory of God, that the wages of sin is death, but that the gift of God is eternal life through Jesus Christ our Lord."

Chang sat looking at her. "It's always something different," he said. "I can't tell you how many stories I've heard about people becoming believers, and each one is unique. I mean, they all get to the same place, but for some it was the disappearances. For you, it was your mother, really."

"We just can't wait to see her again, Chang. And it won't be long."

+ + +

Chloe couldn't tell whether she had actually been dozing or was just zoned out when Florence made a loud entrance about midnight. She unceremoniously poked the energy bar through the cage and let it drop. Chloe wanted to leap on it, tear it open, and gobble it down, but her pride was still working. She turned to look, but she didn't move.

"Dinner, honey," Florence said. "I recommend a white wine, like tap water."

Chloe didn't move until she left. She ate half the bar, which was flat and tasteless. But Chloe had always been told the greatest seasoning was hunger. She wrapped the rest, determined to save it for breakfast. But the few calories she had just ingested merely triggered her appetite. She was able to hold out for about another half hour, then ate the rest.

Though she was still hungry, the bar had taken enough of the edge off that she was able to doze. She dreamed first of her family. Buck and Kenny were close enough to smell, but she couldn't reach to hold them, to touch or kiss them. Then images danced of their horrified faces, repulsed by her. Did she have the mark? Was she hideously ugly? They grimaced and turned away.

Chloe ran to a mirror and found herself headless. She fainted, and when she hit the floor, she woke up. She sat on the cot, her face in her hands, rocking. This was going to be harder than she had ever imagined. She would not for an instant be fooled or even tortured into giving the GC an iota of what they wanted. She just prayed that if she was not going to be sprung somehow—and she couldn't imagine how anyone could pull that off—her execution would be quick.

+ + +

"I've come to a hard decision, Buck," Rayford said. It was two o'clock in the morning in the underground compound. Rayford sat with Buck in Rayford's quarters, where Buck would spend the night. Ming was staying at his and Chloe's place so Kenny could be in his own bed. Sebastian and a young associate were on watch.

"I don't want to hear it, do I?" Buck said.

"Probably not. But for some reason God put me in this position, and even though I'm biased and have almost as much vested interest as you do, I need to take leadership on this one. Mac is asleep. When he is fully rested, he's going to Wisconsin to pick up Zeke. He'll drop him in Petra to start work on our next assignment."

Buck hung his head. "Our next assignment is not right here?"

"Hear me out. Mac is going to go on to clear out of Al Basrah and move to Petra. On the way I'll have him call Otto Weser, the guy I told you about. He'll be in the palace and should be able to dig up what's going on in Al Hillah. Carpathia's assistant knows Nicolae's planning a meeting in Baghdad of the ten heads of state from around the world. We believe that's when he'll add all the other regions' manpower to the armies he's already marshaling in Israel."

"Dad, I'm sorry, but I don't really care about anywhere but right here at the moment. It looks like everything is coming together for all kinds of activity over there, but meanwhile, we're hanging Chloe out to dry."

"Buck, we've both been without sleep way too long. Believe me, I've done as much crying and praying and worrying as you have, which is—"

"I doubt that."

"—exhausting. I need to rest, and so do you."

"Dad, I'm not going to be able to sleep."

"I didn't say anything about sleeping. Get your clothes off, stretch out, put your feet up. Give your body a break even if you can't turn your brain off. We need you sharp, Buck."

"You're telling me I'm not going out with George tonight."

"I'm not even letting George go, Buck. Talk about somebody we don't want to burn out. He's got a good team that can track the GC if they show tonight.

All we want to know is where they're starting their canvasing. I'm impressed that people have already started packing, getting ready to go. Lionel's got planes and pilots lined up. We have to be ready to go at a moment's notice."

Buck leaned forward and rested his elbows on his knees. "I trust you, Dad, and I know you have Chloe's and my best interests at heart. But I don't get this. When do we start scoping out headquarters, figuring how to get in there or how to get next to somebody who would know something about the place?"

"You and I can see how close we can get tomorrow night. If George is available, we'll take him."

"But time's wasting."

Rayford sat back and sighed. "Job one with me is conserving resources, and that includes human ones. Our minds tell us we have energy because we can think of nothing else, but running on adrenaline like that will wear us down quicker, make us rash, ineffective. Trust me on this, Buck. I want her out of there as much as you do, but she's not the only person we're accountable for."

"But I want to know as soon as the reconnaissance party knows anything about—"

"No, now I've left word that we are not to be disturbed until midmorning except in an emergency."

"Dad!"

"Knowing something you can't act on right away anyway is no help. Now no more talk. Let's get some rest."

+ + +

Like everyone else in Petra at high noon, Chang preferred working inside. He had discovered, through much trial and error, that he was able to tap into everything in New Babylon from where he was. The problem was, all the decision makers were gone to Al Hillah. When the plan to beat them there and bug the place had fizzled, he had been assigned to come up with a way that Otto Weser could feed him information. That all depended on what hardware might have been left that could be tapped from Petra.

Chang worried that he might have become too obvious in his interest in Naomi, wanting to spend every spare minute with her. He decided not to assume anything and stayed at his computer over lunchtime. He was hungry, but he could also wait for the evening manna.

Chang was thrilled when Naomi approached shyly with a basket. "Hey, workaholic," she said. "Don't go starving on me."

"Hi," he said.

"Brought you some honey wafers."

\+ + +

"Hail Carpathia" had become just part of the background for Chloe by now. She guessed it was about four o'clock in the morning. She had tried to keep her ears covered as she dozed, but when she drifted off, her hands fell away. That was why she heard the door and held her breath.

From the heavy footsteps and the jangling keys, she could tell it was Florence. What could she want? It sounded as if she was close to the cage, and Chloe smelled food. A burger with all the trimmings. And the sound of a straw, probably in a cold soft drink. Right then it all hit Chloe as the nectar of the gods.

She slowly turned and in the low light saw Florence sit on the floor and lean back against the cage. Chloe rested on one elbow and let out her breath.

"You awake?" Florence said.

"'Fraid so."

"Want me to turn off that music?"

"Do you care what I want?"

"Don't be sassin' me again."

"If you really want to know what I want, yes, I want the music off."

"I'm not all bad, you know," Florence said.

She set next to the cage her half-eaten burger and soft drink and another tall paper cup with a lid and moved to the door. The music stopped.

When Florence returned, Chloe said, "Thank you."

"Mm-hm," she said, sliding to the floor again. "Just having a burger."

"So I gathered."

"Brought you something."

"You did not."

"See, why you wanna be that way all the time? Can't a person do something nice for somebody?"

"I wish."

"Well, your wish has been granted, if you like chocolate."

"Who doesn't?"

"How about a chocolate shake?"

"I'm still dreaming, right? No more music, and now a chocolate shake in the middle of the night. What's gotten into you?"

"I told you. Ain't all bad. Nobody is."

I can think of someone. "If you're really going to give me a chocolate shake, all I can say is I'm grateful."

"I'm a mama too, you know."

"That so?"

"Mm-hm. Brewster. Almost three."

"Have a picture?"

"I do! You wanna see it, really?"

"'Course I do."

"Jes' a minute. Can't get in trouble turning on the lights when it's only just us." She finished her meal, leaving the chocolate shake on the floor while throwing away the trash. Chloe wanted the shake so badly she trembled. Was it possible she could get next to this woman somehow, mother to mother?

Florence went out again and turned on the lights. When she returned and shut the door, it clearly locked behind her, which Chloe had already learned was protocol. The shake was not going to fit through the mesh of the cage, so if the cage door was going to be open, of course the outer door could not be unlocked. But that also told Chloe that Florence was lying about being there alone. Otherwise, how would she get back out?

"Now if I unlock this cage, which is totally against the rules, you're not going to pay back my kindness by trying something, are you? I'm bigger and stronger than you, but even if you—"

"Yeah, I know. Heard it from Jock. We're still both locked in."

"Exactly."

"So if I behave and take the shake and you lock me back in here, how are you getting out?"

"I buzz 'em, and they let me out."

"So we're not really alone."

"Well, no, not after I buzz 'em."

"What if they see what you gave me?"

"Then I'm in trouble, so if you want it, you better take it now."

"I want it."

"Stay right where you are. Don't be standing up when this door opens, or I'll be shutting it again."

Florence unlocked the cage, handed Chloe the shake, then quickly locked it again. It was the first time Chloe had noticed emotion in her. Florence looked excited, maybe scared. Maybe flush with the feeling of doing something nice when she wasn't supposed to.

Chloe sucked eagerly at the straw and was not disappointed. The shake was still cold, thick, rich, and—if anything—too chocolaty. Which, as she used to laugh about with her friends, was like saying something tasted too rich.

Florence stood watching her. "Whoa, girl. 'Member you're doing that on an empty stomach. Better pace yourself."

"I will. And I don't want brain freeze."

Florence laughed.

"And don't forget to show me the picture of Brewster."

"Oh, I will. Soon as you're finished."

Why not now? Chloe wondered as she attacked the straw again. The sugar and caffeine were going to keep her awake, but it wasn't like she had anything to look forward to in the morning. Maybe Jock would show up and eat his breakfast in front of her again.

"Jock," she said, giggling.

"What?" Florence said.

"Eggs in front of me."

"What you going on about?"

"Jock. Jack. Jick. Jeck . . ."

"Hm?"

Chloe was dizzy. The cup was slipping. She reached with her other hand to steady it, but the shake fell to the floor and splashed. It hit her as the greatest tragedy she could recall, and she began to weep.

Her eyes were trying to shut. She forced herself to keep them open and deliberately lifted her chin so she could see Florence, who just stood watching. Florence pressed her buzzer. The outer door opened, and both Nigel and Jock entered, pushing a gurney.

"I'll get this cleaned up," Florence said, unlocking the cage.

"Great work, Flo," Jock said. "Loved the bit about you having a kid."

"Oh, honey, they easy when they hungry."

10

BUCK WAS AWAKENED midmorning by soft but insistent knocking on Rayford's door. He reached up from the foldout couch and opened it.

"I was kinda hoping I'd wake your father-in-law," Sebastian said.

Suddenly Buck was wide awake. "What time is it?"

"Almost 1000 hours."

"What's the deal? What'd your guys find?"

"Buck, I got to go through channels."

"What're you, kidding me? You can't tell me anything about my wife?"

"I report to Rayford, Buck. So do you."

"You beat all, George. You know that?" Buck rocked himself up off the couch and banged on Rayford's door. "Sebastian's here with a briefing, Dad. Let's go."

Rayford emerged, looking foggy. "Hey, guys," he said. "How'd you sleep?"

"Same way you did," Buck said. "Now let's get to this."

Buck stuffed sheets and blankets between the mattress and the back of the couch, closed it, and sat. Rayford joined him.

"I have my guy in the hall," Sebastian said. "Wanted to make sure you two were presentable."

"Your call," Rayford said. "Here we sit in our Skivvies."

George opened the door. "Razor?" he said. "You're on."

Razor was Hispanic, early twenties, and very military. He saluted everybody and Buck waved him off. "Come on, come on," he said. "It's just us. What've you got?"

"Sirs, I was on watch, as you know, and noticed motion-detector activity at approximately 0300 hours. One of my team of three is a female, so I asked if she would check the periscope in the Williamses' quarters, due to the fact that a female was in there alone—well, with a baby, and I didn't want to breach protocol by—"

"We know why, Mr. Razor," Buck said. "Please."

"Yes, sir. She checked and reported enemy activity within two blocks of the compound and secured permission from Mrs. Toy for me to enter your domicile."

Buck glanced at Rayford, shook his head, and stared at the floor. *For the love of all things sacred . . .*

"I personally observed similar activity and so marshaled my team. We went out in fatigues and greasepainted faces, armed with lightweight, high-powered automatic weapons. Our objective was to observe, get close enough to listen, if possible, and—if necessary—either defend the compound or somehow misdirect the enemy to a neutral area, thus giving the occupants of said compound—"

"Time to evade," Buck said. "Yeah, what happened?"

"We observed two separate platoons of GC canvassing the area; however, they appeared to have started about two blocks west of us and were proceeding in a westerly direction."

"Meaning they were moving away from us rather than toward us?"

"Yes, sir, but that is not all entirely good news. Observing their direction and relative speed, we were able to flank them, and the two of my party on their south side had enough flora-and-fauna coverage to get close enough to hear them. They came away with the distinct impression that the objective for that particular mission was to begin where they had recently left off—in my estimation, Mr. Williams, what you and Mr. Sebastian had observed approximately twenty-four hours before—and were to survey a wide area leading to where Mrs. Williams was apprehended."

"I'm praying you followed them to that point," Buck said.

"We did, sir. We also overheard them saying that tomorrow night at the same time, they would be backtracking and going past where they started, which obviously would include our compound again. We expect them to be quite thorough, and thus if at all possible, we should be evacuated before 0200 hours tomorrow."

"You have informed the right people, and the move is on pace?"

"Yes, sir, but there's more. Near where they indicated Mrs. Williams was apprehended, our people recovered her Uzi and ski mask."

"What's that tell you, Buck?" Sebastian said.

"She ditched them."

"But we also—at least my people—heard two GC discussing her disposition."

It was all Buck could do to contain himself. "Please, Officer Razor, tell me what you heard about the disposition of my wife."

"They seemed to indicate that she was to be moved, sir."

"When?"

"Within the hour, sir. Something about getting it done before Carpathia starts calling for troops from this region."

"Back to the 'within the hour' business, Razor," Buck said. "Within an hour from now or then?"

"Then, sir."

"All right, quit with the 'sir' stuff, please. I know you were in the military, but I wasn't and it makes me crazy. You're telling me Chloe was to be moved at about four this morning?"

"Yes, s—"

"To where?"

"The best my people could gather, s—Mr. Williams, was 'somewhere back east.'"

"Somewhere back east." Buck stood and held his open palms to Rayford and George. "They moved her somewhere back east, which implies an aircraft—" he looked at his watch—"going on six hours ago. Tell me, Razor, did anyone think to get to GC headquarters and see if there was a chance to abort this move?"

"No, sir."

"No one thought this might be an emergency worth waking Mr. Steele or Sebastian or me?"

"By the time I got the report, sir, um, sorry, the move would have been already in progress."

"You assume."

"Yes, that's an assumption."

"The one time they might be more vulnerable than another, taking a woman out of a cell, out of a building, into the open air to a vehicle so they could get her on an airplane, and we all sleep through it."

"I apologize, sir, but in my judgment nothing effective could have been accomplished, given when we overheard this and the, ah, assumed timing of the maneuver."

Buck could not stand still. He paced the apartment, looking expectantly at the three others. "We sat on it," he said. "We had a window of opportunity, and we were asleep."

"Buck, please," Rayford said, but Buck would not be appeased.

"Somewhere back east," Buck parroted. "That narrows it down, doesn't it? Maybe if we all just start walking east, we'll overtake them, huh?"

"Thank you, Razor," Sebastian said. "If there's nothing else, you may go."

"Thank you, sirs," Razor said.

"Yeah, thanks for nothing," Buck said.

"I apologize, sir, if—"

"Oh, just go," Buck said.

Rayford nodded at the young man, and he hurried out.

"Buck," George said, "he probably made the right decision. Racing down there in the wee hours, hoping to get there in time to do something without a plan—"

"Would have at least been an effort, wouldn't it?" Buck kicked a chair that flew into the kitchen and banged off the table and a cabinet. "I guess if I ever want to see my wife again, I'm going to have to be a one-man commando unit."

"And get yourself killed," Rayford said. "Now you've vented. That's enough."

"It'll never be enough until I have Chloe back."

+ + +

Chloe had fallen off the metal shelf and into the chocolate mess on the floor. Since she was unable to break her fall, her head banged on the tile. She lay there with one leg tucked awkwardly beneath her, her head lolling, and fighting sleep. Whatever had been in the shake had tranquilized her so thoroughly that she wanted only to go with the feeling and sleep the deep sleep of the drugged. It reminded her of how she felt after giving birth to Kenny.

Florence unlocked the cage and knelt to clean up the spill. She rolled Chloe onto her side and pulled her foot down so both legs were straight. She held Chloe with one hand as she cleaned the floor, then let go, and Chloe rolled onto her back.

Her eyes fell shut and her breathing became deep and regular, but she prayed desperately. "God, let me stay conscious. Let me hear. Help me listen."

"That floor dry?" Jock said.

"Give it a second," Florence said.

"Put the sheet down there, Nigel, and take her ankles."

Chloe felt Jock's hands under her armpits and Nigel's at her feet. "On three," Jock said, and they lifted her off the floor and a few inches over to the sheet. Then they lifted the sheet to the gurney, and Chloe was glad her eyes were closed. She had lost equilibrium and felt as if she could pitch off the cart any second.

"Out to the truck quickly now."

The gurney rolled across the big room, through the door, and stopped. Chloe heard elevator doors open. She was rolled aboard, and the car lifted one floor. Soon she was outside and could not open her eyes as hard as she tried. Uncovered, she felt the cold air, but something didn't allow her even to shiver. She wanted to press her legs together and rub them and massage her arms with her hands, but she couldn't move.

"Lord, please. Keep me awake."

"A hearse?" Nigel said. "Whose idea was that?"

"Mine," Jock said, chuckling. "People don't want to look if they think there's a stiff in here."

"You going with her?" Florence said.

"Yup," Jock said, and Chloe heard pride. "It's my deal right up to the end."

"When's that going to be?" Florence said, and Chloe felt the vehicle moving.

"Not sure. They're going to milk it. We may still get some information out of her. Truth serum is next."

"That always works, doesn't it?"

"Usually."

Not this time. "God, don't let me say anything you don't want me to." Chloe was immobile from her toes to her scalp, yet God seemed to grant her wish of consciousness. She could hear and she could smell. Touch and sight were a different matter, but she had certainly felt the chill of the predawn air.

She guessed the mostly smooth ride at a little less than an hour. Then the gurney was lifted out of the hearse, rolled maybe a hundred yards, and carried by hand up some stairs and into what she assumed was a plane. And when the engines began to whine, she knew she was right. Chloe heard the congratulations and good-byes from Nigel and Florence. Then Jock and, she assumed, another man laid her out along several seats with armrests raised. The men somehow belted her in at the torso and the knees by using parts of seat belts from adjoining seats.

From their voices she could tell they sat in the row ahead of hers. She had the impression it was just the three of them and the pilots on a jumbo jet. She didn't know of another plane that had enough seats together to allow her to stretch out.

"How long is this flight anyway?" a man with a Spanish accent said.

"Four hours, I think, Jess," Jock said. "Then we've got about a fifty-mile drive from the southwest. Whole Chicago area was nuked, you know, so we'll be about as far north as we dare."

The conversation deteriorated into the mundane, and Chloe succumbed to the drowsiness.

+ + +

Buck knew he was being a nuisance, but he couldn't help himself. While everyone else in the compound was preparing for the big move, he badgered people. Had anyone worked at GC headquarters before becoming a believer? Did anyone know anybody who had or did now? Any connections, any leads, any inside information? Somebody, anybody to talk to who might know someone who could be bluffed into giving out information about Chloe's whereabouts?

He tried calling headquarters himself from a secure phone, pretending to be from GC International. Nobody was buying. He scripted a speech for Ming to try while he played with Kenny. She struck out too.

Rayford finally tracked Buck down and told him, "Do what you have to do, but be ready to go when everybody else is."

"I'll be traveling light anyway, boss," Buck said. "Don't suppose one of Lionel's guys could just drop me back east somewhere?"

Rayford shook his head and moved on.

"Hey, Dad," Buck said, "your place unlocked?"

"Yep. And empty except for your stuff."

"I'll clear it out now."

On his way to Rayford's place, Buck passed Razor in the corridor. "Sir," the young man said, saluting self-consciously.

"Hey, son, hold up. I owe you an apology."

"No, that's all right. I understand what you're going through."

"That's a reason, but it's not an excuse. I want you to forgive me. I was way out of line."

"Of course, sir. Don't give it a second thought."

"Well, thank you. And can I ask you a question?"

"Anything."

"Where's the name come from?"

Razor flushed and looked down. "Snowmobile accident."

"Ouch. Do I want to hear it?"

"First time on. In Minnesota. Not exactly like Mexico, you know? Didn't see the razor wire. Should have been killed. It caught my helmet and luckily dug in rather than sliding down and slicing my head off. It ripped that helmet off as I went underneath. People watching said the wire somehow wrapped itself around the helmet. The wire never broke, and after I had stretched it as far as it would go, it flew back and came forward again like a slingshot and flung the helmet at me, hit me in the back of the head, and knocked me out."

"But here you are. And no matter how I sounded earlier, I'm glad to have you with us."

Of all things, that crazy story got Buck obsessing about decapitation. Losing Chloe was his main concern, of course, and he worried about her suffering. He couldn't stand to think of her being violated, abused, tortured—he didn't want to even consider all the possibilities. It was no consolation to know that even if she was martyred, he would see her in less than a year. What would that mean to Kenny?

Worst of all, all he could think of was how Chloe would most likely die. Death was death and it shouldn't make any difference, he knew. But if it came to that, if the GC made a public spectacle of her, as they certainly would, there was no way he could watch it. The idea of his beloved dying such an ugly, grotesque death made him ill.

No question she would stay true to her faith to the end. He had heard stories of others, even watched as his old friend Steve Plank thumbed his nose at Carpathia and honored God before he died. Buck also knew that if it came to that, Chloe's body would be new one day in heaven. But still, he was repulsed by the idea that the person most precious to him in the world might die in the worst possible way he could imagine.

If he couldn't push it from his mind's eye now, how would it be if it actually happened? He sought out Rayford.

"I'm really busy," his father-in-law told him, "and you should be too. I'm not saying it'd take your mind off Chloe; it sure hasn't mine. But you'd be more productive."

"I know, but I need a minute."

He told Rayford of his tormenting daydreams. To his surprise, Rayford's lip began to quiver. His voice was thick. "I've been going through the same thing, Buck. I didn't want to tell you."

"Really? This whole idea?"

"Exactly. A father has a different take, you know. Imagine how you feel about Kenny. I was there when Chloe was born. Seems like yesterday she was a little red ball of squealing girl who could be comforted only by being tightly wrapped in a blanket and put on her mother's chest. Then, to us, she was the most beautiful creature we had ever seen. We would have done anything for her, anything to protect her. That's never changed. She's grown up to be a beautiful woman, and somehow, even with all her injuries and disfigurements, I still see her that way."

"So do I."

"So, yes, Buck, I know what you're thinking. We just have to be strong and try not to dwell on it. I don't know what else to do."

\+ \+ \+

Chang was walking Naomi to her quarters late at night. "I want to show you something on my computer tomorrow," he said. "I discovered that the GCNN production chief's solution to the plague of darkness was, I guess, to feel his way into the control room and find the switch that allows the international network feed to be remotely accessed by three or four of the major affiliates."

"Ingenious," Naomi said. "Isn't it?"

"Oh, I was impressed. But I'm also excited. There is no block on my accessing it too, and I can override the affiliates with the system David Hassid had set up in New Babylon."

"I can't wait to see it."

"It has unlimited capabilities, Naomi. When Cameron Williams gets here, we'll work together and counteract the lies that the GC broadcasts, and we can do it immediately."

"Nothing they can do about it?"

"Not that I can think of, short of starting a whole new network. They may think they have time to do that, but the end is closer than they know."

+ + +

"So you drew the short straw, eh there, pardner?" Mac said.

"I am sorry, Mr. McCullum," Ree said, "but I do not understand that expression."

"Well, without getting into specifics, it means you got grunt duty."

They had studied the area through the periscope an hour before and determined they could get the Hummer out of the vehicle bay without being detected.

"Driving you to the plane? No problem. I like to do it. I only wish I was flying you to Wisconsin. I have flown a Gulfstream only once before, and I liked it."

"If you've got so little experience, I'm glad you're not flying me, know what I mean?"

A little more than three hours later, Mac touched down in Hudson, Wisconsin, where he was met by the hulking Gustaf Zuckermandel Jr., better known as Zeke.

"I wish you could meet everybody in Avery," the twenty-five-year-old said. "But even the guy who drove me has already headed back. Took us an hour to drag my stuff into the underbrush."

Mac followed him to his cache of boxes and trunks. "You sure we want to be lugging this stuff all the way to the plane in broad daylight, Zeke?"

"Unless you want to wait till dark, but there's no need. This is the part of the country the GC forgot. I haven't seen a Peacekeeper since I got here."

As they were loading, Mac said, "No second thoughts about leaving? You must be close to these people."

"Lots of second thoughts, but I figure a guy's got to go where he's called. I was called here, and now I'm being called there. Who woulda thought a no-account like me would ever get called anywhere?"

"Well, you're the best document and appearance man I ever saw, and I hear you really blossomed here."

"Oh, that's not true if you want to know the actual fact, Mr. McCullum. Thing is, there wasn't anything for me to do here as far as disguises and documents and such, because we flat didn't need 'em. So I got real involved in the Bible studies, improved my reading and all that, and pretty soon the leader took me under his wing. I never got to teaching or preaching, but I helped out all I could. I liked it, like to stay busy. They gave me that assistant pastor title sort of as a gift."

"Honorary, eh?"

"Yeah, like that."

"Well, I hope you were honored, because that really means something."

"I'm gonna miss everybody, but I got to tell you, I'm ready to get to Petra and just see the place. And to hook up again with Dr. Ben-Judah and Dr. Rosenzweig and you and all the others, well . . ."

"And you've got a big job."

"You're supposed to tell me about it."

✢ ✢ ✢

Chloe more than woke up after almost four hours in the air. The drugs had worn off and she came to. And she was ravenous. An energy bar and whatever portion of shake she ingested before the Mickey kicked in had been all she'd eaten since seven the evening before she was abducted. That made it easy to pretend she was still unconscious.

"What time is it here?" Jock's companion said as the plane landed.

"Coming up on noon, and I'm hungry," Jock said. "You?"

"Oh yeah."

"I'm going to feed the prisoner finally. Play a little good cop. Shoot her a little truth juice. See if we can't get her to sing."

"She's been a tough bird, hasn't she?"

"Tell me about it, Jess. I'd have been doing the 'Hallelujah Chorus' solo by now."

"What if she doesn't flip? How long do you give it?"

"If you can't get to 'em somehow in the first forty-eight hours, more of the same isn't going to be any more effective."

"Starvation isn't a motivator?"

"Would be for me, but I guess they've proved it with prisoners of war. The ones who can survive that first round of psychological and physical torture aren't likely to ever break, no matter how long you keep it up."

As Chloe was being carried down the jetway, Jock said, "This facility never had woman prisoners before we took it over. We'll keep her in solitary. That's the only real way to keep her separate from the rest of the population."

Chloe was laid out across the backseat of a large SUV, which she noticed had wire mesh on the windows and no locks or door handles on the inside. Jock handcuffed her anyway. "She'll be coming to soon," he explained. "Can't be too careful."

When they stopped along the way, Chloe racked her brain for any idea of escape.

Jock said, "I'll get the food. You stay with her."

Chloe sat up. "I need to use the rest room."

Jock stared at her. "Seriously."

"I'd say."

"Well, I got no matron who can go with you. You'd have to use the men's, and one of us would have to be in there with ya."

"Forget it."

"You want me to buy you one of those adult diapers?"

"How far are we from where I can go?"

"Half an hour."

"I'll wait."

While Jock was inside, she tried to strike up a conversation with the man she had not gotten a look at until now. His mark was a *0,* which meant he was from the United South American States. He was strikingly dark with perfect teeth. "You remind me of my husband," she said.

"That so?" he said.

"Yeah, except he's not ugly."

The man found that hilarious and turned to face her. "You're funny," he said. "Why would you want to antagonize me?"

"You're one of the people who are going to wind up killing me. Doesn't look like I'm going to get to fight back, do any physical damage, so . . ."

"Makes sense."

"Jock calls you Jess."

"Yeah. Jesse," he said.

"Hmm. Named after Jesus. That your real name? Jesus?" Chloe pronounced it in Spanish.

"Matter of fact, yes, and I have a sister Maria."

"Is she also a Carpathianist?"

"Of course."

"How disappointing that must be to your namesake."

Jock brought food and uncuffed her. The men tore into theirs, while Chloe sat behind the cage that separated her from the front seat. She said aloud, "Lord, thank you for this food. I pray that you will help me eat it slowly so it doesn't make me sick, and that you will override any poisons Jock might have put in it. Give me strength to resist any efforts on the part of Jock or Jesse to get me to say anything I shouldn't. In Jesus' name I pray, amen."

11

"I LIKED ALBIE a lot," Zeke said as Mac piloted them across the Atlantic. "He was a good man."

"You got that right, Z," Mac said. "And for the life of me I can't understand it, but I'm afraid he did something royally foolish to get himself killed."

"Doesn't sound like him. You and Captain Steele and everybody used to listen to his ideas all the time."

"But everybody's human. Let your guard down for a second, get overconfident, who knows? He was determined to see this lowlife he used to know, and even when he and I agreed I should go on to Petra and fly Rayford back to the States, Albie still wanted to go through with his little mission. It's just as much my fault. Both of us thought it was something that had to get done—and fast. Now look where we are."

"Rayford said Tsion and Chaim are taking it hard."

"We all are. As much of this as we've gone through, it never gets easier. They're planning a little service for Albie at Petra once everybody gets there from San Diego."

"When will that be?"

"Oh, first wave ought to be arriving around three in the morning tomorrow. You and I got about a thirteen-hour jump on 'em. Once I drop you off, I got to get to Al Basrah and clear out Albie's and my apartment, make sure we didn't leave any clues for anybody. I'll be taking a bigger plane from Petra 'cause I got to bring back this Otto Weser guy and his people."

"Captain Steele told me about him. So you're bringing them back to Petra because of that Scripture about God's people getting out of Babylon before God destroys it?"

"Exactly."

Z sat staring at the ocean seven and a half miles below. "What must that have looked like when it was all blood?"

"You can't imagine."

"Hey, Mac, you think Rayford ought to be trusting Carpathia's secretary?"

"The way he tells the story, I guess. You don't think so?"

"I don't trust anybody who isn't a believer. What if she has second thoughts, sets a trap, gets you and this Otto ambushed?"

"A pleasant thought."

"You said yourself, you can't be too careful."

"Well," Mac said, "we've got to know what's happening in Al Hillah, and as much as possible what's coming after that, and we don't know how else to do it."

An hour later, Zeke dug through one of his bags and brought out a book. He looked self-conscious. "Something I wouldn't even have been able to read when you knew me in Chicago."

"I was gonna say—"

"But now that I'm reading better, I think I can do more things, you know, scientifically."

"Such as?"

"Such as I'm guessing you guys are asking me to come up with new looks and identities for a bunch of people."

"Right. All our old aliases and appearances have been compromised."

"Found this book in an abandoned library just across the Minnesota border. There's all kinds of stuff in here I never even heard of before. New ways to change skin and eye color and all that. Fake scars and blemishes. How many people are we talking about?"

"I think just five," Mac said. "I think Ray wants getups for him and Buck and Sebastian and Smitty and me."

"Really? That's it? I brought way too much stuff."

"What'd you bring?"

"Everything I had left over from Chicago. GC uniforms at all levels, IDs, documents, stuff for women and men. This is going to be easy. I mean, it'll take time, but I was afraid you'd need ten or twelve. The hardest one is going to be Mr. Sebastian, but I've already got an idea for him."

"Tell me."

Zeke put his book down, apparently so he could gesture with both hands. "The problem with your big people is that no matter what you do with them, you can't make 'em smaller. You can make a small person big with padding and whatnot, but you can't take pounds off the big ones.

"But what I can do, see, is give George a whole new look, the look of an older man. So his size doesn't look so threatening. It looks like it came on him from getting old, rather than from working out and military training. Might even give him a cane, glasses. Make him look like one of those old middle-aged guys who have gone to seed. Chop off that blond hair, give him a rim of white, put some lines in his face. All of a sudden instead of being a guy in his late twenties in perfect shape and huge, he's thirty years older, slowed down by food, maybe diabetes, bad knees, bad feet, stooped a little. Add some padding around his middle, front and back, so he waddles. He's not gonna threaten anybody."

"Brilliant. What do you do with me?"

"Biggest giveaway with you is your Southern accent. Can you fake others? Can you be a Yank or a Brit?"

"A Brit easier than a Yankee, that's for sure."

"If you can be British, I can make you look that way. Tweeds and all."

+ + +

Chloe's guess about where she was headed was confirmed when Jock radioed ahead and the SUV was met by a phalanx of GC motorcycles and squad cars. They escorted the celebrated prisoner to the grounds of what had once been known as Stateville Correctional Center in Joliet, Illinois.

The place was a gothic house of horror that had been converted from a state penitentiary to one of the GC's largest international prisons. It had both male and female prisoners. In fact, the female population was second largest only to the Belgium Facility for Female Rehabilitation (Buffer).

The first thing to hit Chloe was the crowd of media trucks jamming the entrance. Cameras pointed toward the SUV from every conceivable perch, and once the vehicle had passed, she looked back to see the crews scrambling for position in the vast courtyard.

The yard had become legendary at Stateville during the last two and a half years. Prisoners were allowed there for only two reasons. They were herded past a gigantic bronze statue of Carpathia three times a day, where they were stopped in groups of thirty to fifty and allowed to kneel and worship, or they were in the yard to be executed. The yard had seven guillotines about thirty feet apart and positioned so that the sun baked them from dawn to dusk.

Jock stopped the SUV just inside the yard. "Look at 'em there, sweetie," he said. "Those blades get sharpened every night, but not a one of 'em's ever been cleaned. No scraping, no washing, no rust inhibitors.

"And you know those slots on each side, where the big blades slide down? Back when we were more humane, those were lubricated every time they were used. No more. Now the blades scrape along the sides, sometimes get hung up, get crooked, slow down. I mean, they still weigh enough that, even on a bad day, by the time they reach your neck, they're gonna dig in at least three inches.

"In the old days, a blade didn't do its job, too bad for us. The sentence was to stick your head in there until the blade dropped. If it somehow didn't kill you, well, you had taken your punishment. And don't think that didn't happen more than once. Lots of people walking around with severe neck wounds.

"But now, blade doesn't kill ya, we just hoist 'er again and let 'er go. Two, three times with a rusty, blood-caked blade that, like I say, is sharpened every night—that'll do the trick."

About twenty feet before each guillotine stood a rickety wood table, also gray and weathered by the sun and wind. Each had two incongruous Bank of England chairs behind it, burnished redwood significantly less wind worn.

"Processors and mark applicators get to sit," Jock said. "The condemned stand in lines. Once their information is recorded and any personal belongings have been confiscated, they're issued a plastic laundry basket they hand to the executioner. He or she sets it on the other side of where the blade comes down.

"Head drops in the basket, body stays where it knelt. Lifers without parole do collection duty. Come on, I'll show you."

"Spare me."

"Oh, you'd like that, wouldn't you?"

Jock got out. "Cuff her, Jess," he said.

Jesse turned and opened the cage. "Hands," he said.

"Better dope me again," Chloe said.

"Say what?"

"You think I'm going to voluntarily be cuffed so you guys can take me somewhere I don't want to go?"

Jock opened the back door.

"Hold on, Jock!" Jesse hollered. "She's not cuffed yet!"

"What the—?"

Jock, seeming to Chloe to show off for the cameras, leaped into the backseat. Chloe sat with her fists balled under her thighs. "You like to be difficult, don't you?" he said.

Jock grabbed her wrists and jerked her hands up and together where Jesse could reach them. As soon as she was cuffed, Jock slid back out of the car, pulling her by the cuffs and letting his body weight drag her out. She came out hands first, head banging the door, knees scraping the floor and then the ground. Jock pulled her to her feet.

Chloe hurt all over, but she was glad she had made them work. Someone else could go gently into that good, good night of death. Not her. Jock clamped a hand around her elbow and led her to the middle death machine. "This is going to be yours tomorrow if you don't cooperate today."

The stench overwhelmed her, and both men covered their mouths and noses with handkerchiefs. Chloe, mercifully cuffed in front this time, bent her elbows and held her nose closed with her fingers.

"As you can see," Jock said, "we don't wash the platforms or the ground either. I mean, who would that benefit?"

The area around the middle machine, like the others along the sixty-yard row, looked to Chloe like a slaughterhouse. The ground around it was black, caked with blood. "See that Dumpster back there?"

Directly behind the middle machine, maybe a hundred feet back, sat a Dumpster that looked half the size of a boxcar. It had no lid. "One collector takes the basket and dumps the head in there. Two collectors drag the body to the same place. See those black trails from each station to the Dumpster? You know what that is."

Chloe knew all right. She tried to hold her breath, but Jock kept pulling her arm so her hands came away from her nose. She prayed he would not take her out and make her look in the Dumpster. "It gets emptied about once a week."

The GC held the media back, but they yelled questions. "What's that on her jumpsuit? Did she soil herself?"

Chloe, mortified, hollered, "Chocolate!"

Jock whirled and batted her in the forehead with the back of his hand. "You say nothing to anyone but us, understand?"

"They drugged me with a choco—!"

Jock slipped around behind her and clamped his hand over her mouth. When she tried to bite him, he drove a knee into her lower back, knocking the wind from her. "Give me the tape, Jess."

"It didn't have to come to this, ma'am," Jesse said, pulling a three-inch roll of duct tape from his jacket pocket. "I was hoping we wouldn't have to."

Jock reached to pull a length of tape off the roll, freeing Chloe's mouth. "Tell the truth for once! I was drugged! They—"

Jock pressed the tape under her nose so tight her upper lip bulged, and when he pressed the sides against her cheeks, she couldn't move her jaw, let alone speak.

"God," Chloe prayed silently, "help me be strong. I don't want to go easy. I don't want to be beat or scared into submission. And if they kill me, let me speak first. Remind me of all the verses I've memorized. Please, God, let me speak your words."

Jock and Jesse took her back across the yard toward a steel door in the wall of one of the cell blocks. The door was at ground level, but she assumed stairs would lead below the ground to solitary confinement.

They stopped about ten yards from the door, and the media was about the same distance away on the other side. "Has she spilled any more?" a woman called out.

"Oh yes," Jock said. Chloe vigorously shook her head. "More all the time," he continued. "Of course we had to tell her there would be no trading leniency for, ah, physical favors as it were. She can only help herself by telling the truth. I'm confident we'll get there. We've already gained more knowledge about the Judah-ite underground and the illegal black-market co-op from her than from any other source we've ever had. And as you know, she gave up Mr. Al Basrah, the leading subversive in the Middle East, and he is already dead."

Chloe continued to shake her head, but she had no illusions that would be shown on GCNN that evening.

"That's all for now, folks. We have a few more prerequisites for Mrs. Williams to qualify her for a life sentence rather than death, but our daily executions here will be held tomorrow at 10 a.m., regardless. We do not foresee having the full house they did yesterday, with every machine busy for nearly half an hour, but the latest count is thirty-five on the docket, so five for each machine."

The press began to disperse, but still Jock and Jesse stood there with Chloe. "I am going to finish my tour-guide speech, little lady, and you're going to hear me out," Jock said. "Some of the best days of my life have been spent in this yard, seeing people get what's coming to them. Frankly, I was disappointed when I was transferred to San Diego, but the brass assured me a huge Judah-ite cell was suspected there. They told me I could cart them back here if we rooted them out. Here's hoping you're just the first."

+ + +

Mac was glad to have Zeke for company on the long flight. Though uneducated, the young man was smart and inquisitive. He never ran out of questions or things to talk about.

"Abdullah's kinda tough because he's already so ethnic. He's not good with accents, so I've got to keep him Middle Eastern but obviously something different than Jordanian. Rayford's pretty easy, 'cause I can go any direction with him. Buck's the hardest, with all the facial scars. But anyway, let's say I make you five guys into totally different people. What're you gonna do?"

"I'm not totally sure myself, Z," Mac said. "Rumor has it Carpathia's calling in the ten kings—'course, he calls 'em regional potentates, but we know what's going down, don't we?"

"I do."

"If Otto succeeds in New Babylon, we find out where the big shindig is gonna be before it happens, and we get in there and bug the place. We're not going to try to stop prophesied events, of course, but it'll be good to know exactly what's happening."

"What happens to Carpathia's secretary?"

"Krystall? If I had a vote, I'd say we convince her we know what's going to happen to New Babylon and get her out of there."

"To Petra?"

Mac shook his head. "Much as we might like to do that, God has set that city aside as a city of refuge for his people only. Sad as it is, she made her decision, took her stand, and accepted the mark. Getting her out of New Babylon just keeps her from dying in that mess when God finally judges the city. She's going to die anyway, sometime between then and the Glorious Appearing, and when she does, she's not going to like what eternal life looks like.

"That doesn't mean we can't befriend her and be grateful for her help. Or that we can't feel sorry that she waited too long to see the truth."

"I still wonder if we can trust her though," Zeke said.

+ + +

The San Diego evacuation deadline was moved up to midnight, partly because preparations were ahead of schedule and partly to be safe. No one knew for sure when the GC would begin their next round of canvasing.

Buck was in the vehicle bay on a walkie-talkie with Ming, who was in his apartment watching Kenny and also manning the periscope. When she said the coast was clear, Buck sent loaded vehicles to the airstrip, where planes and pilots arranged by Lionel Whalum met them.

At 6 p.m. Ming radioed. "Buck, Chloe's on TV."

"Kenny watching?"

"I'll get him into his room."

Buck sprinted back, and by the time he got to his quarters, Rayford had shown up too. The news showed Chloe trying to communicate to the press and Jock backhanding her. Buck felt murderous, especially when they taped her mouth shut. He was used to the lies, but he couldn't stand to see her mistreated.

"Where's that look like to you, Ray?" he said.

Rayford shook his head. "Studying it."

One of the woman reporters said, "Here in Louisiana prisons are notoriously hard, and none harder than Angola. International terrorist Chloe Williams will rue the day she pushed the Global Community to the point where she was sent here. The guillotine will be sweet relief compared to hard labor for the rest of her life."

"Angola, Louisiana!" Buck said. "That's where I'm going. I want to take

Sebastian and Razor, and you'll want to come, of course, Dad. Who else do you think we should—?"

"Hold on, Buck," Rayford said. "We're not going to Louisiana."

"What? You send three of your top people to Greece to get George, and you're going to let the GC do what they want with Chloe?"

"No way she's in Louisiana."

"You just heard it!"

"Think, Buck. They want us to believe she's in Louisiana. They moved her from San Diego to keep away from a raid. They wouldn't be announcing where they took her."

Buck knew Rayford was right. "She's at a prison though, isn't she? They're not faking that."

"I wouldn't put anything past them."

"Ray, I can't fly to Petra and leave her here. If I stay somewhere closer to back east, at least I'd have a chance to—"

"But how are we going to find out where she is?"

"I'd never forgive myself if I jetted off to safety and left her to die alone. I don't know how you could either."

"I'm not about to, if you must know."

"C'mon, Dad, we're in this thing together. Don't be holding out on me."

"I've got a call in to Krystall to see if she's heard anything. Problem is, it's four in the morning over there, and she doesn't think anybody has a clue anyway. The people who would know are in Al Hillah, and we have no access to them. It's going to look pretty suspicious if Krystall starts asking them about Chloe."

+ + +

It was the middle of the evening in Illinois, and Chloe was surprised to have been left alone for hours. She had been right about solitary. The stairs led below ground, and she had been ushered into a small cell with no cot, no sink, no toilet, no chair, no bench, no nothing. Including no light or window. The duct tape had been removed from her mouth, and when the solid metal door was shut, she was in pitch darkness.

A small square hole in the door opened and was filled with Jock's face. "I'm going to let you get some rest," he said, "and I'm going to get some too. Think about anything you can tell me that will benefit you, because when I come back, we're going to see if we need to give you an injection to help you open up. Your little shenanigans today bought you this. You're not going to like it in there if you're claustrophobic or afraid of the dark."

Chloe was both, but she was not about to admit it. She feared she would panic or go mad, but as she heard Jock's footsteps retreat, she was overcome with a sense of peace. "Thank you, Lord," she said. "I need you. I'm willing to die, but I don't want to shame you. I need you to override the truth serum. Don't let me give away anything or anybody, and keep me strong so I won't worry so much about myself. Help me keep my mind, my focus, and my priorities. And be with Kenny and Buck and Dad."

Just thinking about them brought a sob to her throat. Chloe pressed her back against the wall and lowered herself to the cold floor. "God, please, bring to mind Scriptures you want me to hear right now. Don't let hunger or fatigue or fear keep me from remembering. You know who I am and who I'm not. I just want to be what you want me to be. You know better than I that you're working with imperfection here."

She lay on her side with no heart palpitations from the closed-in space or the darkness. That alone was evidence that God was hearing her. She began rehearsing in her mind her memory verses, starting as far back in the Bible as she could remember. But when she stalled, she panicked. "Lord, keep my mind fresh. Don't let me forget. I want to be quoting you when I see you."

Her mind became a jumble. *How will I remember? What if my mind goes blank?* "Lord, please."

And suddenly, light. Was she dreaming? She blinked. The rusted, filthy chamber was bright enough to make her shield her eyes. A vision? A dream? A hallucination?

Then a voice. Quoting her favorite verses. She repeated them, word for word. "Is this your answer, God? You'll speak them and I'll repeat them? Thank you! Thank you!"

Loud banging on the door. "Keep it down in there!"

"Yes, peace, be still." *That voice came from the corner!*

Chloe pulled her hands from her eyes and jumped at a figure, sitting, a finger to his lips.

"Is it you, Lord?" she said, breathless.

"No one can see God and live," he whispered.

"Then who are you?"

"He sent me."

"Praise God."

"Yes, please."

"Can anyone else see you?"

"Tomorrow. Not until then."

"You'll remind me of what God has promised?"

"I will."

"You make me want to sing."

"Do so."

"Sing with me."

"I am not here to sing but to speak. You sing."

Chloe began singing. "'When we walk with the Lord in the light of his word, what a glory he sheds on our way! While we do his good will, he abides with us still, and with all who will trust and obey.'"

"Shut up in there!"

Chloe sang louder. "'Trust and obey, for there's no other way to be happy in Jesus, but to trust and obey.'"

"If I have to open this door, you're going to wish I hadn't!"

"'Then in fellowship sweet we shall sit at his feet. . . .'"

That brought knocking—it sounded like with a stick—and Chloe laughed aloud. "They don't like my voice," she told her new friend.

"Or the words," he said, and she laughed all the more.

"You going crazy in there?"

"No! Do you have any requests?"

"Only that you knock it off!"

"Sorry!" And she began again. "'Standing on the promises of Christ my King, through eternal ages let his praises ring; glory in the highest I will shout and sing, standing on the promises of God.'"

"All right!" The small door flew open. The room went dark again. "You got a light in there?"

"Sure! The light of God."

"I'm serious! What've you got in there?"

"Just the light of his presence."

"If Jock gets back and finds you with something in there, you'll regret it."

"Regret the chance to surprise him? I don't think so. Do you know how to sing harmony? Sing with me. 'Standing on the promises that cannot fail . . .'"

The guard slammed the door.

12

RAYFORD HAD ONLY an inkling of what Buck must be going through. It had to be different for a husband than for a father. But he couldn't put his finger on it.

"Here's what we'll do," he told his son-in-law. "I have arranged with Lionel to leave us a two-seater. It's fast, but it holds only so much fuel. We'll have to take on more en route, maybe in Cypress. We'll help get everyone else out of here; then we can sit at the airstrip for all I care. Fly to the Midwest somewhere, the South. Wherever you think we'd be closest to Chloe."

"And do what?"

"We can take that little satellite TV and keep in touch with Mac and Otto and Krystall, see if we can get a clue," Rayford said.

"You just want to be on the same continent when she dies, is that what you're telling me?"

"Well, uh, no—"

"Dad, think about it. I don't fly planes. You don't have a backup pilot. Neither of us is military. You've got a two-seat plane for two guys, so there's no thought of springing Chloe and bringing her along."

Rayford sat and held his head in his hands. "I don't know what else to do, Buck. I'm not leaving the States with her still in custody. But unless we find out where she is, I'm not putting a crew on it either."

"Where're we going to go?"

"How about Wisconsin, where Zeke was? He tells me the GC never nose around. It's fairly central, so if we do get word, we can be on our way quick."

+ + +

Jock led Chloe to a dimly lit room about a hundred paces from her cell. "It's just you and me tonight, ma'am. No playing off the other cop, no bright lights in your eyes, no pressure."

But when she saw where she was supposed to sit, a steel chair bolted to the floor with leather straps on the legs and armrests, she said, "No, it won't be just you and me, Jock."

"What do you mean?"

"You alone cannot strap me into that chair."

"I think I could, but you wouldn't like it."

"And I'd make you wish you hadn't done it alone. I'm not getting strapped down for any reason unless I'm overpowered. Uh-uh."

"How about we try this the easy way?" he said. "How about we just talk awhile and see if you need restraining?"

"No truth serum?"

"Not if you cooperate."

"I can tell you right now I won't."

"I can't persuade you to rethink this, be nice, help yourself?"

"No sir. For one thing, I have to use the ladies' room, and I won't even be sitting, let alone strapped in, until then."

Jock sighed and walked her farther down the hall. "As you can imagine," he said, "there's no window in a prison john. The only way out is the way in, and I'll be waiting."

+ + +

Mac was on the phone to Rayford from high over the Atlantic in the middle of the night. "When is Weser going to be at the palace?"

"By 8 a.m. their time."

"I'm guessing top priority is anything on Chloe."

"Right."

"And then Carpathia's plans."

"Exactly."

"I'll try him a half hour after he's supposed to have gotten there. I'll call you as soon as I know anything."

+ + +

Chloe emerged from the dingy Stateville bathroom to find Jock with three guards, a woman and two men.

"So it's not just the two of us, Jock?"

"Could have been. When you're all strapped in and not happy, look in the mirror. At least by telling me up front, you saved wasting my time trying to talk you into anything and then having to rassle you into the chair."

As Chloe walked down the hall, the woman grabbed her right hand and twisted it up behind her, while one of the men did the same with her left. She thought about protesting; she had made it clear to Jock she wasn't going easy. As soon as they entered the small room, the third guard bent and scooped her off the floor by her ankles. The wrenching pressure on her shoulders made her cry out, but within seconds she was strapped in the chair.

The guards left, leaving a hypodermic with Jock. He shut the door and approached. "Last chance," he said. "You're not going to tell the truth without this?"

Chloe's pulse sprinted until she noticed her friend from solitary sitting in Jock's chair. "I'm not going to tell you the truth with it," she said.

"Oh, this has broken stronger subjects than you," Jock said.

He began by inserting a receptacle in a vein in her forearm. He did it with such precision it was clear he had experience. Chloe felt no pain, and he deftly taped it in place. Then he inserted a tube that ran to his side of the desk.

Jock sat and Chloe's new friend stood behind him. She fought a grin, peeking at him over Jock's head. "What are you looking at?" Jock said.

"Nobody you know," Chloe said. There was some truth, if he wanted it.

Jock inserted the hypodermic into the tube. "When I push the plunger, it will inject 15 cc's of serum, half an ounce, into your veins. You should feel little more than a relaxed mood. You probably know how this stuff works. It counteracts a chemical in your brain that inhibits overfrankness. But, of course, that is precisely what I want from you."

"I can't wait to hear what I have to say."

"Say enough, and it's life rather than death for you."

"Oh, Jock, I think someone else here needs truth serum more than I do."

"You doubt me?"

"You know as well as I do that no matter what I say, I still die."

"Not necessarily."

"You're a liar. I know that, and that's the truth, and if I'm not mistaken, you haven't even injected me yet."

"No, but enough of this. Here we go."

Chloe's visitor motioned from behind Jock like a music director, and Chloe began to hum. Then she sang quietly. "'There shall be showers of blessing; this is the promise of love. There shall be seasons refreshing, sent from the Savior above.'"

"The serum doesn't act that quickly, so don't assume you're singing the truth."

"'Showers of blessing, showers of blessing we need. Mercy drops round us are falling, but for the showers we plead.'"

"Nice tune."

"Thanks. Nice lyrics too."

Within a few minutes, Chloe felt the effects of the serum. It was strange. A sense of well-being, of trust, that she could feel free to say anything, anything at all. If she didn't know better, she would want to help this man by answering his questions. No harm would come to her, and everything would be all right.

Except that she knew better. She looked past Jock. "How long will you be with me?" she said.

"As long as necessary," the invisible man said.

"Hm?" Jock said. "As long as this takes. I got some rest. I can hang in here as long as you can."

"Bet you can't."

"Try me."

Chloe smiled. "I think you'll find me very trying."

"How are you feeling?"

"Mellow."

"Good. That's progress. What is your name?"

"Chloe Steele Williams, and proud of it."

"What is your father's name?"

"Rayford Steele."

"And your husband?"

"Cameron Williams. I call him Buck."

"Do you have a child?"

"Yes."

"What is his name?"

"His name is very special to Buck and me, because he was named after two dear, dear friends and compatriots who died."

"And what were their names?"

"If I answer that, you will know the name of my son."

"And why should I not know the name of your son?"

"The less you know about him, the harder it will be for you to gain access to him."

"I have told you we mean your son no harm."

"That is a lie."

"Anyway, you mentioned his name to your father on the phone. Kenny."

Jock pushed the hypodermic plunger again, and maybe it was psychological, but Chloe seemed to feel an immediate rush. Strange, but the stuff did seem to be making her tell the truth, even if the answers were not what Jock wanted.

He was more red-faced than usual. Was she making him mad? She hoped so.

"Are you a member of an underground group subversive to the Global Community government and its supreme potentate, Nicolae Jetty Carpathia?"

"Yes."

"Is it true that you do not believe the potentate is worthy to be called a deity?"

"Yes, and beyond that, we believe he is the Antichrist of the Bible."

"Are you aware that that statement alone is punishable by death?"

"Yes, as well as I know that God desires truth, God's law is truth, Jesus is the truth, and if you know the truth, it can set you free."

Where did that come from? Thank you, Lord.

"Are you a member of a Judah-ite faction with a large cell group residing in San Diego, California?"

"Are you asking me who I am?"

"I am asking you are you a—"

"I am a follower of Christ, the Son of the living God. He is the one who is mightier than I, whose sandal strap I am not worthy to stoop down and loose."

"What?"

"Did you not hear me?"

"Did the Judah-ites or a faction of the Judah-ites called the Tribulation Force have anything to do with the darkness that envelops New Babylon?"

"That was the work of God himself."

"Do you or the group you represent seek to overthrow the government of this world?"

"That has already been done. It has simply not been played out yet."

"The Global Community government has been overthrown?"

"It shall become known."

"Do you worship the image of Nicolae Carpathia at least three times a day?"

"Never."

"Will you tell me the whereabouts of your compatriots or any information leading to their capture? Primarily I am talking about your father, your husband, Dr. Tsion Ben-Judah, and Dr. Chaim Rosenzweig."

"I would die first."

Jock pushed the rest of the serum through the apparatus and sat picking at his fingernails for about five minutes. Chloe sang, "'Amazing grace! How sweet the sound, that saved a wretch like me! I once was lost but now am found, was blind but now I see.'"

Jock stood and looked out the door, breathing heavily. Presently he moved to Chloe's chair and removed the surgical tubing and receptacle. He unstrapped her.

"We're finished?" she said.

"No, but you have ingested the maximum dose. I've never seen anything like it. We can sit and chat for a few minutes, and if that last hit kicks in and makes you come to your senses, you let me know."

"Let's talk about you, Jock. What got you so fired up about Carpathia?"

"Oh no, we're not going there. You can just leave me alone. You obviously believe what you believe. That's impressive, I'll give you that. Misguided, but impressive. That's the problem with religious extremists."

"Oh, that's what we are?" she said.

"Of course."

"You'd like to lump us with people who kill in the name of their faith, wouldn't you?"

"You're as extreme as they come, ma'am."

"We don't kill people who don't agree with us. We don't erect statues of our God everywhere and require by law that everyone bow and scrape before them three times a day. We offer the truth, show people the way, call them to God. But we don't force them."

Jock sat heavily. "Do you realize you're going to die tomorrow?"

"I had an inkling."

"And that doesn't bother you?"

"Of course it does. I'm scared."

"And you're never going to see your husband, your baby, your loved ones and friends again."

"If I thought that was true, that would be a different story."

"I get it. Pie in the sky by-and-by. You're all going to be floating around on clouds someday, playing your harps and wearing white robes."

"I hope you're right about the pie but not the harps."

Jock shook his head. "You know we're going to televise this to the world."

"Spread some more lies about me first?"

"We say what we have to say to save face."

"And you need to save face with me because this operation was a colossal failure, wasn't it?"

"Could have gone better."

"Could have? It couldn't have gone worse! What'd you accomplish?"

"Well, when we find out where the rest of the cowards are hiding, we'll have accomplished something."

"You calling them cowards because they're in hiding, or do you mean the rest of the cowards like me? You find me cowardly?"

"Actually no."

"Do I get any last words tomorrow?"

"In your case we might not allow that. I can just hear you trying to preach a sermon, going off on Carpathia, trying to get people saved."

"So, I get to say my last words only if they pass muster with the Global Community."

"Something like that."

"We'll see about that."

"We? Who's we?"

Chloe stood and realized her friend was gone. She plunged on. "Jock, do you realize that the day is coming—and much sooner than you think—when everyone will have to acknowledge God and his Son?"

"Think so?"

"'It is written: "As I live, says the Lord, every knee shall bow to Me, and every tongue shall confess to God."'"

"Well, honey, not me."

"Sorry, Jock. 'Each of us shall give account of himself to God.'"

"My god is Carpathia. That's good enough for me."

"What about when Jesus wins?"

"He wins?"

"'Therefore God also has highly exalted Him and given Him the name which is above every name, that at the name of Jesus every knee should bow, of those in heaven, and of those on earth, and of those under the earth, and that every tongue should confess that Jesus Christ is Lord, to the glory of God the Father.'"

"I hope all that gives you some comfort when you're standing in the hot sun tomorrow morning, smelling that smell, seeing heads roll, and knowing yours will be next. Maybe I'm not the interrogator I thought I was, and maybe you paid a lot of money to be trained and prepped for truth serum. But there's nothing that brings clarity to the mind like knowing you're next in the guillotine line.

"I'll be watching you in the morning, girl. My money says you'll be shaking and wailing and pleading for one more chance to save yourself."

\+ \+ \+

At 8:30 a.m. Palace Time, Mac was still about seven hours from Petra. He called the number Rayford had given him for Otto Weser and identified himself.

"He is risen," the German said.

"Christ is risen indeed," Mac said. "What've you got for me?"

"I gotta tell you, Miss Krystall has been a gem. I wish she was on our side. She let me listen in on a conversation from a man named Suhail Akbar, head of Sec—"

"I know who he is, Mr. Weser. All due respect, cut to the chase."

"Carpathia has assigned him and his people to do two things. First, get the government running in Al Hillah, and second, prepare for a real Oktoberfest for all the leaders of the world in Baghdad six months from now."

"So, not in October?"

"That was just an expression. It's going to be what you Yanks would call a big blowout. All the pomp and circumstance, flags, banners, light shows, bands, dancers, everything. If the lights come back on in New Babylon, the government goes home. But even if they do, the big deal still happens in Baghdad."

"Exactly where? Do we know?"

"It's a brand-new building, Mr. McCullum. On the site where the Iraq Museum used to be, before the war. It's supposed to be state-of-the-art, plush accommodations, room for the meetings and the pageantry. I mean, there are only ten other heads of state, but apparently besides the private meetings with his cabinet, Carpathia wants some festivities open to the public.

"To his people he is referring to the meetings with the sub-potentates, however, as the final solution to the Jewish problem."

"To a German, that has to resonate with your history books, eh, Mr. Weser?"

"Frankly, sir, our history books don't read the same as those of others who write about us, but I know what you mean, yes. We've been down this road before."

"Anything on Chloe Williams?"

"Krystall says she's at Angola Prison in Louisiana."

"She basing that on the same news we saw, or does she have inside information?"

"Let me ask."

Otto came back on a few seconds later. "Both. She says she heard that newscast but that she's also heard Security and Intelligence people talking about Chloe being there. Latest word is that she is to be executed at 1000 hours Central Time."

+ + +

"We've got to go and take George and a few others with us, Rayford," Buck said.

"It still makes no sense," Rayford said. "Why would they broadcast where she is?"

"Maybe to trap us."

"Then it's *less* likely she's there."

"You think they're on to Krystall?" Buck said. "Giving her bogus info to test her?"

"Let's get Sebastian in on this."

+ + +

Since before dawn, Chang had been at his computer in the tech center. When Naomi arrived, she stood behind him, hands resting lightly on his shoulders.

"Troops, troops, and more troops," he said. "The ones from Greece could overpower Israel, let alone those from all over the Carpathian States. And this is just the beginning."

"What's the latest on Mr. Williams's wife?"

"Everything I'm getting from communications going into the palace from Al Hillah puts Chloe in Louisiana and sentenced to death at 6 p.m. our time."

"Oh no."

"That's not the worst of it, Naomi. They let that out over international television, and they never tell the truth. If they want to lure the Trib Force, they could have left her in San Diego. Rayford and Buck are in the thick of the evac from San Diego, but they're not going to know what to do now. I hope they can see through this. For all we know, Chloe is an hour from San Diego. All the GC has to do is have her somewhere where a GCNN affiliate can send a live feed."

Naomi pulled up a chair and sat next to Chang. "If ever there was a newscast you'd want to interfere with, it has to be that one, doesn't it?"

"No way I want the world to see it."

"But we *would* want them to see and hear what Chloe might say."

"Definitely. I'll just be ready to flip it when they've lost patience with her."

+ + +

Rayford found that Sebastian agreed with him. "No way they're letting out where she really is," he said. "It would be a major gaffe."

"Then where are we?" Buck said. "I'd rather know the worst than not know anything."

"Let's see if Krystall's ready to take a chance," Rayford said. "I'll call her."

When she came on the line, Rayford said, "I need to ask you to do something bold for me."

"I could be executed for what I've given you people already."

"I'm going to trade information with you that will prolong your life."

"What are you talking about?"

"You're a visitor to Dr. Ben-Judah's Web site, right?"

"I told you I was."

"Then you know he has shown from the Bible, in advance, all these plagues and judgments that have hit the earth."

"Yeah, it's spooky."

"It's spooky, but it's real, and we know the next thing that's going to happen in New Babylon, only we don't know exactly when."

"And what is that?"

"God is going to destroy the entire city in the space of one hour."

"Oh my—"

"He will call his own people—like Otto and his friends—out of there so they will be spared. You need to get out too."

"Where will I go?"

"Anywhere but New Babylon."

"And you're sure this is going to happen?"

"If it doesn't, it will be the first time one of these prophesied events hasn't happened. Now, Krystall, I can't promise you'll be safe just because you leave New Babylon. The rest of the world will suffer as well, but maybe not as severely and quickly as New Babylon. Getting out of there will be your only hope."

"Is Carpathia sending all these armies into Israel one of the prophecies too?" Krystall said.

"Ever hear of Armageddon? This is it. But the end of New Babylon comes first."

"And for that fair warning, you want me to do what?"

"Call someone. Someone who would know. And I want you somehow to work Chloe Williams into the conversation. Tell him you saw it on the news or whatever, but you're just curious. Is she really going to be executed and where? Can you do that?"

"You don't believe it's going to be in Louisiana?" she said.

"Finding that hard to swallow."

"No promises, but I'll see what I can find out."

+ + +

"What're you doing tonight, Jock?" Chloe said as he walked her back to solitary.

"Sleeping like a baby. Big day tomorrow. We tell the world you sang like a canary, but that in the end you refused the mark and wouldn't pledge allegiance to Carpathia. Our hand was forced."

"And you're the hero."

"Probably promoted. Shipped off to International."

"Which is where now?"

"What do you care? You can't tell anybody or do anything about it."

"Then what's the harm in telling me?"

He cocked his head at her. "Rumors say I'll be assigned to the Jezreel Valley."

"Oh? What's going on there?"

"Not at liberty to say."

"But you know?"

"Well, yeah, 'course I do."

"Congratulations."

"Thank you."

"Sky's the limit, huh?"

"I guess," he said.

"Want a little inside information?"

"You're a little tardy with that, but I'm listening."

"New Babylon is never getting back to normal."

"And you know that for a fact."

"Sure as I'm standing here," Chloe said.

"Well, I doubt you're right, but you won't be around to find out. And I will."

"I wouldn't be so sure of that either."

"See you in the morning, ma'am."

Chloe sat in the dark chamber and asked quietly, "Are you still here with me?"

"Always," came the reply. "To the end of the age."

Chloe prostrated herself on the floor and prayed the rest of the time, unable to sleep. She sang, she quoted Scripture, she praised God, and she listened.

Mostly she listened. As he comforted her heart.

13

"I'M NEVER GOING to let this happen again, Dad," Buck said. They stood outside their two-seater jet in remote western Wisconsin at dawn, monitoring a miniature TV and a radio and waiting for Krystall's call. "We could find out Chloe was half an hour away in St. Paul, and there wouldn't be a blessed thing we could do about it. No car, no disguises, no IDs, nothing. Never again, Dad, and I mean it."

Rayford didn't appear to have anything to say, and Buck felt sorry for him. "I don't know what else could have been done," Buck said. "But anything more than sitting on our hands, waiting for something to happen."

"I don't know why Krystall hasn't called," Rayford said. "She's had all day." He looked at his watch. "It's the middle of the afternoon in New Babylon."

"You'd better hope they're not onto her, haven't bugged her phone or something. They'd know about Otto, know we know where the big confab is going to be, everything."

"I don't know," Rayford said. "David and Chang have always said the GC doesn't tap its own phones."

"So everybody in Al Hillah's been in meetings all day and there's no one to tell Krystall the truth about where Chloe is? You should have given her some kind of a time frame. Doesn't she assume we'd like to know before the execution?"

"It's not like she works for us, Buck. She's been a godsend."

"Interesting thing to say about someone bearing the mark of the beast."

* * *

Mac dropped off Zeke in Petra at about two in the afternoon. Abdullah had already readied the bigger plane for Mac and then took charge of getting Zeke settled. "I plan to get in and get out of that apartment as fast as I can," Mac said. "Then I'm picking up Weser and his clan and getting back here. I'd like to get all that done before the GCNN goes on the air with Chloe. I won't watch 'em kill her, but I want to see what leads up to it anyway."

+ + +

In pervasive darkness, Chloe had no idea of the passage of time. Occasionally she pressed her ear against the steel door to listen for activity in the solitary unit. So far, nothing.

She thought waiting for one's execution would be like waiting to see the principal or facing a punishment you knew was coming, only multiplied on a mortal scale. And yet she found herself relatively calm. Her heart broke for Buck, not so much for the prospect of his missing her, but for how wrenching it would be to have to explain this to Kenny.

He was too young, and there would be no explaining it, she knew. But the daily questions, the need of a boy for his mother, the fact that no surrogate could love him like she did . . . all that worked on her.

Chloe felt the presence of God, though she didn't see the messenger she had the night before. Her muscles ached from the positions she found herself in for prayer and then just trying to get comfortable. Hunger was a distraction she succeeded in pushing from her mind. Soon, she told herself, she would be dining at the banquet table of the King of kings.

Most gratifying was that she had fewer doubts and more assurance as the hours passed. She had put all her eggs in this basket, she had always liked to say. If she was wrong, she was wrong. If it was all a big story, she had bought it in its entirety. But for her the days of questioning and misgivings were gone. Chloe had seen too much, experienced too much. She had been shown, like everyone else on the planet, that God was real, he was in control, he was the archenemy of Antichrist, and in the end God would win.

Early on in her spiritual walk, Chloe had entertained a smugness, particularly when people berated or derided her for her beliefs. She was too polite to gloat, but she couldn't deny some private satisfaction in knowing that one day she would be proved right.

But that attitude too had mercifully been taken from her. The more she learned and the more she knew and the more she saw examples of other believers with true compassion for the predicaments of lost people, the more Chloe matured in her faith. That was manifest in a sorrow over people's souls, a desperation that they see the truth and turn to Christ before it was too late.

She didn't even know what to do with her feelings of love and concern and sympathy for people who had already taken Carpathia's mark and were condemned for eternity. They were beyond help and hope, and yet still she grieved for them. Flashes of humanity in Florence, in Nigel, in Jesse, in Jock . . . what did those mean? She couldn't expect unbelievers to live like believers, and so she was left without the option to judge them—only to love them. Yet it was hopeless now.

While Chloe couldn't understand how there could still be uncommitted people in the world, she knew there were. Those were the ones she would try to reach with whatever freedom God made the GC give her to make a last comment. How someone could see all that had gone on during the last six years and not realize that the only options were God or Satan—or worse, could know the options and yet choose Satan—she could not fathom.

But no doubt this was true. Ming had told her of Muslims who were anti-Carpathia because they were so devout in their own faith. Some practicing Jews who did not believe in Jesus as Messiah also rejected Carpathia as god of this world. George knew of militia types who refused to give allegiance to a dictator yet had not trusted Christ for their salvation either.

Was it possible, after all this time, that there were still spiritually uncommitted people who simply hadn't chosen yet? Chloe couldn't imagine, but she knew it had to be true. Some simply chose to pursue their own goals, their own lusts.

Chloe wondered about the others in Stateville who would die that morning. Many would be bearers of Carpathia's mark, but surely many would not. Would she, as the prize arrest, be last on the docket?

"Clarity, Lord," she said. "That's all I ask for. You have already promised grace and strength. Just let my mind work better than it should under the circumstances."

\+ \+ \+

Mac dug through his luggage and found his wino outfit. No one cared to look for the mark of Carpathia under the stocking cap of a smelly man down on his luck. It had become the only ensemble Mac dared go out in during the day. He found his scooter where he had left it in the underbrush near the airstrip and rode to the outskirts of Al Basrah, chaining it securely before staggering into town.

Mac was greeted only by real drunks. He acted as if he was just wandering, but he was on a clear route. And when he got to within a block of his and Albie's place, he ducked into an alley and found himself alone. He jogged the rest of the way and started up the stairs when he heard voices. Mac stopped and sat on the landing at the top of the stairs. Two men stood in front of his and Albie's dingy rooms.

"You can't be in here, old man!" one of them shouted. "Get out."

Mac mumbled and let his head fall back, snoring.

The men laughed. "Anyway," one said quietly, "I'm guessing he'll come after dark. Double-M wants him alive."

Mac recognized the nickname.

"I got two guys who can watch the entrance starting about an hour before sundown. You're sure he wouldn't come earlier?"

"He's got no mark, man! Who would risk that?"

When the men moved on and Mac was sure the way was clear, he sprang to his feet and unlocked his door. The place was empty. Not a lick of furniture. None of their stuff. Now it just sat as a trap for him to return to.

Mac bounded down the stairs and ran back to his scooter, sped to the airstrip, and headed for New Babylon. He had arranged with Otto that he bring his people to the New Babylon airstrip. "Better to load up where no one can see us," he said.

The thirty or so men and women in Otto's charge tried individually to thank Mac, but he just smiled and kept moving them into the plane. He wasn't going to feel at ease again until he was in Petra. Then, with a new identity courtesy of Zeke, he'd be ready for any caper Rayford could think of.

Otto was bouncing on the balls of his feet at the back of the crowd. "Once you're on," Mac said, "we're off."

"Mac, we can't go yet."

"Why? What now?"

"She's dead."

"Who?"

"Krystall."

"What are you talking about?"

"Go see for yourself. After I was here this morning, I went back to our underground place and helped get everybody ready to meet you. When we got here, I told them to wait for you and that you would be the only person who could see enough to land. I went to thank Krystall, and that's when I found her."

"How do you know she's dead?"

"I'm not a doctor, sir, but there was a stench like someone had tossed something in there. She was on the floor with the phone buzzing. I let it lie. I checked her pulse. Come see for yourself."

"Mr. Weser, we don't have time. If she's dead, she's dead, and I'm sorry. And Rayford getting her mixed up in all this may have caused it. But there's nothing I can do for her, and we might jeopardize this mission if you and I go running off with all your people waiting on the plane."

"You think they were onto her? Sent somebody to kill her?"

"I don't know how they would do that if they couldn't see."

"I was thinking maybe they had someone who knew the palace come back and feel his way up there, make sure she was there by talking to her, and then toss poison gas or something in there."

"Could be. That explains why Rayford never heard from her. Did you let him know?"

"I should have, shouldn't I? I didn't know what to do. I was so upset."

"Get aboard. I'll call Rayford."

+ + +

Buck looked on as Rayford took a call from Mac and covered his eyes with a hand. "What is it?" Buck said.

Rayford held up a finger to tell Buck to wait, and his knees buckled.

"What? Is Chloe already gone?"

"No, Buck," Rayford said, on his knees in the grass. "But she might as well be." He told him the news.

Buck sat and pulled his knees to his chest. "I can't believe I'm stuck here in the middle of nowhere, waiting for my wife to die, not even knowing where she is."

Rayford looked ashen. "We should get started for Petra."

"But what if someone—"

"No one who knows is going to tell us, Buck. It's time to give it up."

"Give up, you mean."

"Yes, Buck," Rayford said, standing, emotion in his voice. "I have given up. She's in God's hands now. If he chooses to spare her somehow, he's apparently decided to do it without our help."

As Rayford boarded, Buck stood and spread his palms on the fuselage of the aircraft, his head hanging. "Chloe," he rasped, "wherever you are, I love you."

+ + +

After a long night of praying, Chloe actually drifted off. She was awakened, she wasn't sure how long later, by the unmistakable *thwock-thwock-thwock* of helicopter blades. More than one chopper. Maybe as many as three. For an instant she allowed herself to wonder if her deliverance had come.

Deep inside she knew her husband and her father, and perhaps many in the Trib Force, would work to free her until the end. But she also knew that without a miracle there was no way they could know where she was. That had been the whole point of her transfer.

Had they somehow found out? She never ceased to be amazed at the resources available to so many of her compatriots. Should she prepare to flee in the event they did break in and look for her? Did they know more than where she was? Did they know the architecture and layout of the prison, where solitary was, somehow which cell she might be in? And how many were there? Could they overpower the GC?

Her questions were answered in an instant when her friend reappeared and the darkness of her cell was turned to noonday.

"May I know your name?" she said.

"You may call me Caleb."

"I am not to be rescued today, am I, Caleb?"

"You will be delivered, but not in the manner you mean."

"Delivered?"

"Today you will be with Christ in paradise."

That drove Chloe to her knees. "I can't wait," she said. "There are so many here I will miss desperately, but not much else. How I long to be with Jesus!"

Besides the choppers, Chloe heard only the loudest noises from outside and none from inside. Vehicles. Metallic hammering. Shouts. Construction of some sort. In spite of herself, she began to grow nervous. "I want to be the picture of a child of God," she said, trying to control her emotions.

"God will keep you in perfect peace if your mind is stayed on him."

"Thank you, Caleb. But suddenly I feel so fragile."

Finally Chloe heard sounds from inside solitary. A rap on the steel door, the smaller door sliding open. Jock's face appeared. "How we doing this morning, missy? Bathroom break."

"Give me a minute, please."

"Oh, tough girl."

She looked desperately to Caleb.

"'Peace I leave with you,' says your Lord Christ," he said. "'My peace I give to you; not as the world gives do I give to you. Let not your heart be troubled, neither let it be afraid.'"

Chloe knocked on the steel door. "I'm ready," she said.

A guard opened the door. When Chloe emerged, she found Jock in his dress blues, gold buttons, the whole bit. She also faced a woman wearing a GCNN blazer and carrying a leather bag. "My, my," the woman said. "That won't do. Let me know when I can join you in the bathroom. And, Jock, get her a clean jumpsuit."

"Dressing me for the kill?" Chloe said.

"All pageantry, my dear," the woman said. "Justice will be served, but it will be clear you were not mistreated."

"I see," Chloe said, as the woman followed her. "Snatched from my family, starved, drugged, flown halfway across the country, injected with truth serum, and held in solitary confinement overnight is your idea of fair treatment?"

"Hey, I'm just the makeup artist. Call for me when you're ready."

"For what?"

"I'll fix your hair, make you up a little."

"Don't bother."

"Oh, I have to."

"You don't have a choice?" Chloe said.

"If you were presentable, maybe, but look at you."

"Surely I have a choice. I ought to be able to look however I want."

"You'd think. But no."

Chloe caught a glimpse of herself on the way past the mirror. She did look awful. Her face was greasy and smudged. Her hair a tangle. *Bizarre. When was the last time someone fixed me up?* And here it was, free, when her appearance was the last thing on her mind.

"Don't dawdle," the woman called out. "We're on a TV schedule, you know."

Chloe shook her head. TV people. They expected even the condemned to play team ball.

"I'm putting a fresh jumpsuit on the sink! Tell me when you've changed!"

Chloe changed but said nothing. When she came out, the woman said, "You were going to tell me when you were ready."

"No, I wasn't."

"Let's go back in there so I can use the mirror."

"Feel free. I don't need it."

"Come on! I have to get you ready."

"I'm ready."

"Wait, stop! Hold still."

Chloe looked the woman full in the face. "Do you not see the absurdity of this? It's not bad enough that I'm to be put to death? You have to make a spectacle of it?"

"I have a job and I'm going to do it."

"Then you're going to do it right here and right now."

The woman bent to set her bag on the floor and rose with a comb and brush. She worked vigorously on Chloe's hair. Then she used a wetnap to wash Chloe's face and dabbed rouge on her cheeks. When she produced mascara, Chloe said, "No. Now that's it. No mascara, no lipstick. We're done."

"You know, you're really quite an attractive girl."

Chloe arched an eyebrow. "Well, thank you so much. When I look back on this, that's going to be the highlight of my morning." *What a comforting thought. I have a chance at having the best-looking head in the Dumpster.*

When Chloe was delivered back to Jock, he said, "Do I need to cuff you, restrain you?"

"No."

"That's my girl."

She gave him a look.

"Nothing personal," he said. "I'm just doing what I have to do."

"Then make sure I get a few last words."

"If it was up to me—"

She spun and faced him. "It *is* up to you, Jock, and you know it. Anybody who could tell you what to do is thousands of miles away. Take responsibility once, would you? Make a decision here. Announce that I'm going to speak and then let me. In the end I'm gone, and you're headed for your promotion. What's the harm?"

Jock avoided her gaze. He led her up the stairs and into the morning sun. She shielded her eyes. Not only was the Carpathia-run press out in full force, but stands had been set up and apparently the public invited. Chloe wondered what all the noise was about until she realized the crowd apparently recognized she was the main attraction and was applauding and cheering.

The other prisoners, mostly men, were already in their respective rows, waiting behind the tables. Some bounced nervously. Others seemed to hyperventilate. Officials sat at each table, one with a mark applicator. What was the point? At this stage, even the ones who took the mark still endured the blade. Did they think the mark gave them some sort of an advantage in whatever afterlife Carpathia offered?

Cross-legged on the ground around each guillotine sat prisoners in dark denim. These, Chloe realized, were the lifers Jock described as collectors. They would dispose of the remains. They looked excited, smiling, joshing with each other.

Jock led her to the back of the line at the middle table. "Well, I guess this is it," he said, and to Chloe he sounded apologetic. "You can still—"

"We should have made it a bet yesterday," she said.

"Ma'am?"

"You were sure I would be making last-minute pleas about now."

"You win that one," he said. "You're a strange woman."

Chloe was aware of lights on high poles, scaffolding that supported cameras and cameramen, technicians wearing headphones running here and there, people checking their watches. In line at the table to her right, a middle-aged man bearing Carpathia's mark—which meant he had been sentenced for some other capital crime—had fallen to his knees, shuddering and sobbing. He grasped the pant legs of the man in front of him, who laid a tentative hand on his shoulder and looked ill at ease.

An older woman, yet another line beyond, stood with her face buried in her hands, swaying. Praying, Chloe assumed. In every line were Jews, identified with stenciled Stars of David or wearing self-made yarmulkes, some made of scraps of cloth, some of cardboard. The people were wasted, scarred, having been starved, beaten, sunburned.

Chloe knew enough from Buck's research and the inside stuff from David Hassid and Chang to know that Carpathia wanted these to be tortured to within an inch of their lives but not allowed to die before their public beheadings.

Chloe had been as alarmed as anyone when television had gone from bad to worse and from worse to unconscionable. The worst possible perversions were available on certain channels twenty-four hours a day, and literally nothing was limited. But when studies showed that by far the most-watched television shows every day of the week were the public executions, she knew there had been one more far corner for society to turn after all, and it had turned.

The bloodlust was apparently insatiable. It had come to the point where the most popular of the live-execution shows were those that lasted an hour and included slow-motion replays of the most gruesome deaths. When guillotines malfunctioned and blades stuck, victims were left mortally wounded and screaming but not dead. . . . This was what the public wanted to see, and the more the better.

Each execution was preceded by a rehearsal of the misdeeds of the recalcitrant. The more sordid the past, the more satisfying the justice, the logic went. Chloe knew what kinds of stories circulated about her. She could only imagine what was said about the truly guilty.

Chloe watched Jock make his way back toward the stands and a single microphone. What appeared to be a stage manager quieted the crowd, waited for a cue, then signaled them to applaud while he read from a script, introducing Jock Ashmore. He called him one of the Global Community's crack lead investigators, single-handedly responsible for the capture and arrest of Chloe Steele Williams, the highest level anti-Carpathian terrorist apprehended to date. The people cheered.

"Thank you," Jock began. "We have thirty-six executions to carry out for you today—twenty-one for murder, ten for refusing to take the mark of loyalty, four for miscellaneous crimes against the state, and one for all those charges and many, many more."

The crowd cheered and shouted and whooped and whistled.

"I am happy to say that though Chloe Steele Williams did not in the end agree to accept the mark of loyalty to our supreme potentate, she did provide us with enough detailed information on her counterparts throughout the world to help us virtually eradicate the Judah-ites outside of Petra and put an end to the black-market co-op."

The crowd went wild again.

"But more on her when she becomes today's thirty-sixth patient of Dr. Guillotine."

When the crowd finally settled, Jock said, "We begin this morning in line 7 with a man who murdered his wife and two infant sons."

Chloe caught a glimpse of a monitor where the mutilated bodies of the boys were shown in ghastly detail. "God, give me strength," she said silently. "Keep me focused on you."

A woman directly in front of her, pale and sickly and with no mark of loyalty, turned suddenly. "Are you Williams?" she said.

Chloe nodded.

"I don't want to die, and I don't know what to do!"

Thank you, Lord. "If you know who I am," Chloe said, "you know what I stand for."

"Yes."

"Your only hope is to put your faith in Christ. Admit you're a sinner, separated from God. You can't save yourself. Jesus died on the cross for your sins, so if you believe that, tell God and ask him to save you by the blood of Christ."

"I will still die?"

"You will die, but you will be with God."

The woman fell to her knees and folded her hands, crying out to God. A guard pointed to a collector and then to the woman, and the man jumped up and ran toward her. Just as it appeared he was about to bowl her over, Chloe lowered her shoulder and sprang toward him.

Her elbow caught him flush in the mouth and snapped his head back. He flopped in the dirt, screaming and spitting teeth and blood. The woman continued to pray. Finally she stood. The man made a move toward the woman again, but Chloe merely pointed at him and he skulked away.

"I prayed," the woman said, "but I am still scared. How do I know it worked?"

"Let me have a look at you," Chloe said, and she saw the mark of the believer on her forehead. "What do you see on my forehead, ma'am?" Chloe said.

"A mark, as if in 3-D." She reached to touch it.

"I see the same on you," Chloe said. "Only the children of God are sealed with this mark. No matter what happens to you today, you belong to God."

The crowed roared as collectors dragged the first man to the guillotine by his hair. He dug in his heels; he kicked and screamed. He let his legs go limp and had to be carried into position. The man squirmed and fought so much that extra collectors were called in to hold him down. When the executioner made sure everyone's extremities were clear, he pulled the cord and the great blade fell.

The rusty thing, blackened by blood, flipped at an angle just before it bit into the victim's neck. Chloe recoiled as it sliced only halfway into the man, causing him to lurch and pull back, flailing at the collectors who tried to hold him.

He somehow broke free and spun and staggered, flinging blood and gore. The collectors ducked and laughed and made sport of him as the executioner quickly banged at the blade, straightened it, and raised it again.

Two collectors grabbed the man and pushed him headlong into position again, whereupon the cord was pulled yet again and the job done right this time. The reaction of the crowd showed they thought it was the perfect way to start the day.

"Next," Jock said, "we begin with the first of ten in a row who refused to take the mark, minus our guest of honor, of course, as we save the best till last."

But before he could say anything else, Caleb appeared in all his brightness in the middle of the courtyard, between Chloe and Jock. He appeared fifteen or sixteen feet tall in raiment so white that when Chloe turned to see the crowd's reaction, it was clear it hurt people's eyes.

They shrieked and froze. Chloe saw Jock turn to see what scared them so. He fell, holding the microphone, and stared, seemingly unable to move.

When Caleb spoke, the ground shook and a wind blew dust about. Chloe was sure everyone wanted to flee, but they could not.

"I come in the name of the most high God," he began. "Hearken unto my voice and hear my words. Ignore me at your peril. 'Oh, that men would give thanks to the Lord for His goodness, and for His wonderful works to the children of men!'

"For He satisfies the longing soul and fills the hungry soul with goodness. You who sit in darkness and in the shadow of death are bound in affliction because you rebelled against the words of God and despised the counsel of the Most High.

"Cry out to the Lord in your trouble, and he will save you out of your distress. He will bring you out of darkness and the shadow of death and break your chains in pieces.

"Thus says the Son of the most high God: 'I am the resurrection and the life. He who believes in Me, though he may die, he shall live. And whoever lives and believes in Me shall never die.'

"But woe to you who do not heed my warning this day. Thus says the Lord: 'If anyone worships the beast and his image, and receives his mark on his forehead or on his hand, he himself shall also drink of the wine of the wrath of God, which is poured out full strength into the cup of His indignation. He shall be tormented with fire and brimstone in the presence of the holy angels and in the presence of the Lamb.

"'And the smoke of their torment ascends forever and ever; and they have no rest day or night, who worship the beast and his image, and whoever receives the mark of his name.'"

14

CHANG SAT DEEP in the bowels of the tech center at Petra, finally understanding the Western expression about having one's eyes glued to the TV screen. He was prepared to take over the broadcast, to yank it off the air before anyone anywhere saw Chloe's execution.

Yet the appearance of this messenger of God, warning the undecided against taking the mark, pleading with them to receive Christ—this was something the globe needed to see and hear yet again.

For months reports had come from around the world that angels were showing up at mark application and guillotine sites. Some accounts were hard to believe, but Tsion Ben-Judah said they fit perfectly with the loving-kindness he knew of God.

Chang glanced over to where the elders sat before a big screen, and beyond them, hundreds of computer keyboarders awaited instructions. The fading late-afternoon sun cast slanted rays through the door a hundred feet from Chang, and he was moved nearly to tears by the gently falling manna. Providing food for his chosen, protecting and thrilling Chang, comforting Chloe, and sending messengers with the everlasting gospel . . . God was the ultimate multitasker.

A phone rang and Naomi answered. Chang read her lips as she leaned close to Tsion. "It's Buck for you."

"Cameron, my friend! How difficult this must be for you. . . . No, I am sorry, son. I know of no instance where the bearer of the everlasting gospel has intervened in the sentencing. . . . Yes, of course God could miraculously deliver, but I caution you to be prepared for either result. . . ."

\+ + +

Rayford second-guessed his decision to be in the air during the broadcast. He put the jet on autopilot and watched, but he dreaded the moment that was surely to come and wondered when he would recover enough to trust himself with the controls. Well, he decided, he had no choice. Maybe this was the best therapy.

Unless he was willing to see Chloe and Buck and himself die the same day, he had to stay disciplined regardless.

Poor Buck. On the phone with Tsion and apparently not hearing what he hoped. Rayford wanted to comfort him, but Buck was not the type who took soothing until well after a crisis was over. Right now he was arguing his case. As the messenger of God stared down at the apoplectic crowd and saw the nine remaining undecideds on their knees, weeping, Buck pressed Tsion.

"But he has his man right there, Doctor! How hard would it be to intervene? Why can't he just sweep her out of there and deliver her back to us? You know he could! He could have arranged for us to get word of where she was too. What have I done or not done that makes me so unworthy of a little consideration?"

+ + +

Chang turned back to the screen to be sure he didn't miss anything, but he could still hear Tsion earnestly counseling Buck.

"Cameron," Tsion said, "that is your emotion talking. You know as well as anyone that this whole period, the entire Tribulation, is not about us individually. God has a master plan. It is the culmination of the battle between good and evil that has spanned millennia. He is reconciling his people to himself. We should be grateful we have been included. He has a bigger picture in mind, but it is also evidence of his eternal love for us. Trust him, my friend. Trust him no matter what."

+ + +

Chloe felt as if she were already in heaven. Caleb's glow had blocked from her vision the hideous death of the first victim. She watched Jock struggle to his feet and dust himself off.

"Please, people, no one leave. We have had reports of these apparitions at other sites, though this is the first visit we have had here. This is a trick perpetrated by the spiritualists within the camp of the rebellion. Perhaps we should ask permission of the intruder if we may proceed with our program." He turned to look at Caleb, pretending to be even more afraid than he was. Chloe could tell he had not persuaded the crowd that this was other than real.

"Kind sir," Jock said, his voice dripping with sarcasm, "may we continue?"

Caleb's voice, louder than ever, resounded off the prison walls. "You have been tried and found guilty for your crimes against the most high God. That you bear the mark of the evil one condemns you to death. Nothing you do can improve your fate. Because you have worshiped the beast and his image and received his mark, you shall drink of the wine of the wrath of God. You shall be tormented with fire and brimstone in the presence of the holy angels and in the presence of the Lamb. And you shall have no rest day or night.

"That which the Lord God even thinks shall surely happen, and what he decides shall never change, for as the Scripture says, 'The Lord of hosts has sworn, saying, "Surely, as I have thought, so it shall come to pass, and as I have purposed, so it shall stand."'"

Jock stared up at Caleb with brows raised, then looked back at the crowd with a shrug. "Ask a simple question . . . ," he said, and they laughed nervously. "I'll take that as an indication that we may proceed, because, hey, bottom line, if he's right and God's got us in his sights, he can pull the trigger anytime he wants. But look who's dying here today. Huh? Are you with me? Who's dying? Let me hear you!"

No one responded.

"The so-called people of God!" Jock said. "The ones who chose him instead of the real god and our supreme potentate, Nicolae J. Carpathia! Come on, people, don't be intimidated by big, shiny, transparent ghosts. Yeah, he's scary. But all he's done is interrupt a TV show and—get this—make it better! Is this great theater or what? The enemy shows up to rattle his saber, but he hasn't changed a thing! You came to see heads chopped off, and that's what you'll see. These people can cry and pray and beg all they want, but they're still gonna die!"

Chloe was thrilled to see the formerly undecided nine rise and find that six of them had the mark of the believer on their foreheads. Something within them must have confirmed this, because they lifted their hands and smiled despite their impending fate. The other three looked miserable, and Chloe assumed they were among the hard-hearted who may have been desperate to change their minds but had waited too long.

Jock, for all his bluster, was either more intimidated by Caleb than he let on or he still had the TV schedule in mind. "Let's shake things up a little, shall we?" he said. "I want one of the ten without the mark of Carpathia at each of the guillotines, all at the same time. Now! Move! Collectors, see to it! We'll do them all at once and get back on schedule. Any of you who still want the mark, say so now."

The woman ahead of Chloe and the six others she had seen with the mark of the believer stayed where they were, while the other three scrambled to the mark applicators.

The collectors grabbed the remaining seven without Carpathia's mark, including the woman ahead of Chloe. She turned and they embraced. "Be strong and trust God," Chloe said. They dragged the woman to the middle machine.

Not one of the seven struggled or fought or had to be forced to kneel and lay their necks in place. "We'll do it on three!" Jock shouted, and the crowd, though still clearly wary of the huge, glowing stranger, began to come alive with anticipation.

Chloe lowered her head and closed her eyes, determined not to be one who watched the execution of children of God. But even with her eyes shut, she noticed something and looked up to see that Caleb had filled the entire courtyard with a light so bright that no one could see anything. It wreaked havoc on the TV cameras, and cameramen and technicians began hollering for help, pleading with Jock to wait.

"We will not be delayed by this trick of the enemy!" Jock said and counted to three. The sickening sound of the heavy blades echoed, and the people cheered, but because of the blinding light, no one saw the deaths, there or on television anywhere in the world.

+ + +

Chang sat back and studied the screen. He signaled to Naomi to come over. "Did you see that?" he said. "If the angel does that for Chloe as well, we won't need to switch the feed. He'll accomplish the same thing for us."

"But he's gone," Naomi said. "Look."

She was right. The prison courtyard looked normal again. The executions proceeded on schedule for the next half hour, each death preceded by the typical preliminaries—graphic depictions of the condemned's crimes.

With the absence of Caleb, the crowd had returned full-throated—hissing, booing, cheering, applauding. The collectors were filthy with splattered blood and dust, and they seemed drunk with the thrill of their task.

Chloe had stood in the hot sun for more than an hour, mostly averting her eyes from the ghastly panorama of horror. Weak from hunger, parched with thirst, and dizzy from standing, she fought to maintain her emotions. She prayed and prayed that God would grant her an opportunity to speak for him, and that she would be able to articulate what was in her mind.

Chloe missed Caleb. When he was there it seemed she basked in the glow of glory and felt the presence of God. Now she knew God was with her, but it took more faith. She tried to anticipate that she was just moments from the presence of almighty God, and she thrilled to the idea that she would soon fall at Jesus' feet.

But now she stood in the heat of the day, dust kicking up around her, and noticed the sympathetic looks of the mark applicators and the other officials at each desk who had processed the condemned. They had been through this before, had seen the so-called guest of honor ridiculed and humiliated, as if beheading weren't enough.

More than thirty minutes after Caleb had interrupted him, Jock was full of himself. He had warmed to the task and, Chloe assumed, could taste his promotion, could picture himself in the corridors of power in Al Hillah with the potentate himself.

Still facing the crowd, Jock switched to a cordless microphone and began moving toward Chloe. "And now the moment we have all been waiting for," he announced, and the people began to clap.

As he reached Chloe, he touched her shoulder and turned her to face the stands. He stood there with his arm around her, and though repulsed, Chloe was struck by how gentle he was. His fingers were spread, palm open, as he enveloped her shoulder. In her flesh she wanted to wrench away and spit at him, but she was aware of the international television audience and that this was her last opportunity to impact anyone for Christ.

"It's often customary to give a celebrated case a few last words," Jock said. "But I have been debating this. What do you think?"

Some screamed, "Get it over with! Kill her! Let's see that pretty little head in a basket!"

Others clapped and yelled, "Let her speak!"

Jock looked at a stage manager, and Chloe saw the woman signal that he had time to fill.

"I don't know," he said. "Should I or shouldn't I?" The crowd started in again. "While we're thinking about that," Jock continued, "let's watch this tape of the crimes we're avenging today."

The assembled hooted and hollered as monitors showed a lavishly produced history attributing all sorts of evils to Chloe, the Judah-ites, the Tribulation Force, and the International Commodity Co-op. Chloe was surprised to see that many of the plagues and judgments that had come from heaven the past six years were somehow charged against her and her compatriots' accounts.

Finally, the phony charges against her father and her husband were shown, along with the bogus picture of a two-year-old boy she had supposedly named after Jesus and claimed was God reincarnate.

"Despite all this," Jock said, "this little lady did an almost complete about-face when confronted with her own mortality. In order to take some of the heat off her family, particularly her god-in-human-flesh child, she sang like a canary behind closed doors. She gave us so much information that we have to concede that Chloe Steele Williams has done more than we ever could to help wipe out the last vestiges of the most significant rebellion the New World Order has ever faced."

The people cheered.

"So, maybe she's said enough! Maybe she's said too much already! Maybe we should just get on with this! What do you say?"

More applause, stomping, shouting.

"Mrs. Williams gave up her friends and relatives and coconspirators, but in the end she still refused to pledge her loyalty to the real god of this world, the resurrected Nicolae Carpathia."

Boos filled the courtyard.

"And so, Mrs. Williams," Jock said, turning toward her, "unless you're ready to change your mind about that, I believe we're ready to proceed with justice."

Chloe reached for the microphone, but Jock held it tight. "Ah, ah, ah!" he said. "No speaking privileges for you unless you're ready to take the mark of loyalty to the throne of the leader of the Global Community."

But she continued to reach, and now both their hands were on the mike. "Are we witnessing a historic moment here, folks?" Jock said. "You understand, Mrs. Williams, that taking this microphone also means taking the mark of Carpathia?"

She took the microphone, and Jock turned to the crowd with both arms extended, then led them in a huge ovation.

"Sir, you told me if it were up to you, I would get to say a few words. Is it up to you?"

Jock reached for the mike. "That is not the arrangement! You may speak only if you surrender to the mark."

Caleb appeared behind Chloe again and merely raised a finger and gestured no to Jock. Jock froze in place and toppled backward, his arm outstretched, still reaching. In spite of themselves, the crowd laughed while Jock reddened and perspired, rigid.

Chloe turned to the people and spoke softly. "A famous martyr once said he regretted he had but one life to give. That is how I feel today. On the cross, dying for the sins of the world, my own Savior, Jesus the Christ, prayed, 'Father, forgive them, for they do not know what they do.'

"My personal preference? My choice? I wish I could stay with my family, my loved ones, my friends, until the glorious appearing of Jesus, who is coming yet again. But if this is my lot, I accept it. I want to express my undying love to my husband and to my son. And eternal thanks to my father, who led me to Christ.

"A famous missionary statesman, eventually martyred, once wrote, 'He is no fool who gives what he cannot keep to gain what he cannot lose.' He was talking about his life on earth versus eternal life with God. In my flesh I do not look forward to a death the likes of which you have already witnessed thirty-five times here today. But to tell you the truth, in my spirit, I cannot wait. For to be absent from the body is to be present with the Lord. And as Jesus himself said to his Father at his own death, 'Into Your hands I commit My spirit.'

"And now, 'according to my earnest expectation and hope that in nothing I shall be ashamed, but with all boldness, as always, so now also Christ will be magnified in my body, whether by life or by death. For to me, to live is Christ, and to die is gain. . . . For I am hard pressed between the two, having a desire to depart and be with Christ, which is far better.'

"And to my compatriots in the cause of God around the world, I say, 'Let this mind be in you which was also in Christ Jesus, who, being in the form of God, did not consider it robbery to be equal with God, but made Himself of no reputation, taking the form of a bondservant, and coming in the likeness of men. And being found in appearance as a man, He humbled Himself and became obedient to the point of death, even the death of the cross.

"'Therefore God also has highly exalted Him and given Him the name which is above every name, that at the name of Jesus every knee should bow, of those in heaven, and of those on earth, and of those under the earth, and that every tongue should confess that Jesus Christ is Lord, to the glory of God the Father.

"'Now to Him who is able to do exceedingly abundantly above all that we ask or think, according to the power that works in us . . . and to present us faultless before the presence of His glory with exceeding joy, to God our Savior, who alone is wise, be glory and majesty, dominion and power, both now and forever.'

"Buck and our precious little one, know that I love you and that I will be waiting just inside the Eastern Gate."

Chloe bent and laid the microphone on Jock's unmoving chest and without escort found her way to the base of the middle guillotine. As she knelt and laid her head under the blade, Caleb's glow blinded the eyes of the world. Chloe heard only the pull of the cord and the drop of the sharpened edge of death that led to life eternal.

Interlude

FIFTEEN HOURS LATER Buck staggered from Rayford's plane, jet-lagged and bleary-eyed, but more than anything aching to hold his son. Abdullah had driven to the airstrip just outside Petra, and Ming had ridden along, holding the boy. Buck gathered him up and held him tight, his tears streaming down Kenny's back.

As the five rode toward the Siq that led into Petra, Abdullah radioed ahead their estimated time of arrival. "I hope you don't mind, Buck," he said, "but Dr. Ben-Judah would like to hold the memorial as soon as you and Rayford get there."

Buck was overwhelmed at the turnout. Several hundred had gathered at the high place, within the sound of rushing water from the stream. Acquaintances had made way for Buck's and Chloe's closest friends to gather in the front. Hard as it was with Kenny's arms still wrapped tightly around his neck, Buck sat on a rock shelf and took in the scene.

Tsion and Chaim stood in the middle, waiting for people to settle. In an inner half circle, facing Buck and Kenny and Rayford, were George and Priscilla Sebastian and Beth Ann. Ree Woo and Ming Toy held hands close by. And fresh in from Illinois were Lionel Whalum and his wife, Felicia, along with Leah Rose and Hannah Palemoon.

Buck nodded to Zeke, who stood near Abdullah and Mac. Not far away Chang sat on a rock with his new friend Naomi. They appeared very comfortable with each other already, which Buck noticed seemed to catch the eye of Naomi's father, Eleazar Tiberias, standing nearby.

Tsion raised a hand for silence. He began quietly, but Buck got the impression everyone could hear him over the rushing water. "I brought with me today my personal Bible. As you can understand, the elders and particularly Dr. Rosenzweig and I are constantly studying the Scriptures and commentaries and Bible dictionaries, trying to make sense of what is happening in these last days.

"These are academic pursuits, and while they bear on everyday life here, they can also be devotional exercises. Every day on every page we see the fingerprints of God himself, working his will in our midst and in this world.

"But today I bring the Word of God that is not just part of my theological library but rather is the text I have studied since a few years before the Rapture. As you know, my life changed when I discovered that Jesus was the Messiah I had so long sought, and I discovered that not only because of the Rapture, but also because I had been commissioned to study the prophecies concerning Messiah.

"To do this, I had to purchase a copy of both the Old and New Testaments, which was to me—at the time of the purchase—more than an embarrassment. I worried I would be an anathema not just to my colleagues but to my God as well.

"I was onto the truth before it was proved to me by the Rapture, and soon after that I made the knowledge of the true Messiah my own faith. And suddenly this book—" he held it aloft—"became my very life's bread. It had gone from a necessary piece of textual research, which I bought apologetic and red-faced, to my most prized possession.

"When my family was massacred, I clung desperately to it for life. It became a physical symbol, a talisman if you will, of the Word of God that signified to me Jesus, the Christ, the Messiah, the Son of the living God, the Lamb who was slain to take away the sins of the world. I once read of a great theologian whose personal Bible became so precious to him that at times he found himself reaching out and patting it, almost caressing it as he would a son or daughter or spouse. That seemed strange to me, but I grew to understand it, to identify with it.

"I love this book! I love this Word! I love its author, and I love the Lord it represents. Why do I speak of the Word of God today when we have come with heavy, heavy hearts to remember two dear comrades and loved ones?

"Because both Albie and Chloe were people of the Word. Oh, how they loved God's love letter to them and to us! Albie would be the first to tell you he was not a scholar, hardly a reader. He was a man of street smarts, knowledgeable in the ways of the world, quick and shrewd and sharp. But whenever the occasion arose when he could sit under the teaching of the Bible, he took notes, he asked questions, he drank it in. The Word of God was worked out in his life. It changed him. It helped mold him into the man he was the day he died.

"And Chloe, our dear sister and one of the original members of the tiny Tribulation Force that has grown so large today. Who could know her and not love her spirit, her mind, her spunk? What a wife and mother she was! Young yet brilliant, she grew the International Commodity Co-op into an enterprise that literally kept alive millions around the globe who refused the mark of Antichrist and lost their legal right to buy and sell.

"In various safe-house locations over the past half-dozen years, I lived in close proximity to Chloe and to her family. It was common to find her reading her Bible, memorizing verses, trying them out on people. Often she would hand me her Bible and ask me to check her to see if she had a verse correct, word for word. And she always wanted to know exactly what it meant. It was not enough to know the text; she wanted it to come alive in her heart and mind and life.

"To those who will miss Chloe the most, the deepest, and the most painfully until we see her again in glory, I give you the only counsel that kept me sane when my own beloved were so cruelly taken from me. Hold to God's unchanging hand. Cling to his Word. Fall in love with the Word of God anew. Grasp his promises like a puppy sinks its teeth into your pant legs, and never let go.

"Buck, Kenny, Rayford, we do not understand. We cannot. We are finite beings. The Scripture says knowledge is so fleeting that one day it will vanish. 'For we know in part and we prophesy in part. But when that which is perfect has come,' and oh, beloved, it is coming, 'then that which is in part will be done away.

"'When I was a child, I spoke as a child, I understood as a child, I thought as a child; but when I became a man, I put away childish things. For now we see in a mirror, dimly, but then face to face.'

"Did you hear that promise? 'But then . . .' How we can rejoice in the *but thens* of God's Word! The *then* is coming, dear ones! The *then* is coming."

Tsion sat and opened his Bible in his lap. "Let me close with this, as we mourn, not as the heathen, but as we mourn the loss of our beloved brother and sister in Christ. The psalmist writes: 'Precious in the sight of the Lord is the death of His saints. O Lord, truly I am Your servant; I am Your servant, the son of Your maidservant; You have loosed my bonds. I will offer to You the sacrifice of thanksgiving, and will call upon the name of the Lord.

"'I will pay my vows to the Lord now in the presence of all His people, in the courts of the Lord's house, in the midst of you, O Jerusalem. Praise the Lord!

"'Praise the Lord . . . laud Him, all you peoples!

"'For His merciful kindness is great toward us, and the truth of the Lord endures forever. Praise the Lord!

"'Oh, give thanks to the Lord, for He is good! For His mercy endures forever.

"'Let Israel now say, "His mercy endures forever."'"

15

Six Years, Five and a Half Months, into the Tribulation

A FEW DAYS after the memorial service, Ree and Ming had been married in a small ceremony officiated by Tsion. Chang and Naomi's relationship had blossomed, but they were counseled to delay their engagement until after the Glorious Appearing.

Over several months, Rayford had reorganized the Tribulation Force. Mac, Abdullah, and Ree became the principal pilots. Lionel Whalum, after months of duty in the air, volunteered to take over the direction of the Co-op with Ming assisting and Leah and Hannah joining the staff.

Chang had come up with a brilliant plan to bug the Baghdad site of the international confab of GC heads of state. By checking the main computer in New Babylon daily, he discovered that Leon Fortunato was having someone remotely transmit records of the daily activity of the government for duplication and dissemination. The big break came when Chang learned the government was bidding out the job of wiring the conference hall for sound for the big event.

He told Naomi of his scheme. "It's brilliant," she said, "and I think Captain Steele will think so too. You'd better include him in your thinking soon, don't you think?"

Late one night, Chang invited Rayford to the tech center. "Here's my plan," he told him. "Ree Woo's identity has never been compromised, and his name is not known to the GC. I have formulated a dossier on him that tells his entire background in technological college and his small sound-engineering firm in South Korea, Woo and Associates."

"Which I assume does not exist."

"Of course. As you can see, I have him registered as a loyalist in good standing from Region 30, with a list of satisfied customers. If you cross-check those customers, their endorsements are all in order. I already know what all the other bids are on the sound job, so I can easily underbid them and get Woo the job."

"Then what?"

"I put in a bunch of caveats about how he prefers to use a small crew and work quickly at night when no other sounds would interfere with his adjustments. Setting up the main room and working with GCNN will be easy. I can teach Ree and you how to do that in a day or two. We tell the GC the job will take about twice as long as it really will, giving you access to the main conference room off the big hall, where we know Carpathia and his cabinet plan to meet with the regional potentates. Bugging that room is trickier, but I can also teach you that.

"I'd love to come and do it myself, but it would take too much for Zeke to make me unrecognizable to people I worked with for so long. So I propose teaching Buck and George how to do the bugging work, and while you and Ree are doing the basic sound stuff in the big hall, they can slip into the conference room and get that done."

"Ree's the only one who's going to look Korean, Chang. The rest of us are too big."

"That's easy. The whole crew has to be approved in advance anyway, so whatever looks and nationalities Zeke can come up with, I can plug them in and have them cleared. I'll have Mr. Woo explain that he's using his all-star international crew to do the best job possible."

"I like it, Chang. Let me make sure everybody's on board, especially Zeke. He's going to have to make company uniforms and get everyone's disguises and documents in order."

It went off without a hitch. Zeke was masterful in turning both George and Rayford into much older men. Buck he made a ruddy-faced Aussie. All were quick studies in electronics. Chang found Buck the easiest to teach because, he believed, Buck so badly needed to immerse himself in a new project.

+ + +

It seemed a small break at the time, but in retrospect, Rayford believed it was major. The only representative of the GC cabinet responsible for letting Woo and Associates into the conference hall was a woman who had not been in place when Rayford and Buck had worked for Carpathia.

She was not suspicious anyway, but interacting with a stranger put them both at ease. The rest of the government was still ensconced at Al Hillah, but the woman let on that as soon as the hall was ready for the big meetings in a few weeks, the government would move there and prepare.

Rayford was impressed by Ree's ability to bluff about electronics. He had learned enough from Chang to know the lingo, and he made sure to keep it over the head of the woman with the keys. She rarely stayed long, and since the Woo crew all had ID tags and company caps riding low on their foreheads, they were never carefully checked, and the job went smoothly.

Chang had worked closely with Lionel in bartering for parts, and the men lugged in with them everything they needed to transmit from every station around the big conference table, as well as put video transmitters in half the light fixtures.

Ree Woo and his associates finished the job ahead of schedule, and to their credit, the GC electronically deposited full payment via the Internet. "We are now on Carpathia's payroll," Chang told Rayford.

+ + +

Nicolae's cabinet moved from Al Hillah to palatial quarters near the conference hall in Baghdad, and in a matter of days, the heads of the ten regions would join them. Rayford told Buck one night, "It's been months since the world has heard directly from Carpathia. Now at least we'll know what's in that mind of his."

Carpathia had lain low since the darkening of New Babylon. The government was in chaos and many employees had died. The potentate seemed to have done little but instigate the massive troop buildup in Israel. Rayford speculated that Nicolae was actually embarrassed and humiliated by his inability to counteract the latest plague.

"That's when he's most dangerous though, right?" Buck said. "When given time to think and plot. You can bet he's cooking up something spectacular."

Carpathia hinted at that "something" the first time Chang tapped into the conference room when it was just Nicolae and his inner circle. Chang recorded it for Rayford. "I have news," the potentate said. "And it is so dynamic and delicious, I can hardly wait to share it. But I must. I will make you wait until our colleagues from around the globe are here. I have a trio I want to introduce to everyone, three who will help us accomplish our goals."

"Where are they from, Excellency?" came the clear voice of Viv Ivins.

"That is also a secret for now."

"Oh, Lordship, why must you toy with us?" Leon said.

"Be glad I only toy with you, confrere. The rebel forces will rue the day they ever dreamed of opposing me."

+ + +

Rayford was about to retire late one evening when he received word that Tsion wanted to see him. "He's willing to come to your quarters," Rayford was told.

"Oh no, I'm happy to go to his."

When Rayford arrived, Tsion began, "Before I get to my request, I want you to know that I am at your disposal. The elders and I are fully aware that when you are in Petra, you are the head of the Tribulation Force, and I am merely, how shall we say it, the chaplain of that."

"I'm glad you raised this, Tsion, because I had been meaning to talk to you about your deference to me. It makes me uncomfortable. I do not see Petra as the headquarters for the Tribulation Force. Yes, I feel God has put the mantle of leadership on me in regard to them, but clearly he has chosen you to lead the Remnant of his people, now a million strong. You must not feel you answer to me. You have your elders and your colleague Chaim, and however the Lord leads you through them is fine with me. In fact I prefer it."

Tsion reached and squeezed Rayford's shoulder. "I very much appreciate your confidence, Captain Steele. But you must not denigrate your own leadership responsibilities. I was about to ask you about my next internationally televised message."

Rayford was puzzled. "Your messages have been going out daily via the Internet, haven't they?"

"Of course. But occasionally God lays on my heart a message that I believe he wants addressed to believers and unbelievers alike. And while I know the Web site is available to all and that many unbelievers stumble across it, if we were again able to pirate the international airwaves, I would be grateful for the opportunity. I believe God has given me a message he wants even the god of this world and his minions to hear. When people hear the truth of God preached on the Carpathia-owned networks, well, it is like taking the gospel into the very pit of hell."

"'And the gates of hell shall not prevail against it,'" Rayford quoted.

"Excellent. So, what do you think? Can we do this, and when?"

"First, Tsion, you don't need my permission."

"Consider it informing you then."

"Fair enough. Just know that we have the best techies in the world here, and that means more than just Chang. He's tops, but Naomi is right there, and they've developed a team that can do anything. They work as much for you as they do for me, so anytime you want them to do anything, just say so."

"You have such wonderful rapport with them, Rayford. And with me. I would prefer to go through you."

"As you wish. All I'm saying, Tsion, is that no matter when we do this, it is pirating. It *is* illegal."

"You have a problem with that?"

"None whatsoever. Not even a second thought. We are at war, and I am prepared to use any means necessary to gain an advantage. All I'm saying is that this does not have to be planned. Chang has built his system in such a way that it's simply a matter of throwing a switch. Then they're off and we're on. Say when and say the word."

"Well, I should think we would want to do this at a most opportune time, when the most people are watching. Maybe during some official pronouncement from Carpathia, or one of the most popular programs."

"You know what those are."

"Don't remind me. I suppose one time is as good as another. How about tomorrow at noon, our time?"

"Consider it done."

"I shall call a meeting of everyone, as I am energized by a live audience."

"A million strong? I can't imagine why. We'll have the cameras set up and Chang in position."

+ + +

The next day Tsion found himself uncharacteristically nervous. Petra had many newcomers, and he never knew what to expect from the crowd. The elders had prayed for him and encouraged him, and Chaim had introduced him. And sure enough, when he emerged to speak and Master Chang gave the cue that he was on live international television, Petra erupted into an ovation.

It was just what Tsion had feared, and though he called for quiet and tried to transfer this outpouring of emotion to the Lord by pointing up, the people would not be deterred until they got it out of their system. Rayford must have noticed how uncomfortable and displeased Tsion was, for he rushed to the rabbi and whispered, "They are just loving you and thanking you, Tsion! They are so grateful for what you have meant to them. Just acknowledge it and it will subside."

"But, Captain Steele! In Isaiah 42:8 God is clear! He says, 'I am the Lord, that is My name; and My glory I will not give to another.'"

"And I'm telling you these people are not trying to glorify you. They are merely thanking you for pointing them to him."

But Tsion could not acknowledge the people, as much as he wanted to believe Rayford was right. He'd rather the earth had swallowed him right then. He merely hung his head and stared at the ground for several minutes until the people apparently grew tired of cheering.

+ + +

Chang had ducked back into the tech center once the transfer was made, and he enjoyed listening in on the chaos in Baghdad. "What is going on?" someone shouted. "How did this happen? It's impossible!"

Someone else ordered the control team to shut off all the affiliates. "We can't," came the reply. "All our systems have been overridden."

And so it wasn't just the million strong at Petra who heard the message of God through Tsion that day. It was billions around the world.

\+ + +

"God has laid on my heart a message that I believe he would have me share with you," Tsion began. "I shall not whitewash or sugarcoat it, as we are at the most perilous time in the history of mankind. We are nearly into the last six months of life as we know it. The battle of the ages that has raged since the beginning of time is about to reach its climax.

"The evil ruler of this world, the Antichrist, is spewing his anger and vengeance primarily on God's chosen people. All over the world innocent men and women are being tortured, even as we speak. Their crime? They are Jewish. Some are believers in Jesus as Messiah, and many are not. Regardless, they refuse the mark of loyalty to Nicolae Carpathia, and he makes them pay every day.

"You have seen the footage, and you know the glee with which the evil one watches his plan carried out.

"Many years ago I began proving the truth of God's Word by telling you in advance of the judgments and plagues to come, things clearly prophesied hundreds, yea thousands of years ago. We saw the fruition of the prophecy of a rider on a white horse, promising peace but bringing a sword. The red horse, World War III, followed that. That brought the black horse of famine, then the ashen horse of death. Next came the martyrdom of many saints before the Wrath of the Lamb earthquake.

"Those six judgments had been foretold in Scripture, and the seventh ushered in the next seven. Hail and fire rained on the earth. Then the burning mountain fell into the sea. Wormwood poisoned the waters, and then the sun, moon, and stars were dimmed by one-third. Demonic locusts attacked those who were not sealed by God, and then we were plagued by an army, two hundred million strong, of demonic horsemen who slew much of the population. The fourteenth judgment ushered in the last seven, five of which have already befallen us.

"Millions suffered from boils, and then the sea turned to blood, then the rivers. The sun scorched people to death and burned a third of the earth's greenery. The darkness that has fallen on New Babylon has been defended, rationalized, and explained away. But no one can account for the fact that it is so pervasive that it causes those caught in it to gnaw their tongues from the pain.

"Many have speculated how long this will last. I tell you nothing in Scripture indicates it will abate before the end. That is why the ruler of this world has moved out of his own kingdom. He may think the day will come when he and his people can move back in, but I proclaim he never will. Two more judgments await before the glorious appearing of our Lord and Savior, Jesus the Christ.

"Hear me! The Euphrates River will become as dry land! Scoff today but be amazed when it happens, and remember it was foretold. The last judgment will be an earthquake that levels the entire globe. This judgment will bring hail so huge it will kill millions.

"I am asked every day, how can people see all these things and still choose Antichrist over Christ? It is the puzzle of the ages. For many of you, it is already too late to change your mind. You may now see that you have chosen the wrong side in this war. But if you pledged your allegiance to the enemy of God by taking his mark of loyalty, it is too late for you.

"If you have not taken the mark yet, it may *still* be too late, because you waited so long. You pushed the patience of God past the breaking point.

"But there may be a chance for you. You will know only if you pray to receive Christ, tell God you recognize that you are a sinner and separated from him, and that you acknowledge that your only hope is in the blood of Christ, shed on the cross for you.

"Remember this: If you do not turn to Christ and are not saved from the coming judgment, this awful earth you endure right now is as good as your life will ever get. If you do turn to Christ and your heart has not already been hardened, this world is the worst you'll see for the rest of eternity.

"For those of you who are already my brothers and sisters in Christ around the world, I urge you to be faithful unto death, for Jesus himself said, 'Do not fear any of those things which you are about to suffer. Indeed, the devil is about to throw some of you into prison, that you may be tested. . . . Be faithful until death, and I will give you the crown of life.'

"What a promise! Christ himself will give you the crown of life. It shall be a thrill to see Jesus come yet again, but oh, what a privilege to die for his sake.

"The good news is that I believe that the enemy, whether he admits it or not, knows his time is limited. That too has been prophesied. Revelation 12:12 says, 'Therefore rejoice, O heavens, and you who dwell in them! Woe to the inhabitants of the earth and the sea! For the devil has come down to you, having great wrath, because he knows that he has a short time.' Lest you doubt me, remember that everything this man has done was foretold. Revelation 13:5-8 says, 'He was given a mouth speaking great things and blasphemies, and he was given authority to continue for forty-two months. Then he opened his mouth in blasphemy against God, to blaspheme His name, His tabernacle, and those who dwell in heaven. It was granted to him to make war with the saints and to overcome them. And authority was given him over every tribe, tongue, and nation. All who dwell on the earth will worship him, whose names have not been written in the Book of Life of the Lamb slain from the foundation of the world.'

"You can have your name written in the Book of Life! That is the good news.

"Now I must tell you there is also bad news. The wrath of the evil one will reach a fever pitch from now until the end. There will be increasing demands for all people to worship him and take his mark. To you who share my faith and are willing to be faithful unto death, remember the promise in James 5:8 that 'the coming of the Lord is at hand.'

"Oh, believer, share your faith and live your life boldly in such a way that others can receive Christ by faith and be saved. Think of it, friend. You could pray to be led to those who have not yet heard the truth. You may be the one who leads the very last soul to Christ.

"Second Peter 3:10-14 says that 'the day of the Lord will come as a thief in the night, in which the heavens will pass away with a great noise, and the elements will melt with fervent heat; both the earth and the works that are in it will be burned up.

"'Therefore, since all these things will be dissolved, what manner of persons ought you to be in holy conduct and godliness, looking for and hastening the coming of the day of God, because of which the heavens will be dissolved, being on fire, and the elements will melt with fervent heat? Nevertheless we, according to His promise, look for new heavens and a new earth in which righteousness dwells.

"'Therefore, beloved, looking forward to these things, be diligent to be found by Him in peace, without spot and blameless.'

"I urge you to imitate our Lord and Savior and say with him, 'I must be about My Father's business.'

"Some have legitimately questioned how a loving and merciful God could shower the earth with such horrible plagues and judgments. Yet I ask you, what else could he have done after so many millennia to shake men and women from their false sense of security and get them to look to him for mercy and forgiveness?

"Think of how merciful he has been. He removed his church before the Tribulation began. He sent two supernatural witnessing preachers to Jerusalem to communicate his love. He poured out his Holy Spirit in power, as he promised through the prophet Joel, to convince mankind of its need to receive Christ rather than serve Satan and his demons.

"He sealed 144,000 Jewish evangelists to fan out across the globe and reach what the Bible calls 'a great multitude which no one could number' with the saving knowledge of the Son of God. He sent three angels of mercy to help people make their decision for Christ. And he has promised to supernaturally warn mankind before he destroys Babylon.

"Most of all, in his mercy, God still allows people to decide their own eternal destiny, whether to choose Jesus Christ as Lord and Savior or to believe Satan.

"The most wonderful news I can share with you today is that God has prompted us to use the brilliant minds and technology we have been blessed with here. Anyone who communicates with us via the Internet will get a personal response with everything you need to know about how to receive Christ.

"Yes, I know the ruler of this world has outlawed even visiting our site, but we can assure you that it is secure and that your visit cannot be traced. We have thousands of Internet counselors who can answer any question and lead you to Christ.

"We also have teams of rescuers who can transport you here if you are being persecuted for the sake of Christ. This is a dangerous time, and many will be killed. Many of our own loved ones have lost their lives in the pursuit of righteousness. But we will do what we can until the end to keep fighting for what is right. For in the end, we win, and we will be with Jesus."

+ + +

Near the end of Tsion's message, Rayford picked his way through the throng and made his way to the tech center. He stood behind Chang, watching as the young man chuckled and kept track of the frustration in Baghdad and at the affiliate stations around the world.

When he noticed Rayford, Chang said, "Here, listen to this." He clicked on a session he had recorded in the conference room where Nicolae was demanding to know whom to fire or kill because of the TV disaster.

"Where is Figueroa?"

"He has not been seen since we left New Babylon, Excellency."

"What about his people? The Asian kid. The Scandinavian young man."

"The Asian is unaccounted for. The Scandinavian died from the heat, remember?"

"I cannot keep track of everyone who dies from one of these plagues. Who is running television now?"

"It has been farmed out to the affiliates. Things are impossible in New Babylon."

"I *know* that, Leon! I want someone assigned who can put an end to this. What will people think?"

Fortunato cleared his throat. "Begging your pardon, Highness, but they will wonder what some on the cabinet are wondering. They are asking, 'What about the fact that so many of these things we have suffered through were foretold? Is there some truth to all this? Who is Carpathia anyway?'"

"They want to know who Carpathia is?" Nicolae said, his voice rising. "My own cabinet?"

"Yes, sir."

"And what about you, Leon? Who do you say that I am?"

"I know who you are, sir, and I worship you."

"Are you implying there are those in my inner circle who do not?"

"I am telling you only what I hear, Majesty."

"Maybe it is time we tell them, Leon. Maybe it is time they know who I am, if they truly do not know."

+ + +

Chang knew he would be unable to sleep. He and Naomi walked toward her quarters, their pace slowing more and more the closer they got. "What an incredible time to be alive," he said.

"Really?" she said. "If I could choose, I'd rather have known Jesus earlier and gone to be with him at the Rapture."

"Well, sure, if we had that choice."

"We had it."

"Yeah."

"Actually, Chang, in my mind the greatest time to be alive will be after the Glorious Appearing. Besides getting to be with Jesus in a time of peace on earth, I'll get to live with you for a thousand years."

Chang was staggered by the thought. He stopped and took both her hands in his. "I wonder what I'll look like when I'm a thousand and twenty years old," he said. "A wrinkled-up little old Chinese man, I guess."

"You'll still be cute to me. I'll be an old Jewish lady with lots of kids between the ages of five hundred and nine hundred-and-something years old."

He cupped her face in the moonlight. "I am so grateful to have found you."

+ + +

Buck lay on his cot, across the room from Kenny's, his arms aching from holding his Bible up to read it. He was studying everything he could find on the coming battle. Rayford had promised he would be assigned to Jerusalem, and at first he was disappointed, thinking all the action would be outside Petra or in the Jezreel Valley. But from what he could tell, those were just staging areas for the armies of the world. Much of the conflict would be in Jerusalem.

And there was no place he would rather be.

16

RAYFORD WAS ASTOUNDED that things could get worse. Just when he thought there was nothing Carpathia could do to top his evil exploits, reports flooded into the computer center that made it clear Carpathia had turned up the heat all over the world. More persecution, more torture, more beheadings.

Tsion's appeal to people to contact the Internet counselors at Petra had generated an overwhelming response. This necessitated that the elders train more counselors and Naomi and Chang train more teachers to get more people up to speed on the computers.

Tsion had been preaching for ages that the world was speeding headlong toward Armageddon, but Rayford had never felt it so personally. He began really looking forward to seeing his Savior face-to-face and to reuniting with his loved ones and friends.

But there was much to do yet. Mac, Abdullah, and Ree recruited pilots and planes from all over the world to continue the massive airlift to Petra. There were days when Rayford wondered if they could even begin to catch up to the demand. The only prerequisite for a free ride to safety was the mark of the believer. It was assumed a person without the mark of Carpathia would be persecuted or executed.

Most amazing to Rayford, as he studied the Scriptures every day, was that the end of the strange prediction in Revelation 16:10-11 regarding the plague in New Babylon proved true of Carpathia's followers all over the world: "His kingdom became full of darkness; and they gnawed their tongues because of the pain. They blasphemed the God of heaven because of their pains and their sores, and did not repent of their deeds."

How could it be, Rayford wondered, that all these plagues and judgments could fall and yet the vast majority of people would not change their ways?

+ + +

Chang had, of course, mercifully ceded control of international television back to the Global Community. And it was clear from Carpathia's public pronouncements that he was taking the credit for "finally having this thing under control."

"The next time he says that," Chang told Rayford, "I'm going to immediately switch to this commercial we devised last week."

The tape showed a particularly strong clip from Tsion's last broadcast speech and closed with a voice-over: "Proclamations from your potentate are allowed only by the goodwill of Tsion Ben-Judah and your friends at Petra."

Chang had for several days been testing the bugging job Buck and George had done in the private conference room in Baghdad. He got to where he could coordinate the video with the audio, switch to whoever was talking, and even follow Carpathia as he moved at the head of the table. Two of the hidden video devices had the ability to follow a person around the room.

+ + +

The arrival of the ten regional potentates from around the world was broadcast by GCNN, and Buck couldn't remember such pomp and circumstance since Carpathia had mocked the Stations of the Cross in Jerusalem. Parades, marching bands, light shows, dancing girls, announcements, and pronouncements. Stands full of cheering supplicants lined the routes, as representatives from each of the regions preceded their potentate.

Finally the dignitaries and a few thousand sycophants lucky enough to get tickets were ushered into the great room of the new conference hall, where Carpathia was to hold forth on an exciting new chapter in world history.

The Most High Reverend Father of Carpathianism, Leon Fortunato, was tapped to make the royal introduction, of course. He was in full regalia, which started at the top with a brimless fez of cardinal-red felt with a flat top adorned by a tassel of alternating gold and silver strings with mirrored bits that reflected the stage lights all over the auditorium. He wore a new robe of purple and iridescent yellow with six bars of brocade on each sleeve.

Fortunato was so obsequious and fawning in his introduction that anyone but Antichrist himself would have been ill with embarrassment. Carpathia stood in mock humility, clearly fighting a smile, and bathed in the worship from his toadies.

"Thank you, thank you, thank you, one and all," Carpathia said, arms outstretched. "You are too kind to this humble servant from modest beginnings who has found himself thrust into a responsibility far beyond what he ever dreamed, only to discover by a spark of the divine that he was truly god—even to the point that he resurrected himself from the dead.

"And yet you—yes, each and every one of you—have made my task easier, in spite of crushing opposition and obstacles on every side. Every region has been well served by dynamic sub-potentates who have pulled together in times of crisis and helped make our fractious world a truly global community."

Carpathia was interrupted countless times by tumultuous applause, and each time he seemed to bask in the glow of it. "This," he said, "may be the most momentous and historic occasion in the history of our world. Despite the decimation of our citizenry—and our government—by relentless plagues and what our enemies glibly refer to as 'judgments from heaven,' I have called the top leaders together from every corner of the earth. Tomorrow, in a highly secure, private meeting, I will outline my marvelous, truly inspired plan to once and for all lead us to our goal of true global harmony.

"Our detractors have been given ample opportunity to see the error of their ways and to join our international family. I truly believed for too long that they were merely misunderstanding our aim and were ignorant of the benefits of standing shoulder to shoulder with us. Imagine what we could accomplish with everyone on board!

"Well, that day will soon come, my friends. We shall work together to enlist our enemies as fellow laborers, or we will eradicate them from our midst and be left with only loyalists . . . loyalists who share a common goal and purpose: true utopia, paradise on earth.

"No doubt all—even the opposition—have to agree that we have been fair. We have been patient. We have tried. But the time for tolerance has come to an end. Do you detect an end of patience? I freely admit it. It is time to get on board or be eliminated. Within half a year, I pledge to every loyal citizen of our Global Community, the opposition to peace will be destroyed. You will be living in the peaceful wonderland of your dreams."

Representatives of the sub-potentates from the ten regions, when interviewed by TV reporters, all played a variation of the same tune: "This is the privilege of a lifetime. What I wouldn't give to be in the private conference that follows this."

When the ceremonies were over, so was the broadcast. But the best part would come early the next morning at the meeting of potentates—which everybody in the Global Community assumed, because it was a closed-door session, was also private.

But it was as if selected members of the Trib Force were in the room. Gathered around a big-screen TV deep in the caverns of Petra, Rayford's hand-selected lineup of colleagues watched every moment through the miracle of technology and Chang's expert maneuvering.

Chang sat in the back, manning the controls. Rayford sat with Buck on one side and George on the other. Tsion and Chaim were also there. All would fill in the other key members, who were busy with Co-op and airlift duties.

As the room in Baghdad was filling, Rayford asked Chang to pan the room. "Let's get a look at who's there."

The big conference table had room for three at each end and six on each side. Each spot had a microphone, and all but the three at the far end also had a name card. Only two places were set at the head of the table, one for Carpathia—who was not there yet—on the left and the other for Fortunato—who was nervously tapping his gigantic ruby ring on the first of two luxurious leather notebooks to his right.

To the left of Carpathia's spot and proceeding to the other end were the potentates from the United African States, the United European States, the United Great Britain States, the United South American States, the United North American States, and Viv Ivins.

Each wore the epitome of a themed outfit from his or her respective region, from the colorful dashiki of the African potentate to the wide sombrero and gauchos of the South American and the ten-gallon hat and embroidered cowboy suit of the North American.

Viv Ivins wore her customary powder-blue suit, which nearly matched her hair color, but for the first time her outfit was completed by a gigantic diamond brooch and a blouse so white it played havoc with the video feed.

To Fortunato's right and extending to the other end of the table were the potentates from the United Carpathian States, the United Russian States, the United Indian States, the United Asian States, the United Pacific States, and Suhail Akbar.

Again, these potentates were dressed in their finest regional garb, the most dramatic of which was a jet-black-and-silver kimono worn by the Asian leader. Suhail wore his most formal dress uniform of the Global Community military Peacekeeping forces, topped by a navy cap with gleaming gold braid.

The three chairs at the end of the table opposite Carpathia and Fortunato were filled with three males who looked to Rayford like triplet manikins. All wore plain black suits, buttoned up, with black ties. No jewelry, no headwear, nothing else. They sat with their hands clasped before them on the table, not moving and looking neither right nor left.

"I don't recognize those three, Tsion," Rayford said. "You?"

The rabbi shook his head. "Oddly, they seem to be not even blinking. Everyone else certainly seems to be stealing glances at them frequently. Do you think they are real? Could they be cardboard cutouts?"

"Chang," Rayford said, "focus on just them, could you?"

He did, and also reported, "They are real. I taped them sitting down. You want to see it?"

"As long as we don't miss Carpathia's entrance."

"You won't."

Chang ran back the tape, showing the three taking their seats. They seemed to be one, moving in unison.

"Which door did they come in?" Rayford said.

"I missed that part. They seemed to simply appear."

"Okay, back to live."

A short buzz made Fortunato jump and reach inside his robe, as if to turn off a pager. He stood quickly and straightened his robe, removing his fez. "Ladies and gentlemen," he said, "please rise for your supreme potentate, His Highness, His Majesty, His Excellency, our lord and risen king, Nicolae Carpathia, the first and last, world without end, amen."

Except for the three mystery men, who still didn't budge, all stood, removing headwear. A military man in dress blues opened the door and Carpathia entered, whereupon Fortunato fell, rather loudly, to his knees. Nicolae was dressed in a black, pin-striped suit with a white shirt and a bright turquoise tie.

While Leon knelt, face buried in his hands on the floor and rear end aloft, displaying more expanse of his robe than anyone might have wished to see, Nicolae stopped a couple of feet behind his own chair and allowed the assembled to approach him one by one.

Individually they bowed and shook his hand with both of their own. Many kissed his hand or his ring, and more than one briefly knelt like Leon, whispering expressions of devotion and deference. They returned to stand behind their chairs.

When all had finished there was an awkward silence, as apparently Leon was next on the docket and unaware of his cue. Finally Carpathia cleared his throat, Leon looked up suddenly and clambered to his feet, catching the hem of his robe under the toe of his shoe. A distinct rip could be heard as he straightened up, stumbling and catching himself on Carpathia's chair, which was on rollers and nearly pitched him into his lord and risen king, first and last, world without end, amen.

Fortunato grabbed Nicolae's hand and pulled it toward his lips, almost making Carpathia leave his feet. At the last instant, Leon realized he had grabbed the wrong hand, dropped it, grabbed the other, and loudly kissed the potentate's ring.

"Your Excellency, sir," he said, pulling Carpathia's chair out with one hand and grandly gesturing toward it with the other.

"Thank you most kindly, Reverend," Carpathia said, sitting. "And, ladies and gentlemen, you may be seated."

Leon had left him a foot from the table, so Carpathia grabbed the edge and pulled himself forward. Fortunato, realizing his gaffe, quickly reached behind to push, and now Carpathia's chest pressed against the table. While Leon busily opened one of the leather notebooks and slid it in front of His Highness, Carpathia backed away to a more comfortable distance.

Nicolae thanked them all for coming, as if they had a choice, and said, "Down to business. Let me begin by reminding you that this is not a democracy. We are not here to vote, and neither are you here to give me input. If there is something you believe I need to know, feel free to say so. If you have a problem with my leadership or have any questions about why I have done anything or about the plans I will reveal today, I remind you of the disposition of three former potentates to the south who have been replaced due to their untimely deaths.

"Questions? I thought not. Let us proceed.

"Ladies and gentlemen, the time has come for me to take you into my confidence. We must all be on the same page in order to win the ultimate battle. Look into my eyes and listen, because what you hear today is truth and you will have no trouble believing every word of it. I am eternal. I am from everlasting to everlasting. I was there at the beginning, and I will remain through eternity future."

Nicolae stood and began to slowly circle the table as he spoke. No one present followed him with their eyes. They just sat as if catatonic. "Here is the problem," he said. "The one who calls himself God is not God. I will concede that he preceded me. When I evolved out of the primordial ooze and water, he was already there. But plainly, he had come about in the same manner I did. Simply because he preceded me, he wanted me to think he created me and all the other beings like him in the vast heavens. I knew better. Many of us did.

"He tried to tell us we were created as ministering servants. We had a job to do. He said he had created humans in his own image and that we were to serve them. Had I been there first, I could have told *him* that I had created *him* and that it was *he* who would serve me by ministering to my other creations.

"But he did not create anything! We, all of us—you, me, the other heavenly hosts, men and women—all came from that same primordial soup. But no! Not according to him! He was there with another evolved being like myself, and he claimed that one as his favored son. He was the special one, the chosen one, the only begotten one.

"I knew from the beginning it was a lie and that I—all of us—was being used. I was a bright and shining angel. I had ambition. I had ideas. But that was threatening to the older one. He called himself the creator God, the originator of life. He took the favored position. He demanded that the whole earth worship and obey him. I had the audacity to ask why. Why not me?

"Did I incite insurrection? You bet I did. And why not? What does seniority have to do with anything when we all evolved from the same source? There is plenty for everyone, but if preeminence is to be gained, I shall have it! About a third of the other evolved beings agreed with me and took my side, promised to remain loyal. The other two-thirds were weaklings, easily swayed. They took the side of the so-called father and his so-called son.

"Am I Antichrist? Well, if he is Christ, then yes! Yes! I am against the Christ who was falsely crowned by the pretend creator. I will ascend into heaven; I will exalt my throne above the stars of God. I will ascend above the heights of the clouds; I will be like the Most High.

"But because he got there first and I was the one with the audacity to challenge him, I got cast out! Where is the justice in that? We have been mortal enemies ever since, that father and that son and I. He even persuaded the evolved humans that he created them! But that could not be true, because if he had, they would not have free will. And if he created me, I would not have been able to rebel. It only makes sense.

"Once I figured that out, I began enjoying my role as the outcast. I found humans, the ones he liked to call his own, the easiest to sway. The woman with the fruit! She did not want to obey. It took nothing, mere suggestion, to get her to do what she really wanted. That happened not far from right here, by the way.

"And the first human siblings—they were easy! The younger was devoted to the one who called himself the only true God, but the other . . . ah, the other wanted only what I wanted. A little something for himself. Before you know it, I am proving beyond doubt that these creatures are not really products of the older angel's creativity. Within a few generations I have them so confused, so selfish, so full of themselves that the old man no longer wants to claim they were made in his image.

"They get drunk; they fight; they blaspheme. They are stubborn; they are unfaithful. They kill each other. The only ones I cannot get through to are Noah and his kin. Of course, the great creator decides the rest of history depends on them and wipes out everyone else with a flood. I eventually got to Noah, but he had already started repopulating the earth.

"Yes, I will admit it. The father and the son have been my formidable foes over the generations. They have their favorites—the Jews, of all people. The Jews are the apples of the elder's eye, but therein lies his weakness. He has such a soft spot for them that they will be his undoing.

"My forces and I almost had them eradicated not so many generations ago, but father and son intervened, gave them back their own land, and foiled us again. Fate has toyed with us many times, my friends, but in the end we shall prevail.

"Father and son thought they were doing the world a favor by putting their intentions in writing. The whole plan is there, from sending the son to die and resurrect—which I proved I could do as well—to foretelling this entire period. Yes, many millions bought into this great lie. Up to now I would have to acknowledge that the other side has had the advantage.

"But two great truths will be their undoing. First, I know the truth. They are not greater or better than I or anyone else. They came from the same place we all did. And second, they must not have realized that I can read. I read their book! I know what they are up to! I know what happens next, and I even know where!

"Let them turn the lights off in the great city that I loved so much! Ah, how beautiful it was when it was the center for commerce and government, and the great ships and planes brought in goods from all over the globe. So it is dark now. And so what if it is eventually destroyed? I will build it back up, because I am more powerful than father and son combined.

"Let them shake the earth until it is level and drop hundred-pound chunks of ice from the skies. I will win in the end because I have read their battle plan. The old man plans to send the son to set up the kingdom he predicted more than three hundred times in his book, and he even tells where the son will land! Ladies and gentlemen, we will have a surprise waiting for him.

"The son and I have been battling for the souls of men and women from the beginning. If you rulers and I join forces from all over the world and act in unison from a single staging area, we can once and for all rid ourselves of those forces that have hindered our total victory up to now.

"The so-called Messiah loves the city of Jerusalem above all cities in the world. He even calls it the Eternal City. Well, we shall see about that. That is where he supposedly died and came back to life.

"This strange affection for the Jews resulted in what he tells them is an eternal covenant of blessing. If we, the rulers of the earth, combine all our resources and attack the Jews, the son has to come to their defense. That is when we turn our sights on him and eliminate him. That will give us total control of the earth, and we will be ready to take on the father for mastery of the universe."

Nicolae had made two rounds of the table and returned to his chair, looking spent. "It is in their Bible," he said. "And they claim never to lie. We know right where he will be. Are you with me?"

"We are with you, Excellency," the South American said, "but where will that be?"

"We rally everyone—all of our tanks and planes and weapons and armies—in the Plain of Megiddo. This area in northern Israel, also known as the Plain of Esdraelon or the Plain of Jezreel, is about thirty kilometers southeast of Haifa and one hundred kilometers north of Jerusalem. At the appointed time we will dispatch one-third of our forces to overrun the stronghold at Petra, and I shall do it this time without so much as one nuclear device. We shall overcome them with sheer numbers, perhaps even on horseback.

"The rest of our forces will march on the so-called Eternal City and blast through those infernal walls, destroying all the Jews. And that is where we shall be, joined by our victorious forces from Petra, in full force to surprise the son when he arrives."

Fortunato sat shaking his head as if overcome with the brilliance of the strategy. "Questions for the potentate?" he said. "Anyone?"

The potentate of the United Asian States timidly raised his hand. "I don't know about the rest of you," he said, "but our army of hundreds of millions is led by many independent generals who are not easy to meld. Their staffs and their platoons have been devastated and greatly reduced by plagues, boils, and many other unbelievable tortures. Over half my population is dead or missing. How are we going to get these armies and their leaders to follow us?"

Many heads nodded.

"That is a question I do not shrink from, my friends," Carpathia said. "But before I tell you how together we shall accomplish that, let me tell you what your military leaders' first order of business will be. As you will remember, when I first came to power nearly seven years ago, I collected from all the world governments 90 percent of their weaponry. This was stored at a secret location I am now willing to reveal. In massive armories in and around Al Hillah, just under one hundred kilometers to the south of us, we have enough firepower to destroy the planet.

"Needless to say, we do not want or need to destroy the planet. We simply want your soldiers to have more than what they need to wipe out the Jews and destroy the son I have so long opposed. So once I tell you how we will get your military leaders on board, your next assignment will be to get them to Al Hillah, where our Security and Intelligence director, Mr. Suhail Akbar, will see that they are more than fully equipped."

"How long will this take?" the Indian potentate asked.

"You have less than half a year, ladies and gentlemen, so begin today. I have had Carpathian States troops pouring into Israel for months already. And when our Global Community army is in place, I want the armories of Al Hillah empty. Is that understood?"

"Understood," the Russian potentate said, "but like my colleagues, I am eager to hear how we are to persuade discouraged, sick, and injured leaders and troops."

"Reverend Fortunato," Nicolae said, rising. Leon leaped to his feet, his chair rolling back. "Ladies and gentlemen, the time has come to introduce you to three of my most trusted aides. No doubt you have been wondering about the three at the end of the table."

"Wondering why they seem not to have so much as blinked since we sat down," the British potentate said.

Carpathia laughed. "These three are not of this world. They use these shells only when necessary. Indeed, these are spirit beings who have been with me from the beginning. They were among the first who believed in me and saw the lie the father and son were trying to perpetrate in heaven and on earth."

"Leon," Carpathia said, and they walked down either side of the table to the other end. "Excuse me, Ms. Ivins," Nicolae said, and she stood and pulled her chair out of his way.

"Excuse me, Director Akbar," Leon said, and Suhail did the same.

+ + +

Rayford jumped when Tsion snapped everyone to attention by calling out, "Chang, get this! This is Revelation 16:13 and 14!"

The camera angle changed, and those assembled in Petra had a clear view of both Nicolae and Leon from behind the three seemingly lifeless bodies at the end of the table.

+ + +

The Antichrist and the False Prophet leaned in from either side, resting their elbows on the table and looking into the eyes of the robotlike creatures. Leon and Nicolae exhaled hideous, slimy, froglike beings—one from Leon and two from Nicolae—that leaped into the mouths of the three.

The three suddenly became animated.

Nicolae smiled.

+ + +

"Let's see them from the front, Chang," Buck hollered, and Chang made the adjustment.

+ + +

The three now bore a striking resemblance to Carpathia. They sat back casually, smiling, nodding to the potentates all around. The leaders looked stunned and frightened at first, but soon warmed to the personable strangers.

"Please meet Ashtaroth, Baal, and Cankerworm. They are the most convincing and persuasive spirits it has ever been my pleasure to know. I am going to ask now that we, all of us, gather round them and lay hands on them, commissioning them for this momentous task."

The three backed up their chairs to make room for the potentates, Viv, Suhail, Leon, and Nicolae to surround and touch them.

Nicolae said, "And now go, you three, to the ends of the earth to gather them to the final conflict in Jerusalem, where we shall once and for all destroy the father and his so-called Messiah. Persuade everyone everywhere that the victory is ours, that we are right, and that together we can destroy the son before he takes over this world. Once he is gone, we will be the undisputed, unopposed leaders of the world.

"I confer upon you the power to perform signs and heal the sick and raise the dead, if need be, to convince the world that victory is ours. And now go in power. . . ."

Ashtaroth, Baal, and Cankerworm disappeared amid a huge bolt of lightning that struck the middle of the conference table and temporarily blacked out the TV monitor in Petra. As the picture returned, a huge peal of thunder made Chang rip off his headphones.

Nicolae and Leon returned to stand behind their chairs, as did the rest of the potentates and Viv and Suhail. As they stood there calmly, Nicolae said, "Farewell, one and all. I will see you in six months in the Plain of Megiddo on that great day when victory shall be in sight."

+ + +

Buck sat stunned but quickly came to his senses. "Somebody read that passage Tsion mentioned!"

"I've got it right here," Chaim said. "Revelation 16:13 and 14 say, 'And I saw three unclean spirits like frogs coming out of the mouth of the dragon, out of the mouth of the beast, and out of the mouth of the false prophet. For they are spirits of demons, performing signs, which go out to the kings of the earth and of the whole world, to gather them to the battle of that great day of God Almighty.'"

"Read the next two verses too, Chaim," Tsion said.

"The first quotes Jesus himself," Chaim continued. "'"Behold, I am coming as a thief. Blessed is he who watches, and keeps his garments, lest he walk naked and they see his shame." And they gathered them together to the place called in Hebrew, Armageddon.'"

17

RAYFORD TOLD BUCK and George to scout out a new meeting room, somewhere in Petra that would not draw curiosity seekers. "It needs to hold maybe twenty, at most," he told them, though he knew it was unlikely to see half that.

He met with Tsion in the tiny living room in Tsion's quarters. "I need you to teach my top guys," he said. "They all know by now what went on in Baghdad, and everybody has questions about what it all means and what our roles should be. Nobody wants to just sit here in safety while the rest of the world goes to hell."

"I can identify with that, Rayford, and I will gladly do it. I have just this morning turned over all administrative and teaching duties of the Remnant here to Chaim."

Rayford shot him a double take. "You did *what?*"

"I do not want to stay here either."

"What are you saying?"

"If I am to teach your top little military band, I want to be part of it. I want to be taught to fight, to use a weapon, to defend myself, to keep my comrades and my fellow Jews alive."

Rayford stood and walked to the unscreened window that looked out on endless skies. "I'm dumbfounded," he said.

"Do not think I have not consulted the Lord on this."

"It's not enough you're a rabbi, a teacher, a preacher? Now you want to be a soldier?"

"Rayford, listen to me. I identify with my Lord, my Messiah. I cannot sit here when Antichrist and his worldwide forces are closing in on Jerusalem. I will not stand by as innocent Jews are killed. The Bible teaches that a third of the remaining Jews will turn to Messiah before the end. That means many, many more than there are now, and they need to be reached. I want to preach in Jerusalem, Rayford. That is what I am trying to tell you."

"You'll get yourself killed."

"I would rather wake up in heaven a few days early and join the army coming the other way with Messiah, knowing I died with my boots on, than sit here in Petra watching it on television."

"I don't know if I can allow it."

"If the Lord allows it, I do not see that you have a choice. Oh, Rayford, sit down. I do not want to go foolishly, to go unprepared. I am just into my fifties now, not an old man. Not young, I know, but I am in shape. If Mac McCullum can do these kinds of things at his age, surely I can too. I know my hands are soft like those of a scholar, but how long can it take to develop calluses and learn to handle a weapon?"

"You're serious."

"I will not be dissuaded. I am more than willing to teach your team what I know about what is going on. But my price is to also become a student of your Mr. Sebastian."

Rayford sat and shook his head. "You may not be an old coot, but you're stubborn."

"Is that not part of the makeup of the warrior?"

"Oh, you're a warrior now."

"I hope to be."

"Have you consulted the elders?"

"Did I inform them? Yes. Were they happy? No. Will they pray about it? Yes. Do I care what they come back with? Only if it is a yes."

+ + +

Buck couldn't believe it. "But I have to admire his spunk. I'll never forget the night he and I first talked to the two witnesses at the Wailing Wall. That was before I even knew Dr. Ben-Judah was a believer. I was pretty new at this stuff myself, but I recognized John 3 and the nighttime conversation between Jesus and Nicodemus. It was moving."

"I'd never forgive myself if I let him go and something happened to him," Rayford said.

"He's a tough guy. He stood up to Carpathia on international television, telling what he thought about Jesus being the Messiah. And after his family was massacred, I know he'd rather have been carrying an Uzi than a Bible. He could be a valuable addition to this team. And the only one who can preach and teach. I'd vote for him."

"I'm not taking any vote."

"You just got one. Anybody voting against?"

"I might," Rayford said.

"You're more of a coward than he is."

+ + +

Mac got a kick out of the whole thing. He was all for Tsion learning to be a soldier and coming with them to Jerusalem. He sat under Tsion's teaching in the private chamber every week for the next several months and learned more about the very last days than he thought there was to imagine. He saw the fire in the rabbi's eyes and knew, Rayford's misgivings aside, that Tsion was going.

Tsion began one evening's lesson by reading Jude 1:14-15: "'Now Enoch, the seventh from Adam, prophesied about these men also, saying, "Behold, the Lord comes with ten thousands of His saints, to execute judgment on all, to convict all who are ungodly among them of all their ungodly deeds which they have committed in an ungodly way, and of all the harsh things which ungodly sinners have spoken against Him."'

"Did you catch that, people? The word he repeats so many times? It sinks in, doesn't it, when a prophet of God refers to the ungodly four times in one sentence? These enemies of ours are the enemies of God. They are out to steal and kill and destroy anything that is of God. But Jesus himself says in John 10:10 and 11, 'I have come that they may have life, and that they may have it more abundantly. I am the good shepherd. The good shepherd gives His life for the sheep.' Oh, to be a shepherd called to give your life for your flock!

"Many of you have asked where I get the idea that one-third of God's chosen people will turn to him before the end. Turn in your Bibles to Zechariah 13. That is the second-to-last book in your Old Testament. In verses 8 and 9 the prophet is talking about the Remnant of Israel: '"And it shall come to pass in all the land," says the Lord, "that two-thirds in it shall be cut off and die, but one-third shall be left in it: I will bring the one-third through the fire, will refine them as silver is refined, and test them as gold is tested. They will call on My name, and I will answer them. I will say, 'This is My people'; and each one will say, 'The Lord is my God.'"'

"Now as I have told you before, calling this final conflict the Battle of Armageddon is really a misnomer, as this is just the staging area of the world's armies. The actual conflicts will take place here at Petra, or near here, as God has proved this city is impenetrable, and at Jerusalem. To be precise, this should be called the War of the Great Day of God the Almighty."

Buck raised his hand. "I've been hearing you teach this stuff for years, and I still don't think I have the sequence down. What's going to happen when?"

Tsion chuckled. "Scholars have debated that since time immemorial. I found that the only way I could make sense of it was to have my Bible and all my books and commentaries open at the same time and try to make a list of the various stages of the events.

"In my opinion, eight events will take place sometime after the sixth Bowl Judgment, the drying up of the Euphrates River. That event, by the way, makes it possible for the kings of the East to bring their armaments of war directly into the plain of Megiddo on dry land, saving them the time of shipping them all the way around the continents. There is no biblical corroboration for this next assertion, but in my humble opinion, this is a trap set by almighty God. He's luring these rulers and their armies right to where he wants them.

"Regardless, once the Euphrates has dried up, we see the assembling of the allies of the Antichrist. Next, I believe, comes the destruction of Babylon. Isaiah 13:6-9 says, 'Wail, for the day of the Lord is at hand! It will come as destruction from the Almighty. Therefore all hands will be limp, every man's heart will melt, and they will be afraid. Pangs and sorrows will take hold of them; they will be in pain as a woman in childbirth; they will be amazed at one another; their faces will be like flames.

"'Behold, the day of the Lord comes, cruel, with both wrath and fierce anger, to lay the land desolate; and He will destroy its sinners from it.'"

"Wow," Buck said. "I don't know if I want to be there to see that."

"You're going to be in Jerusalem by then, Buck," Rayford said.

"Me too," Tsion said. "Following the destruction of Babylon comes the fall of Jerusalem. That will encourage the allied troops of Antichrist, and they will surge to join their compatriots here at what the Bible calls Bozrah. Immediately following that comes what I call the national regeneration of Israel.

"In Romans 11:25-27 the apostle Paul writes, 'For I do not desire, brethren, that you should be ignorant of this mystery, lest you should be wise in your own opinion, that blindness in part has happened to Israel until the fullness of the Gentiles has come in. And so all Israel will be saved, as it is written: "The Deliverer will come out of Zion, and He will turn away ungodliness from Jacob; for this is My covenant with them, when I take away their sins."'"

"Then comes the good stuff," George said. "At least the way I read it."

"Exactly," Tsion said. "The Glorious Appearing. Jesus Christ appears on a white horse with ten thousand of his saintly army, and regardless of what Antichrist thinks is going to happen, his end is near.

"Want to hear a bizarre word picture? When John talks about this in his Revelation, he says in verses 19 and 20 of the fourteenth chapter: 'So the angel thrust his sickle into the earth and gathered the vine of the earth, and threw it into the great winepress of the wrath of God. And the winepress was trampled outside the city, and blood came out of the winepress, up to the horses' bridles, for one thousand six hundred furlongs.'

"Think of that! When Jesus and his holy army finally slay the world allies of Antichrist, the slaughter will be so great that the flow of blood in Israel's central valley could be as high as a horse's bridle. How high is that? Four feet or more."

"And how far is one thousand six hundred furlongs?"

"I am so glad you asked, George," Tsion said, "because I happen to have studied it. It is about one hundred and eighty-four miles, the approximate distance from Armageddon to Edom."

"But that's only six events," Buck said. "Are there really two more?"

"Yes. There is the end of the fighting in the Jehoshaphat Valley, which is basically the area from here to just south of Jerusalem, west of the Dead Sea. Because Petra is safe, all Antichrist's armies can do is fight outside.

"Then, finally, comes Jesus' victory ascent up the Mount of Olives. I want to be there for that."

"You may be there," Rayford said. "But whether you'll still be alive is a different story."

18

Six Years, Eleven Months, into the Tribulation

WITH JUST WEEKS to go to the culmination of the final events, Rayford had finally gotten used to the idea that Tsion was going to Jerusalem.

"That I'm acceding to this doesn't imply that I support it, does it, Tsion?"

"I know you better than that. But I may also know you better than you know yourself. After all this talk, you would be disappointed if I pulled out now."

"Disappointed? Relieved. I somehow feel I'm going to have to answer to God for what happens to you."

"Trust me. I will let you off the hook."

"Let me see those hands, old man."

"I told you," Tsion said, extending his hands. "I am not that old."

"Older than I am, so ancient in my book," Rayford said. "But those are impressive calluses. And George and Razor tell me you're actually starting to hit targets with that Uzi."

"I do not see how anyone can miss. It shoots so many bullets in so short a time, to me it is like using a garden hose. If you miss your mark, just swing it back and forth until you hit it."

"What do you plan to do, seriously, Doctor? Stand somewhere and preach with a weapon hanging from your shoulder?"

"If I must. Rayford, we have known each other long enough that we should be free to be frank. I feel such a compulsion to plead with my fellow countrymen to give their lives to Messiah that I do not believe it would be physically possible for me not to. I must get there, and I must preach. I do not want a disguise. I cannot imagine the GC even caring about me anymore."

"Are you serious? The leader of the international Judah-ites—"

"That is their term for us, not ours, and certainly not mine."

"But, Tsion, everybody knows you. If they thought my daughter was a prime catch, imagine if they got hold of you."

Tsion shook his head. "But if God has laid this so heavily on my heart, maybe he is telling me that I will be supernaturally protected."

"Well, is he or isn't he?"

"All I know is that I must go."

"I'm sending Buck with you. I promised him duty in Jerusalem. I can't think of a role with more action than what you're going to draw."

"I would be honored to have him as my bodyguard. Is he the military man George is?"

"Who is? But George is otherwise engaged, you know."

"Defending the perimeter here, yes, he told me. My question is, why don't we ignore the perimeter if our borders are impregnable?"

"Because people are seeking refuge here all the time, and they are not safe until they get inside."

"And yet they are safe in the air. How do you figure that?"

"I've quit trying to figure out God, Tsion. I'm surprised you haven't."

"Oh, Rayford, you have just stepped into one of my traps. You know how I love to quote the Word of God."

"Of course."

"Your mention of figuring out God reminds me of one of my favorite passages. Ironically, it leads into a verse that justifies my going in spite of the danger."

"I'm listening."

"Romans 11:33-36: 'Oh, the depth of the riches both of the wisdom and knowledge of God! How unsearchable are His judgments and His ways past finding out! "For who has known the mind of the Lord? Or who has become His counselor? Or who has first given to Him and it shall be repaid to him?" For of Him and through Him and to Him are all things, to whom be glory forever. Amen.'"

"Impressive."

"But, my friend, that leads into the first verse of the twelfth chapter, which is my justification: 'I beseech you therefore, brethren, by the mercies of God, that you present your bodies a living sacrifice, holy, acceptable to God, which is your reasonable service.'"

"Just hope it's a *living* sacrifice, Tsion."

+ + +

Chang had concluded that Carpathia believed the prophecy about the drying up of the Euphrates, because he had sanctioned sensitive devices in the river that recorded information that was fed into and evaluated by the GC mainframe computer. Chang, of course, was monitoring that from Petra. Nearly four weeks later, he knew when the event occurred before the GC did.

"It's happened!" he shouted, standing at his computer. Everyone nearby jumped and stared, and Naomi came running. "There was water in the Euphrates a minute ago, and now it is as dry as a bone. You can bet tomorrow it will be on the news—someone standing in the dry, cracking riverbed, showing that you can walk across without fear of mud or quicksand."

"That is amazing," Naomi said. "I mean, I knew it was coming, but isn't it just like God to do it all at once? And isn't that a fifteen-hundred-mile river?"

"It used to be."

Mac's and Abdullah's reconnaissance flights over the area showed that weaponry had been taken from the armories in Al Hillah until they had to be empty. Within days, great columns of soldiers, tanks, trucks, and armaments began rolling west from as far away as Japan and China and India.

"And here," Chang told Naomi, "is the break Tsion has been looking for, whether he knew it or not. Look at this." He printed out a directive from Suhail Akbar himself, instructing Global Community Peacekeepers and Morale Monitors to cease and desist with all current assignments and consider themselves redeployed to the GC One World Unity Army. "Your superiors have been similarly assigned, and you will report to them in the staging area in twenty-four hours or face AWOL charges."

"What happens to the streets?" Naomi said.

"I can't imagine, love. The inmates will be running the asylum. But that means people without Carpathia's mark can come out from hiding."

"If they dare. There's still a bounty on their heads. The loyalists will kill them and stack their bodies, waiting for the end of the war to cash in."

"Won't they be disappointed."

+ + +

"I must go as soon as possible," Tsion told Rayford. "What is the fastest way Cameron and I can get to Jerusalem?"

"Helicopter, I suppose, if I can find you a pilot."

"What are you doing right now?"

"Uh, well—I guess nothing. Anything else?"

Tsion laughed. "I cannot wait. I have packed foodstuffs and a change of clothes, and if Cameron has done as I requested, he will have done the same. Who would know if a chopper is available?"

"Meet me at the helipad in half an hour."

+ + +

Priscilla Sebastian made a valiant effort to distract Kenny Bruce as Buck tried to extract himself from the boy's embrace.

"I'll be back soon," Buck said. "Got to go with Uncle Tsion."

Kenny said nothing. He just hung on.

"Grandpa's going to come see you after he drops us off, okay? You're going to stay with him while I'm gone."

Kenny lightened his grip and pulled back to look at Buck. "Grandpa?"

"That's right."

"Plane ride?"

"I bet so."

"When?"

"Soon. Soon as he gets back."

"I wanna go."

"Not enough room. Now you be a good boy and play with Beth Ann, and Grandpa will be here soon. Okay?"

"'Kay."

+ + +

Mac was working with Otto Weser and George on planning the evacuation from New Babylon, as soon as the word came that believers were to move out. No one, not even Tsion, seemed to know how that would be supernaturally announced or even whether anyone outside New Babylon would hear it.

"I know of a few other cells there," Otto said. "I have left instructions with one of the leaders to call me once she gets the word. I don't know what else we can do. I'll tell them to meet us at the palace airstrip and hope we have a plane big enough to get them all out of there."

"All we can do is all we can do," Mac said.

Naomi interrupted their meeting. "Want to say good-bye to Tsion? Everyone is turning out for the farewell."

"He's going already?"

She told Mac why.

"Tsion never lets any grass grow on an idea, does he?"

He and George and Otto followed Naomi to a clearing near the helipad, where it seemed hundreds of thousands had shown up. "Word travels quick round here, doesn't it, Otto?"

"Mr. McCullum, many of these people are weeping. He's only going to Jerusalem, isn't he? That can't be more'n a hundred miles, can it? And surely he's coming back."

"That's what they're cryin' about, Otto. Most folks wonder if he will be back."

Rayford waited on firing up the chopper so Tsion could be heard. The rabbi pulled a white cloth from his pocket and waved it vigorously at the people as

Buck boarded behind him. "These people are going to want your neck when you come back without him, Rayford," Buck said.

"Which, of course, I plan to do in an hour or less."

"*I'd* just better not come back without him," Buck said.

"People! People!" Tsion shouted. "I am overwhelmed at your kindness. Pray for me, won't you, that I will be privileged to usher many more into the kingdom. We are just days away now from the battle, and you know what that means. Be waiting and watching. Be ready for the Glorious Appearing! If I am not back before then, we will be reunited soon thereafter.

"You will be in my thoughts and prayers, and I know I go with yours. Thank you again! You are in good hands with Chaim 'Micah' Rosenzweig, and so I bid you farewell!"

He continued waving as he boarded. Rayford noticed the rabbi's tears as he buckled himself in.

+ + +

"Something's on your mind," Naomi said, as she and Chang walked hand in hand. He had just finished transmitting to Rayford's helicopter a schematic of Jerusalem with various potential put-down spots.

Chang shrugged. "Sometimes I'm glad I'm here and safe and can sleep—unlike at the palace—but other times I feel I'm taking the easy way out. Everyone else is gearing up for the battle."

"Oh, Chang. Don't say that. You put in your years of frontline work. And anyway, you know full well you're much more valuable here in the center than out there shooting or being shot at. I don't know what we'd do without you."

"You were getting along fine before I got here."

She dropped his hand and put her hands on her hips, cocking her head at him. "You have a short memory, Chang Wong. How can you forget that I spent a good portion of every day on the computer with you, though we were more than five hundred miles apart? I would have been nowhere without your teaching me, which is the way I feel now."

"Everything's up and running here. I could be gone a few weeks."

"I wasn't talking technically, Chang. Call me selfish, but I'm glad you're not venturing out. Father loves me, but not like you do."

"I should hope not."

She smiled. "And I enjoy spending time with him, which is something a lot of women my age can't say about their fathers. But I would rather be with you. Remember, we want to survive so we can be together for a millennium. Let's not risk that for the sake of your conscience."

"You don't think I'd be good in combat."

"Actually I do, Chang. I know you're half the size of that Sebastian character and much more rational than Buck Williams. But I believe a person's personality and character come out when the pressure is on, and I've seen you under pressure. With a little training, you could hold your own."

+ + +

Rayford was studying Chang's transmissions and trying to discuss with Buck the best place to land. Buck was busy digging through what he'd brought and said, "It's your call, Ray. I can't imagine one spot is going to be any less treacherous than another."

"Remember that all these GC are expected to be in Megiddo tomorrow," Rayford said. "Not today. They might still like a plum arrest."

"I disagree," Buck said. "Their directive told them to immediately cease and desist and head toward where they had to be. I don't know a guy in uniform who wouldn't take them up on that."

"Just take me to the Wailing Wall, Rayford," Tsion said. "I want to be preaching when I get off this thing."

"Could you think of a more dangerous place?"

"Danger is not the issue now, Captain. Time is. The Day of the Lord is at hand. Let us not be setting up camp when the enemy attacks."

"Easy for you to say," Rayford said.

"Not unless I am on the ground. Now, for once, do what I ask."

Rayford came within sight of the Temple Mount. It was crawling with people. "Agh!"

"They will move," Tsion said. "Trust me. Put this thing down, and they will get out of the way. Wouldn't you?"

19

THE INSTANTANEOUS DRYING up of the Euphrates proved good news to only the kings of the East, who transported their weapons directly into Israel across dry land. The rest of the Fertile Crescent was no longer fertile. Irrigation dried up, hydroelectric plants shut down, factories closed. In short, everything that depended on the massive power of the great river was immediately diagnosed as terminal.

Chang's prediction of GCNN's carrying accounts of reporters standing in the middle of the dry riverbed proved accurate. But all the fancy pronouncements and isn't-it-something-that-I'm-standing-here-where-yesterday-I-would-have-been-a-hundred-feet-below-the-surface did not amuse millions who depended upon the Euphrates for their very existence.

\+ \+ \+

It didn't surprise Buck that Tsion proved to be right. When Rayford lowered the chopper into a clearing at the Temple Mount, hundreds of angry people scattered, raising their fists at him.

Buck grabbed his bag and tucked his Uzi behind his back and under his jacket. He leaped from the chopper and scampered to safety in underbrush near the Wall. He looked back to see Tsion doing the same and was amazed at the agility of this newly trained guerilla.

They knelt, catching their breath and watching Rayford lift off. The chopper whirling out of sight took the attention off them. Buck looked around. "This is where I saw the two witnesses taken into heaven three and a half years ago," he said.

\+ \+ \+

That old curiosity was back. Rayford couldn't shake it. No way he could be this close to Armageddon—he guessed less than seventy miles—and not do a flyover. It was crazy, he knew. He might find himself in an air traffic jam. But the possibility of seeing an aerial view of what he had been hearing and reading and praying about drew him like an undertow. And if the result was that he plunged into the abyss like a rafter over the falls, it was worth the risk.

+ + +

"Cameron, look," Tsion said. "Look at all the unmarked men! They proudly parade around, beaming at each other, as if defying the GC."

Global Community Peacekeeping and Morale Monitor forces were nowhere to be seen, of course. But war was in the air. For all the posturing of the devout Jews at the Temple Mount, it was clear that terror pervaded the place. These people knew where the GC were, and they knew they would soon be Carpathia's targets.

"The old men are at the Wall," Tsion said, "praying fervently and openly as they have not been able to do for so long. How my heart breaks for them. The young men are talking, planning, looking for arms. They are determined to defend this city, as I am."

"But the city is to fall, Tsion," Buck said. "You've said so yourself."

"Only temporarily, and the more of these people we can keep alive, the more can come into the kingdom. That is all I care about."

+ + +

Mac was still not sure what to make of Otto Weser. He was a good man, no doubt, but he was amateur in his thinking. He may have been a successful timber businessman in Germany, but Mac would not want to have served under him in combat.

"But don't you see, Mr. McCullum," Otto was saying, "if we are already on the ground at the palace airstrip when the supernatural announcement comes, we'll be that much more ready to quickly get people on board and out of there."

"And what if we never hear that announcement, or people can't get to the airstrip? There we sit with the city coming down around us."

"But will we not be protected as believers?"

"Think, man! If believers were protected, why would God be calling his own people out of there before he levels the place?"

+ + +

"I want to wait no longer, Cameron. I'm going to the Wall, and I will simply begin preaching."

"But what if—"

"There is no more time to think things through," Tsion said. "We are here for one purpose, and I am going to do it. Now are you going to cover me? Go with me? What?"

"I'll go with you. No one will give me a second glance, once you open your mouth."

Tsion pressed a yarmulke onto his head and handed one to Buck. "No sense getting stoned for a technicality," Tsion said. "We are going to a holy place."

They stuffed their bags between a tree and a black wrought-iron fence. Wearing loose-fitting, canvas-type clothing and jackets, Uzis at their sides, they crawled out of the bushes and jogged toward the Wall.

"Hey, old man, two hundred Nicks for that gat!"

"I'll go three hundred!" someone else said.

"The weapon is not for sale!" Tsion hollered. "Come hear what I have to offer!"

The area before the Wailing Wall was crowded with people in traditional garb, eager to push their prayers into the cracks between the stones. Many began praying even before they got close. The place would have been deserted the day before. And anyone caught in religious clothing, even with the mark of Carpathia, would have been sent to a concentration camp or executed.

As soon as Buck and Tsion began to shoulder their way toward the Wall, men glared at them and grumbled. Tsion did not hesitate. He bellowed, "Men of Israel, hear me! I am one of you! I come with news!"

It was clear people thought it was news of the impending attack, as they immediately began gathering. Tsion climbed a short precipice, where he could better be seen and heard.

"We will fight to the death!" someone shouted.

"I know you will, and so will I!" Tsion said. "You see me with my head covered and no mark on my forehead or hand."

The men cheered.

"Many of us will die in this conflict," Tsion continued. "I am willing to give my life for Jerusalem!"

"So are we!" many shouted in unison.

"We need arms!"

"We need information!"

"What you need," Tsion boomed, "is Messiah!"

The men cheered and many laughed. Others murmured. This was plainly not what they expected to hear.

"Many of you know me! I am Tsion Ben-Judah. I became persona non grata when I broadcast my findings after being commissioned to study the prophecies concerning Messiah."

Many remembered and applauded. Although they obviously disagreed with his conclusions or they would have been believers, they seemed to admire him.

"My family was slaughtered. I was exiled. A bounty remains on my head."

"Then why are you here, man? Do you not know the Global Community devils are coming back?"

"I do not fear them, because Messiah is coming too! Do not scoff! Do not turn your backs on me!" Many did not. "Listen to our own Scriptures. What do you think this means?" He read Zechariah 12:8-10: "'In that day the Lord will defend the inhabitants of Jerusalem; the one who is feeble among them in that day shall be like David, and the house of David shall be like God, like the Angel of the Lord before them. It shall be in that day that I will seek to destroy all the nations that come against Jerusalem.

"'And I will pour on the house of David and on the inhabitants of Jerusalem the Spirit of grace and supplication; then they will look on Me whom they pierced. Yes, they will mourn for Him as one mourns for his only son, and grieve for Him as one grieves for a firstborn.'"

"You tell us what it means!"

"God is saying he will make the weakest among us as strong as David. And he will destroy the nations that come against us. My dear friends, that is all the other nations of the earth!"

"We know. Carpathia has made it no secret!"

"But God says we will finally look upon 'Me whom they pierced,' and that we will mourn him as we would mourn the loss of a firstborn son. Messiah was pierced! And God refers to the pierced one as 'Me'! Messiah is also God.

"Beloved, my exhaustive study of the hundreds of prophecies concerning Messiah brought me to the only logical conclusion. Messiah was born of a virgin in Bethlehem. He lived without sin. He was falsely accused. He was slain without cause. He died and was buried and was raised after three days. Those prophecies alone point to Jesus of Nazareth as Messiah. He is the one who is coming to fight for Israel. He will avenge all the wrongs that have been perpetrated upon us over the centuries.

"The time is short. The day of salvation is here. You may not have time to study this for yourselves. Messiah is God's promise to us. Jesus is the fulfillment of that promise. He is coming. Let him find you ready!"

+ + +

Rayford's was not the only craft over the Plain of Megiddo. It was all he could do to pick his way through the traffic, but he also found it difficult to avert his eyes from the ground. He climbed to where he could see the 14-by-25-mile valley in its entirety, some 350 square miles.

The dust seemed to rise a mile as tanks, trucks, personnel carriers, missile launchers, cavalries, and ground troops moved into the area. Rayford had never seen as large an assembly of people in one place. It appeared as if an army of millions was marshaling in the vast staging area. From there he could also see the bustling seaport at Haifa, where great ships filled the harbor and fanned out in massive lines, waiting to disgorge armaments and troops.

From every direction personnel and equipment flooded into the region. Massive as it was, there seemed no way it could hold more. And yet the armies kept coming.

\+ + +

Buck feared at first that Tsion was only offending the devoutly Jewish crowd. Many tried to shout him down and many walked away, but others tried to hush the rest, and still others called more to come and hear him. The crowd kept growing, despite the noise and confusion.

Tsion seemed energized. He began quoting Scripture and explaining it, not waiting for the crowd's response. His message went from dialogue to monologue, and yet people seemed riveted.

"Yes, the armies of the world are coming. Even as we speak, they are rallying to the north. They aim to destroy Jerusalem and destroy us. But I beg of you, 'do not fear those who kill the body but cannot kill the soul. But rather fear Him who is able to destroy both soul and body in hell.' Yes, you know of whom I speak. Messiah is coming! Messiah shall overcome! Be ready for his arrival!

"If you want to know how to be prepared for him, gather here to my left and my associate will tell you. Please! Come now! Do not delay! Now is the accepted time. Today is the day of salvation."

Buck was stunned. He had not been prepared for this, but as the Jews gathered around him, looking expectant, he breathed a desperate silent prayer, and God gave him the words.

"When Jewish people such as yourselves come to see that Jesus is your long-sought Messiah," he said, "you are not converting from one religion to another, no matter what anyone tells you. You have found your Messiah, that is all. Some would say you have been completed, fulfilled. Everything you have studied and been told all your life is the foundation for your acceptance of Messiah and what he has done for you."

Buck moved into the plan of salvation, telling these hungry and thirsty men to tell God they acknowledged that Jesus was Messiah. "He comes not only to avenge Jerusalem but to save your soul, to forgive your sins, to grant you eternal life with God."

+ + +

"Naomi!" Chang called out. "Come watch this."

She joined him to see Carpathia being interviewed by GCNN. It was clear he was not at Armageddon yet, but he was on a colossal black stallion and brandishing a sword so wide and long it appeared its weight alone would have pulled a smaller man from the saddle. He wore thigh-high boots and leathers, and he seemed unable to quit grinning.

"We have the absolute latest in technology and power at our fingertips," he shouted as the reporter reached as high as she could with her microphone. "My months of strategy are over, and we have a foolproof plan. That frees me to encourage the troops, to be flown to the battle sites, to mount up, to be a visual reminder that victory is in sight and will soon be in hand.

"It will not be long, my brothers and sisters in the Global Community, until we shall reign victorious. I shall return to rebuild my throne as conquering king. The world shall finally be as one! It is not too early to rejoice!"

+ + +

As word spread that Tsion Ben-Judah was at the Wailing Wall preaching to the Jews, more and more streamed in.

"These Scriptures foretell what is going to happen soon!" he said. "Listen again to the words of Peter: 'The day of the Lord will come as a thief in the night, in which the heavens will pass away with a great noise, and the elements will melt with fervent heat; both the earth and the works that are in it will be burned up. Therefore, since all these things will be dissolved, what manner of persons ought you to be in holy conduct and godliness, looking for and hastening the coming of the day of God, because of which the heavens will be dissolved, being on fire, and the elements will melt with fervent heat? Nevertheless we, according to His promise, look for new heavens and a new earth in which righteousness dwells.'

"That is our promise, what we have been looking for! For how many generations have we prayed for peace? Soon, after the conflict, eternal peace!

"Messiah will return as King of kings. He promised to return, to conquer Satan, and to set up his millennial kingdom, reestablishing Israel and making Jerusalem the capital forever!

"With probably a billion of Messiah's followers already removed from this earth, and with the disappearances of seven years ago that were predicted more than two thousand years before, many Jews and Gentiles have turned to Jesus Christ as the true Messiah.

"Our own prophet Joel foretold of these very days. Listen to the words of Holy Scripture: 'It shall come to pass afterward that I will pour out My Spirit on all flesh; your sons and your daughters shall prophesy, your old men shall dream dreams, your young men shall see visions. And also on My menservants and on My maidservants I will pour out My Spirit in those days.

"'And I will show wonders in the heavens and in the earth: blood and fire and pillars of smoke. The sun shall be turned into darkness, and the moon into blood, before the coming of the great and awesome day of the Lord. And it shall come to pass that whoever calls on the name of the Lord shall be saved. For in Mount Zion and in Jerusalem there shall be deliverance, as the Lord has said, among the remnant whom the Lord calls.'

"You are that remnant, people of Israel. Turn to Messiah today! Listen further to the prophecy of Joel and see if it does not reflect these very days! 'For behold, in those days and at that time, when I bring back the captives of Judah and Jerusalem, I will also gather all nations, and bring them down to the Valley of Jehoshaphat; and I will enter into judgment with them there on account of My people, My heritage Israel.'

"This massive international force that the evil ruler of this world calls the One World Unity Army will break up from its staging area and pass through the very Valley of Jehoshaphat Joel writes of, and when they find the city of refuge impossible to overthrow, the fighting will spill back into that valley."

+ + +

Rayford had to head back. There was nothing he could do high above the assembled hordes of Antichrist. He knew it was from this area that the great mass would divide two-thirds and one-third, and that the latter would begin its inexorable march toward Petra.

His best guess was that it would take almost a full day for the force to cover that much ground and begin its offensive. In just a few hours, however, the two-thirds assigned to Jerusalem might already be engaged in battle.

+ + +

Buck was answering questions, praying with people, and all the while trying to listen to Tsion, who seemed to have found a second wind.

"The Day of the Lord is upon us," he said. "And lest there be any among you who still doubt, let me tell you what the prophecies say will happen after the armies of the world have gathered at Armageddon—which, as we all know, they are now doing. How many of you know Peacekeepers and Morale Monitors who have been called there? See? Yes, many of you. We have no illusions. They are rallying now, planning our destruction.

"And yet the Scriptures say that when they have gathered there, it will be time for the seventh angel to pour out his bowl into the air. Do you know what this refers to, men of Israel? The drying of the Euphrates was the sixth Bowl Judgment of God on the earth, the twentieth of his judgments since the Rapture.

"This seventh Bowl Judgment shall be the last, and do you know what it entails? When this bowl has been poured out, the Bible says 'a loud voice came out of the temple of heaven, from the throne, saying, "It is done!"' How like the pronouncement of the spotless Lamb of God on the cross when he cried out, 'It is finished.'

"'And there were noises and thunderings and lightnings; and there was a great earthquake, such a mighty and great earthquake as had not occurred since men were on the earth.'

"Let me warn you, my countrymen. This earthquake will cover the entire world. Think of it! The Bible says that 'every island fled away, and the mountains were not found.' The mountains were not found! The elevation of the entire globe will be sea level! Who can survive such a catastrophe?

"The prophecy goes on to say that 'great hail from heaven fell upon men, each hailstone about the weight of a talent.' Beloved, a talent weighs between seventy-five and one hundred pounds! Who has ever heard of such hailstones? They will crush men and women to death! And the Scriptures say men will blaspheme God because of the plague of the hail 'since that plague was exceedingly great.' Well, I should say it will be! Turn and repent now! Be counted among the army of God, not that of his enemy.

"Do you know what will happen here, right here in Jerusalem? It will be the only city in the world spared the devastating destruction of the greatest earthquake ever known to man. The Bible says, 'Now the great city'—that's Jerusalem—'was divided into three parts, and the cities of the nations fell.'

"That, my brothers, is good news. Jerusalem will be made more beautiful, more efficient. It will be prepared for its role as the new capital in Messiah's thousand-year kingdom."

By now the crowds at the Temple Mount had ballooned as word of Tsion's preaching continued to spread. Hundreds and soon thousands wept aloud and fell to their knees, repenting before God, acknowledging Jesus Christ as Messiah, pledging themselves to the King of kings.

Buck was weary but kept ministering, amazed at so many, steeped in their centuries-old religion, finally seeing that Jesus Christ fulfilled all the Old Testament prophecies concerning the coming Messiah.

Tsion thundered, "How will we know when this is about to come to pass? It will be preceded by the destruction of Babylon. Yes, the destruction of Babylon! Listen: 'And great Babylon was remembered before God, to give her the cup of the wine of the fierceness of His wrath.'

"Awful! It will be horrible! The loving, merciful patience of God will have been pushed beyond the brink by that wicked city, and he will not hold back his anger. The plague of darkness has not been enough to satisfy his wrath. He will allow her to be attacked and plundered, destroyed in but one hour's time. So great will be the power of the calamity that befalls it that its repercussions will be felt around the entire globe as all nations mourn the death of what had become the capital of the world."

+ + +

Knowing the time was short and what Buck had promised Kenny, Rayford radioed ahead to Petra and had Abdullah bring the boy to the helipad. He gave Kenny a quick ride, pretty much straight up and straight down, which Kenny loved.

Rayford was grateful the boy didn't ask about the ragtag platoons George and Razor were amassing below at the perimeter of the rock city. Compared to what Rayford had seen north of Jerusalem, it was plain that the few thousand Petra troops would not have a chance without supernatural intervention.

Rayford spent the next couple of hours with Kenny, then ventured out to check on George and his fighting band.

+ + +

"Mac, come quick," Otto said. "I've got a colleague on speakerphone, but she's nearly speechless."

When Mac arrived at Otto's quarters, he heard the woman try to recount what had happened. "I don't know how much time we have," she said, out of breath, "but it's time to go."

"How do you know?" Mac said.

"An angel," she said.

"You're sure?"

"Bright, white, shiny, big, very big. And it was a man, at least this one was. He was so bright that the darkness in this city is gone. It is as bright as noon here still."

"What did he say?"

"He spoke so loud that everyone here had to hear it, and I will never forget one word of it. He said, 'Babylon the great is fallen, is fallen, and has become a dwelling place of demons, a prison for every foul spirit, and a cage for every unclean and hated bird!

"'For all the nations have drunk of the wine of the wrath of her fornication, the kings of the earth have committed fornication with her, and the merchants of the earth have become rich through the abundance of her luxury.'"

"We're on our way, ma'am. Get everybody to the palace airstrip, and if you hear from any more groups of believers, send them there too."

"That's not all, sir."

"Excuse me?"

"I heard another voice from heaven. It said, 'Come out of her, my people, lest you share in her sins, and lest you receive of her plagues. For her sins have reached to heaven, and God has remembered her iniquities.'"

+ + +

"I hardly have enough people to encircle this place," Sebastian said.

Rayford avoided George's eyes. "I don't know what to say. The way I read it, we aren't expected to even hold our own."

"I don't want men and women to suffer, though, Captain. I'd rather we just line up above and pick a few off."

"Look at it this way, George. This is where Jesus is supposed to come first. We could be among the first to witness the Glorious Appearing."

"Tell that to a fighting force outnumbered a thousand to one. They may be in heaven before Jesus leaves there."

+ + +

Mac had no idea what to expect in New Babylon, so at the last minute he enlisted Lionel to also bring in a large jet. Between the two of them he figured he could evacuate up to two hundred people.

When they landed at the palace, he found it eerie. The place was no longer dark, but the wounded souls within the boundaries didn't know what to make of it. They had been in pain and darkness for so long they were disoriented and still hadn't found their bearings. Most still limped and staggered around.

But waiting for the planes of refuge were more than one hundred and fifty believers, cheering their arrival. They carried their belongings in sacks and boxes and were eager to get aboard, which made the whole process quick and easy. Mac and Lionel had their planes loaded and turned around and headed down the runways when two invading armies attacked.

Before Mac was even out of New Babylon airspace, black smoke billowed into the heavens. He circled the area for an hour, and Lionel followed, as their charges watched the utter destruction of the once great city. Within those sixty minutes every building was leveled, and Mac knew that every resident was slaughtered. When the mysterious armies who had invaded from the north and northwest pulled out, they left the entire metropolis aflame. By the time Mac turned toward Petra, the only thing left of New Babylon was ash and smoke.

+ + +

Chang watched, confused, as GCNN reports came in of fighting within the ranks of the One World Unity Army. Carpathia's forces apparently had to strike back at nations who became drunk with power and ambition when armed with resources that had been stored at Al Hillah. The majority of Nicolae's allies banded together to crush the resistance, and by the time all were assembled at Armageddon, they had all been persuaded, by the demons or by Carpathia or by the realities of war, to join together against the people of God.

The sheer number of troops swelled well beyond the Valley of Megiddo and spilled north and south and east and west, past Jerusalem and down toward Edom. Some estimates included an almost unimaginable mounted army alone of more than two hundred thousand. Aerial views shot by GCNN aircraft could show only a million or so troops at a time, but dozens and dozens of separate such pictures were broadcast.

Chang sensed panic on the part of the people at Petra. Those who saw the news could not imagine standing against such an overwhelming force. Those who didn't see the news heard it from others, and the word swept the camp. Many ran to the high places and could make out the clouds of dust and the dark masses of humanity, beasts, and weaponry slowly making their way across the desert.

Chaim took the occasion to call the people together, just before the evening manna was expected. "My dear people, brothers and sisters in Messiah. Be of good cheer. Fear not. I am hearing wonderful reports out of Jerusalem, where our brother Tsion preaches the gospel of Jesus Christ with great boldness and, I am happy to report, great results as well.

"I only ten minutes ago talked with a very exhausted and still very busy Cameron Williams. He tells me thousands are repenting of their sins and turning to Christ, acknowledging Jesus of Nazareth as Messiah. Praise the Lord God Almighty, maker of heaven and earth!"

The people seemed encouraged and cheered and wept and raised their hands.

"We are not ignorant," Chaim continued, "of what is to come. New Babylon has fallen, utterly destroyed in one hour, fulfilling the prophecies. That leaves only two events on the prophetic calendar, my friends. The first is?"

And the people shouted, "The seventh Bowl Judgment!"

"And the second, oh, praise God?"

"The Glorious Appearing!"

Chaim concluded, "We serve the great God of Abraham, Isaac, and Jacob, the deliverer of Shadrach, Meshach, and Abednego. We lived through the fires of the Antichrist, and we have been delivered from the snare of the fowler. Do not be afraid. Stand still, and see the salvation of the Lord, which he will accomplish for you. For the enemy whom you see today, you shall soon see no more forever. The Lord will fight for you, and you shall hold your peace."

20

DARKNESS HAD FALLEN in Jerusalem, yet still the Temple Mount teemed with people. Buck thought Tsion appeared weak and tired, so he broke away and went to their stash to bring him some foodstuffs. But their bags were gone. He ran back to where Tsion held forth, but now he himself felt dizzy with hunger.

"I need something with which to feed the rabbi!" he called out.

"I am fine!" Tsion said and continued preaching.

"Someone, please. A morsel. Bread, fruit."

"Five loaves and two fishes?" someone suggested, and everyone laughed.

An elderly man tossed an apple to Buck. Others passed him a round of bread, crusty and warm. Someone donated a block of cheese. Someone else a couple of oranges.

"Help me persuade this stubborn teacher to take a break!" Buck said, and many urged Tsion to at least sit. And so he did.

Talking now, teaching rather than preaching, Tsion took questions and nibbled between answers. The crowd only grew. "I had no idea how hungry I was," Tsion said. He looked at Buck. "I am grateful, my friend." Someone passed him a container of water, and he drank deeply.

Suddenly someone held up both hands to shush the crowd, and everyone fell silent. The rumble of a moving army was clear. Buck felt the vibration throughout his body.

"We need to get the rabbi to shelter," someone said. "We can meet over there."

Tsion appeared to start to protest, but the audience was leaving en masse, so he and Buck followed. They were led into a massive stone structure that could easily have accommodated a thousand people. About half that many crowded near the front.

"What are we to do when the enemy arrives?" someone asked. "We are more outnumbered than Gideon."

"We can do only what we can do," Tsion said. "If you have an inkling what I am trying to do here today, it is to usher as many of my fellow Jews into the kingdom of Messiah as possible before it is too late. Because of that I feel a compulsion to keep as many candidates alive as I can. If you agree with my mission, go out into the city proper and invite anyone who wants to, to come and join us. The enemy will begin to conquer Jerusalem and plunge people into captivity, but I believe their main objective is the Old City. What better meat to his pride than for Carpathia to think he can invade this holy place and set up his headquarters here?

"If we are attacked before you can return, take what you have learned here and tell everyone you know. They need not come back here to pray the prayer of faith and become a member of Messiah's kingdom."

Someone shouted, "Better yet to have them come back already decided and carrying a weapon!"

"Well," Tsion said. "Yes."

✠ ✠ ✠

As was so often true when spending the night at Rayford's, Kenny was nearly impossible to get to sleep unless he began by lying atop his grandfather. Rayford lay gingerly on the small cot designated for the boy and reached for him. Kenny climbed aboard and laid his cheek just under Rayford's chin.

Rayford fought fatigue, not wanting to fall asleep with Kenny asking questions, singing, praying.

"Mommy's in heaven," Kenny said.

"That's right. And we miss her, don't we?"

"I do."

"I do too."

"Gonna see her real soon."

"Very, very soon, Kenny." Rayford knew Buck had been showing him the calendar.

"Tomorrow?"

"Maybe. Or the next day. Not too many days."

"Where's heaven, Grandpa?"

"With God."

"And God is with Mommy?"

"Yes."

"And Jesus?"

"And Jesus."

"I want them to come here."

"Soon."

Rayford had arranged with Priscilla Sebastian that she would come by for Kenny before dawn, when Rayford was expected to join the troops on the perimeter.

Kenny soon stopped talking and moving, and his breathing became regular and deep. Rayford prayed for him and waited a few more minutes before delicately sliding out from under him.

A few minutes later Rayford lay on his own cot across the room and studied the boy. How thrilled Irene would have been with her grandson. Had Kenny grown up during any other period of history, he would be starting school within the year. Rayford wondered what form education would take in the millennial kingdom.

He also wondered how it worked. Would he and Buck and Kenny grow old while Irene and Raymie and Chloe remained the age they were when they went to heaven? And what about Amanda? He feared that reunion with his wife might be awkward, but would those situations matter when everyone was in the presence of Jesus?

Rayford had been so busy for so long that he had not allowed himself the luxury of daydreaming about it. What would it be like to see the Glorious Appearing and then to actually be with Christ? Rayford was more emotional than he had been as a younger man, and often the mere thought of the change Christ had made in him made him choke up.

To imagine the sinless Son of God caring enough about him to die for his sins . . . Rayford could still hardly fathom it. And to have the opportunity to thank him, to worship him, face-to-face. For a thousand years. And then for eternity. He hadn't even begun trying to imagine what heaven would be like.

+ + +

In the wee hours of the morning in Jerusalem, Buck and Tsion found themselves taken in by an elderly father named Shivte and his two sons in their forties. They were all thick, beefy men, and soft-spoken.

As soon as Shivte's wife opened the door to her husband's coded knock, she blanched and nearly fainted. "Praise God! Praise God!" she said. "You are Tsion Ben-Judah! And you!" she added, looking first at her husband and then at her sons. "You have the mark of God on you! Can you finally see mine?"

They smiled and nodded, embracing her one by one.

"I cannot tell you how much we appreciate this," Tsion said. "Our belongings have disappeared, and we made no provisions for lodging."

Shivte's wife told him, "We made no provisions for lodging either. But we have blankets and some food."

"The Lord will reward you," Tsion said.

"He already has," she said. "To see you with my men when they came through the door, that is enough for me. I am humbled to offer hospitality to God's servants."

"Tell me how you came to Messiah, ma'am," Tsion said.

She sat heavily. "Micah," she said, and Tsion and Buck looked at each other. "I had waited so long to take the mark of Carpathia. I did not want to. My men were not going to. They were going to hide out here during the day so as not to be detected by the GC. But I believed someone had to take the mark in order to buy and sell and keep us alive. I was willing, but the idea of worshiping that statue made me want to vomit. Forgive me."

"Please, continue."

"I was at the Temple Mount, planning to go through with it, even though in my heart I believed in the one true God. I did not know what else to do. I worried about my eternal soul, but I believed I was laying down my life for my family, and I could think of no nobler act. I did not realize at that time that I would be selling my soul to the evil one. Not even these men are worth that."

Her husband and sons smiled.

"I was in line that day, Rabbi, actually in line. I don't know how many people were between me and the mark applicator. But I saw a commotion and slipped out of line. I watched from the back of the crowd. I saw the gunshots that did not kill the man of God. I escaped back to our home, and my men will admit they ridiculed me. They had liked my plan of one of us—me—having the mark so we could eat. Now what were we going to do?

"I told them they could go out in the dark of night and find food, but I was going to find out more about the man of God. One of my young friends had a computer, and we found your Web site. That is how I came to believe Jesus was Messiah. Now I was an outcast in my own home. My men were devout enough Jews to resist Carpathia, but they were not ready for Messiah.

"I tried and prayed and pleaded and begged, but finally we agreed to quit talking about it. Enough, they said, and I had had enough of their rejection and ridicule anyway. But still I could pray. And God answers prayer. Here you are, and here they are, with the mark of God."

+ + +

Rayford had trouble sleeping and felt compelled to check in with Buck. He tiptoed to the other room so as not to wake Kenny and placed the call. After asking about Kenny, Buck brought him up to date.

"Amazing," Rayford said. "What's Tsion saying about timing now?"

"He expects a predawn attack. Maybe there as well."

"We're kind of on that schedule too, Buck, but the combat part of this is so futile."

"Temporarily, you mean."

"Of course, but I just don't know that I see the value of risking people's lives when they could stay inside here and—"

"—and wait for Jesus?"

"Exactly."

"Come on, Dad. Who wants to do that? I'd kinda like to have him find me on the job. Wouldn't you?"

"I know, but you should see the crew we're going to have on the perimeter. A couple of thousand I don't know at all. Then Otto and a few of his people, none of them with any business manning a weapon. Ree, Ming, Lionel, Hannah, Zeke. Not exactly soldiers. Mac, of course, and Smitty. They can take care of themselves, and there's no question about Razor and George. Unless George tries to be a hero. He's so military, Buck, you should see him, trying to make the best of it. You can just tell he thinks his street smarts ought to carry the day, but then he realizes how few soldiers are under his command, and those eyes go glassy."

"You've got directed energy weapons and fifty-calibers yet, right?"

"Yeah, but against nuclear power? Come on."

"Do some damage. Stall till the Calvary cavalry gets here."

"The what?"

"Thought of that the other day. Jesus is going to appear from heaven on a horse. That's literal, according to Tsion. Ten thousand saints with him. The Calvary cavalry."

"Too much time on your hands."

"Hey, Rayford?"

"Yeah."

"We can hear the armies coming. Can you?"

"Not the way this city is laid out. Maybe when they get closer. They're sure easy to spot from the high places, though. Pretty ominous. I'd be looking for a way out of here if I didn't know better."

"Sort of like watching a delayed ball game where you already know the final score, isn't it?"

"I guess," Rayford said. "That's the kind of thing only a mind like yours would come up with."

"Thanks, I think."

+ + +

Unable to sleep, Chang made his way to the tech center and his computer at about four in the morning. Idly checking the GCNN affiliate feed out of Haifa, he heard a report of troop deployments.

"Supreme Potentate Nicolae Carpathia has made no secret of his strategy," the reporter intoned. "In fact, it seems as if he would just as soon enemy targets know what's coming. I spoke with him late last night at his bunker, somewhere near the Sea of Galilee."

"You see," Carpathia said, "we have such an overwhelming advantage in manpower, firepower, and technology, it really makes little difference what we encounter. I have not hidden that we have two main objectives aiming toward the same goal. We want to lay siege to the city of Jerusalem, where the majority of the remaining Jews reside. And we want to eliminate Petra once and for all, where what they like to call 'the Remnant' remains in hiding like scared children.

"They know we are coming, and they will see us coming, and there is little they can do about it."

"You expect no casualties?"

"Oh, there are always casualties," Carpathia sniffed. "But my people are honored to give their lives in service to me and the Global Community. I will see that they are appropriately rewarded. Of course, there is the possibility of no loss of life or limb on our part. That is, if the enemy sees what is coming and realizes it has no hope. An unconditional surrender would be the prudent course, and naturally I would accept that with utmost face-saving respect for them."

"Seriously? What accommodations would you make in that case?"

Carpathia could not answer over his gales of laughter.

+ + +

Rayford was up, dressed, and armed before dawn. He opened the door before Priscilla knocked.

"I'll stay here with him until he wakes up, Rayford, if that's okay."

"Perfect. Thanks, Priss. Make yourself at home."

"Uh, Ray? You're going to be sure my husband comes home tonight, aren't you?"

"As much as it's up to me."

"That's not very reassuring."

"Well, I take it that was a serious question. A serious answer is that there are no guarantees. I'm hoping he'll make sure I come back."

"He feels obligated to everybody," Priscilla said, sitting.

Rayford stood by the open door. "Price of leadership. He volunteered for this command."

"Like there was another choice."

"There wasn't in my mind, Priscilla."

"Well, I'm just saying—"

"I know. Sometimes, though, seems a guy like me trying to keep an eye on a guy who knows what he's doing can just get in the way. You know, of course, that even if—"

"Don't say it, Rayford. Too many of the wives try to comfort themselves with that stuff about how their man will only be in heaven a day or two, maybe less, then he's coming back. That doesn't help."

"It's true."

"I know. But it isn't the living without him that worries me right now. It's his getting hurt, suffering, dying a hard way."

+ + +

Buck and Tsion and their hosts drank the thickest, bitterest coffee Buck had ever had. It was still pitch-black outside. Shivte's wife was already sniffling and trying to hide it.

"Cameron," Tsion whispered, "I would like you to go with the old man, Shivte, at first."

"Now, wait. I came here to be your bodyguard, no one else's."

"Do me this favor. I worry about him. Even his weapon is ancient. The sons believe the invaders will come from the northwest and try to come through the Damascus Gate."

"Based on what?"

"The Unity Army could probably easily overrun any of the gates, but the Jaffa Gate and the Citadel are well fortified with many rebel troops."

"But beyond that," Buck said, "they could try to storm any of the gates, and the most likely, in my opinion, would be the Golden Gate. Their first priority has to be the Temple Mount, no?"

"I don't know, Cameron. Just do this for me, please. Take the old man to the Citadel. Once he is settled there, then come and find me. I will be with the other two near the Damascus Gate."

Buck would rather have followed his hunch and gone straight to the Golden Gate, but he was here for Tsion, and he would do him this favor. He didn't know why the brothers were even guessing. If two-thirds of Carpathia's troops were concentrating on Jerusalem, it wouldn't take many of them to take over the tiny Old City.

As soon as he and Tsion and the other three men were out the door, they heard gunfire. Tsion and the brothers jogged northwest, Buck and Shivte, west. Rebels ran everywhere, shouting what they knew. The enemy was on the Jaffa Road. Damascus Gate was under siege. The Yad Vashem Historical Museum to the Holocaust victims had been destroyed. Hebrew University, the Jewish

National and University Library, and Israel Museum were in flames. The Old City would be next.

Thousands were dead and many more captured and held. Buck knew, if the rumors could be believed, that he and Shivte were in the worst possible place. In essence, they had cornered themselves inside the walls of the Old City.

+ + +

Rayford was impressed with Sebastian's strategy, though they both knew tactics were out the window in the face of such odds. The third of Carpathia's troops assigned to Petra carried every type of weapon in the potentate's arsenal. At least two hundred thousand mounted troops slowly moved into position, far outflanking Sebastian's forces and virtually surrounding them and the city.

"I have so few DEWs," George told Rayford. "In retrospect, if I had known they were going to start with this horse trick, I'd have had Lionel find me more."

"What do horses have to do with it?"

"Horses are not armored, and the riders can't really hide. See how lazily they're moving into position?"

Rayford took the field glasses and saw thousands of horsemen cantering into place. They were a mile from Petra's massed troops. "They act like they've got all day."

Suddenly, George seemed animated. "We're going to get in the first blow in this thing, and we're going to have the advantage, at least temporarily."

"How?"

"Those horses are trained to not spook under artillery fire. We could pop a few fifty-caliber rounds at 'em and get them stirred up a bit. Maybe take out a few horses and a few riders. But I'll bet they haven't dealt with DEWs yet. You ready for some action?"

"Sure."

"I've got only about a hundred DEWs, but at least I was smart enough to assign them all positions inside on the rim. I need them pretty evenly spaced, all around the top of the city. Can you handle that?"

"On it. Then what?"

"Tell them all to wait for my command. If we can hit anywhere close to a hundred horses or riders with DEWs from this distance, we could cause a stampede that would put all their horses out of commission for a while."

"Brilliant."

"Only if it works. Thing is, we've got to do this before they really know where we are. We could have them on the run right off the bat and see how they like being on their heels."

+ + +

Buck got Shivte settled well inside the crowded Citadel, where it appeared many scared younger men had decided to hole up as well. While Buck could hear activity on the Jaffa Road, the invaders had indeed ignored the Jaffa Gate for the very reason Buck guessed. Why do more work than you had to?

Buck guessed the Damascus Gate was a little over a quarter of a mile away, but getting there through the crowd of petrified and wild-eyed rebels made it seem farther. And of course, Tsion and the brothers were nowhere in sight. "Lord, come quickly."

+ + +

Rayford scampered to a four-wheel-drive ATV and charged to the nearest high place. It took nearly half an hour with the vehicle and his walkie-talkie to get the hundred or so DEW operators spread out evenly and coordinated.

At George's command, they would fire invisible beams of directed energy at the enemy. In essence, they heated soft tissue past the tolerance point in less than a second, and if the rider or horse didn't elude the ray, their flesh would burn.

With Petra surrounded by a couple of brigades of mounted troops, the result had the potential to be maddeningly confusing to the enemy. The strategy was to try to hit horses only, making them bolt away and causing the steeds around them to do the same. No question some riders, especially their legs, would be hit in the process, hopefully causing them to kick and achieve the same result. If the beam hit higher on a rider's body, he would likely scream and yank the reins. George, Rayford thought, was a genius.

+ + +

"Dung Gate is giving way!" someone shouted. "Let's kill us some One World Army!"

Buck prayed it wasn't true. The Dung Gate was the southern gate closest to the Western Wall. It was the long way around to get to the Temple Mount, and that's why he had assumed the Golden Gate on the east side would be the Unity Army's first choice. If they got through the Dung Gate, they might try battering through the Wailing Wall to get to pay dirt.

Unable to raise Tsion by phone or find him or either of the brothers at the Damascus Gate, which seemed to be holding for the time being, Buck ran toward the Dung Gate, a mile away. All along the route he heard rumors and fears. If any of it was to be believed, it wouldn't be long before half the greater city of Jerusalem was in captivity. His goal was to stay alive until the good guys showed up.

✣ ✣ ✣

Rayford figured Petra was fewer than fifteen minutes from sunrise when he let George know the directed energy weapons were in place and awaiting his command. "I'd really like to make sure the targets are where I want them before we commence," George said.

"Only one way to do that as fast as you need it done," Rayford said.

"ATV?"

"Too much ground to cover. You'd have to circle the whole perimeter up top."

"Helicopter?"

"Bingo. If you want to risk it."

"They wouldn't believe it was us," George said. "Who'd be stupid enough to make himself that kind of a target?"

"You would."

✣ ✣ ✣

Buck had run almost half a mile and was sucking wind when he saw Carpathia's Unity Army troops coming the other way. Now he was desperate to find Tsion and get him out of the Old City.

Rebels, some shooting over their shoulders, ran past him for their lives, but Buck noticed the GC were not firing. They were moving in a colossal battering ram that looked as if it would make short work of the Wailing Wall. Now that was a tragedy. After millennia of prayer, could such a sacred site be wasted in just moments?

Suddenly, all those rebels who had flooded past Buck turned and came back. Shouts resounded: "Not the Wailing Wall!" "Not the Wall!" "Sacrifice yourselves!" "Fight to the death!"

The word spread throughout the Jewish Quarter and into the center of the Old City, and instantly hundreds became thousands. Buck joined the fray. They charged the GC, shooting, throwing rocks, fighting hand to hand. The rebels overcame those on the battering ram and turned it back toward the Dung Gate.

As more and more rebels joined, at least for that brief skirmish, the Jews had the Unity Army on the run. They pushed the battering ram up to the Dung Gate, chased out the army, and managed to shut the gate with the ram inside. Great cheers rose, and so, it seemed, did the rebellion's confidence. Someone assigned a large group to guard the gate, while others were sent to the Golden and Lion's Gates on the east side.

Buck's phone chirped. "Tsion! Where are you? I tried to call you!"

"My phone is dead. I am borrowing this one. Is it true the rebels turned the army away from the Dung Gate?"

"Yes! I'm here now! Where shall we meet?"

"Do you know the Church of the Flagellation?"

"Near the Muslim Quarter?"

"Just west of there, yes!" Tsion said. "Hurry! I have lost the brothers."

+ + +

"You know we've always been protected in the airspace around here," Rayford said as he lifted off.

"I'd rather not test that," Sebastian said. "Just straight up and give me a three-sixty so I can see if the horses are where I want them. Then straight back down."

"Oh no!" Rayford said. "Incoming!"

"What?"

A missile was streaking right at the chopper. Rayford tried to evade it, knowing that was hopeless. A whirlybird simply didn't have the maneuverability or speed to dodge a missile.

"My idea and a bad one, George. Sorry."

"Just stay away from the city, Ray!"

Rayford had toyed with the idea of dropping onto a high place, but if the missile tracked him, it could injure or kill more than just the two of them.

He banked and let the chopper roll out past where Petra troops were stationed, which only brought him face-to-face with the missile that much faster.

"Sorry, Priscilla," Rayford muttered, shutting his eyes as the warhead met the chopper.

+ + +

It didn't make sense to Buck that he should get to the rendezvous point before Tsion, despite the difference in their ages. Buck figured Tsion had started from at least twice as close. He searched the crowded church, but once again, no Tsion. This was getting old.

"Herod's Gate!" someone shouted, and hundreds of rebels headed toward the northernmost gate in the city. It was amazing to see the zeal in their eyes when their ancient holy sites were threatened. That had to be where Tsion went too. Buck couldn't think of another option.

It was just over an eighth of a mile from the church, but there was no running this time. Buck found himself pressed on all sides, wall-to-wall rebels. Maybe it was for the best. He was exhausted already, and his pulse raced uncontrollably.

He couldn't call Tsion if the rabbi's phone was dead. All he could think to do was bend his knees occasionally and leap high enough to see over the crowd.

But when he spotted Tsion Ben-Judah, he didn't like where he found him.

21

THE CHOPPER SHUDDERED and stayed on course.

"Thought we were goners," Rayford said. "I never get used to that."

"Where'd that missile go?"

"Right through us, as usual."

"Nothing usual about that," Sebastian said. He scanned the horizon. "Over there."

Rayford saw a plume of black smoke about a mile south of Petra.

"They may have hit their own people!" George said and got on his radio. "Big Dog 1 to southern perimeter, over."

"Mac here, Dog. What was that?"

"Just missed us. What did it do?"

"Found one of their transports just beyond the equestrian line. Had to have some casualties. They look pretty exercised."

"Wait till they find out it was friendly fire. Attention all DEW operators, open fire immediately!" George ordered.

Within seconds, the black rim of horses and horsemen surrounding Petra disintegrated, and steeds charged away in all directions.

"A masterpiece, George," Rayford said. "Well done."

"Some of that horse meat is probably well done. Hey, Ray, did I hear you mention my wife's name when we were about to buy it?"

"Guilty."

"What's that about?"

"I told her I'd look out for you as much as was possible."

"And that's your idea of looking out for me?"

"As much as was possible. What say we bounce back up and see if we can get them to shoot at us again, maybe take out some more of their munitions on the other side?"

"Not funny, Rayford."

\+ + +

Every time Buck leaped over the heads of the crowd, he caught sight of Tsion being borne along on the shoulders of zealots. He wanted to scream at them to put him down, but no one would be able to hear above the din. What were they trying to do, get him killed? Maybe they saw him as a hero. Maybe they thought by getting him to the head of the pack he could inspire the troops. Regardless, it was insanity.

Buck lowered his shoulder and bulled his way through until he was almost up to Tsion. "Hey!" he shouted. "Hey! Put him down!"

"He will lead us to victory!"

"He is our leader!"

"Well, he's my responsibility, and you're going to get him killed!"

Buck grabbed Tsion's ankle, which slowed the crowd, and as they lost their grip, Tsion tumbled headfirst. Buck dived beneath him to break his fall, and now both of them were being trampled. It was providential, however, as Unity Army troops had scaled the wall above Herod's Gate and opened fire. Rebels fell all around Tsion and Buck, heads slamming the ground, blood spattering.

Buck wrapped his arms around Tsion's head and buried his own, waiting out the fusillade. With the zing of bullets ricocheting and the explosion of the pavement around him, he tensed for the killing round that would hit his or Tsion's head or neck or spine.

But they were spared.

When the burst let up, Buck dragged Tsion to his feet and hustled him toward the legendary healing pool of Bethesda. "I was not hit, Cameron! No need for healing!"

Millimeters from death and the rabbi jokes.

\+ + +

Rayford and George landed and were racing down to George's post via ATV. "They've got to retaliate," Rayford said. "What form will that take, and what do we do?"

"They've got mortar launchers in range. I want to see if the riders can persuade their horses to return. If they can't, that's going to be chaos. The key is keeping them out of the Siq. I don't want a one of 'em thinking he can infiltrate this place."

"You'd think Carpathia would have learned his lesson. Imagine how much money he wasted trying to get at us here," Rayford said.

"Yeah, but every military commander thinks he's better than anybody else, so whoever's in charge of this offensive is going to have to learn for himself."

"The DEWs and his own missile should have taught him something."

"Should have," George said. "But you can bet he'll try everything in his arsenal before he gives up."

"What would be the hardest to defend against?"

"Sheer numbers. When they start rolling this way, we're going to be chased back inside."

"Where, so far, it's been safe."

"True. But retreating is not my idea of warfare. That missile was God's protection, but wasn't it fun to attack with the directed energy weapons?"

+ + +

A young woman gestured frantically from a small cavelike structure near the pools, and Buck hustled Tsion to her. "There is room for two more," she said.

As they pushed their way in to safety, Buck realized about twenty others were in the echoing chamber. "Is it the rabbi?" someone called out.

"I am here," Tsion said.

"Praise God. When do you expect Messiah?"

"Actually, I expected him about five minutes ago. Or maybe I should say he should have been expecting me."

"I want to believe he is coming to save the day and rescue us."

"He is if you are ready," Tsion said.

"I am ready. I just want to be alive when he gets here."

"So do I," Tsion said. "But we did not choose the best place to ensure that, did we?"

"What is this talk of Messiah?" someone grumbled. "We have been waiting for him to rescue us for generations."

Tsion ran through his teaching as fast as he could. Three of the terrified men and the young woman prayed to accept Jesus as Messiah, but the skeptic did not. "When he comes," he said, "I will believe."

"'Blessed are those who have not seen and yet have believed,'" Tsion said.

The gunfire suddenly ceased. Buck peered out past the woman. Was this it? Had Messiah returned and saved the day?

Young men raced by, screaming. "We have won! We have won! They are pulling back! The gates are secure!"

"Wait! It's a trap! Don't believe it! They are just regrouping!"

Buck and Tsion's bunker mates piled out and warily looked around, weapons at the ready. "I don't like it," someone said. "They have bombs that could annihilate us. What are they doing?"

"Toying with us."

"We should go on the offensive! Open the gates and attack! Kill them while they are retreating."

"They are not retreating. This is a trap. They want us to open the gates. We should regroup while they are regrouping. Be ready for them."

+ + +

There was a lull at Petra too, and Rayford took a call from Mac McCullum. "Can you and Razor spare me a minute, George?" Rayford said. "Mac wants me to come and see something."

It was half an hour's ride by all-terrain vehicle to get to Mac, and when Rayford arrived, Mac was studying the enemy through powerful field glasses. "You know they can see us plain as day by now, Ray, just like we can see them. What are they waitin' on?"

He handed Rayford the binoculars. "Looks like they've got most of the horses under control. That must have been a mess. And I know, Ray, that our DEWs caused the stampede. But what's making them squirrelly now? I don't get it."

Rayford studied the enemy in the distance. It didn't appear it was as simple as horses being shy of where they had been burned. They weren't even close to that. It was more like the riders could not get the horses to do anything they wanted them to.

"It reminds me of a verse, Ray. Something Tsion taught us. What was it?"

"I don't recall. Want to ask him? I need to check in on him and Buck anyway."

+ + +

The silence was more than eerie. Buck and Tsion moved close to the wall by Herod's Gate. Buck answered the phone and handed it to Tsion.

"Yes, here too," Tsion said. "I have the strange feeling it is the lull before the storm. Horses? Yes. Zechariah 12:4: '"In that day," says the Lord, "I will strike every horse with confusion, and its rider with madness; I will open My eyes on the house of Judah, and will strike every horse of the peoples with blindness."' You know, Mac, that may be what has happened here too."

As soon as Tsion was off the phone, people around him wanted to know what he was talking about. He told them.

"Let's check it out," one said. "The rabbi believes the Unity Army is blind or mad."

"Could be," Tsion said. "That is the only explanation I can think of for what is going on."

Some of the younger men boosted each other and began climbing. Two reached the top of the wall. "I see nothing! They're hiding, maybe."

"Rabbi! Teach us some more."

Buck looked to Tsion, who shrugged. "That is why I came. If they want to listen, I want to preach."

As soon as he began, curious crowds gathered again. And as Buck watched and listened, he was overcome with the privilege of being where he was and when it was. He sensed he could see Jesus at any time. And Chloe.

To hear God's man in God's place at God's time—what an unspeakable privilege. Scared? Of course he was. Wondering if Jesus would really come when he said he would? Not even a question. Buck couldn't wait. He just couldn't wait.

+ + +

Back with George, Rayford was out of ideas. "Don't ask me," he said. "If you want to fire the Fifties, fire them."

"I know we could kill horses and men from this distance and take out a few of their vehicles," George said. "But I also know that would bring return fire. I'm not concerned about inside the city. But I'm afraid we're vulnerable out here at the perimeter."

"What would be the purpose of going on the offensive when you know you can't win?"

"Exactly. But I just hate sitting here, waiting for stuff to happen. We need to make something happen."

"Fire a Fifty or two and plenty will happen."

+ + +

One of the young men on the wall interrupted Tsion, yelling, "They're raising some kind of a giant bullhorn. Maybe they want to negotiate."

"You don't want to negotiate with the devil," Tsion said, and the crowd roared.

"Maybe he's offering a truce!"

"A truce," Tsion said, "is worth the character of the man on the other side of the table."

"Attention, people of Jerusalem! This is your supreme potentate!"

"Boo! Boo! Our only potentate is the God of Israel!"

"Shut up! Hear him out!"

"Please listen, citizens. I come in peace."

"No! You come with weapons!"

"Come, let us reason together!"

"Listen. Shh! Listen to him!"

"I come to offer pardon. I am willing to compromise. I wish you no ill. If you are willing to serve me and be obedient, you shall eat the good of the land; but if you refuse and rebel, you shall be devoured by the sword. I will rid myself of my adversaries and take vengeance on my enemies. I will turn my hand against you and thoroughly purge you.

"But it does not have to be this way, citizens of the Global Community. If you will lay down your arms and welcome me into your city, I will guarantee your peace and safety.

"This will be your sign to me. If at the count of three I hear silence for fifteen seconds, I will assume you are willing to accede to my requests. A single gunshot into the air during that time will be your signal that you would rather oppose me. But I warn you, half of Jerusalem is in captivity already. The entire city could be overthrown easily within an hour. The choice is yours at the count of three."

But before Carpathia could utter the first number, thousands of weapons fired into the air, including Buck's and Tsion's.

+ + +

The enemy's attempt to control the horses and surround Petra was still not working. Rayford stood on a precipice and watched through binoculars as more Unity vehicles were deployed. The horizon was full of dust and smoke, and the mass of munitions and hardware looked like a black, roiling mass, filling his vision and oozing toward him like lava.

"I'm going to let them advance only so far," George said. "Then it's DEWs again and fifty-calibers."

"Like trying to dam a tsunami with BBs," Rayford said.

+ + +

When the shooting stopped in Jerusalem, the ghostly silence returned. The One World Unity Army did not immediately attack, but Buck almost wished they had. The quiet was disquieting. He feared the next sound would be the proverbial freight train that tornado victims always mentioned, only this twister would consist of an unending horde of marauders who would stomp Jerusalem to dust.

But if that's what it took to usher in Jesus, well, bring it on.

Strangely, the crowd wanted to hear more from Tsion, and Buck was impressed that the rabbi was ready. "It is not too late!" Tsion cried. "Make your stand for Messiah now! Repent, choose, and be saved!" And many did.

\+ + +

Now even Sebastian seemed alarmed. The massive flow of horses, men, and weaponry advancing toward Petra was so enormous that as it spread and separated and filled in again, it blocked out the horizon, the desert sands, the rocks.

It was as if a cloud of locusts were blotting out the sun. No human could have imagined the scope of the enemy. They had somehow rallied, somehow overcome their madness and blindness, somehow broken out of their lull. And here they came.

They fanned out and flanked Petra on all sides, slowly filling in as far as the eye could see. And while their front lines were still a mile or so from the perimeter, there was no end to the swarm. The eye could not reach the back of column after column after column of millions strong that kept coming and coming and coming.

And when they were in place, they merely stopped and waited. For what was anybody's guess. But even when they stopped, there was no gap, no holes in their coverage, no end of their ranks.

"That, Rayford," Sebastian said, "is just a whole lot of army. If every one of our weapons fired every one of its bullets and each one was a flat-out kill, we wouldn't put a dent in that wave."

"What do you think about riding out there about a half mile and seeing if you can smoke a peace pipe with somebody?"

"You watch too much TV, Captain."

"Seriously, how about another round of DEW rays? See if we can push 'em back a bit."

"If I thought they'd react like dominoes I would. There really isn't far for them to go, because they'll run into their own replacements. Think we can get millions to stampede?"

Rayford shook his head. "I wouldn't mind seeing what that would do to them. Maybe they wouldn't be so eager to get closer."

"But, Ray, there's so many of them."

\+ + +

Tsion was still holding forth when a sound like a bomb shook the area, and people scattered for cover. Within seconds came the report that a second battering ram had penetrated the Old City. This time the Unity Army had eschewed any gate and had broken through the northeastern wall of the Old City, about halfway between the Lion's Gate and the northeast corner.

Hundreds of Jewish rebels raced toward the site, and to Buck's dismay Tsion took off behind them, not even discussing options. Buck had no choice but to follow, trying to catch Tsion in the melee. By the time he caught up, the battle was in full swing, and amazingly, the Jews seemed to have the upper hand again. They were pushing the army back, and fierce hand-to-hand combat over the battering ram almost saw it fall into rebel hands again.

Just as the rebellion was forcing the army back through the wall, several on the Unity front line turned and opened fire with high-powered automatic weapons, a grenade launcher, and what looked to Buck like a bazooka. He joined in returning fire, and the invasion was briefly squelched, but he was horrified to see more than a hundred dead or wounded Israelis all around him. He wondered how close he had come to deadly fire himself.

The hole in the wall seemed to be secure for the moment, so Buck turned to grab Tsion and pull him back toward the Bethesda pool. But the rabbi was on his knees, feet tucked awkwardly beneath him. His Uzi had slipped off his shoulder, the strap near his elbow now, the weapon dragging.

Buck grabbed the shoulder of his jacket to help him up, but when he pulled, Tsion pivoted on one knee and flopped to the pavement. "Tsion! Come on! Let's go!"

But he was a deadweight.

"Are you all right?" Buck demanded, turning Tsion's face toward him.

"I do not think so, friend."

"Are you hit?"

"I am afraid I am."

"Where?"

"I am not sure."

"Can you move?"

"No."

"Can I move you?"

"Please. You had better try."

Buck didn't have time to even think about being fancy. He grabbed Tsion's weapon and strapped it on his left shoulder, then got around behind the rabbi's head and thrust both hands under his arms. He bent his knees and lifted, walking backward, dragging the older man through the streets. He was grateful the shooting had stopped, if only temporarily.

Buck was cramping, having pulled his friend about an eighth of a mile, but he didn't want to stop until they were safe in the little chamber he remembered at Bethesda. He kept looking behind him to make sure the way was clear, but when he turned back he realized Tsion was also leaving a thick trail of blood.

Buck stopped to rest and check Tsion. He hurried around and opened the man's jacket. There he found the source of blood. Tsion could not have been shot in the heart or he would be dead already. But he had lost a lot of blood, which had flowed from near his sternum, down his belly, under his jacket, over his crotch, and into the street.

Tsion was pale, and his eyes threatened to roll back in his head. Buck leaned close to hear his shallow breathing. "Stay with me, friend," he said.

"Let me go, Cameron. Find shelter. I could do worse than die in the streets of my beloved city."

"You're not going to die, Tsion. You're going to hang on to see this victory, all right?"

"I wish."

"Don't wish! Work with me!"

Buck whipped off his jacket and his shirt, rolled up his shirt, and stuffed it into the wound. The hole was nearly the size of Buck's fist. "I have to get you to shelter," he said. "You up for a few more feet?"

"I am feeling nothing anymore, Cameron. You go. Please."

"I will not leave you here."

"Come, come. I will not be here long. We both know that."

"I'm taking you to the shelter."

"Do not do it for my sake."

"Then for mine."

Buck knew he was doing Tsion no good. The shirt popped out, and a great mass of blood gushed. Tsion moaned. Life seemed to be escaping him. His eyes were watery and pale, his lips blue. He had begun to shake all over.

Buck wrestled him into the shelter and tried stanching the blood flow again, but Tsion reached for him with weak, fluttery hands. He finally got hold of one of Buck's hands and pulled it toward him.

"Do not, friend. Please. It is too late."

"I don't want to lose you here, Tsion!"

"Come close," he whispered. "Listen to me." He was rasping now, taking labored breaths between words. "I can say . . . with Paul, 'I am already . . . being poured out . . . as a drink offering, and the time of my departure is at hand. . . . I have fought the good fight, I have finished the race, I have kept the faith. . . . Finally, there is laid up for me . . . the crown of righteousness, which the Lord, the righteous Judge, will give to me on that Day, and not to me only . . . but also to all who have loved His appearing.'"

"Tsion, don't! Stay with me!"

"Cameron . . . because of Jesus . . . my wife and children . . . forev—"

\+ + +

Sebastian had ordered another round from the DEWs, and Rayford had to admit it was something to watch as the front line of the pervasive mass fell back in agony, and the ripple effect could be seen for miles. Razor had the fifty-calibers ready in the event of a counterattack, but none came. That just made things weirder. The city of refuge, a million strong, sat like a pea in the middle of an ocean of enemies that seemed waiting to squash it.

Rayford's phone chirped, and he saw on the readout it was Buck. "Talk to me."

Buck's voice was thick. "He's gone."

"Tsion?"

"Hit in the chest. Nothing I could do."

"You need to get back here, Buck. We'll send somebody."

"They'll never get in, and I can't leave him."

"Buck! Come on. He's gone. I hate it too, but like you said, there was nothing you could do, and certainly nothing you can do now."

"Nobody could get in here, and I can't imagine getting out."

"You all right?"

"Didn't foresee this, frankly."

"Keep your phone handy. No sense doing anything foolish now. We've got to be very close to the end."

\+ + +

Buck crossed Tsion's feet at the ankles. He closed his jacket over the death wound and pulled Tsion's hands together, interlocking the fingers at his waist. Buck smoothed Tsion's hair, closed his eyes, and took a last look at his face. "You almost made it, friend," he said. He draped his jacket over Tsion's torso and face.

Brandishing both Uzis now, he headed for Herod's Gate, where two young rebels seemed to have a decent vantage point. It wasn't the safest spot, and it sure didn't fit Rayford's advice of not doing anything foolish. But Buck didn't know what else to do.

\+ + +

Mac was on the phone from the other side of the perimeter. "Rayford, if I was to ask Sebastian to lend you to us, you think that would be doable?"

"He'd probably be glad to get rid of me. Let me ask."

"What's he need?" George said.

"Mac? Sebastian wants to know what for."

"Don't want to say."

"That's not going to cut it with him; you know that."

"I'm supposed to tell him the truth?"

"Never hurts."

Mac whispered, "I need somebody to talk to. Smitty's about two hundred yards to the west, and Otto's drivin' me bats. Plus, for real, we could use some manpower here. Like I could use an ATV to check on my troops, east and west. You got as many Carpathia troops out your way as we do back here?"

"There's no end to them, Mac."

"I'm countin' on Jesus real soon. But in the meantime, could you come?"

22

GETTING TO THE TOP of the wall of the Old City, particularly by Herod's Gate, was no easy task. Buck didn't feel that old, but the two rebels already there were at least fifteen years younger. They nodded to him and pointed in the distance.

Unity Army troops were amassing on Jericho Road, on Suleiman Street, and in the garden where the traditional site of Jesus' tomb lay. Foot soldiers stretched as far as Buck could see—from the Rockefeller Museum on his right to the Church of St. Stephen past the garden, even as far as Hel Ha Handasa.

He and the two rebels were in plain sight, but the enemy seemed content to let them stay there. Buck wondered if Christ would return only in the middle of an active siege, or if he might appear any moment. He hoped the Remnant at Petra would not even have to know about Tsion until after the Glorious Appearing.

Buck worried about the troops behind the Rockefeller Museum. They seemed quieter, more clandestine than the others. And they were harder to see. He detected movement, but it was not hurried. He would have to keep an eye on that area.

Buck watched the sky. At the coming of Jesus he expected a heavy cloud cover to roll in, the sun to go dark, the earth to convulse. All that could happen in an instant, he knew, and when he allowed himself to dwell on it, the atmosphere seemed to crackle with tension.

+ + +

Sebastian told Rayford to "go ahead and hold Mac's hand. I swear, sometimes he's like an old woman. But let him wait. Go see Chang on your way. You can go up and in and then down and out and avoid the long way around."

"What's Chang need?"

"Just buck him up. The way he was talking to me the last few days, it was obvious he'd rather be out here than in the tech center. Tell him how crucial he is to us, all that. 'Course it's true, you know."

The route Sebastian suggested was tougher than Rayford expected. He had become fairly proficient on the machine, but the terrain was treacherous. He used the brake and lower gears more than ever and a couple of times found himself in rock formations that didn't allow him through. He had to put the ATV in neutral, ease back down, and try another route.

By the time he got to the tech center, he was exhausted and glad to have a break.

+ + +

A lot of quiet talk and planning seemed to be going on inside the Old City. Buck noticed several groups of particularly young rebels making their way toward the walls. He liked his perch and what he could see, but he wasn't so sure it was a good idea to put the front lines up top all the way around. And the more he watched, the clearer it became that that was precisely the decision someone had come to.

There was still a good strike force in the center of the city as well, but it was made up of the older men and some women. The prime fighting men, the teenagers and those in their early twenties, were taking their places at the top of the wall. Something about it niggled at the back of Buck's brain. There was a vulnerability about it, an all-or-nothing quality. He liked the idea of having options, but that was just for himself. He wasn't charged with defending the whole place.

+ + +

Chang had resigned himself to his role, but still he appreciated Rayford's comments and the fact that he had taken the time to stop in. Naomi came by, and the three sat before Chang's screen.

"We all believe the Millennium starts soon," Rayford said. "No later than tomorrow. That's why it's important the populace here not know what's happened to Tsion."

"Tsion?"

"He was killed."

"No!"

Rayford told what he had heard from Buck. Naomi hid her face in her hands, and while Chang wanted to comfort her, he too was overcome. "And Buck is all right?"

"So far, but they were in a very precarious location, and Buck still is."

"Can we get him out?"

"Wouldn't be worth the risk. He's pretty self-sufficient. Like everybody else, he's trying to keep Jews alive and, of course, himself, until the event the world has been anticipating for thousands of years."

Chang pointed to the screen, and they watched the latest GCNN newscast.

"Global Community Supreme Potentate Nicolae J. Carpathia has assembled the largest army in the history of mankind. As you can see in this aerial view, the One World Unity Army consists of all the soldiers, livestock, rolling stock, and munitions available anywhere. The fighting force of untold millions covers the plains of Israel from the Plain of Megiddo in the north to Bozrah in Edom in the south and stretches east to west almost the entire breadth of what was once known as the Holy Land.

"The ground forces are supported by air bases as far away as Cyprus and by aircraft carriers in the Mediterranean Sea, and troop transport ships in both the Gulf of Suez and the Gulf of Aqaba off the Red Sea.

"At this hour one-third of Carpathia's forces have surrounded Petra in Edom to the southeast in Jordan, hideout of the Judah-ite rebels. Global Community Security and Intelligence Director Suhail Akbar says Tsion Ben-Judah himself is ensconced at that location, and while the goal of the Unity Army is annihilation, there may be value in taking the leader alive.

"The other two-thirds of the Unity Army is poised to overtake the city of Jerusalem. Potentate Carpathia himself reports that nearly half the city has been occupied and that it is just a matter of time before the Old City is overrun.

"Earlier today in a press conference held while on horseback, the potentate was upbeat about the potential outcome."

Carpathia's face appeared on the monitor. "We are confident that these are the last two rebel enclaves in the world," he said, "and that once they have been thoroughly defeated and our enemies scattered, we will realize what we have so long dreamed of: an entire world of peace and harmony. There is no place in a true global community for rebellion. If our government was anything but benevolent or did not have the attitude of 'citizen first,' there might be cause for dissention. But all we have ever attempted to do was create a utopia for society.

"It is most unfortunate that it comes to this, that we have to resort to bloodshed to achieve our goals. But we will do what we have to do."

Someone asked, "Doesn't the size of your global army seem like overkill?"

"An excellent question," Carpathia cooed, his leathers squeaking as he reset himself on his horse. "No effort in the cause of world peace is wasted. The rebel factions have proved surprisingly formidable. We have decided at the highest levels to be sure we leave nothing to chance this time. We will use whatever we need, everything that is at our disposal, to succeed."

"Is there any truth to the speculation that you are overarmed in anticipation of running into surprising support for the opposition, that perhaps their God might intervene on their behalf?"

Carpathia chuckled. "I do not worry about fairy tales, but even if they did have supernatural help, they would be no match for our fighting machine. By our numbers alone, even unarmed, we could win any war by continuing to replenish our ranks. But we also happen to be fully equipped with the best and latest technology."

"Why not win this war all at once? What's the delay?"

"I am a man of peace. I always believe first in diplomacy and negotiation. The window of opportunity for settling this peacefully is always open. I had hoped that the enemies of peace would be persuaded by our size and would come to the bargaining table. But our patience is running out. They seem markedly uninterested in any reasonable solution, and we are prepared to use any means necessary. So it is just a matter of time now."

+ + +

By midday, with the sun riding high, Buck was famished. He gingerly made his way down from the wall when volunteers brought foodstuffs in for the fighters. He gulped fruit and bread and cheese, and climbed up again. The army seemed to be taking a lunch break too. Buck wished the rebels had larger weapons. Maybe a surprise attack would do some damage. On the other hand, a sleeping giant was a gentler giant, and perhaps it made sense to leave things as they were.

He hated the idea of just waiting for the other side to attack, but with the front lines atop the wall now, at least that wouldn't be a surprise when it came.

+ + +

Rayford started down the back side of Petra, finding it even more harrowing than coming up. He had stayed with Chang and Naomi a little longer than he had planned, so he assumed Mac would be looking for him and that George thought he had already arrived.

From his vantage point he had a good view of the army a mile off. He was reaching for his phone to reassure Mac when it became clear something had happened. The front lines were recoiling again, so George must have initiated another burst of the directed energy weapons.

This time, however, despite the ensuing chaos, the Unity Army didn't take it sitting down. Rayford heard the booms of retaliatory fire, like thunder from a storm head a hundred miles wide. He knew enough about munitions to know that Carpathia's forces were a little far away to be using the mortar cannons and shooting at high angles. He guessed the shells would drop short of the Petra perimeter.

He was wrong. Maybe their cannons were bigger than the typical unrifled short barrels. The shells flew past the perimeter and began dropping all around him. When one exploded right in front of him, Rayford was nearly pitched off the ATV. Grabbing for the handlebar with his free hand, he saw his phone go flying, bouncing a hundred yards down the rocky steep.

And now his vehicle was out of control. He bounced high off the seat and realized he was soaring through the air with only his hands attached to the ATV. He came down hard, and the contraption bounced and rolled sideways. To hang on or not was the only thing on his mind, and quickly that option was gone too. The four-wheeler hit yet again, ripping his grip away. As he bounced and rolled, he kept picking up the sight of the vehicle disintegrating as it smashed into rocks all the way into a valley.

Rayford reminded himself not to try to break his own fall. He tucked hands and arms in and tried to relax, fighting his natural instinct for all he was worth. The grade was too steep and his speed too fast to control himself. The best he could wish for was a soft landing place.

A shell deafened him from about ten feet to his right, knocking him into a sideways roll. Rayford felt his temple smash into a sharp rock and was aware of what sounded like rushing water as he rolled toward thorny overgrowth. Scary as the thorns looked, they had to be softer than what he had been hitting.

Rayford was able to shift his body weight as he slowed and backed into the thorns. It was then he realized what the liquid sound was. With each beat of his heart, galloping now, his life's blood spurted six feet from the wound in his temple.

He pressed his palm hard against his head and felt the gush against his hand. He pressed with all his might and felt he might be containing it somewhat. But Rayford was in danger now—mortal danger. No one knew exactly where he was. He was without communications or transportation. He didn't even want to inventory his injuries, because regardless, they were minor compared to the hole in his head. He had to get help—and fast—or he would be dead in minutes.

Rayford's arms were gashed, and he felt sharp pains in both knees and one ankle. He reached with his free hand to pull up his pant leg and wished he hadn't. Not only had something sliced the flesh from his ankle, but something had taken part of the bone too.

Could he walk? Dare he try? He was too far from anywhere to crawl. He waited for his pulse to abate and for his equilibrium to return. He had to be a mile from Mac and his people, and he could not see them. There was no going back up. He rolled up onto his feet, squatting, one hand desperately trying to keep himself from bleeding to death.

Rayford tried to stand. Only one leg worked, and it was the one with the nearly totaled ankle. He may have broken a shinbone in the other. He tried to hop, but the incline was so great, he found himself pitching forward again. And now he was out of control one more time, trying to hop to keep from falling but picking up speed with every bounce. Whatever he did, he could not take his hand from his temple, and he dared not land on one more hard thing. "Lord, now would be a most appropriate time for you to come."

+ + +

Chang sensed something was about to give. He had succeeded in intercepting signals from geosynchronous satellites that supported communications among the millions of troops. They were about to move, and his key people needed to know.

He called George. "Expect an advance within sixty seconds," he said.

"We've already been shelled," George yelled. "You mean more than that?"

"Yes, they will be coming."

"Rayford see you?"

"Left a little while ago. On his way to see Mac."

"Thanks. Call Mac, would you? I'll inform the others."

Chang called and told Mac the same.

"Hey," Mac said, "I can't raise Sebastian, and Ray is overdue."

"On his way," Chang said.

He called Buck. "Expect ad—"

But he was cut off. He redialed. Nothing.

+ + +

"They're coming! They're coming!"

Buck heard a young rebel shrieking just as his phone chirped and he saw an incendiary device hurled over the Rockefeller Museum, right at his position. He saw Unity Army troop movement from every side, and he grabbed his phone and held it up to his ear just as the bomb hit the wall right in front of him and clattered to the ground outside.

He recognized Chang's voice just before the bomb blew a hole in the wall. Rock and shrapnel slammed his whole right side, killed his phone, and made him drop one Uzi. He felt something give way in his hip and his neck as his perch disintegrated.

One of the young boys near him had been blown into the air and cartwheeled to the pavement. Buck was determined to ride the wall as it fell. He reached for his neck and felt a torrent of blood. He was no medical student, but he could tell something had sliced his carotid artery—no small problem.

As the wall crumbled, he danced and high-stepped to stay upright, but he had to keep a hand on his neck. The remaining Uzi slid down into his left hand, but when he stabbed it into something to keep his balance, it fell away. He was unarmed, falling, and mortally wounded.

And the enemy was coming.

+ + +

Rayford could break his fall only with his free hand, not daring to take pressure off his temple. His chin took as much of the brunt as the heel of his hand as he slid at what he guessed was a forty-five-degree angle. There would be no walking. All he could do was crawl now and try to stay alive.

+ + +

Buck's feet caught in a crevasse of shifting rock, and his upper body flopped forward. He was hanging upside down from the crumbling wall over the Old City. His hip was torn and bleeding too, and blood rushed to his head.

+ + +

Even inside the tech center of a city made of rock, Chang felt the vibration of the millions of soldiers advancing on Petra. He was clicking here and there, flipping switches, and trying to make calls. How far would God let this go before sending the conquering King?

+ + +

Fighting unconsciousness, he tried gingerly edging along, one hand ahead of him, the other occupied. Each inch made the angle seem steeper, the way more unstable. With every beat of his heart, every rush of blood, every stab of pain, he wondered what was the use. How important was it to stay alive? For what? For whom? "Come, Lord Jesus."

Dizziness overwhelmed, pain stabbed. A lung had to be punctured. His breath came in wheezes, agonizing, piercing. The first hint of the end was the crazy rhythm of his heart. Racing, then skipping, then fluttering. Too much blood loss. Not enough to the brain. Not enough oxygen. Drowsiness overtook panic. Unconsciousness would be such a relief.

And so he allowed it. The lung was ready to burst. The heart fluttered and stopped. The pulsing blood became a pool.

He saw nothing through wide-open eyes. "Lord, please." He heard the approach of the enemy. He felt it. But soon he felt nothing. With no blood pumping, no air moving, he fell limp and died.

GLORIOUS APPEARING

To the memories of Frank LaHaye and Harry Jenkins,
whom we shall again see

Special thanks to David Allen for expert technical consultation and to John Perrodin for additional biblical research

1

MAC MCCULLUM SCANNED the Petra perimeter with high-powered field glasses. Rayford should have reached him by now.

Mac's watch showed 1300 hours—one in the afternoon, Carpathia Time. It had to be more than a hundred degrees Fahrenheit. Sweat ran down his neck from the grayish red hair peeking out from under his cap, soaking his shirt. Mac detected not even a wisp of wind and wondered what his freckled, leathery face would look like in a few days.

Without taking his eyes from the lenses, Mac unholstered his phone and punched in the connection to Chang Wong in the computer center. "Where's Ray?"

"I was about to ask you," Chang said. "He left here forty-five minutes ago, and no one else has seen him either."

"What do we hear from Buck?"

Mac noticed the hesitation. "Nothing new."

"Since when?"

"Uh, Rayford heard from him late this morning."

"And?"

Another beat. "Nothing to speak of."

"What're you sayin', Chang?"

"Nothing."

"I gathered. What's wrong?"

"Nothing that won't be cured in a little—"

"I don't need double-talk, buddy." Mac continued surveying the rocky slopes, feeling his pulse quicken despite his years and experience. "If you won't tell me, I'll call him myself."

"Buck?"

"Well, who else?"

"I've tried. My sensor shows his phone inoperable."

"Turned off?"

"Unlikely, Mr. McCullum."

"Well, I should guess so. Malfunctioning? Damaged?"

"I'm hoping the former, sir."

"Global Positioning System active, at least?"

"No, sir."

+ + +

Chaim Rosenzweig had not slept, and after only two light meals of manna, he expected to feel the fatigue. But no. The best he could calculate, this was the day. He felt the swelling anticipation in both his head and his chest. It was as if his mind raced as his heart ached for the greatest event in the history of the cosmos.

The old man's senior advisers, a half-dozen elders, sat with him deep in the stone compound of Petra. Eleazar Tiberius, a broad globe of a man, offered that the million-plus pilgrims under their charge "are clearly as restless as we. Is there nothing we can tell them?"

"I have an activity in mind," Chaim said. "But what would you have me say?"

"I am newer to this than you, Rabbi, but—"

"Please," Chaim said, raising a hand. "Reserve such a title for Dr. Ben-Judah. I am merely a student, thrust into this—"

"Nonetheless," Eleazar continued, "I sense the populace is as eager as I to know the exact moment of Messiah's return. I mean, if it is, as you and Dr. Ben-Judah have for so long taught, seven years from the signing of the covenant between Antichrist and Israel, does that mean it will be to the minute? I recall the signing being at around four in the afternoon, Israel time, seven years ago today."

Chaim smiled. "I have no idea. I do know this: God has His own economy of time. Do I believe Messiah will return today? Yes. Will it trouble me if He does not appear until tomorrow? No. My faith will not be shaken. But I expect Him soon."

"And this activity you mentioned?"

"Yes, something to occupy the minds of the people while we wait. I came across a videodisc of a dramatic sermon from before the turn of the century by an African-American preacher, long since in heaven, of course. I propose calling the people together and showing it."

"The Lord may come while it is playing," an elder said.

"So much the better."

"There remain unbelievers among us," Eleazar said.

Chaim shook his head. "I confess that puzzles and disturbs me, but it also fulfills prophecy. There are those who enjoy the safety of Petra, even many who believe Jesus was the most influential person who ever lived, who have not yet put their faith in Him. They do not recognize Him as the long-awaited Messiah, and they have not acknowledged Him as their Savior. This sermon is also evangelistic. Perhaps many of the undecided will take their stand before Messiah appears."

"Better than waiting until the event itself," someone said.

"Gather the people for a two-o'clock showing," Chaim said, rising. "And let's close in prayer."

"Begging your pardon," Eleazar said, "but do you feel the absence of Dr. Ben-Judah as keenly as I do?"

"More than you know, Eleazar. Let's pray for him right now, and I will call him in a few minutes. I would love to share his greeting with the people and hear what has been happening in Jerusalem."

✢ ✢ ✢

Mac's magnified vision fell upon colorful, metallic pieces glinting in the sun, perhaps a mile from his position. *Oh no.*

A red fuel tank and a tire looked very much like parts from Rayford's all-terrain vehicle. Mac tried to steady his hands as he panned in a wide arc, looking for signs of his friend. It appeared the ATV could have been hit by a heat-seeking missile or smashed to bits by tumbling. Perhaps, he thought, no sign of Rayford nearby was good news.

Mac raised Chang again. "Sorry to be a nuisance," he said, "but what does your sensor say about Ray's phone?"

"I was afraid you'd ask. It's inoperable too, but its GPS is still pulsing. My screen shows it deep in a narrow crevasse a little over forty-five hundred feet below you."

"I'm heading down there."

"Wait, Mr. McCullum."

"What?"

"I've got a lens pointed that way, and there's no room in the opening for a person."

"You can see the phone?"

"No, but I know it's there. It can be the only thing there. The opening is too narrow for anything else."

"So have you seen his ATV too?"

"I'm looking."

"Well, I have. If that phone is due south of me, look about twenty degrees east."

"Hang on . . . I see it."

"But no sign of Ray, Chang. I'm going to look."

"Sir? Could you send someone else?"

"Why? I'm twiddling my thumbs here. Big Dog One has the troops under control."

"Frankly, I'd rather you go to Jerusalem."

"You gonna tell me what's goin' on?"

"Come see me, Mr. McCullum. I was honoring the confidence of Captain Steele, but I think you—and Dr. Rosenzweig—should know."

Mac arrived at the tech center, deep in the bowels of Petra, a few minutes after one thirty in the afternoon. Chaim rose to meet him while Chang acknowledged him with a look but kept turning back to his numerous screens. Finally Chang pulled away and the three sat, far from the ears of others. Mac noticed, however, that many techies and others frequently stole glances in their direction.

"There's no delicate way to say this," Chang began. "Captain Steele told Naomi and me this morning that Mr. Williams had told him that Dr. Ben-Judah was killed in the fighting at Jerusalem."

Mac stiffened.

Chaim buried his face in his hands. "I hope he did not suffer terribly," the old man said.

"With Captain Steele missing now and—"

"What? Him too?" Chaim said. "And I am unable to raise Cameron on the phone. . . ."

"I felt you both should know. I mean, I know this may all be moot by this time tomorrow."

"Perhaps even by four this afternoon," Chaim said. "The question now is what to say, what to do."

"Nothin' we *can* do," Mac said. "I've got Abdullah Smith looking for Ray. Chang here thinks I ought to go to Jerusalem."

Chaim looked up in apparent surprise.

"I do," Chang said. "From the looks of what's left of his vehicle and his phone, odds are all Mr. Smith is going to find are Captain Steele's remains. I'm sorry to be so blunt."

"But a flight to Jerusalem now?" Chaim said. "Just to see whether Cameron—"

"It's what I would want if it was me," Mac said. "I know he may be dead, and either way, Jesus is comin', but with Tsion gone, I'd just as soon get Buck outta there and back here with us."

"Even for as little as an hour," Chaim said, more a statement than a question.

"Like I say, that's what I'd want."

"And what do we tell the people?" Chaim said.

Minutes later, Mac was in Gus Zuckermandel's quarters. He filled in the young man on his plans. "And here's the hard part, Z. I want to leave in ten minutes."

"Can you give me twenty?"

"Fifteen."

"Deal."

"What've you got, Z?" Mac said, as the forger yanked open a file drawer, riffled through several folders, and slapped one open on his desk.

"Your new identity," Zeke said, moving to a closet, which he opened with a flourish. There were two dozen black-on-black Global Community Unity Army uniforms, from tinted eye-shield helmets to calf-length boots. "Find one that fits while I'm working on your documents. Don't forget the gloves. Nobody's checking for marks of loyalty anymore anyway, but just to be safe."

"How do you do this, Z?" Mac said, approaching garments that looked his size.

"With lots of help. Sebastian's boys have killed a few of 'em, and I got me a little crew that runs out and gathers up their stuff—papers, clothes, and all."

"Weapons?"

"'Course."

When Mac emerged with the uniform a perfect fit, he found Zeke mixing some sort of a brew.

"You look good, Mac," he said. "Problem is, you got to be black."

"And you can manage that in a few minutes?"

"If you're game."

"Whatever it takes."

Mac whipped off his helmet, jacket, shirt, and gloves. Zeke used the mix to paint him dark brown from the shoulders to the hairline. "Keep the helmet on, 'cause I haven't got time to make the hair authentic."

"Check."

"And let's do your hands, just in case." Zeke dyed Mac's skin from mid-forearm to fingertips. "This should dry in two and a half minutes. Then an instant photo, and you're on your way. Give my best to Buck and Tsion."

Mac hesitated. "You betcha. Zeke, you're a genius."

The younger man snorted. "Just here to serve."

Mac was sprinting to a chopper when he reached Abdullah Smith by phone.

"Nothing yet, Mac. I will let you know as soon as I discover anything."

As Mac lifted off, he saw multitudes streaming from all corners of Petra and gathering at the central meeting place.

+ + +

Chaim was alarmed at the mood of the throng. It was the biggest crowd he had ever drawn at Petra, and it was noisy, clearly preoccupied, antsy. He heard nervous laughter, saw lots of embracing. When one or two would look to the skies, hundreds—sometimes thousands—did likewise.

"My beloved brothers and sisters in Messiah," he began, "as well as the seekers and undecided among us, please try to quiet yourselves and settle for a moment. Please! I know we all expect the imminent return of our Lord and Savior, and I can think of no greater privilege than to have Him appear as we speak. But—"

He was interrupted by thunderous applause and cheering.

Chaim gestured that they should be seated. "I share your enthusiasm! And while I know that there will be nothing else on your minds until He comes, I thought there might be value in focusing specifically on Him this afternoon. I know there remain among us many who are withholding their decisions about Him until He appears. Consider this my last effort to persuade you not to wait. We do not know what may befall us at that moment, whether God will allow scoffers and mockers and rejecters to change their minds. Pray He will not harden your heart due to your rebellion or unbelief. Surely there has been more than enough evidence than anyone could need to reveal the truth of God's plan.

"While we watch and wait, consider the thoughts of a great preacher from decades past. His name was Dr. Shadrach Meshach Lockridge, and his message is entitled 'My King Is . . .'"

Chaim signaled for the disc to play, and it was projected off two white walls of smooth stone, each several stories high, where all could see it. The sound system carried it to the ends of the seated masses.

Lockridge proved to be animated and thunderous, interrupting his own cadence of shouts and growls with whispers and huge smiles. The disc caught him near the end of his sermon, and he was picking up steam.

"The Bible says my king is a seven-way king. He's the king of the Jews; that's a racial king. He's the king of Israel; that's a national king. He's the king of righteousness. He's the king of the ages. He's the king of heaven. He's the king of glory. He's the king of kings. Besides being a seven-way king, He's the Lord of lords. That's my king. Well, I wonder, do you know Him?"

Hundreds of thousands applauded, and many stood, only to sit again as Lockridge continued.

"David said, 'The heavens declare the glory of God, and the firmament showeth His handiwork.' My king is a sovereign king. No means of measure can define His limitless love. No far-seeing telescope can bring into visibility the coastline of His shoreless supply. No barrier can hinder Him from pouring out His blessings.

"He's enduringly strong. He's entirely sincere. He's eternally steadfast. He's immortally graceful. He's infinitely powerful. He's impartially merciful. Do you know Him?"

Many shouted their agreement.

"He's the greatest phenomenon that has ever crossed the horizon of this world. He's God's Son. He's the sinner's Savior. He's the centerpiece of civilization. He stands in the solitude of Himself. He's honest and He's unique. He's unparalleled. He's unprecedented.

"He is the loftiest idea in literature. He's the highest personality in philosophy. He is the supreme problem in higher criticism. He's the fundamental doctrine of true theology. He's the core, the necessity for spiritual religion. He's the miracle of the ages. Yes, He is. He's the superlative of everything good that you choose to call Him. He's the only one qualified to be our all-sufficiency. I wonder if you know Him today."

As the preacher continued, more and more listeners stood, some raising their hands, others shouting agreement, others nodding.

"He supplies strength for the weak. He's available for the tempted and tried. He sympathizes and He saves. He strengthens and sustains. He guards and He guides. He heals the sick. He cleanses the leper. He forgives the sinner. He discharges debtors. He delivers the captive. He defends the feeble. He blesses the young. He serves the unfortunate. He regards the aged. He rewards the diligent. And He beautifies the meek. I wonder if you know Him.

"Well, this is my king. He's the key to knowledge. He's the wellspring of wisdom. He's the doorway of deliverance. He's the pathway of peace. He's the roadway of righteousness. He's the highway of holiness. He's the gateway of glory. Do you know Him?

"Well, His office is manifold. His promise is sure. His life is matchless. His goodness is limitless. His mercy is everlasting. His love never changes. His word is enough. His grace is sufficient. His reign is righteous. His yoke is easy and His burden is light. I wish I could describe Him to you."

That elicited an ocean of laughter and more applause. The same had happened with his original audience, and Lockridge had paused, allowing it to fade before he continued.

"He's indescribable. He's incomprehensible. He's invincible. He's irresistible.

Well, you can't get Him out of your mind. You can't get Him off of your hand. You can't outlive Him and you can't live without Him. The Pharisees couldn't stand Him, but they found they couldn't stop Him. Pilate couldn't find any fault in Him. Herod couldn't kill Him. Death couldn't handle Him, and the grave couldn't hold Him. That's my king!"

Everyone was standing now, hands raised, many applauding, shouting, some dancing.

"And Thine is the kingdom and the power and the glory forever and ever and ever and ever! How long is that? And ever and ever! And when you get through with all the forevers, then amen! Good God Almighty! Amen!"

+ + +

By the time Mac found himself within sight of the rocky Judean hills where Jerusalem lay smoking in the early afternoon sun, he had begun to despair of finding Buck. If he was all right, would he not have borrowed a phone to check in? The latest intelligence from Chang was that Buck had reported Tsion's death to Rayford from inside the Old City.

Though the colossal armies of the world—now amalgamated into Carpathia's Global Community Unity Army—stretched by the multimillions from north of Jerusalem to Edom, it was clear from the air that the current major offensive focused on the Old City.

Mac looked for a place to land. He had to look like a GC officer on assignment and head on foot to the Old City as if he knew what he was doing. In fact, he didn't have a clue. The Old City was only a third of a mile square. And if he found Buck alive, what was he to do? Arrest him and muscle him to the chopper? Finding Buck dead or alive, Mac decided, would be like discovering a patch of dry ground in the Louisiana bayou.

Mac's phone chirped, and he saw it was Chang. "Give me some good news."

"Such as?"

"Such as Buck's dead phone all of a sudden started showin' his position."

"No such luck. But I do have something. Carpathia's on the rampage about the destruction of New Babylon, and he's taking heat from all over the world."

"Heat?"

"Everybody who depended on New Babylon is crying over the loss. I'm picking up televised reports from everywhere of leaders, diplomats, businessmen—you name it—literally weeping, decrying what's become of New Babylon and their own interests. Some are committing suicide right on camera."

"No way the GC is puttin' that stuff on the air."

"No, *they* aren't, but yours truly still has his ways."

"Attaboy, Chang, but how does that help me find Buck?"

"You're not going to find Buck, Mr. McCullum."

"What? You know that for sure?"

"I'm just stating the obvious."

"Ye of little faith."

"Sorry. But I figured as long as you're there and undercover, you might want to know where Carpathia is."

"I don't care where he is. I'm here to find Buck."

"All right then."

"But just for smiles, where is he? Last I heard he was on a bullhorn outside Herod's Gate. Moved there from his bunker near the Sea of Galilee. Unless they were just broadcasting his voice."

"No, it was him all right. He's moved his entire command post inside the Old City."

"Impossible. I'm lookin' down on it right now, and the place is crawling with—"

"I thought so too until I heard where. Underground."

"You don't mean—"

"Solomon's Stables."

"How do I get in there?"

"Follow somebody. Carpathia's got an entire regiment there, and I got your new name on the list."

"That might not have been prudent, Chang."

"Why?"

"What if I choose not to go, am discovered missing, and someone sees me elsewhere?"

"Well, there *is* that possibility, yes. Tell them you're on your way."

"What if I'm not? I mean, I'd love to be your eyes and ears here, Chang, but my priority is Buck. And nothin' we know about Carpathia now is going to amount to a hill of beans anyway. What's gonna happen is gonna happen. Can you get me off that list?"

"Not without looking suspicious. Sorry, Mr. McCullum. I thought I was doing the right—"

"Don't worry about it. None of it will matter tomorrow, will it?"

Mac saw GC activity and other choppers putting down at the Tombs of the Prophets, south of the Mount of Olives, east of the Old City. Caravans of jeeps quickly loaded the disgorged personnel and raced them toward the conflict. As soon as Mac stepped out of his copter at 2:45 p.m., an officer directing traffic pointed him to an armored personnel carrier. Mac saluted and jogged that way.

He joined a dozen other like-uniformed soldiers, who merely nodded at each other, tight-lipped, and rode in stony silence.

The cavalcade headed north on Jericho Road and turned west in front of the Rockefeller Museum onto Suleiman Street.

"We headed to Herod's Gate?" someone said.

"Is it open?" someone else said.

"Damascus Gate," the driver announced.

As they passed Herod's Gate, Mac joined the others in pressing against the windows on the south side of the vehicle. Somehow the resistance continued to hold the gate.

"If you're assigned to the potentate," the driver said, "follow me to the entrance to the stables. Everybody else head for the staging area at the Church of the Flagellation. When we have enough personnel, we'll attack the insurgents from behind and blow 'em out Herod's Gate."

Mac felt himself swelling with pride over what Tsion and Buck had apparently accomplished before the rabbi was killed. If they had been at Herod's Gate, they were responsible for helping hold that position against overwhelming odds. *And neither of them battle trained.*

Mac assumed Buck would agree that Tsion would not want his body removed from the Old City. He only hoped Buck had found an appropriate spot for the rabbi. Bodies fallen in an active battle had a way of getting trampled beyond recognition. That wouldn't matter tomorrow either, but Mac knew he and Buck would be on the same page.

Mac found himself fighting anguish. No way Buck would let them worry and wonder for this long. Surely he could have found a way to check in if he was alive.

When the vehicle stopped and the driver gave the order, Mac and the soldiers got out and moved as directed. Mac dropped several paces behind his group and phoned Chang, speaking quietly. "Anything?"

"Nothing."

"I'm not going to succeed, am I?"

"What do you want to hear, sir?"

"You know."

"I'm past pretending, Mr. McCullum."

"I appreciate that. Maybe I should just proceed to my assignment."

"To the compound?"

"Yeah. I know I should have my head examined, but I'd love to be with ol' Nick when Jesus gets here."

+ + +

Chang felt Naomi's strong fingers on either side of his neck.

"You're tense," she said.

"Aren't you?" he said.

"Relax, love. Messiah is coming."

Chang couldn't turn from the screens. "I'd like to lose no one else before that. No matter how much I tell myself they'll be dead only a short while, it all seems so pointless now. I don't want anyone hurt, let alone suffering, then dying. Mr. McCullum's going was my idea."

"But he sure jumped on it, didn't he?"

"I knew he would. I wish I could have gone."

"You know this place can't function without your—"

"Don't start, Naomi."

"You know it's true."

"Regardless, I sent him for my own vicarious thrill. No way he's going to find Buck, and if he does, Buck will be dead. Then what's Mac supposed to do? If he gets found out, he's history. And for what? He could be here watching for the return with everyone else."

Naomi pulled a chair next to Chang and sat. "What do you hear from Mr. Smith?"

Chang sighed. "That's turned out to be a waste of time and manpower too. So far he hasn't found a thing. Either Captain Steele was obliterated by a missile or he was buried in the sand."

"Could he have crawled to safety?"

"There's no safety in that sun, Naomi."

"That's what I mean. Maybe he found shelter or built himself some shield against the heat."

Chang shrugged. "Best-case scenario, I guess. But wouldn't he think to leave some sign for us?"

"Maybe he was hurt too badly or simply had no resources."

"He could arrange sticks or rocks, even a piece of clothing."

"If he was able," Naomi said.

Chang's phone chirping made them both jump. "Yes, Mr. Smith?"

"I'm on his trail. He was on the move for a while, at least."

"What did you find?"

"Blood, I'm afraid."

2

MAC HAD NEVER SEEN the ancient walls of Jerusalem in such a state. While Herod's Gate (some still called it the Flower Gate) was somehow still held by the resistance, places on either side of the walls had been blasted from their normal forty-foot height to half that. It would be only a matter of time before the Unity Army pushed through.

But for now the invading force seemed to be concentrating elsewhere. Mac would make sure he was last in line when the unit he was with jogged through the Damascus Gate. That way he could peel off at any time. He could find the entrance to the underground stables somehow, but not until he had at least tried to locate Buck.

Past sixty now, Mac remained fit with a daily run. But while the borrowed uniform looked as if it were made for him, the boots were going to leave blisters. As he hurried along, invisible in a sea of similarly attired plunderers, he recognized the irony that he could easily take a bullet from snipers who didn't realize he was on their side of the conflict.

Mac had seen enough carnage in seven years to last an eternity, but nothing could have steeled him against the images that came into view as his little unit mince-stepped into the Old City. The narrow cobblestone streets that snaked through the markets and crowded houses were so full of broken and dead bodies that he had to keep his focus to keep from tripping over them. His eyes darted everywhere, looking for Buck, praying he was not already on the ground.

Mac's nostrils were assaulted by smoke, sweat, gunpowder, burning flesh, manure, and the sickly sweet stench of overturned fruit and vegetable carts. He recoiled at two quick gunshots until he saw it was a Unity Army commander putting a horse and a mule out of their misery.

A bullhorn announced that Unity forces had occupied the Armenian Quarter to the south, the Christian Quarter to the west, and much of the Jewish Quarter outside the Temple Mount. The insurgents still held the Temple Mount to the southeast and the Muslim Quarter to the northeast, from Herod's Gate to just east of the Church of the Flagellation. Mac wondered how Carpathia and his staff had access to Solomon's Stables beneath the Temple Mount.

He prayed that Buck was somewhere in the Muslim Quarter or the Temple Mount, knowing that if he found him anywhere else, Buck was likely dead. If only Mac could "capture" Buck and convincingly drag him out of the Old City . . .

Unity Army foot soldiers were filling the west side of the Church of the Flagellation, avoiding the other side, which was taking fire from the rebels. A GC commander shouted that the assembled were to be ready to storm the Pools of Bethesda after the next artillery volley.

"The rebels have apparently constructed a makeshift shrine to a dead rabbi there. They'll be easy to spot. The body is hidden, but they have surrounded it with personnel and cardboard signs pleading that no one defile his resting place. We're less than five minutes from a mortar launch that will obliterate that whole site. We will shell the enclave in such a way that there will be no escape through the Lion's Gate to the east. Survivors will be pushed north toward Herod's Gate, and we'll be right behind them. The gate they have so ferociously held since yesterday they will now open themselves."

The commander assigned various troops and platoons, some to follow the shelling of the pools and others to attack the fleeing rebels as they headed toward Herod's Gate.

Mac racked his brain. There was no escaping now. He was deep inside this. While he would not, of course, fire upon the Unity Army's enemies, neither could he risk being seen shooting GC forces. Surely it was Tsion's remains the rebels were foolishly trying to protect, and he couldn't imagine Buck having a part in that. Buck would have tried to entomb the body, but he would know the futility and meaninglessness of staying to guard it.

Was there a prayer that in the midst of the chaos Mac could raise his visor and be identified as a believer by even one of the rebels? Not all were believers themselves, of course. He could be seen by one and shot by another. What was he doing here? His odds were infinitely smaller than he dreamed, and getting worse every second.

"Come, Lord Jesus."

+ + +

Chang had broadcast the S. M. Lockridge presentation all over the world, having hacked into the Global Community's broadcast center. The GC had been getting better at countering such invasions, but the sermon was short enough that it was over by the time they reacted. Chang also monitored the reaction to the message by those assembled at Petra.

Naomi said, "It's time to step out into the sun to see for yourself."

"I'm kind of locked in here," he said.

"There's nothing more you can do now," she said. "And you don't want to be inside when Jesus comes, do you?"

He looked at his watch. "If the elders are right, we've still got some time. Believe me, I'll be out there before four. I'll tell you what's most bizarre about all this: the reports from all over the globe that Carpathia won't allow to be broadcast."

"Everybody crying over the destruction of Babylon?"

"Exactly. They have no clue what's coming, so they can't think of anything worse than that."

"But look," she said, pointing to the screen monitoring the Petra crowd. "Hundreds, maybe thousands, are kneeling. Let's go see if they need people to counsel or—"

"In a minute. Let me show you some of these . . . look."

But in the reflection of the screen, Chang saw her leaving. Her priorities were right, he knew, and he stood to follow. He quickly realized how long he had been sitting in one spot. He ached head to toe and stretched as he continued to watch his screens. "I should check with Mr. Smith!" he called out.

"He knows your number," Naomi shot back.

"I'll be right with you," he said.

"I'm not waiting."

"I'll find you."

"I hope so."

From New York, Brussels, London, Buenos Aires, the Persian Gulf, Tokyo, Beijing, Toronto, Moscow, Johannesburg, New Delhi, Sydney, Paris, and other major cities came the laments of those in power. As they began their prepared remarks about the difficulty of suddenly being ripped away from New Babylon, of losing computer contact with the source of commerce and leadership, to a man or woman each began to weep. Their shoulders heaved, their lips quivered, their voices caught. From everywhere came vivid pictures of giants of commerce disintegrating into sobs.

"All is lost!" the woman in charge of the Tokyo Exchange wailed. "Had we been able to restore our connections within twenty-four hours, this might have been salvageable, but our entire economy is tied to New Babylon, and to see the pictures of her lying in utter ruin, smoke rising into space, well, it's just, just . . . hopeless!" And she fell apart. Moments later came the report that she had committed suicide, as had many in the sub-potentate's cabinet there.

A captain of industry from Europe announced that he had thousands of ships at sea that would virtually be dead in the water before the next sunrise.

Unity Army officials in the United North American States submitted their resignations en masse, "knowing that we face court-martial and execution," because they had lost all their resources and would not be able to send reinforcements to Armageddon. "And wait until the millions of troops already marshaled there realize that no more food is coming, let alone any pay."

As countless such reports flooded GC broadcast headquarters, some opportunistic official there kept forwarding them to Carpathia and asking what should be done.

Chang intercepted all such interactions and was amused at Carpathia's obvious rage. "Do not make me say it again," Carpathia shot back. "No such reports are to be made public. I am not to be quoted except to say that this seemingly devastating loss will be remedied by our victory in the Jezreel Valley, in Edom, and especially in Jerusalem, where I shall establish my eternal kingdom as the one and only true god. The temporary losses of finances and commerce will be forgotten once I have ushered in the ultimate New World Order. There will no longer be a shred of opposition from man or spirit, and this planet will become a paradise of bounty for all."

Chang hurried out and joined Naomi. "Sometimes I think I'm looking forward to the end of all this just so I can get some rest."

Naomi laughed and mimicked him. "Good to see You, Lord. Can I get back to You after a nap?"

+ + +

"Go now, now, now!" the Unity Army commander hollered, rousting Mac and the other troops and their platoons out of the Church of the Flagellation. "You will be exposed only briefly! The mortars will be launched from behind you, and by the time the rebels take aim, they will be struck. Go! Go! Go!"

The troops, most half Mac's age or younger, looked wide-eyed and panicky, but they seemed to gather strength and courage from one another. Again Mac maneuvered so he was at the back as they sprinted toward the Pools of Bethesda. "Ten seconds!" came the bullhorned announcement from behind them, but it came too late. Those in the front, clearly terrified that they had come within firing range of the resistance, slowed and many stopped, crouching and aiming.

That caused those behind to run into them, and many were trampled. Mac heard swearing and screaming just before the rebels opened fire. Unity forces quickly retaliated, but every second without supporting mortar fire made them more vulnerable. To Mac it seemed as if the crowd was about to turn back in a rage, firing upon their own superiors.

And the mortars were launched. Because so many in front of Mac had dropped, he had a clear view of the scruffy rebels, their faces mirroring the terror of seeing mortar shells arcing directly at their positions. They were shoulder to shoulder, not uniformed, pale and wasted from surviving more than most of their comrades had been able to endure. They had proudly stood their ground and defied the GC to overrun them and their shrine, but in an instant it would all be over.

They could see it coming, see it happening, and Mac read it in their eyes. None turned away. There would be no escaping. Many apparently decided to go down fighting. They death-gripped their Uzis, rattling off loud bursts even as the first mortar shell hit and sent dozens of them flying in pieces.

The next hit a split second later and the place became a crater, with a hundred dead or dying and three times that many scurrying for the closest gate. As had been the plan, those who opted for the Lion's Gate to the east were quickly killed or sent scampering back by yet another mortar round. Now, as scripted, those resistance forces remaining were running for their lives toward Herod's Gate. The last vestiges of those guarding the gate had heard the blasts and seen the bloodbath, clearly realizing their compatriots had nowhere to go but toward their own positions. With the invaders on their heels, the gate had to be opened or they would all be pinned to the wall and slaughtered.

From Mac's vantage point he could plainly see what awaited the fleeing rebels outside the gate. While he and the others had entered the Damascus Gate, surreptitious Unity personnel had slipped into place with what appeared to be colossal Gatling guns on massive caissons. From the looks of the barrels, Mac guessed the guns could accommodate fifty-caliber shells.

Those in the front of the advancing Unity forces were now shooting the rebels in the back, and the more who fell, the more were fired upon. Mac stole a glance behind him. He was bringing up the rear. "Lord, forgive me," he breathed, spraying his Uzi and dropping at least a dozen GC from behind. He felt no remorse. *All's fair* . . . It was only fitting, he decided, that the devil's crew were dressed in all black. *Live by the sword, die by the sword.*

Unity personnel in front of him parted like the Red Sea as their counterparts outside the walls opened fire with the big guns. Mac, too, dived for cover, watching in horror as dozens of rebels were ripped to pieces.

It seemed to be over as quickly as it had begun. Rogue GC stepped among the bodies shooting this one and that who seemed to still be moving. Others fanned out and began helping themselves to weapons and whatever keepsakes they could find on the shattered bodies. This was Mac's chance.

He quickly pretended to do what the GC were doing, but he was pickier. He used his weapon or his boot to roll over only those dead or dying who were the right size to possibly be Buck. Mac picked up a weapon occasionally and rifled a pocket or two, just in case anyone was watching. He didn't really want to find Buck now, not unless he remained alive in the Temple Mount. No rebels had survived in the Muslim Quarter, as far as he could see.

+ + +

It was the strangest battle George Sebastian had ever been part of. One could hardly call it a battle at all. It was just he and his ragtag bunch of earnest, impassioned believers, ringing part of the Petra perimeter with a handful of fairly sophisticated armaments—some directed energy weapons that burned the skin of soldiers and horses from long distances, and too few long-range fifty-caliber rifles—against the largest fighting force in the history of mankind.

The Global Community Unity Army, spearheaded by Antichrist himself, filled the horizon, even when George backed up onto the slopes and looked through solar-powered uberbinoculars. Hundreds of thousands of black-clad troops on horseback seemed to undulate under the shimmering desert vapors, steeds champing at the bit and high-stepping in place, appearing eager to carry their charges in an attack on the hopelessly outnumbered defenders.

Yet Sebastian felt little fear. He couldn't deny a certain trepidation, scanning the tanks and armored personnel carriers, the foot soldiers, the fighters and bombers and choppers that backed up the cavalry as far as the eye could see. It was no exaggeration to call his enemy a sea of humanity, and he could not imagine a throng so massive ever having gathered in one place before. More than once he had seen most of the million-plus gathered at Petra, and impressive as that was, it was nothing compared to this.

Sebastian's occasional volleys of DEWs and Fifties had proved a nuisance for the Unity forces. He had even caused several dozen casualties, which sent Gustaf Zuckermandel's crazy underlings scampering into the field to harvest weapons, IDs, and full uniforms. And the supernatural protection of Petra seemed to hold, even out here. Sebastian had lost nary a troop.

Yet he knew well that if that great army merely advanced upon his position without firing a shot, his entire cache of ammunition would make not one serious dent in the overall force aligned against him. The enemy had begun advancing at a snail's pace, and while they were neither firing nor launching artillery of any sort, the mere size of that force directing its momentum his way caused the earth to tremble and the footing to become unsure.

And of course he was worried about Rayford. He had seen the man protected like the rest of them, heat-seeking missiles appearing to fly directly through aircraft without harming a hair on anyone's head. What could have caused injury to him now, and why? Some had speculated that the pieces of his vehicle found in the hills might have evidenced damage from an incendiary. But the latest report from Abdullah Smith was that the damage appeared to be the result of a loss of control, that the ATV had rolled and tumbled, smashing to bits.

What, then, about the blood trail that could have been only Rayford's? It was way beyond Sebastian to question God, but he had to wonder. Could a missile God caused to miss Rayford have still caused an accident that mortally wounded him? And who was to blame for that? Ray himself? The enemy?

The bigger question now, of course, was what would come of this advance by the invaders. Sebastian believed with his whole heart that Petra was impregnable. What was he doing out here with his band of resisters then? Presumably giving latecomers a chance to benefit from the safety of the place. Before they came within the saving influence of the stone city, Sebastian would try everything in his power to pave the way for them. Yet none had come, and he saw none on the way.

Surely in a matter of hours—some said minutes—this would all be meaningless. Christ would appear, He would win the battle, and Rayford and Buck and even Tsion—dead, alive, or somewhere in between—would be reunited. Still, Sebastian couldn't get Rayford off his mind. He had been trained to never leave a comrade on the battlefield, regardless. It made no sense that Smitty could find the blood trail of a man severely wounded and thus moving slowly and yet not be able to find the man himself.

The best Sebastian could determine, there were no enemy personnel behind Rayford. He could not have been captured. Worst-case but most likely scenario: Ray had dug himself a shelter against the sun and died there. Did it make a difference, given that he would be with Christ—just like the rest of them—when it was all over? Of course it did. Because you don't leave a man.

How long had it been since he had checked in with Smitty? He looked at his watch. Too recently. And Abdullah said he would let him know at first opportunity. But Sebastian had to do something, short of heading to the hills himself—clearly an impossibility. He called Chang.

"No, I haven't heard a thing yet," the young man reported. "I sure wish you could be here, though. Thousands are turning to Christ, right here in Petra."

That was wonderful, but Sebastian couldn't bring himself to say so. Frankly, he carried a bit of resentment, even disgust, for those who had waited this long. Where had they been when all the judgments had come down? All the miracles? No sane person could deny that for the past seven years, God and Satan had waged war. Had these people really been undecided about which side they wanted to join? Any doubt about the reality of God and both His mercy and His judgment had long since been erased.

"I've got a call coming in," Chang said.

"So do I," Sebastian said. "Later."

"Big Dog One, this is, Camel Jockey."

"Go ahead, Smitty," Sebastian said.

"And, Techie, are you there?"

"Roger," Chang said.

"I've spotted Captain Steele."

+ + +

Enoch Dumas awoke just after seven thirty in the morning. His musty mattress in the basement of an abandoned house in Palos Hills, Illinois, was warm where he had slept and cold where he hadn't. And he hadn't slept much. All night he had told himself that today was the day. He couldn't imagine sleeping past 4 a.m., but the truth was, that was about the time he finally dozed. Eight in the morning, Central Time, would mark seven years to the minute since the signing of the covenant between Antichrist and Israel, a covenant that had been broken years earlier, but which marked the years before the Glorious Appearing of Christ.

The Place, his little church of thirty or so down-and-outers from the inner city of Chicago, had incongruously burgeoned since they had been scattered to the suburbs with the compromising of the Tribulation Force safe house. They no longer had a central meeting place. While knowing that they should trust no newcomers, every time they got together, more were added to their number. And because they recognized the seal of the believer on the foreheads of the newcomers, Enoch knew they had not been infiltrated. They now numbered nearly a hundred. While some had been martyred, a surprising majority had eluded detection and capture, though they busied themselves every day trying to gather more converts—"getting more drowning people onto the life raft," Enoch called it.

Sometimes he even found himself urging caution to passionate new believers and warning them that the enemy was constantly on the lookout, eager to devour them, to make them statistics. And yet he was often reminded, usually by one of his own flock, that there was no other choice now than to be overt in their witness.

His favorite times were when the floor was opened and people who risked their very lives by assembling in secret would exude the joy of heaven when they spoke. He could not, nor did he want to, erase from his mind's eye the testimony of Carmela, a fiftyish, heavyset Latina. In an abandoned laser-tag park about ten miles west of Enoch's quarters, she had stood telling her story with tears running down her generous cheeks.

"I once was blind but now I see is the only way I can say it," she said. "I was blind to God, blind to Jesus, selling my body to buy drugs and food. I had left everything and everybody important to me. Before I knew it, I only cared about me and my next high. It was all about survival, kill or be killed, do what you gotta do.

"But then one day one of you came to me. And it was her, right there." Carmela had pointed to an older woman, an African-American named Shaniqua. "She handed me one of the brochures, about the meetings and all, and she said, 'Somebody loves you.'

"I thought, *Somebody loves me? Tell me somethin' I* don't *know! Men tryin' to love me all day.* But I knew better. Nobody loved me. Fact, they hated me. Used me. I meant nothin' more to them than their next meal or their next high. Just what they meant to me. Nobody loved me since my mama, and she died when I was little.

"I knew the brochure had to be somethin' religious, but her saying that about somebody loving me, and her havin' the courage to give me the brochure when she knew it was against the law . . . that was the only thing made me not throw it away or cuss her to her face.

"I read it that night, and I'm glad the Bible verses were in it, 'cause I ain't seen no Bible for years. What got me was that it wasn't fancy, wasn't hard to understand, didn't get all complicated. It just told me God loved me, Jesus died for me, and Jesus is comin' again. All them Scriptures sounded true to me, 'bout being a sinner, being separated from God, and Jesus being the way back to Him.

"Before I knew it, that was the only thing I wanted. I didn't know how I'd live, what I'd eat, nothing. But I knew I wanted Jesus. Next time I saw Shaniqua, I just about attacked her, didn't I, honey? I told her she had to tell me how to get Jesus in my life. She told me it was simple. All I had to do was pray and mean it. Tell God I was sorry for the mess I'd made of my life and take Jesus as my Savior. It ain't been easy, but know what? I'm ready for when Jesus comes."

The believers wanted to be together by eight this morning, and they had settled on a parking lot of a former shopping center. Enoch had warned that a daylight assembly of that size would surely bring out the GC, and they would be looking for marks of loyalty.

"Let 'em be checking us when Jesus appears," someone said, and the rest applauded.

As Enoch quickly showered and dressed, he found himself less worried about interference. The destruction of New Babylon in the space of one hour had so thrown into chaos the international economy that it seemed nothing else mattered to nonbelievers. Suicides were at an all-time high, and he sensed an anti-Carpathian spirit among the formerly loyal.

Social and community services already devastated by the population loss of the last few years were now virtually nonexistent. And rumor had it that even local GC enforcement personnel would be hamstrung without fuel or money for more. Salaries had been frozen for two years as it was, and now it seemed clear to the populace that there would be zero pay for government employees until further notice.

The private sector—what was left of it—was in disarray as well. Carpathia's tentacles had reached so far into every avenue of life and commerce that the virtual bankruptcy of the international government was certain to cripple everyone within days. Enoch had read of great depressions and bank failures throughout history, but no one had seen anything as far-reaching as this. Muggings, robberies, break-ins—all the unsavory acts that had been the purview of the underworld—now had become part and parcel of everyday life for all.

It was every man for himself now, and any vestige of politeness or manners or even lawfulness would soon be history. Enoch prayed Jesus would return right on schedule.

+ + +

It was nearing 1600 hours, four o'clock in the afternoon, in Jerusalem. Mac felt slimy in his GC Unity Army uniform and had to fight the temptation to shout his true identity and open fire without worrying about who was watching. He could take out a few dozen more Carpathian troops, but what was the use? They'd be gone soon enough as it was.

The resistance, except behind the walls in the Temple Mount, had been virtually obliterated. Unity forces congratulated each other as they combed through rebel casualties, gathering the spoils. Mac pretended to do the same in a desperate last-ditch effort to find Buck, though he ignored the eyes of people who thought they were his compatriots. Nothing would give him greater satisfaction than seeing Buck standing tall on the Temple Mount when the end came.

Mac was near the half-crumbled wall just west of Herod's Gate when a phone hit the ground next to him and he heard someone curse above him. The phone looked familiar, but as he reached for it he heard, "Don't waste your time! Nothing left of it!"

Mac looked up to a young Unity soldier bending over a fallen rebel. "Nice boots, though, and my size. He left one of them in the wall here." The soldier untied the other boot and was wrenching it off the body when it pulled free and slipped from his hands, dropping toward Mac. He snatched it from the air and recognized it as Buck's.

"Hey, toss that up here, will ya?" the soldier said, digging the other boot from a crevasse where Buck had apparently left it as he struggled free.

Trembling, Mac tightened his fists around the boot. "A little help, huh, pal?" the soldier said, briefly turning back to the stuck boot.

Mac took a step to get a good angle. Just as the young man freed the boot from the crack and turned toward him, Mac harkened back to his sporting days as a youth. He fired the matching boot so hard that the raider had no chance to react. The sole caught the bridge of his nose and sent him catapulting back over the wall.

To be sure he wouldn't have to face him again, Mac hurried through the gate. He found the young man splayed on the ground, clearly dead. He ran back in and found enough holes and protrusions to hoist himself up to where Buck lay. He wanted to do something—anything—but he could think of nothing. Whatever he did besides appearing to ransack the body would only give him away, and what would be served?

Mac sucked in deep breaths as he surveyed Buck's injuries, gaping wounds that left Buck in a deep pool of black blood so sticky that it had barely begun to run down the wall when it coagulated. His whole right side had been torn open, and wounds also disfigured his hip and neck.

A bullhorn called for assignees to the potentate, and Mac knew he might be identified as an imposter if he didn't report. As he reluctantly pulled away from Buck he prayed that the same fate had not befallen Rayford. It just wouldn't be right if no one from the original Trib Force had survived to see the Glorious Appearing.

It was four o'clock.

3

DESPITE HIS SUBSTANTIAL INJURIES, Rayford had managed to crawl several hundred yards to an outcropping of rock. With his free hand—though its heel had been scraped raw—he somehow had scooped away enough topsoil from behind the rocks to allow himself to stretch out away from the relentless sun and beyond anyone's view.

He had exhausted every reserve of strength and had to trade the hope of being seen by his own people for fighting off dehydration and blood loss long enough to survive until the Glorious Appearing. He gingerly positioned his body in the shallow grave in such a way that if he lost consciousness, his gashed temple would remain pressed against his hand. Every time he thought he had stanched the blood flow long enough for it to stop pulsing, he was proven wrong when he released his palm for even an instant.

It was a relief to be out of the sun, but the benefit of the slightly lower temperature with the topsoil gone did not last. Within half an hour Rayford's mouth and tongue were dry, and he felt his lips swelling. He fought drowsiness, knowing that unconsciousness was his enemy. His wounds stabbed, and he worried about going into shock.

Delirium soon followed, and Rayford daydreamed about people spotting the ATV and following the trail of blood, only to find his lifeless body being pecked at by vultures. At times he discovered he had roused himself to consciousness by singing, praying, or just babbling.

As he stiffened and his temperature rose, he began to feel the deep pang of each injury, and he prayed God would just take him. *I wanted to see it from this side of heaven, but what's the difference? Relief, please. Relief.*

He wasn't sure, but he didn't think he could bleed to death from any wound other than the one to his temple. When it seemed everything had ebbed from him but his last breath, Rayford considered releasing his hand and letting his life's blood slip away too. But he could not.

He quickly lost all sense of time and had to remind himself that his watch seemed to be functioning properly, despite his fast-fading ability to focus.

Rayford was stunned to see how little time had passed since he went careening. The sun was still high in the sky, but he would have bet hours had passed. It had been a mere fifty minutes.

When he awoke groaning, he realized he had actually dozed with enough presence of mind to keep the pulsing temple dammed. His neck was stiff, and he had the feeling he would be unable to stand or even roll into a crawling position if his life depended on it. If someone didn't find him soon, his life *would* depend on moving yet again. But that simply wasn't in the cards.

It seemed hours later, and Rayford was bereft of hope. He heard the advancing Unity Army and was surprised to see the sun still nearly directly overhead. It would remain that way until late afternoon, he knew, but he wouldn't have been surprised to open his eyes to dusk. No such luck.

Far in the distance he heard the high-pitched whine of a powerful dirt bike, the type Abdullah Smith rode. The Jordanian would buzz about Petra, careful in the crowds, then find his way out to the desolate slopes, where he would really open it up. Rayford could only pray that what he heard was Smitty searching for him. He tried to sit up but could not. If he had to guess, he'd have said Smitty was in the area where the ATV had finally landed. That was a long, long way from Rayford's meager shelter. He tried to stay conscious so he could call out if the dirt-bike sound grew nearer, but he knew it would also have to be shut off if the rider was to hear him.

Rayford realized his pain had spread past the spots that had taken the most direct abuse. His head throbbed all over. His eyes had become supersensitive to light, and he could barely open them to peek at his watch. His neck hurt, his shoulders were tight and achy, his back felt as if hot pokers were piercing his ribs. He was hungry, nauseated, and alternated between overheating and shivering. His leg muscles and even his toes cramped.

In and out of consciousness now, when he finally heard the dirt bike slowly approaching, Rayford was certain he was imagining it. When the engine died, Rayford tried to move, to grunt, to do anything to let Smitty, or whomever, know he was there.

"Big Dog One, this is Camel Jockey. . . . And, Techie, are you there? . . . I've spotted Captain Steele. Or at least I think I have. The trail stops here, and I do not expect to like what I see. Hold on."

Rayford's breathing was so shallow he was certain Abdullah would not be able to tell he was alive. He couldn't move a muscle, let alone turn his head, wave, or wiggle a foot. When he heard Smitty's steps in the sand he fought to open an eye. Nothing was working. Was Smitty really there, or was this some sort of a near-death experience?

"Agh, I think he is gone," Abdullah said. "I mean, no, he is here, but I do not think he made it."

Rayford felt the index finger on his free hand bouncing, but clearly Smitty wasn't looking at it. "Oh, Captain Steele," the Jordanian said as he gently rolled Rayford onto his back. He sounded so grief-stricken that Rayford was moved.

Rayford kept his palm locked against his temple, but rather than persuading Abdullah he was alive, it must have made him think rigor mortis was already setting in. And so Rayford did the only thing he could manage. He pulled his hand away an inch. By now the blood had clotted enough that it did not immediately squirt from the wound.

And Abdullah apparently had not noticed the movement.

Rayford felt the pressure building in his temple, and as Smitty straightened Rayford's legs, the wound broke loose.

"Well, hello!" Abdullah said. "Dead men do not bleed. You are there, are you not?"

Rayford clamped his hand over the wound again and managed a "Yeah. Good to see ya."

"Do not talk, Captain. I do not want to lose you before the big event."

"Thought this *was* the big event."

But Abdullah was back on the phone. "Chang, he is alive. I need help here as quickly as you can send it. . . . Yes, Leah would be perfect. Ask her to bring everything she can carry. I will launch a flare in ten minutes."

+ + +

Mac fell in with Unity Army troops in the Muslim Quarter of Jerusalem's Old City and followed them to an obscure but lavishly guarded entrance underground. No one even got close without proper credentials, and Mac fought to maintain his composure as two sentinels held his photo ID next to his cheek and studied it. He could only hope none of Zeke's dye had worn off in the skirmishes.

He and those with him were directed to a pressed-dirt path at least thirty feet wide and lined on either side with narrow wood steps that led deep under the northern wall and past the Temple Mount. They continued directly beneath the only ground in Jerusalem still held by the resistance, and it was, of course, surrounded by the Unity Army. Were the rebels holding their own, or were they virtually imprisoned?

Mac worried about Rayford and wished he'd had an opportunity to call Chang or Sebastian or Abdullah. Ree Woo was leading a platoon on the opposite side of Petra's perimeter. Maybe he'd seen Rayford. But now Mac had to turn off his phone.

The passageway to Solomon's Stables was so dimly lit that he and the others were immediately forced to raise their tinted visors. Still the effect was like coming into a dark theater from the bright sun, and the soldiers slowed and felt their way along so as not to fall down the stairs. Mac was grateful the edge of his helmet rode low over his eyebrows, not exposing that he bore no mark of loyalty.

Being a few steps out of the afternoon sun cooled his face and neck, and he was tempted to remove his gloves. He was nearly overcome by the reek of horse manure and urine, which grew worse as they neared the stables.

As they reached the southeast corner of the Temple Mount, some forty feet underground, they came within sight of Solomon's Stables, a series of pillars and arches that had once supported the southeastern platform of the courtyard above. The halls, made up of a dozen avenues of pillars, were a little over thirty yards wide, sixty yards long, and nearly thirty feet high. At least a hundred men, not in uniform, seemed to be tending more than a thousand horses.

The odor alone took Mac back to his childhood, and he wondered how he had ever grown used to it.

"Attention!" someone shouted. "Silence for your potentate!"

Everything and everyone stopped, and Mac wondered where Nicolae could be. Mac and several other uniforms had their backs pressed up against a wall, standing at attention. He recognized Carpathia's voice coming from inside a pillared room. "Gentlemen and ladies, you will be pleased to know that several months of renovations here were accomplished in the space of fewer than three weeks. The sanitation facilities are second to none, at least for humans, and best of all—per my instructions—they empty into the legendary Cradle of Jesus."

Leave it to Carpathia to sicken Mac with his first words. Mac had never heard of the Cradle of Jesus, at least in the context of the Temple Mount. Many others apparently hadn't either, for Leon Fortunato was called upon to explain.

"Thank you, Excellency. The Cradle of Jesus can be accessed down a winding staircase in the southeast corner. This leads to a chamber approximately fifty by seventy feet where in the past there have been both a basilica named for Saint Mary and a mosque. There is also, on the west wall, some ancient Byzantine art. Should you care to view the chamber, be forewarned of its current use, which we feel is more appropriate to something bearing its name. You will want to hold your nose. You'll be glad to get back to the odor of mere horses."

Suhail Akbar was next, Carpathia's chief of Security and Intelligence. "Having just arrived from Mount Megiddo," he began, "I am pleased to report that everything and everyone is in place for our soon unequivocal victory. Despite reports of discord due to the destruction of New Babyl—"

Suddenly a shout, more of a scream, but Mac clearly recognized Carpathia's voice. He cursed and cursed again. "Tell me, Suhail!" he raged. "Tell me you are not going to violate my specific order to never again mention the name of—"

"But, sir, I merely meant to—"

"You dare interrupt me? Do you see yourself above corporal punishment?"

"No, sir, I—"

Something slammed the table. "I should have you executed this instant! I should do it myself!"

"Excellency, please! I was saying that *despite* what we have heard, the truth is—"

"The truth is that *I* will rebuild New Babylon right here in Jerusalem. She shall be restored to a thousand times her former beauty and majesty. I have decreed there shall be no more mention of what has become of her."

"My humble apologies, Potentate. I—"

"Silence! I have spoken. Back to your quarters, Chief Akbar. Your services will not be required again until further notice."

The commander in charge of Mac's unit quickly stepped forward and conferred with a colleague at the entrance to the meeting room. He backed away as a half-dozen guards led out an ashen Suhail Akbar. The commander then silently pointed to six uniformed men at attention, including Mac, and directed them inside to replace those who had left.

+ + +

Rayford's lucidity had returned somewhat after Abdullah slowly worked a liter of water into him. Leah arrived on a small ATV with two coolers full of supplies and tossed a clipboard to Abdullah. "Would you do the honors, sir?"

"The honors?"

"Take notes."

"Of course."

Rayford kept interrupting her. "What's the buzz at Petra? They think Jesus is late?"

"Hush."

"C'mon, Leah. I gotta know if we've all been off by a day."

"Nobody's off," she said distractedly, coolly inventorying his injuries. "Chaim has everyone calmed down."

"How? What's he saying?"

"God's ways are not our ways. He's on His own clock. That kind of thing."

"Leah, you love this, don't you?"

"Sorry?"

"Having me at your mercy."

"I don't know what you're talking about."

"Yes, you do. We—"

"Mr. Smith," she said, "I'll be suturing the head wound. The chin, the arms, the right hand, and the knees can wait. The left shinbone may be broken, but I won't attempt to set it until we can be sure. I'm going to need to study the right ankle and probably suture that too. And we're going to need some kind of conveyance to get him back up to the compound, probably within half an hour."

"You *love* this, Leah! I can tell."

"You're delirious."

"What kind of conveyance, Miss Rose?" Abdullah said.

"I need him prone."

Abdullah got back on the phone.

"You could be just a little rougher with me than you might be with another patient, just to get back at me."

Rayford was teasing and trying to smile, but Leah clearly wasn't biting. "Back at you for what?"

"For how I used to talk to you."

"Well, maybe you owe me too," she said.

"Maybe I do, but I'm in no position to exact revenge."

"And I have your flesh wounds in my hands. Now keep quiet and let me work."

+ + +

It was all Mac could do not to burst out laughing when he saw Carpathia. Had the man been wearing a black hat, he would have looked like Zorro. A shirt with a frilly collar represented the only white in his ensemble. Everything else, from his knee-length boots to his leather pants, vest, and thigh-length, capelike coat, was black.

Leon was in his most resplendent, gaudiest, Day-Glo getup, including a purple felt fez with multiple hangy-downs and a cranberry vestment with gold collar, appliquéd with every religious symbol known to man, save the cross of Christ and the Star of David. A turquoise ring on his right middle finger was so large it covered the adjoining knuckles.

If only God had scheduled the Glorious Appearing on Halloween . . .

Carpathia stood at the head of an enormous, polished wood table, around which sat—if Mac could guess from their native garb—the sub-potentates from each of the ten international regions, their entourages, and Carpathia's brain trust, sans Chief Akbar, of course. There had to be more than fifty gathered.

Viv Ivins sat demurely in her customary sky blue suit (with hair to match) six chairs from Nicolae on his far left side. She seemed even paler than Mac had remembered, and he thought he detected a trembling in her fingers as she busied herself taking notes. The others, despite their positions of high authority on Carpathia's cabinet and around the world, also seemed tentative in his presence. The outburst against Suhail Akbar had clearly shaken them all.

Mac was near the entrance, one of the last few to have entered, and he realized that the six sentries he and his platoonmates had replaced had filled out a contingent of another fifty or so who lined the walls of the long room. Knowing what it had taken even to be allowed underground, he had to wonder against whom they were protecting Carpathia. Was he afraid of his own people?

+ + +

Chang had walked Naomi back into the tech center. "What am I going to do?" he said. "I'll never sleep tonight, and I'm wasted."

"Surely you don't think we'll have to wait another day."

"I don't know what to think."

"Today is the day, love. There's no question."

"I hope you're right. I'm wired, but at some point I'm going to crash. Dr. Rosenzweig wants me to get him on international TV just before dark. You may have to prop me up."

"You'll rise to it. You always do."

+ + +

The wall at his back, made of large blocks of stone, cooled Mac through his uniform jacket. He desperately wanted to peek at his watch. He knew it was well after 1600 hours now, and he believed Jesus could come any second. This was the last place he wanted to be when that happened, but being here was part of the price he paid to find Buck. And there was the prospect of seeing the look on Carpathia's face.

Mac tried to appear focused on his menial task—providing showy security where none was needed—but when he ran through his mind what he really wanted to be doing, he found it difficult to concentrate. Besides being in broad daylight in the Holy City when the Lord Christ appeared, Mac's second choice was opening fire on Carpathia from his perfect vantage point. There would be none of that, he knew. It fit no prophetic scenario, but how fulfilling it would be!

Nothing would come of such foolhardiness, of course. The man had been murdered once, and was he now even a man? Drs. Ben-Judah and Rosenzweig had said he was now indwelt by Satan himself, a spirit-being using a human body—albeit a dead one.

In addition, Mac simply wanted to take a load off. The idea of sliding to his seat on the floor, of stretching out with his hands behind his head . . . well, that was something that would come once Jesus had taken His rightful place. Mac's friends and comrades often talked about what kind of a world they would live in soon, but he kept to himself the idea that what he most longed for was simply rest.

He was certain he was not alone in this. Others had hinted at it. They had all been so busy, so stressed, so sleep deprived, and all that had only worsened as the days grew nearer to the Glorious Appearing. The idea of living in a world of peace and safety so appealed to Mac that he could barely imagine it. To be able to sleep without half an eye or ear figuratively open to danger . . . well, talk about heaven on earth.

And to be reunited with friends and loved ones. It was nearly too much to get his mind around. Best of all, of course, would be to see Jesus personally. Would he get to touch Him, to speak with Him? Mac felt so new as a believer, so limited in his knowledge of the things of God. He felt as if he had been attending seminary under the Tribulation Force's spiritual leaders ever since Rayford had led him to faith. But there was so much he didn't know.

All he knew was that Jesus loved him, had died for his sins, and was the reason he did not have to fear death and hell.

\+ + +

Chang had been called before Dr. Rosenzweig and the elders.

"Of course I can do it," he said, "but the GC has been improving on wresting back control of the airwaves. The shorter the broadcast, the more likely I can keep it on without interruption."

"I plan to be brief," Chaim said.

"And if, ah, if—"

"You're wondering what happens, hoping as I am, if Messiah returns first?"

"Or in the middle of it," Chang said.

"Well, I should think that event would take precedence, wouldn't you?"

Chang smiled as the elders laughed.

"Rabbi Rosenzweig is attempting," Eleazar Tiberius said, "to persuade the rest of the Jewish population—those who have refused the mark of the beast and yet who have not acknowledged Jesus as Messiah—to do just that. He, and we agree, estimates that this may constitute a third of the remaining Jewish population. You understand that these are God's chosen people, His children from the beginning of time. All of Scripture is His love letter to them, His plan for them."

"Understand it?" Chang said. "I can't say that I do. But I believe it."

Chaim stood. "We must not delay. As I have said so many times, we know the day—today—but we do not know the hour. If we thought we did, we were wrong, were we not, Eleazar?"

The big man smiled. "I acknowledge it. But is it not also true that we know the sequence of events, so we have some idea what follows by what comes next?"

"That is what I will be talking about on the broadcast, my friends."

✣ ✣ ✣

Before the anesthetic took effect in his temple, Rayford fought to keep from recoiling from the thrust of the needle. He was amazed that a new twinge of pain could supersede all the others, and he was also struck by Leah's gentleness as she cradled his head and assured him the sting would soon fade.

"You're being much better to me than I deserve," he said, knowing he sounded groggy and hoping she understood.

"Will you stop with that now, Captain? I have work to do, and while I know you're trying to keep things light, I don't need to be worrying if you're serious."

He reached for her hand. "Take a minute, Leah. I am serious. When you first came to us you know that we sniped at each other. I wasn't used to your types of questions and probably was threatened by them. I never made that right, but as far as I could tell, you never made me pay."

She pressed her lips together. "And I'm not about to now. Listen, Ray, you're hurt more badly than you know. My job is to stabilize you, keep you from going into shock. The fact that you haven't already is a miracle. But you apparently need to hear this, so let me tell you. My failure was that I never cleared the air between us either. Fact is, you eventually won me over. Everybody could see how much you cared for all of us, how tireless you were, how you put everybody else ahead of your own needs."

Rayford was embarrassed. He hadn't meant to elicit this, nice as it was. He squeezed her hand. "Okay, okay," he said. "We're friends again."

"Think of the people who will be in heaven because of you," she said.

"All right, enough," he said. "I was just trying to thank you for not rubbing it in."

"Now will you hush?"

"I will, ma'am."

+ + +

Mac noticed Viv Ivins look up with a start but then recover quickly. Carpathia had asked, "Photographers in place and ready, Ms. Ivins?"

"Yes, Excellency."

"I shall be on horseback," he said. "All Global Community Unity Army personnel in this room, plus their superiors, shall also ride. Your mounts are being saddled as we speak."

Mac panicked. How long had it been since he had ridden? Was it like riding a bicycle? Would it all come back to him? He had never been atop a steed the size of the Thoroughbreds in the stables. Any horse responded to a sure, confident hand. The beast had to know the rider was in charge. He might have to fake that bravado.

"Are you looking directly at me, soldier?" Carpathia demanded.

"No, sir," the young Brit next to Mac said, eyes darting everywhere but at Nicolae.

"You most certainly were! You would have done better to admit it and beg forgiveness."

"Affirmative, sir. I was, and I regret it and offer my sincerest abject apologies."

"That is the second time you have referred to me as sir! Have you not been instructed neither to look directly at me nor to refer to me in any manner except as—"

"Yes, Excellency! My apologies, Supreme Pot—"

"And now you deign to interrupt me?"

The Brit's voice was quavery and Mac believed his legs were about to fail him.

"Sorry," the young man whispered.

"I cannot hear you, soldier!"

"I'm sorry, Excellency. Forgive me."

"Who is your superior officer?"

"Commander Tenzin, sir—Excellency!"

Carpathia cursed the man. "Commander Tenzin!"

The Indian commander rushed in, bowing. "At your service, Excellency!"

"Commander, have you taught your men who I am?"

"I have, Lord Potentate."

"All of them?"

"Yes, my king."

"And the privilege of serving god on earth?"

"Absolutely, divine one."

"Even this man? Your name, son?"

"Ipswich, Excellency," he said, tears flowing now.

Mac wanted to shoot Carpathia dead and feared he just might if the potentate approached.

"Commander Tenzin, what is that in your hand?"

"A rattan rod, Excellency. I so look forward to the privilege of riding with you today."

The rod was an inch thick and appeared to Mac about four feet long.

"If I told you that Mr. Ipswich has flouted your training, could you think of an appropriate use for your rattan rod, Commander Tenzin?"

"I could, Your Grace."

Ipswich was whimpering.

"And would you do me the honor of employing it in my presence, for my entertainment and for the education of all?"

Without another word, Tenzin stepped forward and drew back the rod. Before Ipswich could even recoil, his commander lashed his face with such speed and force that the stick caught him just to the left of his nose, splitting both lips, cracking some teeth, and slicing his left eyelid.

Ipswich screamed and grabbed his face with both hands, bending at the waist. Tenzin brought the rod down on the back of his neck, just above the hairline, opening a gash that spattered blood on Mac's face and chest. It was all he could do to keep from attacking the Indian.

As Ipswich pitched forward, Tenzin cracked him twice across the backside in quick succession, the second blow tearing his uniform pants. That drove him to the floor, and as he tried to scramble away, his commander followed, raining blows on his back.

Carpathia howled in delight. "When he can crawl no more, Commander Tenzin, spare the rod and put him out of his misery!"

Another soldier was quickly enlisted to replace Ipswich in line. He entered pale and shaky and quickly came to rigid attention.

"Ooh," Carpathia moaned, clasping his hands and gazing upward. "What a way to start the day! Leon . . ."

"Yes, holy one?"

"Ask Commander Tenzin to pay a visit to Chief Akbar."

"Certainly, lord."

"But instruct him to punish him only to the point of *near* death."

4

ENOCH DUMAS LED more than a hundred of The Place followers around the back of the abandoned Illinois shopping center. Just before eight in the morning he had begun to teach, trying to inform his people and a few interested others what should precede the Glorious Appearing. None of the heavenly preliminaries had begun, and he sensed the disappointment, doubt, and fear on the part of his little band of believers. But mostly he found himself looking over his shoulder at the main road.

Though there were few vehicles of any type about, given the fuel shortage and the crippled economy, he knew the local GC had not shut down completely. They would have to investigate a meeting of this size. And the discovery of that many people, not one bearing the mark of loyalty to Carpathia, would result in a bloodbath.

There was no longer any earthly excuse not to bear the mark, and punishment was execution on the spot by any means. Even a civilian had the right to put to death an insurgent. All that was required for exoneration from the crime of homicide was either to drag the victim to a local GC headquarters and prove he or she bore no visible mark, or to flag down a patrolling Morale Monitor or GC Peacekeeper and get him to confirm the same.

In fact, there was a healthy bounty on such offenders, and citizens loyal to the potentate competed for cash prizes. Many made their living as vigilantes, and some were famous for their impressive number of kills.

Perhaps that was why Enoch found his usually bold congregation willing to follow him from the public light of day to the relative seclusion of the other side of the empty mall. "If we knew Jesus would get here before the GC, we could stay where we are. But I, for one, do not want to have survived seven years, only to die just before He comes back."

The group crowded into an inner court, where it was obvious they all felt safer. But they had questions.

"When's it gonna happen?"

"What'd we miss in the prophecies?"

"Did you only *think* the 'weeks' meant 'years,' or what?"

"Could we be off by a long ways?"

"I don't think so," Enoch said. "But I don't know. I was never a scholar or a theologian. I'm sort of a blue-collar student of all this, just like you all are. But I have been reading and studying for years. While there is a lot of disagreement and debate, so far everything, every element of the prophecies, has been fulfilled literally, the way it was spelled out. I have to believe today is the day."

"Ho'd on!" a woman shouted from the back. She was peering into a tiny TV. "Look like somebody done took over the GC's airwaves again."

People crowded around.

"That Micah guy," she said, "runnin' things at Petra, is gonna speak about what comes next."

Others pulled mini-TVs from their pockets and bags. "Should we listen, Brother Enoch? Will you be offended?"

"Hardly," Enoch said, digging out his own TV. "What could be better than this? Dr. Rosenzweig is a scholar's scholar. Let's have church."

The assembled put their tiny screens together on a concrete bench and turned them up so the combined volume reached everyone.

\+ \+ \+

Mac saw the narrowing of Carpathia's eyes and feared someone else was about to catch his rage. His attention had been drawn to the entrance of the room.

"Yes, what is it?" Carpathia said.

An underling said, "Begging the potentate's pardon, but, Excellency, you asked to be informed."

"What? What!"

"The zealots at Petra, the Judah-ites—"

"I know who is at Petra! What now?"

"They have pirated their way onto GC television again."

Carpathia flushed and leaned over the table, resting on his palms. His jaw muscles tightened. "Turn it on," he said through clenched teeth.

Leon nearly toppled trying to pull out a chair. He sat heavily and made a show of reaching far up under his robe and producing a remote-control laser, which he aimed at the wall behind Nicolae. A screen descended and the picture appeared: Chaim Rosenzweig seated on a simple set, deep in the confines of Petra. His open Bible was before him, and he bore a pastoral smile. A timer showed that he would begin in less than a minute.

Carpathia looked over his shoulder at the screen, then turned back and slammed both fists on the table. "First," he shouted, "confirm that Ipswich is dead! Then tell Tenzin I have changed my mind about Akbar! I want him dead too! Finally, get hold of Security at Al Hillah. Inform them of the demise of their chief and tell them the following order comes directly from me.

"Whatever it takes, I want Security to take over our broadcast center. I want the management personnel shot to death through both eyes, one administrator at a time, from the top down through the chain of command, one every sixty seconds until someone has wrested back control of the airwaves. Understood?"

No one moved or spoke.

"Understood?!"

"Yes, Excellency!" Leon said, reaching for his phone.

"I'm on it," Viv Ivins said, phone already to her ear.

Carpathia whirled and faced the screen. "Does no one understand?" he railed. "Does no one recognize this man? This is the one who assassinated me! And while I raised myself from the dead and reign as your living lord, he remains a thorn in my side. Well, no longer! Not after today! A third of our entire army will overrun Petra tonight, and he shall be my personal target!"

+ + +

With hydration and an IV started by Leah, Rayford at last began to feel he might make it. He still felt as if he had been run over by a tank, and there would be no walking or helping himself get off this godforsaken slope. But his mental faculties were returning, and he came to believe that Leah and Abdullah could somehow get him back to the compound.

"Two things, Miss Rose," Abdullah said.

"Shoot."

"According to Miss Palemoon, we have a problem with the conveyance."

"What problem? There's a stretcher in the Co-op. And a gurney too."

"She checked with Mrs. Woo, and they both believe these will be impossible to transport to this location."

Leah sat back, and Rayford saw her scan the hills above her leading to Petra. "She may have a point. What's number two?"

"She says Micah is on GC television and that we might want to tune it in."

"Do you have a TV, Mr. Smith?"

"Of course."

"Well, the captain is as stable as I can make him, and we may be here a while. Let's have a look."

Abdullah pulled a small TV from a leather bag attached to his bike.

"You want to see this, Captain?" Leah said.

✣ ✣ ✣

Chang was glued to his monitor, but he asked Naomi to gather around him the rest of the techies on duty.

"Check this out, people," he said. "Look at the counter in the upper left of the screen."

Whistles and back slaps and exultations followed the speeding numbers, racing upward by the tens of thousands a second but having already surged far past the largest television audience in history. Nothing Carpathia ever broadcast had come close; in fact, the previous three records had all been held by Tsion Ben-Judah.

"Dearly beloved," Chaim had begun, "I speak to you tonight probably for the last time before the Glorious Appearing of our Lord and Savior, Jesus Christ the Messiah. He could very well come during this message, and nothing would give me greater pleasure. When He comes there will be no more need for us to fight Antichrist and his False Prophet. The work will have been done for us by the King of kings.

"But as He did not return seven years to the minute from the signing of the covenant between Antichrist and Israel, many are troubled and confused. I wish to speak to that here, but mostly I need to be brief, for as you know, we commandeer these airwaves against the wishes of our archenemy, and you must believe that he is doing everything in his power right this very instant to bump us.

"More important than discussing the timing of Messiah's return, however—which I can summarize in a sentence: I believe He will be here before midnight, Israel Time—is the spiritual state of my fellow Jews around the globe. If you have never listened before, lend me an ear this day. This is your last chance, your final warning, my ultimate plea with you to recognize and accept Jesus as the Messiah you have for so long sought.

"You have heard many times the proclamations of my dear friend and colleague, Dr. Tsion Ben-Judah, who outlined the numerous prophecies that soon came to pass. If these never persuaded you, hear me now and know that it is likely this very day that you will see the signs in the sky heralding the Glorious Appearing of Jesus.

"The Bible says in Matthew 24:29 and 30 that 'immediately after the tribulation of those days the sun will be darkened, and the moon will not give its light; the stars will fall from heaven, and the powers of the heavens will be shaken.

"'Then the sign of the Son of Man will appear in heaven, and then all the tribes of the earth will mourn, and they will see the Son of Man coming on the clouds of heaven with power and great glory.'

"This *is* the last day of the Tribulation that was prophesied thousands of years ago! Today is the seventh anniversary of the unholy and quickly broken covenant between Antichrist and Israel. What is next? The sun, wherever it is in the sky where you are, will cease to shine. If the moon is out where you are, it will go dark as well because it is merely a reflection of the sun. Do not fear. Do not be afraid. Do not panic. Take comfort in the truth of the Word of God and put your faith in Christ, the Messiah.

"What does it mean that the powers of the heavens will be shaken? I do not know, but beloved, I cannot wait to find out! The Bible says God 'will show wonders in heaven above and signs in the earth beneath: Blood and fire and vapor of smoke. The sun shall be turned into darkness, and the moon into blood, before the coming of the great and awesome day of the Lord.'

"I expect a show like I have never witnessed, but I will be safe as He has promised. Will you be safe? Are you ready? Are you prepared? Do not put it off another second.

"What is the sign of the Son of Man? Again, I do not know, but I know who the Son of Man is: Jesus, the Messiah. His sign could take any form. Might it be a mighty dove, as descended upon Him when John baptized Him? Might it be the form of a lion, as He has also been called the Lion of Judah? Might His sign be a lamb, as He is also the Lamb of God? The cross upon which He died? The open tomb, in which He conquered death? We do not know, but I will be watching. Won't you?

"Who are these tribes of the earth who will mourn when they see Him coming? Those who are not ready. Those who have lingered in their rebellion, their disbelief, their sloth.

"Zechariah, the great Jewish prophet of old, foretold this thousands of years ago. He wrote, quoting Messiah: 'I will pour on the house of David and on the inhabitants of Jerusalem the Spirit of grace and supplication; then they will look on Me whom they pierced. Yes, they will mourn for Him as one mourns for his only son, and grieve for Him as one grieves for a firstborn.'

"Imagine that, people! Historians tell us Zechariah wrote that prophecy well more than four hundred years before the birth of Christ, and yet he quotes the Lord referring to Himself as 'Me whom they pierced.'

"Zechariah goes on: 'In that day there shall be a great mourning in Jerusalem. . . . And the land shall mourn, every family by itself: the family of the house of David by itself, and their wives by themselves . . . all the families that remain, every family by itself, and their wives by themselves.

"'In that day a fountain shall be opened for the house of David and for the inhabitants of Jerusalem, for sin and for uncleanness. And it shall come to pass in all the land . . . that two-thirds in it shall be cut off and die, but one-third shall be left in it.

"'I will bring the one-third through the fire, will refine them as silver is refined, and test them as gold is tested. They will call on My name, and I will answer them. I will say, "This is My people"; and each one will say, "The Lord is my God."'

"Can there be any doubt, friends, that He is who the Bible says He is? If you can still reject Him after seeing the sun snuffed out, the heavens shaken, and His sign appear, surely you are past hope, past saving. Do not wait. Be part of that one-third whom the Lord God has promised to bring through the fire.

"One of our first-century Jews, Peter, said, 'It shall come to pass that whoever calls on the name of the Lord shall be saved.' I cannot choose more appropriate words than his when I speak to fellow Jews, saying, 'Men of Israel, hear these words: Jesus of Nazareth, a Man attested by God to you by miracles, wonders, and signs which God did through Him in your midst, as you yourselves also know—Him, being delivered by the determined purpose and foreknowledge of God, you have taken by lawless hands, have crucified, and put to death; whom God raised up, having loosed the pains of death, because it was not possible that He should be held by it.

"'For David says concerning Him: "I foresaw the Lord always before my face, for He is at my right hand, that I may not be shaken. Therefore my heart rejoiced, and my tongue was glad; moreover my flesh also will rest in hope. For You will not leave my soul in Hades, nor will You allow Your Holy One to see corruption. You have made known to me the ways of life; You will make me full of joy in Your presence."

"'Men and brethren, let me speak freely to you of the patriarch David, that he is both dead and buried, and his tomb is with us to this day. Therefore, being a prophet, and knowing that God had sworn with an oath to him that of the fruit of his body, according to the flesh, He would raise up the Christ to sit on his throne, he, foreseeing this, spoke concerning the resurrection of the Christ, that His soul was not left in Hades, nor did His flesh see corruption. This Jesus God has raised up, of which we are all witnesses. Therefore being exalted to the right hand of God, and having received from the Father the promise of the Holy Spirit, He poured out this which you now see and hear.

"'Therefore let all the house of Israel know assuredly that God has made this Jesus, whom you crucified, both Lord and Christ.'

"Beloved," Chaim raced on, "the Bible tells us that when they heard this, they were 'cut to the heart, and said to Peter and the rest of the apostles, "Men and brethren, what shall we do?"'

"Do you find yourself asking the same today? I say to you as Peter said to them, 'Repent, and let every one of you be baptized in the name of Jesus Christ for the remission of sins; and you shall receive the gift of the Holy Spirit. For the promise is to you and to your children, and to all who are afar off, as many as the Lord our God will call.'

"Oh, children of Israel around the globe, I am being signaled that our enemy is close to wresting back control of this network. Should I be cut off, trust me, you already know enough to put your faith in Christ as the Messiah.

"Not knowing when this signal shall fade, let me close by reading to you one of the most loved and powerful prophecies concerning Messiah that was ever written. And should my voice be silenced, you may find it and read it for yourself in Isaiah 53. And remember, this was written *more than seven hundred years* before the birth of Christ!

"'Who has believed our report? And to whom has the arm of the Lord been revealed? For He shall grow up before Him as a tender plant, and as a root out of dry ground. He has no form or comeliness; and when we see Him, there is no beauty that we should desire Him. He is despised and rejected by men, a Man of sorrows and acquainted with grief. And we hid, as it were, our faces from Him; He was despised, and we did not esteem Him.

"'Surely He has borne our griefs and carried our sorrows; yet we esteemed Him stricken, smitten by God, and afflicted. But He was wounded for our transgressions, He was bruised for our iniquities; the chastisement for our peace was upon Him, and by His stripes we are healed. All we like sheep have gone astray; we have turned, every one, to his own way; and the Lord has laid on Him the iniquity of us all.

"'He was oppressed and He was afflicted, yet He opened not His mouth; He was led as a lamb to the slaughter, and as a sheep before its shearers is silent, so He opened not His mouth. He was taken from prison and from judgment, and who will declare His generation? For He was cut off from the land of the living; for the transgressions of My people He was stricken. And they made His grave with the wicked—but with the rich at His death, because He had done no violence, nor was any deceit in His mouth.

"'Yet it pleased the Lord to bruise Him; He has put Him to grief. When You make His soul an offering for sin, He shall see His seed, He shall prolong His days, and the pleasure of the Lord shall prosper in His hand. He shall see the labor of His soul, and be satisfied. By His knowledge My righteous Servant shall justify many, for He shall bear their iniquities. Therefore I will divide Him a portion with the great, and He shall divide the spoil with the strong, because He poured out His soul unto death, and He was numbered with the transgressors, and He bore the sin of many, and made intercession for the transgressors.'"

During the broadcast, Chang had superimposed on the screen a Web site where those who were making decisions to receive Christ could let Dr. Rosenzweig know at Petra. Even before the GC reclaimed control of the television network, the Web site was being overrun with such messages. Millions around the world, most of them Jews, were acknowledging Jesus as the Messiah and putting their faith in Him for their salvation.

+ + +

Mac was always moved by Scripture, and all the more so now to see Nicolae Carpathia, Antichrist himself, and his False Prophet, Leon Fortunato, squirm so.

"I wonder," Nicolae said, "how many died in Al Hillah before we succeeded in pushing the pirates off the gangplank. Who was the next one standing, now in charge?

"Well, let me tell you something. These people can say what they want, preach what they want, believe what they want. But if they have not taken my mark, not sworn their allegiance to the living god of this world, they shall surely die. This man appeals to the Jews, the dogs of society, the ones I have declared my enemies from the first. Meanwhile I have cut them down like a rotted harvest all over the world.

"And while my assassin sits temporarily free, hiding like a coward behind stone walls, my armies are decimating his wretched brothers and sisters in their so-called Holy City. After we have stormed Petra and laid waste to our enemies there, we shall return to complete the taking of Jerusalem. The resistance thinks they own the surface above where we even now reside, but their options are gone. They have nowhere to run, nowhere to hide.

"Let their *Savior* appear! I welcome Him. I will cut Him down like a dog and ascend to my rightful throne."

Mac's thighs ached and quivered with fatigue. The wall behind him had lost its coolness, and he couldn't figure it. Had his body heat finally tempered the subterranean effect? No, something was happening. The temperature was rising. How could that be? What would cause it?

Even Carpathia, immune to hunger and fatigue and thirst since his resurrection, if the reports could be believed, noticed. He tugged at his collar. "What has happened to the air-conditioning?"

"None is needed, Excellency," Leon said. "We are forty feet below the sur—"

"I know where we are! I want to know why the temperature has risen. Do you not feel it?"

"Of course I do, exalted one. But there is no source of heat here. It has always remained a constant of—"

"*Will* you silence yourself! The temperature has risen, and even our collective body heat should not have resulted in that much difference."

Could it be? Mac wondered. Was there a chance this was a sign of the imminent return? Might Jesus appear even here, in the lair of His enemy? "Lord, please!"

Maybe outside the sun had darkened.

+ + +

Rayford shielded his eyes and squinted into the sky. Not one cloud. The sun had finally coursed far enough to see the temperature drop, perhaps more than ten degrees, since its brutal noontime peak. Rayford gratefully accepted Abdullah's offer of his cap, which was a little small but served its purpose.

"If we're not going to be able to carry you to Petra," Leah said, "we at least need to sit you up. Can you manage it?"

"I can't imagine," Rayford said. "But I know you're right. I'll need help."

"You're going to be dizzy," Leah said, which proved an understatement. When she and Abdullah sat him up, blood rushed so quickly from Rayford's head that he felt he'd lost his bearings, though he was still firmly planted—albeit on his seat now—in the shallow grave of his own making.

"Whoa," Rayford whispered.

"When you're steady," she said, "tell me what hurts most."

"I can tell you that now. The ankle. Then the shin. Then the hand."

"I'll take them in order," she said, "but it's all going to be temporary and makeshift. It's not what I would want done if I had you in a sterile environment and could do an MRI."

As Leah cleansed and anesthetized the ankle, which had a gaping gash and obvious damage inside, she said, "A surgeon will want to work on the bone before closing this up, but you don't need sand and air in it." She cut away dead and damaged skin that could not be salvaged and sutured it in such a way that it could easily be accessed again.

"This is going to hurt," she said, cutting away his khaki pants below the left knee and examining his shin with both hands. "No doubt you have a fracture, but this is not an easy bone to set. I can give it a try, but only before I numb it. You up to it?"

"I have a choice?"

"No. We may have to try to put you on one of our bikes, and without this set and splinted, you'll pass out from the pain."

"And what about the pain from your trying to set it?"

"No promises."

Rayford had been severely injured before, but he could not remember agony like this. Leah failed in her first attempt to set the shinbone, but she simply said, "Sorry, I can get it," and took another run at it. Despite a wad of gauze to chew on, Rayford screamed loud enough—he feared—to alert the Unity Army. Even once the bone was clearly in place, his leg hurt so badly that it jumped and quivered for more than ten minutes as he fought to keep from whimpering.

"I'll let that settle down some before applying a splint," Leah said.

"You're so kind," he said, and elicited a smile from her.

The splint, fortunately, was inflatable plastic and once in place provided enough stability that the pain finally started to subside. Leah busied herself cleaning and dressing the wounds on the heel of his hand, his chin, and on both arms and both knees.

"I'm going to look a sight," he said. "Better not let Kenny see me until some of this stuff is off."

+ + +

George Sebastian was relieved to know that Rayford had been found alive, but he had to wonder how busted up his boss must be. More pressing, he was uneasy about what the Unity Army was up to. They had closed the mile gap by half, advancing on his position so slowly that the maneuver had taken hours. And now they were stopped. If it was some sort of psychological warfare, it was working. Sebastian's people were spooked.

It was as if this roiling armada, fronted by the hundreds of thousands of mounted horsemen, was just waiting for one word from Antichrist to either open fire or charge. Bothering Big Dog One most was that he now had to turn his head more than 120 degrees just to take in the breadth of the fighting force he faced. And regardless of how high he could place himself, he could never see its full depth. The end of this army literally blotted out the horizon.

+ + +

Mac was as stunned as Leon clearly was when Carpathia said, "I need a chair. Get me a chair!"

Nicolae rarely sat anymore. He was known not to have eaten or slept in three and a half years, persuading loyalists he was the true and living God, and confirming to his enemies that he was indeed Antichrist, indwelt by Satan. His rage was legendary. But no one had seen a weakness or physical frailty in him.

And now he needed a chair?

Leon Fortunato leaped from his own and slid it behind the potentate, who shakily sat. Nicolae tore at his collar and unbuttoned his shirt, feebly fanning himself with his hand. "Allow me, Excellency," Fortunato said, and he knelt and grabbed the hem of his own ostentatious robe, lifted it to his waist, and began fanning the potentate.

Normally Carpathia would quickly tire of such obsequiousness, but he actually appeared panicky and grateful. But when Leon turned to ask Viv Ivins to pour Nicolae a glass of water, his garish fez slipped off and landed in the blousy folds of his skirt. His next tug tightened the fabric and launched the hat into Carpathia's lap.

"Oh!" Leon cried out. "Oh, Majesty! Forgive me!" He lurched forward and tried to retrieve the fez, succeeding only in knocking it out of Nicolae's lap and onto the floor on his other side. Leon's momentum carried him over the potentate, and now he was stretched out across the ailing world leader, his ample belly in his boss's lap. He grabbed the hat with both hands, and as he rocked back to his feet he jammed it atop his head again, uttering every apology imaginable.

Mac was certain Nicolae would execute his right-hand man for such a breach of etiquette, but he appeared to have hardly noticed. Carpathia was in trouble. Viv Ivins finally got a glass of water in front of him, but by now his hands were at his sides and his usually ruddy countenance had paled.

Leon grabbed the water and held it to Carpathia's lips as the fez began to tumble yet again. This time Leon angrily batted it away with his free hand and it toppled to the floor behind them. Carpathia could barely manage to open his mouth, water sloshing down his chin.

"Get paramedics in here!" Leon squealed. "Someone, please! Hurry!"

5

SWEAT TRICKLED DOWN Mac's back. The temperature was rising, almost as if there was a fire below the Temple Mount. With Carpathia having his own problems, Unity Army sentries fell out of attention and wiped their brows, tugged at their shirts and jackets, and traded looks as if to ask what was going on.

Mac turned and leaned out the arched opening at the sound of shouts. Whatever this was, it was widespread. And suddenly, the stables were in chaos. Unfettered horses broke free from their handlers, neighing, spooking each other into a stampede that had nowhere to go. Stablemen tossed lassos but found themselves pulled off the ground when the steeds reared, and then thrown to the ground when they took off, horses jostling horses, fighting for space to get through the arches.

Men and women were trampled, some to death, but when a shortsighted soldier fired into the air, things only got worse. More than a thousand full-size Thoroughbreds were manic and terrified. Following their instincts, they tried to flee, crushing anything in their path, including each other.

Mac saw great equine shoulders ripped open as horses were crushed against the stone walls. He heard legs snapping, saw horses nipping and biting each other, and soon it was a free-for-all.

"Where's the fire?" someone shouted. Many must have heard only "fire," for it was repeated and repeated, soldiers screaming it all over the underground. Mac saw no flame, smelled no smoke. But he heard "Fire!" "Fire!" "Fire!" and like the rest, his instinct was to head for the surface.

But a commander nudged him back into the room with the barrel of a nuclear submachine gun. "There is no fire!" he announced. "Every soldier in this room has a job, and that is to protect the potentate. That is what we shall do. No one enters; no one leaves."

"Permission to speak, Commander," came from a corner.

"Granted."

"What is causing the heat?"

"No idea, but let everyone else kill themselves trying to escape a fire that doesn't exist. You're not going to best a twelve-hundred-pound horse that wants your space anyway, so stay here and do your job."

"What's wrong with the potentate?"

"How should I know?"

"Are the paramedics coming?"

"I don't know how they'd get here. But you can bet no one else will get in. If this is a plot against His Excellency, it stops right here. Now come to attention! Weapons at the ready!"

Mac had never liked being underground, but up till now this foray had not brought on claustrophobia. The sheer size of the area had given him room to move and breathe. But now, outside the only room where everyone remained still, pandemonium reigned. There would be no escape, no freedom, no daylight, no air, no lessening of the heat, even if he opened fire and killed everyone around him and made a break for the surface. What was happening on the dirt ramp and the wood stairs dwarfed mass tragedies due to fire in crowded buildings. Even without an actual fire, this was going to be catastrophic.

With his safety turned off and his firing finger on the trigger, Mac fought to maintain his composure, remaining at attention, staring straight at Carpathia, sweat running freely now inside his uniform.

Nicolae looked wasted. His formerly full head of hair appeared somehow sparse now. His clear, piercing eyes were bloodshot and droopy. His face was sallow, and though it made no sense, Mac believed he could see veins spidering across the man's face, framing his hollow eyes.

Carpathia's fingers looked thin, his skin papery, his shoulders bony. It was as if he had lost fifty pounds in minutes. His pale, bluish lips were parted, and his teeth and gums showed . . . the mouth of a dead man.

"You must drink, Excellency!" Fortunato whined.

"I am spent," Carpathia said, and though Mac could barely hear him, his was clearly not the voice Mac had come to recognize. His words seemed hollow, faint, echoey, as if he spoke from a dungeon far away. "Hungry," Carpathia said flatly. "Exhausted. Dead."

No doubt he meant that last as a figure of speech, but to Mac he did look dead. Were his skin any worse he could have passed for a decomposing corpse. Even his ears had lost color and appeared translucent.

In the next instant, Mac found himself on his knees, shielding his eyes from the brightest light he had ever experienced. It reminded him of a science experiment in junior high more than fifty years before when he and his classmates wore heavily tinted goggles as they ignited magnesium strips.

Mac peeked to find that he was not the only soldier on the ground. Most had pitched forward onto their stomachs, weapons rattling to the floor. Whatever the source radiating from the middle of the table, it lit the room like the noon sun.

"Beautiful! Beautiful!" people whispered, interlaced with the oohs and aahs associated with fireworks displays. All the dignitaries had thrust their chairs back from the table and covered their eyes, peeking through fingers to gaze on this magnificent appearance, whatever it was.

Mac pushed himself up and rocked back on his haunches, his eyes gradually becoming accustomed to the initially blinding radiance. As he squatted there, hands on his weapon again, it was clear why so many thought this . . . this apparition was so striking. It seemed to hover inches above the table, directly in the center, such a bright gold-tinged white that you could not take your eyes from it. It shone with such brilliance that no detail was clear, from the bottom to the top of what appeared to be a roughly six-foot human form. There was no way to tell whether it—if it was a humanoid being—wore shoes or clothes or was naked.

Gradually Mac realized he was looking at the back of a being that faced Carpathia and Fortunato. Flowing blond hair came into view, but it appeared that the rest of the body would remain a mystery to the human eye. Clearly, this was not the Glorious Appearing of Christ, as Mac knew He was to return on the clouds with His faithful behind Him.

Viv Ivins's chair was empty, but Mac could hear her moaning in ecstasy on the floor.

Leon was also on the floor, head buried in his hands, rocking, weeping.

Carpathia had fallen forward in his borrowed chair, his cheek on the table, arms outstretched, palms flat. "Oh, my lord, my god, and my king," his death-rattle voice repeated over and over.

From outside the room Mac heard the awful, terrifying sounds of death. Panic, screams and screeches, pleading, bones being crushed, air pushed from lungs, horses snuffling and caterwauling as other, smaller creatures might do.

Pitiful, lonely cries could be heard from grown men and women. "Save me! Oh, God, save me! I don't want to die!"

And yet die they did. Without even being able to see, it was clear to Mac that the carnage between him and the exit would be unlike anything he had ever encountered. Shooting began, and he could only guess it was the few remaining soldiers putting horses or comrades out of their misery and trying to pave themselves some macabre exit route over dead bodies.

Carpathia raised his pathetic head, his Zorro getup hanging as if on a cadaver. "Lucifer," he managed in that rasping, hollow voice, appearing to squint into the eyes of the being. "My lord king, why have you forsaken me? Why have you withdrawn your spirit from me? Have I not given myself wholly to you, to serve you with my entire heart and being?"

"Silence!" came the response in a voice so phantasmagorically piercing and awful that it made Mac recoil and want to cover his ears. "You disgust me! Look at you! You dare suggest you have anything to offer *me* besides your pathetic frame?! You are drunk with a power whose source is far beyond your own! You are merely a vessel, a tool, a jar of clay for my purposes, and yet you parade yourself as if you had a shred of value!"

"Oh, my king!" Carpathia gasped. "No! I—"

"You do not even understand the meaning of the word *silence*! You are nothing! Nothing! You had no power to rise from the dead! You were a carcass, stiff and decaying. Look at you now. Aside from my grace, you would return to the earth, ashes to ashes and dust to dust."

"Spare me, oh, my lord! I love you and long to serve you! I will do anything for—"

"Oh, spirit of nothingness, mere speck of my imagination. I will borrow your otherwise worthless skeleton yet again. But you must know, and if you cannot fathom it, I must myself remind you who you are and who you are not. You are not me! I am not you! You are mere inventory, goods and services. You are a piece of equipment, and you must never dare imagine otherwise."

"I have never, divine one! Never! I am humbly at your serv—"

"I am the lord your god, and I will not share my glory!"

"Absolutely," Carpathia said, panting. "O king of heaven and earth."

"Do not think it was by accident that my Adversary, in His own words, acknowledged that I originated in heaven and called me the son of the morning! Do you not know, as He knows, that it is I who have weakened the nations?"

"I know," Carpathia sobbed. "I know!"

"I, not you, not anyone else in all of the evolved world, am the one who shall ascend into heaven. I will exalt my throne above the stars of God; I will also sit on the mount of the congregation on the farthest sides of the north; I will ascend above the heights of the clouds. I will be like the Most High."

"Yes, precious master. Yes!"

"Yet my Enemy claims I shall be brought down to Sheol, to the lowest depths of the pit."

"No, lord, no!"

"He claims that those who see me will gaze at me and consider me, saying, 'Is this the man who made the earth tremble, who shook kingdoms, who made the world as a wilderness and destroyed its cities, who did not open the house of his prisoners?'"

"May it never be so, my sovereign!"

"Oh yes, my Enemy derides me! He claims all the kings of the nations, all of them, die in glory, every one in his own grand tomb, but that I—*I*—shall be cast out of my grave like an abominable branch, like the garment of those who are slain, thrust through with a sword, who go down to the stones of the pit, like a corpse trodden underfoot. *I* will be buried like a common soldier killed in battle?"

"Never!" Carpathia sobbed. "Never! Not as long as I have breath!"

"Are you so thick you do not understand? It is *I* who give *you* breath!"

"I know! Yes, I know!"

"And what shall be your contribution, knave, when the Enemy attempts to make good on His promise that no monument will be given me, for I have destroyed my nation Babylon and slain my people? He taunts me that my son will not succeed me as king."

"Oh, let me be your son," Carpathia blubbered. "And you shall be my father!"

"But *no*! The Enemy derides me. He says, 'Slay the children of this sinner. Do not let them rise and conquer the land nor rebuild the cities of the world. I, myself, have risen against him,' and He has the audacity to call Himself the Lord of heaven's armies."

"But that is you, O beautiful star! It is you alone!"

"He has already destroyed my beloved Babylon, but He will not be content until He makes her into 'a desolate land of porcupines, full of swamps and marshes.' He promises to 'sweep the land with the broom of destruction,' this so-called Lord of the armies of heaven."

"We shall never let that happen, Your Grace."

"But He has taken an oath to do it! He says this is His purpose and plan. He has decided to break the Assyrian army when they are in Israel and to crush them on His mountains, saying, 'My people shall no longer be their slaves. This is My plan for the whole earth—I will do it by My mighty power that reaches everywhere around the world.'"

"But His power is nothing compared to yours, conquering king! We will prove it even today, will we not?"

"We? *We?*"

"You! You, exalted one!"

"Who are you to speak? What have you to offer me when the Enemy, who calls Himself the Lord, the God of battle, has spoken—who can change His plans? When His hand moves, who can stop Him?"

"You can, all-powerful one. I believe in you."

"I can. And do not forget it. Who does He think stood up against Israel and moved David to number Israel, when clearly his God had forbidden it?"

"He knows. I know He knows!"

"Of course He knows! It is I who have gone to and fro in the earth, walking up and down in it. It was I who tested and tempted Job to nearly abandon and curse his God. When Joshua the high priest stood before the Angel of the Lord, it was I who stood at his right hand to oppose him. It was I who tempted the Enemy's own Son in the wilderness."

"And you nearly succeeded."

"Success comes today."

"I believe it, my lord."

"I am the one who took the Enemy's Son up into the Holy City and set Him on the pinnacle of the temple. I said to Him, 'If You are the Son of God, throw Yourself down. For it is written: "He shall give His angels charge over You" and "In their hands they shall bear You up, lest you dash Your foot against a stone."' But He would not! He Himself did not believe! He countered as a coward, with mere words. He tried to tell me, as if *I* did not know, that 'It is written again, "You shall not tempt the Lord your God."' Well, He is not *my* Lord or God!"

"Nor mine, prince of the power of the air."

"It was I who took Him up on an exceedingly high mountain and showed Him all the kingdoms of the world and their glory. I offered Him all of these if He would but fall down and worship me. But He would not."

"He was a fool."

"But I did not bow to Him either."

"And you never will."

"I never shall. He spoke the truth and told it well when He called his own disciple Satan. I had hold of Peter for a time then. The Enemy's Son rightly accused him of not being mindful of the things of God, but of the things of men."

"May it ever be so!" Carpathia gushed.

"Oh, the Son knew well that when men heard His message, it was I who came immediately and took away the word that was sown in their hearts."

"That has always been your strength."

"It was I who entered Judas, who was numbered among the Son's disciples. And it was I who asked for Simon Peter yet again, that I might sift him as wheat. He was so weak that night."

"I will not be weak in your hour of need, master."

"I do not need you! I will not be weak! You, sad one, are unteachable."

"Forgive me, lord."

"It was I who filled Ananias's heart to lie and keep back part of the price of his land for himself."

"A masterpiece!"

"Silence! I am wearying of you. I am preparing for battle with the One who calls Himself the God of peace and claims He will crush me under His feet. I, the one who takes advantage when men are ignorant of my devices. I am the god of this age, able to blind the minds of those who do not believe—as I do not—in what my Enemy calls the light of the gospel of the glory of Christ, who is the image of God. I am more than His image. I am His superior and shall be His conqueror. I was crafty enough to deceive Eve, His second creation. Am I not up to this task?"

"You are, and the universe shall sing your praises and call you blessed."

"You have well said that I am the prince of the power of the air. I am the spirit who now works in the sons of disobedience toward the Enemy. I work among them to fulfill the lusts of their flesh, fulfilling the desires of the flesh and of the mind. None shall stand against my wiles. They do not wrestle against flesh and blood, but against my principalities, against my powers, against my rulers of this age, against spiritual hosts in the heavenly places."

"That is you, O blessed one."

"I have fiery darts that cannot be quenched."

"Amen and amen!"

"I hindered even the Enemy's favored servant, Paul, thwarting his plans time and again. And in his absence from his followers, I tempted them from their faith. I was their adversary, and they referred to me as akin to a roaring lion, seeking whom I might devour."

"Today shall be a feast for you."

"The Enemy who calls Himself God has decreed that His Son was manifested, that He might destroy my works."

"Blasphemy!"

"He called me the great dragon, called me that serpent of old, called me the devil and Satan, and acknowledged that it is I who deceives the whole world. But He erred when He cast me to the earth and my angels with me."

"He made an eternal blunder, lord. How excellent is your name in all the earth! Be exalted above the heavens. Let your glory be above all the earth. You, my lord, are high above all nations, and your glory above the heavens. Who is like unto you who dwells on high?"

"I have need of your shell again for a brief season."

"I am yours," Carpathia said.

And with that the light disappeared and Nicolae stood, chin lifted, arrogance restored. His color returned as he buttoned his shirt and straightened his clothes. It was as if he had come back to life, his voice again crisp and sure.

"Return to your seats, ladies and gentlemen, please. Ms. Ivins, please. Reverend Fortunato." He deliberately moved the chair Leon had provided for him and held it as the holy man awkwardly disentangled himself from his garments and stood, then sat.

"Sub-potentates, generals, assistants, sit, please. Soldiers, return to attention."

It was plain to Mac that the room was full of shocked and shaken people. Their eyes shone with fear. Their bodies were hesitant and unsure. They returned to their places fearful and stunned.

"Your discomfort will soon cease," Nicolae said. "When you are all in place, I shall tell you what you just witnessed and what you will remember."

An Asian dignitary raised a hand, consternation on his face.

"Please hold all questions, just for a moment."

An African stood, hand also raised.

"Please honor my request, sir," Carpathia said. "I will get to you in a moment if you will extend this courtesy."

The African sat, clearly troubled. Others looked at each other, eyes narrow, shaking their heads.

"Ladies and gentlemen and soldiers," Carpathia began, but he was interrupted by a man at the door. "What is it?"

"Because of the carnage outside, Excellency, we have been unable to find a paramedic unit for this room."

"Thank you. No longer needed."

"And, your grace, neither have we been able to determine the source of the heat that caused the stampede."

"I believe that issue is moot now, is it not? Anyone uncomfortable?"

"Not from the heat," an Aussie said, "but I have some serious questions about what just—"

"I shall ask you too, sir, to hold all questions and comments for another moment. Thank you. And, sir?" he added, addressing the one in the archway. "Would you mind staying as I offer an explanation?"

The man moved past Mac and stood behind those seated at the far end of the table from Carpathia.

"Ladies and gentlemen," Nicolae began in his most mellow, persuasive tone, slowly scanning the room and looking briefly but directly into the eyes of everyone. "Do not feel obligated to look away this time. I am choosing to connect with you visually. You have just been privileged to enjoy a unique experience. You were present when I left this mortal body and took on my divine form.

I charged you with all the rights and privileges that attend your station as loyal followers and encouraged you in the battle to come.

"You shall become aware as we leave this place and mount up to ride into our glorious victory that the enemy has succeeded in penetrating the ground above, essentially our ceiling. I divinely protected myself, you included, but they caused a stampede that has caused many casualties among our troops and our livestock, which, as you know, we value as highly as our human resources. But do not be alarmed. Do not fear. Our resources are limitless. I shall lead you up and out, and there will be enough mounts for all. Now, there were some comments and questions?"

The Asian stood, bowing. "I just wanted to thank you, Excellency, for the privilege you have extended to me and my party. To have been here for this most momentous and historic moment will become the memory of a lifetime, and we are most grateful."

"Thank you. Yes, sir?"

The African stood. "I would like to echo that sentiment, your holiness, on behalf of my staff. You are most worthy to be praised, and we look forward to joining you in your ultimate victory, after which the world shall see you for who you truly are."

Mac wanted to shout an amen. If he was the only believer in the room—and he couldn't imagine otherwise—he was the only one not hypnotically hoodwinked by Carpathia.

The exit to the surface was surreal. The men and women were led and followed by contingents of the soldiers, giving Mac a perfect view of their response to what had befallen everyone else. The place was worse than any war zone. Hundreds of horses and even more men and women lay dead in hideous repose, broken, trampled, crushed, torn to pieces. The stench of the stables was nothing compared to the steaming entrails of human and beast, and yet the men and women from the meeting room stepped on and over the remains as if traipsing through a meadow.

No one made a face, held his nose, or had a comment. It was as if they could not see the slaughter that soaked their shoes and caused dirt to adhere to the blood. As they reached the surface they blithely stamped their feet and thanked the soldiers for their assistance. The mood was festive as great steeds were moved into line for them and each was helped into the saddle.

Bound for Armageddon, they smiled and laughed and chatted as if on their way to a day at the races. Mac noticed for the first time that day that puffy, fluffy clouds had begun to dot the sky. The sun was still visible, turning orange on the horizon. All he wanted was to slip away and be with his brothers and sisters in Christ when the end came.

\+ + +

Rayford had his misgivings about both the vehicles. There was room on Abdullah's for the both of them, but not much. And it was a thin, whiny, violent machine built for speed, hardly comfort. Leah's ATV was wider and sturdier and slower, but unless they left her supplies behind there would not be room for two people. As the second rider, Rayford needed stability. And speed would be his enemy. The angles, the inclines, the acceleration, the turns and bounces and jostling would be torture.

The alternative was not acceptable. He didn't want to stay in the barren, rocky hills any longer. Who knew what the global earthquake would do out there? He didn't expect to die in it, but he hadn't expected to be pitched off his ATV either.

His ATV. Now there was a solution. Not his, of course. It lay in ruins. But there were more where that came from. They called Sebastian.

"Camel Jockey to Big Dog," Smitty said.

"This's Dog, Jockey. Go."

"Can you get us an ATV to transport Captain Steele to Petra?"

"If I can drive it."

"Affirmative, but should you leave your troops?"

"Kidding, Smitty. I'll send Razor."

"You know our position?"

"Affirmative. Chang zeroed you in for me. Rayford going to make it?"

"If he survives the trip. How does Mr. Razor drive?"

"I think he knows what's at stake. What do you make of the clouds?"

"First ones all day, Big Dog. I think Somebody's coming."

\+ + +

"I've got to get out of here," Chang said, rubbing his eyes.

"That's all I need to hear," Naomi said, virtually lifting him from his chair.

"Let me log off first," he said, resisting.

"Not on your life. Now let's go. Nobody's going to suffer if you don't log off. This is supposed to be a spectacular sunset."

"With no clouds? How do you figure?"

"You'll see. You've been so busy, you don't even know what's going on."

When they got outside, Chang was stunned. The sun was dropping, big and wide, and there were indeed clouds. They seemed to appear from nowhere, more and more by the minute. There was something festive about them—bouncy, fleecy, and yet moving quickly as if there were strong winds high in the atmosphere. Before long they were joining each other, making shadow-forming canopies south of the sun while individual clouds continued to form to the north.

These, too, soon began to join. Chang and Naomi went to their favorite high spot and lay on their backs, hands behind their heads. "I've never seen that before," Chang said, pointing straight up. Clouds seemed to be forming directly above, not on the horizon as usual. They began as long, narrow formations in the stratosphere, quickly forming into stratocumulus.

"We're getting high-, mid-, and low-level formations all at the same time," Chang said.

"They're gorgeous."

"Yeah, now. Wait till they start developing vertically. They can reach heights of more than seven miles and generate incredible energy."

"How do you know all this?" she said. "All I know is computers."

"I know everything," Chang said.

Naomi punched him. "Hey," she said, turning on her side and gazing at his face. "You're going to fall asleep."

"Not likely," he said. "Too much happening up there. Too much to look forward to."

6

"BROTHER ENOCH," a Hispanic man said, "if you can concentrate, we can concentrate."

"I don't follow," Enoch said, again looking through trees and windows at the edge of the mall's courtyard to be sure the GC had not found them out.

"You seem distracted, brother. I mean, we're all waiting for the same thing. We want to be ready. We want to be here when Jesus comes. But in the meantime we want you to teach us. You keep saying you're no scholar, but you've been our pastor for years. Something's working."

"Yeah," another chimed in. "I don't feel like I've got a handle on what all's happened and what's going to happen. I know we'll soon be with Jesus—or anyway, He'll be with us—but I wouldn't mind going into all this with more understanding. You got more for us?"

Enoch had to smile. "I do," he said. "I just didn't expect to have the time to cover it, and I certainly didn't expect you to have the patience for it."

"Beats waitin' around. I can't wait till Jesus gets here, but the clock moves slow when nothin's happening."

"Fair enough. I've got my Bible and my notes, if you're game."

"We're game. But, Pastor, have you looked up lately?"

It was coming up on noon in the Midwest, and the sun was riding high. Enoch shielded his eyes. "Clouds," he said.

"Clouds that weren't there an hour ago. If I'm not mistaken, we woke up to blue skies."

"Totally blue."

"They're not threatening clouds," Enoch said. "I don't expect we'll get rained on."

A woman laughed. "I just wanna see clouds Jesus can ride in on."

+ + +

Razor showed up on a 750cc ATV plenty big enough to accommodate Rayford if he were healthy. But he had not been sitting up long, let alone standing or bouncing along on a vehicle.

"You didn't happen to bring any food, did you?" Rayford said.

"Sir, yes, sir," Razor said in the maddening military formality of which Rayford had been trying to break him.

"Miz Leah here didn't care if I starved to death."

"Hydration was most important," she said. "And I didn't expect you to be stuck here this long."

"I'm kidding, Leah. You saved my life. Now what've you got, Razor?"

"An energy bar, sir."

"One of those Styrofoam jobs that tastes like cardboard?"

"One and the same."

"Flavor?"

"Corrugated chocolate, I believe, sir."

Kidding aside, Rayford was famished. He tore open the wrapper and took a huge bite.

"Easy there, cowboy," Leah said. "Your system's been traumatized."

"Well, this ought to help," Rayford said, following orders and slowing down. He was stalling. Climbing aboard an ATV was going to be an ordeal, but that would be the least of it. The path back to Petra, such as it was, looked like a sheer cliff from his vantage point. "It's going to be a beautiful sunset," he said idly.

"And probably the last one before Jesus comes," Leah said.

+ + +

Sebastian sat on the hood of a Hummer that had been idle for hours, but whose metal had only just cooled enough to allow him there. The Unity Army seemed distracted, if that characteristic could be applied to such an expansive gathering. Ever since they had advanced half a mile and stopped, they had sat staring menacingly at him and his troops.

George had decided not to antagonize them with directed energy weapons or fifty-caliber fire, and in the last half hour they had grown, well, somehow less threatening. It was as if they had lost focus. Earlier, the hundreds of thousands of mounted troops alone had seemed to act in concert to stare him down, and now he heard their squeaky saddles in the distance. They had stopped staring and had begun wheeling in their saddles, chatting with each other.

Was it possible the rumors had reached the battlefield? Did these soldiers know that they might not be spelled by reinforcements or that, even if they were, it was unlikely they would be paid on time, if at all? The grapevine was remarkably accurate, quick, and—if this proved true—resilient enough to reach across the desert sands.

Could Big Dog One take advantage of this lapse? He couldn't imagine how.

A volley of shells or DEW rays would succeed only in getting the enemy re-engaged, setting them back on course. For now, hopelessly outnumbered as he was, Sebastian liked his adversary just the way it was. If he could choose, he'd have moved them back about a mile and a half. But they couldn't pull that off even if they wanted to, even if they were ordered to. Backing up the front lines meant backing up the rear, and coordinating that would take weeks. This was a fighting force that could go only one way, and Sebastian and his excuse for a defending force were directly in their path.

He got on the phone. "Chang, what're you doing right this instant?"

"You don't want to know."

"'Course I do."

"I'm lying on my back, watching the clouds."

"And you're not alone, are you?"

"Of course not," Chang said.

"Priscilla and I are going to be apart when Jesus comes," Sebastian said.

"You want me to send her and Beth Ann to be with you?"

"Hardly. We've arranged a meeting spot for when this is over."

"I hope Captain Steele will be up to watching all this when he gets here and the time comes," Chang said.

"Oh, he will be. Just hope the time doesn't come before Razor gets him there."

+ + +

"As you know," Enoch told his people, "the whole theme through my teaching of the events of the end times has been the mercy of God. To many of you this seemed inconsistent with what was prophesied and what came to pass. But as I have said, all of this, all twenty-one judgments that have come from heaven in three sets of seven, have been God's desperate last attempts to get man's attention. Make no mistake about it, however; the last seven judgments in particular also evidence His wrath.

"In fact, the angels who carry out these judgments are depicted as turning over and emptying out bowls or vials, so that every drop of judgment is poured out on the various targets of God's anger. Notice the focus of these judgments:

"The first bowl was poured out on the *earth* in the form of horrible malignant sores on the bodies of those who had taken the mark of the beast.

"The second was poured out into the *sea,* turning the water to blood and killing every living thing in it.

"The third was poured into the *rivers* and *springs* so that all remaining freshwater was turned to blood. You'll recall that this was God's initial and partial response to the martyrs' prayers in Revelation 6:10 that their deaths be avenged:

'And they cried with a loud voice, saying, "How long, O Lord, holy and true, until You judge and avenge our blood on those who dwell on the earth?"'

"The fourth bowl was poured out on the *sun* so that it so increased in power that extraordinary heat burned men with fire. And how did those who survived respond? Revelation 16:9 tells us they 'blasphemed the name of God who has power over these plagues; and they did not repent and give Him glory.'

"The fifth bowl was poured out on the *throne of the beast.* Who knows what that means?"

"New Babylon."

"Yes! And we know that mighty city was plunged into a darkness so great that it caused physical pain so severe that men and women gnawed their own tongues. And once again, what was their response? 'They blasphemed the God of heaven because of their pains and their sores, and did not repent of their deeds.'

"The sixth bowl was poured out on the great river, the *Euphrates,* and it dried up. That allowed the leaders from the east to bring their armies to the mountains of Israel for the battle of Armageddon. Here God was clearly luring Antichrist into His trap. Joel 3:9-17 prophesies this, and though scholars disagree about when the book of Joel was written, it is generally agreed that it was more than eight hundred years before Christ:

"'Proclaim this among the nations: "Prepare for war! Wake up the mighty men, let all the men of war draw near, let them come up. Beat your plowshares into swords and your pruning hooks into spears; let the weak say, 'I am strong.'"

"'Assemble and come, all you nations, and gather together all around. Cause Your mighty ones to go down there, O Lord.' Let the nations be wakened, and come up to the Valley of Jehoshaphat; for there I will sit to judge all the surrounding nations. Put in the sickle, for the harvest is ripe. Come, go down; for the winepress is full, the vats overflow—for their wickedness is great."

"'Multitudes, multitudes in the valley of decision! For the day of the Lord is near in the valley of decision. The sun and moon will grow dark, and the stars will diminish their brightness. The Lord also will roar from Zion, and utter His voice from Jerusalem; the heavens and earth will shake; but the Lord will be a shelter for His people, and the strength of the children of Israel.

"'So you shall know that I am the Lord your God, dwelling in Zion My holy mountain. Then Jerusalem shall be holy, and no aliens shall ever pass through her again.'"

Enoch continued, "The seventh Bowl Judgment, the one we still await, will be poured out upon the *air* so that lightning and thunder and other celestial calamities announce the greatest earthquake in history. It will be so great it will cause Jerusalem to break into three pieces in preparation for changes during

Christ's millennial kingdom. It will also be accompanied by a great outpouring of hundred-pound hailstones.

"And what will the general response be from the very ones God is trying to reach and persuade? Revelation 16:21 tells us that 'men blasphemed God because of the plague of the hail, since that plague was exceedingly great.'"

"And this is what's coming next?" someone said.

"In advance of the Glorious Appearing," Enoch said. "Yes."

"And you believe this?"

"Without question."

"Then what are we doing outside while the clouds gather?"

"Do you not recall that believers have been spared injury under all these judgments? I rest in that."

"Amen!"

"Praise the Lord!"

"Come, Lord Jesus!"

"I rest in something else, beloved," Enoch said. "One of the most beautiful and reassuring passages in Scripture is John 14:1-6, where Jesus is comforting His disciples. I believe we can take these promises for ourselves and stand secure, knowing they were made by One in whom there is no change, neither shadow of turning. Let me read them to you.

"'Let not your heart be troubled; you believe in God, believe also in Me. In My Father's house are many mansions; if it were not so, I would have told you. I go to prepare a place for you. And if I go and prepare a place for you, I will come again and receive you to Myself; that where I am, there you may be also. And where I go you know, and the way you know.'

"'Thomas said to Him, "Lord, we do not know where You are going, and how can we know the way?"

"'Jesus said to him, "I am the way, the truth, and the life. No one comes to the Father except through Me."'"

+ + +

Rayford noticed a lull in the activity and assumed it was because both Razor and Leah needed Abdullah's help to load him aboard the big ATV. And Abdullah was fifteen feet or so down the rocky slope with his back to them, on the phone. When it appeared he was finished, he called someone else.

The energy bar, distasteful as it was, had its desired effect, and Rayford was ready to get going. He'd felt better in his day, but despite numerous ailments, he had a renewed sense of purpose and drive. *Let's go; let's go!* he thought, but he said nothing.

Presently Abdullah returned. "Many people worry about you, Captain," he said. "Ree Woo for one, but especially Chaim himself. He wonders what your plans are."

"My plans? To keep breathing. To survive the trip."

"He is wondering if you would be up to his visit at your quarters when you arrive."

"Of course," Rayford said. "Know what he wants?"

"Again," Leah said, "let's not get ahead of ourselves, shall we? You joke about surviving the trip, and frankly I am quite worried about that. You have no idea how you'll feel when you arrive. You likely have a broken rib on top of everything else, maybe more than one. It's nearly impossible to tell without an X-ray or MRI."

"What're you saying, Doc?"

"I'm just a nurse, but moving you the way we're planning is just about the worst possible scenario for you right now."

"Just about?"

"Staying here would be worse, but at least you're stable."

+ + +

Mac gingerly climbed aboard the biggest, blackest, most powerful horse he had ever seen. It had been years, but he knew enough to plant his left foot firmly in the stirrup before swinging his right leg up and over. If anyone was looking, he might appear to have a clue.

Unfortunately, he was more concerned with mounting than he was with his dangling Uzi, and before he settled firmly in the saddle, the barrel of his weapon poked the horse in the back, just above the saddle horn at the base of the neck. The beast started and stepped about quickly, causing Mac to panic and stiffen. That made the horse rear. Mac pulled on the reins with all his weight, desperate to hang on and not be chucked off onto his head.

As the steed whinnied loudly and reared higher, spooking other horses and riders, Mac slid out of the saddle and the stirrups slackened. Mac pushed his legs straight as hard as he could, tucked his chin to his chest, and held the reins for all he was worth. That pulled the horse's muzzle down and nearly made him topple backward. Mac was almost upside down, all his weight pulling against the horse, and he could imagine pulling the animal down atop him.

Somehow the horse balanced itself with a few well-placed steps with its back feet, then slammed down to all fours, thrusting Mac hard into the saddle and throwing him forward to where he was now hugging the horse around the neck. The animal still felt unsure beneath him, and Mac knew he had done the opposite of showing it who was in charge. If a message had been sent to the horse, it was that the rider was scared to death and hanging on for dear life.

Mac's "superior" appeared not to have noticed. He cantered up and pointed to several soldiers, Mac included, directing them to position themselves off the flanks of Carpathia's horse. Leave it to the potentate to have a monster creature that put the rest to shame. His horse was at least two hands taller and a hundred pounds heavier than the others. It had a spot of white between its eyes and four white feet. Its tail seemed to shoot straight up before the rest of it cascaded down in a smart flow. The mane was somehow longer and thicker as well. Mac had heard of the hound of heaven. This was the horse from hell.

It even seemed to have attitude. It snuffled loudly whenever another horse invaded its space, and it nipped and kicked to keep its place. Carpathia appeared to have been raised around horses, deftly controlling the thing with a light grip and decisive hands, knees, and feet. He rode ahead several feet and turned his horse to face the others.

"Let me remind you all," he said, "that we are merely feet from an active battleground. The resistance currently holds the Temple Mount, aboveground, and they are capable of firing from atop the wall. Be vigilant. This is not a press junket or a sightseer's safari. I am most disappointed to tell you that I have just been made aware of an insurgence within our own ranks from both the south in Egypt and below and from the northeast. Ironically, some who pledged their allegiance now call themselves 'Revitalized Babylon' and condescend to assert their independence. These uprisings shall be crushed posthaste. As we speak, portions of our more than extravagantly outfitted fighting force will peel off to these locations to lay waste to the pretenders. They will regret their insolence only as long as they have breath, and then they will be trampled and made an example of.

"Meanwhile, we will figuratively set out for Petra. I say figuratively, because I do not plan to waste the hours it would take to actually ride some sixty miles on horseback. The Global Community media will get what it needs as we strike out from here, leave the occupied Muslim Quarter, and head southwest through the Jewish and Armenian Quarters—both also having been easily taken by our forces—and leave the Old City through the Zion Gate. There you will transfer to ground vehicles capable of covering the distance at well over a hundred miles an hour. I will set out a few minutes later with my generals and cabinet in aircraft that will actually transport us and our horses to the area slightly in advance of your arrival.

"We have mounts similar to those you are on now waiting for you outside Petra, and you shall have the privilege of witnessing my leading our troops to victory over what shall by then be one of only two remaining enclaves of opposition to the New World Order. Smile for the cameras!"

Mac finally felt he had control of his horse, but he had no intention of following Carpathia in one of the ground vehicles. If any portion of the security detail was assigned elsewhere, Mac would find a way to join them, and then peel off to his own helicopter. He wouldn't mind seeing what went down at Petra, though he had been taught that the actual fighting would take place twenty miles north in Buseirah, Jordan—the modern name of the city of Bozrah, ancient capital of Edom—when Messiah chased the Unity Army back toward Jerusalem.

✢ ✢ ✢

Besides the dizziness that came with trying to stand for the first time in hours, Rayford found himself wholly dependent upon the small but wiry Abdullah Smith and the broader, stronger, and younger Razor. Leah had brought everything, it seemed, but crutches. She did her bit to help too, but she could not support him and mainly directed traffic, trying to keep his most vulnerable injuries isolated.

Rayford could put zero weight on the broken shinbone, splint or not. Hopping was out of the question, so the two men had to bear all his weight as they moved him to the ATV. Even his good foot touching the ground occasionally sent shock waves of pain throughout the rest of his body. The anesthetic in his temple was wearing off, and Leah had decided not to add more.

Straddling the ATV was a delicate operation. Leah rolled up a towel and bunched it under the knee of his broken leg in an attempt to keep his foot from touching the vehicle. That left him able to balance himself only with his good foot and leg, with his painful arms latched tightly to Razor's waist. Rayford dreaded what he knew was coming. At some point his weight would shift to the broken shinbone side, and he would either have to wrestle Razor the other way or plant that foot to keep from flying off the ATV.

Once he was in place, Leah insisted he just sit there and get his bearings. "You okay?" she said.

"Think so," he said, already exhausted. He shut his eyes and rolled his neck, hearing it pop and crack. Then he stole a look at the sky. Clouds covered half the visible canopy now, and they were beginning to roil in all different colors. The sun was half below the horizon, wide and flat and at its most burnt orange, painting the clouds in pinks and reds and yellows. Were he not fearing for his life, he'd have thought it one of the most beautiful skies he had ever seen.

Leah had final instructions for Razor. "I'll lead the way," she said. "Mr. Smith will follow you, should we have a problem and need to lift Captain Steele again. My machine has a lot of weight on it too, so if I can make it through a certain area, you should be able to as well. I'll be trying to avoid ruts, bumps, even the smallest rocks, but of course we can't avoid them all. Try to take the steep areas as slowly as possible, but you'll need some power and momentum. Rayford, you'll just have to hang on and grit your teeth. The first fifty yards or so are pretty clear, so I'll try to keep an eye behind me to make sure you're both doing okay."

Rayford had always considered himself a man's man. Six-four and thickly muscled, he had played sports through pain of all sorts. And since the Rapture, he'd endured his share of serious injuries. But as he sat there, vise-gripping Razor's belt, he wanted to scream like a baby. Everything hurt. It was as if the pain had a life and mind of its own and threatened to kill him itself. It dug deep, mostly in his temple and shin, and it vibrated, throbbed, prodded.

When Razor so much as fired up the engine, the hum alone flashed through Rayford's body and made him instantly light-headed. Razor would likely be able to tell if he passed out, just from the change in his grip. But Rayford was determined to gut this out.

Leah slowly pulled ahead, the pair of coolers hanging off the sides of her ATV like mismatched saddlebags. Razor turned his head. "Just say the word, and I stop."

"Go," Rayford managed, and the four-wheeler began rolling. "Lord, have mercy."

"Okay?" Razor called back.

"Don't ask, son. I'll let you know. You just keep moving."

+ + +

Sebastian was struck by the grandeur of the early evening sun casting its glow over the black-clad enemy. Who'd have thought this evil mass of humanity could be seen in an attractive light? He had been joined by Otto Weser, the German who had maintained a small band of believers inside New Babylon until nearly the end.

"Ever dream you'd have this privilege, Otto?"

"Privilege? This is my definition of the awesome and terrible day of the Lord."

"But to be standing here, facing Antichrist's army on the last day of the earth as we know it . . ."

"I'd rather have acted on the truth when I had the chance and be in heaven already, if you want complete honesty."

"Well, 'course," Sebastian said, "but given that we missed it, there's no place I'd rather be right now. I just wish my wife and daughter could be with me."

"You wouldn't want them out here," Otto said, the understatement so obvious that Sebastian could not think of a retort. "You're not bothered by an enemy close enough to look up our nostrils?"

Sebastian shook his head. "If they wanted to kill us and God allowed it, it would have happened long ago. I've been in aircraft that missiles had no business missing. I feel invulnerable standing here. I can't beat this army, I know that, not on my own. But Dr. Ben-Judah and Dr. Rosenzweig and lots of other teachers have me convinced that this whole fighting force is going to make like the Midianites before Gideon and turn tail and run by the time this night is out. I can't wait to see that."

"It's a little hard to believe, though, isn't it? I mean, looking at their sheer numbers?"

Sebastian turned and studied the older man in the twilight. "God changed a cloudless day into a cloudy one a little while ago. And you. You watched while the entire city of New Babylon was laid to ruins in the space of sixty minutes. And you say something's hard to believe?"

+ + +

Rayford hated it most when Leah stopped and Razor had to do the same. There was no smooth way to do that, not on these inclines. Sometimes Razor was forced to stop without having found a flat place. There Ray sat, hanging on tight to keep from slipping off the back of the ATV.

"This is where the going gets tough," Leah said.

And the tough get going, Rayford thought. "What do you call what we've been doing so far?" he said.

"Easy street," she said. "From here on out, we can't stop. We can barely slow down. We're going up steep angles and we need to keep moving. You just have to gut it out. Let's go."

She took off faster than Rayford had thought possible or prudent, and while Razor eased into his speed a bit more carefully, he was soon gunning the engine to make the grade. A couple of sharp turns made Rayford cry out, but when Razor backed off the throttle Rayford assured him with a shout that he was okay.

Soon they hit the steepest climb and Rayford felt as if he were hanging upside down. He scanned the area around him and realized if he lost his grip here he would be in serious trouble. He would tumble farther than he had initially. Abdullah's bike whined up beside them and he flashed a thumbs-up. Rayford shook his head. All he needed was to yield to the temptation to let go with one hand and return the gesture, and he'd be a dead man.

He rested his forehead in the middle of Razor's back. Where did these kids get the steel muscles today? In his prime Rayford was never cut like this specimen.

The sun was fast fading, and all three vehicles' automatic lights came on at the same time. They finally rounded a curve that put them on an actual path, and Rayford realized the rest of the way would be relatively easy.

What he was not prepared for, however, was the welcome he received. Tens of thousands of residents were out gathering the evening manna and watching the heavens. Word must have passed far and wide about his predicament, because everyone seemed to know the makeshift motorcade was his transport home.

People waved and shouted and whistled and raised their hands. He could not acknowledge them except to nod. Meanwhile, Smitty was waving as if it were his own ticker-tape parade.

Rayford could only imagine the welcome Jesus would receive.

7

THE SUN HAD DIPPED below the horizon, leaving a bright, nearly full moon to illuminate an otherwise inky, cloud-scattered sky. The cloud colors had seemed to change in an instant, pastels giving way to deep blues, purples, lavenders, and traces of a fast-fading burnt orange.

Abdullah, Razor, and Leah helped Rayford to his quarters. He insisted on waiting, uncomfortably, in a side chair, while they moved his bed to face the open window. That way, on his back, he could take in the entire vista of the beautiful night sky. Something was brewing and, of course, he knew what it was.

Razor appeared eager to get back to his post and was quickly gone. Leah said she would be close by in the infirmary and that either she or Hannah would be available at a moment's notice with just a call.

Abdullah said he was worried about Mac, then looked as if he shouldn't have said anything.

"Where *is* Mac, Smitty?" Rayford said.

Abdullah told him.

"If anything's happened to Buck," Rayford said, "I don't want Kenny knowing. And I don't want him seeing me this way. Can you confirm Kenny's still with Priscilla Sebastian?"

Abdullah got on the phone, updated Priscilla on Rayford, and nodded to Ray. "Kenny is about to go to sleep for the night," he said.

"That'll be one to tell his grandchildren," Ray said. "'I slept through the Glorious Appearing.'"

Rayford was grateful to be off the four-wheeler and in his own bed, but he had not realized how much the day had taken out of him until he was lying flat. "I may sleep through it myself," he said. "Would you keep me company, Smitty? Keep me awake?"

The Jordanian looked ill at ease. He had never been one for confrontation, but it was obvious he didn't want to accede to Rayford's request.

"Hey, it's all right, man," Rayford said. "You've got stuff to do, places you need to be."

"It is not that, Captain. But Dr. Rosenzweig is due soon—"

"Oh, that's right!"

"And, yes, I would like to be in the air when all these things come to pass. If you do not mind."

"You kiddin'? You know that's where I'd love to be if I could. You go right ahead, buddy. Really. I'll be fine."

"Oh, there is no way I would leave you alone. I can stay until Dr. Rosenzweig arrives."

Rayford carefully put his hands behind his head and folded his pillow double to prop his head a bit more. From his vantage point he had a wide view of the heavens, with the moon far to his left and the rest of his field of vision filled with heavy, colorful, moving clouds. As the sky grew darker, the moon seemed brighter, the clouds denser, and the stars clearer. As usual, when his eyes grew accustomed to the night sky, a deeper layer of stars came into view. But as he studied them, they disappeared and he had to search between clouds for more.

Chaim arrived with a small entourage, and Rayford was surprised when he dismissed all of them. "I will call if I need you," he said.

And as Abdullah Smith left, Rayford exacted from him a promise that he would call with anything new about Mac or Buck.

"Are you sure you want to know?" Abdullah said.

"Of course. Don't protect me. Even if it's the worst, we'll reunite with them soon."

Chaim settled into a tilting chair next to Rayford's bed and leaned back. "Magnificent," he said. "Like a front-row seat to eternity."

It wasn't like Chaim to stall. Though well past seventy now, he was a brilliant man of seemingly unbridled energy, and no one knew him to waste time. Yet here he sat, studying the skies of Israel, with apparently nothing to say.

"Something on your mind, Doctor? I mean, more than a million people here would give anything to spend this night with you. To what do I owe the pleasure?"

\+ + +

Global Community news-media cameras were trained on the Carpathian cavalry that emerged from the Dung Gate. Mac was relieved to discover he was not nearly the only member getting used to his steed. An equal number of men and women, most representing other sub-potentates, overreacted to their horses and wound up steering them in circles or being nearly chucked off. At first this was greeted with smiles all around, but it quickly became obvious that Carpathia was no longer amused. He dismissed the press and urged his generals to get everyone to their various means of conveyance to Petra.

Mac watched for his opening and was disappointed when his commander chose him as one to accompany Carpathia's cargo plane, big enough for several horses and vehicles. If those in charge only knew that Mac was once Nicolae's chief pilot . . .

Mac had once prided himself on keeping cool in a crisis, particularly when undercover. But as he dismounted and went through the motions of turning his horse over to a swarthy young man in a loud T-shirt who would walk it aboard the plane, he could think of nothing more creative than to simply try to talk his way out of it.

"Say, I've got a problem here, sport," he said.

"Yeah? What might that be, *sport?*" the young man said, his accent that of a New Zealander.

"Got myself in the wrong group. Is it too late to catch up with the others?"

"You mean the ones being carried by Hummers and such?"

"Right."

"I don't know, but you'd better try. You get on board this plane when you're not supposed to, and there'll be blood to pay. Anyway, I got no room for even one extra horse."

Mac took the horse back and mounted, and when someone called after him asking what he thought he was doing, he hollered, "Following orders! Going where they point me!" He looked over his shoulder to confirm that the voice was not that of his commander. He was otherwise engaged, which Mac found comforting. He didn't want to have it out with anybody in the GC this close to the return of Jesus. All he needed was to be arrested or shot just before the end.

The animal beneath him seemed to respond to Mac's sense of purpose. Mac knew where he was going now, and he wanted to get there fast. The first thing he wanted to do, once out of anyone else's sight, was to call in the news about Buck and about Carpathia's plans and see if there was any word on Rayford. Then he wanted to get into his own chopper and out of this infernal Global Community Unity Army uniform. His own plain and baggy clothes had never seemed so inviting.

+ + +

Sebastian felt the fatigue, not of boredom but of inactivity. Tension and anticipation would carry him until midnight or even dawn, if necessary. He hoped it wouldn't come to that.

He was grateful for the International Co-op and the job Lionel Whalum had been doing with it since Chloe Steele Williams's death. Behind Sebastian stood three gargantuan searchlights, equipment only the Co-op could have located and transported. Without the lights, Sebastian's eyes could play tricks on him. In the moonlight alone, he might have imagined the Unity Army beginning to advance again. He sensed the rumble, felt the vibration, knew something was happening, but all he needed was to flip the switches, train those gigantic beams toward the enemy, and determine that they were merely holding their ground half a mile away.

Razor's ATV came skidding up behind him in a cloud of dust. Razor approached with a salute and stood at attention.

"You've really got to quit that, boy," Sebastian said. "I'm as military and gung ho as the next guy, but what am I going to do with you? Court-martial you and put you in the brig for what—an hour or two?"

"Sorry, sir," Razor said, fully reporting on what he called his Captain Steele detail.

"Well, I'm just glad to know it was only you making the ground rumble. Had me thinking the enemy was on the move again."

"Oh, they are, sir."

"They are?"

"Yes, sir. From up on the slopes I could see them advancing. You can't see them at this level, but they've moved a good bit, sir. They surely have."

Sebastian dispatched Otto Weser to flip the switches on the big lamps. "I'd trust my night-vision goggles, but I don't mind the Unity boys seeing what we've got. Anyway, their horses can't be accustomed to this."

"Standing by, Big Dog One," Otto called in.

"Fire 'em up," Sebastian said, and the high beams ripped across the desert sand. "Mercy."

The enemy had advanced at least eight hundred yards in the darkness, and the front line of their seemingly endless mounted troops now stood silently about eighty yards away. It was plain they were merely waiting for orders to attack.

"We should attack them, sir," Razor said.

"Say again?"

"We should—"

"I heard you, Razor. I just can't believe I heard you. In any other situation, that would be brilliant. Seriously. Sucker punch them. Like taking the first swing at the bully. You know they wouldn't be expecting it."

"But?"

"But two things: First, if everything we threw at them found its mark, we'd cause a ministampede, kill a few soldiers and horses, then get massacred.

Second, we're invulnerable where we stand, as far as we know. We may not be out there."

"There is one other thing," Razor said.

"I'm listening."

"This battle's already been won, and without us lifting a finger."

"Well, there is that, yes."

Sebastian's phone chirped. It was Mac. "Yes," George said, "Rayford's back in his quarters with Chaim and will apparently pull through. And Buck? . . . I'm sorry to hear that. You talked to Chang? . . . Probably monitoring the world. We'll spread the word."

✠ ✠ ✠

"I sense we are a lot alike, Captain Steele," Chaim said.

That drew Rayford's gaze from the window for a second. He couldn't imagine many people he was more different from than Chaim. They were Jew and Gentile, old and not so old, Middle Eastern and American, botanist and aviator, leader of a million people and leader of a small band.

"I sense," Chaim said, "despite our cultural and professional differences, that we are both normal men thrust into decisions and roles not of our own making. Am I right?"

"I guess."

"It may be even more surprising that I am a believer in Messiah than you are. But both of us took the long way to get here, didn't we?"

"We did."

"As you know, in my current position I have more company—more friends and associates and elders and advisers—than anyone would ever need. True, I had no shortage of options as to with whom I would spend this evening. Frankly, if I could have chosen from the whole universe, I would have chosen your son-in-law. We go back a long, long way. I knew him before he was a believer, and he knew me so long before I was that I daresay he still finds it hard to fathom. My hope is that if Cameron returns tonight, he will join us and feel welcome."

✠ ✠ ✠

Chang was, in fact, monitoring the world. He had seemed to catch his second wind. He knew he should be in bed, but who could sleep at a time like this? He sat at his computer, staring at the reports coming in from all over the world about people, especially Jews, putting their faith in Jesus Christ as their Messiah. Tens of thousands every few minutes were totaling in the millions now, and Chang had the feeling it wouldn't stop until the Glorious Appearing. There were to be signs in the heavens before that, and more were prophesied to come to Christ.

+ + +

Rayford and Chaim got the news about Buck from Sebastian a few minutes later. Rayford didn't know what to feel. He knew Buck was fine, better than he had ever been, and that he would see him soon. But he hated the thought that the young man, the father of Rayford's grandson and the husband of his daughter, had suffered so. Rayford had lost many friends and loved ones, none so close as his daughter and now son-in-law. But in the past he had somehow been able to come to terms with the losses, to tell himself it was the price of war, the inevitable result of what they had been called to do.

It was not so easy now, not when it struck so close to home. He called Mac.

+ + +

The clouds parted and the moon shone brightly, all the way to the Dead Sea, directly beneath Mac.

"I'm not gonna lie to you, Ray. Yeah, it looks like Buck came to a rough end. But he was doing what he wanted to do. He worked at it, trained for it, and if you remember the first reports we got from him, he and Tsion got done what they hoped to."

"How's the resistance?"

"'Bout finished. Unity's got 'em pushed into the Temple Mount, and it's clear the GC has hardly scratched the surface of their resources yet. They could take the whole city anytime they wanted."

"You're heading back, I assume."

"Not all the way," Mac said. "I want to see what happens on the Petra perimeter from the air. Then I want to head back up to Buseirah and see how that plays out."

"You know I'd give anything to be there with you."

"Holy mackerel! You see that, Ray?"

"I see it. I'll let you go. Time to watch the show."

+ + +

A cloud had now covered the moon. It was bright and nearly full and had been highlighting the dancing clouds. Suddenly, it had seemed to disappear, as if someone had turned it out like a light. Rayford knew the moon merely reflected the sun anyway, thus it was the sun—far below the horizon now—that had lost its light. The sky was pitch.

Rayford asked Chaim to douse all the lights.

"We will see nothing, Captain," Chaim said. "Nonetheless, the better to see what is coming."

Once the lights were off, Rayford could tell Chaim stood by the window only by the sound of his voice.

Rayford said, "Have you ever seen blackness so thick?"

"I have seen many wonders in the last seven years," Chaim said. "This is like seeing nothing. But the mere anticipation it engenders causes a buzz from the top of my head to the soles of my shoes."

Lightning ripped through the sky, and Rayford was stunned to see the clouds briefly again. "I think I saw a shooting star," he said. "I love those."

"That was more than a shooting star," Chaim said, "which, as you know, is not really a star anyway. What you saw was truly a falling star, maybe a meteor. Soon stars and meteors will fall, but you will only hear them. Isaiah foretold that the stars of heaven and their constellations would not give their light. The sun will be darkened and the moon will not shine.

"God is saying, 'I will punish the world for its evil, and the wicked for their iniquity; I will halt the arrogance of the proud, and will lay low the haughtiness of the terrible.

"'I will shake the heavens, and the earth will move out of her place, in the wrath of the Lord of hosts and in the day of His fierce anger.

"'Everyone will flee to his own land. Everyone who is found will be thrust through, and everyone who is captured will fall by the sword.'"

Rayford shook his head. "There's another difference between us, Chaim. I've never been able to memorize like that."

"What else have I to do, Rayford? As I say, I was thrust into this position, and the teacher became the student. My former protégé, Dr. Ben-Judah, would not hear of my giving short shrift to the Scriptures. He discipled me, pushed me, grounded me in them. Most of all, God gave me a love for His Word. Now there is nothing I would rather do than study it every spare moment and commit as much of it as possible to memory."

+ + +

Enoch's people leaped to their feet and cried out when the early afternoon sun disappeared from the suburban Chicago sky. Though he knew it was coming, Enoch himself was spooked when the light of day turned into the darkest night and the temperature immediately dropped.

He heard a roaring, whistling sound and thought of the cliché that people always used when recounting a tornado: "It sounded like a freight train." Well, this sounded like a plane about to crash. They were close enough to the airport that it could have been, but Enoch did not recall hearing a jet.

Something was coming, and it was getting closer.

"Don't be afraid!" Enoch called out, but he couldn't hide the fear in his own voice. "This was prophesied. We just talked about it. It's all part of God's plan."

But when whatever was falling finally crashed into the main road on the other side of the mall, there was no stopping the gathering from bolting to take a look. Enoch jogged along behind them, grateful for the light-sensitive streetlights that began popping on all over. A meteor about three feet in diameter had bored a ten-foot-wide hole twenty feet deep in the road.

And here came another.

People screamed and scattered, but Enoch held his ground. "I believe we're protected!" he said. "None of the judgments from heaven harmed God's people! We bear His mark, His seal! He will protect us!"

But his body of believers had taken flight. Enoch smiled. He would chide them tomorrow when all were unscathed. How strange it seemed to be walking around in midnight darkness early in the afternoon. The next meteorite, which Enoch guessed was twice the size of the first, obliterated one of the former anchor stores in the deserted mall. It caused such an explosion he had to cover his ears. While he truly believed he would not be hurt, he found himself ducking and expecting debris to crack him on the head.

Enoch ran back to where he had met with the people, but he was alone now. He sat on a concrete bench and watched the show. Mostly he listened. Had he been a caveman, he would have believed the sky was falling, that the stars would all eventually hit the earth.

\+ + +

If anything, the rate of incoming reports of Jewish people turning to the Messiah increased dramatically over the next half hour. Chang beckoned Naomi to his side and sat with his arm around her waist as she stood. They couldn't decide what was more entertaining—the myriad camera feeds from all over the dark world, or the racing meter giving evidence of the fulfilling of the prophecy that a third of the Jewish remnant would come to believe in Jesus as their Messiah by the time of the end.

Chang could only think back to the horrific scenes he had monitored when Carpathia was at the height of his murderous fury against the Jews. He had had them rounded up, put in death camps, starved, tortured, beaten, humiliated with psychological warfare—you name it. That any survived was a miracle. That many became believers was something else.

"This is sure different from the last time Jesus came," Naomi said. "Besides that we weren't ready, it happened in the twinkling of an eye. Apparently God's going to play this one out for all it's worth."

+ + +

Mac had the strangest sensation. He had been trained to fly by instruments, of course, but still he found it disconcerting to see nothing above. And the only light on the ground was man-produced. Gradually he picked up boat lights, lights on other planes, headlights of cars and trucks and military vehicles. He heard the scream of falling meteorites over the usually deafening *thwock-thwock-thwock* of the blades and even heard the explosions when they blasted the earth. That was new. Mac had never been able to hear anything inside the chopper cockpit, especially with his earphones on.

Now, even above the cacophony of GC aviators demanding to know what was going on, the earth resounded with the wrath of God, with the literal falling of the heavens. A meteor at least ten feet in diameter fell within a hundred feet of Mac's helicopter. His lights picked it up, and he followed it until it hit a building, sending a shower of fire and sparks into the air. He had no idea what the building might have been, but it gave him pause. Was he protected from these free-falling monsters of stone or metal? Even a small one would demolish a chopper, and now they began to fall all around him. People on the ground, particularly Unity Army troops, had to be terrified. Mac wondered how many wished they could change their marks of loyalty now.

He was fairly certain he would be protected, as believers had been since the judgments began seven years before. But *fairly* certain wasn't enough for him to follow through with his plan. Mac made for Petra, knowing that airspace was secure. He could have been killed there many times over, but he had been miraculously spared every time.

+ + +

Rayford was having the time of his life. The news about Buck had set him back, of course, and despite what he knew about the future, it gave him that ache in the pit of his stomach, as had his loss of Chloe. But to lie in his bed watching the heavens shake as they had been prophesied to do thousands of years before . . .

And to have his old friend, Chaim Rosenzweig, the one God had chosen to be a modern-day Moses, standing there quoting those prophecies from memory, well, it almost made him forget his grief and his wounds.

"'I saw another angel coming down from heaven,'" Chaim said, "'having great authority, and the earth was illuminated with his glory. And he cried mightily with a loud voice, saying, "Babylon the great is fallen, is fallen, and has become a dwelling place of demons, a prison for every foul spirit, and a cage for every unclean and hated bird! For all the nations have drunk of the wine of the wrath of her fornication, the kings of the earth have committed fornication with her, and the merchants of the earth have become rich through the abundance of her luxury."'

"That is what has Carpathia so enraged today, Rayford. It was one thing to lose his beloved city and to see the rest of the kings of the earth and the merchant moguls weeping crocodile tears over her. But to have it rubbed in like this, to have an angel pronounce it, to know that it was the fulfillment of an ancient prophecy by his archenemy . . . no wonder he is on the rampage now. He has a plan, a scheme he thinks is foolproof, even though he is no fool and has read the Book. But he will fail, and we will witness it."

"I so wish I could be out there right now," Rayford said. "Why did this have to happen today, of all days?"

He could not see Chaim, but he heard the smile in his voice. "The leader of the Tribulation Force is not going to start questioning God now, is he? You of all people. You have been delivered by His hand as many times as I have. You walked through the fire just like Shadrach, Meshach, and Abednego when the GC launched their bombs on Petra, and you are going to whine about having to play inside on a rainy day?"

Rayford had to laugh.

"Listen to this from the prophet Joel," Chaim said. "'I will show wonders in the heavens and in the earth: blood and fire and pillars of smoke. The sun shall be turned into darkness, and the moon into blood, before the coming of the great and awesome day of the Lord.'"

"I saw that," Rayford said. "When the moon was turned to blood. That was not long before I lost Amanda."

"I know," Chaim said after a pause. "We have all lost so much. And yet so much will be restored. Here is the best part, also from Joel: 'And it shall come to pass that whoever calls on the name of the Lord shall be saved. For in Mount Zion and in Jerusalem there shall be deliverance, as the Lord has said, among the remnant whom the Lord calls.

"'For behold, in those days and at that time, when I bring back the captives of Judah and Jerusalem, I will also gather all nations, and bring them down to the Valley of Jehoshaphat; and I will enter into judgment with them there on account of My people, My heritage Israel, whom they have scattered among the nations.'"

All Rayford could do was grunt. Sometimes Scripture had that effect on him. There was nothing more to say. At least not by him.

"We are those captives," Chaim said. "My brothers and sisters, the children of Israel."

"Makes me wish I were," Rayford said.

"Oh, you *are,* of course, by adoption. Gentile believers are His adopted sons and daughters."

"But you all are His chosen people."

"Not that we have proved worthy. Maybe that is why we are always referred to as the *children* of Israel."

"What's that reference to the Valley of Jehoshaphat?"

"Oh, that is where the judgment will take place, in a valley created by the splitting of the Mount of Olives when He sets foot on it. Jesus Himself will judge all men, and prophecy states it will be right there. The Bible says more about Him than that He is just the returning King and victorious Warrior. It also calls Him the Judge. The Gospel of Mark says, 'Then they will see the Son of Man coming in the clouds with great power and glory.' And Revelation says, 'Now I saw heaven opened, and behold, a white horse. And He who sat on him was called Faithful and True, and in righteousness He judges and makes war.'"

+ + +

Sebastian stood next to his Hummer with Otto and Razor, straining his eyes to see what he could see. Meteors were raining upon the enemy, and the sounds of panicking soldiers and horses washed over him. Was it possible the hundreds of thousands of steeds would stampede, and what would that do to the plans the Unity Army had for Petra?

Vehicles were smashed, exploding into flames and offering the only light to give him a clue how far back the front lines had been driven. It seemed they were still virtually atop him, but Sebastian needed to know.

8

"DO WE KNOW the timing?" Rayford said. "I know we know *what* comes next, but do we know when?"

"We never have," Chaim said. "I was one who thought the Glorious Appearing would be exactly seven years from the signing of the covenant between Antichrist and Israel, but clearly we were wrong about that. We know that following the phenomena in the sky comes the sign of His coming, but nothing tells us whether that will be immediate. God has His own timetable."

"A thousand years is as a day, and all that," Rayford said.

"And vice versa."

The booming of the meteorites shook Rayford's little shelter, and as they increased in frequency, his bed moved. He felt every injury. The anesthetic in his temple had long since worn off, and the pain pierced and throbbed. His chin bothered him too, though he had considered that the least of his wounds. Every nick and scrape and gash was sensitive, and the aching ankle, which had caused his foot to swell, made his muscles tense. He felt it in both legs, all the way to his hip.

Rayford spread his pillow flat and laid his head back, stretching. He had no idea what was keeping him awake. On the other hand, of course he did.

+ + +

Mac overflew Buseirah, where he saw little but scattered lights on the ground, and was soon at the edge of Petra. He checked in with Chang to let him know he would be putting down. The last thing he wanted was to be mistaken for enemy aircraft and be fired upon by Big Dog One and his own people. Would God protect him even from them?

"Hey!" Mac shouted into the phone. "What's that? What's Sebastian doing?"

"Using his big torches to light up the sky," Chang said. "He wants to know how much damage the meteorites are doing to the Unity Army."

"Looks like he's more fascinated with the clouds."

"So am I."

"I hear you, Chang. Me too. If you're in touch with Sebastian, tell him to leave those babies pointing straight up."

+ + +

Sebastian wouldn't have dreamed of doing anything else. The searchlights had the enemy looking up too. The clouds blanketed the entire sky, bubbling and roiling and joining one another to form a ceiling unlike anything anyone had ever seen. Far in the distance Sebastian heard the low rumble of long, echoing explosions and finally deduced it was thunder. Did that mean lightning was striking somewhere? Or was it just streaking through the heavens among the clouds?

"Cut the lights a minute," he radioed, eliminating the possibility that they would cost him a view of the lightning. Sure enough, above the clouds—and who knew how thick they were?—tiny pulsating bursts of light seemed to try to peek through. Suddenly the artificial light lost its allure. If a storm was coming his way, Sebastian wanted to see it in all its natural glory.

+ + +

Mac landed and hurried to Rayford's quarters, surprised to find them dark as midnight. He considered refueling and heading out again. Regardless of Rayford's view, if he was here after all, nothing would compare with watching from overhead when the Antichrist got his due.

He knocked lightly. "Anybody in here?"

"Mac!" he heard. It was Rayford, but Chaim greeted him when the door opened.

After embraces all around in the dark and a quick retelling of both men's day, Rayford told Mac there was another chair in the other room. Feeling about, Mac noisily banged his way back with it and sat himself in front of the window. "Nice show," he said. "But you ought to see it from a chopper."

"You're breaking my heart," Rayford said.

"Sorry."

"No, I want every detail. You going back out?"

"Thinkin' about it, pardner. Seems risky."

"I'd think you'd be throwing caution to the wind at this point."

"I want to be alive when it happens, Ray. That's all."

"I'll bet old Chaim here would even be tempted to go with you, once the sign appears in the sky."

"Oh no, gentlemen," Chaim said, chuckling. "My place is here. I want the entire remnant out in the high places, watching for the return. We must all be in place, singing, praying, ready to worship Him in spirit and in truth, and best of all, in person."

"I've at least got to be *there,*" Rayford said. "Mac, can you make sure of it?"

"Unless you talk me into getting back in the air, sure." All three men jumped when lightning shot from straight overhead to the ground, followed by an immediate resounding roar. The strike had to be less than half a mile away. It shook the dwelling and echoed for half a minute among the surrounding mountains and hills.

"Here we go," Chaim said. "Keep your eyes on the heavens."

"Don't need to tell me that," Mac said.

+ + +

"Supposed to rain?" Sebastian said. "Looks like it might, but I didn't count on that."

"Don't think so," Otto said. "I don't recall hearing that in any of the teaching, but that may say more about my attention span than the prophecies."

"I don't want my guys out here in a downpour," Sebastian said. "'Specially if we have a choice."

"What's the choice?"

"Got me there. We don't have nearly enough vehicles, and no one wants to be back in Petra when everything goes down."

"Speak for yourself, Big Dog," Otto said. "I'm into creature comforts. I mean, I want to see what there is to see. But I have nothing against a poncho and an umbrella."

Sebastian threw his head back and guffawed. "'Here am I, Lord,'" he mocked in a bad German accent. "'Put galoshes on me!'"

That made even Razor laugh, but he quickly recovered. "Begging your pardons, sirs," he said. And soon all three were howling.

+ + +

After leaving Rayford's quarters, Abdullah had taken a small jet with a large Plexiglas hood over the cockpit, giving him a panoramic view. He flew over the masses assembled near Petra, then rocketed north, all the way to Jerusalem, nearly overcome by the expanse of the Unity Army. He knew. He'd heard. He'd been taught. But to see it for himself made it hard to breathe.

How far he'd come in just a few years! He'd made it a practice not to show his emotions in public. It was his culture, the way he was raised. Oh, he had been amused, mostly by Mac, and he had been prodded to anger—also by Mac. But to ride above the elements that made up the final chapter of history and realize how easy it would have been to miss it all, Abdullah couldn't stem the tears.

He had been raised in another religion altogether, and to convert to Christ was to turn his back on his family and, it seemed, his country. Yet the truth had pressed in upon him. His decision for Jesus was a towering leap of faith, yet from the beginning the rightness of it, the truth with a capital *T,* had become clear. He had always been a student, after all.

Abdullah had been amused that his friends, particularly the Americans, seemed to think him intellectually limited because of his broken English. Something about his speech patterns, with his Jordanian accent, rendered his sound childlike to Americans. He could tell in how they looked at him, how they responded to him. Sometimes, he admitted, he played to it. One could garner more information by sounding young and innocent.

He was anything but, however. Abdullah had been put through the rigors of military training to where he was certified to fly jets of almost any type. Did his friends really think all Jordanians were so childlike and stupid that they would entrust a young man of limited mental capabilities to pilot fighter-bombers worth tens of millions of dinars? It was laughable. He had been a celebrated pilot, eventually a trainer himself.

Abdullah wondered what Rayford and the others thought of his serious study of prophecy under Tsion Ben-Judah and Chaim Rosenzweig. Unlike the others, he was mostly quiet and didn't ask many questions. But he put to use the same gray matter that allowed him to understand the myriad technical specifications of sophisticated modern aircraft and had made him an accomplished pilot.

Perhaps because they were humble Middle Easterners themselves, neither Dr. Ben-Judah nor Dr. Rosenzweig acted surprised at Abdullah's intellectual proclivities, evidenced in private e-mails and conversations. And while the teaching could be heavily theological and deep, the most persuasive parts of all were the almost daily fulfillments of prophecy.

Abdullah had no doubt that the ancient Scriptures were authentic, penned thousands of years before the birth of Christ. Hundreds and hundreds of prophecies had been fulfilled, many before his eyes. In spite of his grief over the loss of his family, in the midst of constant fear of being discovered without the mark of Carpathia, and yes, even with his private offense over his friends' clearly assuming he was not as bright as they, Abdullah's fledgling faith had grown more solid every day.

He knew Mac and Rayford and Buck and the rest really loved him. Perhaps he could educate them in the next chapter of this unfolding of history and then they would see that, while they no doubt did not even realize they were doing it, there was no reason to condescend to him.

The lightning had increased, and Abdullah loved it. It cast eerie, intermittent bursts of light upon the restless troops below. And it lit up the clouds, which he otherwise could not see due to the absence of moon and starlight. Oh, what a glorious, frightening scene!

Abdullah prayed, thanking God for how far he had come, for allowing such an unlikely prospect into His kingdom, for protecting him even now from the killing power of the enemy.

Over Jerusalem Abdullah noticed tiny campfires dotting the city, many at the Temple Mount. The lightning revealed Unity troops surrounding that area, which he now knew was the last stronghold of the stubborn resistance. He had to chuckle. If only they could see their plight from his vantage point. It was as if a parakeet believed he had commandeered his own cage. Still, he admired them. He was on their side. They were God's chosen people, and in the end, Jesus Christ would give them the victory.

Oh, Jerusalem was to fall, Abdullah knew. But because every one of the other prophecies he had ever studied had literally come true as it was spelled out, he also had zero doubt that Jesus would make things right again. With a full fuel tank and a lightning show to illumine the playing field, he felt he was in the prime spot for the greatest show on earth.

With a steep left bank and a flyover of the millions of troops in the great Valley of Megiddo, Abdullah turned his screaming craft back to the south. Next on the agenda was Carpathia's showing up in Edom to lead a third of his forces against Petra. Unity Army searchlights from the ground crisscrossed the sky and occasionally locked onto Abdullah's craft. But he was fearless. "Launch your surface-to-air missiles," he whispered. "They will bounce off this plane like shuttlecocks."

+ + +

Rayford was speechless. He'd never been considered particularly quiet, but among this trio, he might have been a church mouse. Chaim had always loved to talk everything to death—every truth, idea, or concept. It was his way. And Mac was his Texan counterpart, maybe not as articulate and intellectual but always prepared to weigh in with a homespun opinion on everything.

But now it was eerie. All three were silent. The lightning had become almost constant; long, thick streaks of gold fired from cloud to cloud, cloud to ground, and—Rayford knew—though beyond detection of the human eye, often from ground to cloud.

The length and severity of the bolts varied, but they snaked through the heavens with such speed and abundance that the air crackled and snapped. *Boom! Boom! Boom!* came the deafening crashes of thunder that rattled the walls of Rayford's flimsy quarters.

The flashes lit up the clouds. Rayford could not have imagined them getting larger or more active, and yet they had. They seemed miles wide and deep now, gray and black and pregnant with moisture, as if about to burst. And these blotted out everything above. Were it not for his faith, this would be a horrifying scene. Indeed, the power and wrath of the God of the universe were being unleashed, and those without confidence in His love had to be terrified.

"Astounding," Rayford whispered, but the other two men, silhouetted in the constant flashes, neither moved nor responded. His lame summary must have hit them as feebly as it had him.

+ + +

Sebastian trained his night-vision goggles on the skies, reminding himself to breathe. He felt Otto pressing in on one side and Razor on the other, and strange as that might seem in any other circumstance, it reminded him of his childhood when he and his younger brother hugged each other in fear while watching a thunderstorm from their bed, a storm a thousandth the size of this.

And just when Sebastian believed the sky could contain itself no longer, the lightning seemed to ratchet up to a ridiculous speed. Hundreds, thousands of bolts crashed to the desert floor every second, deafening roars of thunder piling atop each other in such an overwhelming invasion that he was forced to let the goggles drop and dangle from his neck as he covered his ears with both hands. The sky from east to west and north to south was ablaze, blinding streaks firing every which way. The ground heaved and rolled, and Sebastian knew that had to be from a combination of the lightning, the thunder, and the thorough panic of Antichrist's mounted forces.

He sent Otto to check on Ree Woo's troops on the other side of the perimeter and Razor to check his own on this side.

+ + +

Enoch sat in Illinois with his Bible tucked under his arm, trying to protect it should the rain come. But when the lightning seemed to lose all sense of proportion, all he could do was stand, thrusting the Bible over his head in both hands, offering it to God as a form of worship. What a show! The awful and terrible wrath of the Lord on display for the whole world!

Enoch thought of Old Testament Scriptures he had bookmarked and quickly sat again, riffling through the pages and reading them by the almost constant light of the electrical extravaganza, shouting them to the heavens.

"'Enter into the rock, and hide in the dust, from the terror of the Lord and the glory of His majesty. The lofty looks of man shall be humbled, the haughtiness of men shall be bowed down, and the Lord alone shall be exalted in that day. For the day of the Lord of hosts shall come upon everything proud and lofty, upon everything lifted up—and it shall be brought low.

"'They shall go into the holes of the rocks, and into the caves of the earth, from the terror of the Lord and the glory of His majesty, when He arises to shake the earth mightily.'"

Finding the prophetic warnings in the books of Hosea and Joel, Enoch read of the enemies of the Lord. "'They shall say to the mountains, "Cover us!" and to the hills, "Fall on us!"

"'The Lord gives voice before His army, for His camp is very great; for strong is the One who executes His word. For the day of the Lord is great and very terrible; who can endure it?'"

I can endure it, Enoch thought, *just like anyone who sees past His wrath and trusts God's mercy.*

He read from Joel 2:12: " 'Now, therefore,' says the Lord, 'turn to Me with all your heart, with fasting, with weeping, and with mourning.'"

Turning to Nahum 1:6, Enoch read: "'Who can stand before His indignation? And who can endure the fierceness of His anger? His fury is poured out like fire, and the rocks are thrown down by Him.'"

The very next verses offered hope and yet another dire warning: "'The Lord is good, a stronghold in the day of trouble; and He knows those who trust in Him. But with an overflowing flood He will make an utter end of its place, and darkness will pursue His enemies.'"

Near the end of the Old Testament, Enoch came to Zephaniah and read from chapter one, verses 14 to 17: "'The great day of the Lord is near; it is near and hastens quickly. The noise of the day of the Lord is bitter; there the mighty men shall cry out.

"'That day is a day of wrath, a day of trouble and distress, a day of devastation and desolation, a day of darkness and gloominess, a day of clouds and thick darkness, a day of trumpet and alarm against the fortified cities and against the high towers.

"'I will bring distress upon men, and they shall walk like blind men, because they have sinned against the Lord; their blood shall be poured out like dust, and their flesh like refuse.'"

+ + +

Beyond all comprehension, Chang thought, the Global Community News Network ignored the nature show. He knew from pirating the feeds from all over the globe that the constant lightning was a universal phenomenon. From Sri Lanka came visual feeds of a metropolitan area ablaze, the downtown having been ignited by thousands of lightning strikes. People rioted, trampling each other, screaming, pleading for mercy.

A GCNN cameraman, or his brave producer, transmitted images of a tiny band of anti-Carpathia Jews kneeling amid the lightning flashes beneath an ancient Israeli flag, a Star of David, and a rough-hewn cross. They were thumbing their noses at the god of this world, boldly showing that they had never received the mark of loyalty to the supreme potentate, but had now staked their claim with Messiah.

From South America came the same. Regardless of where the feed originated, it came as if at midnight. The only light came from the lightning and artificial sources. Citizens were hysterical. Even many with Carpathia's mark screamed obscenities at him through the cameras and demanded to know where he was and what he was doing about this. Chang asked a Hispanic coworker to translate what the South Americans were shouting.

"They are saying," she said, "that this is obviously an offensive from God Himself, and so what does the potentate have to say about that? Who will win? They want to know, who will win?"

Even the producers, who worked directly for the GC, sent in harshly worded demands to know why GCNN was ignoring their feeds. What, they asked, was more important than a cosmic disturbance like this, one that saw global panic and devastation? People were being killed, committing suicide, looting, rampaging. Yet GCNN ran wall-to-wall coverage of the war effort.

"Unity Army troops assigned to Egypt are already on their way back to the Valley of Megiddo," intoned an anchorwoman, showing clips of overwhelming victories for the GC. "Reports from the northeast mirror these, and Unity generals report they will have their platoons back to Israel in plenty of time for the siege on Jerusalem."

An interview with Carpathia himself showed the folly of the so-called objective coverage. The potentate was shown mounting his enormous horse, just outside the cargo plane that had delivered him and his generals to Ash Shawbak, about halfway between Petra and Buseirah. That put Carpathia and his people about ten miles east of the edge of his massive Unity Army that extended to the border of Petra.

"I am pleased with the reports from the south and from the northeast," he said. "And now we are about to embark on one of our most strategic initiatives. A third of our entire fighting force will advance upon the rebel stronghold cowering in Petra. Intelligence tells us that a paltry defensive unit has rung the city round about, but they are hopelessly outnumbered and have already offered to surrender."

Carpathia was interrupted by nearly continuous crashes of thunder, which he and the reporter appeared to ignore.

"Was this enclave not attacked twice before, Excellency?"

"*Attacked* would not be the proper term," Carpathia said, making Chang laugh aloud. The first failed attempt saw the GC bring huge numbers of troops and weapons, only to see them miraculously swallowed up by the earth. The second was a double bombing that produced a spring of water that provided sustenance for the people to this day, and which also resulted in the inhabiting Jewish remnant and a few of the Tribulation Force being supernaturally protected from the ensuing firestorm.

"In fact," Carpathia continued, "we made peaceful overtures to the leadership, offering amnesty for any who would voluntarily leave the stronghold and take the mark of loyalty. Our understanding is that many wished to make this move, only to be slaughtered by the leadership. Many will recall that it was this very leadership who assassinated me, serving only to give me the opportunity to prove my divinity by raising myself from the dead.

"Well, this time around, there will be no negotiating. Loyalists to our New World Order have either been murdered or have escaped, so intelligence tells us Petra is now inhabited solely by rebels to our cause, murderers and blasphemers who have thumbed their noses at every attempt to reason with them."

The cameras homed in on the potentate as he was handed an almost cartoonishly oversized silver sword with gold rococo inlays and a garishly overdone handle. He strapped it around his waist, then theatrically unsheathed it with a long, slow, metallic screech. He pointed it skyward.

Chang couldn't help praying silently that just one of those bolts of lightning would find that tip and roast the enemy where he sat.

"Therefore," Carpathia said, "our plan is annihilation. I shall personally lead this effort, with the able assistance, of course, of my generals. We shall rally the troops as soon as we arrive, and the siege should take only a matter of minutes."

As Carpathia yanked the reins and turned his mount to the east, racing off at a gallop, the reporter called after him, "All the best to you, holy one! And may you bless yourself and bring honor to your name with this effort!"

Chang called Mac and filled him in on the lunacy. "You guys ought to turn this on," he said. "Things are coming to a head."

\+ + +

Abdullah had heard the broadcast over the radio and flew over Ash Shawbak. Carpathia's planes and rolling stock were visible, but Abdullah was a little high to make out individuals or horses. He could, however, see the Unity Army to the west and knew it wouldn't take Nicolae long to get there.

The lightning exposed an army in disarray. The horses, naturally, were spooked by the light show and thunder, and it appeared to Abdullah that riders were fighting to keep their mounts from heading for the hills. What Carpathia thought he could do with this mess was a mystery.

And just like that, the lightning ceased.

As before, the sky was as black as coal. Unity searchlights looked pathetic, peering feebly into the murky blackness. They reached the thick, stewing clouds that hovered menacingly over the whole earth.

The cessation of the rolling thunder made the relative silence of the cockpit unearthly. Abdullah looked all around for what was to come next. And the longer he looked, the more he wondered how long the Lord would tarry. Those horses would be controllable now. Carpathia would surely believe victory was at hand.

\+ + +

Rayford directed Mac to find his radio in the other room. Mac brought it in, feeling his way in the utter darkness.

"You could turn on a light," Rayford said, the ghostly silence unnerving him.

"Oh, please don't," Chaim said. "This darkness is of the Lord. Can you not feel it?"

"I feel it all right," Rayford said. "Every part of me wants to be out in it. I would give anything to be at Carpathia's side right now. I'd love to see the look on his face when he is chased back to Buseirah and then to Jerusalem."

"How would you see anything at all?" Mac said.

Chaim said, "This is just a preliminary. At some point this darkness will turn to daylight. Carpathia will turn tail and run from the Son of Man, who will be the only source of light. Anyone near Nicolae will be able to see him, all right, and I am with Rayford in wishing I could be there. But I will be here, watching, worshiping, singing. And then we will all follow, tracing the route that brought us here. We will sweep across the great expanse and join Messiah when He triumphs in Jerusalem and then ascends the Mount of Olives, from which He was transfigured so long ago."

"I've got to be on that trip," Rayford said.

"Not in your condition," Mac said.

Rayford shook his head in the darkness. "It's going to be mighty lonely here."

\+ + +

The sudden silence and abject blackness made Enoch fear rain again, and it sent him searching for his car. His ears still rang from the cacophony of the last hour, and as he staggered along, feeling his way with his toes, he finally picked up the faint glow of a few streetlights. He drove toward home, planning to drag a chaise lounge out of the cellar and enjoy the rest of the show from the yard.

Somehow Enoch had to find a way to get to the Holy Land as soon as possible after Jesus returned. He was confident he would see it in the sky—the return and all—but Jesus would apparently confine Himself to an earthly body once again, and believers from around the world would want to see Him. He would govern from Jerusalem, and the pilgrimages would begin immediately. He and the people from The Place would have to start raising money to finance this trip.

\+ + +

Sebastian was up to speed and debating what to do. His night-vision goggles were virtually worthless in this kind of darkness. That meant it had to be supernatural, because he had successfully used these underground where there was no source of light. He could make out nothing of the clouds now, and only the occasional vehicle light in the Unity Army ranks provided visual clues.

What was he to do if Global Community forces attacked before Jesus returned? He knew he and his people, and the entire remnant at Petra, were prophesied to be delivered in the end. But what about in the meantime? Was he to fight? to retaliate? to shoot? He knew he could do some damage because he and his forces already had. Would his people take fire, and would they be wounded or killed?

He was a military man, but this was as much a theological decision as a tactical one. Sebastian could consult with Dr. Rosenzweig, but the old man had enough on his mind. His purview was the remnant. Sebastian's was the defense of the perimeter. Might it be as effective strategically to let the Unity Army overrun his position, knowing they were advancing into a trap of cosmic proportions?

It wasn't the way he was trained, but then it wasn't as if he had much of a choice anyway. Sure, he could stall them, slow them with surgically designed strikes from his directed energy weapons and fifty-caliber rifles. But no one could tell him whether that would do any good, or for how long he should try to hold them off.

Clearly there would be no holding back a force of that size for long. Ten minutes? Twenty? Surely no more than that. He could do some damage. But once the Lord arrived, Sebastian's puny efforts would be meaningless. The question was, were they meaningless regardless?

9

COMING UP ON the two-hour mark of the utterly silent blackness covering the face of the earth, Rayford sensed a restlessness in Chaim.

"I had better get to the elders," the older man said. "This cannot go on much longer, and once the sign of the Son of Man appears, who knows how long it will be before the event itself?"

"'Who knows' is right," Mac said. "Once that comes, I think I've talked myself into goin' back out. You don't mind, do ya, Ray?"

"'Course I mind, but I wouldn't deprive you of that. I can handle the loneliness. It's the jealousy that'll be the issue."

"You'll forgive me," Mac said.

"I will."

"Want me to send Leah or Hannah or somebody to keep you company?"

Rayford pondered that. "Don't think so," he said. "Anybody else here might just prove to be a distraction."

"I am going," Chaim said. "This has been a wonderful memory."

"Suit yerself, Doc," Mac said. "I could take you for the ride of your life, you know."

"I know. I am grateful. But until Messiah appears, I have responsibilities."

Rayford heard him approach in the darkness and reached for his hand. Chaim took Rayford's in both of his. "Mr. McCullum," Chaim said, "join us, won't you?"

Mac stepped close and Rayford felt a hand on his shoulder and assumed the other was on Chaim's. "Revelation 1:3 says this," Chaim said. "'Blessed is he who reads and those who hear the words of this prophecy, and keep those things which are written in it; for the time is near.' Amen."

Rayford and Mac repeated the amen.

"Let me pray for us," Chaim said, but before he could, Rayford's eyes popped open, first at the sound, then at the light of something new in the sky. Rayford could compare the sound only to a downed high-tension power line he'd once seen bouncing and popping.

"O God, O God," Chaim prayed as he too turned to look. Rayford could only stare.

He rocked up into a sitting position and leaned forward, peering out at what appeared to be lightning but was like none he had ever seen. Thick, jagged, and pulsing, a vertical yellow streak extended from about a hundred feet above the horizon to what he estimated was at least ten miles into the sky. Two-thirds of the way up it was crossed by a horizontal streak of the same thickness and half its length.

Rayford could not speak. He could barely breathe. Here, clearly, was the cross of Christ, emblazoned in the heavens in lightning that lingered, crackling with unbridled energy, yet striking nothing. He squinted at its brightness but could not turn his eyes from it. He felt full of awe, of wonder, of the love of God Himself. This was the sign of the Son of Man, and it was there for the whole world to see. But it was also personal, burning into his heart.

The blazing radiance of it lit the room. Chaim finally pulled away and left without another word.

Rayford stole a glance at Mac and nearly fell off the bed. Mac was black! And he appeared to be trying to say something. "Well, I'll be," was all Mac could manage, then, apparently noticing Rayford's reaction, said, "It's me, Ray. Zeke's handiwork."

"Mac, something's happened to me."

"Me too, buddy. It's a-standin' there plain as day."

"No, something's happened."

"What're you goin' on about?"

Rayford slipped quickly off the bed and stood next to Mac at the window. "I'm standing," he said.

Mac turned. "Don't get ahead of yourself there, Ray. Let's take this one step at a time."

"I'm fine," Rayford said.

"Are you sayin'—?"

"That's what I'm saying, Mac. No pain. No wounds. Look at me."

Rayford tore off his bandages. Even the hole in his temple was gone, though where Leah had shaved around the stitching, he still had no hair. He bent and yanked at the ankle wrap. Not even a scar. He jumped up and down, then loosened the plastic shin splint and kicked it free.

"You don't say."

Rayford whooped and hollered. "I do say! Let's get out there, Mac! Get me into the air."

"Now I don't know about that, Ray."

"Then sit here and watch, man, because I'm going!"

+ + +

Enoch was cozy under a light blanket in his chaise lounge in the backyard when the sign appeared. He burst into tears and lifted his arms. "Praise God, praise God," he said, and began singing every worship song he knew. The cross that extended from sky to sky towered, as the hymn writer had put it, "o'er the wrecks of time." Something about the overwhelming majesty of it simply communicated victory.

For how long had he prayed and carried a burden for the inner-city people to whom God had sent him to minister? And for how long had he preached and taught and warned of this very day, this very event? He'd had no idea what form it would take, but this was perfect. "In the cross of Christ I glory," he said, his voice thick.

Enoch slid off the cheap, rickety lounge chair and onto his knees, bowing before God. Though he lowered his head and closed his eyes, still the image of the cross in the sky stayed with him, as if burned onto the insides of his eyelids.

+ + +

As soon as Chang saw the cross on every screen in the bank of monitors before him, he shouted for Naomi and she came running. Hand in hand they raced outside and up to their favorite spot. They didn't speak. There were no words for this. They stretched out on their backs and stared and stared.

+ + +

"Thank You! Thank You, God!" Abdullah exulted. At the first appearance of the sign he had pointed the jet directly at the cross and throttled to full power. Was it there, right in front of him, as 3-D objects had appeared to be in movie theaters when he was a child? It was as if he could reach out and touch it, but though his craft reached top speed in seconds, the cross never appeared to grow closer. Its horizontal arms, like those of Jesus Himself, seemed to welcome the entire world into its embrace.

The only logical follow-up was the Lord Himself, and Abdullah couldn't wait.

+ + +

For two hours Sebastian had not known what the enemy was waiting for, and maybe the enemy didn't either. But the sign became an impromptu trigger, and suddenly the frisky horses of the Unity Army were on the move. Their riders, now clearly visible because of the pulsating cross in the sky, urged their mounts to full gallop.

And here they came.

"Big Dog One to all units," Sebastian intoned into his radio. "Hold your fire. Wait. On my command."

Protests from every side crowded his ears. "Hold, hold, hold," he said, though platoon leaders from all around the perimeter reported the enemy literally yards away.

"Have you lost your mind?" Otto squealed from a quarter mile to Sebastian's left.

"Have you lost your faith, Otto?"

"Ree Woo to Big Dog: It's time, sir."

"Hold."

"Permission to speak my mind, sir," came an urgent transmission from Razor.

"Denied. Follow orders."

The front line of the Unity Army closed the gap in seconds. Sebastian stood his ground, facing horsemen with rifles pointed at him and others with swords drawn. He knew he was as visible to them as they were to him, the Petra perimeter suddenly bright as day. Only the sky behind the rugged cross was black with cloud cover.

The Unity Army opened fire and Sebastian winced, but he did not turn or seek shelter. A couple hundred of his own troops stood between the army and the hillside that led almost straight up to the rose-red city of Petra, and all were fired upon. Shooting from a galloping horse was no small chore, but surely some of the bullets should have found their marks.

The pings of shrapnel ricocheting off rocks filled the air, and the looks on the faces of the horsemen were priceless. Swordsmen steered their horses behind the mounted riflemen and one, clearly troubled but determined, came straight for Sebastian. George raised a hand and wiggled his fingers as if in greeting—or farewell—and the blade-wielding soldier swung his rapier in a wide arc while brushing past. It was as if the blade went right through Sebastian at the waist.

Sebastian was now adrift in the middle of the Unity Army, and horseman after horseman rode straight at him—some shooting, some hacking with their swords. None so much as jostled him. One stopped and spun his horse around to try again, only to be overrun by a wave of his own comrades who had nowhere to retreat to.

George turned and watched the assault on the hillside leading to Petra. The army had apparently underestimated the riders' ability to stay aboard their mounts as the horses managed the steep terrain, and everything slowed to a halt. Those on the plain below kept coming, causing a traffic jam of biblical proportions. Soldiers shouted at one another. Commanders screamed orders that could not be followed.

Meanwhile, Sebastian and his people blithely walked through the midst of the enemy, unscathed.

* * *

Chang ignored his phone as long as he could. He had considered turning it off, deciding his work was finally over. But a sense of duty prevailed. He tore away from the magnetic sign in the sky, shot Naomi an apologetic smile, and answered.

It was his assistant. "You'll want to see this," he said.

"I'm already seeing what I want to see," Chang said.

"But you're still interested in the Jewish question, right?"

"The Jewish question?"

"What Dr. Rosenzweig called the 'worldwide turning to Messiah'?"

"Of course, but that's been going on since Chaim's broadcast."

"And it picked up with the lightning storm."

"Exactly," Chang said. "So what's new?"

"You must come and see. *Massive* doesn't begin to describe it. There must have been millions still undecided, but no more. They're all coming to the Lord, and it seems every one of them is letting us know."

* * *

Rayford had never thought about what one wears to meet Jesus. He dug through his closet, finding—also as prophesied—three-and-a-half-year-old but good-as-new khakis, socks, and boots. He was dressed in seconds.

"You thinkin' what I'm thinkin', Ray?"

"What?"

"That we got no business skedaddlin' out of here if you're healthy enough to fight. There's a battle comin', and the both of us were supposed to be in it."

"Don't do this to me now, Mac."

"I don't want to be here any more'n you do, Ray. But Sebastian and Razor and Otto and them are all tryin' to hold the perimeter."

"Oh, man! Well, Abdullah's gone." Rayford was transported back to his childhood when he would plead his case with his parents. "Why does *he* get to do it?"

"Abdullah can answer to his own conscience."

"And I've got to answer to yours?"

"Just do the right thing, Ray."

"You staying, either way?"

"Got to. It's the way I'm made."

"You *would* have to get parental on me all of a sudden."

"Do what you got to do, Ray. I'll understand."

"I'm not flying without you, Mac. You really think God healed me so I can help in a battle He's already promised to win?"

Mac shook his head. "I didn't say it made sense. I just told you what I thought."

"I'm calling Sebastian."

+ + +

"This is Big Dog One!" Sebastian shouted. "Talk to me!" When he heard Rayford's question he laughed loud and long. "You and Mac get yourselves in the air right now, and if you don't I'll come up and shoot you myself."

He told Rayford where he was and what was happening.

"Then you'll believe it when I tell you that when the sign appeared, God healed me."

"I'd believe anything right now, buddy. If it didn't mean leaving my people, I'd go with you. So you remember every detail, hear?"

+ + +

Chang had been told enough, by Naomi—whose love for him made him wonder about her objectivity—and by the leadership, that he had served a crucial function not just for the Tribulation Force, but also for the entire remnant in Petra. He was gratified to hear it, and while he was relieved to be out from under the daily pressure of living as a mole in the Antichrist's own lair at New Babylon, he had found Petra an unusual challenge.

Naomi had been the bright spot, of course. But his work, sometimes fourteen to sixteen hours a day, could be both a grind and invigorating. It motivated him because he was—he couldn't deny it—somewhat of a prodigy in technical things. Associates told him that was an understatement, and some even held that he might be the leading computer expert in the world, despite his youth.

All well and good, but when he examined himself and tried to decide what was troubling him about his current work, it was the old real-estate agent's adage: location, location, location.

Computers had come a long way in his lifetime alone, but they still largely had to be housed inside, out of the weather. It seemed to Chang that he was still a mole, living mostly underground—or at least indoors. His forays out were always on breaks or at the end of the day, or when he was stealing a moment or two with Naomi, as he had just done.

Now here it was, just before the Glorious Appearing of Christ, and he was back inside, sitting before a bevy of screens, keeping tabs on the whole world. It was a privilege, sure. Who else was doing it or knew how? And he knew he brought a lot to the table, like the ability to hack into the enemy's transmissions, both computer and television. And while he would rather be with the rest of the remnant, marshaling outside and being directed to various high places, Chang knew this was where he would sit for the end of the world.

He could cry and moan or he could do his job, and he would do the latter. There would be time to be a frontliner, able to take in every detail of the millennial kingdom. For now he would monitor and coordinate the activities of his compatriots. They had to be kept in touch with each other.

Sebastian was in the midst of the Unity Army's attempted invasion, as were Razor and Otto and Ree.

Abdullah was in a jet, who knew where?

Chaim was working with the elders to coordinate the people.

Last word Chang had heard was that Rayford had been healed and that he and Mac were looking for four-wheeled ATVs so they could rejoin the fray.

Lionel was in Chang's same situation, tied to a desk, still managing the far-flung exploits of the International Co-op from Petra with the help of Ming Woo.

And Leah and Hannah were running the infirmary, a polite term for a medical facility as large as most hospitals.

More fell to Chang than he felt should be under his purview, but with the leadership otherwise engaged, he would have to make some executive decisions. Abdullah had radioed in, asking permission to rejoin the masses at Petra.

"I understand the resistance to the Unity Army on the perimeter has already been overrun," he said. "But they are still safe and protected, and we know extra help is not needed there."

Chang couldn't blame Abdullah for asking. It was the very thing he wanted to do and to be—a camper instead of a counselor, for lack of a better description. "Come on ahead," Chang told him. He also explained why Abdullah was having trouble reaching Rayford and Mac, but a minute later that all changed too.

"Chang," Rayford said, "Sebastian doesn't need us and can't use us. I've instructed him to bring his troops in to join the remnant. Their work is done."

"But won't they have to come through the Unity Army to get here now?"

"They're in the middle of 'em already, and the enemy has no power over them. Once Chaim and the elders get everyone in place, the population here can look down on the plains all around Petra. They'll have a perfect view of the sky and the earth."

"And you and Mac?"

"Mac's going to take his chopper and I need an ATV."

"You sure you want to go back out on one of those?"

"What are the odds, Chang? Gotta climb back on the horse, as they say."

Chang checked his records and told Rayford where Lionel Whalum kept the best units, "full of fuel, charged up, and ready to go. And where will you go, or do I want to know?"

"I'm going to go where Mac tells me. He'll be hovering over the Unity Army, trying to spot the leader himself. I want to be close enough to see and hear Carpathia. He's got to be somewhere out there behind the horde that has swept past Sebastian's position and is on its way up to our western border."

Chang filled Rayford in on what everyone else was doing, including Abdullah. "And you know where I'll be."

"We couldn't survive without you, Chang."

"Yeah, yeah."

+ + +

Enoch got on his phone, shaking his head. He couldn't blame his little flock for cutting and running. He'd been scared too, but there was nowhere to go and, really, nothing to fear. That was easy to say but quite another thing to act upon when the powers of heaven had been shaken. But it didn't seem right to be apart from his people, not now.

How surreal it felt to be stretched out on a chaise lounge in a suburban backyard, trying to reach parishioners on the phone while a cross of lightning miles tall and wide vibrated in the sky. He finally reached Florence, a late middle-aged black woman who seemed to have the most influence with the congregation.

"Florence, where is everybody?"

"About half of us are right here, Pastor. A little embarrassed, but okay."

"And where's *here*?"

"'Bout three blocks from you, I reckon. We came back to the mall, but your car was gone, so we figured you was at home."

"I'm home. Why don't you all come here and be with me when the Lord returns."

"You told us never to give away your hideout. How we all gonna fit in your cellar, anyway?"

He told her where he was. "Of course we don't want to draw the attention of the neighbors or the GC, but don't you think they're preoccupied with the sky right now?"

"Watch for us. We'll be comin'. Only a few of us have cars, and we'll leave those here."

* * *

Mac stood talking with Lionel Whalum while refueling the chopper. "Haven't been outside all day," Lionel told him, hands on his hips, studying the cross in the sky. "Except to get Captain Steele his ATV, of course."

"Not even for the lightning storm? That was something."

"Heard it. Saw it on a monitor. Tell ya, Mac, you'd think Co-op stuff was over now, but we've never been busier."

* * *

Chaim missed Tsion in the worst way. The younger man commanded respect, maybe because he was a rabbi, maybe because he simply exuded a walk with God that was newer to Chaim. It wasn't that Chaim couldn't get his elders' attention. It was just that he had to raise a hand and ask for the floor. Tsion never had to do that. Merely leaning forward or taking a breath or opening his mouth seemed to draw attention to him and quiet everyone else.

Eleazar Tiberius, not that much older than Tsion had been but a much bigger, rotund man, had become a wonderful ally. Twenty years younger than Chaim, his deep bass voice and the gray invading his sparse rim of black hair and beard lent him an air of authority. And he was appropriately deferential to Chaim's leadership, frequently calling for order and requesting—demanding, really—that his colleagues listen to Dr. Rosenzweig.

That was crucial now when the elders were about to split up and coordinate the various group leaders for all the Petra citizens in their respective areas. "We must have order," Chaim said. "We must keep people moving and under control. Notice the chart here. Gentlemen, please. Notice the chart where the groups are to go. Please! Each of you is responsible for undershepherds who will have a total of a hundred thousand men, women, and children in their charge."

Chaim stopped and looked down. He feared the elders were not listening. He could understand that they wanted to get back outside so as not to miss the Glorious Appearing. But that was what this was all about. He didn't want anyone to miss it. He looked at Eleazar, who used his voice to fix the matter.

"Gentlemen! If you do not at least glance at the chart, you will not know where to tell your group leaders to go! Group number one, as you can see, you are taking the southern route to the high places on the western border. Our engineers have determined there is enough room for everyone, if all cooperate. The first forty groups of a thousand each can move to within ten feet of the edge, but they must all be willing to sit once they get there. And it is of crucial importance that the sixty groups behind them not press forward or we could lose tens of thousands over the side. Understood?"

Chaim was pleased to see Abdullah rush in. As Eleazar continued the instructions to the other elders, Chaim pulled the Jordanian aside and embraced him. "How is my prize student?"

Abdullah told him where he had been and what he had seen. "As you know, Doctor, I am not a man of outward emotion, but I do not mind telling you, I was moved to tears by what the Lord showed me. It was such a privilege."

"I cannot imagine your wanting to leave the sky."

"I had an overwhelming desire to be with you and the people for what comes next. I have the strangest feeling that it could be any second, even before we get everyone assembled."

"We fear the same," Chaim said. "The Unity Army is at our doorstep, and the only reason our people have the confidence to look down over the sides into their gun barrels is that we saw them swallowed up by the earth the first time they dared approach, and we danced in the fire they sent us the second time."

+ + +

Rayford loved the feel of the monster ATV. Any fear that he would be tentative had vanished when he took it for a spin inside Petra, leaning this way and that as he gradually accelerated and made right and left turns, eventually at high speeds. He didn't plan to be careless. He would use the headlights, even with the illumination from the cross above, and keep his eyes on the ground to avoid ruts and rocks.

The loud, staticky humming in the sky both thrilled and unnerved him, because while he knew the portent of it, he also believed Jesus could appear at any time. The only thing better than being here when that happened was to be close enough to Carpathia to see his response. In truth, Rayford assumed he himself might be so overwhelmed that he would no longer give a rip about Carpathia.

Having given Lionel Whalum a thumbs-up, he pointed the vehicle toward the steep grade that led to the western flats. He would accelerate for as long as he felt in control, and at the first sign the bike was getting squirrelly, Rayford would ride the brake.

+ + +

Mac ascended vertically several hundred feet before leaning the helicopter away from Petra airspace and swooping directly over Unity Army forces. He had to watch for their own aircraft, but it appeared no one on the ground paid him any mind.

He knew Carpathia and his entourage had come from the east, so he flew to the eastern edge of the massive army. There, perhaps a quarter mile from the mounted troops, was an encampment of vehicles and horses and what appeared to be comfortable chairs. Dignitaries sat watching the action on television. He'd have liked to have been there when the cross first appeared, because he imagined it quickly drew their attention away from the TVs.

But they now appeared to have grown used to the ominous sign and were apparently trying to follow the exploits of their leader. Wait till they saw what was coming next in the sky.

Meanwhile, Mac wondered how he was supposed to locate Nicolae Carpathia in the sea of black below.

10

LEAH ROSE HAD thought she was past impressing. She had been with Rayford, after all, when the judgment of 200 million demonic horsemen had invaded the earth and wiped out a third of the remaining population. And she had seen and endured, firsthand, all the judgments that followed.

Leah and Hannah Palemoon, the younger nurse who had become such a close friend, were the first to run from the infirmary when word came that the sign of the Son of Man had appeared. It was not the first time they had ventured out that evening. They had also seen the lightning show.

They had been discussing their collective guilt over leaving Lionel Whalum to handle things at the Co-op. He had help, sure, but they had been his assistants for months and were only recently pressed back into nursing duties because of various ailments, injuries, and illnesses throughout Petra. These maladies were solely among the spiritually undecided, which Leah thought should be a lesson to all.

But if there was one thing she had learned since becoming a fugitive from the Global Community, it was that people learned slowly. She had been taught and had heard over and over that mankind would be blind to the acts of God: they would see His mighty works and yet still reject Him and choose their own path. It was no longer a matter of unbelief. That was clear. No one in his right mind could see all that had gone on over the last seven years, starting with the Rapture, and still claim not to know this was the ultimate battle between good and evil, heaven and hell, God and the devil.

So if it was not unbelief, as had been Leah's own problem in the pre-Rapture world, what was it? Were people insane? No, she decided, they were self-possessed, narcissistic, vain, proud. In a word, *evil.* They saw the acts of God and turned their backs on Him, choosing the pleasures of sin over eternity with Christ.

God had, in the meantime, hardened many hearts. And when these unbelievers changed their minds—or tried to—they were not even capable of repenting and turning to God. That had seemed unfair to Leah at first, but as the years rolled by and the judgments piled up, she began to see the logic of it. God knew that eventually sinners would grow weary of their own poverty, but His patience had a limit. There came a time when enough was enough. People had had way more than enough information to make a reasonable choice, and the sad fact was they had made the wrong one, time and time again.

Well, today was really the end. No question God's mercy still extended to His chosen people. He, through His servants like Tsion and Chaim and the 144,000 witnesses, still pleaded with unbelievers in the final remnant to come to Him. And to hear it from Chang's sources, millions were doing just that.

But Leah was intrigued to see that she was not, after all, unable to be further impressed. For when she and Hannah finally returned to the infirmary, she was staggered to find that everyone there had been healed. Everyone. No one was sick, hurt, or lame. All were up and about, congratulating each other, getting dressed, and leaving without even checking themselves out.

Best of all, many of the formerly undecided were on their knees, crying out to God to save them. And all around them were remnant volunteers, counseling them, praying with them.

"We, Hannah," Leah said, "are out of work."

She called Rayford, only to find that he was already up, dressed, and looking for action.

+ + +

When he came within striking distance of the slowly advancing Unity Army, Rayford applied all three brakes to his ATV—the ones on each handlebar and the one under his right foot. He had been merrily cruising down the side of the rocky hill, hearing the advance. But when he swung around some underbrush and realized the army could see him, his eagerness was checked.

Many of the soldiers were on foot, vainly urging their horses upward. Those still mounted struggled to keep their animals pointed in the right direction. The soil was loose, the going rough. They didn't look happy, but they sure looked intrigued to have a target.

"Identify yourself," one barked, reining his horse and stopping ten feet in front of Rayford.

"Citizen of Petra," Rayford said, his voice not as confident as he had expected.

"You're now a prisoner of war."

"You're taking prisoners? There are more than a million of us."

"Only you. You can be of help to us. We need to know where everyone is, the best way in, all that."

"And then I can go?"

"Don't be smart."

"Well, as for where almost everyone else is, they're inside. But you knew that.

The best way in is all the way around the other side from where you are, but of course you're not allowed. I'm curious, though. Why didn't you take one of the perimeter guards hostage and ask these questions?"

"Massacred them all."

"That so?" Rayford pulled a walkie-talkie from his belt and mashed the button. "Big Dog One, this is your captain. Over."

"One, here. Hey, Rayford."

"How're we doing? Any casualties?"

"Not a one."

"Then if I wanted to thumb my nose at the Unity Army, I should be confident that—"

"Where are you, man?"

"About a mile south of the western border."

"I'm about a half mile down from you and on my way up."

"In the middle of the enemy, Big Dog?"

"Exactly. Their bullets are no good here. Their blades either."

"Kill him," the soldier said, and half a dozen weapons opened fire.

Except for a ringing in his ears, Rayford did not suffer. "Maybe you all can tell me something," he said. "I'm looking for your leader, the big man, the top guy. Where's Carpathia?"

But the soldiers had paled. It was as if they were wondering what was the use. If they could not kill the rebels, what was the sense of storming their fortress? And what did the rebels need a fortress for, anyway?

"That's all right," Rayford said. "I have my sources. 'Scuse me," he said as he let the ATV roll on down the way. "'Scuse me." A few more soldiers shot at him and a couple of others thrust swords at him, but soon commanders were instructing personnel to save their ammunition for the siege of the stone citadel.

\+ \+ \+

Finding Carpathia was not as difficult as Mac had feared. In the middle of the churning mass of humanity that pushed its way across the flatland toward the gridlock on the hill was a circle of lights pointed at a man on a bigger-than-average black stallion. Only Carpathia needed lights shined his way, so the worldwide television audience could see him in action.

As Mac watched from his chopper, Nicolae spent a lot of time holding his sword aloft and appearing to shout commands. Then he would sheath the weapon and engage in angry conversation with those around him, presumably his generals. He was clearly not happy with the slow pace, but when the sword was unsheathed again, he worked up a determined expression.

Mac called Rayford and gave him the coordinates where he might find the potentate.

"Thanks, Mac. I expect to run into Sebastian and some of his people first."

As Rayford picked his way through the Unity Army, he found more and more soldiers who must have learned the futility of trying to attack their enemy outside Petra. They looked at him, raised weapons, then wearily moved on.

But soon there was a new development. Word came through the commanders that all personnel on the hill were to execute an immediate right-face and clear the area. Some grumbled, but most looked relieved. "About time," Rayford heard one say.

As the thousands of horses and riders cleared the area, the rest of the Unity Army stopped at the foot of the hill. An area fifty feet wide was cleared in the middle of them, and Mac told Rayford that was the avenue Carpathia and his people would use.

"Looks like they're planning to take over this operation themselves," Mac said, "and it's gonna happen as soon as he's in place at the head of the line."

"Their horses won't have any more luck on this incline than the others did," Rayford said.

"They're gonna get rid of the horses, I think," Mac said. "Nick himself is in the big Humvee, but they've also got the smaller Hummers, SUVs, and armored personnel carriers. Uh-oh, somethin' else too. Grenade and missile launchers are comin'."

"What do you mean, 'uh-oh'? Why should those work any better here than bombs?"

"Good point. I'm just sayin'—"

Rayford came upon a Hummer carrying Sebastian, Weser, and Razor. It had little trouble managing the ascent, especially now that the Unity Army had abandoned the area. Rayford pulled up to the driver's side and shut down his engine.

Sebastian lowered the window. "How exciting is this?" he said.

"You know you're showing the enemy how to handle the terrain."

"So it'll be my fault if they crash through on top and kill everybody, and all the prophecies are proved wrong?"

"I'll hold you responsible," Rayford said. "Wanna have some fun? Follow me down and around. I'm going to settle in behind Carpathia's mobile command center and tag along."

Sebastian sighed. "I'm tempted," he said. "Make it an order so I don't have a choice."

"What's your best assessment of what you should be doing, George?"

Sebastian looked at Weser and Razor, then back at Rayford. "What I'm doing right now. I want to get all of my people back up there and inside so they have the best view of what's next. I can't abandon them now."

"Then that's what you ought to be doing." Rayford slapped the hood of the Hummer. "Carry on."

\+ \+ \+

Abdullah was back on his dirt bike, noisily picking his way through tens of thousands of people. He supervised and advised elders as they directed under-shepherds and group leaders in getting more than a million people to their places. The going was slow, but it was getting done.

Abdullah had scouted an area to the northeast and decided that was where Chaim and the elders should stand when everyone else was in place. At least 80 percent of the populace would be able to see Chaim from there. And in case he had any last words for the citizens, he had access to the public-address system. "But I expect all attention will be on the sky anyway," he said.

\+ \+ \+

Chaim could not hide his apprehension from Eleazar. "What is it?" the younger elder said.

"Lack of faith," Chaim said.

"Surely not. Not you. The Lord has brought us too far, showed us too much. Can there be any doubt that He will appear and rescue us at the appointed time?"

"But what is that time, brother? Chang's people tell me the Unity Army has cleared the western slope for a rolling armada with Carpathia himself in charge."

"All the more reason to believe Messiah is coming soon. He will not fail us, will not break His promises. Antichrist cannot prevail, and the closer he comes, the sooner we shall be delivered."

"I believe that, Eleazar."

"Of course you do. So what troubles you?"

"Things have been left unsaid."

"By you?" Elder Tiberius said with a twinkle. "I cannot imagine it."

"I wanted to explain the imagery of the Glorious Appearing. Tsion and I both have spent so much time insisting on a literal approach to the Scriptures that I fear I have neglected some of the clearly symbolic references in the Glorious Appearing passages."

"Perhaps there will still be time," Eleazar said, "but why don't we discuss it outside? The Lord may get here before you do!"

"But I must make notes."

"Do you want to be in here scribbling when it happens? Bring pen and paper with you, Chaim, but come, please!"

+ + +

For months Enoch had hidden his car a few blocks from the home where he lived in the cellar. He never turned on lights upstairs, and the basement windows were boarded over. The neighbors in Palos Hills never saw him out in the light of day because he would have been unable to hide the fact that he did not bear the mark of loyalty to the potentate. He sneaked in and out of the seemingly abandoned house in the wee hours of the morning.

But now here he sat in the high-fenced backyard, hearing neighbors quizzing each other, discussing the astronomical phenomena in panicky tones. What would they think of strangers invading, gathering in his yard? Would they take the time and trouble to check and see if he and his friends were renegades, fugitives, outlaws? Would there be time for the neighbors to put them to death?

Since the neighbors had to assume his place was uninhabited, nothing else would arouse suspicion in the dark. Why would they have to assume anything about him or his people? *Ah,* he thought, *that's naïve. What would we all be doing here?*

+ + +

Mac had a clear view of the latest Unity Army maneuver, and he had to hand it to the leadership. Someone knew how to fix a problem. Whether it was Carpathia or one of his henchmen, the plan was working. The thousands from the front lines who had begun storming up the western slope found the going impossible and had already moved south, then west, then back northeast again, and had begun reinserting themselves into the ranks.

Meanwhile, the quarter-mile-long and fifty-foot-wide corridor had opened before Carpathia's private unit—and also about fifty yards behind it. He and his people were transferring to rolling stock. A convoy of ten vehicles was maneuvered into position, trailed by two carriers of heavy armaments. If Mac had to guess, he would say Carpathia would lead the charge, the munitions right behind, and that the rest of the army—other than those on horseback—would bring up the rear.

From where Mac sat, it was obvious that under other circumstances Petra wouldn't have had a chance. They were unarmed and outnumbered three or four to one by only a third of Carpathia's total fighting force. Unity Army vehicles could easily traverse the terrain, and the front line of this new unit could be on the other side of the walls of Petra in less than half an hour.

Mac called Chang. "You able to crack into Carpathia's communications yet?"

"Almost. I can pick up everybody but him, but I've got a rapid decoder screaming through it, so it shouldn't be long."

"Patch it through to me as soon as you get it, hear?"

"You got it. Rayford wants the same."

"Roger."

+ + +

Rayford waited at the base of the hill, facing the Unity Army about ten degrees south of the opening that had been left for Carpathia's unit. Rayford was virtually ignored as the rest of the troops had quickly become aware of the VIP in their midst. All eyes were on Nicolae.

Rayford's plan was to fall in with Carpathia as he swept past, hoping not to attract attention. That would have been sheer folly aside from what had already occurred. The Unity Army had finally seemed to concede that they had no power on the perimeter against the meager defense. Why they thought they had a prayer inside Petra itself, given their futile history against God's people, was a mystery. Carpathia's ego knew no bounds.

+ + +

Enoch's fears proved unfounded. His people were sly enough to appear silently in twos and threes, and they found their way to the backyard without drawing notice. The neighbors drifted to their own homes eventually anyway, and Enoch was left in the yard with more than forty of the hundred or so that had joined him at the mall that morning.

They gathered around his chair and sat in the grass, no one seeming to grow tired of gazing at the cross adorning the horizon. "Come, Lord Jesus," several whispered, and others joined in. "Come, Lord. Come soon."

"Everything that's gonna happen is going to be over there, right, Pastor?" a young man said.

"Over there?"

"In the Holy Land. You said Jesus was going to fight for the Jews in Petra first, then save Jerusalem. How we gonna know when He's come?"

"Well," Enoch whispered, "the Bible says the whole world will know when He comes. Revelation 1:7 says, 'Behold, He is coming with clouds, and every eye will see Him, even they who pierced Him.'"

"How's He gonna 'complish that? Holy Land's on the other side of the world."

"Don't you think they're seeing what we're seeing now?"

"I guess, but like when the moon is out, people over there see the other side of it, right?"

"They could be seeing the other side of this cross too. We have no idea how massive it is."

"Or if there's more than one," someone said.

"How's that?" Enoch said.

"God can do what He wants, right?"

"Right."

"He could put ten crosses in the sky to make sure ever'body sees one."

"But there's only one Jesus."

"Yeah, but He can show up anywhere He wants, all at the same time. Just like He was only one man but He died for everybody, He can appear to everybody too."

"Now you're talking," Enoch said.

"Is He gonna kill a bunch of people here, like He is over there?"

"I'm afraid He is. If they're working for the Antichrist, they're in serious trouble."

\+ + +

"Rayford, you should see this from where I'm sittin'," Mac said.

"I kind of like where I am," Rayford said.

"Yeah, but it's pretty. The red-stone city is lit from the cross above, and I feel like I'm in one of those blimps that used to hover over the football stadiums at night. Everybody's just about in place, ringing the top of Petra. In front, people are sitting so the ones standing behind them can see. Most of 'em'll be able to see the Unity Army attacking and the Lord returning. I hope He gets here soon."

"I imagine He'll be right on time, don't you?"

"I imagine. I can see Chaim and the elders makin' their way to a spot where most everybody can see them. You gotta wonder if anybody is scared to death out there on the edge."

"I would be, and I've lived through it all."

"Me too, Ray. Guess it's human nature to feel like you're testin' fate one time too many. Hey, looks like Chaim's addressin' 'em. I'm gonna see if Chang can patch us in—oh, he's way ahead of us. Here it is. Talk at you later."

\+ + +

". . . and sisters in the Messiah," Chaim was saying. "We gather here in this historic place, this holy city of refuge provided by the Lord God Himself. We stand on the precipice of all time with the shadow of history behind us and eternity itself before us, putting all our faith and trust in the rock-solid goodness and strength and majesty of our Savior.

"May the Lord appear as I speak. Oh, the glory of that moment! We stand gazing into the heavens where the promised sign of the Son of Man radiates before us, thundering through the ages the truth that His death on the cross cleanses us from all sin.

"Within the next few minutes, you may see the enemy of God advancing on this fortified city. I say to you with all the confidence the Father has put in my soul, fear not, for your salvation draweth nigh.

"Now many have asked what is to happen when Antichrist comes against God's chosen people and the Son intervenes. The Bible says He will slay our enemy with a weapon that comes from His mouth. Revelation 1:16 calls it 'a sharp two-edged sword.' Revelation 2:16 quotes Him saying that He 'will come to you quickly and will fight against them with the sword of My mouth.' Revelation 19:15 says that 'out of His mouth goes a sharp sword, that with it He should strike the nations.' And Revelation 19:21 says the enemies 'were killed with the sword which proceeded from the mouth of Him who sat on the horse.'

"Now let me clarify. I do not believe the Son of God is going to sit on His horse in the clouds with a gigantic sword hanging from His mouth. He is not going to shake His head and slay the millions of Armageddon troops with it. This is clearly a symbolic reference, and if you are a student of the Bible, you know what is meant by a sharp, double-edged sword.

"Hebrews 4:12 says the Word of God 'is living and powerful, and sharper than any two-edged sword, piercing even to the division of soul and spirit, and of joints and marrow, and is a discerner of the thoughts and intents of the heart.'

"The weapon our Lord and Messiah will use to win the battle and slay the enemy? The Word of God itself! And while the reference to it as a sword may be symbolic, I hold that the description of the result of it is literal. The Word of God is sharp and powerful enough to slay the enemy, literally tearing them asunder."

+ + +

Anticipation surged through Rayford. He turned to look up at Petra when the cheering and applause drowned out Chaim, who was apparently finished. Emotion swept over Rayford as he took in the scene. Rimming the very top of the fortified city was the remnant of God, slowly turning from Chaim to face the sky and then the enemy below them.

From that distance they were mere specks, but there were so many that Rayford could tell they were raising their hands and clasping them together. He heard the strains of hymns from their collective voices, faint at first, then with growing volume. First they sang "I Sing the Mighty Power of God." Moments later they sang "A Mighty Fortress Is Our God."

When they broke into the "Hallelujah Chorus," Rayford wished he could stand and join in. And when the echoing truths washed down the mountainside—"For the Lord God omnipotent reigneth"—he thought he would shed his skin.

At that moment Chang apparently solved the encryption coding of the potentate's audio transmission, and it came crackling through the earphone in Rayford's left ear. So at the same time he was hearing the magnificent *hallelujah*s in one ear, he heard Antichrist in the other.

And Nicolae was not happy. "Let us roll! The fools are singing!" He cursed and cursed again. "They sing in the face of their own deaths!"

The caravan began rolling, the cross above it bouncing waves of light off the dust that ensued. "Take me to the highest and closest point," Nicolae ordered, "with our munitions settling in behind where the angle is optimal. I shall stand on the roof of the vehicle so all can see me: my troops to be inspired, and the enemy so they know the author of their doom."

At the mention of Carpathia's intended destination, Rayford glanced again up the slope to where hundreds of thousands swayed and sang and looked down. The immense cross shone on the entire hillside, as if pointing the enemy to the spot where God Himself wanted them.

Rayford had to wonder if any in Petra had second thoughts, doubts. He was happy to say he had none. He had come too far. His own pride and laziness had cost him his wife and son at the Rapture. He'd felt responsible for the fact that his own daughter had shared his jaded view of people of faith and had followed his example, thumbing her nose at God.

And while he was grateful beyond expression for his own salvation and Chloe's, seeing her and her husband martyred was merely the capstone of the tragedy that resulted from his having missed the truth in the first place. So many friends and loved ones had suffered over the past seven years. New friends, old friends, a new wife, spiritual mentors, dear compatriots had been injured, killed, tortured for their faith.

Yet God had proved faithful and true to His Word. Every prophecy had been fulfilled. While there had to be those who wondered why the Lord tarried even now and whether there was any sense or logic to allowing Antichrist to reach the very boundary of the city of refuge, Rayford found himself simply trusting. God had His plans, His ways, His strategy. Only when Rayford stopped questioning God had he finally come to grips with the confusing, sometimes maddening, ways of God—which the Scriptures said were "not our ways."

Some things still didn't make sense, and many would not become clear, he knew, until he saw Jesus face-to-face.

The evil motorcade thundered within yards of Rayford. He gunned his ATV engine and joined them, a couple of vehicles behind Carpathia's and ahead of the rumbling armament carriers. A general tried to wave him off. Rayford smiled and waved back. The general reached for a weapon from an aide and aimed it out the window. Rayford winked at him, and the man opened fire.

The general blanched when the burp of bullets he'd fired at point-blank range seemed to go right through Rayford.

"No shooting!" Carpathia screamed. "Ignore any enemy outside the walls of the city!"

+ + +

Abdullah studied his copy of the location charts and slowly picked his way through narrow pathways and crowds until he found the area where George Sebastian's wife, Priscilla, should be with her daughter, Beth Ann, and Rayford's grandson, Kenny Bruce. Once there, he had to ask several people, but finally he found them.

Priscilla had Beth Ann next to her, holding her hand, and her free arm held a lanky, incongruously sleeping Kenny, draped over her shoulder.

"Let me take him," Abdullah said.

"Oh, would you, Mr. Smith? He's getting so heavy."

"Come here, big boy," Abdullah said, taking him in his arms. He gently put Kenny's head on his shoulder and began to rock him, but when Abdullah also tried to quietly join in the singing, the boy roused.

"Uncle Smitty," he said.

"Hi, Kenny."

"Jesus comin'," the boy said.

"Yes, He is, buddy. He sure is."

11

AT LONG LAST, there was nothing more Chang could do. It seemed likely that he and Zeke were in the same boat. Both might have to find a new trade or be out of work for the next thousand years of Christ's rule on earth.

Chang knew where everyone was, had them all in place.

Abdullah was back in the fold.

Chaim and the elders were with the people, waiting and watching.

Hannah and Leah had shut down the empty infirmary and were outside, as were Lionel and Ming—the Co-op finally dark.

Mac was in the air, Rayford on the ground, and Sebastian, Otto, Razor, and Ree should be entering Petra at that very moment, joining their own people and urging the rest of the rebel soldiers to do the same.

Chang had patched the enemy's radio transmissions to Mac and Rayford and wore an earphone himself so he could stay posted. He sat back and sighed, then stood quickly. It was time to find Naomi and get outside where they belonged.

"Taking the rest of the day off?" she said, taking his hand when Chang found her.

"The rest of my life," he said.

+ + +

Mac kept an eye on Sebastian's vehicle and the hundreds of remnant rebels following him into Petra. "Looks like they're all safe, Ray," he reported. "Ever'body's home and accounted for but you and me."

"Wish I could be with Kenny right now," Rayford said. "Priss says he was asking for his dad earlier, and all she could think to tell him was that they'd see him tomorrow."

"Good thinkin'. Hey, Ray, ol' Nick's leaving nothing to chance."

"How so?"

"He's got the rest of the troops fanning out to surround the city."

"I didn't hear that order, Mac."

"Musta been something he decided on before we could hear him."

"The mounted troops must just be in the way. Not to mention all the meteor craters."

"Some of the trails on this side are navigable. Remember they used to have donkeys bring tourists in."

"Rally the planes," Rayford heard. Carpathia's voice.

"What's he doing, Mac?"

"I'll watch, but it looks like he's bringing everything he's got in this region."

"A third of the total, just like the Bible says."

"He can't get out from under the prophecies, can he, Ray?"

As Rayford surged up toward Petra in the evil procession, he heard jets screaming. "Fighter-bombers?"

"Nah," Mac said. "Fighters but not bombers. Guess they know better than that. He'll have to learn the hard way that the guns don't work here either."

When Carpathia's Humvee reached the last particularly steep stretch, it was nearly pointed to the sky. "Find me a place," he told the driver, "where I can stand on the roof and see all my troops on this side and can also see the enemy."

"I believe we're almost there, Excellency."

Rayford left the formation and shot right about twenty yards to where he had a good view. He shut down his engine and swung his left leg over the seat, using the ATV as a bench. "Attack, you coward," he whispered, hoping that would bring Jesus from heaven. *Yeah, I know. He'll be here in His own time.*

"How's this, Your Highness?"

Rayford heard the squeak of Carpathia's leathers as he moved to look this way and that. "Perfect."

His door opened and simultaneously generals opened their doors and piled out the back. One held Carpathia's door and offered his hand so the potentate could mount the hood. But Nicolae ignored him. He leaped onto the front of the truck and stepped atop the roof. The vehicle was at such an angle that he began sliding. He caught himself, loudly drew his sword, and raised it above his head. "Lights!"

A beacon pulled by a Jeep lit him with a harsh, garish beam that cast a one-hundred-foot shadow on the rocks behind him.

"Loyal soldiers of the Global Community Unity Army, observe your commander in chief!"

The singing inside Petra ceased and the people peered down at him.

"You are privileged to be part of the greatest fighting force ever assembled on the face of the earth! You will be lauded for time immemorial for the victory we are about to win. The plan is foolproof, our resources unlimited, your leader divine. Once we have crushed the resistance here, you will occupy the city and enjoy the spoils while I proceed to Jerusalem to lay siege to it.

"And if there really is a God of Abraham, Isaac, and Jacob, and if He truly has a Son worthy of facing me in combat, I shall destroy Him too! When I have been informed that all elements are in place and at the ready, be prepared to advance upon Petra on my command. Leave no man, woman, or child alive. The victory is mine, says your living lord and risen king!"

From out of the back of Carpathia's vehicle stumbled Leon Fortunato, still in his ridiculous regalia. He failed in his first attempt to climb the hood, then finally hiked his skirts and clambered aboard. Stepping onto the windshield to mount the hood, he stepped on the hem of his robe and had to back down and take another run at it.

When he was finally sharing the roof with Carpathia, Leon reached under his robe and produced a small decanter and began sloshing it about. "Praise to the resurrected lord," he chanted, and then began to sing, "Hail Carpathia, our lord and risen king."

"Leon, what *are* you doing?" Carpathia demanded.

"Leading the assembled in worship, Highness."

"This is a battle, man! And lose the holy water!"

Leon bowed and apologized and loudly stepped down to the hood, then slid off the side onto the ground. "Oh yes!" he said. "Almost forgot. I was to tell you that everyone is in place and at the ready."

"Get in the car, Leon."

"By your grace, Excellency."

As soon as Leon's door was shut, Carpathia stomped twice on the roof. Nothing happened. He stomped twice again. Still nothing. "Go!" he shouted. "Go!"

"You want me to drive with you on the roof, Potentate?" the driver said. "I thought I was supposed to stay—"

"Go! Now!"

The vehicle's engine raced, and when it began virtually climbing the wall, it was all Carpathia could do to keep his balance. "Attack!" he screamed. "Attack! Attack! Attack!"

Rayford watched Carpathia's vehicle bounce up and over while planes let fly their bullets. As far as Rayford could see, the Unity Army surged while the remnant peering over the wall stood in silence, holding hands.

The siege was deafening. Jet engines, Jeeps, cars, trucks, Hummers, transports, armaments, munitions, rifle fire, machine-gun fire, cannons, grenades, rockets—you name it. But when the panoramic cross disappeared from the sky, the world went black again. It reminded Rayford of what he had heard about the darkness that had descended upon New Babylon. The only sound was the clicking of weapons that would not fire. Nothing produced light. No headlights. No matches or lighters.

"Light!" Carpathia screeched. But everything was dark. "Fire!" he raged. Still nothing. "Take the infidels by hand!"

But the soldiers could see nothing and would not know whether their victim was friend or foe. The clicking tapered and then quit. All Rayford heard were frustrated shouts and the nickering of thousands of horses waiting below.

And then, as if God had thrown the switch in heaven, light.

But that wasn't enough of a word for it. This was not light from above that cast shadows. This was a brightness that invaded every crevice and cranny. Rayford had to shield his eyes, but it did no good, as the light came from everywhere.

It exposed a Unity Army in chaos. On the plains, horses bucked and reared, whinnying and throwing riders. On the hillsides leading to Petra, soldiers examined weapons that did not work. On the border of the city, Carpathia stood exposed atop his personnel carrier, sword at his side, stared at by saints standing side by side.

"You can see them now! Charge! Attack! Kill them!"

But as his petrified, lethargic soldiers slowly turned back to the matter at hand, the brilliant multicolored cloud cover parted and rolled back like a scroll from horizon to horizon. Rayford found himself on his knees on the ground, hands and head lifted.

Heaven opened and there, on a white horse, sat Jesus, the Christ, the Son of the living God.

Rayford could not explain how he could see his Savior so clearly. It was as if He appeared within inches of Rayford, and he knew that had to be the experience of everyone everywhere.

Jesus' eyes shone with a conviction like a flame of fire, and He held His majestic head high. He wore a robe down to the feet so brilliantly white it was incandescent and bore writing, something in a language wholly unfamiliar to Rayford and something else he easily understood. On His robe at the thigh a name was written: KING OF KINGS AND LORD OF LORDS. Jesus was girded about the chest with a golden band. His head and hair were white like wool, as white as snow. His feet were like fine brass, as if refined in a furnace.

Jesus had in His right hand seven stars, and His countenance was like the sun shining in its strength.

The armies of heaven, clothed in fine linen, white and clean, followed Him on white horses.

An angel appeared in the light and cried with a loud voice, saying to all the birds in the midst of heaven, "Come and gather together for the supper of the great God, that you may eat the flesh of kings, the flesh of captains, the flesh of mighty men, the flesh of horses and of those who sit on them, and the flesh of all people, free and slave, both small and great."

"I am the Alpha and the Omega," Jesus said, "the First and the Last, the Beginning and the End, the Almighty."

When Rayford first heard the voice of Jesus, he understood what John meant in Revelation when he compared it to both a trumpet and the sound of many waters. It pierced him, reaching to his heart. It was as if he was not hearing with his ears but rather that the voice came alive within him and communicated with his very soul. Rayford was certain every believer on earth heard Jesus in the same way, deep within his or her own being.

This was the One who is and who was and who had finally come, "the faithful witness, the firstborn from the dead, and the ruler over the kings of the earth. This was Him who loved us and washed us from our sins in His own blood, and has made us kings and priests to His God and Father, to Him be glory and dominion forever and ever."

And with those very first words, tens of thousands of Unity Army soldiers fell dead, simply dropping where they stood, their bodies ripped open, blood pooling in great masses. "I am He who lives, and was dead, and behold, I am alive forevermore. Amen. And I have the keys of Hades and of Death."

With that Carpathia scrambled down from his perch and slid in the passenger-side window. "Retreat! Retreat! Retreat!" he shouted, but the driver must have been dead. "Leon, drive! Get this carcass out!" The driver's door opened and a body flopped out. Soon the vehicle was bouncing down the hill toward the desert.

"I am the Son of Man, the Son of God, the Amen, the Faithful and True Witness, the Beginning of the creation of God. I am the Lion of the tribe of Judah, the Root of David, the One who prevailed to open the scroll and to loose its seven seals."

With every word, more and more enemies of God dropped dead, torn to pieces. Horses panicked and bolted. The living screamed in terror and ran about like madmen—some escaping for a time, others falling at the words of the Lord Christ.

"I am the Lamb that was slain and yet who lives. I am the Shepherd who leads His sheep to living fountains of waters. I am the God who will wipe away every tear from your eyes. I am your Salvation and Strength. I am the Christ who has come for the accuser of the brethren, who accused them before our God day and night, the one who has been cast down."

For miles lay the carcasses of the Unity Army. The manic, crazed survivors ran and staggered and drove over and through them, fleeing for their lives.

"I am the Word of God. I am Jesus. I am the Root and the Offspring of David, the Bright and Morning Star."

+ + +

It was hard to kneel and look up, but somehow Enoch found a way. And all his parishioners did the same. He couldn't articulate his feelings, even in the quietness of his own heart and mind. To see Jesus, clad in white, riding the white horse, and speaking with the authority of the ages, and knowing that He was slaying the enemy in the Holy Land at the same time . . . it was just too much to take in.

Enoch believed that Jesus was the lover of his soul, and seeing Him return on the clouds, knowing He was there to set up His thousand-year kingdom reign, completed Enoch somehow. The psalmist said that as a deer pants after water, so the soul pants after God. Enoch somehow knew that his panting was over. His Savior had come.

He was only vaguely aware that neighbors had burst from their homes in terror, screaming and calling to each other. The light blinded them and they ran to and fro, some jumping in cars and careening down the street. Enoch knew that the news the next day—if there would be news—would report hundreds of thousands of employees of the ruler of this world having mysteriously been slain at the time of the phenomenon in the sky.

And the ruler of this world was himself now running for his life.

+ + +

The all-encompassing, pervasive light that preceded the opening of heaven had fully awakened Kenny Bruce, and Abdullah quickly turned him to face the sky. When Jesus appeared, Abdullah awkwardly knelt, careful not to drop the boy.

"Me too, Uncle Smitty," Kenny said. And he too knelt, first intertwining his tiny fingers as if to pray, then reaching out to Jesus.

"My Lord and my God," Abdullah said, and Kenny repeated him.

"Jesus!" Kenny cried, standing and waving. "Jesus!"

+ + +

Rayford stood atop the seat of his ATV, his attention divided between the Lord on the clouds and the Unity Army breaking for cover across the sandy plains. But there was nowhere to run, nowhere to hide. As the words of Jesus trumpeted throughout the earth, they could not be avoided. He could not be ignored.

Something about Jesus' appearing struck Rayford so deeply that he was glad no one else was around. He would not have been able to utter a sound. There were no words for the thrill, the magnetism, the overwhelming perfection of the moment. Jesus was the culmination of his whole life, and not just since he had been regenerated. Rayford realized that Jesus was whom his soul had been seeking since he was old enough to think and reason. Jesus was the source and the point of all life.

Rayford knew that somewhere in that heavenly band of white-clad saints behind Jesus were his wife and son, and that his daughter, his second wife, and many friends and loved ones would soon be brought forth to join them. How sweet those reunions would be, and yet how the very thought of them paled next to his fulfilled devotion to Jesus.

As the Global Community minions threw miles-long clouds of dust as they scattered, Jesus continued to speak. And the enemies of God continued to die.

"I am able to save to the uttermost those who come to the Father through Me! I live to make intercession for them. I come from above and am above all. My Father has delivered all things to Me. He put all things under My feet and gave Me to be head over all things. I am the anchor of your soul, sure and steadfast. I am the Lord's Christ."

As Rayford slowly made his way down to the desert plains, though he had to concentrate on missing craters and keeping from hitting splayed and filleted bodies of men and women and horses, Jesus still appeared before his eyes—shining, magnificent, powerful, victorious.

And that sword from His mouth, the powerful Word of God itself, continued to slice through the air, reaping the wrath of God's final judgment. The enemy had been given chance after chance, judgment after judgment to convince and persuade them. To this very minute, God had offered forgiveness, reconciliation, redemption, salvation. But except for that now-tiny remnant of Israel that was seeing for the first time the One they had pierced, it was too late.

"I am the vine, you are the branches. He who abides in Me, and I in him, bears much fruit; for without Me you can do nothing. If anyone does not abide in Me, he is cast out as a branch and is withered; and they gather them and throw them into the fire, and they are burned.

"I am the Apostle and High Priest of your confession, God manifest in the flesh, justified in the Spirit, seen by angels, preached among the Gentiles, believed on in the world, received up in glory.

"I am the Son whom God has appointed heir of all things, through whom also He made the worlds; who being the brightness of His glory and the express image of His person, and upholding all things by the word of His power, when I had by Myself purged your sins, sat down at the right hand of the Majesty on high, having become so much better than the angels, as I have by inheritance obtained a more excellent name than they."

Rayford saw soldiers kill themselves at the sight of their slain comrades. Others looked like cartoon characters on speed, using any implement they could find to dig holes and bury themselves, trying to hide from the piercing light and convicting words of Christ.

Carpathia was radioing ahead to generals and commanders in the middle of his army that still extended miles from Petra to the north. "Reinforcements! Reinforcements! Spare no expense or equipment! Meet us at Buseirah!"

The royal Humvee, with the ubiquitous Leon at the wheel, far outraced Rayford's ATV until it ran into the rest of the army trying to flee on horseback and on foot. About half the original caravan trailed the Humvee, minus the munitions carriers that remained inoperative just outside Petra.

Rayford raced up behind the fleeing potentate and his panicked entourage, and turned to see what was happening with the rest of the Unity Army that had been encircling Petra. All he could see for miles were craters; overturned vehicles; clouds of dust; dead and dying soldiers and horses; personnel walking in a daze, running, staggering. And above them great clouds of ravenous birds, getting their fill of man and beast. Strangely, though, the swarming flocks that would have otherwise blocked out the sun cast no shadow on the ground. The light of Christ permeated everything.

"How we doing up there, Mac?"

"Oh, Ray! I can hear every word, and it's like God's in the cockpit with me, looking right into my eyes."

"I know the feeling."

"Listen, I'm going to head to Buseirah, 'cause that's where what's left of the front lines here seem to be headed. From up here it looks like the worst of the damage and casualties is within five miles of Petra. The rest of the one-third is steering toward Buseirah, and farther north the other two-thirds is pretty much intact and trying to regroup."

+ + +

One of the women told Enoch, without taking her gaze from the sky, that it seemed "as if Jesus is lookin' right at me."

"Me too," another said, and another.

"Just fellowship with your Savior," Enoch said quietly, not wanting to speak while Jesus was speaking. It should have been no surprise, he decided, that Christ would supernaturally make personal to every believer the truth of His coming, as if He had come for each individually. Enoch had once heard an old saint say, "He loved us every one, as if there were but one of us to love."

Jesus said, "Look unto Me, the author and finisher of your faith, who for the joy that was set before Me endured the cross, despising the shame, and sat down at the right hand of the throne of God.

"God now commands all men everywhere to repent, because He has appointed this the day on which He will judge the world in righteousness by Me, the Man whom He has ordained. He gave assurance of this to all by raising Me from the dead.

"I am Jesus Christ the righteous, your Advocate with the Father. And I Myself was the propitiation for your sins, and not for yours only but also for the whole world. I am the Prince of life, whom God raised from the dead. I am the Word that became flesh and dwelt among you, and you beheld My glory, the glory as of the only begotten of the Father, full of grace and truth.

"I, being in the form of God, did not consider it robbery to be equal with God, but made Myself of no reputation, taking the form of a bondservant, and coming in the likeness of men. And being found in appearance as a man, I humbled Myself and became obedient to the point of death, even the death of the cross.

"Therefore, Enoch, God also has highly exalted Me and given Me the name which is above every name, that at the name of Jesus every knee should bow, of those in heaven, and of those on earth, and of those under the earth, and that every tongue should confess that Jesus Christ is Lord, to the glory of God the Father."

Enoch's jaw dropped. Sitting there in the brilliance of God's glory, his Savior Jesus had spoken directly to him by name. "Did you hear that?" he said, and the three dozen plus kneeling around him dissolved into tears. "He used my name."

"He used *my* name," a young man said.

"He called me by name," a woman said.

"Me too."

"Me too."

\+ \+ \+

Rayford sat in the middle of the carnage surrounding Petra, his heart bursting, the love and adoration he felt for Jesus coming right back at him from the clouds. Christ had called him by name, and as Rayford gazed at Him he had the feeling that it was true that the very hairs on his head were numbered, that Jesus knew everything there was to know about him. It was as if He had returned just for Rayford.

"Ray, this's Mac."

"Yeah, Mac."

"You're not goin' to believe this, but—"

"I know."

"You too?"

"Everybody, I think, Mac."

"Incredible."

Even knowing that the same phenomenon had happened to others, Rayford longed to hear Jesus say his name again. It came with such love, compassion, and knowledge that it was as if no one had ever uttered it before or would again.

"Rayford—" there it was again—"you know My grace, that though I was rich, yet for your sake I became poor, that you through My poverty might become rich."

"I know, Lord," Rayford said, tears streaming. "I know."

"I have delivered you from the power of darkness and conveyed you into the kingdom of the Son of God's love, in whom you have redemption through My blood, the forgiveness of sins. I am the image of the invisible God, the firstborn over all creation.

"For by Me all things were created that are in heaven and that are on earth, visible and invisible, whether thrones or dominions or principalities or powers. All things were created through Me and for Me. And I am before all things, and in Me all things consist.

"I am the head of the body, the church, the beginning, the firstborn from the dead, that in all things I may have the preeminence. For it pleased the Father that in Me all the fullness should dwell, and by Me to reconcile all things to Himself, whether things on earth or things in heaven, having made peace through the blood of My cross."

Again Rayford slid to the ground, raising his arms. "My Lord and my God, I am so unworthy."

"And you, Rayford, who once were alienated and an enemy in your mind by wicked works, yet now I have reconciled in the body of My flesh through death, to present you holy, and blameless, and above reproach in God's sight."

"Unworthy, unworthy!" Rayford cried.

"Justified by faith," Jesus said. "Justified."

+ + +

It seemed to Abdullah that all in Petra were on their faces and yet still somehow able to see Christ. And when the Savior had called Abdullah by name, he could tell from the response around him that Jesus had called each person by their own name. Even better, Jesus had spoken to Abdullah in his native Arabic.

Kenny shouted, "He *knows* me!"

And Beth Ann wrapped her arms around George's neck and squealed, "He said my name!"

From that moment, Abdullah heard everyone conversing with Jesus as if He were speaking to each of them alone.

12

MAC LOOKED DOWN on Bozrah, the modern-day Jordanian city of Buseirah. It lay thirty miles southeast of the Dead Sea and about twenty miles north of Petra. He told Rayford, "It's a remote village in the mountains here, and access is gonna be difficult."

"Especially if the Lord doesn't want the Unity Army to get there safely."

"And He doesn't."

"Mac, didn't Chaim say the remnant is supposed to go with Jesus to Jerusalem?"

"I believe so."

"How're we going to get a million people sixty miles in one day? We don't have enough vehicles or planes."

"I don't guess it's our problem, Ray."

"So the question remains."

"Look up, brother. Look up. Hey, you're not gonna try to chase Nicolae all the way to Jerusalem on that little buggy, are ya?"

"I've been reconsidering that, Mac."

"I've been in touch with Chang and Lionel. I don't want to be this far from the action myself. What say we get back to Petra and commandeer us a Hummer?"

"We'd better hurry. I don't want to miss what happens in Bozrah."

"You're drivin', Ray."

"No you don't. You're driving."

"Let's get Smitty. He loves to drive. Plus I'll bet he'd love to be along."

By the time Rayford had scooted back up to Petra, Mac had already landed the chopper and found Abdullah. The three embraced. "What do you call it again," Abdullah said, "when someone states the obvious?"

"I call it statin' the obvious," Mac said. "And it's usually done by a Jordanian. You about to state somethin' obvious, Smitty?"

"I am, sir."

"Well, let 'er fly."

"This is the greatest day of my life. How about you?"

\+ + +

Chaim was nearly overrun with people peppering him with questions. He wanted to give them his full attention, but how could he with his Savior in the clouds? The people were preoccupied with Jesus too, of course, but until they could talk with Him face-to-face, they asked Chaim for answers while looking past him into the heavens.

"Why are the saints behind Him wearing white? To signify their purity?"

"I believe so," Chaim said. "And also because they are not really going to be involved in the war at all. Jesus will do all the work, and the battles—three more following this one—will not really be battles at all, but rather one-sided slaughters."

\+ + +

Rayford longed to see Kenny, but he didn't want to upset him by then pulling away again so quickly. He also wanted to talk to Priscilla Sebastian about how she planned on keeping the kids, her daughter and his grandson, from seeing the horror outside the walls. Abdullah assured him that Kenny was fine for now—he was as enamored of Jesus as they all were—and that Priscilla indeed had a plan.

The million-strong in Petra had fallen far out of their original formation by now and were milling about, most with their necks craned toward the sky but somehow also intuitively migrating toward the exits. They knew they were to be delivered by Jesus, not just from the attack of Antichrist, but back to their homeland, their home city, the City of God, Jerusalem.

\+ + +

"Are we free?" someone asked Enoch.

"I think we are," he said. "No way the Lord will allow Antichrist's forces to kill us for not having the mark of loyalty, now that He is here and is to rule the nations. Even ours."

"How will God do that from over there?"

"I have no idea," Enoch said. "But after today, I will simply believe it, won't you?"

"That's in the Bible, Jesus rulin' the nations?"

"It is. Revelation 12:5 says, 'She bore a male Child who was to rule all nations with a rod of iron. And her Child was caught up to God and His throne.' That's Jesus. And He's here now. That rod of iron sounds like He's going to take no baloney from anybody, doesn't it?"

"I heard that."

"Then I think we're free to live and move about without fear," Enoch said.

"I'm gonna fear a little for a while, but that sure sounds good to me."

+ + +

The only downside of having Abdullah drive the Hummer was that Rayford would have to trade off with Mac for the privilege of riding shotgun. That transported him back to college when he and his fraternity brothers would compete to call the favored seat, sometimes as much as twenty-four hours before a trip. That also reminded him how far he had been from being a believer back then. Had someone predicted where he would be thirty years later and painted this scene, Rayford would have laughed in his face.

The tight, compact, stiff-riding Hummer made its way out of the city under Abdullah's careful control. Tens of thousands of pilgrims filled the pathways and stone stairways, walking arm in arm, hand in hand, singing, praying, praising God, and gazing at Jesus in the sky.

"This had to be what the Exodus looked like," Abdullah said.

Mac laughed long and loud.

"You know," Abdullah added, "the original one. The children of Israel leaving Egypt."

"I know what the Exodus is, Smitty!" Mac said. "You think those people were happy then?"

"Well, no, I guess not. And they would have had children older than seven too, wouldn't they?"

Finally outside Petra, Rayford was impressed that Abdullah was able to find stretches where he could reach speeds of more than sixty miles an hour. Most of the time he had to be careful of rocks and ruts and craters from the meteorites, and he slowly found ways around the carcasses of horses and soldiers. But clearly he was a man on a mission, wanting to get to Bozrah soon after Carpathia did. And from what Rayford had seen of where the former potentate's convoy had stalled, he thought Smitty might just get them there first.

About four miles from Petra and flying along before a huge cloud of dust, the three of them rolled down their windows and gazed into the clouds when Jesus began speaking again.

"I will surely assemble all of you, O Jacob, I will surely gather the remnant of Israel; I will put them together like sheep of the fold, like a flock in the midst of their pasture; they shall make a loud noise because of so many people.

"I am the One who breaks open, and I will come up before you. You will break out of the city of refuge, pass through the gate, and go out by it. I, your King, will pass before you. I, the Lord, will be at your head."

"He's going to lead the people to Bozrah," Abdullah said.

"Statin' the obvious again, Smitty," Mac said.

But within minutes, Rayford and the others understood Jesus' plan. "Look behind us," Abdullah said.

Abdullah was in a particularly slow patch, carefully picking his way through numerous obstacles, but still a great dust cloud followed them.

"What's that?" Mac said.

"No idea," Rayford said, studying it and becoming alarmed. Something was gaining on them. Something huge and ominous.

Seconds later Abdullah found a smooth stretch and hit the accelerator. Soon they were hurtling along at more than seventy miles an hour. Still the great dust ball caught and overcame them, and the three quickly rolled up their windows. The ground trembled and the wind shook the Hummer.

"It's people!" Rayford shouted above the din. "It's the remnant!"

"They're following the Lord!" Mac said. "Running faster than we're driving!"

"Look at them go! Smiling, laughing, singing! Even little kids!"

"We wouldn't have needed the car!" Abdullah said.

"Statin' the obvious!" Mac yelled, laughing.

✣ ✣ ✣

It had been Hannah Palemoon's idea that the Tribulation Force try to stay together on the trek to Bozrah. She feared that with the move from Petra and the reunions of so many with loved ones, they might never be together in the same way again. No one knew how long the trip would take, and she foresaw the possibility of a very long day. All around her people had questions about how they would get all the way to Jerusalem when Bozrah itself was far enough—really too far to walk.

She didn't care. It began as fun, and everyone was so blessed and full of gratitude, looking at Jesus and seeing Him look back, seemingly directly at each one. Leah was there, and the Sebastians with their daughter and Kenny. By staying in the middle of the huge throng, the kids were spared the ugliness of what was left in the desert. And the children seemed preoccupied with Jesus anyway. Razor was along, and Lionel, Chang and Naomi, Zeke, and the Woos.

Hannah didn't know who first got the idea of walking faster, but suddenly a laughing and smiling group was pushing them. They stepped along as quickly as they could, then began jogging, trotting, and soon they were in a full sprint. Hannah felt light as air, and while it wasn't that she was actually off the ground, it felt that way. Each step carried her farther and farther, and soon she was running faster than she ever had.

To her amazement, she was not out of breath. Her strength and endurance remained, and so, apparently, did that of the old and the young alike. Ahead,

George Sebastian ran faster than she, and he was carrying Beth Ann! Priscilla kept up though carrying Kenny.

When the group caught and passed a speeding Hummer, Hannah knew they were running at miraculous, supernatural, superhuman speeds. And of all things, the kids wanted to be let down so they too could run. She passed the Sebastians as they slowed to lower the children, but within minutes they had passed her again, the kids running as fast as the adults.

+ + +

Half an hour later the entire mass of a million was past the Hummer and nearing Bozrah. By the time Abdullah pulled up to a narrow entryway to the mountain village, Unity Army troops had straggled in. They looked defeated before the battle began.

What was left of their vehicles and armaments was pathetic, but Rayford was surprised how many soldiers remained alive. Several thousand horses too. He had to wonder whether any of these, who were part of the original one-third of Carpathia's fighting force, would remain to join the others in the north.

How strange to see the entire remnant gathered again as Abdullah drove around the edges of the great crowd. The Lord and His white-clad heavenly army hovered over them, and despite the trip, everyone appeared fresh and clean and none the worse for wear. No one was even breathing heavily. Which was good, Rayford thought, because they still had another journey ahead of them, twice as far.

"Wonder where ol' Nick is this time," Mac said. "We haven't heard from him in a while, have we?"

"If I were him," Abdullah said, "I would leave this battle to someone else."

"Me too," Mac said. "I don't see him anywhere."

Rayford directed Abdullah to a high place just northeast of the city. From there they could look down upon the remnant and out across the plains, where several hundred thousand troops were aligned and apparently ready for a fresh attack. Rayford studied the horizon through binoculars, and soon he heard radio transmissions from Carpathia's generals.

"Standing by for your word, Excellency." The voice sounded weary, defeated.

There was a throat clearing. "And the southern platoons?" Carpathia's voice.

"Ready, Supreme Potentate." Rayford detected a note of sarcasm.

"Ready, holiness. May we know your position?"

"For whatever reason?"

"So that we avoid the danger of friendly fire, great one."

"Suffice it to say that I and my cabinet are to your northwest."

So much for visibility and inspiration. Apparently Nicolae was fully aware how close he'd come to being bird feed at Petra. "Right behind you, boys," seemed to be his mantra for this skirmish. But it would prove to be more than a skirmish.

"It appears the entire population of Petra is here," a general broadcast.

"If you are addressing me," Carpathia said, "you will take care to use proper approbation."

"I'm addressing those crucial to this operation, *sir.*"

"Your commander in chief *is* crucial, General, and you would do well to remem—"

"I will remember that when this begins, you are hiding in the northwest, away from the action."

"Identify yourself, infidel!"

"Front lines, sir, which is more than I can say for the commander in chief."

"Dissension among the ranks!" Mac crowed. "What could be better?"

"We'd better move now, Excellency," another general weighed in. "We do ourselves no favors allowing the enemy to study us."

"They are unarmed!" Carpathia said. "This should be a walk in the park!"

"They were unarmed in Petra, *Commander,*" the first general said. "Have you forgotten *their* commander in chief remains overhead? And have you questioned how they got everyone here so fast?"

"Attack!" Carpathia shouted.

And what was left of the southern third of the Unity Army slowly began moving upon Bozrah.

To Rayford it appeared the operation was a suicide mission. As soon as Global Community forces came within range of the remnant of Israel, the soldiers seemed to launch every last projectile in their arsenal. He could not imagine a more earsplitting fusillade, and yet the bullets and missiles and rockets and mortars fell harmlessly, even in the midst of the mass of people. Millions and millions of rounds continued to pour from barrels of all sizes as the army slowly continued to advance.

Yet despite the din, the words of the Lord could be heard clear and plain.

"Come near, you nations, to hear; and heed, you people! Let the earth hear, and all that is in it, the world and all things that come forth from it. For the indignation of the Lord is against all nations, and His fury against all their armies; He has utterly destroyed them, He has given them over to the slaughter."

Rayford watched through the binocs as men and women soldiers and horses seemed to explode where they stood. It was as if the very words of the Lord had superheated their blood, causing it to burst through their veins and skin.

"Also their slain shall be thrown out; their stench shall rise from their corpses, and the mountains shall be melted with their blood. All the host of heaven shall be dissolved, and the heavens shall be rolled up like a scroll; all their host shall fall down as the leaf falls from the vine, and as fruit falling from a fig tree."

Tens of thousands of foot soldiers dropped their weapons, grabbed their heads or their chests, fell to their knees, and writhed as they were invisibly sliced asunder. Their innards and entrails gushed to the desert floor, and as those around them turned to run, they too were slain, their blood pooling and rising in the unforgiving brightness of the glory of Christ.

"For My sword shall be bathed in heaven; indeed it shall come down on Edom, and on the people of My curse, for judgment.

"The sword of the Lord is filled with blood. It is made overflowing with fatness. For the Lord has a sacrifice in Bozrah, and a great slaughter in the land of Edom.

"Their land shall be soaked with blood, and their dust saturated with fatness."

It was as if Antichrist's army had become the sacrificial beasts for the Lord's slaughter. Carpathia screamed, "Bring me a plane, a chopper, a jet—anything! Get me to the north! Now! Now!"

And Jesus said, "For today is the day of the Lord's vengeance, the year of recompense for the cause of Zion."

"Where's Carpathia's ride going to come from?" Rayford said.

"Ash Shawbak," Abdullah said.

"That's right, Smitty," Mac said. "That your hometown?"

"Hardly. Amman; you know that."

"'Course I do. Wasn't Ash Shawbak where the dignitaries were, on their 'zecutive safari, sippin' cordials and s'posed to be watching Nicolae bring home the victory?"

"That is the place," Abdullah said. "I would love to see their faces now."

"Lookie there," Rayford said, nodding toward the sky to the southeast. A jet helicopter was screaming to the northwest, at the edge of the decimated army.

Rayford raised the binoculars again and studied the area. "There they are," he said. "That big old Humvee is just sitting there alone. Looks like Carpathia's not going to even risk getting out until he absolutely has to."

"His army's gone," Mac said. "'Least this part of it. Not a shot bein' fired from anywhere."

It had grown deathly quiet. As Rayford watched, the chopper put down several yards from Carpathia's position. Only he and Leon disgorged from the vehicle. Leon held the hem of his robe at his waist and ran as fast as was possible for him. Nicolae seemed to catch his great scabbard on the way out of the

Humvee, and it hung him up for a second before he angrily freed himself. He dashed to the helicopter, overtaking Leon and elbowing him out of the way to be the first one on.

As soon as Leon was aboard, having been pulled in by assisting hands, the craft lifted off and headed north. Rayford panned left and right with the field glasses and saw no movement among the wreckage of the Unity Army. Bodies were strewn for miles and the desert floor was red with blood.

"Oh, look at this," Rayford said, scrambling to open his door and leap out. Mac and Abdullah followed and the three climbed atop the Hummer, watching as Jesus descended from the sky. His horse gracefully touched the ground in the plains to the west of Bozrah, and as the entire Jewish remnant watched from the mountain, Jesus dismounted. The army of heaven remained perhaps a hundred feet above Him, following as He strode through the battlefield, the hem of His robe turning red in the blood of the enemy.

The saints above Him began a responsive recitation, asking questions in unison that He answered for all on earth to hear. "Who," they began, "is this who comes from Edom, with dyed garments from Bozrah, this One who is glorious in His apparel, traveling in the greatness of His strength?"

And the Lord said, "It is I who speak in righteousness, mighty to save."

"Why is Your apparel red, and Your garments like one who treads in the winepress?"

"I have trodden the winepress alone, and from the peoples no one was with Me. For I have trodden them in My anger, and trampled them in My fury; their blood is sprinkled upon My garments, and I have stained all My robes.

"For the day of vengeance is in My heart, and the year of My redeemed has come.

"I looked, but there was no one to help, and I wondered that there was no one to uphold; therefore My own arm brought salvation for Me; and My own fury, it sustained Me.

"I have trodden down the peoples in My anger, made them drunk in My fury, and brought down their strength to the earth."

And the vast thousands on horseback above Him in the heavens praised Him in unison:

"We will mention the lovingkindnesses of the Lord and the praises of the Lord, according to all that the Lord has bestowed on us, and the great goodness toward the house of Israel, which He has bestowed on them according to His mercies, according to the multitude of His lovingkindnesses."

And Jesus said, "Surely they are My people, children who will not lie. And so I became their Savior."

With that He turned toward the multitude watching from Bozrah. "When you see Jerusalem surrounded by armies, then know that its desolation is near. Then let those who are in Judea flee to the mountains, let those who are in the midst of her depart, and let not those who are in the country enter her.

"For these are the days of vengeance, that all things which are written may be fulfilled. . . . Now look up and lift up your heads, because your redemption draws near."

+ + +

"What do you think is happening right now, Brother Enoch?"

Enoch wasn't sure, but he had an idea. In Illinois, as he knew was true everywhere, regardless of the hour, the day was as bright as noon without so much as a shadow. The glory of the Lord was the light of the world. But Jesus was no longer visible in the sky.

"Will we see Him again? Or do we have to go there for that?"

"I believe we *will* see Him again," Enoch said. "Even today. He is probably fighting one of the battles that precede the fall of Jerusalem and His delivering of the Jews there. But the prophecies say that when He delivers Jerusalem and ascends the Mount of Olives, every eye shall see Him. Obviously, that includes us."

"But pretty soon, like after today, we're going to have to get ourselves over there, right?"

"I sure want to," Enoch said. "But it won't be cheap."

"Well, look at it this way: we got us a thousand years to raise the money."

"I don't want to wait that long."

"Me either. How about a car wash?"

+ + +

"Head west of the Dead Sea and south of Jerusalem," Rayford told Abdullah. He settled into the backseat of the Hummer, letting Mac have the front. "Carpathia's not happy, Mac. You been listening?"

"Yeah," Mac said. "Guess he expected the northern two-thirds of his army to be ready. Sounds like they'd rather cut and run."

"He could lose a bunch of them and still have plenty. He's trying to get them organized to annihilate the Jews at Jerusalem."

"But Jesus won't let them get that far, will He?"

"Actually, He will," Rayford said. "At least a lot of them. But many soldiers are going to die between here and Mount Megiddo. If I read it right and Tsion and Chaim were correct, that's next."

As they traveled, they followed Jesus now riding horseback on the ground,

His army above and behind Him, and the Jewish remnant running along en masse. Again, they covered more than seventy miles in an hour, and the whole way Jesus spoke to them as if to each individually.

"I am the King who comes in the name of the Lord," He said. "I am the Mediator of the new covenant. I am the one who bore your sins in My own body on the tree, that you, having died to sins, might live for righteousness—by whose stripes you were healed.

"I am the Bread of God who came down from heaven and gives life to the world. Therefore keep the feast, not with old leaven, nor with the leaven of malice and wickedness, but with the unleavened bread of sincerity and truth.

"I created all things in heaven and on earth, visible and invisible, whether thrones or dominions or principalities or powers. All things were created through Me and for Me. I have come to do the will of God. I came into the world to save sinners, not to be served, but to serve, and to give My life a ransom for many."

Rayford had been taught over the past seven years that the Word of God was quick and powerful and sharper than any two-edged sword. He had also learned that the Word would never return void. Now, as it was being burned into his heart and soul by his Redeemer, he felt filled to overflowing and ready to burst.

What a privilege to hear the Word *from* the Word! He and his friends rolled through the desolate land, hearing what everyone else in the world was hearing, and yet Rayford knew each was taking it as if for him or herself. He certainly was. And just about the time he forgot that truth, Jesus would refer to him by name.

"Rayford, for this cause I was born, and for this cause I came into the world, that I should bear witness to the truth. Everyone who is of the truth hears My voice. I can do nothing of Myself, but what I see the Father do; for whatever He does, I also do in like manner. I am the stone the builders rejected, yet I have become the chief cornerstone, having been built on the foundation of the apostles and prophets."

"Lord, I worship You," Rayford whispered, hearing Mac also praying. Abdullah drove along with tears pouring down his face.

13

RAYFORD HAD TO SMILE. Here were the southern flanks of the remaining two-thirds of Antichrist's Global Community Unity Army all right, but they looked little more organized and ready to fight than did the corpses left in Edom. Perhaps that's why Carpathia was nowhere to be found, and from the transmissions they could hear, he was on his way farther north to the center of his fighting force in Megiddo.

Both Tsion Ben-Judah and Chaim Rosenzweig had been telling Rayford for years that of all the prophetic passages in Scripture, the final four battles between Jesus and the Armageddon armies were the most difficult to understand and put in sequence.

"Our best bet is to follow Jesus," Rayford said.

"There's a sermon if I ever heard one," Mac said.

"These battles are going to take place where they're going to take place, and the only thing I'm sure of is who wins."

"Well," Abdullah said, "I am sure of a little more than that."

Rayford saw Mac shoot Abdullah a double take. "Ya don't say, Smitty. Pray tell."

"I have been studying."

"Studyin' what?"

"Geography mostly. On my own."

"That can be dangerous."

"I have found it most informative."

"And I'd like to hear it, Abdullah," Rayford said.

Mac shook his head and settled back. "Oh, boy. Here we go."

"I had been most curious," Abdullah said, "why all of history pointed to Armageddon for the end. I mean, what is Armageddon? It is a place with many names and actually covers a lot of ground."

"You shoulda been a perfessor, Smitty," Mac said.

"Hush, Mac. Teach on, Abdullah."

"Well, you are both fliers, and you have many times seen the mountain ranges that run the length of Palestine."

"Sure, off the Mediterranean coast."

"You know the break where the mountains all of a sudden drop to altitudes of about three hundred feet or less?"

"Up there where the highlands split off from the northern hills of Galilee?"

"Exactly. That is the Jezreel Valley."

"I always thought that was the Plain of Esdraelon," Mac said, "or however you say it."

"Very good, Mac," Abdullah said. "Gold star for you. *Jezreel* is the Hebrew word for it. *Esdraelon* is the Greek."

"Well, I'll be. You *have* been studyin'."

"There's more. Some people call it the Plain of Megiddo, because of the city immediately to the west of it. And that's where we get the word *Armageddon.*"

"Where?" Mac said. "You lost me, teach."

"*Armageddon* comes from the Hebrew *Har Megiddo*, which means Mount Megiddo."

"You have been doin' your homework, boy."

"Experts say Megiddo has been the site of more wars than any other single place in the world because it is so strategically located. Thirteen battles by the end of the first century alone. Some say Megiddo has been built twenty-five times and destroyed twenty-five times."

"Isn't Jesus' hometown up there somewhere? Nazareth?"

"On the northern side of the valley," Abdullah said. "Imagine how it will feel for Him to fight an entire army that close to home."

Indicative of the uncertainty of the Unity Army forces, their Hummer was virtually ignored. The army seemed to have its eyes trained on Jesus, just like everyone else, warily watching Him with His saints behind Him. The way news traveled on battlefields, no doubt these troops were also aware of the slaughters in Edom.

Rayford advised Abdullah to steer clear of the army. Though he remained confident that they were invulnerable now, nothing would be gained by drawing fire.

"I'm probably gonna regret askin' this, Smitty," Mac said, "but what'd you learn about Megiddo and all that, besides the names? I mean, what *is* so strategic about it?"

Rayford was amused at how Abdullah warmed to the topic. Mac had to be even more surprised than Ray. It wasn't often that Abdullah was in a position to teach his elders. But he seemed to have this down well.

"It is the perfect stage of history," Abdullah said. "Mount Megiddo is really not much more than a hill. For centuries it was the place from which the strategic pass was guarded—the international highway that went from the east all the way down to Egypt.

"Over the last several months, the enemy armies have been amassing into one, as you know. The ones that came from the west, from the revived Roman Empire, landed at Haifa and went directly up to the Valley of Megiddo.

"The armies from the east came through the dried-up Euphrates and straight down to the same place. It is the perfect staging ground. The armies from the north swept past Mount Hermon and down into the land of Israel, ending up in the Jezreel Valley at Mount Megiddo."

"Makes sense," Mac said. "Boy, you missed your callin'."

+ + +

Chaim could not keep from grinning. Tsion Ben-Judah, first his protégé and eventually his mentor, once told him that prophecy was history written in advance. Here he was, in his seventies, *living out* that history.

No manna had fallen since Jesus appeared in the clouds. While Chaim knew that eventually he and all the other mortals would have to eat, he was certain no one felt any more twinge of hunger than he did. The Bread of Life was here.

It was as if fifty years had melted away. Chaim knew he looked the same, but he did not feel fatigue, aches, or pains. He had no serious maladies that had to be healed, but if Rayford was made whole despite his wounds and the infirmary had been closed in an instant, it only made sense that Chaim himself had been delivered from the ravages of age.

He was impressed enough that he had been able to get out of Petra and on the way to Bozrah under his own steam. But when he had begun hurrying, then running, then virtually flying over the terrain, Chaim knew this was no longer of himself. He had neither grown weary nor suffered from joint pain. If he had not had his full attention on his Savior, he might have been tempted to try his favorite childhood game: soccer. *Imagine,* he thought, *an old man cavorting with children.*

As the remnant from Petra followed the Lord and His army north toward Jerusalem, Chaim felt himself swelling with appropriate pride and gratitude. Though there had been hundreds of thousands under his authority and care over the past three and a half years, many whom he had never even met let alone gotten to know, he felt a love and responsibility for each. God had been faithful, feeding them, providing water for them, protecting them.

Now, what was next? Would they be expected to go with Jesus to the battle at

Armageddon, or would they be directed to Jerusalem? Word from the Holy City was that the Unity Army was merely toying with what was left of the resistance, and that whenever it wanted to and was ready, it could storm the Old City and complete the fall of Jerusalem.

That, Chaim knew, was prophesied and would happen, even with Jesus on the scene. But He would quickly avenge the loss and reverse it, and many more remnant Jews would come into the kingdom.

Most thrilling for Chaim was any time Jesus spoke. How He addressed the entire globe and yet made it so personal was a mystery. But somehow it satisfied that soul hunger Chaim felt for a personal audience with his Lord. Even knowing that everyone else was hearing the same thing, to Chaim it was as if Jesus were—every time—saying, "Chaim, come here. Let Me tell you something." And, of course, Chaim heard Him in Hebrew.

+ + +

It was one thing to have flown over the Unity Army and seen it en masse. It was another to ride along on the outskirts of it, seemingly never to come to the end. Rayford had to be impressed by the sheer accomplishment of outfitting such a fighting force. Millions of uniforms, weapons, munitions, vehicles, and various and sundry pieces of equipment made the whole operation appear perfectly supplied for its task. In human terms, they could not lose. They could have overwhelmed any mortal enemy on the planet.

But they faced one Man, the Son of the living God. And they were defeated before they began.

The remnant on the ground that accompanied Jesus and the heavenly hosts began to sing praises as they ran. But they quickly quieted when Jesus responded.

"For the suffering of death, I was crowned with glory and honor, that I, by the grace of God, might taste death for everyone. I was the Deliverer who came out of Zion, and I turned away the ungodliness from Jacob. I was the seed of David, raised from the dead, the Mediator of the new covenant. I suffered once for sins, the just for the unjust, that I might bring you to God, being put to death in the flesh but made alive by the Spirit."

Amazingly, there was not even a battle transpiring at the moment, yet thousands of Unity Army soldiers were slain simply by the Lord's words as He passed by. They were not fighting, not threatening, not advancing or even moving. But they had long since made their decision. They had pledged their loyalty to the god of this world, had willingly taken the mark of Antichrist and bowed the knee to him. For them there was no recourse.

Rayford thrilled to the powerful words of the Master and was horrified by the carnage that resulted from them. His heart was full, and yet he found it difficult to tear his eyes away from the bloodshed on the ground. Oh, what this portended for the army as a whole when the actual fighting ensued! How any of the surviving men and women could see their companions die such horrible deaths—simply from the words pronounced from the sky—and still be willing to stay in the fray was beyond Rayford.

"My enemies have become My footstool," Jesus said. "Not with the blood of goats and calves, but with My own blood I entered the Most Holy Place once for all, having obtained eternal redemption. I am the Son of God who has come to give you an understanding, that you may know God who is true.

"I am the living bread which came down from heaven. If anyone eats of this bread, he will live forever; and the bread that I gave is My flesh, which I gave for the life of the world. I am the Word who became flesh and dwelt among you, and you beheld My glory, the glory as of the only begotten of the Father, full of grace and truth. For in Me dwells all the fullness of the Godhead bodily.

"Rayford, take My yoke upon you and learn from Me, for I am gentle and lowly in heart, and you will find rest for your soul. For My yoke is easy and My burden is light."

Every time Jesus spoke his name, Rayford was touched anew. He glanced quickly at his friends and saw that the Lord had communicated to them in the same way. Mac buried his face in his hands, whispering, "Thank You, Jesus." Abdullah looked as if he wished he could pull over and simply worship God.

+ + +

Sebastian, who was running with Kenny's hand in his, felt a tug. He bent to listen and Kenny said, "Jesus's talkin' to me!"

"I know!" Sebastian said. "Isn't it wonderful?"

+ + +

"We need us a proper church, Brother Enoch."

"Great idea," Enoch said. "Who could stop us now?"

"Is it possible all we have to do is find out what's for sale or rent and go get it?"

"Why not?"

"Can we put a cross on it and call it what it is?"

"If Jesus keeps talking to all of us by name, I don't see why not. Anybody who tried to come against that would be due the same treatment His enemies are getting all over the world."

"Let's do it. Churches are going to be springing up all over the place."

\+ + +

Over the next two hours of driving, the scene changed noticeably. The farther north Rayford and Mac and Abdullah traveled, the more obvious it was that the Unity Army had dug in and was prepared for the battle of the ages.

They had to know what their counterparts had suffered, but either Carpathia's broadcasts of encouragement and bravado had succeeded in making them full of themselves, or they were emboldened with the knowledge that they were twice the fighting force their defeated comrades had been. Even with a third of the entire army reduced to nothing, the remainder represented the greatest military power ever assembled.

Maybe they didn't fully know or understand what had gone on. They could see Jesus and His army, and in the core of their being they had to be unnerved that an enemy on horseback and seemingly unarmed—albeit with the ability to defy gravity and move at incredible speed—could compete at all with a foe such as they.

But Rayford saw organization, might, determination. This was going to be anything but a surrender. And yet nothing in Scripture indicated the result would be any different than what they had seen in Edom.

\+ + +

Chang was intrigued that the path they took from the land of Edom to Megiddo bypassed Jerusalem far to the west. It was as if the Lord knew that the remnant would be most curious about their own hometown. Maybe He wanted them to see what happened at Megiddo.

It was strange, Chang told Naomi, to hear Jesus from the sky and hear Antichrist in his earpiece. At times he simply had to remove it. When Jesus called him by name in Chinese it sent chills through him. When that happened to Naomi, he watched as her eyes grew wide with wonder, and she was speechless for several minutes. Maybe the day would come when they could talk about how intimate that felt, but they avoided the subject for now. To Chang it was just too personal, and he assumed it was the same for her.

Bizarre too was the shadowless light that would apparently exist as long as Jesus was in their midst. Chang found himself trying to make shadows with his hands. An omnipresent light source was something science had never approached. Men who loved darkness rather than light were not going to like the millennial kingdom. The piercing glare of the purity of Christ would make easy His ruling the nations with an iron rod. For believers who loved Him and who loved the truth, His rule would be a marvelous change from the last seven years and, indeed, the millennia before that. But for people interested only in their own gain, still thumbing their noses at God, Jesus' rule would be most uncomfortable.

It was fun for Chang to be able to converse with Naomi, even when they were running at superhuman speeds. They didn't have to shout, weren't panting, and when Jesus was not speaking, they were. Mostly they talked about what it would be like to marry and raise children in such an age. Who would perform the ceremony, and would Jesus Himself attend?

Chang always loved when Jesus began to speak again. The entire remnant fell silent, listening, worshiping their Savior.

"I am He whom God exalted to His right hand to be Prince and Savior, to give repentance to Israel and forgiveness of sins.

"I give you eternal life, Chang, and you shall never perish; neither shall anyone snatch you out of My hand. My Father, who has given you to Me, is greater than all; and no one is able to snatch you out of My Father's hand. I and My Father are one."

"Thank You, Lord," Chang said.

But He was not finished.

"My peace I give to you; not as the world gives do I give to you. Let not your heart be troubled, neither let it be afraid."

Chang could not imagine ever being afraid again.

+ + +

Mac wanted to be let off to make his way to Jerusalem on foot.

"Are you sure?" Rayford said.

"Unless you order me not to."

"I don't see it. What's the point?"

"I want to know firsthand what's happening there. I'll stay in touch by radio and phone. And the way I understand it, I won't miss a thing the Lord says."

"You know what's going to happen, Mac. Jerusalem falls, but then Jesus saves the day."

"And why wouldn't I want a front-row seat for that?"

"We'll get back in time to see it."

"And by the time you get here, I will have kept you up to date on the details."

"Suit yourself."

"Thanks." And Mac was out of the Hummer heading toward Jerusalem.

"What might the Unity Army do to him if they catch him?" Abdullah said.

Rayford shook his head. "I'd like to think they have no power over him."

"But we don't know for sure."

"No, we don't. He knows how to take care of himself."

"He is unarmed, Captain."

"In a manner of speaking."

When Rayford and Abdullah finally arrived at the edge of the Valley of Megiddo, it appeared the Lord and His hosts had left the remnant of Israel about halfway between there and Jerusalem. Rayford could only assume that Jesus wanted the remnant with Him for the Jerusalem conquest and what followed but for some reason did not wish them to witness what was to take place here.

Mac reported that a mammoth contingent of the Unity Army surrounded all of Jerusalem and simply seemed to be waiting for orders. "There's a lot of unrest among the army here," he said. "Grumbling. Hunger. Rumors of no pay and no reinforcements. A lot of gossip about what happened in the south."

"Interesting," Rayford said. "There is no division between the forces there and here. The immense army is virtually contiguous from west of the Dead Sea to the Valley of Megiddo, so it's possible some of the ones you see will be put to work here, and vice versa."

"That's a huge stretch, Ray. You sayin' this army's as big as it's been since the beginning?"

"Except for the casualties earlier in Edom."

Mac whistled. "How's my man Smitty doin'?"

"Happy as a clam. Loves to hear the voice of Jesus."

"Don't we all? Tell him Mac says hey."

✣ ✣ ✣

George Sebastian mingled with the Tribulation Force contingent at the resting place north of Jerusalem. He couldn't help but recall how far he had come since the escapade in Greece where he almost lost his life and had to kill to stay alive. "Otherwise," he told Priscilla, "I'd be waving at you from beyond the skies."

"We sure didn't know what we were getting into, did we?" she said.

"Not by a long shot."

"Our days of soldiering are over, aren't they?" Razor said.

Sebastian sighed. "I hope so."

"You tired?" Razor said.

"Actually, no. I should be. Up all day and night, and now, with this light, I have no idea what time it's supposed to be. And all this traveling? The running? I ought to feel like I could sleep for a month, but I've got nothing but energy. Wish I could see what's going to happen up north."

"Me too," Razor said. "I can still see Jesus and hear Him. I don't understand why He doesn't sound farther away than He does. He sounds the same to me."

Priscilla said, "I think it's because we're hearing Him in our hearts instead of with our ears."

Razor shrugged. "Could be. Otherwise, how would everybody hear their own name?"

Everyone fell silent as the Lord spoke yet again.

"No one has seen God at any time. I, the only begotten Son, who came from the bosom of the Father, have declared Him. I am called the Son of the Highest, and today the Lord God will give Me the throne of My father David."

Suddenly another voice cascaded from heaven, and Sebastian knew immediately it was God Himself. "Behold!" He said. "My Servant whom I have chosen, My Beloved in whom My soul is well pleased! I have put My Spirit upon Him, and He will declare justice."

Then Jesus again: "The law was given through Moses, but grace and truth come through Me. Now, George, may the God of peace who brought Me up from the dead and made Me the great Shepherd of the sheep, through the blood of the everlasting covenant, make you complete in every good work to do His will, working in you what is well pleasing in His sight. Amen."

On the amen the whole of the remnant fell to its knees, praying and thanking God. Sebastian knew each had again heard his own name in the benediction Jesus had pronounced, yet that made it no less personal.

+ + +

Rayford climbed atop the Hummer again, Abdullah right behind. They looked out on the vast enemy horde as thousands burst open at the words of Jesus and died before they hit the ground. And the battle at Armageddon had not yet commenced. Rayford heard Nicolae Carpathia trying to encourage and rally the troops.

He barked instructions to the generals and commanders. "This is our true enemy," he said. "Best Him, and victory is ours. Jerusalem will be no obstacle."

How he managed to get so many millions of troops on the same page and pointed in the same direction was beyond Rayford, but somehow Nicolae had pulled it off. Somehow he had orchestrated a half-moon of an army covering hundreds of square miles, all facing Jesus in the sky.

Was he going to have them fire upon the King of kings? How would he determine how far away Jesus was? And if Carpathia's armies had been harmless against mere mortals, what did he expect to accomplish here?

Before a command could be given or a shot fired, Jesus spoke. And while it took only a matter of several minutes, the devastation was enormous.

"Test the spirits, whether they are of God," He said, "because many false prophets have gone out into the world. By this you know the Spirit of God: Every spirit that confesses that I came in the flesh is of God, and every spirit that does not confess that I came in the flesh is not of God. And this is the spirit of the Antichrist."

Rayford heard Carpathia raging, cursing.

And Jesus said, "A mighty king arose who ruled with great dominion, and did according to his will. But his kingdom shall be broken up and divided toward the four winds of heaven, but not among his posterity nor according to his dominion with which he ruled; for his kingdom shall be uprooted.

"Now is the appointed time. The king of this world did according to his own will: he exalted and magnified himself above every god, spoke blasphemies against the God of gods, and prospered until now. But what has been determined shall be done."

The great army was in pandemonium, tens of thousands at a time screaming in terror and pain and dying in the open air. Their blood poured from them in great waves, combining to make a river that quickly became a swamp.

"He regarded neither the true God nor any god," Jesus continued as the soldiers fell and the blood rose, "for he exalted himself above them all. But in their place he honored a god of fortresses; and a god which his fathers did not know he shall honor with gold and silver, with precious stones, and pleasant things. Thus he acted against the strongest fortresses and divided the land for gain.

"Though in the end the king of the South attacked him, and the king of the North came against him like a whirlwind, with chariots, horsemen, and with many ships; he entered the countries, overwhelmed them, and passed through.

"And now he has also entered the Glorious Land, and many countries were overthrown; but these shall escape from his hand: Edom, Moab, and the prominent people of Ammon."

Rayford looked to Abdullah. "Did your geography study tell you where those were? I mean, I know Edom is where Petra is."

"Moab is to the north of there, in Jordan, and Ammon is north of that."

Jesus continued: "He stretched out his hand against the countries, and the land of Egypt did not escape. He had power over the treasures of gold and silver, and over all the precious things of Egypt; also the Libyans and Ethiopians followed at his heels.

"But news from the east and the north troubled him; therefore he went out with great fury to destroy and annihilate many. And he planted the tents of his palace between the seas and the glorious holy mountain . . ."

"He means Jerusalem," Abdullah said.

". . . yet he shall come to his end, and no one will help him."

It seemed to Rayford that the entire Unity Army within his field of vision was dead or dying, and the blood continued to rise. Millions of birds flocked into the area and feasted on the remains.

Carpathia screeched in a frenzy, "I have *not* met my end. I shall take His beloved city and bring it and Him to ruin! Leon, get me out of here!"

14

"SMITTY," RAYFORD SAID, "let's follow Carpathia and Fortunato."

"Are you serious, Captain Steele?"

"They won't even notice."

"Something I do not understand, Captain. Why does Jesus not just capture them? He kills almost the entire army with the words from His mouth, and yet He allows them to run free. I know He is not going to kill them, but it seems He is playing a game with them."

"I'm no theologian," Rayford said, "but as you know, God has His own timetable. All this has been prophesied, scripted. It's going to happen when it's supposed to happen."

As Abdullah steered the Hummer toward the valley and Carpathia's bigger Humvee, for the first time since the appearance of Jesus, the sky began to turn. Dark, menacing clouds formed on the horizon and quickly rose, filling the heavens except where the Lord and His army hovered.

"You feel that?" Mac radioed. "Temperature musta dropped ten degrees in the last minute!"

"Something's brewing," Rayford said.

"Now *you're* understatin' the obvious. I'm heading for cover, Ray."

"Keep in touch."

"Don't worry."

Rayford and Abdullah rolled up their windows. "Do you not want me to lose Leon?" Abdullah said, nodding far across the killing grounds to where the Humvee was picking up speed, apparently trying to find a path through the massacre toward Jerusalem.

"Just try to keep an eye on him," Rayford said. "He's going to have a rough time heading that way. Hey, hit the heat."

Abdullah stopped just the other side of a ravine that separated the high country from the valley where thousands of bodies lay. Although they were dead and their blood had ceased flowing, it seemed to ooze from their bodies and quickly filled the lower areas.

Frost appeared on the windshield. "That's the first time I've seen that in this part of the world," Abdullah said. "In America, yes, but not here." He turned on the wipers, but they merely spread the ice crystals and blocked the view.

Rayford played with the controls until he got the heater and defogger blasting, quickly clearing the window. But even with the heater on full, he was chilled. And the sky turned darker. Strangely, there were still no shadows on the ground. The light of Christ continued to permeate, except for the blackness of the sky that ringed Him and His mounted followers.

Suddenly a voice came from the sky, loud and authoritative, but it was not Jesus'. "It is done!"

Lightning burst from the clouds and explosions of thunder followed. And then came hail—if you could call it that. These were not mere ice chips—not even golf-ball or softball size. The first chunk Rayford saw looked the size of a dining-room table, half a foot thick. It landed about twenty feet below the Hummer and embedded itself a couple of feet into the ground. The concussion sounded like a bomb.

The few remaining Unity Army soldiers behaved like madmen, tearing their hair, some shooting themselves, others begging comrades to shoot them. Another chunk of ice hit a grenade launcher and flattened it. Soon hundred-pound blocks of ice began pelting the entire area, smashing bodies, destroying trucks and cars and Jeeps.

The royal Humvee, with Leon driving erratically, narrowly escaped three chunks, one of which caught a running aide squarely atop the head and crushed him to the ground. The gigantic hailstones were soon dropping steadily, and there was no escape. It was as if God were burying the bloody battlefield in a thick layer of ice.

"You getting this hail in Jerusalem?" Rayford radioed Mac.

"Nope. No hail. Looks like it's threatening rain or snow, but so far we're just freezin' our tails off."

Survivors remained only in scattered spots, but instead of trying to find cover or protecting their heads or even falling to their knees and begging for mercy, they lifted their faces to the sky, shouting, apparently railing against God, flashing obscene gestures at Jesus and His army. Soon they were crushed under the monstrous hailstones.

The temperature returned to normal as quickly as it had dropped, and the clouds rolled away and disappeared. The whole of creation seemed bright as day again, and while the sun still had not been seen since before Jesus came, the desert was soon toasty again. Rayford turned off the heat and opened the windows, and he and Abdullah lit out after Leon and Nicolae.

The ice quickly began to melt, and the water mixed with the torrent of blood. "Stop here," Rayford said, as they watched the blood-and-water mixture rise higher than the tires on the potentate's Humvee. The vehicle was soon bogged down in a reddish brown mud. Rayford heard Carpathia shrieking at Leon to get them out of the mess and on toward Jerusalem. But they quickly found all avenues of escape blocked by the rising muck. When it reached the middle of the door of their vehicle, Carpathia ordered Leon out to push while he climbed into the driver's seat.

"But, Excellency, I will drown!"

"You will do no such thing. Do you want your king to get out?"

"No, my lord, of course not. But I-I, ah—"

Leon pushed open the door and the liquid invaded the vehicle. "Hurry, man!" Nicolae shouted. "Shut the door!"

Leon stepped gingerly into the drink, which reached his waist and made his robe balloon out. He had wisely left his fez in the Humvee. "It's freezing!" he squealed. "My legs are going numb!"

"Of course it is freezing! It has ice in it! Now start pushing!"

"It stinks!"

"Push!"

It took Leon a moment to make his way behind the vehicle, and the footing beneath the surface was clearly uneven. Once he nearly plunged all the way under and had to grab the fender to stay upright. His robe was a mess, his hands and face pale, his hair mussed. Rayford could see he was shivering to his core.

When he got behind the Humvee, Carpathia apparently floored the accelerator, for all he accomplished was to kick up a rooster tail of liquid and steam that covered Leon. The Humvee didn't move.

"Try to rock it!" Leon shouted.

"That is what you are there for! Grab under the bumper and lift!"

"Lift a Humvee!?"

"Rock it!"

Finally they coordinated Leon's lifting and pushing and Carpathia's alternated gunning the engine and letting up, and the big thing began to sway. When it finally started to move, Leon lost his balance and pitched forward, going completely under. He came up sputtering and trying to wipe his face.

Nicolae pulled the Humvee to slightly higher ground and Leon rushed to get in the passenger side. But when he opened the door, Carpathia was already there.

"I am *not* driving, Leon! How would that look?"

Leon trudged around in front of the car and yanked open the door. Just before climbing in he pulled his sodden robe over his head and left it in the rising river of blood. He clambered aboard in his underwear, assuring Nicolae that he had other clothes in the back.

"Well, put them on immediately!"

The Humvee rocked and bounced as Leon found dry clothes and dressed in the car. Apparently deciding his ornate cap would not work with the new outfit, he tossed it out the window as he slowly pulled away, looking for yet higher ground. The blood had already risen more than four feet.

+ + +

When the skies cleared and the temperature rose, Mac rubbed his bare arms and emerged from what had been meager cover under sparse trees not far from the Temple Mount. Though not in the uniform of the Unity Army, he must not have looked like a rebel either, as he was virtually ignored. Many of the normal nonfighting citizenry were milling about among the thousands of soldiers, who spent much of their time sitting around. Some platoons were moved here and there, seemingly on the whim of a general or a commander, but all fighting had ceased. The Global Community forces had occupied all of Jerusalem except the Temple Mount, and they had that surrounded. Occasionally a general with a bullhorn tried to persuade the tiny band of rebels inside to surrender and avoid inevitable bloodshed.

Mac was amused that the general assumed the rebels had no access to outside information. But having talked with them, he knew they had radios and even some televisions. They would know what had happened at Petra and Bozrah, and soon they would probably even know the outcome of the battle at Armageddon.

It seemed weird to Mac that soldiers could sit around smoking and playing cards, only occasionally glancing into the sky to see what Jesus was up to. Maybe this was all part of the hardening of hearts, but Mac thought that he, in the same situation, would recognize that his end was near. Theirs was clearly a supernatural foe who had not even been slowed by the most powerful army in history. The war was as good as over.

And yet Nicolae Carpathia, the great deceiver, despite winning not even a skirmish since the appearing of Christ, had somehow convinced his troops that Jerusalem was the key. If they could take the Holy City, he would be returned to his rightful throne, the Son of God would be defeated, and all would again be right with the world.

The only thing that argument had going for it was the current situation in Jerusalem. The idea of the rebels holding anything when they were surrounded and outnumbered a thousand to one was laughable and pathetic. Except, as Mac knew, they were on the right side.

* * *

Rayford had assumed he was way past being shocked by now. What could he see that would be more surreal than the last several hours? Yet as Abdullah kept a careful but watchful distance from Carpathia's Humvee, all Rayford could do was stare at the result of the last so-called battle. Of course, there had not been a battle at all. The Unity Army had rattled its sabers, loaded its weapons, and made a lot of noise. And Jesus had killed them all, with mere words.

Of course those words were the words of God, and the effect was overpowering. Mile after mile after mile, Abdullah drove next to a river of blood several miles wide and now some five feet deep. Carpathia's whole-world fighting force of several million troops had been reduced to perhaps a million. That was still huge, of course, and from a human standpoint the rebels could never match it. But the devastation to the Unity Army in a short period should have made plain to Carpathia that his days were numbered.

Rather, to hear him talking earnestly to Leon in the car and to the remaining troops by radio, what had happened served as mere motivation. "Our goal remains," Carpathia said, "and our task is clear. Take the Father's city, wipe out His chosen people, and kill His Son. This has been our design from the beginning. We have drawn Him out, and we will soon have Him where we want Him. Remain loyal, remain true, remain vigilant, and you will be rewarded."

Jesus, meanwhile, had turned to the remnant and addressed them directly as Rayford and Abdullah listened.

"You are of God, little children, and have overcome Antichrist, because He who is in you is greater than he who is in the world. He is of the world. Therefore he speaks as of the world, and the world hears him. You are of God. He who knows God hears Me; he who is not of God does not hear Me. By this you know the spirit of truth and the spirit of error.

"Beloved, love one another, for love is of God; and everyone who loves is born of God and knows God. He who does not love does not know God, for God is love. In this the love of God was manifested toward you, that God has sent His only begotten Son into the world, that you might live through Him. In this is love, not that you loved God, but that He loved you and sent Me to be the propitiation for your sins.

"Rayford, if God so loved you, you also ought to love one another."

Rayford was always pierced when he heard his name, as he knew Abdullah and all the others had to be. Then Jesus moved from the personal exhortation to clearly explain what had just happened.

"And they gathered them together to the place called in Hebrew, Armageddon.

"Then the seventh angel poured out his bowl into the air, and a loud voice came out of the temple of heaven, from the throne, saying, 'It is done!' And there were noises and thunderings and lightnings. And great hail from heaven fell upon men, each hailstone about the weight of a talent. Men blasphemed God because of the plague of the hail, since that plague was exceedingly great.

"An angel came out of the temple of heaven, crying to Me with a loud voice, 'Thrust in Your sickle and reap, for the time has come for You to reap, for the harvest of the earth is ripe.' So I thrust in My sickle on the earth, and the earth was reaped.

"Then another angel came out of the temple which is in heaven, he also having a sharp sickle. And another angel came out from the altar, who had power over fire, and he cried with a loud cry to him who had the sharp sickle, saying, 'Thrust in your sharp sickle and gather the clusters of the vine of the earth, for her grapes are fully ripe.'

"So the angel thrust his sickle into the earth and gathered the vine of the earth, and threw it into the great winepress of the wrath of God. And the winepress was trampled outside the city, and blood came out of the winepress, up to the horses' bridles, for one thousand six hundred furlongs."

+ + +

The remnant, full of the glory of God, had been turned and was pointed toward Jerusalem. Chaim believed the Lord would protect them, but strangely, Jesus now moved on ahead with His army. And while the children of Israel seemed to be moving supernaturally fast again, they fell far behind Him and soon lost sight of Him.

Chaim noticed others looking at each other with concern, and he wanted to reassure them. But his place as leader and spokesman had been taken, and he felt no prompting to try to reassert himself. His job was done, and he felt he was just part of the remnant now. They would go where God pointed them and trust the Lord to be their rear guard.

+ + +

Mac was surprised to discover that the radio waves—and he assumed television as well—were still controlled by the Global Community. That, he knew, would not last long. As he made his way throughout Jerusalem, trying to give Rayford and Abdullah a picture of what they'd find when they arrived, he listened to GC reporters and anchors putting Nicolae Carpathia's spin on everything.

There was no mention, of course, of what could have at least been described as an apparition in the sky—some trick by the enemy to scare everyone. Talk about the proverbial elephant in the room. Mac was certain everyone on earth knew who rode on the clouds. The question was what Jesus was going to do and when He was going to do it.

Jerusalem was replete with makeshift jails and prisons and holding tanks where the captured rebels were starved and tortured. GC personnel reported on these with apparent glee as evidence that victory was at hand. One commentator said that the rebels who thought they were holding the Temple Mount area were themselves in only a larger prison of their own making, for they were helpless to stand against the Unity Army, and there was nowhere they could flee.

It was apparent to Mac that word was beginning to spread throughout the city that the potentate was on his way. The place became a center of activity. Card games ended. Sitting around became a thing of the past. Platoons were coming to attention, areas policed, and the path to the front lines cleared. Every few minutes the news carried a fresh, live quote, right from the commander in chief's own vehicle.

"As we approach what many have referred to as the Eternal City," Carpathia said, "I am pleased to announce that following our victory here, this shall become the new Global Community headquarters. My palace shall be rebuilt on the site of the ruins of the temple, the destruction of which is on our agenda.

"As beautiful as New Babylon was, in truth it has been my objective all along to one day relocate the seat of government, commerce, and religion to this city, which has meant so much to so many for so long. So, loyal citizens of the New World Order, I trust you will watch with great satisfaction as we complete our takeover of this place, as we root out and destroy the last pocket of resistance, and as we render impotent the One whom the enemy reveres as the reason they have never been able to join our noble cause.

"This One who flits about in the air quoting ancient fairy-tale texts and forcing sycophants to mindlessly run along worshiping Him will soon meet His end. He is no match for the risen lord of this world and for the fighting force in place to face Him. It does not even trouble me to make public our plan, as it has already succeeded. This city and these despicable people have long been His chosen ones, so we have forced Him to show Himself, to declare Himself, to vainly try to defend them or be shown for the fraud and coward that He is. Either He attempts to come to their rescue or they will see Him for who He really is and reject Him as an impostor. Or He will foolishly come against my immovable force and me and prove once and for all who is the better man.

"While I do not expect this to be an extended campaign, as this is the last battle I ever hope to wage, I am bringing in the whole of our resources. Every man and woman under my command and every armament and munition at our disposal shall be employed to make this the most resounding and convincing military victory in history.

"My pledge to you, loyal citizens of the Global Community, is that come the end of this battle, no opponent of my leadership and regime will remain standing, yea, not one will be left alive. The only living beings on planet Earth will be trustworthy citizens, lovers of peace and harmony and tranquility, which I offer with love for all from the depths of my being.

"I am but ten miles west of Jerusalem as we speak, and I will be dismissing my cabinet and generals so they may be about the business of waging this conflict under my command. The Most High Reverend of Carpathianism, Leon Fortunato himself, will serve as my chauffeur for my triumphal entry. Citizens are already lining the roadway to greet me, and I thank you for your support."

Mac hurried into position where he could get a look at the Humvee and the motorcade of military vehicles following it. He stood on a rise on the west side, where he could see the parading army that extended to the horizon. As the procession neared the city, he could hear drums and trumpets, and if he was not mistaken, even from that distance, the royal Humvee looked a mess. Rayford had told him it had been sloshing through the blood in the Valley of Megiddo, but apparently no one had reminded the potentate to get it cleaned.

When it came into view, Mac's suspicions were confirmed. It was ringed with mud and blood to the windows. But sure enough, civilians lined the roadway on either side, cheering, waving, clapping, saluting, and throwing flowers. Carpathia opened the moonroof, stood on the front seat, and appeared in the open air, waving with both hands and blowing kisses.

Enjoy it while it lasts, pal.

+ + +

"Mac, do you see us?" Rayford radioed over the secure frequency.

"No. Where are you?"

"Third row, behind the Humvee."

"Nobody cares?"

"It's as if they don't even see us."

"What's the plan?"

"As the Humvee reaches Jaffa Road, it will head for the Jaffa Gate, along with a third of the fighting force. The other two-thirds will split off north and south, surrounding the Old City. Once everyone is in place, Carpathia will lead the charge through the occupied Armenian and Jewish Quarters to the Temple Mount. They plan to batter through the Western Wall and overtake the rebels."

"Plan to."

"Exactly."

\+ + +

Mac finally spotted Rayford and Abdullah's Hummer and was struck by how much it looked like it belonged in the procession. As the cavalcade approached Jaffa Road, Mac began jogging that way, hoping to catch up with his friends when they peeled away from the group.

The cheering crowds grew larger as the cars neared the Old City, and as they slowed, the marching band caught up, its music blaring and drums pounding. Mac was reminded of Memorial Day parades as a child when his father had hoisted him on his shoulders and he had thrilled to the *rat-a-tat-tat* of the snares and the thumping undercurrent of the big bass drums. Back then, of course, he never heard "Hail Carpathia."

The music had stirred the crowd to a fever pitch, and the army that followed was clearly something unlike any of them, loyalists or rebels, had ever seen. There would not be room in the Old City for a fraction of the force. Mac wondered how even Carpathia and the rest of the rolling stock were going to navigate the narrow cobblestone streets.

\+ + +

"I've been wondering the same thing, Mac," Rayford said. "This is some festival, eh?"

"Ridiculous!"

"Frankly, I love it," Rayford said. "The more and the louder the better."

"I don't follow."

"The more pomp and circumstance, the greater the humiliation later."

"Well, that's for sure."

"You find us yet, Mac?"

"I'm headin' your way. When you gonna split off?"

"We're not."

"You're *not?* What? You're gonna go paradin' into the Old City with Carpathia?"

"Why not? See if you can get in."

"Unlikely."

"Try."

\+ + +

Mac caught up to the parade and had to wonder what all the extra troops were for. The same contingent of soldiers that had been there when he had discovered Buck was more than enough to get the job done from a human standpoint. If they couldn't do it, the rest wouldn't help.

Fortunato steered the wide Humvee through Jaffa Gate, and almost immediately the folly of their plan became clear. There simply wasn't room for the rolling stock to proceed to the Western Wall of the Temple Mount. In his earpiece Mac heard Nicolae trying to enlist engineers to bring in heavy equipment and knock down buildings and walls en route. When told that would take hours, he exploded, swearing and demanding to know who told him his parade through the Old City had been a capital idea.

"Leave the cars where they are!" he announced. "I shall lead the rest of the attack on horseback."

Mac was close enough now to see Carpathia sneak a peek at the sky. Jesus was not there at the moment, and neither was His heavenly army. Mac thought this unnerved Carpathia more than if He'd been there.

Aides immediately attended to Carpathia when he emerged from the Humvee. He straightened his leathers, which seemed no worse for wear since he had not left the vehicle during the debacle at Armageddon. Nicolae also repositioned his garish sword.

But when Fortunato got out, he was wearing plain civilian clothes that made him appear to be on his way to a workday for a local community service club. "Get the reverend a proper uniform and something to clean his face and hair," Carpathia ordered.

Someone ran off, returning presently. "Biggest we have," the man said, handing the folded clothes and a wet towel to Fortunato, who gave him a look that would lift roadkill off asphalt. "Sorry," the man whispered. "Biggest we have."

"You can change in the cathedral," someone else told Leon, and he hurried off with a couple of aides. Meanwhile, more generals and hangers-on and toadies surrounded Carpathia, who asked that they make room for the photographers and TV camera crews.

When Leon returned in the too-short, too-tight Unity Army getup, he looked like Sergeant Garcia trying to fit into Zorro's costume. He had tried to religious-ize the outfit by hanging around his neck a large gold chain with *216* dangling from it.

It was all Mac could do to keep a straight face. He fell into step with Rayford and Abdullah as they approached from their vehicle. They had begun to draw a few stares, though fortunately not from anyone who cared enough to ask questions. All three wore caps pulled low over their foreheads, but without proper uniforms they couldn't pass for Unity Army personnel.

"We'd better split up, eh, Cap?" Mac said.

"I guess. Smitty, you go north. Mac, south. Meet you outside the Eastern Wall at the Golden Gate when this is all over."

* * *

Chaim felt the tingle of anticipation as the remnant fell into place at a high point on the western slope overlooking Jerusalem. It still seemed disconcerting not to see Jesus above them, but he knew the Lord knew best. Antichrist had been crowing about luring the Son of God into his trap, when it was clear to Chaim that the opposite had happened. Carpathia had to have read the Bible. He had to know all this was prophesied. He even had to know the predicted outcome. Yet he brazenly came to the very spot he was supposed to, and in spite of the mass execution of his troops in three other confrontations, he still had the gall to believe he would prevail.

This was going to be something to see, and Chaim wanted to say so to the assembled. He had no means to address them all at once, and from looking at those around him, he knew there was nothing they needed to be told. They, like he, looked on with great expectancy.

Ride on, King Jesus!

15

RAYFORD WAS CLOSE ENOUGH behind Nicolae that he heard him ask a woman general, "What is our equestrian strength?"

She checked via radio and reported, "Excellency, of more than a million soldiers, a little more than a tenth are on horseback."

"Call for as many steeds as we need to get the first wave to the Western Wall, and order Reverend Fortunato and me appropriate mounts."

Within minutes several thousand horses crowded the streets, and Unity Army soldiers were mounting up. A tall, handsome stallion, almost identical to the one Carpathia had ridden out of the city toward Bozrah, was delivered for his use. Cameras clicked and TV crews crowded around as he swung aboard, raising his sword.

He twirled the blade above his head, rousing the troops, who responded with a crescendoing *whoop,* like a football team about to break from the locker room.

Fortunato struggled up onto a smaller black horse and settled himself.

"Follow me to the Western Wall," Carpathia shouted, "and make way for the battering ram and missile launchers! Upon my command, open fire!"

Knowing the Old City by now, Rayford sprinted for side streets, heading toward the Western Wall.

+ + +

Mac was already at the southern corner of the Old City, a few steps north of Dung Gate. Abdullah contacted him by radio and said he had found a perch near Antonia's Fortress and believed he was safe and undetectable, with a good view of the approaching invaders.

"I am high enough to see the surrounding army forces too, Mac," he said. "They have the entire Old City encircled, several thousand deep. I can see why they are so confident of victory, having cut off all escape routes 360 degrees."

+ + +

Rayford set up a hundred yards short of the Western Wall and far enough south that he had some underbrush for cover. He thought he saw Mac but couldn't be sure. Almost everyone inside the Old City but the press was part of the attacking force, but the occasional civilian stood atop anything available, cheering and shouting encouragement as Carpathia came into view, valiant and proud on his huge horse, sword pointing to the sky, microphone wrapped around his ear and in front of his mouth so the entire army could hear his commands.

"For the glory of your risen master and lord of the earth!" he shouted, urging his ride to a full gallop, clacking over the cobblestone ground. Fortunato's horse mince-stepped slowly after, which seemed plenty fast enough for Leon.

The band lagged behind the mounted and rolling and marching troops, loudly clanging out a rousing melody. As Carpathia drew within range of the wall, he peeled off to the south with Fortunato trailing him.

"Horsemen, make way for the armaments!" Carpathia bellowed. "Attack! Break through the wall! Take the Temple Mount! Destroy the rebels!"

But when the horsemen whipped their mounts, they did not make way. Rather, the horses bolted as if blind—nickering, whinnying, braying, rearing, bucking, kicking, spinning into each other, running headlong into the wall, throwing riders.

"Make way!" Carpathia screamed. "Make way!"

The riders not thrown leaped from their horses and tried to control them with the reins, but even as they struggled, their own flesh dissolved, their eyes melted, and their tongues disintegrated. As Rayford watched, the soldiers stood briefly as skeletons in now-baggy uniforms, then dropped in heaps of bones as the blinded horses continued to fume and rant and rave.

Seconds later the same plague afflicted the horses, their flesh and eyes and tongues melting away, leaving grotesque skeletons standing, before they too rattled to the pavement.

"Reinforcements!" Carpathia called out. "Charge! Charge! Fire! Fire! Attack!"

But every horse and rider that advanced suffered the same fate. First blindness and madness on the part of the horses, then the bodies of the soldiers melting and dissolving. Then the falling and piling of the bones.

Rayford stood, mouth agape, noticing that neither Carpathia's nor Fortunato's horses had been affected yet. Leon slid off his mount and flopped to the ground, rolling to a kneeling position and burying his face in his hands.

"Get up, Leon! Get up! We are not defeated! We have a million more soldiers and we shall prevail!"

But Leon stayed where he was, whimpering and wailing.

Plainly disgusted, Nicolae urged his horse back to the middle of the wall and looked past the bones of his decimated troops for reinforcements. He lifted his sword and cursed God, but suddenly his attention was drawn directly above.

Rayford followed his gaze to see the temple of God opened in heaven, and the ark of the covenant plain as day. Lightning flashed and thunder roared, and the earth began to shift.

Carpathia's horse reared and high-stepped, and Nicolae fought to control him. Fortunato's horse scampered away without him.

The earth groaned and buckled, and the city of Jerusalem was fractured into three as the great fissures swallowed up Carpathia loyalists and soldiers. Buildings and walls were left intact, except Abdullah reported seeing the cemented-over East Gate—closed off for centuries—blasted open by the movement of the earth.

Rayford slapped his palm over his earpiece and plugged his other ear to hear reports coming in from all over the world. The earthquake was global. Islands disappeared. Mountains were leveled. The entire face of the planet had been made level, save for the city of Jerusalem itself.

And suddenly the Lord Jesus Himself appeared in the clouds again, and the whole world saw Him. He spoke with a loud voice, saying, "Speak comfort to Jerusalem, and cry out to her, that her warfare is ended, that her iniquity is pardoned; for she has received from the Lord's hand double for all her sins.

"Every valley has been exalted and every mountain and hill brought low; the crooked places have been made straight and the rough places smooth. The glory of the Lord has been revealed, and all flesh have seen it together; for I have spoken.

"Behold, the day of the Lord has come, and your spoil has been divided in your midst. For I gathered all the nations to battle against Jerusalem, but the remnant of the people was not cut off from the city. I went forth and fought against those nations, as in the day of battle.

"And the plague with which I struck all the people who fought against Jerusalem was this: their flesh dissolved while they stood on their feet, their eyes dissolved in their sockets, and their tongues dissolved in their mouths. I sent a great panic over them. Such also was the plague on the horses.

"Behold, I made Jerusalem a cup of drunkenness to all the surrounding peoples, when they laid siege against Judah and Jerusalem. And I made Jerusalem a very heavy stone for all peoples; all who would heave it away were surely cut in pieces, though all nations of the earth were gathered against it.

"I struck every horse with confusion, and its rider with madness; I opened My eyes on the house of Judah and struck every horse of the peoples with blindness.

"I defended the inhabitants of Jerusalem; the one who was feeble among them today is like David, and the house of David shall be like God, like the Angel of the Lord before them. I destroyed all the nations that came against Jerusalem.

"Therefore the curse has devoured the earth, and those who dwell in it are desolate. Therefore the inhabitants of the earth are burned, and few men are left.

"In the midst of the land among the people, it was like the shaking of an olive tree, like the gleaning of grapes when the vintage is done.

"The children of Israel called on My name, and I answered them. I said, 'This is My people'; and each one said, 'The Lord is my God.'"

+ + +

Though the Lord did not speak audibly to the remnant, Chaim felt as if he and they were being drawn inexorably around the Old City to the east side. As the million-plus slowly made their way past the dead and the dying, a fraction of Antichrist's forces remained alive. They struggled and staggered toward shelter, also apparently drawn to the east.

The Lord sat triumphant on the back of His white horse in the clouds, His army behind Him, gazing upon the one-sided victory over the forces that had come against Jerusalem.

+ + +

Mac found Rayford and they went looking for Abdullah. They knew he was all right, because they had radio contact. He too was headed east of the city.

"You should have seen Nicolae and Leon," Rayford said.

"I saw them briefly," Mac said, "when Leon fell off his horse."

"Nicolae galloped off a little while ago, heading back the way he had come. Leon was running after him, pleading to let him ride along, but Carpathia ignored him."

"Figures."

The earth still shifted and moved from aftershocks, and Rayford tried to imagine what it must look like from outer space. No more islands. No more mountains. Virtually flat with gently rolling hills. The whole of Israel, except for Jerusalem, was level.

They found Abdullah, who at first looked past them, then smiled and shook his head. "I was looking for two white men, Mac."

+ + +

Hannah Palemoon caught up with Chaim, who was surrounded by people with questions. She waited until he recognized her, then said, "How long until we are reunited with loved ones who went on to heaven before us?"

"Very soon, I hope," Chaim said. "There are many I wish to see too, but first I want to see Jesus face-to-face."

"What's next?"

"Oh, I think you know. The Lord Himself will set foot on earth again, for only the second time since His ascension. As you know, He came in the clouds for the Rapture, and this time He briefly walked on the ground when He soiled His robe in blood at Bozrah."

"Is the enemy completely gone?" Hannah said.

"Soon," Chaim said. "Very soon."

+ + +

Illinois, flat as it already was, was hardly affected by the earthquake, though Enoch was certain no one doubted what had happened. The long, low rumbling of the earth continued, and he heard Carpathia loyalists screaming for their lives.

After his people had returned to their homes, Enoch had begun moving his furniture upstairs, looking forward to a life where he could look out the window without caring who might see in. Just before the earthquake one of the few Global Community Peacekeeper patrol cars he'd seen in recent weeks raced down the street. As it came around the curve in front of his place it veered off the road and hit a fire hydrant.

Neighbors ran to the car, collapsing in disbelief when all they found were skeletons and clothes in the front seat. The declared enemies of God were being decimated around the world.

Enoch tried calling his parishioners, reaching many and missing several who called while he was on the phone. No one was hurt, though some of their homes were damaged. Several were badly shaken, telling of seeing government employees disintegrating before their eyes. And all wanted to talk about their new church, where it might be and how soon they might move into it. Many also mentioned their pilgrimage to the Middle East.

"I don't know when it's gonna be," one woman told Enoch, "but I'll be along whenever."

Enoch reminded each that sometime after the earthquake, Jesus would set foot on the Mount of Olives, east of Jerusalem, and the whole world would see Him. "Keep looking up."

+ + +

"You still in a teachin' mood, Smitty?" Mac said.

"That depends on whether I have studied whatever you are curious about."

"The Mount of Olives, of course."

"Oh yes, I have studied it thoroughly. You can see it from here, naturally. It is only half a mile from the Eastern Wall of the Old City. It is really more of a hill than a mountain, as you can tell. One of Jesus' most famous sermons was preached there. When He made His triumphal entry, He came from the

Mount of Olives. And He returned there every night of the last week before the Crucifixion, often praying in the Garden of Gethsemane. The Ascension took place there later too."

"So it makes sense that's where He wants to come now."

"It certainly does to me," Abdullah said.

\+ + +

George Sebastian had never seen anything like it. He told Priscilla he would catch up with her and the kids and the rest of the Tribulation Force traveling with the remnant. He lagged, and rather than following the remnant around the devastated city, he decided to cut directly through it on his way to the Mount of Olives.

As a career military man, Sebastian had seen the spoils of war before, of course, on many fields of battle around the world. He could not recall, however, a quaint, beautiful city so devastated. Most peculiar, it was nearly impossible to determine who had won.

Sebastian had been kept up to speed on the conflict from the beginning and knew from Buck and then Mac how the city had been completely overrun by the Global Community Unity Army. Half the residents had been killed or captured. Many were still imprisoned and had been tortured and starved.

But now as he ambled through the narrow streets, George saw some surviving Unity soldiers leisurely dividing the spoils, while others regrouped for an assault on rebels who would try to escape from the Temple Mount. He also noticed piles of clothes and bones where the Lord had decomposed the bodies of His enemies.

So this was not over. Jerusalem, the jewel City of God, had been violated to the point of ruin. It was a wonder God Himself had not leveled it along with the mountains and islands of the world.

Sebastian scanned the entire area as he walked, heading north to Herod's Gate, where he knew Buck had been killed. He climbed the wall and looked out over the rest of Jerusalem. Perhaps a hundred thousand of Carpathia's troops remained. The rebels still held the Temple Mount, guarding the newly opened East Gate rather than choosing to try to escape through it.

He could see the vast remnant slowly making its way past the South Wall, heading toward the Mount of Olives, and knew he had better catch up or risk leaving his wife with the responsibility of two youngsters by herself. Of course, others would help, but that didn't justify his abandoning her.

Just before Sebastian made his way back down from the wall, he saw a flurry of activity outside the New Gate in the northwest corner of the Old City. It appeared the press had surrounded Nicolae and Leon and what was left of the potentate's cabinet of advisers and generals. Sebastian shook his head. He knew what was coming, and Carpathia had to as well. Why wasn't he running for his life?

Some men never know when they're beaten, never know when to fold and walk away. Nicolae Carpathia, proving—as if that were necessary—that he was indeed Antichrist, was the epitome of that kind of a man. In a classic case of cosmic denial, his pride still persuaded him he could not lose in the end.

There he stood, pointing, cajoling, scheming, barking orders, talking to the press. Sebastian fired up his radio, and sure enough, his highness was still trying to sell the citizenry on their eventual triumph. "This city shall become my throne," Carpathia said. "The temple will be flattened and the way made for my palace, the most magnificent structure ever erected. We have captured half the enemy here, and we will dispose of the other half in due time.

"The final stage of our conquest is nearly ready to be executed, and we will soon be rid of this nuisance from above."

✠ ✠ ✠

Rayford, Mac, and Abdullah had also been listening as they watched the crawl of people, mostly the remnant, moving toward the Mount of Olives. Of course, the children of God knew what was supposed to come, and so they kept their distance. No one had any idea of the Lord's timing, but there He remained, hovering over them with His horsemen. And soon He began again to speak words of comfort to His own.

"As you have received Me as your Lord, so walk in Me, rooted and built up in Me and established in the faith, as you have been taught, abounding with thanksgiving. You are complete in Me, the head of all principality and power.

"My Father has said unto Me, 'Your throne, O God, is forever and ever; a scepter of righteousness is the scepter of Your kingdom. You have loved righteousness and hated lawlessness; therefore God, Your God, has anointed You with the oil of gladness more than Your companions.

"'You laid the foundation of the earth, and the heavens are the work of Your hands. Others will perish, but You remain; and they will all grow old like a garment; like a cloak You will fold them up, and they will be changed. But You are the same, and Your years will not fail.'

"And I, the One about whom these things were said by God Himself, assure you, My children, that I will never leave you nor forsake you. So you may boldly say: 'The Lord is my helper; I will not fear. What can man do to me?' I, your Lord Jesus Christ, am the same yesterday, today, and forever. Therefore, holy brothers and sisters, partakers of the heavenly calling, consider Me the Apostle and High Priest of your confession.

"I was faithful to God who appointed Me, as Moses also was faithful. For I was counted worthy of more glory than Moses, in the same way that God, who built the house, has more honor than the house. For every house is built by someone, but He who built all things is God.

"God has set Me as a High Priest fitting for you—holy, harmless, undefiled, separate from sinners, and higher than the heavens. I do not need daily, as human high priests, to offer up sacrifices, first for My own sins and then for the people's, for this I did once for all when I offered up Myself."

Despite all Jesus' magnanimous comments about Himself, Rayford was struck by how lowly, humble, and compassionate He sounded. He was merely speaking the truth, reminding His children what they enjoyed in Him. The truth of the Word of God, coming from the Living Word, again drove Rayford to his knees, along with his friends and the entire Jewish remnant.

As Rayford knelt, his face in his hands on the ground, Jesus continued to speak directly to his heart.

"God willed to make known the riches of the glory of this mystery, which is Christ in you, Rayford, the hope of glory. I am the hope of Israel, the horn of salvation in the house of God's servant David. Most assuredly, I say to you, before Abraham was, I AM."

Jesus fell silent. From the west Rayford heard the Global Community Unity Army marching band. Their weak rendition of "Hail Carpathia." sounded discordant from a distance, and of course it paled in comparison to the murmured prayers of the million on their knees before the Lord in the sky.

The ground rumbled as what was left of the GC's armaments were rolled into position. It was pathetic and laughable to Rayford that Carpathia had not learned anything from the past several hours. There would be no competing with this force from heaven. No damage would be done to Jesus or to His people with weapons of war.

And yet here Carpathia came, horse at full stride, leathers squeaking in the saddle, sword aloft, the pitiable False Prophet bouncing awkwardly along behind him, holding the reins of his horse for all he was worth. The remnant stood as one, not wanting to miss a thing. Rayford looked fully into the face of his Lord and was again reminded of the biblical description of the man on the white horse with eyes like fire.

The conviction that shone in the eyes of Jesus was of one who had finally had enough. His enemy was right where He wanted him, lured fully into the trap that had been set before the foundation of the world. The fulfillment of age-old prophecies was about to take place, despite the fact that the enemy himself had read them, knew them, and had seen every last one of them come to fruition exactly as it had been laid out.

In all his sick, imitative glory came galloping the quintessence of pride and ego, indwelt by Satan himself. Carpathia swung his sword round and round above his head while Fortunato used one hand to attempt some sort of a weird gesture of worship and the other to keep control of his horse and himself in the saddle.

The band, which led the way, played louder and louder and, on cue, split right and left to allow the mounted soldiers, then the foot soldiers, then the munitions and armament platoons in rolling vehicles to slowly come into position.

With the remnant just a few hundred yards to the east, the besieged city of Jerusalem a half mile to the west, and the heavenly hosts hovering directly above, Jesus nudged His magnificent white charger and descended to the top of the Mount of Olives.

As He dismounted, Carpathia shrieked out his final command, "Attack!" The hundred thousand troops followed orders, horsemen at full gallop firing, foot soldiers running and firing, rolling stock rolling and firing.

And Jesus said, in that voice like a trumpet and the sound of rushing waters, "I AM WHO I AM."

At that instant the Mount of Olives split in two from east to west, the place Jesus stood moving to the north and the place where the Unity Army stood moving to the south, leaving a large valley.

All the firing and the running and the galloping and the rolling stopped. The soldiers screamed and fell, their bodies bursting open from head to toe at every word that proceeded out of the mouth of the Lord as He spoke to the captives within Jerusalem. "You shall flee through My mountain valley, for the mountain valley reaches to Azal. Yes, you shall flee as you fled from the earthquake in the days of Uzziah king of Judah. The Lord your God has come, and all the saints with Me."

With shouts and singing, it was as if Jerusalem burst forth; the captives, who had been imprisoned in Jerusalem, came running toward the great rift between the two sides of the Mount of Olives. And as the earth continued to rumble and shift, Rayford watched in awe as the whole city of Jerusalem rose above the ground some three hundred feet and now stood as an exalted jewel above all the surrounding land that had been flattened by the global earthquake.

\+ + +

Mac struggled to his feet and grabbed Rayford. "You see 'em?" he said, pointing. "See Nicolae and Leon lighting out for safety? And look at that big glob of bobbing light bouncin' along ahead of 'em! 'Member what I told you about Lucifer showing up at Solomon's Stables? That's got to be him, and he's deserted ol' Nick again!"

Mac and Abdullah and Rayford stood, arms around each other's shoulders, taking in the spectacular scene. Rebels from the Temple Mount and the captives fled through the new valley, chased by the last feeble vestiges of the Unity Army. But when Jesus spoke, the pursuers died at His words.

"Living waters shall flow from Jerusalem," He said, "half of them toward the eastern sea and half of them toward the western sea; in both summer and winter it shall occur. And I the Lord shall be King over all the earth. Today the Lord is one and His name one.

"All the land has been turned into a plain from Geba to Rimmon south of Jerusalem. Jerusalem has been raised up and inhabited in her place from Benjamin's Gate to the place of the First Gate and the Corner Gate, and from the Tower of Hananeel to the king's winepresses. You, the people, shall dwell in it; and no longer shall there be utter destruction, but Jerusalem shall be safely inhabited."

With that, Jesus mounted His horse and began His final triumphal entry toward Jerusalem. During His first visit to earth He had ridden into the city on a lowly donkey, welcomed by some but rejected by most. Now He rode high on the majestic white steed, and with every word that came from His mouth, the rest of the enemies of God—except for Satan, the Antichrist, and the False Prophet—were utterly destroyed where they stood.

"This is the day of vengeance, that all things which were written have been fulfilled. The loftiness of man shall be bowed down, and the haughtiness of men shall be brought low; the Lord alone will be exalted today."

Loud voices from heaven said, "The kingdoms of this world have become the kingdoms of our Lord and of His Christ, and He shall reign forever and ever!

"We give You thanks, O Lord God Almighty, the One who is and who was and who is to come, because You have taken Your great power and reigned. The nations were angry, and Your wrath has come, and the time of the dead, that they should be judged, and that You should reward Your servants the prophets and the saints, and those who fear Your name, small and great, and should destroy those who destroy the earth."

The remnant trailed Jesus, raising their hands, singing *hosanna,* and praising Him. They fell silent when He spoke again.

"It is a righteous thing with God to repay with tribulation those who trouble you, and to give you who are troubled rest. I have taken vengeance on those who do not know God, and on those who do not obey My gospel. These shall be punished with everlasting destruction from the presence of the Lord and from the glory of His power. I have come to be glorified in My saints and to be admired among all those who believe."

16

KNEELING IN HIS FRONT YARD in suburban Chicago, Enoch wept at the glorious triumphant words of Christ. He also wept because of his deep longing to be in Jerusalem. He had studied these passages for years and knew what was happening. He couldn't wait to get there, to reunite with his friends from the Tribulation Force, and to hear every detail of the great day of God the Almighty.

More than anything, however, he wanted to see Jesus.

\+ \+ \+

With every moment it became more and more difficult for Rayford to take in the magnitude of the supernatural events. Sensory overload was a gross understatement. He never once had to pinch himself to determine whether this was a dream. It was all so real, so massive, that even what he might have considered smaller miracles took their place alongside the global and local earthquakes in importance. Like the fact that he still felt no fatigue, despite no rest—let alone sleep—in he didn't know how long.

But when he and Mac and Abdullah parked the Hummer outside the Old City and followed the vast procession in the newly burst-open East Gate, a new phenomenon awaited him. It was one thing to follow his Lord, the King of kings, on His ultimate triumphal entry into the City of David, but to see what he saw there compared with what he expected to find . . .

Jerusalem, particularly the Old City, should have been filled with the gore of the dead. Hundreds of thousands had been slain here, the majority in most grotesque ways. There should have been stench, blood, and flesh, not to mention the skeletal remains of Unity Army soldiers and horses.

But the earthquake that had rent in two the Mount of Olives and elevated the Eternal City some three hundred feet had accomplished a macabre cleanup operation as well. Jesus led the happy throng in and around the inside borders of the Old City, stretching the parade of singing, dancing, chanting, embracing, praising, worshiping, celebrating people for several miles. Strangely, the walls had been leveled, all of them. No more battle scars, no more jagged edges from bombs and battering rams, no more uneven heights. Where the walls had stood were gently rolling mounds of fine, crushed stone.

Even the Wailing Wall had disappeared, and Rayford had the full-hearted feeling that Jesus had replaced it with Himself. Sure enough, as the head of the procession came within sight of the Western Wall, Jesus began to speak. And while in the saddle He was only slightly higher than the people in line and was facing away from them, Rayford knew all could hear Him as clearly as he himself could, about a third of the way back in the throng.

"There is one God and one Mediator between God and men, I, the Man Christ Jesus. I gave Myself a ransom for all."

Where was the residue of war? Rayford could only guess. It was as if the city had been shaken and tilted this way and that. And while the buildings and landmarks remained, the rubble of the walls had apparently scrubbed the streets and pushed the gruesome evidence—all of it—into crevasses now covered over for the rest of eternity. The City of God was pristine anew, and the people seemed astonished by it.

When the Lord had ridden His horse far enough into the city to allow all those following to also enter in, He circled so that the entire host was in a great circle, thousands deep. Behind everyone, almost as an afterthought, were the hosts of heaven, also still on horseback.

The remnant ignored them, as if temporarily unaware of them. Rayford saw them clearly and knew that everyone else could too. In the back of his mind was the prospect—soon, he hoped—of reunions with loved ones. But having Jesus in their midst made everyone think only of Him. Everything else, pleasant or not, faded to insignificance.

When everyone had finally stopped walking and shuffling and maneuvering into place, Jesus dismounted and stretched out His arms. "O Jerusalem, Jerusalem," He cried, "the one who kills the prophets and stones those who are sent to her! How often I wanted to gather your children together, as a hen gathers her chicks under her wings, but you were not willing! See! Your house was left to you desolate; for I said to you, you shall see Me no more till you said, 'Blessed is He who comes in the name of the Lord!'"

Jesus looked to the remnant, and Rayford knew intuitively that each one had the same feeling he did, that He was looking directly into their eyes alone. Rayford could not contain himself. He took a huge breath and shouted for all he was worth, "Blessed is He who comes in the name of the Lord!" And every soul there had shouted the same thing, bringing the most beatific smile to the face of Jesus.

✢ ✢ ✢

Ming Toy Woo, standing hand in hand with her new husband, Ree, drank this all in with a lump in her throat, her heart full to bursting. She heard every word in her native tongue and had to remind herself that Jesus was doing this for each person in his or her own language. Though she and Ree were at least a hundred deep in the crowd, and everyone was standing, she had a clear and perfect view of Jesus without having to stand on tiptoe or lean between bodies.

Suddenly standing behind Jesus were five heavenly beings, three of whom she recognized: Christopher, the angel with the everlasting gospel; Caleb; and Nahum. These were the three angels of mercy who had delivered her from certain death when she was working undercover for the Global Community. They were also the ones who told her she would not die before the Glorious Appearing of Christ.

The other two angels were quickly identified when Jesus handed the reins of His horse to one, saying simply, "Gabriel." The other set a stone bench in place, and as Jesus sat He said, "Thank you, Michael."

Then the Son of God, Maker of heaven and earth, Savior of mankind, looked directly into Ming's eyes and said in Chinese, "Come to Me, My child."

Ming stared as if struck with paralysis. Finally able to move, she touched her chest and asked, "Me?"

Jesus seemed to look into her soul, concentrating only on her. "Yes, dear one. Come to Me, Ming."

She wanted to run, to push others aside, to leap into His arms. But it was all she could do to put one foot in front of the other. She let go of Ree's hand and slowly began to move, realizing that the entire band, many more than a million now, was moving toward Jesus as one.

✢ ✢ ✢

It had been plain as day and no mistake. Jesus had looked right at Rayford, deep in the crowd, and singled him out. He had called him by name and told him, "Come to Me, My child."

Rayford tore his eyes away and looked to his right and his left. Both Abdullah and Mac looked shocked, also staring at Jesus and questioning, by gesture or word—Abdullah in Arabic—whether He was talking to them.

But He was not, Rayford knew. *He is talking to me.* Rayford pointed at himself with both hands and raised his brows. And Jesus nodded. He began to move toward his Savior. How could this be? How could Jesus give individual audiences before a crowd this size? How much time could He give each person? This could take months! And how was it possible that Rayford was selected first?

As he moved stiff-legged toward Jesus, Rayford's mind reeled. What were the odds? How could he quantify the privilege of locking eyes with the eternal God of the universe? He began to hurry, and Jesus said, "Come unto Me, Rayford, and I will give you rest."

Though his eyes were on Jesus and his body moved forward, Rayford suddenly became aware of everything. He was coming out of a crowd of well over a million. Five angels stood sentry behind the Master. Rayford's friends and family would see him. What had he done to deserve this privilege? Rest—yes, for the first time he felt that need. The fatigue of the last several hours washed over him and he felt as if he could sleep if only given the opportunity.

But as he came within steps of Jesus and saw His welcoming smile, he was struck that the Lord seemed as thrilled to see him as he was to see the Lord. And he was overcome with the shame of his sin. Unworthy. So unworthy. He slowed almost to a stop, fearing he would collapse in disgrace and humiliation.

"No, no," Jesus said, still smiling, and now leaning forward and reaching for him with scarred hands. When Rayford saw that, he nearly dissolved. He forced himself to keep moving, though he had lost control of his own coordination and feared he would stumble and fall into Jesus' lap.

He dropped to his knees at Jesus' feet, sobbing, reminded of every sin and shortcoming of his entire life. Loving hands gathered him in, and he was drawn to Jesus' bosom. "Rayford, Rayford, how I have looked forward to and longed for this day."

Rayford could not speak.

"I knew your name before the foundation of the world. I have prepared a place for you, and if it were not so, I would have told you."

"But, Lord, I—I—"

Jesus took Rayford by the shoulders and gently pushed him back and cupped his face in His hands. He stared into his eyes from inches away, and Rayford could barely hold His piercing gaze. "I was there when you were born. I was there when you thought your mother had abandoned you. I was there when you concluded that I made no sense."

"I am so sorry. I—"

"I was there when you almost married the wrong woman. I was there when your children were born. I was there when your wife chose Me and you did not."

"I—"

"I was there when you nearly broke your vows. When you nearly died, before you knew Me. I was there when you were left behind. And I was waiting when finally you came to Me."

"Oh, Lord, thank You. I'm so—"

"I have loved you with an everlasting love. I am the lover of your soul. You were meant to be with Me for eternity, and now you shall be."

Rayford had so many questions, so many things he wanted to say. But he could not. Looking into Jesus' face transported him to his childhood and he felt as if he could stay kneeling there, childlike, letting his Savior love and comfort him forever.

Jesus put one hand on Rayford's shoulder and the other atop his head. "I pray to My Father, from whom the whole family in heaven and earth is named, that He would grant you, according to the riches of His glory, to be strengthened with might through His Spirit in the inner man, that I may dwell in your heart through faith; that you, being rooted and grounded in love, may be able to comprehend with all the saints what is the width and length and depth and height—to know My love which passes knowledge; that you may be filled with all the fullness of God.

"Now to Him who is able to do exceedingly abundantly above all that you ask or think, according to the power that works in you, to Him be glory in the church to all generations, forever and ever. Amen."

As Rayford seemed to walk on air back to his place among the throng, something deep within him understood that as personal as that had been, Jesus was bestowing the same love and attention on everyone present. He suddenly became aware that Mac and Abdullah were also returning to the crowd, tears streaming, body language evidencing that they had also been with the Master. The three stood again with arms around each other's shoulders, unashamedly worshiping.

As Rayford looked around, he could see from every face that each person had personally encountered Jesus.

\+ \+ \+

The Savior had come to Enoch in his sleep, and yet the encounter was so real and deep that the young man didn't question it for a second. When it was over he found himself on his knees on the floor, feeling as if Jesus had been right there in the room. He had been reminded of significant events in his life, of his journey first away from and then toward true faith. Enoch was able to see anew the hand of God throughout his entire life, and to know that Jesus had known him by name before the foundation of the world. . . .

His phone was chirping, and as Enoch took the first call it began to signal that more and more calls were coming in. An hour later he had heard from almost everyone in his congregation. "I still want to go over there," was a common theme, "but if Jesus is going to come here like that, maybe I don't need to."

\+ + +

Jesus stood and stretched His arms wide, and Rayford was struck that the experience of watching and hearing Him was more personal than ever, despite the numbers of those all doing the same.

"I beseech you," He said, "to walk worthy of the calling with which you were called, with all lowliness and gentleness, with longsuffering, bearing with one another in love, endeavoring to keep the unity of the Spirit in the bond of peace.

"Never again put your trust in men, in whom there is no help. Man's spirit departs, he returns to the earth; in that very day his plans perish. Happy are you who have the God of Jacob for your help, whose hope is in the Lord your God, who made heaven and earth, the sea, and all that is in them; who keeps truth forever, who executes justice for the oppressed, who gives food to the hungry. The Lord gives freedom to the prisoners.

"The Lord opens the eyes of the blind; the Lord raises those who are bowed down; the Lord loves the righteous. The Lord watches over the strangers; He relieves the fatherless and widow; but the way of the wicked He turns upside down.

"The Lord shall reign forever—your God, O Zion, to all generations. Praise the Lord!"

And Rayford did. They all did.

For the first time since His appearing, Rayford saw Jesus speaking and yet did not hear Him. He was conferring with the angelic beings behind Him, and naturally, this attracted the attention of the entire gathering with as much curiosity as when they could hear Him.

The one He had called Gabriel stepped forward. "Remnant of Israel!" he began, with a voice clear as crystal and able to be heard by all. "And Tribulation saints! In truth I perceive that God shows no partiality.

"But in every nation whoever fears Him and works righteousness is accepted by Him.

"The word which God sent to the children of Israel, preaching peace through Jesus Christ—He is Lord of all—that word you know, which was proclaimed throughout all Judea, and began from Galilee after the baptism which John preached: how God anointed Jesus of Nazareth with the Holy Spirit and with power, who went about doing good and healing all who were oppressed by the devil, for God was with Him.

"And we are witnesses of all things which He did both in the land of the Jews and in Jerusalem, whom they killed by hanging on a tree.

"Him God raised up on the third day, and showed Him openly, not to all the people, but to witnesses chosen before by God, even to those who ate and drank with Him after He arose from the dead.

"And He commanded some to preach to the people, and to testify that it is He who was ordained by God to be Judge of the living and the dead.

"To Him all the prophets witness that, through His name, whoever believes in Him will receive remission of sins. Amen."

The gathered repeated the amen in unison. And Jesus once again addressed them:

"In this manner, therefore, pray: Our Father in heaven, hallowed be Your name.

"Thank You that Your kingdom has come. Your will has been done on earth as it is in heaven.

"Give us this day our daily bread. And forgive us our debts, as we forgive our debtors. And do not lead us into temptation, but deliver us from the evil one. For Yours is the kingdom and the power and the glory forever. Amen."

After praying with Him in unison, they opened their eyes and Rayford noticed that only four angels now stood behind Jesus. Michael was gone.

And Jesus said, "I am not alone, because the Father is with Me. In Me you have peace. In the world you had tribulation; but be of good cheer, I have overcome the world."

Jesus lifted up His eyes to heaven, and said: "Father, You glorified Me that I also may glorify You, as You have given Me authority over all flesh, that I should give eternal life to as many as You gave Me.

"And this is eternal life, that they may know You, the only true God, and Me whom You have sent.

"I glorified You on the earth. I finished the work which You have given Me to do.

"And now, O Father, glorify Me together with Yourself, with the glory which I had with You before the world was.

"I do not pray for the world but for those whom You have given Me, for they are Yours. And all Mine are Yours, and Yours are Mine, and I am glorified in them. Those whom You gave Me I have kept; and none of them is lost except the son of perdition, that the Scripture might be fulfilled.

"I do not pray that You should take them out of the world, but that You should keep them from the evil one. Sanctify them by Your truth. Your word is truth.

"O righteous Father! The world has not known You, but I have known You; and these have known that You sent Me. And I have declared to them Your name, and will declare it, that the love with which You loved Me may be in them, and I in them."

Again Gabriel stepped forward. "The Lord is faithful, who will establish you and guard you from the evil one."

\+ + +

With the mention of the evil one, Mac saw commotion in the crowd far behind Jesus and the angelic beings. People were moving aside and murmuring, making way for the archangel Michael. With him were Nicolae Carpathia, in his now disheveled leathers, sans sword; a worn and exhausted looking Leon Fortunato in one of his lesser, simpler robes and no head adornment; and the three ghastly robotic Carpathia look-alikes Mac and the others had seen over the hidden camera when Carpathia and Fortunato had introduced them to the ten kings of the world. These were Ashtaroth, Baal, and Cankerworm, the three froglike demonic creatures who had been sent out to deceive the nations, persuading them to gather together in Megiddo to fight the Son of God.

They were hideous, chalky white beings that had taken on human form and wore identical black suits. They looked defeated, bent, as if crippled by their own evil. They stuck together but separated themselves from Carpathia and Fortunato, and Nicolae and Leon seemed not to want to have anything to do with each other either.

Michael led the five in front of Jesus, and Mac was struck by His countenance. He detected righteous anger, of course, but also what appeared to be disappointment, even sadness. There was no gloating.

The pathetic trio locked arms and knelt before Jesus, whimpering in annoyingly screechy tones. Carpathia turned his back on Jesus and faced the remnant, hands on his hips, defiant and bored. Leon wrung his hands and occasionally fingered his gaudy gold 216 necklace. He half faced Jesus, looking guilty and full of dread, peeking at Carpathia every now and then as if for direction.

Gabriel stepped between Jesus and the three and bent at the waist to get in their faces, and in a loud voice said, "As a fulfillment of age-old scriptural prophecy, you kneel this day before Jesus the Christ, the Son of the living God, who, being in the form of God, did not consider it robbery to be equal with God, but made Himself of no reputation, taking the form of a bondservant, and coming in the likeness of men.

"And being found in appearance as a man, He humbled Himself and became obedient to the point of death, even the death of the cross."

"Yes!" the beings squealed, hissing. "Yes! We know! We know!" And they bowed lower, prostrating their deformed bodies.

Gabriel continued: "Therefore God also has highly exalted Him and given Him the name which is above every name, that at the name of Jesus every knee should bow, of those in heaven, and of those on earth, and of those under the earth—like you—and that *every* tongue, even yours, should confess that Jesus Christ is Lord, to the glory of God the Father."

"Jesus Christ is Lord!" they rasped, and Gabriel stepped back behind Jesus. "Jesus Christ is Lord! It is true! True! We acknowledge it! We acknowledge Him!"

Jesus leaned forward and rested His elbows on His knees. The three kept their faces to the ground, not looking at Him. "'As I live,' says the Lord God, 'I have no pleasure in the death of the wicked, but that the wicked turn from his way and live.'"

"We repent! We will turn! We will turn! We worship You, O Jesus, Son of God. You are Lord!"

"But for you it is too late," Jesus said, and Mac was hit anew by the sorrow in His tone. "You were once angelic beings, in heaven with God. Yet you were cast down because of your own prideful decisions. Rather than resist the evil one, you chose to serve him."

"We were wrong! Wrong! We acknowledge You as Lord!"

"Like My Father, with whom I am one, I have no pleasure in the death of the wicked, but that is justice, and that is your sentence."

And as the three shrieked, their reptilian bodies burst from their clothes and exploded, leaving a mess of blood and scales and skin that soon burst into flames and was carried away by the wind.

Leon flopped to the ground with such force that his palms smacked loudly and his forehead bounced with a crack. He ripped off his necklace and tossed it away. As Jesus sat staring intently at him, Leon rose and tore off his robe, casting it aside and kicking off his shoes. Then he lay face-first on the ground, clad only in plain pants and shirt and socks, his great belly pressing the pavement.

"Oh, my Lord and my God!" he wailed, sobs gushing from him. "I have been so blind, so wrong, so wicked!"

"Do you know who I am?" Jesus said. "Who I truly am?"

"Yes! Yes! I have always known, Lord! Thou art the Christ, the Son of the living God!"

Jesus stood. "You would blaspheme by quoting my servant Simon, whom I blessed, for flesh and blood had not revealed it unto him, but My Father who is in heaven?"

"No, Lord! Your Father revealed it to me too!"

"I tell you the truth, woe to you for not making that discovery while there was yet time. Rather, you rejected Me and My Father's plan for the world. You pitted your will against Mine and became the False Prophet, committing the greatest sin known under heaven: rejecting Me as the only Way to God the Father and spending seven years deceiving the world."

"Jesus is Lord! Jesus is Lord! Don't kill me! I beg you! Please!"

"Death is too good for you. How many souls are separated from Me forever because of you and the words that came from your mouth?"

"I'm sorry! Forgive me! I renounce all the works of Satan and Antichrist! I pledge my allegiance to You!"

"You are sentenced to eternity in the lake of fire."

"Oh, God, no!"

Gabriel said, "Silence!"

Leon rolled and then crawled several feet away, where he lay in a fetal heap, sobbing.

Jesus sat again and Nicolae Carpathia, still facing the assembled crowd, shrugged and thrust his hands deep into his pockets. His eyebrows were raised, a smirk planted, and Mac had to wonder how this would play out. Even Carpathia was to bow and confess that Jesus was Lord, but he exuded no fear and certainly no humility.

Michael advanced to one side of him, Gabriel the other. Michael grabbed an elbow and spun him around as Gabriel shouted, "Kneel before your Lord!"

Carpathia wrenched away from Michael and again stood arms akimbo. Jesus said, "Lucifer, leave this man!"

And with that, Carpathia seemed to shrink. He looked again the way Mac had seen him below the Temple Mount in Solomon's Stables. His leathers were now too roomy for him and hung on him like limp robes. His hands and fingers became bony. His neck seemed to swim inside a collar now much too large.

Nicolae's hair was sparse and nearly colorless, and dark veins appeared on his exposed skin. He was pale and pasty, as if his skin could be easily rubbed away. Again Mac had the feeling that this was what the body of Carpathia would have looked like, had it been moldering in the grave since his assassination three and a half years before.

Nicolae shivered and quivered despite the heat, and he slowly, clearly painfully, reached up and spread his cape around both shoulders, covering himself and seeming to hide within it as if it were a cocoon.

"Kneel!" Gabriel shouted, and he and Michael moved back behind Jesus.

Nicolae nodded weakly and deliberately lowered himself, like an old man, to one knee. It was as if the pavement was too hard for him and his other knee quickly came down, his hands splaying to the sides to keep himself from pitching to his face. There he knelt, on all fours, weak and pathetic and frail, leather cape hanging limply off bony shoulders.

Mac had to contrast the righteousness of Christ with his own humanity. Had he been in Jesus' place now, he would have been unable to resist rejoicing in the triumph. Mac would have said, "Not such a big man now, are you? Where's the sword? Where's the army? Where's the cabinet, the sub-potentates? Now you're only the supreme *im*potentate, aren't you?"

But this was not about winning. This was about justice.

Jesus said, "You became a willing tool of the devil himself."

Nicolae did not protest, did not beg. He merely lowered his head even more and nodded.

"You were a rebel against the things of God and His kingdom. You caused more suffering than anyone in the history of the world. God bestowed upon you gifts of intelligence, beauty, wisdom, and personality, and you had the opportunity to make the most of these in the face of the most pivotal events in the annals of creation.

"Yet you used every gift for personal gain. You led millions to worship you and your father, Satan. You were the cunning destroyer of My followers and accomplished more to damn the souls of men and women than anyone else in your time.

"Ultimately your plans and your regime have failed. And now, who do you say that I am?"

The pause was interminable, the silence deadly. Finally, in a humble, weak voice, Nicolae croaked, "You *are* the Christ, the Son of the living God, who died for the sins of the world and rose again the third day as the Scriptures predicted."

Jesus reached and gestured as He spoke, and Mac had the impression He wished that Nicolae would look at Him. But he did not. "And what does that say about you and what you made of your life?"

Carpathia sank even lower than Mac thought possible. "I confess," he whispered, "that my life was a waste. Worthless. A mistake. I rebelled against the God of the universe, whom I now know loved me."

Jesus shook His head and Mac saw a great sadness in His face. "You are responsible for the fate of billions. You and your False Prophet, with whom you shed the blood of the innocents—My followers, the prophets, and My servants who believed in Me—shall be cast alive into the lake of fire."

The archangels Michael and Gabriel stepped forward, Michael to pull the False Prophet from the ground and Antichrist to a standing position. He stood before Jesus as if awaiting instructions while the wasted Nicolae Carpathia was hunched and elderly looking, hanging his head. Leon Fortunato looked a mess, hair askew, face flushed and tear-stained, hands clasped tightly in front of him.

Gabriel pronounced to the crowd, "And I saw the Beast, the kings of the earth, and their armies, gathered together to make war against Him who sat on the horse and against His army.

"Then the Beast was captured, and with him the False Prophet who worked signs in his presence, by which he deceived those who received the mark of the beast and those who worshiped his image.

"These two were cast alive into the lake of fire burning with brimstone."

Gabriel moved out of the way, and on the spot where he had stood, a hole three feet in diameter opened in the ground and a putrid, sulfuric odor burst forth, making Mac and everyone in the city hold their noses. This was followed by a whistling blue flame that erupted from the hole and rose twenty feet, which Mac could only compare to a monstrous acetylene torch. This added the smell of ether to the mix, and Mac found the front lines of the crowd backing away.

Even as far as he was from the action, Mac felt the tremendous heat emitted by the raging pillar of fire. Jesus and the five angelic beings were apparently immune to the smell and the heat, but both Carpathia and Fortunato tried to back off. Michael held tight to each, still looking to Jesus.

The Lord nodded sadly, and without hesitation, Michael briskly walked the two to the edge of the hole. Fortunato caterwauled like a baby and fought to escape, but with one mighty arm Michael pushed him into the hole. His keening intensified and then faded as he fell. Carpathia did not struggle. He merely covered his face with his forearms as he was dropped in, and then his bawling echoed throughout Jerusalem until he had fallen far enough away. The hole closed as quickly as it had opened, and the Beast and the False Prophet were no more.

17

RAYFORD WAS REELING, and he could only imagine what the rest of the throng must have thought. He knew these things were supposed to happen, and he also knew what was next, but he had never imagined being an eyewitness to all of it. He believed George and Priscilla Sebastian had their ways of shielding the eyes of the children from the gruesome sights, but he also counted on the supernatural power of Jesus Himself to protect Kenny from such images.

How he wanted to see Irene and Raymie and Chloe and Buck, and yes, Amanda. Somehow he understood that the awkwardness of two wives meeting each other in the natural world would not be an issue in the new world. Their full focus and attention would be on Christ and what He had accomplished in all of their lives.

But that would have to come in due time. Gabriel, the pronouncing archangel, appeared ready to speak again. And as soon as he began, Rayford had the feeling that this was the plan of the Lord, to settle the minds of His people after what they had just seen.

"Jesus is the true Light," Gabriel began, "who gives light to every man coming into the world.

"He was in the world, and the world was made through Him, and the world did not know Him.

"He came to His own, and His own did not receive Him.

"But as many as received Him, to them He gave the right to become children of God, to those who believe in His name: who were born, not of blood, nor of the will of the flesh, nor of the will of man, but of God.

"And the Word became flesh and dwelt among you, and you beheld His glory, the glory as of the only begotten of the Father, full of grace and truth. Amen."

"Amen!" the people shouted, and many seemed comforted.

No food, no rest, and now nowhere to sit but on the pavement—so long as one didn't care if he missed some of the action. And of course Rayford did care. Yet once again he felt no hunger, not even the fatigue that had overcome him on his way to see Jesus. And standing was fine.

Again Jesus conferred with the heavenly beings, and Michael disappeared. Would the big event happen this soon, this close to the first judgments? Rayford couldn't imagine, but it was certainly something he didn't want to miss.

Gabriel spoke once more: "But now in Christ Jesus you who once were far off have been brought near by the blood of Christ.

"For He Himself is your peace, and He came and preached peace to you who were afar off and to those who were near. For through Him those both near and far have access by one Spirit to the Father.

"Now, therefore, you are no longer strangers and foreigners, but fellow citizens with the saints and members of the household of God, having been built on the foundation of the apostles and prophets, Jesus Christ Himself being the chief cornerstone, in whom the whole building, being fitted together, grows into a holy temple in the Lord, in whom you also are being built together for a dwelling place of God in the Spirit.

"You, then, who were raised with Christ, sought those things which were above, where Christ was, sitting at the right hand of God.

"You set your mind on things above, not on things on the earth. For you died, and your life was hidden with Christ in God. So when Christ who was your life appeared, then you also appeared with Him in glory.

"And now, dear ones, be sober, be vigilant; because your adversary the devil still walks about like a roaring lion, seeking whom he may devour. You have resisted him, steadfast in the faith, knowing that the same sufferings were experienced by your brotherhood in the world. But now the God of all grace, who called us to His eternal glory by Christ Jesus, after you suffered a while, perfected, established, strengthened, and settled you. To Him be the glory and the dominion forever and ever. Amen."

"Amen!" the crowd shouted, and as they broke into spontaneous worship and singing, Gabriel concluded: "Then I saw an angel coming down from heaven, having the key to the bottomless pit and a great chain in his hand."

The crowd began to cheer.

"He laid hold of the dragon, that serpent of old, who is the Devil and Satan, and bound him for a thousand years."

Hands raised, they were screaming now.

"And he cast him into the bottomless pit, and shut him up, and set a seal on him, so that he should deceive the nations no more till the thousand years were finished."

Rayford sensed apprehension on the part of the people, because anyone who was not up to speed on what was next had begun to figure it out. And when the mighty warrior archangel Michael suddenly reappeared with a gargantuan lion—easily three times larger than any natural king of beasts—the crowd let out a collective gasp and shriek and embraced each other in fear.

But Gabriel quieted them with this assurance: "You are of God, little children. Fear not, for He who is in you is greater than he who is in the world."

The roar of the prodigious carnivore hurt Rayford's ears and echoed off the surrounding buildings. The lion swiped at Michael and snarled, stamping and turning on its ridiculously muscled haunches. But he held it firm. As the lion set itself for another attempt to break free and devour its captor, Michael tightened his grip and twisted the tree-trunk neck further.

Suddenly the lion transformed itself into a titanic, hissing serpent, coiling itself around the angel's arms and legs and squeezing, its tongue darting between shows of its elongated fangs. Michael quickly wrestled it to the ground and tightly clamped its mouth shut. Whereupon the creature transformed itself yet again.

Now it grew and bulged and covered itself with slimy scales, sprouted four thick legs with horny toes, a lashing tail, a long neck, broad head and face, pointed ears, horns, and a fire-breathing mouth full of canines. This was the greatest test for Michael, who seemed to produce from thin air a heavy linked chain with which he was able to hog-tie the monster.

It rolled onto its back, snorting flames, hissing and drooling, struggling against the restraints. Its tail swept again and again at the angel, its great head shaking back and forth. Michael finally succeeded in lassoing the neck with the remains of the chain and with a powerful yank pulled the head toward the torso, rendering the dragon virtually immobile.

It lay there, snorting and writhing, and anyone watching knew what it would do if it could somehow free itself. Finally it appeared to relax, but that only preceded its final incarnation. The dragon gave way to what appeared to be one more angel, brighter than the archangels and the three angels of mercy, including Christopher, the angel with the everlasting gospel. Yet its light paled to insignificance next to that of Christ, whose glory lit the whole world.

Now the being stood docile, the chain having slid into a tall coil on the ground. It looked menacingly at Michael, who did not retreat. Gabriel spoke with a loud voice, "Lucifer, dragon, serpent, devil, Satan, you will now face the One you have opposed from time immemorial."

"Oh no!" the being rasped. "The last time you contended with me, Michael, it was over the body of Moses, and you dared not even bring against me a reviling accusation, but said, 'The Lord rebuke you!' I do not answer to you!"

"No," Jesus said quietly, though Rayford heard Him distinctly. And with the authority of the ages He said, "But you *do* answer to Me. Kneel at My feet."

"I will do no such thing!"

"Kneel."

And he did, shoulders hunched in rebellion and anger.

"I have fought against you from shortly after your creation," Jesus said.

"My *creation*! I was no more created than You! And who are You to have *anything* against *me*?!"

"You shall be silent."

The angel of light appeared to Rayford to try to stand, but he could not. He also appeared to try to speak, straining, shaking his head.

Jesus continued: "For all your lies about having evolved, you are a created being."

The creature violently shook its head.

"Only God has the power to create, and you were Our creation. You were in Eden, the garden of God, before it was a paradise for Adam and Eve. You were there as an exalted servant when Eden was a beautiful rock garden.

"You were the seal of perfection, full of wisdom and perfect in beauty. Every precious stone was your covering: the sardius, topaz, and diamond, beryl, onyx, and jasper, sapphire, turquoise, and emerald with gold. The workmanship of your timbrels and pipes was prepared for you on the day you were created.

"You were the anointed cherub who covers; God established you; you were on His holy mountain; you walked back and forth in the midst of fiery stones. You were perfect in your ways from the day you were created, till iniquity was found in you.

"But you became filled with violence within, and you sinned; therefore We cast you as a profane thing out of the mountain of God; and We destroyed you, O covering cherub, from the midst of the fiery stones. Your heart was lifted up because of your beauty; you corrupted your wisdom for the sake of your splendor; We cast you to the ground, laid you before kings, that they might gaze at you.

"You defiled your sanctuaries by the multitude of your iniquities, by the iniquity of your trading; therefore God brought fire from your midst; it devoured you, and He turned you to ashes upon the earth in the sight of all who saw you.

"All who knew you among the peoples are astonished at you; you have become a horror, and shall be no more forever."

The kneeling angel of fading light seemed to writhe in pain, eager to retaliate.

Jesus said, "You have opposed My Father and Me from before the creation of man. A third of the angels in heaven and most of the population of the earth followed your model of rebellion and pride. This will earn for them and for you separation from Almighty God in the everlasting fire prepared for you and your angels.

"You deceived Eve into sinning. During the next millennia you attempted to pollute the bloodline of Adam, putting it into Cain's heart to murder Abel and thus eliminating Adam's first two sons. You encouraged the cohabitation of fallen angels with human women to produce Nephilim, fallen ones. Because of you, within sixteen hundred years, only eight humans were found faithful and worthy of preserving from the Flood.

"It was you who attempted to establish a universal, idolatrous religion in Babel, then the largest city in the world, to keep mankind from worshiping the one true God.

"It was you who tried to destroy the Hebrew race, filling Pharaoh's mind with the idea to kill the male babies at the time of Moses' birth.

"I lay at your feet all the suffering of mankind. The earth was created as a utopia, and yet you brought into it sin, which resulted in poverty, disease, more than fifteen thousand wars, and the senseless killing of millions. You and your sin of pride spawned the rebellion of mankind against God, hatred, murder, and the damning of billions of souls from the time of Adam.

"You tried to attack Me upon My earthly birth by filling Herod's mind with the idea of killing all the male babies in Bethlehem. You tempted Me in the wilderness and tried to destroy My church through persecution and false teaching. You brought the storm to the Sea of Galilee while I slept. It was you who entered Judas Iscariot, you who filled the heart of Ananias with deceit. It was you, as the god of this evil world, who blinded the minds of those who do not believe.

"You were at work in the hearts of those who refused to obey God. It was you who prevented My servants from ministering, you who sowed discord in the churches, you who attacked the weak, the suffering, the lonely."

By now Satan had toppled onto his side, gasping and snorting, struggling to get back to his feet, to fight back, to speak.

"It is contrary to the will of God not only that humans sin, but also for them to reject Me. It is the will of My Father who is in heaven that not one of these little ones should perish. He is not slack concerning His promise, but is longsuffering, not willing that any should perish but that all should come to repentance.

"During the last seven years," Jesus said, "you have deceived millions with false teachers, false messiahs, a false prophet, and an antichrist. You gave him his power, his throne, and great authority. And all the world marveled and followed him.

"They worshiped you who gave authority to the Beast; and they worshiped the Beast, saying, 'Who is like the Beast? Who is able to make war with him?' And you gave him a mouth speaking great things and blasphemies, and he was given authority to continue for forty-two months.

"He opened his mouth in blasphemy against God, to blaspheme His name,

His tabernacle, and those who dwell in heaven. You granted to him to make war with the saints and to overcome them. And you gave him authority over every tribe, tongue, and nation.

"All who dwelt on the earth worshiped him, whose names have not been written in the Book of Life of the Lamb slain from the foundation of the world. He performed great signs, so that he even made fire come down from heaven on the earth in the sight of men.

"And you deceived those who dwell on the earth by those signs.

"You have a hatred for Me, a hatred for My people. You made war with those who kept the commandments of God. When anyone heard the word of the kingdom and did not understand it, you came and snatched away what was sown in his heart.

"You were the reason My servant had to remind My people that they did not wrestle against flesh and blood, but against principalities, against powers, against the rulers of the darkness of that age, against spiritual hosts of wickedness in the heavenly places. You were why they had to be instructed to take up the whole armor of God, that they would be able to withstand in the evil day, and having done all, to stand.

"I pledged ages ago that I would build My church, and that the gates of Hades would not prevail against it. Your time has come. I have sent out My angels and they have gathered out of My kingdom all things that offend, and those who practice lawlessness, and I will cast them into the furnace of fire. There will be wailing and gnashing of teeth.

"Then the righteous will shine forth as the sun in the kingdom of their Father."

Michael grabbed Satan and pulled him back up to his knees, where he continued to thrash as if he were about to burst.

"It is you who have brought this on yourself," Jesus said. "For you have said in your heart: 'I will ascend into heaven, I will exalt my throne above the stars of God; I will also sit on the mount of the congregation on the farthest sides of the north; I will ascend above the heights of the clouds, I will be like the Most High.'

"Yet you shall be brought down to Sheol, to the lowest depths of the pit. Those who see you will gaze at you, and consider you, saying: 'Is this the man who made the earth tremble, who shook kingdoms, who made the world as a wilderness and destroyed its cities, who did not open the house of his prisoners?'"

\+ \+ \+

Like everyone else, Abdullah was fascinated by this trial and judgment of Satan himself. In all his study of Scripture and prophecy, he never expected to witness it firsthand. He wished he could ask questions, like why the Antichrist and False Prophet were cast forever into the lake of fire, while Satan himself was set to be bound for a thousand years, only to be released again for a time at the end of the Millennium.

But Abdullah had found that most of his questions were eventually answered without anyone's asking them.

He couldn't get over the beauty of Jerusalem, given what had gone on in the previous several days. It looked pristine, scrubbed clean, and even the foliage seemed in full bloom and fragrant. What an impact on the world the presence of Jesus made!

Most of the remnant was made up of people from greater Jerusalem, far beyond the former walls of the Old City. The enemy had been driven out and killed, and so all the dwelling places in the Holy City were available again. People would be going back to their homes. Abdullah didn't know what that meant for him and other Gentile members of the Tribulation Force. They could always go back to Petra, of course. There was plenty of room there.

But for himself, he wanted to be where Jesus was, and he knew that prophecy said He would rule from the throne of David. That meant that when all this public stuff was over, people would still have access to Him, but of course a million-plus would not fit inside the temple. Maybe He would have supernatural audiences with them all at the same time once again. Otherwise, that would be His headquarters for ruling the nations of the world "with an iron rod."

Would Abdullah live with his wife? He couldn't wait to reunite with her, but he did not know all the ramifications of life now. She would exist in her glorified body, while he would bring to the millennial kingdom his mortal frame. There was so much to learn, so much to know.

+ + +

Chang and Naomi, though they stood watching hand in hand, had barely spoken for hours. The day, in fact the whole time since the Glorious Appearing, had flown by. When Jesus had held Chang, and then cupped his face in His hands and spoken to him in Chinese, Chang had realized that everything he had been through was worth it. He would have given anything for that encounter with his Savior.

Jesus had told him that He was there when Chang was born, when he was raised in a godless home and an aberrant religion. He was there when Chang was sent many miles away to school because of his intellect, and it was He Chang prayed to for strength and comfort and companionship, even though at that time he had never heard of Jesus.

"I was there, Chang," Jesus had told him, "when you came to believe deep in your heart that no god existed, certainly not One you associated with capitalists of the West. I was there when you rebelled against your parents and tried to teach them a lesson for sending you away. I was there when you abused your body and your mind with substances not intended for your nourishment.

"I was there when your mind was deceived by philosophy and vain deceit. I was there when you were discovered by the government of this world and pressed into service for the evil one.

"I rejoiced with the angels when you learned of Me and turned to Me and were used for My glory in the lair of Antichrist.

"And I was there when the mark of the beast was forced upon you and you feared you had lost your salvation. I have loved you from eternity past with an everlasting love, and I have looked forward to this day."

Chang was still glowing from that experience, even though he had finally figured out that everyone there had enjoyed their own personal encounter with Jesus. That it was not unique to him made it no less special. The message his Savior imparted was definitely for him alone, and the fearful, ugly things that had happened over the last few hours did nothing to temper the thrill of it.

+ + +

It was time, Rayford realized. Jesus had finished His charges, and nothing was left but to carry out the sentence. Satan rocked on his knees, forcing gasping breaths through clenched teeth.

Gabriel leaned over the angel of light and shouted, "Acknowledge Jesus as Lord!"

Satan had been struck dumb, and as much as it appeared he was trying to speak, no words came out. But it was clear he had no interest in acceding to the order. He vigorously shook his head and clenched his fists before Jesus.

Jesus looked briefly to His left, and Rayford guessed thirty yards in that direction, farther from the angels and from the crowd, a great gaping hole appeared in the ground. Black smoke belched from deep within and nearly blotted out the sky. Again, no shadows were produced, because the light of day no longer came from the sun, but rather from the Lord Himself.

He nodded to Michael, who scooped up the long, heavy chain and draped it over his sinewy forearm. As he approached the condemned, Satan sprang to his feet and began to fight. Again he morphed, first into the dragon, then the snake, and finally the lion. The conflict covered the distance between the remnant and Jesus and the other angels. Every time Michael and Satan tumbled near the crowd, people backed into each other.

Rayford had no misgivings about the outcome of the tussle. Jesus seemed to look on with abject sadness and no concern. Gabriel, who had always served as a herald and not a warrior, looked every bit as capable as Michael and could have stepped in at any time. The three angels of mercy, including the preacher of the everlasting gospel, were close by as well.

Finally, in his form as the lion, Satan was strangely without a roar. Jesus had silenced him, and the curse carried over regardless of his disguise. Michael finally worked the chain about him and drew it tight, forcing the animal into a bound mass.

As he lifted the captive toward the smoking abyss, Satan altered himself yet again, back to the angel of light. With that he slipped out of the chain and made one last feeble attempt to escape. Michael swung the chain and let it slide through his hands until the extended portion was at least twenty feet long. This he flung at the devil, catching him at the midsection and causing the chain to wrap itself around him.

Michael rushed him, tackled him to the ground, completed the chain-wrapping operation, and jumped to his feet, carrying the bound devil. Just before he reached the smoldering, smoke-belching chasm, Michael left his feet and flew—Satan under his arm—about ten feet into the air and then headfirst down into the abyss.

This Jesus did not watch, though the other angelic beings did. The crowd roared and cheered and applauded, but they quieted quickly when Jesus stood and gestured with a hand.

"And now," He said, "to My Father God, the King eternal, immortal, invisible, to Him who alone is wise, be honor and glory forever. Beloved, sin reigned in death, but even so grace reigns through righteousness to eternal life. Even the demons recognized Me as the Holy One of God. I stand before you this day as the King of Israel, He who comes in the name of the Lord."

He gazed above, and from beyond the clouds came a chorus from those Rayford could only assume were gathered around the throne of God. They sang the song of Moses, the servant of God, and the song of the Lamb, saying: "Great and marvelous are Your works, Lord God Almighty! Just and true are Your ways, O King of the saints! And He will reign over the house of Jacob forever, and of His kingdom there will be no end."

Still the smoke poured from the bottomless pit, and Rayford wondered if others, like he, had begun to worry about Michael. But presently he reemerged with a key in his hand. Satan and the chain were no longer to be seen.

Michael rejoined the others behind Jesus, who turned and mounted His horse. He slowly led the white stallion away from the open square and through the crowd toward the Temple Mount, where He would take His rightful place on the throne of King David.

And finally, Rayford felt a twinge of hunger and a new wave of fatigue. Without instruction or a word about it, the remnant seemed to be slowly scattering to return to their homes. Rayford would have to reconnect with his friends and see who might have room for him.

18

RAYFORD COULD NOT THINK of a word to describe how he felt, other than *euphoric.* He knew there would be times when Jesus would not be visible, like now. It only made sense. But he had feared he would have such a longing for Him that he might be depressed, out of sorts, when Jesus was otherwise occupied. Rayford was thrilled to realize this was not the case.

His heart was still with Jesus, of course. He thought about Him constantly. And he wanted to see Him, sure. But because Rayford was so preoccupied with Him, eager to love and serve Him forever, he found himself free from his normal temptations. He had to wonder if this was temporary. Was he free from lust, from pride, from greed only because this was like being in church, in the presence of your pastor? Or did the binding of Satan and the death of his demons have something to do with it? Rather than being tempted by the world, the flesh, and the devil, he had to worry about only two of the three. And the world was new and ruled by Jesus.

Would the novelty of having Jesus physically present eventually wear off? *I mean, a thousand years, and then eternity . . .*

The way Jesus had talked to him, connected with him, made Rayford feel as if He were still right there, even though he couldn't see Him. When he prayed, it was as if Jesus conversed with him immediately. Rayford had so many questions, so many things he would have to ask Chaim.

First, of course, was whether Chaim had any idea where Rayford might find lodging. He was amused to discover, upon reuniting with the rest of the Tribulation Force personnel who had been at Petra, that this had already been thoroughly thought through, discussed, and even decided.

Rayford and Mac and Abdullah had stayed in the public square, searching the crowd for anyone they recognized. "We had better separate," Abdullah suggested. "If any of us finds someone, he can call the others and arrange a meeting place."

Abdullah headed west, Mac east. Rayford stayed in the center, searching faces for the familiar. What a sight! Everywhere he looked, people looked like friends, though they were mostly strangers. He recognized some from having seen them in Petra, but when he asked if they had seen his friends and acquaintances, none had. And yet all wanted to talk. Mostly about Jesus. But about the earthquake too, and the splitting of the Mount of Olives. The slaying of the enemy. The sentencing of Carpathia, Fortunato, and Satan.

Others mentioned the weather—hot, clear, refreshing, as if they were breathing new air. A woman pointed out the trees and bushes and how suddenly full and healthy they looked. "They did not look this way twenty-four hours ago," she said.

Something hit Rayford. He asked where she was from. "Russia," she said.

"And what language are you speaking?"

"Russian, of course. I know only a little English. And you?"

"English. It's all I know."

Rayford kept moving, looking, asking. Here and there groups were praying, singing, some just lifting their hands toward heaven and smiling. Finally he got a call from Mac.

"Seems strange that these contraptions are still workin', doesn't it?" Mac said. "You'd think maybe we could just talk to each other without machines now."

Rayford laughed. "Why?"

"Why not? Anyhoo, you know Christ Church, a tick southeast of David's Tower?"

"Sure."

"That's where we all are."

"Smitty too?"

"Everybody."

The names of all the landmarks had been changed when Carpathia came to power, but the believers knew what was what. Outside Christ Church, at the southeast corner of the building, Rayford found his circle of friends from Petra. All but Otto.

Besides Abdullah and Mac, Chaim was there with Chang and Naomi and her father, Eleazar. Hannah and Leah were there. When Rayford saw Razor chatting with the Woos, he knew Sebastian and Priscilla and Beth Ann had to be close by, and that meant Kenny couldn't be far off. And here he came.

The boy leaped into Rayford's arms. "Grandpa! I saw Jesus! And He talked to me!"

"Isn't that the best?"

"Yeah! Gonna see Mommy and Daddy too."

Rayford looked at Priss. She mouthed, "Soon."

"Yeah, pretty soon," Rayford said.

As he held Kenny, Rayford was brought up to speed on what had been decided. "Otto has somehow secured an abandoned hotel for his people," Chaim said.

"Already?"

"Oh, Rayford, people are eager to accommodate each other. And as you can imagine, a little over a million people will rattle around in this country. Nearly three quarters of a million used to live in greater Jerusalem alone. There are thousands of deserted residences, but most people seem to be returning to their own homes and inviting in those from other places. Eleazar and Naomi have agreed to take the single women and the married couples, and I have plenty of room for the single men."

"Kenny," Rayford said, "you want to stay with Grandpa at Uncle Chaim's? Or with Beth Ann and Aunt Priscilla?"

"Where's Mommy gonna be?"

"Probably with us," Priss said, and Kenny wriggled down.

"Okay, Grandpa?"

"Okay, Kenny. I'll see you a lot."

"I'll get the car," Abdullah said, and he jogged off.

With Rayford crammed all the way in the back, facing the back window with his knees pulled to his chest, they somehow managed to fit Chaim, Chang, Lionel, Mac, and Razor into the Hummer, with Abdullah behind the wheel.

On the way to Chaim's house, Chang spent the whole time on the phone with Naomi. Razor teased him that he had just been with her for days, but Rayford noticed that they weren't talking about each other anyway. Like everyone else in the car, they were talking about Jesus.

"I have so many questions, Chaim," Rayford called out from the back.

"Probably not as many as I do," Chaim said, "but for those who are interested, we will open the Scriptures and try to make sense of all this."

"Are you all seeing what I'm seeing?" Rayford said, studying the landscape and the people and the animals as Abdullah steered through the happy crowds. All the animals were docile. Sheep, dogs, wolves, critters of all types roamed everywhere. Shops had already reopened and butchers were working in the open air. Trucks delivered fresh fruits and vegetables from nearby groves. "Who'd have had time to pick these, and where are butchers getting their meat?"

"That butcher is a friend of mine," Chaim said. "Let me find out."

Abdullah pulled over and everyone got out, Razor heading for a produce stand. Rayford followed Chaim.

"Ezer!" Chaim shouted, embracing the tall, thin man who wielded a cleaver and wore a blood-spattered apron. "I did not know you were a believer!"

"I wasn't," Ezer said. "I resisted and resisted, blind, so blind. But during the fighting to hold Jerusalem I heard a rabbi in the Old City talk of Messiah. And I was spared."

"Back to butchering already! How does this happen?"

"I was driven underground by the GC because I refused to take the mark. I lost this shop and my home. After what we just witnessed in the Old City, I wanted to see what was left. My home is intact. And my shop stood empty. You will not believe it, Chaim, but fattened animals, ready for slaughter and butchering, milled about the place as if volunteering! Cows, sheep! Imagine! I found my tools and got to work immediately. What do you need?"

"A lot of beef and lamb. I have six houseguests, all hungry grown men."

"Take all you need. It's on me."

"Oh no, I couldn't!"

"You don't have money anyway, do you? And I wouldn't want Nicks."

"No, but start a bill for me, and when we discover what shape the economy takes, I will settle up."

"You opposed Carpathia, Chaim. That is all the pay I need."

"No, I insist. How will you live?"

"I told you! The goods cost me nothing, and look!" He pointed behind the shop and Chaim and Rayford stepped to where they could see. From miles around, the sheep and the cows kept coming. Men were already building pens. "My new employees," Ezer said. "I pay them in meat. I have more than I need, and apparently God is providing. Please, do me the honor of taking all you need. They are the freshest, fattest, finest cuts I have ever produced."

Chaim finally relented, and Ezer was resolute in enlisting all the houseguests to take several pounds each. "To hold in your lap on the trip home. Please, please. You are doing me a favor. I have too much and nowhere to store it."

As they returned to the car, Rayford heard Ezer shouting to the crowds in the streets, "Free meat from the hand of God! Come, please, and take all you need!"

Razor returned from the produce stand, laden with sacks of fruit and vegetables. "The woman would take nothing for these!" he said. "She claims they are falling off the trees, not just in the orchards but right here in the city."

"Hold on," Chang said into the phone, then covered it as Abdullah pulled away and headed for Chaim's. "Naomi says it is a widespread miracle. They too have stopped to stock up on fresh meat and produce. She said they gathered oranges and grapefruit from beneath trees and saw the branches ripen again before their eyes."

That evening—Rayford could tell it was evening only by his watch; the brightness of the day never changed—the men settled into Chaim's spacious home, room assignments seeming to take care of themselves. It turned out that

Razor and Abdullah considered themselves cooks and proved it by grilling the meat and preparing heaping bowls of sliced fruit and steaming vegetables.

Rayford had always been impressed with how the Trib Force and Co-op believers worked together, but he had never seen anything like this. In fact, he wondered if a thousand years with zero strife or conflict would get boring. Despite the generally good attitudes of the people under his charge over the last seven years, part of the challenge of his job had been refereeing battles of ego and turf. Now he just watched as people got along and worked together. Admittedly, it was the first day in their new home. They had just witnessed miraculous fulfillments of prophecy and had been in the physical presence of Jesus. And they had been provided the most comfortable lodging they'd had in years, not to mention they were about to eat free food—and a feast at that.

Mac found chairs and tables and enlisted Chang and Lionel in the setup process, while Chaim asked Rayford to help him assess the home he had not seen for three and a half years. All the old man could do was shake his head at the memories. There was no evidence of damage to the place by the GC. He found no residue from three separate earthquakes, including the most recent global upheaval and the raising of the entire city some three hundred feet at the cleaving of the Mount of Olives.

As Rayford followed him about the place, Chaim said, "I am tired of my own disbelief. I must simply once and for all accept that God is the author of all this. He can do anything, and He has done everything. I had heard that the GC took over this house as a command center almost three years ago. Can you imagine, Captain Steele, what it should look like after dozens of different men have lived and worked in it? I expected the stench of tobacco, garbage, a mess. Yet look."

Rayford *was* looking. It was as if a cleaning crew had swept through the entire place. Floors, walls, ceilings were clean. Furniture was in place. Rayford wouldn't have been more surprised if there had been slipcovers draped on each piece. But there didn't need to be. He couldn't find a speck of dust anywhere.

"Well, the refrigerator and freezer and pantry are empty," Chaim said. "And yet look what the Lord provided on our way here."

"Guess He thought you could stock the shelves yourself."

"I do not know. I could get used to all this."

When it was time to sit and eat, Chaim stood at the head of the table. "Let us pray," he said.

And Rayford had the strangest experience. As he prayed along with Chaim, thanking God for the privilege of witnessing what they had seen that day, for the food He had provided, and for the move-in-ready home He had preserved, it was as if Jesus answered audibly and immediately and personally.

"You're welcome, Rayford," He said. "It is My delight to shower you with love in tangible ways." And before Rayford could pray for Kenny, the Lord said, "I know of your concern. He will be reunited with his parents, as will you, very soon."

It was as if Jesus were sitting right next to Rayford, His arm around him, speaking directly to him. It broke Rayford anew and he couldn't stanch the tears. He folded his hands on the plate before him and rested his face on them, worshiping God.

And Jesus said, "I will reign over the house of Jacob forever, and of My kingdom there will be no end. As the Father knows Me, even so I know the Father; and I laid down My life for the sheep. I am the Lamb who will lead you to living fountains of waters, and God will wipe away every tear from your eyes."

Rayford rested there, listening and worshiping, knowing that the tears Jesus mentioned were those of sadness, and his were anything but. He couldn't imagine ever being sad again.

He heard the rest of the men murmuring their praise and knew they had had the same experience he had. While Rayford could smell the delicious food in heaping serving bowls inches from his plate, his hunger could wait. He never wanted this moment of worship to end.

After several minutes, Chaim picked up his prayer again. "And now, O Lord, our Redeemer and Friend, we thank You for this bounty. I confess, Father, that as grateful as I was for the manna, and as satisfying as it was . . ." He didn't have to finish. Rayford sat up and covered his mouth, but he couldn't stifle the laugh. And in his soul he believed with all his heart that he heard Jesus chuckle too. Yes, manna was one thing. This was something else entirely.

Chaim sat down and the men opened their eyes, looking at each other. "Jesus spoke to me again in Chinese," Chang said.

"Spanish," Razor said.

"Hebrew," Chaim said.

"English," Rayford said.

"Sout' side o' Chicago," Lionel said, and they laughed.

"He worked a little west Texan in there too, I believe," Mac said. "That's the language of heaven, ya know."

Rayford cleared his throat. Still no one had reached for the food. "Ah, was it just me, or did any of you hear Jesus laugh at Chaim's manna crack?"

They all smiled and nodded. Chaim said, "No question the Lord has a sense of humor. Gentlemen, can you believe the food is still steaming as if we hadn't left it out here for several minutes?"

"The fruit looks crisp and fresh too," Razor said. "And no flies."

And so they ate. Rayford assumed that for the others it was as it was for him—the tastiest meal he had ever enjoyed. "The real miracle," he said later, "will be eating like this all the time without gaining weight."

During cleanup, Rayford and Chaim spoke with Eleazar by phone. It was great for Rayford to hear that they had enjoyed the same type of time with the Lord and a wonderful meal as the men had. Chaim reminded Eleazar of what they planned to cover that evening from the Scriptures, and they compared notes on difficult passages. "If we are left with confusing questions," Eleazar boomed, "we shall simply ask Jesus, next time we see Him."

Later that evening, the men gathered in Chaim's great room, and he opened his Bible and spread his notes and a couple of commentaries before him. "Books by men seem superfluous now," he said. "Whenever we pray I feel as if Messiah is here with me, answering questions even before I ask. Let us begin with a time of worship and prayer."

As one the men slipped from their chairs and knelt on the floor, each praying in his native tongue.

+ + +

Mac was about to tell the Lord that there were people—particularly from the previous seven years—that he was eager to see. Each had meant something special to him, had made a significant impact on his life. But before he could articulate it, Jesus spoke to him by name. "I know, Cleburn. And you shall see them soon. I long for that reunion as much as you do and will rejoice with you when you see them."

+ + +

As Rayford received answers to prayers he had not yet even uttered, he prostrated himself on the floor and could see the others doing likewise. He decided that what Jesus was trying to tell him was the same as he had heard from Bruce Barnes years before, and the same as he had heard from Tsion and Chaim: Prayer was as much, or more, about listening as it was about talking. Rayford had never accomplished that balance. It seemed he was always beseeching, asking, requesting. Yes, he thanked God for things and often worshiped Him in prayer, but he was starting to get the picture now. It was time to simply be quiet and listen. And even if God said nothing, Rayford was to rest in the peace of His presence.

Rayford lay there on his stomach and basked in the warmth of God's love. And Jesus said, "God is your refuge and strength, a very present help in trouble. Therefore do not fear, even though the earth be removed, and though the mountains be carried into the midst of the sea; though its waters roar and be troubled, though the mountains shake with its swelling.

"There is a river whose streams shall make glad the city of God, the holy place of the tabernacle of the Most High. God is in the midst of her, she shall not be moved; God shall help her, just at the break of dawn.

"The nations raged, the kingdoms were moved; He uttered His voice, the earth melted. The Lord of hosts is with you; the God of Jacob is your refuge.

"Come, behold the works of the Lord, who has made desolations in the earth. He made wars cease to the end of the earth; He broke the bow and cut the spear in two; He burned the chariot in the fire.

"Be still, and know that I am God; I will be exalted among the nations, I will be exalted in the earth!

"The Lord of hosts is with you; the God of Jacob is your refuge."

Suddenly Chaim rose back to his knees and said, "Oh, clap your hands, all you peoples! Shout to God with the voice of triumph! For the Lord Most High is awesome; He is a great King over all the earth. He has subdued the peoples under us, and the nations under our feet. . . . God reigns over the nations; God sits on His holy throne."

Rayford lay communing with God, only vaguely aware of the others. Finally, when it felt as if he actually needed a break from the loving hand of Jesus, he moved back to his chair. Strange how everyone seemed to have the same experiences at the same time and for the same duration.

"Before you start, Chaim, I have a question, maybe more of a confession. This newly close presence of God, through Jesus, is so fresh, so special, that at times I can't seem to get enough of Him. But at other times, like just now, it was almost as if I was so filled to overflowing that if I stayed there, I could take no more."

Others nodded, which Rayford found comforting. Chaim said, "That reminds me of a story I once read of a great evangelist from the nineteenth century, Dwight L. Moody. He wrote of having an experience with the Lord where His presence and fullness were so overwhelming that Moody had to ask God to 'stay His hand.'"

"Exactly," Rayford said.

"I have felt that too," Chaim said. "Perhaps in the presence of Jesus we will build the spiritual muscle necessary to endure such blessings."

Chaim seemed to look at each man individually, as if to ask if there was anything else before he got started. Then he explained that he and the elders had spent the last month vigorously searching the Scriptures for clues to what to expect after the Glorious Appearing.

"Like cramming for a test," Razor suggested.

"I am not familiar with that term," Chaim said, "but it seems self-explanatory and I would have to agree. Not that we are going to be tested. In fact, there was much discussion among the elders at first over how necessary this was. Some held that Jesus would be our teacher and would explain everything along the way.

"Well, maybe He expects us to know this material, hmm? Today we witnessed His victory ascent to Mount Olivet, also known as the Mount of Olives. We saw it split in two. He conquered the invading armies, slaying them with the Word of God. We were with Him for His triumphal entry into Jerusalem, and we saw Him capture and judge demons, the False Prophet, Antichrist, and even Satan himself. And yet never once did He stop and say, 'Beloved, you'll find this on page so-and-so of your text, and it *will* be on the final.'

"These things happened as they were prophesied, and no explanation is forthcoming. That is much the same way Jesus taught and preached the first time He was on earth. Only occasionally did He follow a parable with an explanation. And when He did, it was only enough for those 'who have ears to hear.'

"I suppose there were many in the crowd today who had little idea what was going on. They probably could have figured out who was who and what was what, and in the end they knew that Jesus had won again, conquering more foes. But they are probably wondering where He has gone, what He is doing. Well, gentlemen, the answers are in the Book, and if you are interested, we shall plumb the riches herein and see what we can learn."

Each enthusiastically expressed his interest, and Chaim began.

"I fear that many—and I confess this was true of me and most of the elders—believed that the Glorious Appearing ushered in the millennial kingdom, which, as you know, means the thousand-year reign of Christ on earth. Anyone here in that camp?"

Several nodded, Rayford included. He glanced at Abdullah, who was smiling. It was not the smile of the condescendingly superior, but of one who had apparently done his homework and knew what was coming. Rayford was most impressed that, despite this, Abdullah did not call out, "Not me! I know!"

Rayford raised his hand. "Chaim, I'll bet Smitty knows what you're talking about. He's become quite the student."

"Is that true, Mr. Smith?" Chaim said.

"I am not well versed in it," Abdullah said, "but my studies, mostly with Dr. Ben-Judah, reveal that there is actually a gap between the Glorious Appearing and the Millennium, much as there was between the Rapture and the Tribulation."

"There was?" Razor said.

"Oh yes," Abdullah said. "You'll recall that the seven years did not begin with the disappearances of the believers, but rather with the signing of the covenant between Antichrist and Israel. That came a couple of weeks later, but it could have come a couple of years later, and the signing, not the Rapture, would have been the start of the Tribulation."

"Excellent!" Chaim said. "That is indeed where I was going and what we will discuss this evening. From the Glorious Appearing to the actual beginning of the millennial kingdom, there is a seventy-five-day interval. If it took God just six days to create the heavens and the earth and man himself, imagine how much work Jesus must have if He has been allotted seventy-five days in which to do it."

"Where do you get that out of the Bible?" Rayford said. "I mean, I'm no great student or anything, but I've tried to read a lot."

"Good question. The answer is found partly in Daniel 12:11-12. Listen to the first of those verses: 'And from the time that the daily sacrifice is taken away, and the abomination of desolation is set up, there shall be one thousand two hundred and ninety days.' Rayford, you remember when Antichrist defiled the temple?"

"*Do* I."

"That was the abomination of desolation. And that was one thousand two hundred and *sixty* days before the Glorious Appearing. So we are already talking about thirty more days. And the next verse says, 'Blessed is he who waits, and comes to the one thousand three hundred and thirty-five days.' That's another forty-five days, giving us a total of seventy-five more days."

"What does the first thirty days refer to?" Rayford said.

"Well, the verse is talking about the temple sacrifice and the abomination, so I think it is fair to assume the first interval relates to the temple. I cannot imagine Jesus wanting to take the throne of David in a temple that has been defiled by Antichrist—at least not before He cleanses it. We know from Ezekiel 40–48 that the Lord will establish a temple during the Millennium, so I conclude that the first thirty days of the interval will be devoted to setting up the temple and preparing it for use.

"The other forty-five days are more open to speculation, but notice that verse 12 says that those who make it through that time will be blessed. If that is a personal, individual blessing, it indicates that the person is qualified to enter into the millennial kingdom. Matthew 25:34 says, 'Then the King will say to those on His right hand, "Come, you *blessed* of My Father, inherit the kingdom prepared for you from the foundation of the world."'

"That makes it sound to me as if the seventy-five-day interval is a time for preparation for the kingdom. So much of the globe has been destroyed during the judgments of the Tribulation, I suppose it should not surprise us that the Lord will take some time to renovate His creation for the Millennium. The beautification of Jerusalem was done in an instant with the elevating of the city from the splitting of the Mount of Olives, but imagine the work that needs to be done around the world. The mountains have been leveled, filling much of the seas. Islands have vanished. Surely God wants to put the earth back into its Edenic state for the enjoyment of those who will share it with Jesus for the next thousand years."

19

LEAH ROSE HAD COME a long way from nursing supervisor at Arthur Young Memorial Hospital in Palatine, Illinois. How was she to know what would become of her when she first encountered Rayford Steele and the fledgling Tribulation Force nearly seven years before? She and Rayford had spotted each other's seal of the believer, visible only to others of like faith. Otherwise, she might not have given him the time of day.

To think that since then she had been all over the world with the Force in a variety of roles, mostly medical but not exclusively. She had made new friends, seen them become loved ones, and then seen them die. There had been times when she wouldn't have given two cents for her chances to make it to the Glorious Appearing. At least not until she was assigned duty at Petra, where in three and a half years, no one had died.

Privileged, that's what she called herself. Certainly nothing she had ever done had earned her the benefits she had enjoyed. It had not been an easy life. Hardly. No one who had lived through the Tribulation had it easy. That she had to live through it at all was her own fault—for having heard the message and ignored it for so long. She had not considered herself a rejecter. Leah had seen herself as an intellectual, a thinker, a ponderer.

Evangelists and evangelistic-minded friends had told her and told her that a nondecision was a "no" decision. She had argued. She wasn't saying no, she said; she was still thinking. Well, one of her well-meaning friends had said, don't think yourself into hell. Or into being left behind.

That had been a laugh. While Leah had seriously considered the claims of Christ on her life, that He had died for her sins—of which she acknowledged there were many—the idea of His showing up in the clouds someday, in an instant so quick you could blink and miss it, well . . . come on now.

And then she had been left behind. Leah took care of that issue immediately. Then, while she floundered spiritually, looking for more, looking for truth, looking for answers, she believed God sent Rayford and the Trib Force into her life.

They were all in the same boat, of course, latecomers to the kingdom. But among them were men of the Bible, lifelong students like Tsion Ben-Judah, from whom she believed she had learned more than she had in nursing school.

And now here she was in Jerusalem, in the home of an elder. With friends who had become dear and who had experienced with her, firsthand, the fulfillment of prophecy in the presence of Jesus Himself. Leah had seen it with her own eyes, talked to Him, and met with Him personally. When He embraced her and called her by name and told her how much He loved her, she could not speak. And yet He heard her heart. He had been with her, known her since the foundation of the world, He said. Was with her all her life, at the high and low points, the turning points, loving her, waiting for her, longing to meet her.

Leah was so full of Jesus she hardly knew if she could stand it. And while others cowered and hid their faces and grimaced at the awful reality of Satan and his lackeys getting theirs, she would not turn away. This, she knew, was justice, and she wanted to see it.

Leah had been a victim of Satan, and of course she had suffered under the rule of Nicolae Carpathia. To be made an international fugitive simply because she loved the one true God and His Son was an unspeakable, unforgivable offense. Antichrist, indwelt by Satan, had exalted himself over God, and Leah's lifelong sense of right and wrong—cultivated even before she became a believer—told her he would have to pay. And when the time came, gruesome and graphic as it was, to her it was fitting.

Leah had seen the physical ravages of sin, what war could do to the human body. When she tried to repair dying comrades she couldn't help but lay the blame at the feet of Antichrist and his False Prophet. She didn't avert her eyes from that carnage, and so she didn't when Satan's demons were put to death by the words of Jesus. And when Nicolae and Leon were sent to eternal torment. And especially when Satan himself was locked away for a thousand years.

Leah still didn't understand that one. It was something she could ask Eleazar when he led the group in Bible study that night. Word was that the elders were all teaching the same stuff, wherever they wound up and with whom. She considered it another privilege to have landed in the lovely Tiberius home.

Naomi's late mother's touches remained, even after all this time. The place had been taken over by the GC, just like any home of some worth. The result of that could have been disappointing, yet when the ten of them settled in, unloading their haul of fresh meat and produce in the generous kitchen, no one was more surprised than Eleazar at the state of the place. It looked as if someone had been hired to make it perfect for their stay.

They had found their quarters—just enough space for everyone—and had worked together watching the children, setting the tables, preparing the food. They had prayed and feasted, cleaned up, and prayed some more. Jesus had spoken to them in three different languages simultaneously. Leah then helped Priss Sebastian get the kids to bed, and now it was time to study.

She found the teaching on the next seventy-five days fascinating, having never heard of it before. What Leah appreciated most about Eleazar was his own bright, inquisitive mind and how he didn't pretend to know things he didn't. "Some things," he said in his jolly basso profundo, "are apparently unknowable, at least for now. Other truths are fascinating to ferret out of the Scriptures."

Leah asked her question about why Antichrist and the False Prophet were sentenced for eternity while Satan would be released at the end of the Millennium.

"The binding of Satan," Eleazar said, "restricts him from what he does best, of course. Revelation 20:3 indicates that God's goal in this binding is 'so that he should deceive the nations no more till the thousand years were finished.'"

"Yes," Leah said, "but it goes on to say, 'But after these things he must be released for a little while.' Why must he?"

"I once asked the same question of Dr. Ben-Judah, and I recently asked Dr. Rosenzweig," Eleazar said. "Neither was entirely sure, and neither am I, but they suggested some remarkable things I had been unaware of, and I'll bet you have been too."

"That wouldn't surprise me," Leah said.

"Here's the way I understand it, based on what I have been taught. Look at it this way: If God did not allow Satan one more chance to deceive the nations, all the people who are born and live during the millennial kingdom would be exempt from the decision to follow God or follow Satan. By releasing him one more time, all people are given equal standing before God."

"Interesting."

"But where it gets dicey is that those who reject Christ during the Millennium will all be young people, relatively. You will see when we dig into the Scriptures that anyone born during the Millennium who does not trust in Christ by the time he or she is a hundred years old will be accursed and die."

"I thought you said young people."

"Relatively. You see, those who do trust in Christ will live to the end of the Millennium."

"So someone born today, who becomes a believer, will live to be a thousand."

"Exactly."

"But the unbelievers, whenever they are born during this period, will die at a hundred?"

"Now you've got it."

"I don't know what I have," Leah said. "But it *is* interesting. If I'm figuring it right, what Satan will have to do at the end of the Millennium is try to organize all the people who were born at the nine-hundred-year mark or after—who haven't become believers—and get them to make one last-gasp effort to fight Jesus."

"There you go."

"Wow. And there's Scripture for this."

"There is. Let's read it together from Isaiah 65:17-25: 'For behold, I create new heavens and a new earth; and the former shall not be remembered or come to mind.

"'But be glad and rejoice forever in what I create; for behold, I create Jerusalem as a rejoicing, and her people a joy.

"'I will rejoice in Jerusalem, and joy in My people; the voice of weeping shall no longer be heard in her, nor the voice of crying.

"'No more shall an infant from there live but a few days, nor an old man who has not fulfilled his days; for the child shall die one hundred years old, but the sinner being one hundred years old shall be accursed.'

"Let me just interject an explanation here," Eleazar said. "This is saying that a person who dies at a hundred will be considered a child, because everyone else is living until the end of the Millennium. And that the 'child' who does die at a hundred will die because he is a sinner. Now, let's read on:

"'They shall build houses and inhabit them; they shall plant vineyards and eat their fruit.

"'They shall not build and another inhabit; they shall not plant and another eat; for as the days of a tree, so shall be the days of My people, and My elect shall long enjoy the work of their hands.'

"Again," Eleazar interrupted, "here's what I believe is being said here. We will not be serving landlords and despots. What we build we will enjoy ourselves. And what we plant and harvest will be for us, not a boss or an occupying government. Reading on:

"'They shall not labor in vain, nor bring forth children for trouble; for they shall be the descendants of the blessed of the Lord, and their offspring with them.

"'It shall come to pass that before they call, I will answer; and while they are still speaking, I will hear.'"

"I've already experienced that!" Leah said. "Haven't you all?"

"Yes!" several others said. "Jesus often answers a prayer before I have prayed it."

"Continuing," Eleazar said. "'The wolf and the lamb shall feed together'—we saw that in the street today—'the lion shall eat straw like the ox, and dust shall be the serpent's food. They shall not hurt nor destroy in all My holy mountain,' says the Lord. "

\+ + +

Rayford's brain was spinning. This was new to him, and he assumed it was to the people at Eleazar Tiberius's home as well. He couldn't wait to discuss it with some of them.

Chang raised his hand. "Chaim," he said, "where are all the people who died before the Rapture? The people from the Old Testament, the believers before Jesus came, and the ones who died during the Tribulation? Were they all in the army that appeared with Jesus in the clouds?"

Chaim sat back and smiled. "You have raised an interesting issue," he said. "Do we want to get into this tonight, or are you all ready to pull the shades and see if we can pretend it is dark enough to sleep?"

Rayford was tired, but he was no more interested in going to bed than any of the rest of the men were. And they said so.

"Fair enough," Chaim said. "It all begins with the Bible's teaching about resurrection day. I had always thought there was only one and that it coincided with the Rapture."

"Me too."

"Apparently, this is not the case, for the resurrection that took place at the Rapture was of what the Bible refers to as 'the dead in Christ' and did not include the saints from the Old Testament. When they died, Christ had not yet come to earth, so even though they were justified by faith, they technically cannot be referred to as 'the dead in Christ.' The resurrections in Scripture fall into two categories: the first resurrection, or the resurrection of life; and the second resurrection, the resurrection of judgment. John 5:28-29 quotes Jesus saying, 'Do not marvel at this; for the hour is coming in which all who are in the graves will hear His voice and come forth—those who have done good, to the resurrection of life, and those who have done evil, to the resurrection of condemnation.'

"The first resurrection includes the redeemed of all the ages, but the timing of the resurrection of these people varies, based on whether they are an Old Testament saint, a Christian who lived before or at the time of the Rapture, or a Christian martyred during the Tribulation. All of them will take part in the resurrection of life. The resurrection of judgment will include the unredeemed of all the ages, and this will happen at the end of the Millennium during what the Bible calls the Great White Throne Judgment. The unredeemed will be cast into the lake of fire."

"So let me get this straight," Rayford said. "Christians who died before the Rapture were resurrected at the time of the Rapture."

"Right."

"Old Testament saints will be resurrected when?"

"Soon. During this interval between the Glorious Appearing and the Millennium."

"And Tribulation martyrs?"

"At the same time. Old Testament saints and Tribulation martyrs will live and reign with Christ in the millennial kingdom."

"What about people who become believers during the Millennium?"

"They will be resurrected at the end of the Millennium."

"Even though they're alive."

"Correct."

"And the unredeemed won't be resurrected until after the Millennium either, for the Great White Throne Judgment."

Chaim smiled. "Now you know as much as I do."

"So," Rayford said, "my wife and son, who were raptured, were in that army of heaven behind Jesus."

"Yes."

"But my daughter and son-in-law, who were martyred during the Tribulation, will soon be resurrected."

"Precisely."

"So, we'll get to see our friends and loved ones soon."

+ + +

Enoch Dumas and his people from the tiny The Place congregation, formerly of inner-city Chicago, began discovering a few tiny pockets of fellow believers here and there. Employees of Antichrist or his government, even in America, had died at the words that came from the mouth of the Lord, but apparently it was God's intent that the Millennium start with a clean slate. *All* unbelievers would soon die.

The group reunited, and immediately everyone had the same idea. They should head back into Chicago to reminisce at their old meeting place, see what the former Tribulation Force safe house—where they had been guests before it was compromised—looked like now. Most of all, they needed to see what living accommodations were available in the city. Were the hotels and flophouses and fleabag apartments still around? And what about the high-rent district not so many blocks from where they had plied their trades before they became believers? If everyone else was going to die, what would keep them from living in the fancy hotels downtown?

Chicago had been considered radioactively contaminated for years, and even members of The Place had believed it, feeling forced to live inside, underground. When Chloe Steele Williams had discovered them and convinced them that the nuclear readings in Chicago were phonies planted by a Trib Force mole at the GC palace in New Babylon, they finally ventured out.

Once the GC discovered the scheme, the Trib Force and The Place members had to relocate—and fast. Since then GC operatives had determined Chicago was safe again, and the city had begun to rebuild. But if what was true in Palos Hills and the surrounding suburbs was also true in the city, Enoch and his people would virtually have the place to themselves.

Enoch expected to see the grisly effects of the worldwide slaughter of Christ's enemies, much as he had seen in his neighborhood when the GC car had hit the hydrant. Would there be bodies lining the streets, blood and flesh everywhere? Piles of bones? There were not. The global earthquake had apparently been a work of cleanup. Many skyscrapers had toppled, including the Strong Building, where the Trib Force safe house had been. But even these piles of rubble had been so shaken that they merely buried the ugliness of the bloodbath among Carpathia's employees.

Enoch had to talk with God about what to do. If only believers would be left in the United States, with scriptural prophecy seeming to ignore America, it was going to be one sparsely populated country. The various groups of believers might find each other, but what were they to do? Would there be enough of them to start rebuilding the country as, finally for real, a Christian nation? Was this why God was going to purge it of the unredeemed and had already leveled it, making the entire planet as flat as the state of Illinois? None of the believers had worked in public for years. Anyone responsible for any public service or utility would soon be dead. Maybe this was God's way of drawing all His people to be with Jesus in Israel.

As Enoch slowly drove through Chicago, Jesus spoke to him. "Fear not, Enoch, for you have rightly deduced that you and your flock are to be with Me."

"But, Lord, we—"

"I will transport you. You need not trouble yourselves."

"When? What will we do about clothes and—?"

"Now, Enoch, if God clothes the grass of the field, which today is, and tomorrow is thrown into the oven, will He not much more clothe you, O you of little faith?

"Therefore do not worry, for your heavenly Father knows that you need all these things. Do not worry about tomorrow."

Enoch would never forget the looks on the faces of his people when he reunited them and told them, "We're going to Israel. Don't ask how. God will make a way."

"When?"

"That you *can* ask. I believe we're going tomorrow."

+ + +

Leah was finally tired and longed for sleep, but she wanted to know about the coming judgments. Apparently there were several, and everyone else seemed curious too.

"I remain up to teaching if you remain up to learning," Eleazar said. "I do not yet know how we will sleep with so much light anyway."

"Today was clearly Judgment Day for Satan and his puppets," Leah said. "But there must be more than one Judgment Day."

"There is," Eleazar said. "Actually there are several times of judgment, each with a specific purpose. Drs. Ben-Judah and Rosenzweig and the elders have come to believe that there are different judgments for the sins and works of believers, Old Testament saints, Tribulation saints, Jews still alive at the end of the Tribulation, Gentiles still alive at the end of the Tribulation, Satan and the fallen angels—which we saw today—and all the unredeemed people of all time.

"Christ's death on the cross was where God placed upon Jesus the sin of all who would become believers. Christ paid for our sins and thus we will face only the judgment seat of Christ and not any of the other judgments. Jesus Himself said in John 5:24, 'Most assuredly, I say to you, he who hears My word and believes in Him who sent Me has everlasting life, and shall not come into judgment, but has passed from death into life.'

"Romans 8:1-4 says, 'There is therefore now no condemnation to those who are in Christ Jesus, who do not walk according to the flesh, but according to the Spirit. For the law of the Spirit of life in Christ Jesus has made me free from the law of sin and death. For what the law could not do in that it was weak through the flesh, God did by sending His own Son in the likeness of sinful flesh, on account of sin: He condemned sin in the flesh, that the righteous requirement of the law might be fulfilled in us who do not walk according to the flesh but according to the Spirit.'"

"Then why," Leah said, "do we face the judgment seat of Christ, and what is that?"

"We believe the judgment seat of Christ is distinct from the judgment of unbelievers. Paul told the Corinthian believers, 'We make it our aim . . . to be well pleasing to Him. For we must all appear before the judgment seat of Christ, that each one may receive the things done in the body, according to what he has done, whether good or bad.'"

"But if Jesus took our punishment and paid for our sins," Naomi said, "on what basis will we be judged?"

Eleazar smiled at his daughter. "So young, yet so bright."

"Daddy," she said, blushing, "stop."

"I am sorry. Your question is a good one." He flipped through his Bible. "Listen to what the apostle Paul told the Corinthians: 'For no other foundation can anyone lay than that which is laid, which is Jesus Christ. Now if anyone builds on this foundation with gold, silver, precious stones, wood, hay, straw, each one's work will become clear; for the day will declare it, because it will be revealed by fire; and the fire will test each one's work, of what sort it is.

"'If anyone's work which he has built on it endures, he will receive a reward. If anyone's work is burned, he will suffer loss; but he himself will be saved, yet so as through fire.

"'Do you not know that you are the temple of God and that the Spirit of God dwells in you? If anyone defiles the temple of God, God will destroy him. For the temple of God is holy, which temple you are.'

"He also said, 'Do you not know that those who run in a race all run, but one receives the prize? Run in such a way that you may obtain it. And everyone who competes for the prize is temperate in all things. Now they do it to obtain a perishable crown, but we for an imperishable crown. Therefore I run thus: not with uncertainty. Thus I fight: not as one who beats the air. But I discipline my body and bring it into subjection, lest, when I have preached to others, I myself should become disqualified.'

"Actually, Naomi, 'the judgment seat of Christ' has already taken place. It happened in heaven so that the church that was raptured with Jesus could be adorned as His bride when it descended with Him at the Glorious Appearing. Revelation 19:7-8 says, 'Let us be glad and rejoice and give Him glory, for the marriage of the Lamb has come, and His wife has made herself ready. And to her it was granted to be arrayed in fine linen, clean and bright, for the fine linen is the righteous acts of the saints.' Those of us who remain alive will be judged by Christ soon, before the Millennium actually begins.

"As for us Jews, the Tribulation itself was the time when God made Israel 'pass under the rod,' according to Ezekiel 20. God says, 'I will bring you into the bond of the covenant; I will purge the rebels from among you, and those who transgress against Me; I will bring them out of the country where they dwell, but they shall not enter the land of Israel. Then you will know that I am the Lord.

"'As for you, O house of Israel, . . . go, serve every one of you his idols—and hereafter—if you will not obey Me; but profane My holy name no more with your gifts and your idols. For on My holy mountain, on the mountain height of Israel, . . . there all the house of Israel, all of them in the land, shall serve Me. . . . Then you shall know that I am the Lord, when I bring you into the land of Israel, into the country for which I raised My hand in an oath to give to your fathers.'

"Zechariah 13 says that two-thirds of Israel would die, so that of those left, 'all Israel will be saved.' According to Romans 11:26-27, 'The Deliverer will come out of Zion, and He will turn away ungodliness from Jacob; for this is My covenant with them, when I take away their sins.'

"We elders have estimated that there are between five and ten million of us Jews who will enter the Millennium. But the Tribulation was also a time of judgment of unbelieving Gentiles. That should have been obvious from the twenty-one judgments that came from heaven during the past seven years."

George Sebastian raised a hand. "Elder Tiberius, Tsion and Chaim taught us there would also be a judgment of nations, but either I missed it or we didn't get into it. What's that about?"

"That is yet to come, and likely soon. The Scriptures seem to indicate that the valley created by the splitting of the Mount of Olives is called the Valley of Jehoshaphat, which means 'Jehovah judges.' The forming of that valley buried the rubbish of nearly four thousand years of civilization and runs from the Mount of Olives right through Jerusalem. In that newly purified area it appears the Lord will conduct three judgments: He will restore the Jewish nation; He will judge the sheep; and He will judge the goats."

"I remember studying the sheep-and-goats judgment," Hannah Palemoon said. "But I forget who they are."

"Some call this a Semitic judgment," Eleazar said. "Jesus will judge you Gentiles on how you have treated His chosen people. Those who honored the Jews are the sheep, and those who did not are the goats.

"When Jesus slayed all His enemies by the sword that came out of His mouth—the very Word of God—Antichrist's armies were put to death in preparation for the millennial kingdom. Soon all remaining unbelievers—yes, including those who did not take the mark of the beast and yet who never decided for Christ either—will also face death."

"Just people here in Israel?" Ming Woo said. "Or from all over the world?"

"Oh, from the entire world, I'm sure."

"And they will be judged here? Or in their own countries somehow?"

"Good question. I don't know. The Bible seems to indicate that this all takes place in the Valley of Jehoshaphat."

"So it might be awhile before everyone can get here. And what if they choose not to come?"

Eleazar chuckled. "Did you see anyone at the judgment today who appeared to have a choice?"

"So what you're saying," Ree Woo said, "is that only believers populate the Millennium?"

"It appears that way, yes. At least at the beginning. People born during the Millennium will have to make their choice, of course."

Priscilla Sebastian said, "Then the Great White Throne Judgment, at the end of the Millennium, is the final one?"

"Yes."

"But it doesn't sound like there will be much to judge. People either received Christ as their Savior, or they didn't."

"Right, but we believe that God, being wise and fair and wanting to demonstrate how far men and women fall short of His standard, will judge them based on their own works. Obviously, all will fail to measure up. This will show that the punishment is deserved, and as I have said, they will be sent to the lake of fire for eternity."

"But what about the goats in the coming judgment? Where do they go? And will they also be judged again at the great white throne a thousand years from now?"

"Yes. For now they will be sent to hades, apparently a compartment of hell, where they will suffer until that final judgment, and then they will be cast into the lake of fire."

"Sad."

"Yes, it is. Very. And yet I believe all these judgments will demonstrate to the whole world God's justice and righteousness and will finally silence all who have scoffed."

+ + +

Just before turning in, Rayford called George Sebastian to check on Kenny, hoping the phone wouldn't wake the children.

"He's out cold," Sebastian reported. "Priss is a little surprised, because all he can talk about is Jesus and seeing Mommy and Daddy tomorrow."

"We covered everything from the millennial kingdom to the resurrections and judgments tonight. You?"

"The same. Fascinating stuff."

"Tired, Sebastian?"

"Exhausted. It's about time. I had begun to wonder if I would ever be hungry or thirsty or tired again."

"And were you hungry?"

Sebastian laughed. "After the dinner we had tonight, I'm still wondering if I ever will be again."

"I hear you. I can still taste the lamb."

"I can still taste everything."

Rayford closed the shades and lay on his back, pulling a single blanket over himself. The light streaming through the cracks around the shade was so bright he had to cover his eyes with the crook of his elbow. He began thanking God for the events he had witnessed, beginning with his own healing, but before he could even mention them, Jesus said, "I know, Rayford. I know. I am right here, and I will always be right here. I will never leave you nor forsake you.

"My blood is precious, as of a lamb without blemish and without spot. I am the light of the world. He who follows Me shall not walk in darkness, but have the light of life."

"Thank You, Lord."

And believing Jesus was there, Rayford drifted off into the sleep of the redeemed.

20

LEAH COULD TELL it was morning only because of the dew on the roses and the coolness of the air. It was as bright as it had been at midnight, the last time she checked her watch before falling asleep. She had awakened with the knowledge that she was to go to the new Valley of Jehoshaphat. There was no question in her mind. As she showered and dressed, she knew she was not to eat, not to do anything else. Just go.

Leah had not been aware of Jesus speaking to her again in the night or in the morning, but this inner conviction about what she was to do was so strong and persuasive that He might as well have shown up in person and told her.

She hurried to the front of the house where Eleazar and Naomi were greeting their guests as they emerged from various sleeping quarters. Not a word was said about breakfast or plans for the day. Leah thought about mentioning her urge and asking how she might get there, but she could tell from the looks on the faces of George and Priscilla Sebastian, Hannah Palemoon, and Ree and Ming Woo that they too were on a mission that needed no words. Even the children, Beth Ann and Kenny, seemed eager to get moving.

When everyone was there, Kenny said, "Can we go now?"

Eleazar roared, his bulging eyes twinkling. "And where would you like to go, little one?"

Kenny shrugged. "To see Jesus."

Leah was struck that he didn't mention his mother or dad. For some reason, he too was being drawn to Jesus so forcefully that nothing else seemed to matter.

They all crowded into a vehicle driven by Eleazar, and Leah found herself next to the Woos. "Where're we going, Ming?" she said.

Ming said, "I don't know where anyone else is going. I just hope Elder Tiberius stops within walking distance of the new valley."

Walking distance didn't begin to describe it. Eleazar drove directly to the valley. As they got out, Leah was staggered to see millions and millions of people. They were white and black and red and yellow, and they were all headed the same direction. Leah sensed Jesus was at the end of this rainbow of humanity, and she knew where to find Him as soon as she turned her eyes to the sky. He was not there, but not only was His heavenly army host hovering on horseback, but also tens of thousands of angels flanked them on the sides and behind.

Leah stopped walking, already separated from her friends. She simply had to stare. The sky seemed nearly filled with heavenly beings, forcing her to shield her eyes. But that did no good. The light of the glory of Christ was all about her, and even behind her hands it glared into her eyes. It felt as if she were staggering toward the object of everyone's attention.

Leah had been to professional sporting events where the crowds were so huge going in and out of a stadium that one could not see the end of the people. This was a million times bigger. As she began to walk again, snatches of conversations grabbed her interest.

"I was in my home, minding my own business."

"Where?"

"Johannesburg."

"When was this?"

"Not ten minutes ago!"

"I was asleep in Michigan!"

Leah followed the gently rolling terrain until it opened on an area just enough below Jerusalem that she could look up and see the Eternal City. She also had a view of Golgotha, the site of Calvary, which took away her breath. Again, Leah had to stop and stare.

"Leah," Jesus said.

"Yes, Lord."

"When you see My throne, join those on My right, your left."

"Yes, Lord."

She turned and continued to follow the crowd, realizing that everyone must have been given personal directions. The masses were breaking to the right and to the left and heading for separate destinations.

+ + +

Rayford tried to stay with Chaim. The men had left the Rosenzweig home without breakfast and without a word, as if they all somehow knew where they must go. Rayford decided that whatever was to come, he wanted to be close enough to Chaim to ask questions. The others must have had the same idea, as they all stuck together despite the crowds.

When Jesus told Rayford where he should go, he moved to his left without question, and as waves of people moved both directions, suddenly the view before Rayford became clear. Directly below and centered under the vast heavenly hosts, saints, and angels, a great raised platform stood, bearing a throne on which Jesus sat. Behind Him were the three angels of mercy. On either side of Him stood the archangels Michael and Gabriel.

Rayford knew instinctively that every living person on earth was gathered in that valley. "I'm guessing several million, Chaim, but it's really not many compared to how the earth was once populated."

"Very few," Chaim said, keeping up with Rayford. "Half a billion or more were raptured seven years ago. Half the remaining population was killed during the seal and trumpet judgments during the next three and a half years. Many more were lost during the vial judgments, and millions of believers were martyred. What you are looking at is probably only one-fourth of those who were left after the Rapture. And most of these will die today."

Indeed, Rayford realized, those assembling on Jesus' right were scant compared to those on His left.

+ + +

Enoch was sitting behind the wheel of his car in his Palos Hills, Illinois, driveway, praying. When he finished and opened his eyes, he was sitting in the sand in Israel with millions of people moving past him. Enoch stood and saw the heavenly hosts, the City of God, and the Place of the Skull. And Jesus told him where he should go.

"And, Lord, my flock. Are they—?"

"Of course they are, beloved. I will direct them to you."

+ + +

It took most of the morning for the masses to find their places and settle. To Rayford it appeared that those to Jesus' left were puzzled at best, frightened at worst.

Gabriel stepped to the front of the platform and stretched out his arms for silence. "Worship the King of kings and Lord of lords!" he shouted, and as one the millions on both sides of the throne fell to their knees. In a cacophony of languages and dialects they cried out, "Jesus Christ is Lord!"

Those on the left of Jesus began rising to their feet, while all around Rayford, everyone remained kneeling. "Clearly two different groups of people here, eh, Chaim?"

"Actually three," the old man said. "Those are the 'goats' over there, the followers of Antichrist who somehow survived to this point. You are among the 'sheep' on this side, but I represent the third group. I am part of Jesus' 'brethren,' the chosen people of God whom the sheep befriended. We are the Jews who will go into the Millennium as believers, because of people like you."

+ + +

Hannah Palemoon knelt in the sand, worshiping her Savior. Those millions in the crowd to Jesus' left had acknowledged Him, but she sensed no worship was involved.

Since the moment she had awakened, she had wanted—needed—to be here. To have Jesus speak to her in her native tongue was more than she ever could have dreamed or asked for.

Now people around Hannah began to rise, and she looked to the platform to see why. Gabriel was gesturing that they should stand. When everyone was in place and quiet, Gabriel spoke in a loud voice, saying:

"John the revelator wrote: 'I saw an altar, and underneath it all the souls of those who had been martyred for preaching the Word of God and for being faithful in their witnessing.

"'They called loudly to the Lord and said, "O Sovereign Lord, holy and true, how long will it be before You judge the people of the earth for what they've done to us? When will You avenge our blood against those living on the earth?"

"'White robes were given to each of them, and they were told to rest a little longer until their other brothers, fellow servants of Jesus, had been martyred on the earth and joined them.'

"People of the earth, hearken your ears to me! The time has been accomplished to avenge the blood of the martyrs against those living on the earth! For the Son of Man has come in the glory of His Father with His angels, and He will now reward each according to his works! As it is written, 'At that time, when I restore the prosperity of Judah and Jerusalem,' says the Lord, 'I will gather the world into the Valley Where Jehovah Judges and punish them there for harming My people, for scattering My inheritance among the nations and dividing up My land.

"'They divided up My people as their slaves; they traded a young lad for a prostitute, and a little girl for wine enough to get drunk.'"

Hannah was startled when the larger mass, the group to Jesus' left, immediately fell to their knees again and began shouting and wailing, "Jesus Christ is Lord! Jesus Christ is Lord!"

She wondered if she should be doing the same, but Jesus said, "Hannah, I know your heart."

+ + +

"Thank You, Lord," Rayford said. "I know You do."

+ + +

"Cleburn," Jesus said to Mac, "come, you blessed of My Father, inherit the kingdom prepared for you from the foundation of the world: for I was hungry and you gave Me food; I was thirsty and you gave Me drink; I was a stranger and you took Me in; I was naked and you clothed Me; I was sick and you visited Me; I was in prison and you came to Me."

+ + +

Priscilla Sebastian responded, "Lord, when did I see You hungry and feed You, or thirsty and give You drink?"

+ + +

Enoch said, "When did I see You a stranger and take You in, or naked and clothe You?"

+ + +

Razor said, "When did I see You sick, or in prison, and come to You?"

And Jesus said in Spanish, "Assuredly, I say to you, Razor, inasmuch as you did it to one of the least of these My brethren, you did it to Me."

"Thank You, Jesus," Razor said, bowing his head. But he was distracted by a commotion from those to the left of the throne. He looked up in time to see Jesus stand and walk to the edge of the platform.

With anger and yet sadness, He said, "Depart from Me, you cursed, into the everlasting fire prepared for the devil and his angels: for I was hungry and you gave Me no food; I was thirsty and you gave Me no drink; I was a stranger and you did not take Me in, naked and you did not clothe Me, sick and in prison and you did not visit Me."

The millions began shouting and pleading, "Lord, when did we see You hungry or thirsty or a stranger or naked or sick or in prison, and did not minister to You?"

Jesus said, "Assuredly, I say to you, inasmuch as you did not do it to one of the least of these, you did not do it to Me. You will go away into everlasting punishment, but the righteous into eternal life."

"No! No! No!"

But despite their numbers and the dissonance of their desperate bawling, Jesus could be heard above them. "As the Father raises the dead and gives life to them, even so the Son gives life to whom He will. For the Father judges no one, but has committed all judgment to the Son, that all should honor the Son just as they honor the Father. He who does not honor the Son does not honor the Father who sent Him."

"We honor You! We do! You are Lord!"

"Most assuredly, I say to you, he who hears My word and believes in Him who sent Me has everlasting life, and shall not come into judgment, but has passed from death into life.

"But My Father has given Me authority to execute judgment also, because I am the Son of Man. I can of Myself do nothing. As I hear, I judge; and My judgment is righteous, because I do not seek My own will but the will of the Father who sent Me."

"Jesus is Lord!" the condemned shouted. "Jesus is Lord!"

Gabriel stepped forward as Jesus returned to the throne. "Silence!" Gabriel commanded. "Your time has come!"

\+ + +

Rayford watched, horrified despite knowing this was coming, as the "goats" to Jesus' left beat their breasts and fell wailing to the desert floor, gnashing their teeth and pulling their hair. Jesus merely raised one hand a few inches and a yawning chasm opened in the earth, stretching far and wide enough to swallow all of them. They tumbled in, howling and screeching, but their wailing was soon quashed and all was silent when the earth closed itself again.

Everyone on the platform was back in their place, and from the throne Jesus said, "Surely, as I have thought, so it shall come to pass, and as I have purposed, so it shall stand."

"Astounding," Chaim said.

"Hmm?" Rayford said.

"I know that verse," Chaim said, "but think about it. What He merely thinks comes to pass, and whatever He purposes will stand."

Rayford was spent, as he assumed all the "sheep" and "brethren" were. Despite every horror he had witnessed during the Tribulation and the Glorious Appearing, the death and eternal punishment of millions all at once overwhelmed everything else.

"I know, Rayford," Jesus said. "Now rest your mind. My peace I give to you; not as the world gives do I give to you. Let not your heart be troubled, neither let it be afraid. Listen now as My servant comforts you."

Gabriel came forward again. He said, "God's Son, Jesus Christ our Lord, was born of the seed of David according to the flesh, and declared to be the Son of God with power according to the Spirit of holiness, by the resurrection from the dead.

"Through Him you have received grace. You also are the called of Jesus Christ; grace to you and peace from God our Father and the Lord Jesus Christ. In His gospel the righteousness of God is revealed from faith to faith; as it is written, 'The just shall live by faith.'

"The wrath of God has been revealed from heaven against all ungodliness and unrighteousness of men, who suppressed the truth in unrighteousness, because what may be known of God was manifest in them, for God had shown it to them.

"For since the creation of the world His invisible attributes were clearly seen, being understood by the things that were made, even His eternal power and Godhead, so that they are without excuse, because, although they knew God, they did not glorify Him as God, nor were thankful, but became futile in their thoughts, and their foolish hearts were darkened. Professing to be wise, they became fools, and changed the glory of the incorruptible God into an image made like corruptible man—and birds and four-footed animals and creeping things.

"Therefore God also gave them up to uncleanness, in the lusts of their hearts, to dishonor their bodies among themselves, who exchanged the truth of God for the lie, and worshiped and served the creature rather than the Creator, who is blessed forever. Amen."

"Amen!" the assembled shouted.

"These who have been cast into outer darkness and await the Great White Throne Judgment a thousand years hence were indeed without excuse. God sent His Holy Spirit as on the Day of Pentecost, plus the two preachers from heaven who proclaimed His gospel for three and a half years, plus 144,000 thousand witnesses from the twelve tribes. Endless warnings and acts of mercy were extended to these who continued to be lovers of themselves rather than of God."

It hit Rayford that all who were left were believers, worshipers of Christ, and that he was among those who would populate the Millennium.

Gabriel gestured that everyone should sit. When all were situated, he smiled broadly and pronounced loudly, "Blessed and holy is he who has part in the first resurrection. Over such the second death has no power, but they shall be priests of God and of Christ, and shall reign with Him a thousand years.

"The Mighty One, God the Lord, has spoken and called the earth from the rising of the sun to its going down. Out of Zion, the perfection of beauty, God will shine forth. Our God has come, and shall not keep silent; He shall call to the heavens from above, and to the earth, that He may judge His people!"

With that Jesus stood and Gabriel moved to stand behind the throne with the other angels. And Jesus said, "Gather My saints together to Me, those who have made a covenant with Me by sacrifice! Come forth!"

From everywhere, from the earth and beyond the clouds, came the souls of those who had died in faith, whom Chaim and Tsion had often referred to as "the believing dead," and whom Rayford knew now also included Tsion himself—along with many more of Rayford's friends and loved ones.

All these were gathered around the throne between Jesus and the assembled tribulation saints. They were arrayed in white robes, gleaming and pristine. Rayford looked for Chloe and Buck, for Tsion and Albie, Bruce Barnes, Amanda, Hattie, Ken, Steve, and the rest, but there were too many.

Jesus began by honoring the saints of the Old Testament, those Rayford had only heard and read about. Rather than handling this the way He had the individual audiences with the tribulation saints—supernaturally doing them all in what seemed to be an instant—Jesus this time gave the spectators His strength and patience. The ceremony must have gone for days, Rayford eventually decided, but he felt neither hunger nor thirst, no fatigue, not even an ache or a cramp from sitting in the sand that long. He loved every minute, knowing that when Jesus finished with the Old Testament saints, he would get to the tribulation martyrs. Waiting for his friends and loved ones to be recognized would be akin to waiting for Chloe's name to be called when she graduated from high school, but the reunion afterward would make it all worthwhile.

+ + +

Abdullah drank it all in. He glanced at his watch every few hours and realized how long it had taken to cover most of the Old Testament saints. Many he had never heard of—either he had not studied enough or these were some whose exploits had not been recorded. And yet God knew. He knew their hearts, knew of their sacrifice, knew of their faith. And one by one Jesus honored them as He embraced them and they knelt at His feet, and He said, "Well done, good and faithful servant."

+ + +

Enoch Dumas reveled in the privilege. He was most fascinated by the names he had read about and studied. He perked up when Jesus said of Abel, the son of Adam, "By faith you offered to God a more excellent sacrifice than Cain, through which you obtained witness that you were righteous, God testifying of your gifts; and through that, though dead for generations, your life still spoke."

Enoch was intrigued to finally get a look at these famous men and women. As they came to Him one by one, Jesus said, "Without faith it is impossible to please God, for he who comes to My Father must believe that He is, and that He is a rewarder of those who diligently seek Him."

There was Noah, humbly kneeling, receiving his reward. Jesus said, "By faith, being divinely warned of things not yet seen, you moved with godly fear, prepared an ark for the saving of your household, by which you condemned the world and became heir of the righteousness which is according to faith."

Hours later it seemed everyone roused when it was Abraham's turn. Jesus said, "By faith you obeyed when you were called to go out to the place you would receive as an inheritance. And you went out, not knowing where you were going. By faith you dwelt in the land of promise as in a foreign country, dwelling in tents with Isaac and Jacob, the heirs with you of the same promise; for you waited for the city which had foundations, whose builder and maker was God."

Sarah was right behind him, and Jesus said to her, "By faith you yourself also received strength to conceive seed, and you bore a child when you were past the age, because you judged Him faithful who had promised. Therefore from one man, your husband, and him as good as dead, were born as many as the stars of the sky in multitude—innumerable as the sand which is by the seashore."

Jesus addressed the spectators. "These all died in faith, not having received the promises, but having seen them afar off were assured of them, embraced them and confessed that they were strangers and pilgrims on the earth. For those who say such things declare plainly that they seek a homeland. And truly if they had called to mind that country from which they had come out, they would have had opportunity to return. But now they desire a better, that is, a heavenly country. Therefore I am not ashamed to be called their God, for I have prepared a city for them.

"By faith Abraham, when he was tested, offered up Isaac, and he who had received the promises offered up his only begotten son, of whom it was said, 'In Isaac your seed shall be called,' concluding that God was able to raise him up, even from the dead."

Later Jacob approached the throne, and Jesus said, "By faith, when you were dying, you blessed each of the sons of Joseph, and worshiped, leaning on the top of your staff."

And behind him, Joseph. Jesus told him, "By faith you, when you were dying, made mention of the departure of the children of Israel, and gave instructions concerning your bones."

All around Enoch Dumas, Jews began to stand. Soon everyone was on their feet. Moses himself was kneeling at the feet of Jesus with a man and a woman, and the Lord embraced them and said, "Well done, good and faithful servants. By faith, when your son was born, you hid him three months, because you saw he was a beautiful child; and you were not afraid of the king's command.

"And you, Moses, when you became of age, by faith refused to be called the son of Pharaoh's daughter, choosing rather to suffer affliction with the people of God than to enjoy the passing pleasures of sin, esteeming My reproach greater riches than the treasures in Egypt; for you looked to the reward. By faith you forsook Egypt, not fearing the wrath of the king; for you endured as seeing Him who is invisible.

"By faith you kept the Passover and the sprinkling of blood, lest he who destroyed the firstborn should touch them.

"By faith you led My children through the Red Sea as by dry land, whereas the Egyptians, attempting to do so, were drowned."

A woman knelt before Jesus. He said, "By faith, Rahab, you did not perish with those who did not believe, because you received My spies with peace."

+ + +

By the time Leah had seen all the heroes of the Old Testament, including Gideon and Barak and Samson and Jephthah, also David and Samuel and the prophets, she felt as if she were already in heaven. Jesus stood and said, "These through faith subdued kingdoms, worked righteousness, obtained promises, stopped the mouths of lions, quenched the violence of fire, escaped the edge of the sword, out of weakness were made strong, became valiant in battle, turned to flight the armies of the aliens.

"Women received their dead raised to life again. And others were tortured, not accepting deliverance, that they might obtain a better resurrection.

"Still others had trial of mockings and scourgings, yes, and of chains and imprisonment. They were stoned, they were sawn in two, were tempted, were slain with the sword. They wandered about in sheepskins and goatskins, being destitute, afflicted, tormented—of whom the world was not worthy. They wandered in deserts and mountains, in dens and caves of the earth.

"And all these obtained a good testimony through faith."

21

RAYFORD STEELE'S MIND was on a woman he had not touched in more than seven years. What would Irene look like in her glorified body? What would they say to each other? Had she been aware of him all this time, watching, knowing what he was doing? Did she know he had become a believer?

"Do you realize how long we've been here?" he said.

Chaim looked at his watch. "Days, and yet it seems less than an hour. You know it is unlikely Jesus will handle the tribulation saints and martyrs the way He did the Old Testament saints."

"Why?"

"Think about it. It would take years."

"How many are there?" Rayford said.

"More than two hundred million martyrs alone."

"How can you be so sure?"

"I read the Book. Revelation says the martyrs under the throne who had come out of the Tribulation constitute a multitude no man can number."

"Then how can you say—?"

"Stay with me. Earlier it refers to the demonic horsemen—remember them?"

"Don't ask."

"It refers to two hundred million of them, obviously a multitude that *can* be numbered. So, if there are so many martyrs that they cannot be numbered, how many must there be?"

+ + +

Mac tried to imagine how he would have felt, before the Glorious Appearing, had he sat in the desert this long without food, water, or sleep. *These old bones would be dried up and blowin' away.*

He recalled that as a child he'd worried about the afterlife. His friends, most of them, were church kids, and they talked about dying and going to heaven as if it was simply expected. "Yeah," he had said, "but what'll we *do* there?" His idea of heaven was ghosts in white robes with halos sitting on clouds and playing harps.

His friends could only shrug and say, "Better there than in hell."

He hadn't been so sure. His uncles always kidded about wanting to go to hell, "because that's where all our friends will be."

Needless to say, Mac was grateful to have avoided hell. And if heaven was as fascinating as this interval before the Millennium, it was going to be more than okay.

+ + +

"It might be a little late to be asking this, Chaim," Rayford said, "but what kind of a relationship will I have with Irene now? And Amanda. I know that's the kind of question Jesus was asked when the Pharisees were trying to trip Him up, but I sincerely need to know."

"All I can tell you is what Jesus said. 'In the resurrection they neither marry nor are given in marriage, but are like angels of God in heaven. For when they rise from the dead, they neither marry nor are given in marriage. But those who are counted worthy to attain that age'—meaning this time period right now—'and the resurrection from the dead, neither marry nor are given in marriage.' I cannot make it any plainer than that."

"So only the people who reach the Millennium alive will marry and have children."

"Apparently."

Rayford also looked forward to meeting his heroes from the Old Testament. "We *do* get to interact with those guys, don't we?"

"Absolutely," Chaim said. "In Matthew 8:11 Jesus says, 'Many will come from east and west, and sit down with Abraham, Isaac, and Jacob in the kingdom of heaven.'"

But for now the Old Testament saints were not mingling. They too had become spectators, because the multitude that no man could number was lined up at the throne, awaiting their rewards.

"Those who were killed for the testimony of Jesus," Chaim said, "which pretty much covers any believer who died during the Tribulation, will be honored. But those who were actually martyred will be given a special crown."

Gabriel stepped forward one more time and announced, "John the revelator wrote, 'And I saw the souls of those who had been beheaded for their testimony about Jesus, for proclaiming the Word of God, and who had not worshiped the Creature or his statue, nor accepted his mark on their foreheads or their hands. They had come to life again and now they reigned with Christ for a thousand years.'"

Chaim's assessment proved accurate. Somehow the Lord arranged it so that only those who knew each tribulation saint witnessed them getting their reward. So, rather than Rayford's having to wait through the ceremonies for a million or two strangers to see a friend or loved one, as soon as the festivities began, Bruce Barnes approached the throne.

"Bruce!" Rayford called out, unable to restrain himself, and he stood and applauded. All around him others were doing the same, but they were calling out other names. "Aunt Marge!" "Dad!" "Grandma!"

From that distance, Rayford could tell only that Bruce looked like himself. Of course he had never seen him in a white robe, and he didn't know what a glorified body would be like, but Rayford couldn't wait to see him face-to-face.

Soon he saw Loretta, Bruce's secretary, who had died in the first global earthquake.

And then came Amanda, Rayford's second wife.

He saw Dr. Floyd Charles, who had worked with the Tribulation Force. And David Hassid, the first mole in the Global Community Palace, who had been shot and killed at Petra, just before the remnant began to move in.

T Delanty was there, and sweet Lukas Miklos and his wife, who received a martyr's crown for enduring the guillotine. Soon came Ken Ritz, who had taken a bullet to the head from the GC in an escape attempt.

What memories! How good it would be to reminisce. Jesus honored Ken by mentioning how he had "used your God-given mind and abilities to often thwart the works of the enemy and encourage your brothers and sisters in Christ."

Melancholy washed over Rayford when he recognized Hattie Durham embracing Jesus. How he had misused her and nearly given up on her, but what a brave saint she had become in the end. When she knelt, Michael the archangel handed Jesus a crystalline tiara, which He placed on her head. "My daughter," He said, "you were martyred for your testimony of Me in the face of the Antichrist and the False Prophet, and so you will bear this crown for eternity. Well done, good and faithful servant."

There was Annie Christopher, who had worked underground at the GC palace. Steve Plank, Buck Williams's former boss, who was thought dead in the wrath of the Lamb earthquake, only to resurface undercover as a GC operative under the name Pinkerton Stephens.

"You suffered the blade for My sake," Jesus said, "and maintained your testimony to the end. Wear this crown for eternity."

Albie appeared, Rayford's old friend and faithful compatriot.

And finally, there was Chloe, and right behind her Buck and Tsion. Rayford kept shouting and clapping as his daughter, son-in-law, and spiritual adviser received their *well-done,* their embrace, and their martyr's crown. The entire heavenly host applauded each martyr, but Caleb, one of the angels of mercy, came out from behind the throne to embrace Chloe. Rayford would have to ask her about that.

Of her, Jesus said, "You too suffered the guillotine for My name's sake, speaking boldly for Me to the end. Wear this for eternity."

Of Buck he said, "You and your wife gave up a son for My sake, but he shall be returned to you, and you shall be recompensed a hundredfold. You will enjoy the love of the children of others during the millennial kingdom."

Jesus took extra time with Tsion Ben-Judah, praising him for "your bold worldwide proclamation of Me as the Messiah your people had for so long sought, the loss of your family—which shall be restored to you—your faithful preaching of My gospel to millions around the world, and your defense of Jerusalem until the moment of your death. Untold millions joined Me in the kingdom because of your witness to the end."

Rayford enjoyed Jesus' welcome to dozens of others whose names he had forgotten, underground believers in various countries who had worked through the Co-op, hosted Trib Force people, and sacrificed their lives in defense of the gospel.

Only by the miraculous work of God through Jesus, the honoring of more than two hundred million tribulation martyrs and saints was suddenly over. Jesus stood at the front edge of the vast platform and spread His arms as if to encompass the mighty throng of souls, most with glorified bodies, the rest mere mortals who had survived the Tribulation.

"I will declare the decree," He said. "The Lord has said to Me, 'You are My Son, today I have begotten You. Ask of Me, and I will give You the nations for Your inheritance, and the ends of the earth for Your possession. You shall break them with a rod of iron; You shall dash them to pieces like a potter's vessel.'

"Now therefore, I say be wise, O kings; be instructed, you judges of the earth. Serve the Lord with fear, and rejoice with trembling. Kiss the Son, lest He be angry, and you perish in the way, when His wrath is kindled but a little. Blessed are all those who put their trust in Him.

"I welcome you, one and all, to the kingdom I have prepared for you. Rayford, welcome."

"Thank You, Lord."

How anyone found anyone else in the endless mass of souls was a miracle in itself. Rayford saw Chaim making a beeline to Tsion, who was already in the embrace of his wife and two children. Albie and Mac were laughing and shouting and hugging.

There were Buck and Chloe running to Kenny as he ran to them.

And seemingly out of nowhere, at Rayford's elbow stood Irene. One thing he could say for the glorified body: She looked herself, and as if she had not aged. No way she could say the same for him.

"Hi, Rafe," she said, smiling.

"Irene," he said, holding her. "You're permitted one cosmic I-told-you-so."

"Oh, Rayford," she said, stepping back as if to get a good look at him. "I've just been so grateful that you found Jesus and so thrilled at how many souls are here because of what you and Chloe and the others did." She looked behind him. "Raymie," she said, "come here."

Rayford turned and there was his son. He scooped him up in a tight embrace. "Even you knew the truth that I didn't," he said.

"I can't tell you how great it is to see you here, Dad."

Rayford pointed to Buck and Chloe and Kenny. "You know who that is?"

"Of course," Irene said. "That's my grandson—your nephew, Raymie."

They approached shyly, but it was Buck who broke the ice as Chloe gathered in her parents. "So nice to meet you, finally," he said, shaking his mother-in-law's hand. "I've heard so much about you."

Kenny seemed fascinated to have a real uncle, and one so young.

As they laughed and hugged and praised God for each other and for their salvation, Amanda White Steele approached. "Rayford," she said. "Irene."

"Amanda!" Irene said, pulling her close. "Would you believe I prayed for you even after I was raptured?"

"It worked."

"I know it did. And you and Rafe were happy for a time."

"I was so afraid this would be awkward," Rayford said.

"Not at all," Irene said. "I didn't begrudge you a good wife and companionship. I was so thrilled that you both had come to Jesus. You're going to find that He is all that matters now."

"And I," Amanda said, "am just so happy you made it through the Tribulation, Rayford." She turned back to Irene and took her arm. "You know, your witness and character were the reasons I came to the Lord."

"I knew that was your testimony," Irene said. "But I hadn't recalled making any impression on you."

"I don't think you tried. You just did."

Rayford had the feeling that his family would be close, affectionate friends throughout the Millennium. He didn't understand it all yet, in fact hardly any of it. But he had to agree with Irene: Jesus was all that mattered anymore. There would be no jealousy, envy, or sin. Their greatest joy would be in serving and worshiping their Lord, who had brought them to Himself.

As Buck and Chloe continued to interact with Irene and Amanda, Rayford borrowed Raymie. "There are so many people I want to see, Son. You must meet them all. And we've only got a thousand years."

Epilogue

BUT AFTER THESE things [Satan] must be released for a little while.
Revelation 20:3

About the Authors

Jerry B. Jenkins, former vice president for publishing at Moody Bible Institute of Chicago and currently chairman of the board of trustees, is the author of more than 175 books, including the best-selling Left Behind series. Twenty of his books have reached the *New York Times* Best Sellers List (seven in the number-one spot) and have also appeared on the *USA Today*, *Publishers Weekly*, and *Wall Street Journal* best-seller lists. *Desecration*, book nine in the Left Behind series, was the best-selling book in the world in 2001. His books have sold nearly 70 million copies.

Also the former editor of *Moody* magazine, his writing has appeared in *Time*, *Reader's Digest*, *Parade*, *Guideposts*, and dozens of Christian periodicals. He was featured on the cover of *Newsweek* magazine in 2004.

His nonfiction books include as-told-to biographies with Hank Aaron, Bill Gaither, Orel Hershiser, Luis Palau, Joe Gibbs, Walter Payton, and Nolan Ryan among many others. The Hershiser and Ryan books reached the *New York Times* Best Sellers List.

Jerry Jenkins assisted Dr. Billy Graham with his autobiography, *Just As I Am*, also a *New York Times* best seller. Jerry spent 13 months working with Dr. Graham, which he considers the privilege of a lifetime.

Jerry owns Jenkins Entertainment, a filmmaking company in Los Angeles, which produced the critically acclaimed movie *Midnight Clear*, based on his book of the same name. See www.Jenkins-Entertainment.com.

Jerry Jenkins also owns the Christian Writers Guild, which aims to train tomorrow's professional Christian writers. Under Jerry's leadership, the guild has expanded to include college-credit courses, a critique service, literary registration services, and writing contests, as well as an annual conference. See www.ChristianWritersGuild.com.

As a marriage-and-family author, Jerry has been a frequent guest on Dr. James Dobson's *Focus on the Family* radio program and is a sought-after speaker and humorist. See www.AmbassadorSpeakers.com.

Jerry has been awarded four honorary doctorates. He and his wife, Dianna, have three grown sons and four grandchildren.

Check out Jerry's blog at http://jerryjenkins.blogspot.com.

Dr. Tim LaHaye (www.timlahaye.com), who conceived and created the idea of fictionalizing an account of the Rapture and the Tribulation, is a noted author, minister, and nationally recognized speaker on Bible prophecy. He is the founder of both Tim LaHaye Ministries and The PreTrib Research Center. Presently Dr. LaHaye speaks at many Bible prophecy conferences in the U.S. and Canada, where his current prophecy books are very popular.

Dr. LaHaye holds a doctor of ministry degree from Western Theological Seminary and a doctor of literature degree from Liberty University. For 25 years he pastored one of the nation's outstanding churches in San Diego, which grew to three locations. It was during that time that he founded two accredited Christian high schools, a Christian school system of ten schools, and San Diego Christian College (formerly known as Christian Heritage College).

Dr. LaHaye has written over 50 nonfiction and coauthored 25 fiction books, many of which have been translated into 34 languages. He has written books on a wide variety of subjects, such as family life, temperaments, and Bible prophecy. His most popular fiction works, the Left Behind series, written with Jerry B. Jenkins, have appeared on the best-seller lists of the Christian Booksellers Association, *Publishers Weekly*, the *Wall Street Journal*, *USA Today*, and the *New York Times*.

Another popular series by LaHaye and Jenkins is The Jesus Chronicles. This four-book novel series gives readers rich first-century experiences as John, Mark, Luke, and Matthew recount thrilling accounts of the life of Jesus. Dr. LaHaye is coauthor of another fiction series, Babylon Rising. Each of the four titles in this series have debuted in the top 10 on the *New York Times* Best Seller List. These are suspense thrillers with thought-provoking messages.